THAT LAST MOUNTAIN

The night was bright with stars and icily cold as the snake of skiers wound its heavily laden way down into the valley. A wind was picking up now, moaning through the mountains and polishing the surface of the snow until it gleamed.

Scarcely had the vacating soldiers disappeared from view than a shadow detached itself from the darkness of the treeline.

Nimbly the figure skied through the bushes until it reached the crushed remnants of the observation post. Seconds later the first figure was joined by another. Then another, and then one more.

Without exchanging a word, two of them took up defensive positions, their Kalashnikov AKS-74 rifles at the ready. The other two began a careful rummage through the snow debris for anything that might have been left behind.

There turned out to be only one item, and it had been easy to find. It had been deliberately hung from a branch.

About the author

Terence Strong is a freelance journalist and writer. He has a keen interest in international politics and military affairs, and special forces in particular. This specialised knowledge was used extensively in his previous bestselling thrillers WHISPER WHO DARES, THE FIFTH HOSTAGE, CONFLICT OF LIONS and DRAGONPLAGUE.

Research for THAT LAST MOUNTAIN necessitated learning both Nordic skiing and climbing in order to travel across the icy wastes of Scandinavia known as 'the last wilderness of Europe'.

However, he is returning thankfully to warmer climes for his next thriller, which will be set largely in the Middle East.

That Last Mountain

Terence Strong

CORONET BOOKS
Hodder and Stoughton

Copyright 1989 © by
Terence Strong

First published in Great Britain in
1989 by Hodder and Stoughton
Limited

Coronet edition 1989

British Library C.I.P.
Strong, Terence
  That last mountain.
  I. Title
823'.914   [F]

ISBN 0-340-50605-9

Printed and bound in Great Britain
for Hodder and Stoughton
Paperbacks, a division of Hodder
and Stoughton Limited, Mill Road,
Dunton Green, Sevenoaks, Kent
TN13 2YA (Editorial Office:
47 Bedford Square, London
WC1B 3DP) by Cox and Wyman
Limited, Reading, Berks. Photoset
by Rowland Phototypesetting
Limited, Bury St Edmunds, Suffolk.

FOR
THE SNOWMEN
Members of the Royal Marines,
the Mountain and Arctic Warfare Cadre
and, of course,
22 Special Air Service Regiment.
All of whom give so much about which we
know so little.
If at all.

AUTHOR'S NOTE

Few people are aware that the Americans' much-publicised plans to develop Star Wars space-defence technology were, in fact, initiated in response to the surprise discovery that the Soviet Union was already close to deploying various land-based systems.

It sent shockwaves through the US defence circles, because the existence of such systems would upset the entire international balance of power, affecting strategic planning and negotiations between the super-powers on arms reduction for years to come.

Imagine then the importance of a defecting Soviet scientist able to verify the capabilities of Moscow's space-beam technology. Importance to the Soviet Union that he should be returned, or prevented from ever talking. Importance to the West that he should succeed in his defection – at almost any cost.

Imagine the lengths that both sides would go to in order to succeed. To win or lose the most important military secrets since the advent of the atom bomb . . .

The events that unfold in this story present an authentic account of exactly what might happen. And the pressures that are brought to bear are not exaggerated. They are frighteningly real.

I am indebted to many people for their help in piecing together the likely scenario and the reactions of the various parties: the British diplomatic community in Stockholm; the office of the Swedish prime minister; journalists Erik Månson and Leif Brännström of *Ex-*

pressen; the Finnish Embassy in London; staff of the magnificent Grand Hotel; the International Institute for Strategic Studies, and *Aviation Week & Space Technology* for their assistance.

Very special thanks must go to the Ministry of Defence for its kind co-operation in teaching me the finer points of Arctic survival and warfare. This onerous task fell specifically to the Mountain and Arctic Warfare Training Cadre and the men of L Company, 42 Commando Royal Marines, who had to endure an inquisitive civilian sharing a snowhole with them during their arduous annual exercise in Norway.

This story gives some idea of the severity of the monstrous conditions that these men have to live and fight in every year. And with remarkably little complaint!

Lessons learned there were put to good effect in my later ski-expedition to the wilderness of the Swedish mountains where that last mountain may be found . . .

TERENCE STRONG
LONDON 1987

I am most grateful to the following people who have contributed so much to this story: 'Big Oscar' Oscarsson, who was hijacked on the train to Åre and subsequently proved an invaluable guide and mentor on all things Swedish; Bob Skole, compulsive copy editor, who sorted out Stockholm's nightmare traffic problems for me; Björn Vinberg; Ken Stubbs, intrepid aviator; Hilda and Yvonne in Moscow who unwittingly became the models for Alice and Daphne.

Particular thanks go to the following Royal Marines for their hospitality and patient explanations: Major Graham Langford; Major David Nicholls; Sergeant Nick Holloway; Captain Leo Williams and Warrant Officer 2 (now WO 1) Bill Wright of 'The Cadre'; Steve Reade; the gentlemen from Comacchio, and most especially Sergeant Buster Brown and Captain Tony Newing.

'We are the pilgrims, Master, we shall go
Always a little further. It may be
Beyond that last blue mountain barr'd with
  snow,
Across that angry or glimmering sea.'

Inscription at SAS headquarters from
Flecker's *The Golden Journey to Samarkand*

PROLOGUE

They were up there, somewhere. Watching.

He could sense their presence. And it made him feel uncomfortable.

Sergeant-Major Brian Hunt allowed himself a terse smile beneath the white silk ski-mask that covered his face.

'Uncomfortable'. 'Comfortable'. Such terms were relative just below the Arctic Circle in Norway where the cold would crack the fillings in your teeth if you laughed too long at a joke. Not that there was much to joke about.

Comfort was zero degrees and respite from the unforgiving wind. It was catching four hours' sleep undisturbed, and putting on dry socks in the morning.

And discomfort? Hunt grimaced. That was just about every damn thing else.

Still, being watched was the most uncomfortable thing of all.

He checked himself. His mind was starting to wander. It was better than any watch to tell him that their stag was nearly up.

Their observation post had been created at the head of the mountain valley. From it they had a clear view all the way down to the road. Only the fluorescent marker wands marked its course through the undulating snow dunes.

Hunt's team had moved silently into the position three nights earlier. In the natural glimmer of reflected snow they had stretched out the lightweight white camouflage

11

net and begun burrowing underneath it. At first the hole was scarcely big enough for each two-man shift. Just a six-foot oblong recess scraped away, leaving a twelve-inch parapet and a six-inch observation slit below the netting canopy.

But, as they planned to use the location as a base for some time, the OP grew a little every day. Each stag would do some nest-building; it helped to pass the time. Snow was never thrown out to leave tell-tale signs, but compacted and sculptured. Now it boasted two benches with a six-foot gap between, almost deep enough for a man to stand in and stretch his legs.

Sergeant-Major Brian Hunt had one bench, Corporal Bill Mather the other. Not that it was easy to distinguish his companion in the gloom, even a few feet away. Just a sinister apparition in white from head to foot.

Mather saw Hunt looking and tapped his watch. Time? Hunt nodded.

The two men dropped from the snow benches and met in the middle gap.

Mather's eyes in the apertures of his ski-mask were grey and as icy as the surrounding snow. He kept his voice low; sound travelled easily in these conditions. "They're there again, Brian."

Hunt said: "I know. Have you seen them?"

"I don't need to. I can *feel* them."

"So no sighting?"

Mather shrugged. "I picked up some movement with the nightsight. In the treeline."

"Not a reindeer?"

"No, Brian. Three or four dark shapes. Moving cautiously. Human."

Hunt nodded. It confirmed his own observations over the past half-hour using the lightweight Spylux image-intensifier.

He felt his anger rising. It had been a particularly tough year and his team had been looking forward to this task during the run-down to Christmas. Just over

12

two weeks of reconnoitring locations for the big annual NATO exercise due to start in the New Year. A welcome break from the pressures of routine front-line soldiering as they decided on the siting of firm bases, hides, and food and ammunition caches to meet the demands of the exercise scenario.

With more time than usual available for the task, Hunt had decided to use their vehicle sparingly and travel on skis as much as possible. Two of their number hadn't skied for several years and it was an ideal opportunity to improve their skills whilst getting in some practical Arctic survival experience. In fact, an almost leisurely interlude compared to their more usual assignments.

But it hadn't worked out like that.

For the third time in two weeks they'd found themselves under observation, and had been obliged to make a discreet withdrawal. Standard procedure when a genuine 'hostile' contact is made in peacetime. And, dammit, they'd had to mount stags as if they'd been going tactical!

Some bloody holiday it was turning out to be – thanks to the prying eyes of the four mysterious skiers.

Not that their identity was any longer a total mystery. After the first encounter, Norwegian Intelligence had persuaded the local police to make low-key enquiries at all the remote farms and settlements in the area.

At last they found a semi-reclusive trapper who was able to shed a little light on the strangers. They had, he said, called at his isolated log cabin one night during a particularly ferocious blizzard. In immaculate Norwegian they informed him they were Finns. Three men and a woman. They were on a hunting expedition when one of them, a good-looking young man with fair hair, had badly twisted his knee. They had stayed for two days until the blizzard had died and the youngster's leg had made a substantial recovery.

Pressed by the police, the trapper was unable or reluctant to add much more. They had been, he said, stiffly polite and not given to conversation. Either with him or

13

between themselves. And somehow he had not felt inclined to ask questions.

Why? persisted the police.

There was something about them that was a little sinister, admitted the trapper. Something quietly menacing.

For a start he hadn't believed a word of their story. No one went hunting for pleasure in such conditions, even crazy Finns. Certainly not without a lodge to return to each evening where you could dry out in front of the wood-burner, have a good meal and a bottle of something to warm your insides. Winter backpacking on skis was for the young, strong and partially insane. It was certainly no place for a woman. And yet somehow the trapper had the feeling that it was the woman who was the leader of the party. He sensed that she was the one the others consulted; the one who made the decisions.

And another thing, their clothes. They had come to his lodge dressed in subdued quilted anoraks. Cross-country skiing, even in sub-zero temperatures, is hot work. Lightweight windproofs would be the order of the day.

Later the trapper thought he knew why. When one of the group was unpacking the small khaki rucksack that each carried, he glimpsed the neatly packed set of windproofs. Not in the latest dayglo fashion colours for safety, but cam-whites. Admittedly useful for reindeer hunting, but definitely the sort of thing that soldiers wear.

Their guns, too, were kept hidden in canvas cases. With the avid enthusiasm that fellow hunters usually share for swapping knowledge and examining each other's rifles, the trapper had asked to see them. "What make?" "What calibre?" "What range?" "Is better than my trusty Krag?"

All these questions were stillborn after his first enquiry met with deafening silence and a hostile glare from the eldest man.

But then the glare had softened. The Finn had smiled and produced a flask of vodka from his backpack.

So from then on the trapper had decided to keep his thoughts to himself, and fill his head with alcohol rather than wild imaginings. If this strange group were Norwegian special forces, then so be it. It was none of his business.

Brian Hunt's eyes moved back to the observation slit and the treeline on the opposite side of the faintly luminous valley.

That was how "Volga Olga" had been born amongst the Mountain Troop of his Squadron of 22 Special Air Service Regiment.

For *they* knew that the strange party of Finns were not Noggy "funnies". Not with a woman amongst them. They had to be Soviet. And, operating illegally in hostile territory, they could only be Spetsnaz. Behind-the-lines specialist sabotage and diversionary troops. The cream.

But Volga Olga's team had to be something special. Clearly they were not conscripts. That suggested they were from one of the highly professional headquarters companies which even most other Spetsnaz personnel didn't know existed.

In wartime they would be given the most difficult tasks, such as the assassination of political and military leaders. But in time of peace they would, like their SAS counterparts, train with total realism. No doubt they too had deliberate lapses in navigational efficiency which allowed them to wander across borders. In the vast wilderness of northern Norway, and given their skills, there was little chance that they would ever be found.

The calm way in which they had confidently adopted a cover story for the benefit of the old trapper, and their perfect mastery of Norwegian, was quite chilling.

Corporal Bill Mather's voice broke into his thoughts. "You want we should withdraw again?"

Before Brian Hunt could reply they heard footsteps

behind them. The icy night air had formed a crust on the snow and the relief's boots squeaked noisily.

The white-clad bulk of Sergeant 'Big Joe' Monk slithered down into the OP. "Len's on the airwaves. Heard something that might interest you." He sounded amused.

"And what's that?" Hunt asked.

"There's a Cadre squad doing a mini-exercise to the north. Their BV's got a burnt-out clutch and shed a track. They've left an officer and signalman in the warm" – he raised his eyes as if to say 'Typical!' – "whilst the rest get back to bring in engineer support. Apparently they're stuck in the arse-end of nowhere. Anyway, Len says the team is skiing this way and he wondered if you fancied giving 'em a little surprise? A spot of tactical training, so to speak." There was a distinct hint of mischief in the voice.

Despite his preoccupation with the presence of the elusive Spetsnaz team, Hunt couldn't resist a grin of anticipation beneath his ski-mask.

"Who's commanding the party?"

"Dusty Miller." Knowingly.

The Mountain and Arctic Warfare Cadre were old adversaries. The *real* snowmen. They were a small elite unit of Royal Marines whose main function was to train 'Mountain Leaders' for dispersal to other Marine and Army units, where they would pass on their highly specialised knowledge.

But in times of crisis the 'Cadre' had another role in the Scandinavian theatre, penetrating behind enemy lines on sabotage and reconnaissance missions. Although similar in function to the Mountain Troop of each SAS Squadron, they 'specialised' in Arctic conditions, whereas Brian Hunt's team might find themselves practising their art in mountains anywhere from Norway to Oman, Spain or Africa. Sort of jack-of-all-trades and, the Cadre would undoubtedly provoke, the master of none.

It was the underlying reason why, to Hunt's knowledge, only one SAS man had ever passed the Cadre's gruelling course. The 'failed' candidate would return to the Regiment's barracks in Hereford armed with new knowledge to be adapted to 'the SAS way of doing things'. Over a drink in the mess he would happily relate how the Cadre took themselves too seriously. It would never enter his head to admit that, in the Arctic, the Cadre was simply the best there was.

Hunt said: "Dusty, eh? Hell, it is Christmas." An opportunity to bounce the Cadre could not be missed. Besides, it might just provide a chance to . . .

Mather said: "Our friends are back, Joe. Peel your eyes on eleven o'clock. Just in the treeline."

Big Joe Monk said: "Volga Olga? Shit! She gets around."

Hunt slapped his shoulder. "Bill and I are turning in. I'll send Len down in a few minutes."

Monk showed his large, square teeth, like a row of tombstones. One was missing. "Okay, Brian. There's a brew on."

It took only moments for Hunt and Mather to negotiate the trench to the snowdrift.

The eighteen-inch entrance hole was at the base of the drift, hidden from view by a shallow gully. Hunt went down on his knees and led the way in. Even after years of experience, snowholes still unnerved him. He had to fight back the feeling of claustrophobia as he squeezed his way along the slippery ice tunnel that inclined gently for some twenty feet, before opening up into a snow cave just high enough for a man to stand in. Automatically he waggled the ski-pole that had been poked into the ceiling of smooth snow to provide an airhole through to the top of the drift.

Corporal Len Pope's long frame was sprawled on a shelf the size of a double bed, which had been fashioned out of compacted snow. He grinned as he pulled off the radio headset. "Did Big Joe tell you about Dusty Miller and his bootnecks?"

17

Hunt nodded, removing his fur-lined forage cap and his ski-mask. The warmth and quiet of the snowhole was a stunning and blessed relief. A single stubby survival candle provided light and kept the temperature at a pleasing zero degrees. And, like a miner's canary, it warned if the oxygen supply had been lost. When the candle went out, it meant that there'd been a fall-in and there were just minutes left to dig yourself out. "Give me the details, Len."

Len Pope glanced at his notepad. His accent was broad Hampshire, and he had the infuriating habit of giving gender to inanimate objects. "The BV's stuck fast about forty klicks to the north," he said, using the military abbreviation for kilometres. "She's stuck in some pretty dire terrain. The engineer unit is new out here so they reckon it's easier to show them the way in. If you ask me it's just Dusty's way of giving his lads a bit of extra hard training. A nice night ski-march."

Hunt nodded. Typical Miller, he thought. Pain is character-building. Give them the hardest time of their lives just when they thought they were in for a cosy few days in the warmth of the Volvo Bandvagn tractor.

"If Dusty pushes them at forty klicks a day," Pope added, "then I reckon they'll be here around late morning. They've given the compass-bearing they'll be travelling. I calculate it'll bring them out through this valley."

Hunt helped himself to the steaming mess tin on the two-man Naphtha stove and poured some of the contents into his mug. "There's a problem." The hot chocolate was thick. Sticky and sweet. Glorious.

"How so?" Pope asked.

Mather took the remainder of the drink from the stove. "Volga Olga's back."

Pope clearly didn't believe it, or want to.

"We're sure," Hunt confirmed. "No sane Noggy is going to be out on a night like this."

Pope rarely showed anger. "Sod 'em! It was going to be fun bouncing the Cadre." He looked up. "Another

18

withdrawal, I suppose? Dammit, she's *comfortable* here! It's the first chance we've had to build a decent hole."

Hunt didn't share Pope's enthusiasm. Sometimes he thought the man was really just a frustrated builder, which was his family's business. Personally Hunt hated snowholes. He never slept well in them. Always had one eye on the ceiling. It was disturbing to crash out with it four feet above your head and wake up with it nearly touching your nose.

But he did share his colleague's indignation at having to move again when their scheduled departure was just two days away.

As he drained his chocolate, a thought occurred to him. Being on recce, neither he nor his men had any type of firearm. Miller's men on the other hand, as they were on exercise, would have weaponry equipped with blanks. An idea began to take form.

At length he said: "Well, lads, I for one don't intend to let Volga Olga spoil our fun. We'll jump the Cadre. Then, when Dusty and his merry men are all dead, we'll have a talk to them. Maybe they'd enjoy a little mischief themselves. With double the number and some pyrotechnics, we'll stand a better chance of singeing Olga's knickers for her."

Pope's eyes twinkled, and even the immovable Bill Mather almost smiled.

Sergeant-Major Dusty Miller pressured his right ski into a stem turn and came to a halt across the fall-line.

He thumbed up his goggles and stared through the trees at the clear valley that ran gently away towards the road.

Thank God, he thought, the morning spindrift that had created near white-out conditions was clearing. They would be able to take advantage of the valley and slide effortlessly for some three kilometres, and make up some of the time they had lost.

The faint click of ski-poles echoed through the fir trees, telling him that the first of the Cadre team had nearly caught up. They were a good bunch, but young and still a bit short on really hard skiing experience.

They'd been travelling a punishing route all through the night and now the strain was beginning to tell. Earlier Chalky Appleton, a big, cheerful black Marine from Brixton, had sprained an ankle. They'd shared out his load as best they could, but it still served to slow them up. Now they were in danger of missing the passing supply-truck shuttle on which Miller had planned to hitch a lift back to base. He really didn't want to call up a helicopter, which were in short supply until the main exercise began in the New Year.

Suddenly the rasp of steel edges on crusted snow filled the air as the first man swished down through the trees and drew up alongside. At minute intervals the next three arrived.

All the sinister begoggled faces turned back as they waited for Chalky. It was several minutes before the bulky figure was seen working uncertainly down the track, gathering momentum on the decline.

Miller somehow knew that fate had selected a victim. He could see the exhaustion in Chalky's posture and sense the agony caused by his ankle. Clearly the Marine had realised too late where his comrades had stopped. He tried to slow and turn too quickly. The weight of the Cyclops Roc bergan pack on his back decided to go the other way. With little strength in his injured ankle, the unfortunate Marine failed to take the bend and piled headfirst into a snowdrift.

"Aim for a tree, miss a tree," Miller murmured with good-humoured exasperation.

But the others weren't in the mood. Chalky Appleton's spectacular 'yeti' just meant another five minutes' standing around, cooling off dangerously quickly, whilst the hapless Marine released his bergan and skis and got himself together again.

It was several long, bone-numbing minutes before they were ready to set off, now beginning the downhill run in single file. This time Marine Appleton led, his skis pointed in a wide, brake-action snowplough to prevent a hurtling runaway descent. The others fell in behind with Miller bringing up the rear. He was grinning to himself. Perhaps the mischievous mountain trolls had decided they'd had enough for one day, and would leave them alone now. This was a gentle downhill run. No effort. The mini-exercise nearly done and Christmas only a few days away.

He wasn't sure what he heard first. It may have been Marine Appleton's cry of alarm. Or it may have been the series of thunderflash detonations that blew in fast succession across their path. Smoke and clouds of snow obliterated the slope as Appleton lost his balance and pitched forward in a heap.

The two Marines following had no room to manoeuvre. With angry curses they concertinaed into their prostrate companion. A third avoided the pile-up and slewed to a halt.

Sergeant-Major Dusty Miller performed the most spectacular kneebending Telemark turn of his life. It was the most graceful and difficult manoeuvre to master, but a joy to watch. And if he'd stopped to think, he'd never have executed it. As it was, sheer panic and instinctive reaction from years of training threw him onto automatic-pilot.

By the time he came to a stop, his rifle was ready to return fire.

His finger hesitated on the trigger. Realisation dawned that his weapon was fitted with a blank-firing mechanism. God, was this a prank or for real?

Four white-clad figures appeared from what was evidently an OP. One of them threw back his arm.

The grenade was a hurtling dark shape against the grey sky.

Instinctively Miller ducked, but too late. It exploded

on his head, and he felt the tell-tale icy trickle down the back of his neck.

"A fuckin' snowball!"

Suddenly the air was full of them. Everywhere snow-balls were bursting around the prone men, showering them with crystals.

"It's the bloody Regiment!" Miller bawled, driven by a mixed feeling of relief and anger at being turned over. "C'mon, lads, let's show the bastards! COUNTER-ATTACK!"

Hurling off bergans and skis the Cadre members launched themselves into the fray, pounding up the slope to take on the jeering ambushers. For five minutes the battle raged until all the ammunition was spent.

Miller gasped for breath, his face wet with snow and perspiration.

"Might have known it was you, Brian! You old bugger!"

Hunt grinned. "Your face was a joy, Dusty. And that Telemark . . . Wish I'd had a camera!" He turned to the mass of bodies sprawled in the snow. "There's a brew on, so c'mon and join us for a wet. And I expect we can rustle up something a little more festive to liven it up."

Still chuckling Hunt turned back to Miller. "Listen, Dusty, we're not just playing silly buggers," he said in a low voice. "You remember those reports about a Spets team in the area?"

It took Miller a few seconds to realise Hunt wasn't joking. "Spetsnaz? Yes, I'd heard."

"Well, don't look, but they're watching us now. *Really*, no kid. They've been bugging us during this whole op."

"Is this a wind-up?"

Hunt smiled. "Put it this way. If there *are* any photo-graphs of your Telemark turn, you're going to have to go to Moscow to get them." He hesitated. "What I have in mind is to give them a little surprise. Just so they haven't had it all their own way."

Miller nodded thoughtfully. "You got clearance?"

The SAS man raised an eyebrow. "Now who the hell is going to give me clearance? It's just between us and them. A deniable operation, so to speak." He studied the veteran Marine closely. "Thing is, can I count on you?"

Sergeant-Major Miller sniffed heavily. "Well, we've missed the sodding truck anyway."

They came in slowly, spread in a wide arc like beaters on a grouse shoot.

Whilst Chalky Appleton and Len Pope retained a semblance of activity at the observation post, the mixed team of seven SAS men and Cadre members had slipped one by one into the treeline at the rear. It took them an hour to gain height, taking a wide sweep around the head of the valley to a position some thousand metres behind the believed location of the Spetsnaz position.

The light was beginning to fail, swathing the snow in a fine pink mist. Exactly 1500 hours.

A sudden ferocious hiss came from the OP, shattering the brittle stillness of the valley, as the illumination flare shot skyward. For a moment the dazzling incandescent light glittered like a new-born star. Then slowly it began its descent towards the Spetsnaz hide.

Brian Hunt waved to the next man in the sweep-line. Gradually they all began moving forward carefully, but with deliberate noise. Every now and then those with rifles would discharge a blank round at the sky which was darkening to a deep ruby-coloured bloom in the west.

Another illumination flare blasted from the OP. Then another.

In Hunt's earpiece he heard Len Pope's transmission: *"Hello Red Bear this is Goldilocks. Hello Red Bear this is Goldilocks. Time to go home. Repeat. Time to go home. Please acknowledge. Over."*

The sweep continued at a slow, methodical pace for

some thirty minutes until the line came to a halt amongst the fir and ash trees on the opposite side of the valley to the OP.

Of course 'Red Bear' never had acknowledged, but fifteen minutes earlier Len Pope reported some movement from Volga Olga's suspected position.

Hunt was taking no chances now. As pre-arranged he waved to Dusty Miller, Bill Mather and Big Joe Monk to advance with him whilst the less experienced men waited in support. Carefully he skied between the tree trunks until he could see the shallow depression which was rutted with disturbed snow. He released his bindings and approached on foot.

After several messy scrambles through deep snow from one tree trunk to another, he had a clear view of the site. It was deserted. Behind it a snowdrift had been collapsed where a well-prepared hole had evidently been dug.

"Okay, Brian!" Miller called from the opposite side of the site. "They're gone. There's fresh tracks here. Going like the clappers."

Bill Mather and Big Joe Monk appeared from the trees, sliding down through the remains of the snowhole.

Hunt joined Miller who was studying the ski tracks.

The Marine said: "You know, Brian, I still half-thought you were taking the piss. I didn't really expect to find anything here."

Hunt knelt down. "One of these ski-tracks is definitely *much* lighter than the others. And these boot prints. Smaller and closer together. See how the toes are turned slightly inwards."

"Meaning?" Monk asked.

Hunt looked up and grinned. "It means that maybe Volga Olga isn't just the creation of some randy, homesick soldier. Maybe she does really exist."

Monk smiled broadly; it was clear what he was thinking.

"Hey! Look what I've found!" It was Mather. He'd

discovered something hanging from a webbing strap in a tree.

"Careful!" Hunt snapped. "It may be . . ."

"No problem, boss," Mather replied easily. He already had the cap off the flask. He sniffed it cautiously. "Vodka. Peppered vodka."

Hunt frowned. "You sure?"

"And it's for you."

"What?" Hunt took the flask and the scrap of note-paper that had been tucked into the webbing. The writing was uneven and the ink had run. The letters had an oddly Cyrillic shape to them. *Happy New Year, Brian.*

Miller flashed a suspicious glance at Bill Mather, but instantly realised he wasn't the type given to practical jokes.

Hunt shook his head slowly. "How in hell did they know my name?"

There was a stunned silence. Then Miller said: "I went to this lecture last summer. Some wallah from Intelligence. He reckoned the Soviets work on building a file on every special forces bloke they can. Cadre, SAS, SBS and the like. Follow their careers in Forces' journals, etc. Try and find out where they live."

Hunt felt suddenly cold. "That's not the same as matching faces."

Miller shrugged. "No, Brian, not your face. Your Morse transmission. You know everyone's got their own pattern, like a fingerprint. Individual. Their HQ can probably identify each man in your team by his Morse."

Hunt held the Marine's gaze for several seconds. The very thought of it made his flesh crawl. At last he said: "It's time to go."

The night was bright with stars and icily cold as the snake of skiers wound its heavily laden way down into the valley. A wind was picking up now, moaning through the mountains and polishing the surface of the snow until it gleamed.

25

Scarcely had the vacating soldiers disappeared from view than a shadow detached itself from the darkness of the treeline.

Nimbly the figure skied through the bushes until it reached the crushed remnants of the observation post. Seconds later the first figure was joined by another. Then another, and then one more.

Without exchanging a word, two of them took up defensive positions, their Kalashnikov AKS-74 assault rifles at the ready. The other two began a careful rummage through the snow debris for anything that might have been left behind.

There turned out to be only one item, and it had been easy to find. It had been deliberately hung from a branch.

Beneath her *ushanka* fur pile hat and above her ski-mask, only Valia Mikhailovitch's eyes showed. They were a rich hazel colour and they smarted with the cold as she lifted her goggles. But they showed the hint of a smile as she turned over the returned flask in her hand.

As she unstoppered it she was aware that the smell of vodka had gone. The flask was full of Scotch whisky.

There was no written message. But obviously Sergeant-Major Brian Hunt of the SAS had a sense of humour.

1

When Nikolai Shalayez saw the train standing at Tbilisi station, he felt suddenly like a bird set free.

He shuffled his feet as he waited impatiently for his friend, and glanced nervously towards the line of green coaches with their cream livery stripes. Already the expectant thrum from the engine filled the air as the few remaining passengers climbed aboard. The last call had already been tannoyed.

It was with profound relief that he saw his friend finally extricate himself from the throng around the ticket office.

"Sorry, Niki!" Sergei Chagall gasped, struggling with his heavy leather valise. The flapping grey greatcoat, which had been so necessary when they'd left central Asia, was now a burden in the mild southern climate of Georgia.

"We're the last ones," Nikolai Shalayez replied. "We'd better move."

"It was chaos back there," Chagall explained. The perspiration was dripping from his forehead as he attempted to keep pace with Shalayez. "They are two de luxe carriages short and there's a party of *nomenklatura* from Moscow insisting they have the seats."

Nikolai Shalayez raised his eyebrows. Typical! Senior officials of the Communist Party were a pain in the arse wherever they went. Always demanding the best seats in restaurants and theatres, getting special hospitals,

27

and prized foreign imports that the working masses scarcely knew existed.

"Then it is our good luck that you have the red pass," Shalayez grinned. "What would we do without it!"

"This carriage," Chagall indicated. "It's only first-class, I'm afraid. Even a KGB colonel is humbled by the massed might of our political masters. As it is, I expect we'll have to turf out some poor unsuspecting peasants."

And, after the high climb up into the carriage, Chagall's prediction proved correct. Adopting his un-smiling official face, the KGB officer flashed his red pass with its gold star and informed the four occupants, students with well-connected parents on their way to a recreation camp on the Black Sea, that the compartment was being commandeered for an official party.

Their protests were met by Chagall's glinting eyes and a quiet firm voice that hardly rose above a whisper. "And would you like me to enquire from where you obtained those jeans? Or that T-shirt?"

Hastily the students' gangling leader covered up the *US Marines Rule. Okay?* slogan emblazoned across his chest. Shalayez noticed that his denims were not the despised Dzhinsy brand, but a pair of Levi 501s, much prized in the new youth culture.

Sheepishly the teenager led his comrade students out into the corridor. The last thing he wanted to do was explain how he'd stopped an American tourist on the streets of Leningrad and offered a ludicrous price to buy the shirt off his back.

As the door slid closed, Chagall humped his valise onto the blue plastic seat and roared with laughter. "So much for student power, eh!"

The train started with a jolt and Shalayez half-fell into the seat by the window. He was a tall man with piercing violet eyes and strong lean features. Almost handsome had it not been for the unruly black mane of hair that always looked in need of a pair of scissors – or at least a brush. He shared the same age as his friend – forty-one years – and the same humble village origins. That was really why they'd become friends in the first place, three years ago. Then they discovered that they shared the same sense of boyish humour and mischief – rare qualities for both a mathematical scientist and a KGB officer.

Nikolai Shalayez, however, could never quite accept Chagall's casual abuse of his rank and privilege. "You were a bit hard on them, Sergei. We didn't need all four bunks."

Thankfully, Chagall removed his heavy coat. "Didn't you see those two beauties in the next compartment?"

Shalayez shook his head.

"Acute observation is one of the more useful tricks they teach us in the Department." Chagall grinned wickedly. "We'll be thankful for our privacy before we reach Sochi. Mark my words, Niki, they were two juicy young fruits. And we'll have them plucked before the night is out. After months of enforced celibacy at that godforsaken camp, it can become a habit." He pulled a dumb expression. "I do believe I've forgotten what it's for!"

The lightness of his friend's mood got through. "That's not what I heard, Sergei!"

"And what was that?"

"That you weren't using it for digging up mushrooms, that's what." He raised one eyebrow. "That little flower from Wologda who works in the canteen?"

A satisfied smirk spread over Chagall's face. The alcoholic glow of his full cheeks, when combined with the boyish brown curls of his head, was easily mistaken for the bloom of youth, and took years off his age. "Rumours, my dear friend, can get you into trouble. Leave rumours to the KGB – we're better at it!" He laughed infectiously at his own joke. "I shall now see the lie of the land with those two beauties next door. I'll get us some tea from the conductor." He dug in his pocket and pulled out an empty hand. "Damn, no change. Don't have sixteen kopecks on you, perchance?"

Shalayez shook his head as he reached into his own

pocket. Sergei Chagall really was incorrigible! He handed over the coins and watched as his friend disappeared into the corridor.

Left alone, his gaze shifted back to the vista of Georgian mountains that were rolling by with gathering speed. How green and warm and inviting they looked, even in winter.

He had grown to love them; it hadn't been an instant thing. Like most Russians, he scorned the easy-going and independent people of Georgia with their Mediterranean ways. Like everyone else he'd been brought up on jokes about the country bumpkins from Georgia. The hillbillies. Their gentle climate and all that sun addled their brains! Not like the crisp cold of Russia that kept the mind sharp to concentrate on more serious matters. Georgia was a place for rest and recreation – only good for the annual vacation.

But all that had been before he'd met Katya.

When he closed his eyes he could picture her without difficulty. In fact, she'd changed little during the ten years they had been married. The same almond face framed in straight ash blonde hair, although it had a few silver threads now. Unusual colouring that, for a Georgian girl. She must have got it from her late father who had been a waterways engineer from Moscow. He had met Katya's mother in Tbilisi. And Katya had her eyes. Large liquid brown eyes that showed every emotion she was feeling. They would tell it all. Joy, concern, curiosity, hurt.

Nikolai Shalayez was no longer registering the passing scenery. Hurt. That was the look he'd been seeing lately. Of course, she'd said nothing, it wasn't her way. But then with those eyes she didn't have to.

The carriage wheels clanked noisily as the train slowed. Shalayez cursed. He'd forgotten how interminably long the journey to Sochi on the Black Sea coast could be. It was a single track with only occasional passing points. So inevitably time would drag as they sat on a side-track, waiting for a late train coming up from the south before the journey could continue.

He forced himself to relax. It wasn't easy. Every second's delay would make his eventual reunion with Katya more traumatic.

Already he was a day late. He and his wife should have been travelling down together to Sochi twenty-four hours earlier. But his journey from the high-security compound at Sary Shagan in central Asia had been delayed. Fog had rolled in off the vast Osero Balchasch lake and grounded the Illyushin jumbo jet. For eight hours it sat like a fat impotent slug.

So when he eventually reached Tbilisi he found their flat deserted and a message from Katya to say she'd gone on without him. There were no rail coupons available for days.

A brilliant finish to a brilliant three years, Niki thought bitterly.

For three years he had been a virtual prisoner at Sary Shagan, working all the hours God gave. In all that time he'd only been granted leave for a few days each New Year and a week each summer. And this year even that had been withheld. It was hardly enough to sustain a marriage.

Such was the importance of the Sary Shagan project to the Motherland – according to his officious masters. Development, they said, had reached a critical stage. Especially so, given the stand the American president had taken on his 'Star Wars' defence policy. But now, at last, Nikolai Shalayez's role in the project was virtually complete.

He may have been there still though, had it not been for Sergei Chagall. Dear Sergei! It had been he who had used his influence as the camp's security chief to get him released from the project. Even then it had cost a crate of vodka to persuade the camp's hard-bitten bastard of a welfare psychologist that one of their most brilliant mathematical scientists was in imminent danger of a

31

complete mental breakdown, if he was not reunited with his wife.

Dear Sergei! How would he have coped with those three years of purgatory without his companionship and cynical good humour? It was Chagall who had freed him. And again it was he who had worked wonders in getting seats on the train.

But when they finally reached the holiday chalet at Sochi, he was well aware that it would be down to him alone to save his marriage. That was one area in which even the resourceful Sergei could wield little influence.

The train began to move again. And he thought back to the year before when he had last seen his wife. Going to bed with her had been like going to bed with a total stranger. Tense, fumbling. It had not been successful. They were only just starting to get to know each other again, when it had been time for him to return to the project.

And as for little Yelina . . . Well, she had shown little interest in her father. If anything she appeared to resent his presence, becoming sullen and withdrawn. And how could he blame a child for that when her father only ever bothered to show himself at New Year and for a few days' mushroom picking in the summer.

His thoughts were disturbed as the door slid open with a crash. Chagall stood there beaming triumphantly, an arm around the shoulders of two timid-looking girls in their teens.

"Look what I've found, Niki!"

"I thought you were going for some tea?" Shalayez chided.

"Bah, the samovar's not boiled yet," Chagall retorted with mild irritation. "Besides, plenty of time for tea later. You should meet Anna and Sophia. Would you believe they are drama students? What a coincidence!"

Coincidence? Shalayez didn't follow. But by now he was used to his friend's sudden brilliant ruses. He found

32

himself appraising the young girls. There were few fe-
males at Sary Shagan.

They were pretty enough. Slim young things with
wide innocent eyes. Anna was auburn with a peppering
of freckles on her face. Sophia was black-haired and
looked the more wary of the two.

The girl called Anna stepped forward and offered her
hand. "I am so pleased to meet you. I've always wanted
to be in films."

He could feel the fine bones of her hand in his.
"Films?"

The girl's eyes were bright with eagerness. "I think
it's such a clever idea to go for complete unknowns. It
will make your movie so much more real."

He looked up at Chagall for an explanation. His
friend's face was straight as he hugged Sophia with
rather more than fatherly comfort. "Yes, Niki, I have
told them how we film producers are always on the
lookout for fresh new talent. New faces."

Shalayez's mouth dropped. Chagall had done it again.
But the protest died on his lips as he found the girl Anna
staring at him curiously. He had to admit she was a
beauty. Her eyes were green and bright, and her skin
glowed with the translucent health of adolescence.

Even as his eyes fixed on her moist pink mouth, her
lips drew back to form a shy smile. Small, even white
teeth bit nervously on her lower lip. "I'd do anything to
be in your film. Truly."

Dawn found the train stationary on a passing track for
yet another interminably long wait.

Nikolai Shalayez had gone to the end of the carriage
which was the only place where passengers were allowed to smoke. The acrid bite of the day's first cigarette
tasted good, and lightened his mood. It wasn't that he
hadn't enjoyed making love with young Anna to the
rhythmic motion of the train, because he had. After
almost a year of enforced celibacy her exuberance and

willingness to experiment had been like a fresh breeze on a spring day after the long dark days of winter.

But he had hated the deception. Sergei's story that they were film-producers seemed to him such an obvious confidence trick that he was amazed that the girls had been gullible enough to fall for it.

For his part he felt ashamed that he had said nothing to put them right. Ashamed that he'd had to ask his friend for a two-kopeck *galosh*. And ashamed that he'd deceived Katya. That he had gone and spent the passion he'd been saving for his wife.

He wiped the condensation from the window and peered out. The train had stopped opposite one of the giant bathing stations that disfigured this popular area of the Black Sea coast. Beyond the ugly concrete structures the water was a polished silver plate, blinding in the reflection of the low-angled sun.

Not long now, he thought. Soon the train would creak forward again and the other passengers would begin to stir. Before lunch they would be shunting into the resort town of Sochi, with its hotels and sanatoria at the foot of the Caucasus Mountains. To where he would find Katya and little Yelina waiting for him.

From now on, Shalayez vowed, he would make it all up to them. Now that his work at Sary Shagan was over, everything would be different. Perhaps he might even get that post in Moscow he wanted. He was well aware that his work on the project had earned him renewed respect in Soviet scientific circles, and that could open up many doors and opportunities . . .

That reminded him. He delved in his pocket and extracted a crumpled white envelope with its Swedish postmark. Carefully he pulled out the contents and examined the letterhead.

It was from the Rönkä Society in Stockholm – an independent Finnish-owned international study centre for the furtherance of mathematics and computer science. To the man-in-the-street it was unknown, but to computer scientists the world over it had, since its inception in the seventies, earned a reputation as one of the most respected seats of learning for the discipline.

He smiled wryly. How strange to think that they knew of him. That his earlier theses published in various Soviet scientific journals had been reproduced around the globe. That he, Nikolai Shalayez, was revered by thousands who had never attended one of his lectures, let alone spoken a word of Russian.

What, he wondered, would his fellow mathematicians have thought if they'd seen him with Anna last night?

"Planning to leave us, Niki?"

He jumped at the sound of Sergei Chagall's voice as his friend pushed open the door with his foot. He was carrying two glasses of tea.

"I was deep in thought, you startled me," he laughed. He took one of the glass-holders. "What did you mean?"

Chagall sipped absently and peered out at the sea. "The invitation to lecture at that Swedish place."

"How do you know about that?"

His friend grinned reassuringly. "Niki, as security chief at Sary Shagan, it is my duty to know about such things."

Shalayez felt suddenly annoyed. "You mean you opened it? Read it?"

Chagall rubbed a larger patch in the condensation on the window. "What a beautiful day." He swallowed more tea before adding: "All mail received by people working on the project is screened by my security staff, Niki. It is the rules. Friends or not, I cannot make exceptions. Especially letters from abroad."

"I see." But he didn't sound as though he did.

"And are you going to go?"

"I'd like to visit Sweden. It would be a good break for Katya and Yelina, too."

Chagall smiled. "May I borrow one of your cigarettes? I'm out."

Shalayez rummaged in his pocket. "Sure."

The KGB colonel lit it and blew out a slow steady stream of smoke which burst over the window. "They'd never let you go, Niki, you must realise that?"

"I hadn't thought . . ."

"Not a whole family. Not someone as important as you. And now you've been working on the project, even you might find it difficult to get permission."

Shalayez shrugged easily. "So I won't go."

The other man turned his head to face him. "So I do not have a traitor on my hands? What the West calls a 'defector'?"

The laugh was genuine. "Of course not! I'd love to go to the Society and talk with fellow mathematicians. Exchange ideas. It would be stimulating – you can only get so much from fellow scientists in your own country. And I'd love Katya and Yelina to see another country –" He paused " – But, why should I want to 'defect'? I love my wife, I love my work, and I love my country."

Chagall nodded sagely. "And all the bureaucratic restrictions you have here . . .?"

Shalayez smiled knowingly. "Things were hard on the project, I admit. But that is different now. Science is one area where the bureaucrats have a hard time. How can you bind up something as ethereal as mathematics in red tape? First they have to understand." Again he laughed and realised that, finally, his despondency at having been incarcerated on the project was at last lifting. "Besides, I've been a Party member all my life and now my career is reaching new heights. I have much to look forward to."

Chagall's face was suddenly grim-set. It was almost the official face he used at his work. Except for his eyes. They were sad and serious. "Then you are lucky, Niki. In my line – bureaucracy knows no bounds. The Party understands *my* type of work all too well." His voice dropped to a whisper. "I will tell you something, Niki. Something I have never told anyone before. And I only tell you because you are my trusted friend." He brought

36

his head closer until Niki was aware of the pores on his skin and the bristles on his jowls waiting for the morning blade. "I would 'defect' tomorrow if I had the chance."

Shalayez felt distinctly uncomfortable. He was aware that this was dangerous talk. He tried to make light of it. "But *you're* not married, Sergei. As you said yourself, if I went abroad I wouldn't be allowed to go with Katya. And I couldn't – wouldn't leave her."

Chagall's mouth twitched almost imperceptibly. "I was married once, Niki, a long time ago. I became another divorce statistic. Like so many others, my wife only married me to get out of her parents' house. So the State would give us a flat of our own." There was venom in his words; it was not a side of his character that Shalayez had witnessed before. "What is the lust of some woman compared with a man's freedom, eh? Tell me that."

"I love Katya."

Chagall's brown eyes were only inches from his own. "Is that so? And did my eyes deceive me last night when you were thrashing around with a little nymph who was young enough to be your daughter?"

Shalayez swallowed; he couldn't think of a reply.

"Men are different," Chagall continued in a low growl. "Freedom is what they need. Freedom of choice and action. It is fresh air, bread and water to them. Any hot-blooded male can find the comfort of a woman – anywhere in the world. Not so freedom."

"What are you saying, Sergei?"

The KGB colonel grunted. "Just that I've seen more of the world than you, my friend. I've seen France and West Germany. And Britain. Even Sweden. A lovely place that. You stay there for a week – no, a day – and you'll understand what I mean. You're so used to life here, so used to coping with it – getting around problems, making up shortages on the black market – you don't even begin to *conceive* of how it can be in the West."

He paused. "I tell you, Niki, we are a Third World country whose only claim to anything else is our military might and our missiles."

In a small voice Shalayez said: "I don't like to hear you talk like this, Sergei."

Chagall raised a heavy eyebrow. "Does the truth hurt so much to hear? Lift your eyes above your confounded books of algebra for five minutes, Niki, and look beyond your nose! With your assets, the West would welcome you with open arms. You'd be free to research at any university in the world, on any subject you wished, and name your own price!"

The train started with a jolt, its sudden momentum pushing the two men together. For a second Shalayez clutched at his friend's lapel to prevent himself from falling. It was becoming claustrophobic in the smoky confines of the end-of-carriage section. He wanted to get out, but he was intrigued. There was one question he wanted to ask. "Sergei?"

"Yes?"

"Is that what you are recommending I do?"

Chagall's grin was back to its usual mischievous self. He was like a different man. "No, my dear Niki. I am just saying what I should like to do if I were you. But, as you point out, you have a loving wife, a sweet daughter, and a blooming career." He hesitated. "In fact, I have some news for you on that score." It was suddenly as though his friend had never given the confidence; that it had been a figment of his imagination.

"News?"

Chagall placed a brotherly arm around his shoulder. "You remember you said how you'd like a research post and an apartment in Moscow?"

"Of course. Even mathematicians are given to occasional dreams."

Chagall shook his head. "Not just dreams, Niki. Even our slow-moving system recognises great achievement. Eventually."

"My achievements are not that great, Sergei." Shalayez pulled a bitter smile. "And I'm afraid I do not have many influential friends."

"Maybe not. But *I* do." The KGB colonel laughed aloud at his friend's pessimism. "You underestimate yourself, Niki."

"What are you trying to tell me?"

Chagall grinned smugly. "That you have been offered a post at Moscow University, and a very handsome apartment has been allotted to you and Katya on Mira Prospekt."

Shalayez stared, incredulous. "You have arranged this?"

"I do have a certain amount of *blat*," Chagall admitted modestly. "I just put a word in the right ears."

"I do not know what to say!" He was beside himself with amazement and happiness. "Just wait until Katya hears about this."

Chagall basked in his friend's joy. "She deserves it after all she's put up with. You both do."

Katya Shalayeza admired the smart wooden chalet.

It nestled with others in the pine groves of a holiday complex overlooking the Black Sea on the outskirts of Sochi. Only a few were in use at this time of year, mostly allocated to specially privileged people, and the old *babushka* who opened up for them made it clear that she did not expect to be at their beck and call. She was also acutely suspicious that there was no man with the woman and her daughter.

"And you should wrap that child up properly," was her scolding parting shot. "This may be a resort but it is still December. Her poor knees are blue."

The door slammed leaving Katya and Yelina staring at each other in amazement. Then mother and daughter saw the funny side of it.

Yelina poked her tongue out at the door. "Old busy-body."

Her mother smiled, and unfastened her headscarf. "She means well."

The nine-year-old wrinkled her nose. It was a pretty, pert nose just like her mother's. "She's nosey and bossy like every *babushka*. Don't they remember what it's like to be young? Don't they know we don't feel the cold as they do?"

Katya smiled. "Well, maybe you don't, but this chalet *isn't* very warm."

"I hope you won't be like her one day."

Her mother's eyes settled on the electric fire. "These huts are really for the summer. I don't suppose they need heating then." She knelt down and examined the appliance. She could see that the fragile wire at the end of the element had fractured. "This is no good. We'll have to use the oven to heat the place."

Yelina wasn't impressed. "Just like home."

"Not quite. At home we have food. I've only a small loaf and a jar of pickled herring left over from the journey. That's all until the shops open tomorrow."

"You could ask the old woman. I bet she's got plenty of provisions in her larder. Look at the size of her."

Katya smiled and hugged her coat around her. "I don't think so, do you? I can imagine the reception I'd get. And I can just imagine the roubles clocking up in her eyes like a cartoon character!"

Her daughter giggled, then sighed: "I wish father was here. She wouldn't dare say no to him. Not an important scientist."

Katya paled a little, but tried not to let the hurt show. Nevertheless her voice was terse when she spoke. "Well, little mother, he's not here, is he? Just like he's hardly been here for the last three years."

Yelina pulled a face. "But he *promised* he'd be here in his letter."

"I know, I know," Katya replied. She stood by the window and stared out at the failing sunlight dappling the pine groves and spreading a stain of shimmering gold over the sea beyond. Like the night shadows she felt her own fears closing in on her. "But he had to come a long way, and the weather can be bad in the east. I expect that's what held him up. So you'll have to put up with just me for a day or two more." She looked down at her daughter and smiled. "Now go and make up your bed, there's a good girl."

Yelina looked curiously at her mother, her head tilted to one side. "You *do* still love father, don't you?"

The challenge took Katya aback. It was so unexpected. Yet how could she expect to hide what had happened from her daughter who was so bright and observant? "I love Niki Shalayez as much as ever, and well you know it. Now, go and make your bed."

Yelina was happier now. As she walked lightly towards her bedroom, her mother turned back to the window. In just a few minutes it had become much darker outside. As the fiery sky was quenched by the sea she could see her own reflection in the glass and, momentarily, she imagined she could see the strong, dark features of her lover standing behind her. She shut her eyes and could feel his warm, slightly smoky breath on the back of her neck. His hands on her hips, feel him pressing against her buttocks.

She opened her eyes. He was gone. Hans was gone, and she prayed to God that he would never return. At their last meeting he said he would go back to Leipzig if she was ending their affair. She hoped that he meant it. With him gone she knew that she could cope. In time, she would force him from her mind, until the memory of his very existence became as faded as an old sepia snapshot from the family album. Dutifully she would work at rebuilding her life and her love with Niki. She had loved him since her teens and he had never done anything that hadn't endeared him to her. Only his work had forced itself between them. Now he was coming back. To stay. It would be different.

Outside it was dark. She felt unaccountably cold. Her

heart fluttered and she felt scared. Because, although she was reluctant to admit it, she knew that if Hans should ever walk up to the jewellery counter where she worked, it would start all over again. Their passion had erupted out of nothing, like a forest fire. An explosion of body chemicals. It had recklessly consumed them both, until she was hurtling totally out of control towards emotional disaster.

The knock on the door made her start.

Katya turned. No doubt it was the *babushka* back to complain about something. Or maybe to offer a working electric fire for a small bribe. Gathering her composure, she crossed the linoleum floor and readied herself to stand her ground. She flung the door open.

She was not prepared for the man in the black coat and trilby hat. Although he was no taller than she, his stocky frame seemed to fill the doorway with its dark presence.

"Comrade Shalayeza?"

She gulped. No words came. Malevolent eyes glinted from a swarthy face. The light behind her picked up the tiny droplets of perspiration glistening above his upper lip.

"Comrade Katya Shalayeza?" She was mesmerised by the snap of the words spoken through crooked teeth. His breath smelled of peppermint.

Saliva trickled into her throat and she found her tongue. "Yes. What is it?"

A red card flashed briefly in his hand before he returned it to his overcoat pocket. "Lieutenant Tatlin, KGB. This is official business."

"Oh." For a moment she was flummoxed. Then a thought struck her. "My husband? Is it about Niki? Has something happened?"

Tatlin didn't smile. "Nothing has happened to your husband. I should be obliged if you would come with me. It won't take long." It was very politely said, but the man's terse tone did not invite contradiction.

"Who is it?" Yelina's voice came from the bedroom.

Tatlin peered over Katya's shoulder at the child. "Your daughter, I believe?" The woman nodded, uneasy. "It's all right, little one, I just have to speak to your mother. Alone. It won't take long. We have an official chalet on the complex. Just a few minutes' walk."

"But – "

"She'll be safe here. The *babushka* will keep an eye on your chalet until we return."

Katya Shalayeza was still trying to reassure her daughter as Tatlin's large hand gripped her bicep and propelled her through the doorway. He did not speak as he steered her firmly along the flagged pathway that ran between the chalets. She was petrified at the suddenness of her abduction. Never before had she had such an encounter. The only KGB man she had ever met had been jovial Sergei Chagall, Niki's friend. But rumours of what happened to people in the hands of the organisation were well known to all Soviet citizens. The very mention of the name was enough to instil panic.

She told herself not to be irrational. She had done nothing wrong. There was nothing to be afraid of. Whatever this was about, she *knew* she had done nothing wrong. Perhaps there was some error on the pass they'd issued for her and Yelina to leave Tbilisi . . .? Some bureaucratic slip-up. Yes, that would be it. Hadn't the man assured her that she would return in a short while?

The air was distinctly chill now and she breathed it deeply to help calm herself. They passed the *babushka* on the path and the old woman stepped aside, scowling suspiciously. Katya raised her chin defiantly.

"In here, Comrade Shalayeza," Tatlin said suddenly.

The cabin was no different from her own. Sparsely furnished, the only obvious additions were a telephone and television.

Tatlin closed the door and indicated the uncomfortable looking settee. "Sit down."

Katya obeyed. "I really don't . . ."

For the first time something resembling a smile crossed the man's face. "No, Comrade Shalayeza, I don't suppose you do."

Puzzlement creased her forehead. "What do you want with me? I've all the right papers to leave Tbilisi."

He leaned back against the door and folded his arms across his chest. "Ah, yes. Tbilisi. And in Tbilisi did you know a certain Hans Hellmich?"

The sudden silence in the small chalet was stunning. Instantly Katya felt her cheeks colouring. A thousand and one questions begged answering. How did this KGB man know? Anyway, what did it matter? She could think of no reason, but still she sensed she was somehow in deep trouble.

On impulse she blurted: "No, Comrade."

"Tatlin," the man said easily. "Comrade Lieutenant Tatlin."

"I don't know him."

The hint of a smile died on the man's face. There was no outward sign now that he was enjoying the cat-and-mouse game of interrogation. No hint that he held all the cards. That he knew *all* about the woman's affair with Hellmich. That it had been he himself who had selected the handsome East German actor to play the role of Katya Shalayeza's seducer. Or that Hellmich had been the last of three prospective lovers they had needed to plant in her life before she eventually took the bait. Before they could start to roll the hidden cameras.

All these things Tatlin kept to himself. Instead he warned tersely: "Think very carefully before you repeat your denial."

"I said I don't – "

"*Carefully,*" Tatlin hissed. "Lying to the KGB can get you into a lot of trouble."

Pleading brown eyes looked up at him; her mouth was slack with bewilderment.

"And Flat 10, 33 Besiki Street? Have you ever been there?"

44

"No." Her voice had faded. She cleared her throat. "I don't think so."

"You don't think so?"

She hesitated. "I don't think so. I don't remember."

Tatlin nodded sagely. "The *dezhurnaya* at 33 Besiki Street remembers you, Comrade Shalayeza."

Damn, she would. Katya recalled the old crone in the ground-floor flat and the creak of the front door whenever she had crept past. And for a couple of roubles she'd remember or forget anything you asked – until a higher bidder came along.

Katya thought fast. "I think I may have delivered something there once or twice. The customers who called at my shop."

"Is it usual to deliver jewellery?"

She saw a glimmer of hope. "Sometimes, Comrade Tatlin. If it's been ordered. When it comes in I might take it round to the customer's address."

The man stopped leaning against the door. "I am sure such enthusiasm for work would win high praise from General Secretary Gorbachev. But shall we stop playing games? I'm sure you want to get back to little Yelina."

God, he even knew her daughter's name! How did he know so much?

Tatlin said: "You have been having a secret liaison with an East German national. One Hans Hellmich. We have the evidence, so do you really want to persist with your denial?"

Her heart was hammering in her chest. Tears of fear began to pulse from her eyes. "Have – have I done wrong?"

Slut, Tatlin thought contemptuously. "Morally, that is not for me to say. But Hans Hellmich is believed to have been recruited by West German Intelligence as a spy."

Her eyes widened. "But he's a construction worker . . ."

Tatlin sneered. "Even construction workers have been known to spy. He was recruited in East Berlin."

Katya couldn't, wouldn't believe it. Not Hans. "He comes from Leipzig."

The KGB man gave a snort of disgust. She was more stupid than he thought. "He worked on a site in East Berlin two years ago. He was recruited then."

The room was closing in around her. This was a nightmare. It made no sense. Her face was full of anguish as she looked up. "Even if this is true, Comrade Tatlin – what would a spy want with me . . .?"

No answer came. All Katya heard was her own question ringing in her ears. Then she heard herself say: "Niki, oh my God." Her voice trailed away.

"You have answered your own question. Your husband Nikolai Shalayez is an important Soviet scientist and mathematician. He is engaged on sensitive work."

Katya shook her head vehemently. "But I know nothing of his work. I couldn't tell Hans anything even if I'd wanted to."

For the first time Tatlin removed his trilby hat. His hair was black and thin, strands of it combed across to hide his balding head. "I believe you, Comrade Shalayeza. But ask yourself this: How would it look on the security report of your husband's file?"

Her mouth dropped.

"I will tell you. If word of this got out, it is possible that you would be sent to trial for complicity in treason. You would probably serve in a labour camp on the other side of the Urals. If you were lucky, in view of the questionable morality of your liaison, you might be sent for corrective treatment in a psychiatric clinic."

He watched with gratification as her lips curled in horror at his prediction. "As for your husband, what happened to him would be certain. He would be removed from the list of privileged scientists. He would no longer work on sensitive projects, or be allowed any senior teaching post. His loss of status would mean no housing priority or admission to special shops. The State and the Party would be obliged to treat him as a social leper. Your daughter would not be considered for any special schools. *That* is what would happen if your affair with this Hans Hellmich reached his security file.''

Katya stared gloomily at the floor as she felt the waves of shame flood over her. Slowly, she looked up. "You said *if*. You said *if* it reached his file.''

Tatlin held her gaze with deadpan eyes. "You are a lucky woman, Comrade Shalayeza. You are a lucky woman because we found out about this early enough, and because your husband has friends.''

"Friends?'' She didn't understand.

"I am acting on instructions from Comrade Colonel Sergei Chagall.''

"Sergei?'' It was all moving too fast for her.

"Colonel Chagall is responsible for the security screening of all personnel working on your husband's project. Luckily it was to him that this information was first passed. If we are careful it need go no further.''

For a moment Katya felt her heart lighten. Go no further? Oh, God, if only that was possible! Please, please, God, let that be so. "I'll do anything,'' she breathed.

Tatlin nodded. "That is good. Because we must take precautions. If ever this gets out we must be able to say *why* we did not take it further.''

Katya frowned. "What sort of precautions, Comrade Tatlin?''

"You must leave your husband.''

"What?'' She was incredulous.

Tatlin smirked. "Are you hard of hearing? You must leave your husband. That way we can claim that the security threat has been neutralised and therefore we considered any additional action against you unbeneficial to the State.''

"Never! Leave Niki?'' She stared at Tatlin as though he was mad. "I've been waiting for three years to be back with him again. If he hadn't been away I'd never have got involved with Hans in the first place."

"Exactly," the man said as though she had just made the point for him. "My understanding is that your relationship with your husband is at a low ebb anyway. So it should not be difficult for you to go before you get fond of each other again. You can take your daughter. Go to another city, far away. We thought perhaps Berezniki. We'll fix you up with a good job and a nice flat."

"Berezniki? That's miles away . . ."

"That's the idea," Tatlin said with a sneer.

"I won't do it." Defiant.

Tatlin nodded slowly, then ambled across the room to the television set. "Well, if you won't do it, Comrade Shalayeza, I am afraid we will have to. We will have to tell your husband and make sure that he never wants to see *you* again."

Katya felt angry and defensive. "Niki wouldn't believe you. I hardly believe what I did myself."

"And with Hans Hellmich to testify to your affair?"

"It would be my word against his!" Katya snarled.

Tatlin reached down to a black box set beneath the television and pressed the button to start the tape. Quietly he said: "Not quite, Comrade. Not quite."

The television flickered into life. Katya found her eyes drawn to the screen.

As the fuzzy image settled down, she was horrified to recognise a close-shot of her own face, her mouth wide and eager to take the engorged penis in front of her.

She felt sick with shame. Then suddenly, with startling clarity she saw her whole future spanning the years ahead, a bleak vision of friendless isolation, poverty and desperate unending loneliness.

2

The rain lashed down on windswept RAF Lyneham in Wiltshire all through the night. It was remorseless.

Even as he woke to the early morning call from the wardress of the laughingly called transit 'hotel', Mike Ash could hear the windowpanes rattling.

Instantly his lean six-foot frame sprang from the mattress. Years of Army life had instilled the need to shift smartly on reveille. If you didn't it could mean a missed breakfast or the humiliation of being last on parade. On active service it could make the difference between life and death.

He crossed the spartan room of cream-painted brick to the wash basin and peered at the cracked mirror. Bloodshot eyes registered his own face. A drink too many in the airforce camp's Pegasus Club bar last night. His usual cheerful expression was missing. His perpetual tan which extended to his bald crown was blanched in the stark light. He grimaced at the loss of his hair that had looked so striking in his wedding photographs seventeen years before. He consoled himself that he had a well-sculptured, distinguished skull and put the thought from his mind. After all, he smiled to himself, Yul Brynner hadn't done so badly in his time.

A swift and vigorous ten-minute exercise programme of press-ups, squats and sit-ups to tone up his hard body was followed by an equally rapid wash and shave.

Half an hour after his call he was waiting by the 'hotel' lobby in his DPM camouflage smock and olive lightweights, with his Crusader bergan hooked over one shoulder. He seemed oblivious to its weight.

The RAF orderly was ticking off the names of the motley collection of passengers gathered in the wet pre-dawn gloom. Cap badges were mostly Royal Marines, but there was a selection of insignia denoting everything from signals to artillery units.

"Captain Ash?"

"Yes."

The orderly glanced up and took in the sand-coloured beret with its famous winged-dagger badge. Twenty-two Special Air Service Regiment. "Right, that's all of you then. The bus'll take you round to the Wessex for breakfast. Try not to throw up at the sight of all them poached eggs floatin' in the vat. You're all just passing through, but we have to live here. Bus'll pick you up again at 0600 for your flight which leaves at 0635. ETA at Gardermoen is 0930 UK time."

Inwardly Ash groaned. Virtually three hours just to southern Norway courtesy of the draughty, lumbering RAF Hercules transport. But at least he'd be on his way again to rejoin his advance party from Mountain Troop. And even at the thought he felt the surge of adrenalin. As the bus ground towards the canteen through the curtain of driving rain that eddied across the airfield, he could already anticipate the crunch of snow beneath his feet and breathe the crackling sub-zero air.

Captain Mike Ash was a mountain man.

Over a breakfast of eggs swimming alongside two greasy sausages he recalled how it had all begun, many years before. As the son of a wealthy solicitor he had been introduced to skiing when it was still the sport of the privileged few. He was just into his teens when he first tasted the mountain air on an activity holiday organised by the boarding school that he loathed. Looking back he realised that, hurtling down the Alpine piste, he had experienced the feeling of real freedom for the first time in his life. For long, precious moments he could

50

forget the absurd Victorian disciplines of his father and the equally restrictive regime of the Roman Catholic school.

Hastily he washed down his breakfast with a mug of unsweetened black coffee. As he left for the waiting bus, it occurred to him that it was that same desire for freedom that had later led him to join the Army as an officer cadet. Whilst his contemporaries bemoaned the short-comings of the military, Ash soon discovered that, as with the rest of life, you got out in proportion to what you put into it. Self-discipline and determination came naturally to him, and he shortly found his efforts re-warded. Not just in his military career but also in his sporting activities. His skiing prowess was soon re-cognised, and that was quickly followed by the discovery of the almost masochistic joys of mountaineering.

And it was a continuation of that thirst for freedom and adventure that lured him, inevitably, to take the selection course for the Special Air Service Regiment. That had been twelve years ago, when he'd been just twenty-seven. Since that time he'd returned to the Regi-ment twice more and had also been on several major mountaineering expeditions, including assaults on both K2 and Everest.

The bus splashed over the concrete apron alongside the row of giant Hercules transport aircraft, their massive dark bulks like primeval monsters in the grey dawn drizzle. The bus lurched to a halt in front of one which had its cockpit lights aglow.

Thankfully there were only a dozen passengers so Ash was able to get one of the canvas knock-down seats by the hot air ducts beneath the wings. The cavernous hold was shared with three giant pallets of 105 mm howitzer ammunition and they were treated to the fairly rare sight of a trim female RAF loadmaster checking the cargo net.

Grins were exchanged as the treasures beneath the girl's straining fatigue trousers were imagined, but no one said anything. Conversation was never easy above the roar of four Allison turboprops, and Ash was thankful for that. He had a lot to think about on the trip.

By rights he should have gone to Norway with the recce team in early December to plan for the coming exercise in the New Year. Unfortunately it overlapped with a refresher course in Russian at the Army School of Languages in Beaconsfield. Yet it was the thought of being denied the snow that had really rankled. He had no doubt at all that the Mountain Troop's sergeant-major would make an excellent job of reconnoitring the various exercise locations and would put together a frighteningly realistic scenario.

No, there were no doubts about Brian Hunt on that score. He and Hunt had been good friends since way back and had come to respect each other's judgement and professionalism, as well as each other's company. Even in the Regiment, where the relationships between the various ranks were fairly informal, such close personal friendships between officers and NCOS were not common. At times it disappointed Ash that he could never persuade Hunt to take up mountaineering as a hobby and join him on one of his expeditions to the Alps or the Himalayas. But his friend had been adamant. He loathed the snow and the cold, and hated heights. He'd discovered that years before when he decided to give Mountain Troop a try for the sake of gaining experience. It was a mark of Hunt's professionalism that he'd become an acknowledged expert and veteran in Arctic warfare.

Mike Ash smiled to himself. He was sure he knew why his friend didn't transfer to something less arduous, like 18 Rover Troop. While routine assignments still provided Hunt with the greatest personal challenge to overcome, Ash had little doubt that his friend would continue to endure his own private hell without complaint.

Although he didn't know it yet, Sergeant-Major Brian Hunt was likely to get a sudden and no doubt welcome reprieve. Just before he'd left the Regiment's new barracks at Stirling Lines on the southern outskirts of Hereford, Ash had been summoned in to see the commanding officer.

Something was in the wind, the 'Old Man' had said. He had received a call from Commandant SAS Group in Whitehall asking to put a team on standby immediately after Christmas. The brigadier had been no more specific than that, except that the location would be Sweden.

The head of the Secret Intelligence Service station in Stockholm would meet him in Norway for a fuller briefing.

Mike Ash settled down to sleep through the remainder of the flight. Already next year looked promising.

RAF Flight 5764 touched down to find Gardermoen already firmly in the clutches of the Norwegian winter. As the propeller blades swung to a stop and the doors were opened, the searing cold rushed in.

Ash followed the others out and sniffed the air. Minus twenty centigrade, he decided. The airfield was as flat as the top of a Christmas cake and so brilliantly white that it hurt his eyes. The swirl of spindrift obscured visibility so much that it was hard to distinguish the deep gouges created by the huge wheels of the Hercules.

The dark snake of new arrivals wound itself towards the welcome warmth of the wooden PAX Lounge where travel arrangements were being sorted out by two harassed duty officers.

"Name, sir?"

"Captain Ash."

Deft fingers flicked through a stack of brown envelopes. "Ah, Ash, right. Nice to see that someone's organised. Take the train from Insvol up to Otta. One of your chaps will meet you there. Sign the rail pass please, sir." The man glanced towards the frost-encrusted window. "There's a truck leaving for the station now, sir. Just sling your kit in the back."

Within minutes Ash was hurtling down the road in the canvas-covered Royal Marines truck and was soon enjoying the gliding comfort of Norwegian State Railways as the train sped effortlessly northward.

It was snowing heavily by the time the train pulled into Otta in the mid-afternoon.

Brian Hunt waited by the Land Rover. The duvet worn beneath his camouflage smock made him look enormous.

"Hello, Brian. This is an honour."

Hunt grinned. "Welcome back to Noggyland, Mike. Couldn't risk the safety of our illustrious leader to Big Joe's driving." He took the captain's huge bergan and lifted it easily into the back. "Hope you've got a couple of turkeys in there? And a bottle or two."

Ash laughed. "No need. I've brought a much better gift."

"How's that?" They climbed aboard and Hunt gunned the engine. "Sjoa's only twenty-five klicks down the road. With any luck we'll be there before our balls turn to brass. The heater's U/S."

"Nothing's changed then."

Hunt peered through the slush-smeared screen. "What's this gift you're so smug about? I don't like the sound of it."

Ash said: "How does spending Christmas in Blighty grab you?"

The other man's face dropped. "What d'you mean?"

"There's something on in the New Year. We've been recalled and given Christmas leave."

"Christ, it must be serious. Any gen?"

"Not yet, except it looks like Sweden. There's someone coming up here to brief us."

Hunt concentrated as a massive articulated truck roared past them from the opposite direction, obliterating the road with a spume of slush. "Bloody woofters! – absolute menace." He relaxed again. "So it's a funny job, eh? But why isn't CRW dealing with it?"

"They're committed until February, and under-strength. We're available."

"Sounds interesting, anyway."

"But not the Christmas bit, eh?"

"Afraid not." Hunt smiled thinly. "It was looking good over here. We've some parties lined up and the local Noggy girls'll jump at the chance of coming. Not much else goes on round here."

Ash could understand his friend's disappointment. Since his wife Joan had divorced him, Hunt had buried himself in work. Annual holidays and Christmas just served to reopen old wounds. As an orphan he didn't even have a family to fall back on at such times.

Ash said: "Gabby wants you to come and stay with us again this Christmas. Like last year. The kids would love it, too. Uncle Brian's a firm favourite. Especially with young Jessica."

Memories of the pigtailed seven-year-old with her face full of freckles brought an involuntary smile to Hunt's lips. She was the second youngest of the Ash family's brood of five children. It was obvious, when he'd arrived at their sprawling Herefordshire farmhouse last Christmas, that they'd all been discreetly briefed that Hunt was very sad and lonely because his wife had left him. He could visualise Gabby kneeling down to explain it all to the indifferent and uncomprehending audience. Indifference by all, except perhaps Jessica. She had immediately held 'Uncle Brian's' hand and taken him under her wing. To her it was as natural as her assumed responsibility of Baby Walt, the newly arrived terror of the family. Hunt had been captivated by her and over the long and relaxing break he became painfully aware that Jessica could so easily have been the daughter he and his wife never had.

"How is she?" he asked.

"Fine. She often asks after you," Ash replied. "She's really enjoying her new form at school. By all accounts she's taken over that, too, just like she has the home. Takes after her mum."

He hesitated. "And how is Gabby?"

"Blooming as usual."

Hunt caught the nuance. "Blooming?"

"I'm afraid she's pregnant again," Ash laughed. "That's the trouble with the rhythm method. It's cost me a fortune over the years."

"You never mentioned you had another on the way, Mike."

"We didn't know. He must be a little chap because it didn't really show much and Gabby usually goes up like a balloon. And her timings have always been all over the place."

"Congratulations then," Hunt said. "I suppose it is in order?"

Ash grinned broadly. "Yeah, why not? The more the merrier. After five, one more doesn't make much difference. I just hope he's not like Baby Walt. I couldn't bear another trouble-maker like him. And as far as Gabby's concerned she can't have too many."

Hunt stared ahead. In the bland whiteness that made it hard to distinguish where the road stopped and the shallow embankments began, he kept getting visions of her when they had last met back in the summer.

Gabrielle Ash. Pale-skinned, fair-haired Mother Earth with eyes of robin's egg blue. Eyes that had a way of making you believe they could see right into your soul. Eyes that seemed to understand the truth behind your words, that tried to seek out your personal hurt. Hunt had never before come across such sympathy and understanding in a woman.

But then, perhaps there wasn't any other woman quite like Gabby. Now in her mid-thirties, she had always presided over her household like some queen bee. Ever cheerful she seemed to cope effortlessly with her continually expanding army of offspring, always having time for each and every one of them.

Constantly on the go, she ran the farm virtually single-handed when Ash was, as usual, away on assignment. It wasn't strictly speaking a working farm: the few head of cattle they owned were really pets, like the horses, chickens and geese. Mostly the land was rented out to other farmers for grazing or haymaking. In summer she took in bed-and-breakfast guests for both the pin-money and the company. It made for a hectically busy life.

On more than one occasion Hunt had called round to find her, heavily pregnant, underneath the battered family car or working on the ancient tractor in grease-stained dungarees. Yet despite all that, she still had time for making bread, jam and chutney in such vast quantities that it would have put a factory's output to shame. An output that, nevertheless, the family devoured at a prodigious rate.

But there was, Hunt knew, quite another side to her . . .

"BRIAN! WATCH IT!"

Ash's scream shattered his thoughts. In the nick of time he urged the Land Rover back over to the right-hand side of the road as the giant Norwegian 'woofter' trailer rig emerged from the swirling white-out with its air-horns blasting.

Hunt let out a slow hiss of self-anger. "Sorry, Mike. Didn't realise we were wandering."

Ash made light of it. "Can't see bugger all in this stuff."

"You'll be pleased to know we're almost there," Hunt said sheepishly. He rapidly changed the subject and recounted to the officer the team's encounter with what they believed to be a Spetsnaz undercover group.

Ash was intrigued. "Just like Afghanistan. The she-wolf."

"That's what I thought," Hunt agreed. Back in 1979 he and the captain had served on a clandestine three-man mission into the Russian-occupied territory to advise the *mujahideen* freedom fighters. Rumours that a Spetsnaz team had been sent to capture or destroy the SAS men had been rife. The rebel group leader had been adamant that they were led by a woman. Later intelligence reports suggested that he had been right.

Ash said: "I remember it was a very uncomfortable feeling. Uncanny. One I could do without."

"We're here," Hunt announced suddenly.

They slowed and turned in through the opening in a low wooden fence by a flagpole from which a Union Jack hung forlornly. A collection of snow-topped wooden chalets took shape through the curtain of falling white petals.

Hunt pulled up outside the largest of the buildings which became a self-catering tourist complex during the spring and summer months. "This serves as the mess for the duration."

As his friend went to get out, Ash placed a restraining hand on his shoulder. "So, Brian, what about Christmas?"

Hunt looked back. "Thanks, Mike. But I don't think so."

"Gabby asked me specifically to persuade you." He reached into his pocket. "Oh, and this is a personal invitation from Jessica."

Hunt took the pink envelope with its Snoopy sticker. *To Uncle Brian* was a fragile construction of small and capital letters.

Mike Ash laughed. "It's not too long, but the message is clear." At that moment a shaft of light came from the chalet as the door opened. There was no mistaking the bulk and the jug-ears of Royal Marine Sergeant-Major Dusty Miller outlined against the bright interior.

"Welcome to our home, Mike."

The two men shook hands.

"Good of you to put us up, Dusty."

"Pleasure. As between us we'll be the only British contingent in Norway until the New Year, we'd best

58

stick together." He led the way through the flagstoned room dominated by a vast open fire which threw out the heat like a blacksmith's furnace. "We mess here. You must have a drink before you go over to the bunkhouse and select your pit."

"That'd be welcome."

Instantly he recognised the other three men from Hunt's SAS team.

Bill Mather's ginger moustache and thin hair were immediately identifiable as he emerged from the book he was reading in the enormous easy chair. The veteran's skin had been burnished by the driving sub-Arctic wind so that the ageing freckles were all but unnoticeable. The eyes looked paler and greyer than ever. And as cold as always, except for the momentary glimmer of recognition and the brief smile of welcome.

"Season's greetings, boss!"

The call came from the massive bulk of Big Joe Monk who was hunched in mortal combat over a chessboard on the bench table. The whiteness of his big tombstone teeth was in contrast with the shaggy black moustache and the dark stubble on his chin.

Ash didn't have to look to know who his opponent was. There would be something wrong if it wasn't the long, lanky form of Len Pope. The two of them were inseparable, always together and always watching each other's back. They fought together and drank together; constant companions despite the continual repartee of wit and insult they traded. But if any man mistook that for mutual dislike and picked on one of them, he would be in for a terrible awakening. With names like Monk and Pope it was hardly surprising they'd been nicknamed the Unholy Alliance and many other less reverent names.

Miller had only just finished dispensing generous measures of Scotch all round when they heard a car pull up outside. A few seconds later the door opened to an inrush of snowflakes, and a large black Royal Marine entered.

"Sarn't-Major, taxi with a gent calling hisself Lavender. 'E's on the expected list."

Miller nodded. "Show him in, Appleton."

Next to the wrapped-up bulk of Marine Appleton, the man who entered looked emaciated by comparison, despite the thick sheepskin car coat he was wearing.

Ash stepped forward, offering his hand. "Mr Lavender?"

The man pulled off the fibre pile hat with heavy earflaps to reveal a thin, clean-shaven face already pinched with cold in just the few moments it had taken to walk from the taxi to the door.

His small pink mouth formed into a smile but Ash noticed that the dark eyes remained as hard and bright as anthracite. He could almost hear the hum of the appraising computer beneath the immaculately trimmed hair.

"Ralph Lavender. Visa secretary to our embassy in Stockholm." The voice was as precise and confident as his appearance.

"I'm Captain Mike Ash and this is Sarn't-Major Brian Hunt, my 2IC." He turned to Dusty. "Sarn't-Major Miller of the MAW Cadre. He's our host here at Sjoa."

Ralph Lavender had little time for social niceties. He completed his round of perfunctory handshakes in record time. Clearly he was a man in a hurry.

Declining a drink, Lavender said: "I'd rather get on. I want to return to Stockholm as soon as possible. Sod's law a problem will blow up the minute I turn my back." He smiled with thin humour. "Is there somewhere we can talk?"

Dusty Miller gestured over his shoulder. "Use the dining room. I'll see you're not disturbed."

Lavender didn't look impressed.

Hunt said evenly: "You're amongst friends here. There'll be no one listening at keyholes."

The visa secretary eyed the SAS sergeant-major uncertainly. He'd worked with members of the Regiment before and he never had felt relaxed in their company. They were prone to cynicism and gentle sarcasm which he found disquieting. For his liking they were too fond of nit-picking and finding problems that didn't exist. It had often left him with the feeling that they were questioning his own professionalism – one quality of which he had no doubt.

Without further protest he entered the dining room, and made straight for the carver chair at the head of the table. He removed his coat, tossed it into an armchair and took his seat.

Ash watched with faint amusement. Lavender was younger than he'd first realised. Probably still the right side of thirty. The grey mohair suit and neat woollen tie suggested suave sophistication, but the skinny body on which it hung, and his mannerisms, suggested a man who suffered from nervous tension. And the two-tone grey designer snowboots into which he'd stuffed his trouser cuffs signalled affectation.

Ash was convinced that the man's acerbic, almost aggressive attitude was probably a mask to hide a lack of confidence. Whether in himself or on the subject of the briefing the SAS captain wasn't yet sure.

Hunt closed the door.

Lavender said: "This is supposed to be a one-to-one briefing, Captain. For your ears only."

Ash smiled disarmingly. "Call me Mike. And Brian Hunt will be my second-in-command for whatever you have in mind. He may well end up running the operation. So you can say anything in front of him. It'll save me repeating it all as soon as you've gone."

Lavender smiled but only with his mouth. "Sorry, er – Brian, is it? No offence meant."

Hunt slipped into his chair. "None taken."

The man from Sweden lifted a briefcase onto the table and began unlocking the combination. "As you may have guessed, gentlemen, I'm now running the SIS station in Stockholm." He allowed himself a smug smile.

61

"Visa secretary is a bit less obvious than the usual cultural attaché."

A brief glance was exchanged between the two SAS veterans, but neither gave away their instinctive feeling of unease.

Lavender extracted a file. "I've been running this case from the Russian Desk at Century House in London. With our Stockholm man due for recall it seemed sensible for me to be in the position to see the assignment through, which is why I'm here. A potential defection is expected early in the New Year. That's why we want your team over to arrange a snatch in Stockholm."

"A snatch?" Ash queried. "Are you trying to say that this isn't a willing defection?"

"Oh no," Lavender protested. "It's willing all right. It's just that the defector is a very important figure in the Soviets' scientific community and he's likely to be kept under very close watch. Your job will be to evaluate the best and safest way to get him away from his KGB minders and spirit him out of the country. Then put your theory into practice."

Ash considered for a moment. "Trusted Soviets are usually allowed off the leash enough to slip their guardians. Maybe go shopping to buy something for the wife. Into a department store, change clothes in the toilets and then slip out by mingling with the crowd."

Lavender nodded. "Sure, but I don't think they'll risk it with this one. If we can do that, fine. But you must be prepared to intercede if necessary."

"A real hot potato, eh?" Hunt commented.

Ash said: "I don't need to tell you that Sweden is a neutral country, Ralph. A staunchly neutral country. Painfully so, sometimes. The Swedes aren't going to take too kindly to any sort of snatch on their territory. There'll be a lot of flak."

Lavender's pink mouth contorted into a twist of a smile. "I do know the country and the Government well, gentlemen. I've worked on the Swedish Desk, I speak the language fluently and I have lived there on and off for eight years. I can gauge their reaction. And we can take any flak there is – provided your operation is clean and fast. Once it's over, all they can do is protest about an unsubstantiated claim by the Soviets that one of their people has been taken. We'll simply deny any knowledge of it."

"And who is this extraordinary VIP?" Ash asked.

Lavender pushed across a glossy photograph. It had obviously been taken with a very powerful telephoto lens at the limits of its range. It showed the blurred image of a tall, slightly gangling man in a crumpled raincoat that was too short in the sleeves for his long arms. Ash put the age of the handsome, angular face at around forty. But it was a young-looking forty, and the unkempt mop of black hair gave him a slightly adolescent air.

"Dr Nikolai Shalayez. One of the Soviets' up-and-coming stars in the world of mathematical science. Age forty-one. Height: Six foot one. Weight: about eleven stone. Lots of nervous energy." Lavender paused as he read from the typescript. "Born in the village of Beresnik, about 140 miles south of Archangel. Educated locally but was noted at an early age for his mathematic ability. That led inevitably to Moscow University where he eventually earned a doctorate in pure mathematics. For the past sixteen years he has been engaged on various space research programmes. He has worked alongside the famous physicist Pavlovski at the Kurchatov Atomic Energy Institute in Moscow, and with Dudnikov at the Institute of Nuclear Physics at Novosibirsk. Inevitably there has been a shift from pure to applied mathematics as he has specialised. He has also been named to the Soviet Academy of Sciences for his specialist work and has published several papers which have received much acclaim in the scientific world."

Hunt was mystified. "I thought things like space research were all done by computer nowadays?"

Lavender nodded. "So did I. But Nikolai Shalayez's work is of the type that is so advanced that it is used to actually programme the computers in the first place. In fact that's just why he's so important to the Soviets. That's *exactly* the type of work he's been on for the past three years. First working out the theory and modifying it as the project develops."

"Project?" Ash asked.

"Yes, a very special project," Lavender replied, warming to his subject. "Ever heard of a place called Sary Shagan?" Both SAS men shook their heads. "Well, it's a top-secret research establishment set deep in Soviet Asia. It is there that work began on the charged particle-beam."

Hunt lit a cigarette. "Sounds like the legendary death ray you used to get in kids' comics," he mused. "Or something out of *Star Wars*."

Lavender grimaced as the cigarette smoke drifted in his direction. "You're not far off on both counts. It's in fact a ground-based anti-missile beam. Anything flying into it would be destroyed. Imagine it like an inverted invisible cone. Several of these sites around Moscow, for instance, would form a sort of protective bubble, making it virtually immune to attack from intercontinental ballistic missiles. Like a vast protective umbrella.

"The public don't realise that it was the threat of such a system to upset the old balance of MAD, as the experts call it – or 'mutual assured destruction' – that the Pentagon embarked on its Star Wars policy in the first place."

Ash interrupted. "Perhaps I'm being naïve, but this Star Wars business sounds very expensive. Why don't the Americans install a ground-based beam system like the Soviets?"

"Just restore the balance," Hunt agreed. "It's got to be cheaper than all that Star Wars stuff in space."

Lavender relaxed back in his chair. "Gentlemen, you have, in fact, put your finger on exactly why our friend Shalayez is so important to the Americans. You see, a couple of decades ago the United States began research into the possibilities of charged particle-beam technology under the name of Project Seesaw. After a while it was abandoned as being impractical – both in terms of generating sufficient power and controlling the beam within the atmosphere. Apparently it would have wavered all over the place and have been very inaccurate." Lavender put his elbows on the table and laced his fingers together. "So our American cousins put Project Seesaw on the back-burner. Not unnaturally they decided that if the Russians experimented on the same lines, they too would hit the same snags – and also decide it wasn't worth the candle to proceed. The Americans moved on to the more rewarding area of laser technology. Still with me?"

Ash smiled graciously. "Right behind you, Ralph. Presumably the Americans were wrong?"

"In the summer of '76 they got their first inclination that the Soviets hadn't been so easily deterred," Lavender continued. "A high-ranking physicist, Leonid Rudakov, was visiting the US fusion experiments at the Lawrence Livermore Laboratory when his various observations gave the first clue to US scientists that the Soviets had persevered with their early experiments on the charged particle-beam, and had made great advances."

"And had they?" Hunt asked.

"The Americans couldn't be sure. Their own scientific community was adamant that Rudakov's claims were highly unlikely. They were startled by the magnitude of such a project which would mean transforming laser and electron beams to soft X-rays to compress fusion fuel at low energy levels."

"Lost me," Hunt confessed.

Lavender wasn't to be deterred. "Rudakov let it be known that he was developing a $55 million machine called the Angara 5 to achieve this. Many sceptics put this down to a ruse by the Russians to get the Pentagon in a panic – so the US would divert billions of dollars of defence expenditure into a project that – in the end – just wouldn't work effectively in practice."

Ash nodded. "I believe the Soviets *have* done that before."

"That's true. Given the circumstances, you can understand the sceptics who thought that the Russians couldn't accomplish it. But then other facts emerged."

"Like?" Hunt pressed. He was finding himself increasingly fascinated by the scientific detective story.

"Like the intelligence discovery that the Russians had overcome the transmission of vast amounts of energy without burning up the cables – by using pressurised gas lines actually invented by the American ITT and General Electric companies!

"Then US Air Force Intelligence pinpointed a mysterious new research establishment at Semipalatinsk, near to Sary Shagan. When they studied the photographs the jigsaw fitted with Rudakov's wild claims. Another satellite detected traces of gaseous hydrogen and tritium in the upper atmosphere over the region – all that you'd expect from the testing of a charged particle-beam device.

"At least now some members of the Intelligence community were convinced. And not a little panic-stricken. You see, another test-site was discovered at Azgir near the Caspian Sea. This one was commanded by the PVO Strany – the national air defence force – itself. That suggested that deployment was far nearer than the early trials stage, which would have been under scientific control."

"Wait a moment," Ash interrupted. "All this was some nine years ago. Does that mean that these – what, charged particle-beams – are now deployed?"

Lavender's eyes flashed darkly, as though the SAS captain was asking an improper question. "I'm not at liberty to say. I can tell you that the whole thing is at a very advanced stage in Russia – beyond prototype. Full or partial installation in Moscow can certainly be expected by the end of the decade."

Hunt let out a long, low whistle. "No wonder there's been such a God Almighty rush on the Star Wars initiative in the States. How far behind the Soviets are they?"

Lavender shrugged. "Probably ten years. It took until 1980 for everyone to become convinced of the threat. Now they're falling over themselves to come up with counter-measures. The bottom line is that the Americans are so far behind that there's bound to be a very dangerous gap in defences. A gap which means that the Soviets could strike at the West with impunity because its own charged particle-beam defence would be installed. The threat of that alone would give the Kremlin massive leverage to get its own way in any number of political areas – not least more foreign adventures."

Ash said: "How long will this dangerous imbalance last?"

"Until the US can get its act together on Star Wars – but that's highly precarious state-of-the-art technology. Not to mention the need to win the battle against Soviet propaganda. As you might have noticed, in the meantime, Moscow is doing everything in its power to get the concept discredited, shelved or traded off in some wider peace treaty." Lavender hesitated. "So that imbalance, I'm afraid, is likely to last anything from ten to twenty years."

Hunt stubbed out his cigarette in the ashtray. "So this potential defector – er, Shalayez – would be an extremely important coup for NATO?"

Lavender straightened up in his seat. "Important is hardly the word. Crucial, vital. His breadth of work on the subject and his past co-operation with other experts like Pavlovski, Dudnikov and Rudakov put him in a unique position to crack the secrets of the charged particle-beam. Then the Americans can forget their own Star Wars counter-measures and simply match the Soviets on the far more economical use of ground beams. It would narrow that dangerous period of imbalance down to five or ten years." He stopped talking suddenly as though someone had thrown a switch. The hard black eyes darted between the two men, waiting for a reaction.

Ash said: "If chummy is that important to the Americans, then it figures that he's equally valued by the Soviets."

"Now you can see why I don't think he'll be allowed off the leash in Sweden." Lavender sounded impatient, although his face remained poker straight.

"Then I don't understand why he's being allowed to Sweden at all," Ash said coolly.

Lavender sensed the SAS man's cynicism. "It hasn't been easy for us to arrange. It's taken a long time and a lot of manipulation behind the scenes. Finally the Soviets have agreed to let him lecture at a series of seminars in Sweden, at the Rönkä Society. But he'll only be there for a week."

Hunt lit another cigarette. "And will he be alone? I mean is he married? Defectors can prove very liable to a change of heart if they've left a family behind. In fact the Russians usually insist that there's a close relative remaining on their soil so they can exert pressure if it's needed."

"Apparently his wife's recently left him," Lavender said easily. Then he chopped the subject like a guillotine. "But that's not really your concern." Clearly he didn't intend to elaborate.

Ash's lips tightened imperceptibly. After a thoughtful pause he asked: "So when do we move?"

Lavender's smirk of satisfaction was unmistakable. "First thing in the New Year. On January 4th you fly out to Stockholm as executives in Fiscex Holdings, a major financial group with fingers in all sorts of pies. They have a permanent liaison staff out there with one of the big Swedish investment houses and they've agreed to put you in one of the company apartments. I've a small briefing paper for your team to read so you can hold your own in any short casual conversation without breaking cover. They've seen fit to make you advertising people, so you don't have to worry about technical details." The glimmer of a smile suggested that Lavender thought it amusing to cast a team of burly heavyweights in such a delicate and artistic commercial role.

Ash however appreciated Fiscex's judgement. Many giant corporations collaborated with the security forces in providing cover for a variety of overseas SAS missions. He couldn't be sure if such co-operation was to win favour when it came to profitable Government contracts, or because the chairman always had an eye on future Honours Lists. Electronics firms were favourite because most undercover soldiers could chat authoritatively about either communications or radar.

He asked: "What about contact with our embassy? Brian and I know the head of Chancery there quite well. Matt Brewster's a good man."

The faint smile on Lavender's face faded. "Matt is indeed an excellent diplomat, Ash, but he's not in on this one. No one is. It's strictly need-to-know basis. I'm sure you can appreciate why. I will be your sole liaison. And your team will be giving the embassy a wide berth."

Ash didn't react, but in truth he wasn't happy. Lavender was probably excellent at his job, but somehow the SAS man doubted that he had the mature wisdom and on-the-ground experience of an old diplomatic hand like Matt Brewster. It was men like Brewster who formed the backbone of the British Diplomatic Service in the same way that senior NCOs ran the Army. Ash would have been happier with access to any advice that Brewster might have in handling what was evidently going to be a very sensitive assignment.

Ralph Lavender had reached the end of his briefing. He slid a buff folder across the table to Ash and began locking his case. "That'll fill you in on all the fine details, gentlemen. And if you've no further questions I'll be on my way."

After the intelligence officer left, Mike Ash called his men over to the bunkhouse to announce officially that they would be returning to Britain for the Christmas period. He outlined the general purpose of the job but did not enter into specifics. However it was sufficient to generate a buzz of eager anticipation.

Monk put the question they all wanted answered. "Do we get tooled up for this, boss?"

Ash nodded. "I'll get some suitable weapons driven over from here by a civilian contact; there are virtually no customs checks. We'll have them delivered to a safe house supplied by Fiscex." He picked up a sheaf of papers from the table. "Just one tip. Booze is horrendously expensive in Sweden, so make the most of your duty-frees. There's no Local Overseas Allowance for thugs."

At that moment, Dusty Miller made an appearance. "Sorry to intrude, Mike. But as your lads are off in the morning, we thought we'd throw you a farewell party. We're also holding a court martial for one of our blokes."

Instantly he had everyone's attention. Pseudo court martials were typical of how special forces dealt with internal discipline, and were a lot of fun for all involved – even, perversely, for the defendant.

"What charge?" Big Joe Monk asked.

"He managed to lose my bloody civvy skis on the way over here," Miller said with feeling. "And *then* he had the audacity to nick my bloody Noggy girlfriend. Chatted her up right in front of me in the mess, calm as you like."

"Them's serious charges," Monk decided.

"He'll be wanting a good defence lawyer then," Pope observed.

Miller smiled slyly. "You want the job?"

70

"If I do, then you can do away with the prosecution. He's as good as hung."

"You've got it." Miller turned to Ash. "And we'll want a judge. Someone unbiased and highly regarded."

Catcalls all round.

Miller continued unperturbed: " . . . And someone from outside the Cadre."

Ash agreed. They all knew that the inevitable guilty verdict would at least mean free drinks for all. A good start to the farewell party.

It was a promise that was to be more than fulfilled as the night wore on. Royal Marines and visiting SAS men packed into the bar, together with half a dozen girls from neighbouring villages, who relied on the annual presence of the British Forces to bring some welcome life and high spirits to an otherwise desolate area.

The unfortunate defendant in the 'court martial' wasn't informed of the impending trial until the last moment. His attempt to bolt was blocked by Big Joe Monk and Royal Marine Chalky Appleton who dragged him before the bench to a roar of cheers and jeers from the onlookers. Encouraged by Dusty Miller, the hand-picked jury were already shouting "Hang him!" enthusiastically, as they downed the drinks that kept coming as fast as the barman could serve them.

A very sombre Mike Ash called for order, and proceeded to listen in great earnest to the charges alleged by Miller.

From the back of the courtroom Brian Hunt and Bill Mather sipped their drinks and watched with quiet amusement. Although the 'charges' sounded pretty fatuous, they had arisen from a series of incidents which had displeased the young Marine's colleagues in the Cadre. Social rather than military misdemeanours. It was a light-hearted but effective way of telling a rather cocksure Marine to mend his ways.

"The defendant, having been accused of losing the skis he was responsible for, told the sarn't-major that he didn't consider it to be his responsibility," Monk declared, having assumed the role of prosecutor. "This charge was aggravated by the defendant chatting up the sarn't-major's girlfriend the next night and disappearing with her. He was a member of the Cadre ski team, which was due to compete with a local Norwegian side the next morning. The accused failed to materialise – this charge being related to the last." Monk turned to the audience sporting a wide grin. "To this I add a charge of my own, that the defendant has a big bottom which exceeds accepted Royal Marine specifications!"

A howl of derision rose from the spectators along with more cries of "Hang him!" and "Guilty!"

Len Pope made a deliberately appalling job of the defence, until the defendant dismissed him. The jury's verdict was a foregone conclusion.

Finally someone produced a piece of black rag which Mike Ash placed on his head before solemnly pronouncing sentence: "You shall be taken forthwith from this place, where you shall be stripped naked and rolled in the snow until you are bloody cold. Then you shall be readmitted on condition that you buy all those present one round, while you drink two pints of Elk's Milk . . ."

A groan of sympathy went up from the onlookers. Disgust for the local Norwegian milk was shared by everyone who'd ever tried it.

The guilty man's run for it was short-lived before, inevitably, the sentence was carried out with due ceremony.

From where he stood Hunt could just see through the door to where the young Marine was being held down in the snow.

"Just deserts, eh, Brian?" It was Ash.

Hunt pulled a smile. "Rather him than me. Must be minus thirty out there tonight. Drink, Mike?"

Ash shook his head. "No thanks." He hesitated. "By the way, have you decided what I can tell Gabby? About Christmas?"

"Okay if I let you know tomorrow?"

'Sure."

The riotous proceedings ground on. The defendant returned, dried himself, and bought the expected rounds. Nevertheless, he insisted on remaining dressed only with a towel around his waist while he engaged the Norwegian girls in his well-proven chat-up line. Some time around eleven Hunt noticed that both the defendant and one of the girls was missing.

So much for justice, Hunt mused.

He turned to Mather. "I'm turning in, Bill. I'll have to oversee the packing tomorrow, and I'd like to run a few klicks first thing. Blow the cobwebs off."

Mather smiled. "Anyone ever told you you take soldiering too seriously?"

Hunt shook his head. "Never."

He stepped out into the sudden quiet and stunning cold of the night. The snow was still falling steadily and he crunched across the ground to the bunkhouse.

He paused on the verandah and looked back to the lights of the bar. Just the faintest burble of voices penetrated the eerie muffled silence created by the snow.

Thoughtfully he lit a cigarette and watched the smoke being whisked away into the velvet night. Christmas? Gabby? Her face appeared before him again as it had on the drive from the station. For a second it was crystal clear. A translucent hologram against the black sky. Then gone.

No, he decided, he wouldn't go. He'd decided not to visit Ash's farmhouse again, back in the summer. It just wasn't worth it. And nothing had happened to make him change his mind. He would tell Ash some distant relative had phoned up with an invite and he was obliged to go.

He'd just go back to his bedsit flat in Ledbury. He'd kept it on since the break-up of his marriage. Somehow to have returned to living permanently in the sergeants' mess would have been to admit to himself that it really was all over, without hope of reconciliation. Besides, he sometimes welcomed the privacy it gave him. At times like these.

He decided he would stock up with booze, and drink and sleep his way alone through Christmas. It wouldn't be so bad.

Then he remembered the letter.

He reached in his smock and extracted the crumpled pink envelope. Thumbing it open, he lifted out the matching paper. The childish hand was really remarkably neat:

Dear Uncle Brian,
Daddy says you are not coming to us for Xmas this year. You will be on your own. I want you to come. So does Mummy and Walt. And Sammy and Jason and Toby. And Biff our new dog. Actually he's mine. You will like him. Please, please, come and see me.
Lots of love
Jessica xxx And Biff too xLick!x

Hunt stared at it. Snowdrops melted on the paper and the ink broke into starbursts and began to run. He felt the lump in his throat and swallowed hard.

He carefully replaced the letter in his pocket and went into the chalet.

Alice Tate was a five-foot-one tower of indignant rage.

The slightly balding sable coat, which had been her most prized possession for nearly half the seventy years of her life, added considerable bulk to her frail frame. Unfortunately the presence it created was somewhat offset by the fur hat which had been knocked comically askew when she had struggled with her luggage through the revolving doors of the Hotel Ukraine.

However the sour-faced reception clerk did not find it amusing. "It is no good. We have no reservation for you," she declared loftily.

74

Alice Tate seethed. She had just endured an excruciating Aeroflot flight from Heathrow which had run out of drink before the trolley reached her and her companions. Then followed a two-hour mêlée in the customs hall at Moscow Sheremetyevo Airport whilst each passenger's luggage was searched. She was still smouldering at the confiscation of her copies of *The Lady* and *Country Life* when she arrived at the plush Cosmos Hotel – only to be told that her party had been double-booked. They were redirected to the splendidly Gothic edifice of the old Ukraine which did not even have a bar. And, God, how she needed a stiffener!

Her umbrella rapped sharply on the reception desk. Alice was an old Russian hand; she knew how to deal with the sluggish obstinacy of petty bureaucrats. "Now listen to me, young lady. We are tired and hungry and fed up with being messed about! The Cosmos knew we were to be booked in here, so *you* certainly should. Now look sharp!"

The clerk's sullen features took on the frozen expression of a mask. "I cannot help that. You are not listed. You will have to speak with your Intourist guide."

Alice peered over the top of her spectacles. "We do not have an Intourist guide. We are not with a group."

The clerk scented triumph. "I see. It is better that you come with a group. You will have to see someone at the Intourist desk."

"Where is it?" Alice demanded.

"Here. In the hotel lobby."

Alice's nostrils flared. "Is it open?"

A shrug. "Tomorrow. At nine o'clock."

That did it.

In the long queue that was beginning to form behind her, Daphne Withers sensed that the explosion was imminent. Alarm showed in her kindly liquid brown eyes and in the expression on the face of crinkled white parchment. She knew her companion all too well, and could recall the wartime days when Alice's short temper

75

had landed them in serious trouble. More than once.

Her thin hand reached out in constraint. But it was too late.

Without blinking Alice had resorted to gutter Russian. "Listen, you lazy cow, I've been coming to Moscow since before you were born! I've met you and your sort a million times before. No wonder your country is in such a mess. Have you no pride?" she demanded. "Now fetch the manager this instant before I report you to your commissar. What would dear Mr Gorbachev think if he knew this was how you treated friends of your great nation!"

The clerk's mouth dropped. Never in a million years would she have expected such a tirade of abuse from this genteel old Englishwoman. And all in perfect Russian slang.

"Do go steady, dear," Daphne Withers warned. "Remember your blood pressure."

"There's nothing wrong with my blood pressure," Alice hissed from the corner of her mouth. "At least nothing a good brandy wouldn't put right."

Drawing herself to her full height the clerk prepared for a counter-attack. "If there is no room, there is no room. You are not listed. That is someone's mistake."

Alice bared her pearly white bottom set. "And presumably *not* yours?"

Suddenly a new voice joined the conversation. It was resonant, authoritative, and male. "Can I be of service, madam?"

Alice turned and peered over her spectacles. She had been expecting some officious hotel busybody, not the broad, smiling face with the charming grin and curly brown hair that hardly belonged to a middle-aged man.

"Sergei!" It was Daphne Withers who recognised him first.

"Good Lord!" Alice exclaimed. "What on earth are you doing here?"

76

Sergei Chagall smiled widely. "I was looking for you ladies at the Cosmos. They said they'd sent you here . . ."

"Well, never mind that now," Alice interrupted irritably. "You're here now, that's what matters. So you can help sort out this stupid nonsense. This silly gel says they have no booking for us."

The receptionist was looking on warily. The big, distinguished-looking newcomer in the grey coat looked like someone with *blat*. She decided to hold her tongue, and was immediately thankful that she had.

It was a stern-faced Chagall who turned on her and discreetly flashed the red KGB pass. "You always have reserve rooms. Allocate one to these good ladies immediately. And make sure it is a good one, and that the radiators work."

Daphne Withers ventured forward, a little hesitantly. She wasn't one to push herself. "Actually, Sergei, we had asked for two rooms . . ."

Chagall bowed from the waist. "My dear Mrs Withers, how delightful. A room each is it?"

Her white cheeks flushed petal pink; he was so handsome for a Russian. "You have forgotten, Sergei, this time we have my granddaughter with us. Alice and I will share, but Lucinda will much prefer a room of her own." She leaned forward conspiratorially until Chagall could smell the lilac toilet water. "She thinks we're such old fuddy-duddies."

The reception clerk grunted. "No single woman on her own. It is the rules."

Chagall ignored her, and looked past Daphne Withers to the young girl who stood next in the queue. "This is your granddaughter?"

"Oh, yes," Daphne exclaimed. "How rude of me! Lucinda, dear, this is the nice Mr Chagall I told you about. He always looks after us so well; a good dear friend. Sergei, my granddaughter, Lucinda Marsh."

The Russian blinked. It was amazing. Lucinda must

have been in her very early twenties to have such an unblemished complexion. Sad brown eyes looked balefully up at him from below the blonde fringe that peeped below a stylish, if impractical, wide-brimmed hat. Even the modern shapeless coat failed to hide the fact that it covered a slender figure.

"Mr Chagall." She extended a slim gloved hand. The full, slightly sullen lips broke into a smile that transformed her face.

It was all so familiar. He felt that he'd known her for years. Quite remarkable. He lifted her hand and pressed it to his mouth. "Lucinda. I'm charmed."

"I can see that," Alice muttered out of the corner of her mouth to Daphne.

Lucinda looked coy. "It's lovely to meet you, Mr Chagall. I've heard so much about you from my grandmother and Aunt Alice."

Chagall was reluctant to release her hand. "And none of it true, I assure you . . ."

Alice prodded him with her umbrella. "It's all perfectly true, you old rogue! Now come on and let's get this room business sorted out before this queue stretches all the way to Red Square. They say Lucinda can't have her own room."

Reluctantly Sergei Chagall turned back to the desk. "Miss Marsh has her own room, unaccompanied or not. If there is any trouble with the manager, just refer him to me."

With that the receptionist complied with bad grace and the problem was resolved. With an air of military authority Chagall marshalled two porters to attend to the luggage, then escorted the ladies to the ancient lift and up to their floor.

The room was austere, high-ceilinged and so large that the twin beds, two armchairs and coffee table failed to fill it adequately. Even the long drapes and scatter rugs on the parquet floor did nothing to absorb the hollow atmosphere of a mausoleum.

Alice peered into the bathroom.

Chagall laughed. "You have remembered?"

"I *never* forget certain things when visiting your dear country, Sergei. My late husband always had plans to manufacture and export bath and sink plugs to Russia. Unfortunately he never got round to it, otherwise I would be a millionaire."

Daphne cautiously tested one of the beds. "Oh dear, it's a bit stiff. And the springs squeak."

"You're only going to be sleeping on it," Alice chided testily, "not trampolining. Now first things first. I expect we're all dying for a cuppa."

She took her suitcase which the porter had delivered with astonishing efficiency, opened it and extracted her heating element for making tea. For several minutes she busied herself organising the mugs she'd brought and filling them with murky tap water.

"Alice, this really is against hotel rules," Chagall scolded, unable to hide his amusement.

"Fiddlesticks," she retorted. "We English never go anywhere without our tea. And you of all people should know that rules in Moscow are only made to be broken. Now, no milk for you, right?"

When they were finally seated with their drinks, Alice produced a hip-flask from her suitcase and passed it round.

Daphne and Lucinda declined, but not so Chagall. He smacked his lips appreciatively. "Beautiful stuff. To tell you the truth I much prefer brandy to our native vodka." He grinned happily at the gathering. "And now, ladies, what do you want to do while you're in Moscow?"

"We're here especially for the Winter Festival," Daphne said. "It's always so lovely and Lucinda is so looking forward to it. We wondered if you might be able to use your influence to get us all the best circus and theatre tickets, and for the carnivals at Luzhniki Stadium."

Chagall faked a frown. "And you suggest I should use my *blat* in this way?"

"We'd be most grateful," Daphne said, smiling sweetly.

Alice grunted. "C'mon, Sergei, you old devil, do you want Daphne to sit up on her hind legs and beg? She would too."

"Really!" her companion protested.

The Russian roared with laughter. "Anyone who has belonged to our Friendship Society for as long as you two gracious ladies deserves the best! And no begging." He turned suddenly to Lucinda who sat on the bed. Without her topcoat she now looked very trim in jeans and sweater. "And what would our delightful young lady like to do on her first visit?"

She smiled. "I'd like to do all those things. But I'd also like to meet some real Russian people."

Chagall cocked an eyebrow. "You speak the language?"

"*Da. Eezveenee'te mayo plakho'ye praeznashé-nye.*" Lucinda giggled. "You see I'm still studying!"

"Your pronunciation is beautiful," Chagall reassured. "I'm sure such a pretty and fluent speaker will be a big hit at some of our parties over New Year. I shall see if I can bend the rules and arrange it."

Alice said: "Everyone will be booked up already over New Year, Sergei. Why don't we be very English and have a *Christmas* party?"

"At my *dacha*?"

"Why not, if that's possible. And *if* you can get them to bend the rules to let us go there."

Chagall dismissed the tourist restrictions with a wave. "There is no real problem. I have influential friends – as indeed do you. I can ask all your old acquaintances. Muscovites and those English living here."

"But no one from our embassy," Daphne added quickly. "They're awfully nice, but it will only make your people ill-at-ease."

"As you wish, my dear Mrs Withers."

Sergei Chagall agreed to get everything organised and, after draining both tea and brandy, left the three women to settle in.

Alice stared at the door after he'd closed it. "What a damn charade."

Daphne Withers cocked her head on one side. "But he really is such a nice man. He's always so good to us. And so handsome too."

Her companion looked reproachfully over the top of her spectacles. "It would be much better if you didn't constantly make moon eyes at him, Daphne. It's embarrassing. He's young enough to be your son." She lowered her voice. "Besides, the man's a nasty little shit, as well you know."

Daphne retreated into silence and began to unpack her case.

Lucinda Marsh lit a cigarette and felt relaxed for the first time since her arrival in Moscow. Thoughtfully she crossed to the large window where Alice was now standing, looking out. The wind was rattling the ill-fitting casement, and outside the silver grey waters of the Moskva river drifted sluggishly between the snow-covered embankments.

Lucinda shivered. It all looked so cold. "Did it go as you wanted, Alice?"

The old woman tapped the side of her nose and smiled. Then she touched her ear.

Lucinda nodded, and turned away.

Alice Tate resumed her silent study of the trolley buses rushing over the bridge below. She knew full well that every room in the hotel was wired. If the authorities were suspicious they could plug in whenever and to whoever they wanted.

And no one caught out Alice Tate like that. She'd been at it far too long. She had worked for MI6 ever since 1939. Because of her husband's family and business connections, and her own fluency in Russian, she had been a natural for the Soviet Desk, and that work had assumed even greater importance in the years of frosty peace that followed.

Rarely since the war had she visited Whitehall. Her instructions invariably came by special courier so there had been little to associate her directly with the British Intelligence establishment. She was just a rich, slightly dotty old lady who'd taken Russia to her bosom.

Since her husband's death she'd joined every Anglo-Soviet friendship society and club there was, taking every holiday and cultural exchange going. For ten years now she'd been teamed permanently with Daphne Withers, whose own wartime history had been with MI5. They made an effective, efficient and totally disarming team.

She knew that the lower echelons of KGB operators mocked foreign Russia-lovers like herself and Daphne. *Govnoed*, they called them behind their backs, shit-eaters. And it amused her.

Little did they know, she thought, and she listened to the wind moaning around the towering pinnacle of the Hotel Ukraine.

3

Sergei Chagall picked up the three women in his chauffeured black Chaika and drove them directly to his *dacha*. The log-built country house was situated twenty miles from Moscow, set in a compound of several similar buildings in a picturesque riverside setting.

The two guards on the gate had a brief discussion with Chagall then, after repeated suspicious glances at the female passengers, reluctantly waved them through.

"It's beautiful," Daphne observed, looking at the glistening rows of silver birch lining the snow-covered drive.

"Lovely," Lucinda agreed.

The Chaika drew to a creamy smooth halt before the wooden steps that led to the door of the two-storey building. From inside came the steady hubbub of voices and the strains of Western music.

As they entered a round of applause rose from the gathering of guests who had become friends and acquaintances over the many years that they had been making regular visits. Their welcome was warm and exuberant, suggesting the guests had wasted little time in starting on the vast and colourful array of vodkas, wines and champagnes.

It was all very Russian, despite Chagall's efforts to find fruit cake, turkey pieces and even a Christmas pudding. The overflowing food tables were dominated by red and black caviar, smoked salmon and cold sturgeon in aspic. There were herby salad dishes and pies with meat and cabbage fillings.

"You even have a Christmas tree!" Lucinda exclaimed. "How absolutely delightful."

Chagall smiled. "Actually, I have a confession to make. In fact, it's a *yolka* – a tree for New Year. But the purpose is the same." He glanced around to see if there was anyone close to him. "Lucinda, your grandmother and aunt seem very occupied with old friends. It may be a good chance for you to meet a very dear friend of mine. Would you like that?"

Her smile widened. "Of course."

He put his arm around her shoulder and steered her gently through the crowd. "His name is Nikolai Shalayez. He is a mathematician. A scientist. I believe you have studied mathematics at university?"

Again the sullen lips ripened into a smile. "Yes, yes I have." As she spoke, she was sure that her voice had quavered. Her heart was going like a trip-hammer.

She was hardly aware of what Chagall was saying. "Then he will love to speak to you. He lives for his mathematics – oh, but you will not find him boring. He has a good sense of fun. But he doesn't know many people here. He's only recently back in Moscow, and this isn't his circle."

"Poor man must feel lost," Lucinda said.

"More than you think. I am afraid his wife has left him. So he's a little depressed, although he hides it well. I am sure you will cheer him up. But I'm afraid his English isn't very good."

It seemed to take an age as Chagall led her through the crowd, frequently stopping to introduce her to various guests. She used the time to regain her composure, and to control the erratic thudding of her heart by regular breathing as she had been taught. With difficulty she resisted the urge to seek out Nikolai Shalayez herself. She knew exactly what he looked like. They had taken that precaution against any attempt at subterfuge.

84

Her smile became fixed as she shook hands with strangers, their faces a blur and their names meaningless. She found her mind wandering. What would she think of him? His photographs looked promising, but he was much older than any of the boyfriends in her university crowd.

More to the point, what would he make of her? She knew full well what everyone *hoped*, but it was far from guaranteed. She was fully aware that it was all down to her to make it work. A tall order for the twenty-one-year-old daughter of a retired British Army brigadier.

To think that last summer she was Lucinda Court-Ogg, just another graduate from Oxford with a degree in Russian, and with no more exciting plans for the future than a trans-Europe trek in a battered Land Rover with her old college friends. At the time she couldn't imagine why her father wanted her to come to tea with him at Claridges and to meet one of his old regimental chums. Even more astounding was the distinguished gentleman himself who intimated that there was a way she could help her country for which she was uniquely qualified.

Looking back on it, she had been astoundingly naïve. It wasn't until much later, when she met Daphne Withers at a briefing in a remote country house in Hampshire, that it began to dawn that this was a job for the security service. And a potentially dangerous job at that.

Fresh from university and with only two past boyfriends to her credit, she had found herself cast in the unlikely role of *femme fatale*. Her father, she knew, would have been horrified if he'd known the nature of the assignment; she was fascinated. Her briefing and short training period was as exciting to her as it was unreal. Until now. Suddenly it all seemed frighteningly real.

"Ah, Niki, there you are!" Chagall greeted. "I wondered where you'd been hiding. I might have known you'd be in with the vodka bottles. I'd like you to meet an English guest of mine. Miss Marsh . . ."

She saw it then. The momentarily frozen expression in Nikolai Shalayez's eyes said it all; then the rapid blink of a double-take. Was it recognition, or confusion?

"Pleased to meet you." She offered her hand and the Russian took it. His skin felt warm and dry. The fingers were strong for the hands of an academic.

"Lucinda, this is my good friend Niki."

"Lu-cin-da." The Russian took each syllable at a time, testing them cautiously. Immediately she noticed how striking his eyes were: deep violet. "Lu-cinda? Ah, that sounds like a – er – very pretty name. Yes? I am sorry, my English is not good."

His smile was infectious and she laughed easily. It helped to relieve the tension. "It is very good. Very clear enunciation."

Shalayez raised an eyebrow. "I do not understand."

"Your English is good," she laughed. "*I* understand you."

The penny dropped. "Ah, good, good."

Chagall said: "Lucinda speaks Russian, Niki. How about that?"

He seemed genuinely impressed. "Yes?"

She looked embarrassed and shrugged. "Like your English, I am not too sure," she said in Russian with a fluency that surprised herself. "I have studied it at university."

Instantly, she could tell that Niki was pleased to revert to his own tongue. She suspected that the array of empty vodka glasses on the drinks table belonged to him. If his mind had been clearer, no doubt he'd have done better. "That was very good indeed – especially for one so young. Why did you decide to learn Russian and not, maybe, French or German? Or Spanish?"

Suddenly, Lucinda was back at the country house in Hampshire. The endless hours of repetitious questions had worked. Her answer was almost too pat: "There are so many language students. There's a lot of competition, so I decided to learn one that is more unusual."

Chagall interrupted. "You must excuse me. I see your Aunt Alice is waving to me. I will see you later."

As he disappeared, Shalayez seemed less at ease. He shifted his weight from one foot to the other. She knew then that the personality file had been right, Nikolai Shalayez was no socialite.

It was as though his mind had been miles away and Lucinda's arrival had taken him by surprise. "I forget my manners. You do not have a drink, Lu-cin-da."

She smiled. "Please, call me Lucy."

"Lucy?"

"It's short for Lucinda."

"Lucy. Ah yes, that is easier. I say it right?"

"Yes, and, thank you, I should love a vodka."

"Which sort?"

"Just an ordinary vodka."

Shalayez grinned. "I see this is your first visit to the Motherland – Lucy. You see there are so many vodkas. Cherry or lemon for instance. Or *zubrovka* which is flavoured with a special grass. Then *ryabinovka* which has been steeped in ash berries . . ."

"Goodness." Lucinda was genuinely surprised. "What would you recommend?"

"I think you must try *starka*. A dark, old vodka that is very smooth."

She laughed. "Then I'll try it, thank you, Niki."

She watched, fascinated, as he selected a bottle from the range on the adjacent drinks table and found her a clean glass. It really was quite a relief to find that he was far more attractive than his photographs indicated. His smile looked really genuine and she found his obvious shyness quite appealing. He had evidently had a haircut recently and the shaggy black hair she'd seen in the photograph was now smartly combed.

"There, Lucy, one *starka*. And try this honey-cake from the Ukraine. Always in Russia we eat when we drink."

She raised her glass. "To a happy Christmas."

He clinked her glass with his. "Happy Christmas, Lucy. But in Russia it is New Year we celebrate."

Lucinda nodded. "Yes, of course. Silly of me. That's why I'm here with my aunt. For the Winter Festival."

"Ah yes, you will enjoy that."

She took another sip of vodka, allowing herself a slight frown. "But really I should like to see more of the *real* Russia, you know? I'm not sure who to ask."

A slow smile crossed Shalayez's face. "You could try asking me?"

Lucinda was delighted – success. "Would you show me?"

"Why not?"

"Wouldn't your wife mind?"

He seemed to be staring into her eyes. "My wife? No, I am alone in Moscow . . ." His voice trailed off sadly, and his eyes glazed over as though he were concentrating on some abstract thought. He appeared to come to a decision. "You may as well know. There is no point in hiding it. The truth is I haven't yet come to believe it myself."

"What?" She wondered what he was going to say.

He smiled thinly. "That my wife has left me."

She could feel the hurt in his words. "I am so sorry, really."

The sparkle returned to his eyes. "So you see, I would welcome the chance to show you around Moscow, little Lucy. For me it would be a real pleasure."

For a moment they looked at each other, smiling, and raised their glasses.

"*There* you are, dear!" It was Daphne Withers. "I've been looking everywhere for you."

Nikolai Shalayez waited with growing trepidation.

For ten minutes he had stood beneath the towering yellow stone archway gates to Gorky Park. Although the Moscow sky was unusually clear and blue, the wind was from the north and its cutting edge bit through the woollen trousers where they were unprotected by his heavy overcoat. He turned his face to the sun, stamped his rubber overshoes on the hard-packed snow and thrust his hands deep into his pockets.

Would she come? He knew little about Western women and their ways. Perhaps it was customary not to turn up, if they had second thoughts about a date? He knew he'd been a little drunk at the party Sergei Chagall had thrown for the two little old English ladies. But he had taken care to sound lucid when he spoke to Lucy. He had tried hard to be polite and friendly. He recalled how genuinely pleased she had sounded when he offered to show her around Moscow.

Or perhaps it was *she* who was being polite, and afterwards decided that she didn't want to be in the company of a man old enough to be her father.

He felt his heart sink. That young woman had lifted his spirits for the first time since that dreadful night in Sochi, when Katya had told him she was leaving. For two precious hours he had felt himself mesmerised by her uncanny resemblance to his wife. Yet when she spoke with those same beautiful pouting lips, her words were light and almost musical. Charming. And the pupils in those dark brown eyes had been wide with warmth and curiosity as they began to chat about their lives and interests. Amazingly, one of hers had been mathematics.

An involuntary smile came to his lips as he recalled their shared jokes. God, if Sergei had seen them, he'd never have heard the end of it! Talking to such a sweet creature about mathematics! Yet they had. They had talked, discussed and joked like two old friends, the years between their ages shortening to the point of non-existence.

A sudden thought struck him. Had he really bored her rigid?

"NIKI!"

He turned. His heart soared as he saw the figure,

swamped in a fur coat and snowboots, waving from farther down the avenue.

Lucinda was breathless by the time she reached him. "Oh, Niki, I'm so sorry I'm late. I got lost on the Metro. I can speak Russian better than I can read it. I'm afraid I got on a train going the wrong way!"

He grinned widely with relief. "No, no, Lucy," he protested. "It is my fault. I shouldn't have arranged to meet you here."

Big brown eyes peered up from the small area of face exposed between her collar and the large fur hat. "You didn't want to come to the hotel – I understand that."

He shrugged, uncomfortably. "Perhaps I am silly. But, you know, if we Russians speak to Westerners, we are supposed to report it to the authorities."

She nodded. "Yes, I know. On the Metro I asked a man the way. He was in some uniform and he understood what I asked. He pointed it out on the map, but refused to say a word."

"Yes, that is why. If he didn't speak, he can argue he didn't have to report it. That is why, if we are seen at the hotel, some *stukach* could cause trouble."

"*Stukach*?"

"Informer," Niki replied. He stepped back and looked at her appreciatively. "Lucy, you are looking very fine. Very Russian."

She giggled. "Oh, this stupid hat and coat. They belong to my Aunt Alice. She insisted I should wear them because of the cold. They're miles too big."

"But very becoming. You are certainly warmer than me, I think. Like a big cuddly bear." He laughed as she wrinkled her nose at the suspected insult. "In Russia it is a compliment to be compared with our national symbol, Lucy! I promise you."

She linked her arm through his. "I'm not sure I believe you. But anyway, let's walk and get warmed up. If I'm cold, you must be *freezing*."

But in truth Shalayez had forgotten about the weather.

This girl had that effect on him. A couple of minutes ago, he had thought his memory had been betrayed through alcohol and wishful thinking, their first meeting a badly remembered dream. If that was so, he must pinch himself because he must be dreaming again now.

"So this is your famous Gorky Park." She stopped, huddled against his arm, at the stone parapet overlooking the tree-lined avenue which stretched into the distance. Strains of balalaika folk music floated through the frosty air from loudspeakers, mixing with the faint sounds of a fairground. Beyond the trees, Lucinda could see the slowly turning spars of two Ferris wheels.

"It is beautiful, yes?" he asked her, and she could sense the pride in his voice.

"It's so calm."

Niki nodded. "It gets busier soon over New Year. Many will skate on the lake and children will try out their new skis – Look!" She followed his pointing finger to where a youth was striding in long gliding movements beneath the trees.

"Is that cross-country skiing?"

"Yes. You see how his boots are fixed to his skis only at the toes, so he can lift his heels and kick along. It is easy on the flat, but going down slopes takes much practice." He looked down at her. "You do not ski like this in England?"

"Not much. A little in Scotland, I think. But I've never been."

"In Russia in the country everybody skis. Often it is the only way to get to the next village. That or by horse-drawn *troika*."

Lucinda felt a sudden compulsion to know everything about her companion. "So you ski, Niki?"

He laughed. "Alas, not now. But as a child I would ski everywhere in winter. Sometimes I would go hunting with my uncle for boars and deer. If we were very lucky, sometimes a bear."

"It must have been a wonderful childhood."

His mouth compressed as he stared across the park. "It was, dear Lucy. But it was a long, long time ago."

She was aware of the sadness creeping into his voice. "Let's move on," she said.

There were few others in the park. They passed the raised tile walls of the duck pond with its frozen surface and the petrified fountains which glistened like glass chandeliers in the wintry sunlight. Two children wrapped in woollen balaclavas threw black bread at the ducks who raced for it in competition against huge grey gulls which swooped from the sky. Along the avenue of trees, an old woman in an overcoat and headscarf shovelled lethargically at a pile of wind-driven snow.

"You know we too have a Santa Claus," Shalayez said, "but we call him Grandfather Frost."

"Really?"

"Yes, like yours he has a long white beard and a red suit with all the fur trimmings. But he comes at New Year."

"You still believe in him?" she teased.

He stopped and looked at her with a look of feigned astonishment. "But, yes! Everybody in Russia believes in him. Didn't you wake as a child to find a sack full of toys?"

She looked at him quizzically. "Of course."

Shalayez laughed. "There you are then! How can you not believe in him – the evidence of your own eyes!"

"Oh, Niki, you're pulling my leg. Next you'll be telling me you believe in goblins and elves."

He raised a finger. "Ah, not Grandfather Frost! No pixies for him. He has the Snow Fairy – the ice maiden we call *Sneguruchka*."

"To help!"

His eyes widened. "No, to keep him from the vodka."

Lucinda shook her head in disbelief.

"It's true, I swear. I shall take you along to the Detsky Mir toy shop. In the past I have taken my little Yelina there. This time *you* shall sit on his knee and tell him what you most want him to bring you!"

"Niki, you're incorrigible!"

"No, I mean it. You *will* see the real Russia, I promise. But first I bet that you are hungry?"

"A little," she admitted.

He raised his head and closed his eyes. "Now, sniff the air like this . . . go on, Lucy."

She fell in easily with his mood, and did as she was told.

"What do you smell?"

Her nostrils flared. "Cold! Cold air – ah, and I can smell pinewood. And . . ."

"And?" he persisted.

"Woodsmoke – " She gasped. "Oh, I caught it then. Something cooking. Meat!"

He hugged her to him as he steered her towards an open-air space filled with wrought-iron tables and chairs. As they reached the wooden hut, the pungent aroma of barbecued beef was overwhelming.

"If you've eaten in Moscow," Shalayez said, "you'll know how awful most of our restaurants are. But this, dear Lucy, is the finest meal you will have."

He selected fine fresh chunks of meat from the old *babushka* at the counter of the hut and they watched as she turned and laid the skewers on a metal grill above a bed of glowing coals.

Only a few minutes later, they were sitting at one of the tables trying to manoeuvre the huge chunks of crusty bread close enough to get their mouths around them. The meat was tender and succulent with a delicious smoky flavour.

Lucinda stopped a trickle of juice running down her chin. "Niki," she said, her mouth bulging, "this is exquisite!"

He laughed. "You see, you didn't believe me, I knew it. To enjoy Russia, you must live and think like a Russian." He pulled a leather flask from his pocket.

93

"Some *starka*. The old vodka you tried at the party. Put it in your tea. It will warm your toes."

He was right. After the sizzling kebabs and bread, followed by scalding tea laced with *starka*, Lucinda no longer noticed the cold. Her skin glowed as she snuggled back into her furs.

"Thank you, Niki. That was wonderful."

He tossed a remnant of meat at a scavenging crow. "It is nothing . . ." He hesitated " . . . But I wonder, after we visit Grandfather Frost, it will be the end of the afternoon. I should like to take you to dinner."

She raised an eyebrow.

"I have offended you?" he asked.

"No, Niki, no. Please don't look so *earnest*. I should like that *very* much. I'm just a little surprised."

"You shouldn't be, Lucy, you are a very lovely woman."

It may have been the vodka, but she distinctly felt her cheeks flush. No man had ever described her as 'a woman' before. Girl or lady, yes. But never woman. She found it strangely flattering. "Thank you, Niki."

"I am glad."

She frowned. "And you are really going to take me to Grandfather Frost? With all those kids?"

The violet eyes shone with mischief. "But of course!"

"He really is a lovely man," Lucinda Marsh enthused.

The three of them were sitting in a secluded corner of the half-empty restaurant, which it had taken all of Alice Tate's extraordinary skills to get into. Even now, despite the near blizzard raging in the Moscow street, the uniformed doorman still doggedly maintained the queue of hopeful patrons on the pavement outside.

"Well, don't go and do anything foolish like fall in love with him," Alice warned.

Daphne Withers smiled benignly. "Don't be such an old sauerkraut, dear. I think it's rather nice that Lucy likes him. Just think how awful it would be if she couldn't

94

stand him. If he had dandruff or a hunch-back. Or smelled of garlic, a lot of them do, you know."

Lucinda laughed. "Well, he doesn't have any of those things. But he does have an amazing sense of fun."

"That wasn't mentioned in his file," Alice muttered.

"And a total disregard for petty rules and regulations," Lucinda continued. "I mean, when we went to that children's store yesterday, it was hilarious. The old woman on the turnstile wasn't going to let us in because we didn't have a child with us. So he just grabbed this child outside and asked its mother if we could take him through. Then, when we got to Grandfather Frost, he slipped him a few roubles to let me sit on his knee. It was a riot! Everyone thought it was very funny – except this really po-faced Snow Fairy, who accused him of being a drunken old lech. But the people in the grotto thought it was a huge joke. Niki got a standing ovation."

"Well, his disregard for rules might come in handy," Alice admitted sourly.

"Tell me, dear," Daphne said, "has he said anything of interest to us?"

Lucinda shrugged. "Well, if you mean has he suggested he'd like to leave Russia, I'm afraid he hasn't. Almost the opposite in fact. He's talked of nothing except how marvellous it is. You know, explaining their way of life and all their customs to me."

"Has he asked about you?" Alice intervened.

"Me? Yes."

Relief showed on the old lady's face. "Thank goodness for that."

"But not about England," Lucinda added. "He's interested in me, but he hasn't really asked anything about England. Or the West in general."

"Mmm." Daphne was thoughtful. "However, you are *sure* that he likes you? Really likes you?"

Lucinda's smile was wide. "Oh yes, I'm sure. But he's been very proper about it. No propositions or anything.

Maybe he's looking on ours as more of a father and daughter relationship."

Alice looked horrified. "Oh, we really can't have that. Has he ever touched you, you know?"

"We've linked arms when walking. Just that sort of thing. And he kissed me on the cheek when we said good night yesterday. Very gentlemanly."

"If you ask me, Niki Shalayez is *too much* of a gentleman," Alice muttered. "Time isn't on our side."

Daphne Withers reached across the table and placed her hand over Lucinda's. "Listen, my dear, I really think you have to step up the body language a little. We gels really are so subtle, many chaps just don't get the message. Now, tell me, you say you are seeing him tonight?"

Lucinda nodded. "Yes, he's got tickets for the Bolshoi. *Sleeping Beauty*. I'm looking forward to it."

"Well," Daphne continued, "you must let him know you think more of him than just a father figure. But not too blatant, you don't want to frighten the dear man off. Maybe clutch his arm at the ballet. When he talks to you look deep into his eyes. If you're holding hands, start toying with his fingers and see if he responds. That can be very sensuous."

"Oh, for pity's sake!" Alice was exasperated. "I'm sure Lucinda has a far better idea of how to lure a man into bed than we do. She is a different generation. Their approach is more modern and direct."

Daphne's soft brown eyes became uncharacteristically hard. "We are not just talking of *bed*, Alice. We are talking about an obviously sensitive man. If Lucinda acts the Jezebel she'll get nowhere. He must fall in *love* with her. With his heart, not just his body. And that is something that many gels today have forgotten." She blinked apologetically at Lucinda. "I am sorry, dear."

Alice Tate pouted in disgust. "Something of an expert, are we, Daphne?"

"Believe it or not, I've had my moments, dear. And I

have not forgotten them." She turned back to the girl. "Now, Lucinda, tonight you must be very warm to him. Start saying how much you are going to miss him when you leave. That you wish you could see him again. And if he doesn't ask, you must find a way of telling him what life is like in England. Then, if he doesn't suggest going somewhere private, then invite him back for coffee to your room. I'll speak to Sergei Chagall and make sure the hotel staff don't put any obstacles in your way." She hesitated, searching for the words. "Behind closed doors, my dear, of course, it's up to you. But you must be better than any woman he's ever had before. You have to start a fire burning within him. Be voluptuous, but not obvious. Inventive but gentle and sensitive. Let him think he is taking the initiative."

Lucinda blinked as she felt the blood flush her cheeks. Somehow she had never envisaged that her trip to Moscow would be quite like this. Not being given near explicit instructions on how to seduce a man who, a few days ago, had been a total stranger. If it had been anyone else talking to her other than Daphne Withers, she would have stomped out of the restaurant in disgust. As it was, the words were spoken kindly with the genuine concern of a well-meaning and loving aunt.

"You see," Daphne continued, "you must make him think you really do care for him. Do you think you can do that?"

She didn't reply except with a slight nod of her head. She knew she could do that all right. That wouldn't be at all difficult.

The doorman decided to admit four more huddled individuals into the restaurant. As the door opened an icy draught blasted away the cosy warmth, and Lucinda shivered.

The track to the Ash family farm was rough and pitted, showing up the suspension weakness in Brian Hunt's ageing MG roadster. As the lights of the farmhouse came

97

into view over the crest of the hill, he stopped and killed the headlamps.

It was a clear, still night of typical Christmas Eve calm. Beneath the sprinkling of stars, the ploughed furrows of the field were rigid under a dusting of frost. Somewhere beyond the hills the bells of a village church chimed out a carol.

Hunt lit a cigarette, then climbed out of the open-topped car, and strolled over to the roadside fence. Leaning against its rotting timber, he looked down into the valley where the rambling farmhouse lay. There was something welcoming about its hotch-potch construction. The main two-up, two-down flint construction was supposedly seventeenth-century, but succeeding generations had added a whole new wing here, a conservatory there, and everywhere else a collection of annexes and outbuildings of various styles and quality. The mantle of ivy beneath the undulating slate roof held it all together and gave it a semblance of architectural respectability.

But it was every bit as unconventional and welcoming as the family who had bought it and saved it from dereliction fifteen years before.

Typically, someone had taken the trouble to string coloured fairy lights around the ancient cedar tree at the front of the cottage garden. Hunt had little doubt it was for his benefit. It was probably Gabby's idea.

His eye followed a white shape flapping silently over the field like a ghost. A barn owl that Mike's wife encouraged to nest in one of the outbuildings.

If he was going to turn back, it would have to be now. There was a phone box down the road; he could call from there. He could come up with a thousand-and-one excuses. However lame, he knew that neither Mike nor Gabby would question it. That was not their style. So even at this late hour, it was still down to him.

He inhaled and expelled a cloud of blue smoke and watched it drift aimlessly into the still night. Everything told him that he shouldn't go. It was last Christmas that it had begun and by the end of the summer he had vowed never to return.

So what had made his determination waver? Was it really that note from little Jessica? Or just a reluctance to offend Mike Ash, the truest friend he had ever had? Or was it just the chance to see Gabby again, protected now by the knowledge that she and Mike had a new addition to their brood on the way?

He couldn't answer his own question. Angry with himself, he crushed out his cigarette butt underfoot. As he did his eye caught the elaborately wrapped parcel on the roadster's squab-seat.

No, he told himself savagely, there was no doubt. It was little Jessica who had lured him back. To see the look of delight on her face when she opened her present – that was why he had changed his mind.

He climbed back into the MG and brought it to life.

Just a minute later he was parking between Mike's old Land Rover and the vintage farm tractor. Almost immediately he was aware of a chorus of barking dogs from within the farmhouse. From the stables a horse whinnied and an inquisitive goose appeared from behind the low stone wall, its neck arched and its wings flapping.

Hunt was still lifting out his case when light streamed from the opened front door. A large golden labrador shambled out, barking in a half-hearted effort to let the intruder know that this was private property. In hot pursuit came Jessica, all long legs and gingham party frock.

"Uncle Brian!"

He met her at the front gate and she reached up to kiss him. "Hello, Jessica. Merry Christmas."

"I didn't think you were going to come," she said earnestly.

He laughed. "How could I resist such a charming invitation?"

The goose was closing in with frantic anger, squawking for all it was worth.

"Go away, Emma!" Jessica shouted. "Daddy was going to kill her for Christmas, but we all got up a petition. So she had *better* behave herself."

The labrador sniffed at the goose with cautious curiosity then backed away.

"I suppose this is Biff?"

A look of pure joy came over her face. "How did you know?"

"A lucky guess. He looks a bit ferocious."

"Oh, no." The seven-year-old was adamant. "He's quite a softy really." To prove the point the dog licked at his fingers.

Jessica took Hunt's wet hand and led him through to the flagstoned parlour where Mike Ash was waiting in an apron. "Hello, Brian. Welcome to Hereford's Yuletide disaster area. I was in the middle of stuffing the turkey when Baby Walt decided to tip over the Christmas tree. Bloody little terrorist; I'm sure he's been planted on us by the Baader-Meinhof. I just sorted that out, then I find the cat's eaten half the stuffing." He aimed a half-hearted kick at the dog. "And I'm not sure Biff didn't have a hand in it."

"He wouldn't!" Jessica protested, although the dog had an expression that suggested he knew what the conversation was about.

Hunt said: "Then it looks like reinforcements have come at the right moment."

Ash grinned. "Yeah, how d'you fancy filling up some mince pies?"

"My speciality."

"Can I help?" Jessica asked.

Hunt bent over. "Help? You can show me *how*. I'm used to getting all my food out of tins."

"First things first though, Brian. A drink? Whisky and ginger wine suit? You could do with it if you came in that open-topped contraption of yours."

"Straight Scotch thanks, Mike."

Ash called out to his two eldest sons, who were busy wrapping last-minute presents in the living room. "C'mon, you two Herberts, come and say hello to our guest."

Hunt waited with mild embarrassment. Both Mike and Gabby maintained old-fashioned, middle-class values of politeness and etiquette, which he rarely came across in youngsters of the eighties. It was a bit formal, and reminded him of his own, far stricter background at the orphanage.

Toby, the eldest, shook hands stiffly. He was fifteen now with an immature moustache and a breaking voice that wavered uncertainly.

At eleven Jason was more relaxed and modern in his outlook. Unlike his older brother, he was keen to make the Army his career.

"Samantha's upstairs getting ready," Ash explained, pouring two glasses. "Ten now and a right little lady. Gabby'll be down shortly. She's been taking a nap."

"Unlike her," Hunt observed. He accepted the offered glass. "Cheers!"

"Cheers!" Ash downed his drink in one. "Gabby's been more tired with this new sprog. Usually shells 'em like peas. Poor old love must be getting past it."

Hunt laughed. "That I do doubt."

A new voice joined in from the staircase. "I'll pretend I didn't hear that, Mike!"

That light, mischievous laugh sent a ripple along Hunt's spine. It was a curious mixture of dread and fascination. He had tried to put the thought of their meeting again from his mind; pretended that it no longer mattered to him.

But as he turned around, he knew he'd been fooling himself. She stood on the landing, one hand poised on the banister, with the ceiling lamp behind her transforming her long hair into a golden halo. As she stepped down the light from the room played over her face. It was inevitable that she would be smiling that warm, open smile that made you feel that you were the most welcome person in the world. A smile that crinkled the fine skin around those hypnotic pale blue eyes.

Hunt found his own mouth responding involuntarily, twisting into a boyish grin as he noticed another, different quality about her. Something resembling serenity. Then his eyes dropped to the distinct swell of her belly beneath the maternity frock.

"Hello, Brian."

Hunt nodded. "Gabby – " He was aware of his own hesitation as he searched for something to say. " – I hear that congratulations are in order?"

She pouted mischievously. "You could say that, although I'm not sure Mike would agree. But thank you, yes they are." As she reached to kiss him on the cheek, he almost pulled back. She noticed and a flicker of uncertainty showed in her eyes. "And thank you for coming, Brian. We were beginning to think you'd abandoned us. It's been so long. Is it six months?"

Hunt swallowed. "I've been busy. You know how it is."

Ash intervened. "Well, he's here now, Gabby, that's the important thing. And just in the nick of time. Chaos rules in the kitchen, okay."

Gabby laughed. "So you're about to put our guest to work?"

"Needs must . . ." Ash replied.

"Shame on you. Go and have your drinks by the fire. I'll take over in the kitchen."

Mike Ash watched her go with something resembling awe. "We've been married seventeen years, Brian, and she never ceases to amaze me. Now she's up, she'll take total command of the household, the cooking, everything. And woe betide us if we venture into the kitchen. I can think of a couple of officers in the Regiment who could do with a lesson from Gabby on organisational technique."

102

Hunt sipped at his drink, his mind preoccupied. "She is one remarkable lady," he murmured.

Christmas Day burst on the Ash household like a mad thing.

It took Hunt a few seconds to orientate himself to the sloping ceiling of the tiny dormer bedroom. He glanced at his watch on the bedside table. Christ, it was almost nine o'clock. He fell back on the pillow. It had been all those mellow ports after supper the night before.

There was a timid knock at the door, and he sat up as it creaked open. Jessica stood in a long nightdress, clutching a mug of tea in both hands.

"Are you awake, Uncle Brian?"

A lolloping bundle of golden fur pushed past her and launched itself at the bed. The wet tongue lapped at Hunt's face. "I am now, thanks."

"Biff just wants to say good morning."

"So I see." He rubbed the dog's chest to let him know he'd been noticed, and the exuberance subsided except for the tail which threatened to upset the tea before Hunt got near it.

"Mummy says breakfast is at ten. If we hurry we can take Biff for a walk first."

"That's a good idea," Hunt said. "Did it snow last night?"

Jessica shook her head.

"Pity. Biff would like that."

"He's never seen the snow. He's too young."

"I'll be down in ten minutes, right?"

She grinned. "Great!"

Outside the air was surprisingly mild. The wind had changed direction and dropped. The coating of frost had vanished from the ploughed fields.

"I don't like the cold," Jessica said, straining to keep up with Hunt's strides. "Not like Daddy, he loves it when it's snowy."

He laughed. "Yes, I had noticed. Don't forget I work with your dad in the snow every year."

"Do you like it?"

"Not much. I prefer the tropics to be honest."

Jessica thought for a moment. "So why do you do it, Uncle Brian?"

"Because it's my job. I don't spend all my time in the Arctic."

"Do you like being a soldier?"

"Most of the time."

She wrinkled her nose as she looked up at him, her expression deeply curious. "Have you ever killed anyone, Uncle Brian?"

Her question took him aback. "That's a very personal question, young lady."

She shrugged and walked on. "I understand if you don't want to talk about it. Daddy doesn't like talking about that sort of thing." She sounded very grown up.

"Especially on Christmas Day," Hunt added pointedly, trying to discourage her.

"Daddy *never* wants to talk about it. Never. I mean if you *don't* kill anyone, there's not much point in being a soldier, is there?"

Hunt frowned. "This conversation's getting a bit deep, young lady. But having armies is as much about persuading another country not to attack you, as it is about killing people. And if you've got good soldiers then you win quickly and decisively. That means fewer people get hurt – on both sides."

That seemed to satisfy her for the moment. She threw a stick for Biff, who bounded after it enthusiastically. "Let's go down to Watercress Meadow. We've just got time. You remember we went there in the summer?"

Remember? How in God's name could he forget it? "It's a bit far," he said.

"Oh please, Uncle Brian. We can if we walk faster."

Reluctantly he agreed, and they diverted into a shallow valley that ran between a copse of oaks where a thick carpet of dead vegetation crunched underfoot.

Jessica said suddenly: "I think Daddy *has* killed someone. I heard him talking about it with Mummy a couple of weeks ago. But I don't know why. I mean, there isn't a war or anything, is there?"

Hunt almost stopped dead in his tracks. God knows what was going through the child's mind. Neither Mike nor Gabby were the sort to talk carelessly in front of the children. She must have been piecing together snatches of conversation, mulling it over, and found the answers she got disturbing to her maturing mind.

But how do you tell a child of seven, who still believes in Father Christmas, that beneath the civilised veneer of modern society, there is a seething pool of hatred and barbarism, as virulent as at any time in history? Or that the war against terrorism and subversion is neverending? And that, sometimes, those who fight against it have to venture into the sewers of the secret war themselves.

Hunt guessed what Mike Ash had been talking about to Gabby. It was around the time of their three-day undercover mission to Eire. They had been given the name. And the place. A reclusive millionaire who managed funds for the Provisional IRA. Few more details were available, except the man was orchestrating a major drugs deal to fuel the Provos' campaign of terror and political subversion. He was an "untouchable" that the Government wanted touched.

They had done that all right, Hunt thought grimly. They had broken into the grounds of the country house, tranquillised the guard dogs, and set fire to the building. It had been carefully done to look like an accident, and the next day the local paper dutifully reported that the seventy-two-year-old businessman had been found burned alive in his bed, after a fire caused by an electrical fault.

It was as simple as that. The man had been an evil menace who had to be destroyed by any means possible.

Such radical assignments were rare, and those who carried them out weren't proud of it. It was just an especially rotten job, and this time it had fallen to Ash's team. Necessary as it was, it left a nasty taste. The more so because, Hunt knew, nowhere at either Hereford or Whitehall would there be any record of such a mission having been ordered or executed.

He said: "Listen, Jessica, whatever your daddy does in his job is to make the world safer for you and your brothers and sister. And other children like you, now and when they grow up. Safe from things you're too young to understand." He stopped walking, and crouched down to be on her level. "Sometimes people get hurt when your daddy and I do our job. Sometimes good people, but mostly bad. But it still upsets us. That's why we don't like to talk about it. Do you understand that?"

She looked into his eyes and sighed resignedly. "I think so. I didn't think Daddy would *deliberately* hurt anyone."

Hunt smiled reassurance. "Of course not. He's a very tough soldier, but he's also one of the nicest, kindest men I've ever met."

"I think you are one of the kindest men I've ever met, Uncle Brian," she said emphatically.

He couldn't resist a smile. "Thank you, ma'am." They resumed walking. "So maybe it's best if you don't ask Daddy too much about the things we've been discussing."

She frowned seriously. "No, I think you're right. He'd only be upset."

"Good girl."

They stepped out of the copse at the edge of the watercress meadow. The dog bounded ahead, down the steep grassy slope to where a fast-flowing stream carved its way through the centre of the valley.

"I wonder if there'll be any cress in the stream?"

Hunt shook his head. "No, not this time of year.

Unless you find some brown cress. You can pick that in winter."

Jessica looked disappointed for a moment, then decided to play at throwing sticks for the dog and training him to retrieve. Biff had other ideas, and delighted in getting her to chase after him to get her stick back.

Hunt watched with amusement as they scampered around the meadow which had such strong memories for him. Of course, it looked like a different place now, with the colour of the cropped grass muted by a chill morning mist. Back in high summer the grass had been long and lush, dotted with blue thistles and buttercups.

He had called around to the farm to see Gabby whilst Mike Ash was away. She had suggested that the two of them take a picnic down to the meadow. It had been a perfect still, hot day with the air sweet with pollen and bird song. White wine from the cooler went ideally with the brie cheese and grapes.

They had made love in the long, dusty grass beside the watercress stream. It had been spontaneous, starting with the touching of fingers. He'd never known such a simple act to stoke such fires. It was like an electric spark. He remembered how he'd looked into Gabby's eyes and had seen that she felt it too. As he clasped her hand, their faces had moved closer. As though their mouths had a will of their own. The kiss had been lingering and deep, and almost immediately Gabby had surrendered to him. There had been no pretext of hesitation. No guilt for her, then or later. She had plainly wanted him then and there, with her naked buttocks against the rough grass and the hot sun on his back. He'd taken her in a rage of passion with little finesse, until he felt the sweat running between his shoulder blades and the soft squelch of damp skin where their bodies touched.

It surprised him that she cried out, tearing at his back with her nails. He knew he hadn't spent time coaxing her as he should. Perhaps it had been an act for his benefit? He didn't ask her; he had thought it best not to know.

He rolled off and kissed the sweat that ran between her breasts.

She laughed and ran her hand through his hair. "Has anyone ever told you, Brian Hunt, you're an animal?"

When he looked at her, there'd been a fierceness in his eyes. "I've wanted to do that for a long time."

"I know."

"And you?"

"Since Christmas." She looked at him as if he were something beautiful. "I've always liked you, fancied you maybe. Then last Christmas, after Joan left you, when you stayed. That kiss under the mistletoe."

He shook his head. "I should have stopped coming over before. Not let it come to this."

She frowned. "This? We've made love, that's all. Don't go all guilty on me. God, you've been coming round enough recently. Like a dog on a scent."

"Was it that obvious?"

"To me."

"I don't think I realised myself."

Again her hand in his hair. "Well, don't worry about it. I wanted it too."

Hunt nodded. "It doesn't make it easier. Anyone else but . . ."

She looked suddenly angry. "But?"

"You're Mike's wife, Gabby."

A hand clasped his forearm. "Mike is in love with his bloody mountains, Brian. They see more of him than I do, so don't feel sorry for him on that count. I understand, you see. He *needs* freedom and adventure, it's in his blood. I love him – dearly – but I have other needs too – "

The sudden shrill voice of the child echoed through the meadow. "MUMM-Y! ARE YOU THERE? – UNCLE BRI-AN!"

"Christ!" Hunt rolled over fast into the grass as though

108

he had suddenly come under fire. Stricken with panic he hauled up his trousers awkwardly as he lay on his back. Strands of grass caught in the zipper.

Gabby had only just had time to brush her frock back down over her legs when Jessica appeared through the long grass.

She said: "We'd better get back. Mummy won't be pleased if the breakfast gets spoiled."

Hunt's thoughts were jolted back to the present. He wondered how different Jessica's reaction to him might be now, if she'd arrived a few seconds earlier back in the summer.

"C'mon, then," he said. "I'll race you and Biff back to the farm."

After the huge traditional breakfast, Hunt offered to mind Baby Walt while the rest of the family went to the eleven o'clock church service. Just as the Ash horde had been assembled into some kind of order alongside the battered Land Rover, Gabby announced that she wasn't feeling well.

"What's the problem, love?" Ash asked. "Not morning sickness again?"

"A bit queasy. It *is* expected." She sounded a little sharp.

Ash smiled. "Unusual for you, though. Best stay behind, eh? I'll pass on your best to God."

Gabby hit him softly on the shoulder. "Get off with you, you blasphemer. I expect I'll be over it by the time you're back."

Ash coaxed the cold engine into life as the children fought amongst themselves for their favourite seats. Finally they were on the move, trailing a billowing blue fog of exhaust which hung motionless in the still air.

Slowly, Gabby turned back to the house. Hunt was already halfway through the washing-up.

"Do you do everything with such military precision, Brian?"

He turned. "I thought you were going to church?"

She smiled. "A touch of morning sickness. Nothing much. I thought I'd let them go without me for once."

"Oh?" His voice sounded hesitant. "It's nice to see a family together. All trundling off, smiling and happy."

"You make it sound all sweetness and light. It's all arguments and squabbles before they all do as they're told."

"It's still nice to see."

She picked up a tea-towel. "I keep forgetting you didn't have a family, Brian. Sorry, yes I can see it means a lot to you. I mean, it would, wouldn't it?"

He worked at an egg stain that wouldn't shift. "Well, I've got a family now."

She frowned. "You mean us?"

His laugh was more brittle than he'd intended. "No, Gabby, this is Mike's family. Yours and Mike's. I meant the Regiment. That's my family now."

"Sometimes I think it's more of Mike's family than we are, too," she replied.

Hunt shrugged. "You know how it is."

"Oh, yes, Brian, I know."

For a moment a silence formed between them, broken only by the splash of water and the clacking of crockery. Then Gabby said suddenly: "Does it make you feel awkward, Brian? Being alone with me again?"

Damn you, woman, he thought savagely. But he showed no outward sign as he said casually: "Not at all, why?"

Gabby hesitated. "We haven't seen you for a long time."

"I've been kept busy." Sharp.

Momentarily her eyes closed. "I know that, Brian. It's just that we saw such a lot of you in the summer. And then – nothing. And I know you haven't been abroad for more than the odd week or two. I just thought that, maybe, that time in Watercress Meadow might – might

110

have brought us closer together." She studied the thick set of his neck as he concentrated too deeply on scouring the frying pan. "It seems instead to have driven us more apart."

It was several seconds before he took his hands from the sink and turned to faced her directly. Her eyes were the palest blue he'd ever seen, and her long fair hair glowed with a lustre. "Unless someone deliberately hurts you, I don't think you ever stop loving someone who's really meant something to you. Not if it was ever real."

Her eyes seemed to bore into his mind. "And us, Brian, were we real?"

"Yes, I think so."

A teasing smile played around her lips. "So you do still care?"

It was Hunt's turn to smile. "Too much, Gabby, that's the problem. To be honest I don't fully trust myself. Not after that time in the summer."

"I see."

"That's why I haven't been back. It's not that I didn't want to."

"But you're here now."

Again a wry smile. "I thought I was over you, you know? I thought I could be near you without wanting you."

He was fascinated by the whiteness of her teeth as her lips moved. "And can you?"

Hunt didn't reply: he didn't need to. They both knew.

Gabby raised her head and indicated the light fitting over the sink. Someone had attached a shrivelled sprig of mistletoe.

Her voice was almost a whisper. "It's allowed, you know. An ancient heathen custom."

He wanted to scream at her not to step towards him, but his tongue was tied. His muscles were paralysed as she slid her arms along his, her long fingers curling around the hair at the nape of his neck.

111

And then her lips were brushing against his. Memories flooded back. The firm moist flavour of her mouth. The way she played her tongue along his teeth. It was all the same, only more exquisite than he had remembered on so many lonely nights. That a kiss could stir such longing in a man.

His resistance crumbled and he took her in his arms with a mad possession, his resolution forgotten in the heat of the moment.

She mumbled something breathlessly in his ear, and he felt her hand steering his to her breast.

It was then that something snapped. He pulled back. His voice was hoarse. "That's enough, Gabby. Let's not start it all over again."

She clutched his fist in her two hands. "God, Brian, I can't tell you how much I've missed you. Really. Just to speak to, even. I know it's wrong – at least in the eyes of the Church. But it *feels* right. With you *everything* feels right."

Hunt turned his head from side to side as though seeking some means of escape. "If it's going to be like this, Gabby, then I can't ever see you. I can't betray Mike."

Her eyes pleaded. "And me, what about me? Don't my feelings enter into it? Mike is still a wonderful man, but he isn't you."

"You and Mike made your choice a long time ago, Gabby. For better or for worse."

She tilted her head to one side with a look of curiosity on her face. "You're not quoting the Bible at me? That really wouldn't be fair."

Hunt turned his head and stared blindly out of the window. "No one said anything about life being fair . . ." He looked back at her. "There's nothing in the world I'd like to do more, believe me. To take you now. On the floor. Here in the kitchen. Because I want you more than I've ever wanted any woman in my life."

Her eyes narrowed as though not quite believing. She appeared to tremble.

"But it's not possible, Gabby," he added, his voice fractured. "I want to touch you. You want me, too. But you belong to Mike and you're having his child."

She swallowed hard, her eyes not leaving his. "I belong to no man, Brian. I never have. I love Mike as my husband. At times I have loved others. Because I am a woman, and I do what I know I have to do to be true to myself. *Myself*." Her voice rose slightly as she made her point. "But I'd never deliberately hurt Mike, never."

Ridiculously Hunt felt a pang of jealousy. "You mean lovers? Does Mike know you take lovers?"

"Not like that, Brian. Once, no twice, before you there have been other men. Men who've come into my life, like you did. They fell in love with me, and I with them. While it lasted." She paused. "But it didn't."

Hunt's face darkened. "And if it had? What about Mike then?"

"Then I'd have told him. That he either shared me, or else I would have to leave."

"And what would he have done?"

Still her eyes didn't leave his. "I expect it would have been him who left. But I'm not sure."

"Hasn't he ever suspected?"

Gabby frowned, almost surprised that he didn't understand. "Mike loves me, Brian. If he suspected anything he would never say. His philosophy is a little like mine. He knew what I was like before we married. He's very understanding."

Hunt's smile lacked humour. "Then he's more understanding than I am. My wife – carrying my child – with another man . . ."

She reached out and touched his arm. "Dear Brian, you really are the jealous man, aren't you? Don't you realise how silly that is? Love is a natural gift. God's gift to us all. We must be true to it in whatever way we can – by being true to ourselves."

113

Hunt didn't begin to understand such philosophy. "That sounds like the flower-power crap of the sixties," he muttered.

Gabby's smile was very wide. "I am a child of the sixties, Brian. Or had you forgotten?"

"You take it that seriously?"

"Yes, I do." She looked at him earnestly. "And I believe that the important thing is that a child is conceived in love, and is loved when it is born. You were abandoned as a child, Brian, that's why you're so confused about it all – sorry."

"Meaning?"

Her eyes were moist and she smiled a smile so warm that it could have thawed an icicle. "You don't understand, my love, do you? And I can't tell you, that's the shame of it. But I don't want to lose you, Brian. I don't want you to run away and hide again. If you think about it, each of the three of us loves the other in our own way."

"Christ, Gabby!" Hunt retorted. "Don't talk such bloody nonsense! Wake up, for God's sake, and stop living in that make-believe hippy fairyland of yours! We're not living in some kind of commune. I have to live and fight alongside Mike. How the hell am I supposed to do that, knowing that I've betrayed him? No, I already have to live with that – but to deliberately go on betraying him – "

Her smile was sympathetic. "Mike would understand if he knew."

"I wouldn't bank on it." Hunt fished in his shirt pocket for his cigarettes and lit one. It steadied his nerves as he tried to marshal his thoughts into some semblance of order. "No, Gabby, I'm pulling out of your life," he decided. "Right out."

Her eyes burned into his with a deep hypnotic stare. "No, Brian, don't. You *can't*. I need you too much, and soon I'll need you even more."

When Mike Ash returned from church in the Land

Rover filled with children, he was surprised to find Hunt's red MG gone.

Gabby met him at the door and blurted out quickly that her husband's friend had received an urgent telephone call from a nursing home where his one-time foster father was believed to be dying. They had said that it was unlikely that he would last until Boxing Day.

Ash looked into his wife's eyes and could see the pain in them. He was sure she had been crying. It was so typical of Gabby, that she could feel genuine grief for someone that she had never even met. Especially at a time of year like this.

He hugged her reassuringly. "It comes to us all, sweetheart. But as death comes to some, life comes to others."

She looked at him strangely.

Ash grinned and patted her swollen stomach. "Life goes on."

That afternoon after Christmas dinner, they sat around the log fire and opened their gifts. Hunt's presence was missed and the business was more muted than normal, despite Biff's attempts to liven up the proceedings with his passion for tearing up wrapping paper.

Jessica was particularly withdrawn. She saved Hunt's present until last and opened it carefully. There were two packets inside. A Sindy Doll and an Action Man. The note on the tag said: *They'll be company for each other.*

Ash thought it was a huge joke, but Gabby's smile, he noticed, was a trifle half-hearted. Jessica announced she'd call the male doll Brian and the girl Ann. Her own middle name.

Later that afternoon Gabby was alone in the room, staring out at the fine sprinkling of snow falling in the dim twilight, when Jessica came up to her.

"Mummy?"

Absently Gabby reached down and ruffled her daughter's hair.

"Mummy, will Uncle Brian be coming back?"

115

Her mother stared out as though mesmerised by the fading landscape. "Not this Christmas."

Jessica frowned, thinking deeply. "Not ever?"

Gabby forced a smile and looked down. "Maybe not."

4

Nikolai Shalayez awoke suddenly during the night.

He didn't know why. Immediately he sensed alarm. Perhaps it had been the dream. It had been strange and haunting. He'd been lost in a dark forest and had been floundering in deep snow with voices calling to the right and left of him. Come this way and come that. Menacing, eerie voices. He'd ignored them and pushed on ahead to where the girl had been standing in brilliant sunshine at the far end of a tunnel of interlacing branches.

She was dressed in white like a Snow Fairy with a soft fur hood. He couldn't see her face but he knew it was Lucinda Marsh. The more he struggled to reach her, the deeper he sank into the snow. It was an icy quagmire, but he was sweating with exertion and fear.

Then suddenly he was there, gasping for breath at her feet. But when he looked up at the face in the fur hood, it wasn't Lucinda. It was his wife Katya. She was looking down at him and laughing. Cackling like an old witch.

He climbed out of bed. The mantelpiece clock on the fireplace of his Moscow apartment told him it was five o'clock. He wouldn't get back to sleep now.

Pulling on a thick dressing-gown he made his way through to the small kitchen. Outside snow was beating against the window like small stones, driven by a searing Siberian wind.

He opened the stove and added some logs, leaving the gate open to warm the room. He filled an old kettle with water and placed it on the top to make some tea.

Then he settled on the hard chair before the stove, lit a cigarette and waited for the dawn.

The time would pass quickly enough; he had a lot to think about. Mostly Lucinda Marsh.

He smiled to himself, basking in the sudden surge of warmth as the bark of the new logs flared. Who would have thought that just a week ago he was the saddest man on God's earth? And then a girl would walk into his life to change everything. Not even a buxom Muscovite, or one of the social groupies who wanted to catch a man of power and privilege. But a foreigner. A beautiful, slender young foreigner who spoke excellent Russian, and shared his interest in mathematics, music, the ballet – in fact shared so much with him that he could not believe his good fortune.

Looking back on it, he had not realised that he was falling in love with her. Perhaps he had hesitated because she was so young? In fact young enough to be his daughter. Or perhaps it was because she was a foreigner? You had to be so careful about meeting with them.

Anyway he had risked it and he was glad that he had. Especially since two nights ago after the ballet. During the performance she had taken his hand and squeezed it. An unspoken message. Telling him, discreetly, that she was his.

They were going back to her hotel, but then Lucinda had suddenly changed her mind. She asked if instead they could go to his apartment in Mira Prospekt. Hesitantly he agreed, although he knew it could be a foolish move. The old *dezhurnaya* in the lobby was ever watchful. Sitting behind the glass hatchway of her lobby like some mischievous fat cat. She'd already complained about him trampling snow on her clean floor, complained about his record-player, and even complained about him coming in late at night when he'd been on the town with Sergei Chagall. If she tolerated a foreigner on her premises, it would only be long enough for her to telephone the *Militsia*.

118

Nevertheless he had decided to risk it. And, while he brought a gap-toothed smile to the old crone's face with a box of chocolates for New Year, Lucinda had crawled under her window on all fours and had waited for him by the ancient elevator cage. Now he had to endure the old bat making moon-eyes at him every time he went past.

But that was a small price to pay for the night with Lucinda. When he'd closed the front door of the apartment she had been transformed immediately. She had thrown her arms around him and kissed him in a way that his wife had never done. They had made love with a passion that had taken his breath away. Afterwards he had sat up in bed and looked down, fascinated at the way the perspiration glittered along the full length of her naked back.

"When I leave here I am going home, and then to Sweden," she had mumbled into the pillow.

He lit two cigarettes and gave her one. "Sweden? Why?"

She flicked sweat-damp hair from her eyes. "Stockholm. I have my first job."

"Mathematics?"

Lucinda smiled. "No, translating. With a big investment corporation that has a lot of dealings with the Soviet Union. Russian into English and English into Russian. Miles and miles of boring contracts."

He had blown a smoke-ring at the ceiling. "Stockholm," he mused. "So near yet so far away."

The kettle was starting to boil. He made a full pot and sniffed at its enticing aroma. He'd wait a few minutes.

Stockholm.

He had received her last phone call before he had gone to bed that night. Some confused story about her grandmother feeling unwell. They thought it was angina. It was best that they returned to England immediately if only they could get the Intourist bureaucrats to pull their fingers out.

119

They had met for the last time in a floodlit Red Square. Alice Tate was with Lucinda and had stood watching the midnight change-of-guard at Lenin's Tomb while the two lovers whispered their farewells. They clung to each other in the sub-zero temperature, oblivious of the small knot of tourists watching the immaculate soldiers.

At last the goose-stepping was over and Alice joined them, muttering under her breath.

Lucinda looked at her for confirmation. Alice said: "We must go now. I'll start walking, you can catch me up."

Shalayez had watched her go. "What was she saying?"

"That I must go."

"No, before that. Under her breath."

Lucinda hesitated, and pulled a feeble smile. "She said she's afraid one day someone will take the stake out of Lenin's heart and it will start all over again."

He hadn't understood. And now, in the increasing warmth of his kitchen, he still didn't understand what the old woman meant.

He had just stood there, a diminutive figure dwarfed by the vastness of Red Square, and watched his new love walk out of his life as she receded into the swirling mist of powder snow.

He stood up and splashed hot tea into a mug. Cupping it to warm his hands he crossed to the larder shelf.

Lucinda's note was still there. Two telephone numbers. One in London; one in Stockholm.

Behind it, propped against a plate, was the crumpled envelope with a Swedish postmark. Slowly he lifted it down and extracted the contents. From the Rönkä Society of Stockholm. Inviting him to lecture in mathematics.

There were tears in his eyes. If only it were possible! What was it Sergei Chagall had said to him on the train to Sochi? That they would never let him go. Not unless

120

he left his wife and child behind as insurance. Well, now he didn't even have Katya and Yelina to speak of, so now there would be no chance at all.

In despair he tossed the letter from Sweden onto the wooden table. Damn the letter! Damn the project at Sary Shagan! Damn Lucinda for causing him so much torment! – No, don't *ever* damn her. He grinned foolishly to himself as he thought of her again. Bless you, sweet Lucinda.

He turned then as he heard the noise of the elevator whining outside his front door. Someone was up and about very early. The concertina gate of the cage clanked noisily and shoes scraped on the worn tiles of the landing.

Instantly the feeling of foreboding that had been with him when he awoke from his bad dream returned. Quite distinctly he felt his heart skip a beat. He scolded himself for being jittery for no good reason and sipped at his tea.

The sudden, violent knock at the door made him jump. Hot drink slopped over his hands. Hurriedly he placed his mug on the table, secured his dressing-gown and went into the hall to unbolt the door.

For a second he failed to recognise his friend. Sergei Chagall's face was shaded beneath a trilby hat tilted over his eyes and the dark overcoat was turned up at the collar.

Shalayez opened his mouth to speak, then stopped as he noticed a second, much smaller man, similarly dressed, standing behind Chagall.

"Nikolai Shalayez?"

The welcoming smile froze awkwardly on Shalayez's lips. "Sergei – ? You know who I am . . ."

The red KGB pass flashed briefly in Chagall's hand. "This is official business, Comrade Shalayez." He gestured to the man who stood behind him. "This is Lieutenant Tatlin."

Shalayez found himself nodding politely, then asked

121

hesitantly: "What do you mean, Sergei, official business? Am I supposed to have done something wrong?"

His friend didn't smile. "That's what we're here to find out. I am acting on information received."

It was cold on the draughty landing and Shalayez began to shiver; it may have been through fear. "For goodness sake, Sergei, *what* sort of information? You're starting to frighten me."

"Colonel Chagall," the other replied impassively.

Shalayez blinked. He'd seen the man's official face too many times to know that it was unwise to argue with it. "You'd better come in."

Chagall nodded curtly. "Stay here, Tatlin. Make sure we are not disturbed."

He followed Shalayez in and closed the door. "Go through to your kitchen. We cannot be overheard there."

The man's tone was friendlier now and Shalayez breathed a slight sigh of relief. "Do you want some tea? It's still hot."

"Why not?" The KGB man removed his hat and dusted the snow from its brim. "It's a filthy night."

Shalayez poured two mugs. "Please tell me what this is about. You absolutely terrified me."

Chagall didn't smile as he took his drink. "As well you might be. I have received a report that you have been in the company of Miss Lucinda Marsh."

"Lucy? Why, yes, you introduced me to her."

Chagall looked astonished and shook his head. "Don't you think that was foolish?"

"But *you* introduced me to her," Shalayez repeated.

"But I did not know you were going to have an affair with the woman, Niki, for God's sake! What on earth possessed you? Why didn't you ask my advice?"

Shalayez's mouth opened and closed like a goldfish gulping for air. "S-since when have I asked your advice on such matters?"

Chagall raised a silencing hand. "True, true, Niki. But

122

it does not alter the fact that you are in terrible trouble, my friend. Terrible trouble."

Shalayez did not taste the tea. "Why? What has happened?"

Chagall sat himself on the edge of the table. "Partly I blame myself for not having warned you. But you remember the two old ladies, Alice Tate and Lucinda's grandmother, Daphne Withers? Well, my friend, they are not quite the doddering old half-wits they seem."

Shalayez was lost.

"They in fact work for British Intelligence. They come here regularly once or twice a year. They have good contacts in high places who have been developed over many years since the war."

Shalayez was incredulous. "You are saying they are spies? I cannot believe it!"

Chagall smiled for the first time. "No, not spies as such. More like couriers or liaison agents. Fix-it people. When something important is brewing they will often come to Moscow and take over from British field agents here. You see, there is always a danger that we – the KGB that is – are onto their regular people. Sometimes the old ladies take over, or else they deliver special messages, or make final arrangements. For getting out intelligence information, sometimes messages from important dissidents, or sometimes – " he hesitated " – to organise what they call a 'defection'."

"And you do not arrest them?"

Now Chagall's smile developed into a full, deep chuckle. He placed a consoling hand on his friend's shoulder. "How little you know of my devious world, dear Niki. If you find out that someone is an agent, you don't always arrest them. Otherwise they may be replaced with someone you don't know. Instead you use your knowledge to your own advantage. As it is, whenever the old ladies visit Moscow or Leningrad we know that something is in the air. We take a discreet but keen interest in all their contacts, and their contacts'

contacts. Also friends and families. It can be very enlightening. That's why over the years I have made a point of befriending them – with official sanction."

Shalayez shook his head slowly. "Do they know you are in the KGB?"

Chagall shrugged. "Probably, they are not stupid. It is a game we play. We first met many years ago when I worked in Moscow. I told them I was a minor official at the agriculture ministry. I doubt if they believed me. Over the years I have introduced them to many people who they have thought might be useful. But to whom? Them or me? You see, they never know. Sometimes it works against us, but mostly I think not.

"Of course, I am no longer attached to Moscow District, but my relationship is such that I am still asked to make myself available whenever they come here. Sometimes I have come all the way back from Sary Shagan especially to see them."

It was the first time that Chagall had ever given an insight into any aspect of his work other than security on the project. Although it surprised Shalayez, it was not his concern. He had only one thought in his head. "Lucy? How does she fit into all of this?"

Chagall's eyes were like flint. "How do you think?"

Shalayez gave a brittle laugh. "Well she certainly isn't any spy, that's for sure."

"And what makes you think that?"

He shrugged. "Everything! Everything about her. She's just a university student who studied Russian."

"And mathematics," Chagall pointed out. "Isn't that a bit of a coincidence?"

Shalayez looked pained. "Life is full of coincidences. Even I recognise that life doesn't run to an algebraic formula, Sergei." He thought for a moment. "And I must tell you that she has never asked me about my work. Not once."

Chagall drained his tea. "That in itself is suspicious."

"There you go again!" Shalayez retorted angrily.

"Reading things that aren't there. You're worse than a gypsy woman with her tea-leaves. Of course she asked me what I did. I just said that I was a mathematical scientist working on space projects. She said that must be interesting, and I said yes it was, but I was unable to talk about it because – naturally – it was covered by State security." Now his violet eyes were blazing. "So, *not* being a spy, she did *not* ask me any more about it. I suppose *that* is suspicious too?"

Chagall rubbed his chin. "All right, Niki, I concede that this girl may not be involved in her grandmother's work. Perhaps she is just being used to make even better cover. I remember once the Alice Tate woman brought over her grandson and, as far as we know, he had no connection with the security services."

Shalayez relaxed and for the first time he smiled. "So there we are. There is no problem."

Colonel Sergei Chagall's face remained fixed. "I am afraid, Niki, it is not so easy."

His friend was becoming irritated at the KGB man's continued suspicion. "Why not?"

Chagall selected his words carefully. "Once a detrimental report on your conduct has been lodged with the KGB it cannot be erased. And, however much I believe you as a friend, I know the security and scientific authorities will take an entirely different attitude. They will be obliged to assume the worst in the national interest."

Fear returned to chill Shalayez's heart. "Assume what worst?"

"That it was quite possible for you to have microfilmed formula documents from the project and passed them on to the girl with some verbal explanations that, as a mathematics graduate, she would understand. And if not Lucinda, you could have passed them direct to Alice Tate or Daphne Withers who are *known* agents."

Shalayez's eyes were wide. "But I never used to tell my own wife details of my work, Sergei. I would never betray my country, never!"

Chagall ignored the protestations of innocence. "It is time for you to do some very hard thinking, my friend, and quickly. Time is running out."

"Time for what?"

Chagall took a deep breath. "For getting out of the country."

"What? Never!"

"Do you know what will happen if you stay?"

Shalayez didn't answer. It was not something that he had even thought about.

Chagall said coldly: "Well, I shall tell you. Your work on the project is finished. If ever you were indispensable, that is no longer the case. You will be taken to Lefortovo Prison for interrogation. For days in an isolated cell with just rotten blankets and the stink of your own urine bucket for company. You'll have no sleep because they keep the light on and drag you off for interrogation every time you doze. Food will be bread and cabbage soup – if you get anything. You'll lose all sense of time. You'll become disorientated. You will probably confess to whatever you're asked in the end. But it doesn't really matter, because you will be sent to one of the camps anyway. You may be lucky and be sent for psychiatric treatment. But if you've signed a confession it's more likely to be a labour camp from which you are not expected to return. Only if you are exceedingly lucky will you be shot."

Shalayez felt his knees suddenly grow weak and he reached for the table to steady himself. "Surely this couldn't happen . . .?"

"Unfortunately," Chagall said tersely, "I have first-hand experience of what happens in such cases. Now, time is running out because this report has only just been made. The man outside – Tatlin – made it to me, otherwise I might have been able to hush it up. Now the report is in the system it has to be followed through. I will say that – at this meeting – I was satisfied that it was all a misunderstanding. However, because of your position, I know my superiors will insist on reopening the investigation. If I make full use of internal delays – maybe get my report lost in the typing pool – then I can perhaps delay that moment for ten days. At best two weeks. That will give you time."

"Time?" This was a nightmare.

"Time to arrange to leave the country."

Shalayez shook his head. "I wouldn't know how to begin. I don't even have a passport."

Sergei smiled reassurance. "Let me worry about how we do this." He glanced at the table. "I see you still have the invitation from that society in Sweden. That could be our answer."

Shalayez frowned. "But you said I wouldn't be allowed to go. Certainly not now that Katya and Yelina have left me."

Chagall shifted to stand in front of the stove, warming the backs of his legs. "I don't know," he said thoughtfully. "There are not yet any divorce papers. With a bit of care on my part, and some luck, my superiors may not even be aware that you and Katya have split up. But time is against us. If I move quickly I may be able to get permission for your trip pushed through. Most departments are still operating with holiday relief staff, so maybe I could get it rubber-stamped in short order. I also have a mathematics professor at Moscow University who owes me a favour. I could get him to request that you attend the Society."

Shalayez sat on the edge of the table. The rapid movement of events had left him winded. "Wouldn't that put you at risk, Sergei?"

"No, not necessarily. We in the KGB are experts at covering our tracks. Especially when it comes to getting around bureaucracy."

"But you know, I still don't want to go." He stared down at the floor. "I suppose they will call me a traitor?"

Chagall took his friend's arm. "Listen to me, Niki. What have you left to stay for? Your parents are dead

127

and you have no close relatives. I am your only real friend and I know you are no traitor! So think of yourself. At least you'll be able to see your precious Lucinda."

Shalayez looked at him. In just half-an-hour the mathematician's handsome face had been transformed into that of an old man. His skin was bloodless and waxy; his eyes were sunken with mental fatigue.

Lucy? She was all he had left to cling to – whether she was a spy or not. And she would be in Stockholm, too.

He said: "What do I do in Sweden?"

Chagall considered for a moment. "You'll simply walk to the embassy of your choice and ask for asylum. If you are guarded it won't be so easy, but I'll think of something. The important thing is to get you there. Do you agree?"

Shalayez nodded glumly. "I suppose I have no choice?"

Chagall took his friend's hand and squeezed it with brotherly affection. "Cheer up, Niki. I tell you, I *envy* you. The West is a wonderful place – I know, I've been there. And now you even have a girl waiting. What more could a man want?"

His friend smiled thinly. "I suppose so." He breathed deeply to help clear his mind. "I am so grateful to you again – as usual."

Sergei Chagall laughed aloud, his eyes twinkling. "And so you should be! You are luckier than you think."

"What do I do now?"

"Nothing. Just carry on as normal. I shall be in touch." He glanced at the letter on the table. "May I take that?"

"Of course."

Colonel Chagall put the letter into his overcoat pocket and let a grateful Shalayez show him to the door. He heard it shut behind him as he clattered briskly down the steps. In the lobby he found Lev Tatlin talking to the old *dezhurnaya* in her room.

"How did it go, Colonel?"

"Like clockwork," Chagall replied.

"There's been another letter."

"His wife?"

Tatlin nodded and handed over a crumpled envelope. Immediately Chagall's professional eye could see it had been tampered with. As he opened it and read the contents he was aware that the old woman already knew what was inside.

A plea for forgiveness. Another one. It didn't contain the confession about the East German actor; that had been in the first letter. This was another request for them to be reunited, regardless of the consequences.

"How many does this make?" Chagall demanded.

"This is the fourth that's arrived," the old woman said.

Chagall shook his head. "Stupid bitch." He turned to his lieutenant. "I want you to leave today for Berezniki. Find Comrade Shalayeza and leave her in no doubt what will happen to her daughter if she persists in this foolishness. No more letters. If just one of them got through everything could be ruined."

The two men left then. Outside the howling blizzard froze to the very marrow of the bone, but it was cosy in the warmth of the Chaika limousine.

Brian Hunt was relieved to get to Stockholm.

Christmas had been hell. After he left the Ash farm he'd driven back to his small flat over a grocery shop in Ledbury, stopping on the way to buy a couple of bottles of whisky from his local pub.

Once home he found he had virtually no provisions, and as his downstairs neighbours were away, he couldn't beg any favours. Instead he survived on an unappetising selection from his accumulated hoard of compo rations. By nightfall he was halfway through his first bottle of Scotch and feeling mellow. He went to sleep early and dozed his way through Boxing Day, which was just as well because his television set went on the blink.

He emerged the following day with nothing to show for his hours of soul-searching but a blinding headache. At least the shops were open so he was able to restock his larder, cook a hearty breakfast and then set off to find Big Joe Monk who lived in the next village.

Things improved after that. His oppo was already bored stiff with two days of inactivity and welcomed the chance of some long, hard walks into the bleak winter countryside. Drinking in company at night was vastly more enjoyable than his previous lonely sojourn, and for the first time he was able to put Gabby firmly from his mind.

He hadn't been looking forward to meeting Mike Ash at Heathrow for the scheduled Scandinavian Airlines flight to Stockholm. At first sight he thought the captain seemed less than his usual buoyant self, but Hunt told himself the man had a lot on his mind. Ash hardly looked at him as he enquired after his sick foster father, and just nodded when told of the unexpected recovery. There was no word of Hunt's foreshortened stay. Instead Ash turned his attention to getting his party through the check-in desk.

The captain had easily slipped into the role of a Fiscex marketing executive with a pale grey suit, which was far smarter than the ageing three-piece that Hunt had dug out from the back of his wardrobe. Ever quiet and watchful, Bill Mather looked more menacing than he should have done in a dark pinstripe. More like a ginger-haired Mafia hit man, Hunt thought, and half-imagined a sub-machine gun being toted in his hand luggage.

Both Big Joe Monk and Len Pope looked just too big and bulky to be taken seriously as businessmen, with their little-used suits bulging at the biceps. Pope, he noticed, only carried one item of luggage. He was the team's "kit freak" with an obsession about light and efficient equipment. He would always be begging, borrowing or stealing every new military or civilian item to come on the market. From boots to sleeping bags he would experiment and test everything to destruction. Hunt had never known Pope not to have the lightest and most effective gear wherever he went in the world.

His lightweight Italian Anniel snowboots proved it again when they arrived at sub-arctic Stockholm, close behind a fresh fall of snow. Whilst the others slipped and slid in stout winter shoes, an amused Pope moved ahead as deftly as a chamois antelope.

The city bus took them to the centre along a flat and boring route lined with silver birch, an uninspiring entrance to what Hunt regarded as one of the most beautiful cities in Europe. Whilst the Russians extolled Leningrad as "the Venice of the North", that was an accolade he personally handed to the Swedes without hesitation. A glittering city spanning fourteen islands interlinked with a charming variety of bridges. Everywhere there were creeks and bays filled with a bobbing forest of ships' masts of all shapes and sizes, and overlooked by splendid eighteenth-century buildings, parks and hotels.

However there was none of this to be seen at the bleak inland Central Station where an icy-edged wind had cleared the urban thoroughfare of all but the hardiest pedestrians. From there they took a taxi to the north-west suburb of Bromma where the borrowed Fiscex apartment was situated.

It was the ground maisonette of a timber-clad house standing in a narrow residential street of similar buildings, each with its own neatly fenced garden, currently buried under two feet of snow.

The door was opened by a rotund, pink-faced man with sharply receding black hair and heavily framed spectacles. Thick cord trousers and a Shetland sweater added to his bulk.

"Welcome, gents. I'm the personnel manager for Fiscex here in Sweden. Peter Burke's the name." He extended a pudgy hand and insisted on greeting each man warmly. "Which just goes to show what they think of Personnel – reckon mine's the only department that can spare the time for this sort of caper." Another jolly laugh. "No offence, lads, I'm quite tickled. Beats spending the day interviewing gorgeous Swedish girls for typing jobs."

Big Joe Monk and Len Pope exchanged looks and grinned. They were amongst friends.

Burke burbled on cheerily. "Just dump your kit in the lounge here. All mod cons, see. Telly, vid, stereo – not much of a record selection – all Abba and Elvis Presley, I'm afraid. Obviously your predecessor was a man of odd taste."

Ash glanced around the room. It was bright and airy with a polished pine floor and painted in typically Swedish style with pastel shades. The sofa and chairs looked soft and inviting. "This will be fine, Peter."

The Fiscex executive looked pleased. "We've arranged a couple of extra telephone lines, so you can always keep one free for incoming calls."

He bounced jauntily through the hall to the bedrooms which met with everyone's approval.

"One bed short, I'm afraid, so whoever draws the short straw sleeps on the sofa," he added.

"No problem," Bill Mather grunted. Over the years he'd been so accustomed to living rough that he actually found it difficult to sleep in a bed.

"What about wheels?" Ash asked.

"Wheels? Ah, a car, yes?" Peter Burke beamed. "There's a company Volvo at your disposal. The one parked at the front. It's topped up with juice and there's everything in the boot – snow-chains, mats, shovels. Go anywhere in that." He took a deep breath, satisfied. "Now I've been told to put everything at your disposal. Of course, I don't know what you chaps are up to – " he tapped his nose "– and I don't want to. Let's just say I've read a lot of thrillers and all the books on the Falklands – so I've a shrewd idea who you are and the sort of things you need . . ."

Bill Mather's face suddenly became even more inscrutable than usual.

"You've got my office number," Burke continued, "my home number and my car phone. Any time day or night. Don't hesitate. Nothing's too much trouble, however outlandish. Meanwhile the kitchen's well stocked – I recommend the sil herrings, bit of an acquired taste though – and I've a whole pile of maps, guidebooks, bus timetables, etc."

Finally Ash could restrain his smile no longer. "Really, Peter, you've done a grand job. We're not used to this five-star treatment and we're really grateful."

Burke's face glowed with pride. "Just glad to work with you chaps. A privilege. Now, any other requests?"

Monk toyed with his walrus moustache thoughtfully. "How about one of your gorgeous Swedish secretaries to do our typing?"

Burke's eyes popped. "A secretary? Oh, I never thought . . ."

"He's just joshing," Hunt said.

"I am?" Monk's face was all innocence.

"He is," Ash confirmed.

Monk shrugged. "I am."

"Tell you what though, chaps," Burke said suddenly. "Why don't I take you round Stockholm tonight? Help you get your bearings. It's quite a common thing when new Fiscex people come over, so it wouldn't raise any suspicions. What y' say?"

It proved to be a smart move. Peter Burke was a well-informed and cheerful guide. Most importantly he asked no questions but provided informative and imaginative answers. By the end of the evening the SAS men's natural taciturn attitude to strangers had relaxed noticeably. He was an ally who was likely to prove reliable if asked to do anything. Nothing was too much trouble.

They first crossed and recrossed the city on foot which gave the entire team a good sense of the urban layout, main locations and bearings. He pointed out buildings of interest, as well as bars and hotels which served to add detail to the mental map each man already carried in his head.

It was two in the morning when they were admitted by a suspicious-looking bouncer into the Old Fashion bar off Drottningatan. The warm air rushed at them, filled with smoke and guitar music as they fought their way to the bar.

"Beers are hellishly expensive," Burke explained as he handed round the glasses. "And spirits are prohibitive. So wine's your best bet. I'll stick to lemonade. In Sweden drinking and driving's absolutely taboo."

Hunt glanced around at the long-haired youngsters. Perhaps it was his imagination, but either the entire room was swaying or he was. "Price doesn't seem to have deterred this lot," he observed.

Burke chuckled. "No, it doesn't, does it? They're a hardworking lot, but when they do drink they take it seriously. Sober as judges all week – no lunchtimes down the pub like back home – but come Friday night – Wow! Beer and chasers. Most youngsters are blitzed by nine o'clock. But whereas the Brits will cave in and go to sleep, the Swedes keep going – somehow!"

"You sound quite fond of them," Hunt observed.

Burke laughed. "They're a good bunch. A bit insular till you get to know them, but once you break the ice they're very friendly. Personally I put their drinking habits down to boredom during the long winter months. And the respectability. Despite their reputation for free love and all that, Swedes are very *respectable*. Very natural in their human responses, mind. Things like nudity and screwing are considered respectable."

"Very sensible," Monk muttered appreciatively, wiping froth from his moustache. "I call that civilised. I could get to like it here."

Burke laughed. He liked the big man with the tombstone teeth who reminded him of a caricature Mexican

134

bandido from a Clint Eastwood movie. Burke would have dearly wished to have been like him. Once, years ago when he was still at school, he had thought he'd like to be a commando. But poor eyesight, indifferent health and a lot of academic promise had steered him reluctantly into commerce. Meeting Mike Ash's team had rekindled old dreams. "Listen, chaps, I think it might be an idea if we set up some sort of pattern regarding your cover. Why don't you all come into the office tomorrow morning, just for a coffee, and leave discreetly after an hour or so. Then make a point of at least one of you calling in at Fiscex every day. That'll allay any suspicions anyone may have. It'll also give you the chance to tell me about your latest requirements face-to-face rather than use the phone."

Hunt frowned. "Just how much *do* you know about what we're doing, Peter?"

Burke smiled nervously. "Look, you guys, I know *nothing*! But when a humble employee like me gets a personal invitation from our chairman for a quiet drink, then meets some shady character from some nameless ministry, I get the idea that what you're doing might not be strictly . . ." He lowered his voice to a whisper " . . . legitimate, shall we say? That means it's got to be against someone else's interests. Maybe the Swedes, or maybe someone else. That suggests Eastern Bloc to me. So that means you've got to be covering your tracks against the Swedish police or the Russkies – or both."

Monk said: "All these thrillers you say you read, Pete. Maybe you oughta try writing one."

From Peter Burke's office at Fiscex, Mike Ash's team was able to arrange the hire of two more cars, handing over the money direct to the company from their own funds. It also gave them the opportunity to ask the man a lot of mundane but necessary questions, the answers to which it would otherwise have taken them wasted time to find out for themselves. They also discovered that the company had dark-room facilities which could prove useful.

Whilst Big Joe Monk and Len Pope set off for the island of Lidingo to the north-east of the city to take a look at the Rönkä Society, Bill Mather headed west to take a discreet look at the Soviet Embassy in case their defector was to be kept in residence there after each day's lecture.

Meanwhile Ash and Hunt took the Volvo back to their apartment. Both men were on edge. Shalayez's arrival was only a couple of days away and so far their information was scant to say the least.

As they were spreading out maps over the floor of the lounge, a taxi left the British Embassy on the other side of the city.

In the rear seat was a pale-faced, rather nervous-looking young man who clutched his attaché case as though his life depended on it. Ralph Lavender, visa secretary.

He took the cab to the NK department store, walked through it and left by the lower level under Sergels Torg, before walking the short distance to Central Station. There he joined the queue of passengers waiting at the taxi rank. After a couple of minutes it was his turn and he climbed aboard, giving an address in Bromma suburb.

Captain Mike Ash answered the door.

"There didn't seem much point in ringing first," Lavender said. "The fewer telephone calls the better. Can't be too careful."

"Quite," Ash replied and led him into the lounge where Hunt was poring over the maps.

"I see you're hard at work with planning," Lavender observed.

Hunt nodded in recognition. "But it would be better if we had something to plan on. So far there's sweet FA."

Lavender's smile was icy. "That's why I've come round. At last we've had news. Shalayez arrives the day after tomorrow, Aeroflot from Moscow. I've all the details here." He patted his attaché case. "He'll be driven first of all to the Soviet Embassy for all the usual niceties. To meet their ambassador and no doubt be told that if he puts so much as a toe out of line they'll cut it off at the knee. Usual stuff. Then he'll go on to the Society. Have you checked it out yet?"

Ash said: "A couple of the lads are doing a recce now from the outside. But we need details of the inside layout too. I think we can bluff our way in. Local authority survey or somesuch. It's only a mathematics centre after all, hardly Fort Knox."

"That won't be necessary," Lavender replied evenly. "It'll only serve to draw attention to whoever pays a visit, which is the last thing I want to do. Besides, I've got some fairly thorough floor plans here too. They're not architectural drawings but good enough. One of our Cambridge professors was at the Society recently. At our behest he suggested that they invite Shalayez over, and at the same time he took a good look around."

Hunt grinned. "Ace! As long as they're thorough."

Lavender looked scornful. "Mathematicians always are."

Ash said: "Do I gather you favour a lift from the Society itself?"

The intelligence officer made himself comfortable on the sofa. "Well, you're the experts, but after his initial trip to the embassy Shalayez will be resident at the Society. They have an adjoining apartment block."

Hunt lit a cigarette. "Then maybe he can just walk out?"

"Ah," Lavender said, "that's the bad news. He'll certainly be guarded. And we can't afford to have dead KGB goons all over the place. So you'll have to get it exactly right."

Ash stared thoughtfully at the ceiling. "One thing does seriously worry me, and that's a way of making contact with Ivan direct. If we're to avoid contact with

137

his minders, we're going to need his co-operation."

"We hope to have means of direct contact, Mike – "
Lavender found the first-name familiarity embarrassing
" – That's another reason for me calling. One of our
people got close to him in Moscow. She's now in Stock-
holm. Like you she's using a job with Fiscex as cover.
And I gather she received a call from him last night."

Ash raised an eyebrow. "She?"

Lavender's smile came out as a sneer. "Yes, she. A
woman. What's so strange about that? Anyway, I asked
her to come here this morning. I thought it safer than
debriefing her at our embassy. And, besides, I expect
you'll have some questions you want to ask."

"When should we expect her?"

Lavender glanced at his watch. "Any time now."

Hunt said: "Then I'd better put a brew on."

The aroma of freshly roasted coffee was just beginning
to waft through the apartment when the visitor arrived.

Hunt answered the door. He didn't really know what
he expected but it certainly wasn't someone as young as
Lucinda. Nor someone as good-looking.

"Is this the right place for Mr Lavender?"

Hunt's grin was spontaneous. "Come in. You're just
in time for coffee."

Relief showed as she smiled. Her nerves had been
playing up and it was good to see a friendly face. In the
hall she climbed out of her snowboots and thick coat like
a butterfly emerging from a heavy woollen chrysalis.
The smart grey two-piece flared nicely at the hip, Hunt
noticed. Slim calves and ankles were sheathed in blue
stockings which matched the simple blouse. To all the
world she looked like a young business executive.

He noticed Mike Ash's reaction was similar to his own:
an involuntary smile as he liked what he saw. Only
Lavender appeared totally unimpressed. He didn't wait
until the coffee had been distributed before he pressed
her for details.

"Well, he telephoned me at my flat last night," she

began nervously. "I think he was calling from his flat in Moscow. He sounded very odd. Cagey, I suppose. Talking in a sort of coded way."

"How?" Lavender demanded. He was making no allowances for her inexperience.

"He said he missed me and that he'd be coming to Stockholm the day after tomorrow. He'd go to the Society to lecture and wondered if he could arrange to see me. I said, sure I'd love to. But then he said the problem was he would be escorted. He emphasised that. *Escorted*."

Lavender nodded. "KGB minders."

"I did as I was instructed," she continued. "I said that somehow I would get to the Society, and that he shouldn't try to reach me."

"And he accepted what you said?" Lavender pressed.

"Yes."

"Without question?"

There was a distant look in the doleful brown eyes. "Yes, it was as though" – her forehead creased into a frown – "as though he *knew* what my role in all this is. He sounded distant. There was no warmth when he spoke to me. Not like before."

Lavender's smirk returned. "I shouldn't worry about that. The important thing is that we've achieved direct contact."

Lucinda shook her head. "I don't like it. I feel as though I've betrayed him."

The intelligence officer's eyebrows rose quizzically. "Well, you have, haven't you?"

Her eyes dropped and studied her fingers which were interlaced restively in her lap.

Realising that he'd been too glib, he added: "Don't worry, there'll be time enough for you to explain things to him. Our contact has obviously told him that you're in a position to help – clearly we can't make detailed arrangements like this via Moscow. When you see him tell him your original meeting was genuine. That you've only been contacted by our security services since you've been in Stockholm. Make it sound convincing. He has no way of knowing any different. If it sounds like you've both been used then it'll bring you closer together."

For Hunt this was a rare glimpse into the inner workings of part of the operation that didn't concern them. A tantalising titbit. It was easy to speculate that the girl had been selected for her evident feminine charms. Although he thought she looked too young and immature for such a job.

Ash tried to steer a way to more practical matters. "Tell me, Lucinda, how do you propose to make contact with Ivan?"

Her eyes hardened. "Actually it's Niki," she corrected frostily.

Ash's smile was disarming. "Sorry, force of habit. We like to avoid actual names. Russians are always Ivan to us. Like Germans are Fritz, that sort of thing."

She blushed. "Sorry, stupid of me. I'm not used to this kind of work. It's getting me a bit uptight."

"That's perfectly understandable. Just remember we're friends and here to help. We'll be organising the actual lift so it's important we all understand each other, and get on."

Lucinda welcomed the friendly attitude of the two strangers which was markedly different from that of Lavender, who now sat glowering at what he considered to be unnecessary familiarity. It didn't occur to him that they were merely trying to put her at ease.

Looking at them she guessed they were military men although their hair was less severely cut than was usual. When you were daughter to a brigadier such recognition was second nature. "You're soldiers I take it?"

Ash just smiled and touched his lips with his forefinger.

She looked happier now. No doubt they were what her father called 'Special Forces'. Maybe commandos of some sort, even SAS troops? Whoever they were their presence filled her with renewed confidence. She said:

140

"It's been arranged for me to attend Niki's lectures. I'll be registered in my own name, which is Court-Ogg, so as not to alert the Russians. It's been arranged through my old university. I graduated in Russian and Mathematics, you see."

Hunt was impressed. Beauty as well as brains.

Ralph Lavender interrupted. "It wasn't difficult for us to organise. The Society is very obliging and of course they don't suspect anything. What it does mean is that Lucinda will be in contact with him all the time he's here."

"That's excellent," Ash agreed. "All we need to do now is decide exactly how we're going to do it."

Björn Larsson was feeling depressed.

He blamed it on the weather. He hadn't seen the sun for days and he put his bad mood down to a lack of Vitamin D. That and the fluorescent light in the cramped office he'd been allocated as a junior feature writer on the popular *Expressen* newspaper.

If it wasn't for the fact that his fair skin went lobster-coloured the instant he stepped under a sunlamp, he might have cured his blues by regular visits to a solarium. It was how a lot of Swedes managed to look a picture of health even on the darkest of winter days.

Restlessly he kicked back his chair and walked to the window. On the tenth floor he was almost in the clouds and visibility was so poor he could only just distinguish the outline of the Soviet Embassy far below on the opposite side of the busy Gjörwellsgatan.

He smiled to himself. What stories were in there to be uncovered? Many, he was sure. He was trying to build his reputation on stories of espionage and international intrigue, but little had happened recently. It had been best when the Russian submarines had been crawling all round the Stockholm archipelago. He'd written some stirring stuff then; earned some well-deserved recognition. He'd scared the pants off half the population with his revelations of Soviet infiltration and subversion.

But it had gone quiet again now. He kicked lethargically at the radiator. Just another month and he'd have a week off to go skiing up in the mountains. He looked forward to that. Then, before you knew it, it would be spring, and he'd be able to cycle to and from work again. Tighten the slack winter muscles; he liked to be fit.

Idly he turned and picked up the remnants of the morning post.

Nothing! Christ, why was Sweden so boring? What he wouldn't give for a decent crimewave like they had in other countries . . .

Suddenly his eye caught the headed notepaper of the Rönkä Society of Advanced Mathematics and Computer Science. A press release. Evidently it had been bounced around all the feature writers until it had finally reached him. No one else was interested.

Björn Larsson sat down. Had he not once thought seriously of becoming a mathematical scientist himself – before a youthful and passionate romance distracted him – and had he not once researched a major anti-Reagan article on Star Wars, he may have been as uninterested in the release as his fellow journalists.

Nikolai Shalayez coming to lecture in Stockholm.

He blinked. It must be him. The very same. It had to be!

Larsson smiled to himself. What an interview that could make! He knew all the right questions to ask, too. But would the Soviets allow an interview? He glanced at his watch. The morning's editorial meeting was due in just a few minutes. He'd raise the subject then.

He decided to bide his time until after the most pressing matters of the day had been discussed between the editor and the gathering of staff reporters and writers.

Half-an-hour later everyone had their allotted tasks for the next twenty-four hours. Larsson raised his hand.

"Yes, Björn?" The editor had taken on the young man

two years before and had great hopes of him in the future.

"I understand a famous Russian scientist-mathematician is coming to Stockholm for a seminar. I thought maybe a piece on his work, or even an interview . . .?"

"Who?" the editor interrupted briskly.

"Nikolai Shalayez."

"Never heard of him."

"His works are well-known in scientific circles. He's been working on Russian space defence projects."

The editor sighed; perhaps he'd been wrong about the youngster after all. "Listen, Björn, no offence but our average reader couldn't give a damn about sputniks and death rays. It's over their heads – literally. Now, dogs in space and women astronauts – another story. I suggest you get your feet more firmly on the ground or go get a job with *Svenska Dagbladet*. Meanwhile why don't you take a look at that farmer who reckons he's discovered that cow pats are a cure for baldness? Human interest, that's the stuff we need."

"But – "

"But nothing, Björn, that Russian coming here has to be the non-story of the year." The editor snapped suddenly: "That's it, the meeting's over."

Björn Larsson's headache returned with a vengeance.

Göran Hallberg had almost lost the British visa secretary when he'd switched taxis that morning. He'd been caught wrong-footed when the man had paid off his first cab on Hamngatan and had walked a short distance before disappearing into the giant NK department store.

It was by pure chance that later Hallberg had driven into the forecourt of Central Station just as Ralph Lavender was speeding out of the exit in a second taxi. Despite fierce and skilful driving Hallberg had still not closed the gap sufficiently when they reached the Bromma suburb. He lost the taxi in the back streets.

Again it was pure good fortune that, ten minutes later, he saw the passengerless cab coming back out of one of the narrow residential streets.

Thinking quickly he steered his car into the centre of the roadway, effectively blocking the path of the oncoming vehicle.

He leaped out and rushed over to the taxi driver.

"Hey, excuse me. You have just dropped a man around here from the station?"

The driver looked cautious. "Yes, so what?"

A relieved smile lit up Hallberg's usually impassive face. "It's my brother. I was due to meet him at the station but I got held up. The problem is I don't know the address we're supposed to be going to in Bromma."

Obligingly the driver told him; he liked to be helpful.

He received a ten kronor note for his trouble and waited patiently while Hallberg backed up to let him pass.

Minutes later Hallberg cruised silently over the snow-encrusted road, passing the maisonette. There was a light on in the downstairs window and he could see some men standing, talking together.

Parking his car around the next corner he sauntered nonchalantly back along the street, pausing on the pavement opposite to retie the laces of his stout winter shoes. His training enabled him to memorise the faces he saw framed in the window. The first was the visa secretary from the British Embassy. The second was a tall man, whose handsome sunburnt features were topped by a crown unusually bald for someone in his late thirties. The last man was of a similar age but of a shorter, more powerful build. Instinct told him they were military men. There was something of an aura about them: shortish hair and an upright bearing. An alertness and an assertiveness about the way they moved.

Göran Hallberg's instincts rarely let him down. He had been a Soviet agent since the early sixties when he'd been unwittingly recruited by a college girlfriend who was active in the Communist Party youth movement. He'd been fully ensnared during the time of his military service in the Fältjägarna special forces; he'd resisted at first but the GRU paid well, and money-management had never been one of Hallberg's strong points. Later in civilian life, he set up business as a freelance photographer. It gave him the excuse to go virtually anywhere he chose with a powerful telephoto camera, and mostly he went wherever his GRU chiefs chose. As now, that was often shadowing the known intelligence officers of other nations, because the Soviets were unwilling to use their own people who were likely to be known to the opposition or to Swedish counter-intelligence.

Just then one of the men closed the curtains in the flat, and Hallberg began returning to his car when another vehicle turned into the street. A small Volkswagen Polo. It moved along ponderously as though the driver was looking for a particular house number.

Hallberg slipped around the corner and paused to light a cigarette, watching surreptitiously through the bare branches of an overgrown shrub.

The Polo pulled up outside the maisonette and the driver climbed out. It was a girl. Young, hardly in her twenties. She glanced nervously up and down the street. As she looked in his direction something in his brain clicked like a camera shutter.

The instant recall of a photographic memory. Not that it was that difficult with such an attractive, striking face. Not when he had seen the girl's photograph only a few days before.

He tried to put a name to it. He visualised the page on which he had read it. It had been a routine report on the personnel of foreign companies which had substantial business contracts with the Soviet Union. The shape of the words formed in his mind. Marsh. That was it. Lucinda Marsh.

He smiled. Lucinda Marsh. Recently joined the

Stockholm office of Fiscex Holdings as a Russian interpreter.

Interesting.

He settled down to wait until Ralph Lavender finished his meeting.

5

The Aeroflot jet liner dipped suddenly on the start of its descent to Stockholm.

It did nothing to quell Nikolai Shalayez's stomach which had been churning throughout the flight from Moscow. Nerves, pure and simple. Ever since his friend Sergei Chagall had come to his apartment in the early hours two weeks ago, he had been living on a knife edge. He'd lost his appetite and had survived on tea and the odd biscuit. Always slim, now even his trousers hung loosely on his hips; he'd had to make two extra notches in his belt.

Each day had been agony as he waited to learn if he'd been granted the permit to visit Stockholm. And each day he had waited for the dawn knock on his door. Visitors from Sergei's superiors in the KGB demanding knowledge of his association with a certain English-woman called Lucinda Marsh.

In the event, no knock ever came. Chagall had been as good as his word; he had temporarily taken his damning report out of circulation to give Shalayez the chance to make good his escape.

Only when he was finally packed and waiting for the taxi, with the pass and air tickets in his hand, did he actually accept that he'd got away with it.

He hadn't been expecting the short man with the sallow Mongoloid looks who arrived at his door minutes before he left. The thick grey overcoat and slouch hat was as good as any uniform. KGB.

His smile had been friendly enough. "Comrade Dr Shalayez? I'm your escort to Stockholm. Just to see you don't get into any trouble. Your taxi's downstairs. Shall we go?"

Shalayez swore that his heart had literally stopped for a second. He'd felt its momentary flutter in his chest.

But it was all right. The man was seated beside him now, asleep and snoring lightly, having feasted himself on both his own and Shalayez's in-flight meal, and demolished a hip-flask of vodka. The metallic butt-end of a pistol was just visible at his armpit where his jacket gaped.

Shalayez sighed. The Mongol was due to return with the flight, and he was to be handed over to someone else when they landed. If they too were armed, he didn't rate his chances of being able to get away.

He'd asked Sergei if he should try to give himself up to the airport authorities, as he passed from the Arrivals area to the main concourse. His friend had been impatient with him. On no account should he hand himself over to the Swedes. They would be just as likely to pack him back on the next flight. No, he should just do what he was told: go to the Society and wait to be contacted.

"How will that be?" he'd enquired.

"You'll know – when it happens," was Chagall's reply.

As it was, he doubted he'd even get through the departure formalities at Moscow. The officials had gone through everyone's luggage. One young American girl tourist had been reduced to tears, as her underwear and a box of sanitary towels were scattered with the rest of her belongings in full public view. She became hysterical when she was taken away for a strip-search.

The Mongol had chuckled. "Obviously they liked the look of her. They're not interested about our image abroad – just concerned about getting a good eyeful."

His escort had found the incident highly amusing, but it left Shalayez feeling cold and helpless. When his turn came, his baggage was subjected to the same minute

148

inspection. The official showed special interest in the pages of algebraic formulae that had been prepared for his lectures.

"It's all right," the Mongol assured, flashing his red pass.

The official's face was a stone wall. "I'll have to check."

"Phone this number," the Mongol said, and handed over a card.

It was an agonising half-hour wait before Shalayez could move on; a wait that caused a delay in takeoff. No one seemed to care.

His ears were blocking now as they continued their descent. He held his nose and blew hard until his ears popped. He could hear again, and pressed his cheek against the window to get a better view of the Swedish mainland which must surely be in sight. But there was only leaden cloud below, thick and wintry.

Unlike the American girl, he thought how he wouldn't even feel free when he arrived in Stockholm. For him there were still hours, or probably days to go. And, if that KGB report surfaced before he disappeared, then he would have to wait a lifetime. A lifetime in which he would never see Lucy again. That would be the most painful part of all. Because, despite Sergei's warnings that she could be acting on orders from British Intelligence, he couldn't believe that she hadn't meant what she said to him in their most intimate moments. Even if she'd been acting, there would have been no need for her to say things like that.

And, again, when he telephoned her in Stockholm. She had sounded both surprised and delighted to hear from him. It was he who felt awkward as he asked her to visit him at the Society. She'd laughed happily and said she was sure there was a way. Leave it to her. He had little option to that.

"Goodbye, dear Niki," she had said finally. "And, please, don't be surprised when you see me."

He started to ask her what she meant, but the line

went dead. The cut-off tone rang irritably in his ear as he found himself staring at the mouthpiece in puzzlement.

It wouldn't be long now before he found out.

The chimes and flashing warning lights heralded the run-in to Stockholm. Twenty minutes later the sleep-weary Mongol accompanied him into the terminal, through customs and into the reception area. There he was handed over to a short, stern-faced man in a fur coat and matching hat with earflaps.

"Welcome to Stockholm, Comrade Doctor. My name's Jackov." A fat smile transformed his face. "I'm assigned to look after you while you're here, sir. And a privilege it is, too, to have such a distinguished guest. You'll enjoy Sweden, it's quite one of the best postings we security chaps can get. Is that your case? Let me take it for you."

As they talked, the two men began walking towards the doors and the waiting Volvo with the diplomatic plates.

A tall man seated on one of the concourse seats lowered his newspaper. His ginger moustache gave a slight twitch as his cold grey eyes followed their progress.

Bill Mather had clocked his quarry.

"Well, now we know," Captain Mike Ash said. "Shalayez *isn't* staying at the Society at night."

A murmur of disappointment went round the gathering in the lounge of the Fiscex apartment. Everyone was there: Hunt's four-man Sabre team, Ralph Lavender and the girl.

"That's a shame," Ash continued, "because it would have been ideal. The residential apartment block adjoins the main building in the grounds. There are no fences to speak of, so access wouldn't have proved a problem. Even if he had a guard in the next room, we could have got him out through the window. Two minutes and we'd have been away by car."

Ralph Lavender sniffed heavily; the strain showed in

his pallor. "Presumably that's exactly the reason he's not staying there. So where is he staying, not the Soviet Embassy compound?"

Bill Mather spoke from one of the armchairs. "No, they've installed him at the Grand Hotel."

Lavender looked relieved.

Mather shook his head. "Sorry, but it's not much better. They've selected the location very carefully. He's in 450 which is what they call a junior suite. Unlike most of the other suites it has no interconnecting doors, and it occupies the left-hand corner of the building overlooking the main road and Strömmen waterfront. Inside there's only one door in – through a small hall and reception, where chummy's minders will be, which leads off to the bedroom."

"How did you find out all this?" Lavender asked.

"Used my cover," Mather replied casually. "Said Fiscex wanted a venue for a small drinks party, so they showed me round. I actually looked at the suite below our friend's, but the layout's identical on each floor."

Lavender sucked at his teeth. "Could you go in posing as a waiter? You know, bucket of champagne with the compliments of the management, that sort of thing?"

Mather's look was withering. "You're dealing with armed KGB professionals, mate, not bloody Girl Guides. It's the equivalent of a full-frontal assault, and someone's going to get hurt. And that could be chummy himself if he's standing in the wrong place at the wrong time. Not to mention some passing tycoon or whoever else can afford the Grand's prices." He paused. "Then we've got the problem of getting him out of the hotel unhindered. And that's before we look at transport, etc. It *could* be done, but it could easily be very messy. Not the clean job you want."

For the first time Lavender looked suitably chastened. "Sorry, Bill, I didn't realise."

"What about a Peter Pan job?" Hunt asked. "Abseil down from the roof or another apartment. Tap on his bedroom window and away? In the morning they'd just find him gone."

"That would be plausible at the back where it looks onto a dark street," Mather agreed. "Or even the sides. But the front is bloody well floodlit, not to mention the fact it overlooks the Royal Palace."

A chuckle of mirth went round the room. It was a sense of humour that Lavender didn't share. "So what are you going for?" he demanded.

Ash smiled disarmingly. "Big Joe and Len had a good look around the Society and they think they've got a possible solution."

"Well, I hope to God someone has. This is starting to look desperate."

Ash motioned Monk to take the floor. The big sergeant pinned an elevated plan of the building to the cork message board by the telephone before he began. "You can see here on the drawings you supplied that the Society is housed in a modern three-storey building, standing in some four acres of wooded grounds. Now we've discovered that a lift goes straight up from the reception rooms to the third floor. From there, you can follow a short flight of steps to a small machinery tower on the roof."

"What's the significance of that?" Lavender asked.

Monk shrugged. "Well, for instance, it means that one minute someone could be sitting in the ground-floor lounge having coffee, wander innocently into the next room, and – zap! – be on the tower in under sixty seconds." He smiled, big teeth showing beneath the shaggy moustache; he always enjoyed revealing a master plan, especially when simplicity solved the seemingly insuperable. "If a helo were to rendezvous at that precise moment, our friend Ivan would be away probably even before his guards realised he was missing. At worst, they'd just get to the roof in time to wave him goodbye."

Lavender chewed on the end of his pen. "A helicopter, eh? Would that be feasible? I thought you said the grounds were wooded? Wouldn't the trees cause a problem?"

This time it was Len Pope who answered in his strong Hampshire accent. "We've done a visual. The building, she stands proud of the trees, see? Well, the tower anyway. I'm not saying he wouldn't be a tricky bit of flying, he would. Couldn't land, see. Have to hover and winch chummy up. She's a very small LS – that's landing site – especially seein' how it'll be dark and snow coverin' everything. We'd have to get a couple of our chaps on the tower to guide her in, but I don't see no problem there."

Hunt felt a profound sense of relief; it sounded promising.

Lavender tried to fathom the implications. "You thinking of hiring a civilian chopper to do this?"

"No way," Monk replied. "Len made it sound easy, but it calls for a highly skilled bit of flying. So we'd need our own pilot – not least for security reasons. Can't just drop any old Sven flyer a couple of hundred kronor to do us a favour. And one of our pilots is going to want a machine he's familiar with. More to the point, one that's capable of doing the job."

A look of horror swept over Lavender's face as he realised what was being suggested. "You mean overfly Sweden illegally?"

Monk grinned enthusiastically. "Why not? If we drop chummy in Sweden, we've still got the problem of getting him over the border. And the Russkies are going to be watching every exit point. This is what you wanted – in and out before you can say 'knife'. Chummy will just have disappeared into thin air, literally. There'll be no evidence for the Russkies to wave about. Nothing."

Lavender felt sick in the pit of his stomach. "What about Sweden's air defences? Radar coverage and that sort of thing?"

Ash said: "We'll have to check it out, but Sweden's air defences are concentrated on the east and Russia.

153

They're not going to panic if an intrusion comes from Norway. They might not like it, but their reaction is more likely to be low-key."

Hunt added: "That's only *if* it's picked up on radar. We want a special unit trained in low-level contour flying all the way. That'll take it under most radars, in amongst the ground clutter."

"I think it should work," Ash agreed.

Lavender looked at each of the men in turn. "The idea will have to be sanctioned at high level. If we blew it we'd be compromising Sweden's neutrality as well as violating its airspace." He turned to the girl. "Did you follow all that, Lucinda?"

She nodded. "I think so. Lift Niki from the roof by helicopter."

"Do you think he'd go along with that?"

Lucinda shrugged. "I don't know. Is it dangerous?"

Monk looked at her strangely, as he pondered what her relationship was with the Russian defector. "There's always a danger, love. But we'd be with him. As long as he's got balls and doesn't suffer from chronic vertigo."

"Then I'm sure he'd do it," Lucinda replied.

"Right," Lavender said with the zeal of the newly converted. "I'll put the idea forward and see what happens. But when you see Shalayez tomorrow, Lucinda, don't tell him yet *how* we hope to do it. Just assure him it'll be in the next day or two. And meanwhile, take careful note of the daily pattern at the Society. Coffee breaks, lunchtime, and any social meetings for drinks, etc. We'll want to strike when his KGB guards are feeling relaxed. I'm afraid that side of it is all down to you."

The girl looked very young and pale, Hunt observed. He wondered if she was up to it. He'd gathered that she wasn't a fully trained professional, but a part-time recruit with special qualities, and he had a shrewd suspicion he knew what they were. Already there was a strained and haunted expression in her eyes that he had seen before in others recruited by the Secret Intelligence Service.

"I'll manage," she said.

Brave little bitch, Hunt thought.

"Any problems from now on, and you deal direct with Mike's men here," Lavender concluded briskly. "They'll advise and look after you."

She glanced around with a nervous smile. Big Joe Monk's wide grin was meant to radiate reassurance; it wasn't quite the way it came across.

Grigory Yvon contemplated the overcast sky from his office in the Soviet Embassy. More snow, he was certain of it. The clouds had that pinkish tinge to them. It was a sure sign.

He turned away, a tall gaunt figure reflected in the heavy gilt mirror on the opposite wall. His suit was well made by Götrich, the exclusive Stockholm tailors, but it could do little to hide his skeletal figure. His skull, too, had little fleshy covering, the skin sunken at his cheeks and around the sockets from which his eyes burned with a dark malevolence. Eyes that were fierce and intimidating, yet gave away no emotion of any kind. The receding black hair swept directly back from his steep forehead did nothing to soften his corpse-like appearance.

Indeed he knew his staff called him 'The Cadaver' behind his back. It was his job to know about such things, and it didn't concern him. He found it vaguely amusing. In its way it showed a certain fear and a certain respect. That he could live with.

As the GRU resident in Stockholm, his power alone *should* demand such fear and respect. He was answerable to no one, neither the ambassador himself nor the KGB. Soviet Military Intelligence looked after its own. Only the head of the *Glavnoye Razvedyvatelnoye Upravleniye* and the Central Committee itself could ask him to account for his decisions. And those decisions covered a range of activities that would chill the average Swede to his bones, if only he knew.

From his secluded office in the Soviet Embassy, with its Plexiglass windows that defeated any attempt to eavesdrop, he commanded a vast intelligence network like a fat spider in the centre of a web. It was a web that reached out to every aspect of Swedish life that could be of use to the military. His hand-picked staff recruited and ran an army of informers in all useful walks of life. Government officials, journalists, police, military factory and shipyard workers, servicemen – in fact, anyone who could assist the GRU to penetrate the secrets of Swedish defence planning and its powerful armaments industry.

Whilst Yvon commanded his network from the security of the embassy, many of his officers operated from the Trade Mission, the Aeroflot offices and other cover organisations.

Grigory Yvon liked Sweden. Its population was friendly and gullible. It made his life easier. Often informers didn't have to be paid. They were so trusting and innocent that frequently information would be offered on a plate in answer to a casual enquiry. Those agents who deliberately betrayed their country were more likely to do so out of sympathy for Soviet socialism than for money.

Then there were Yvon's 'illegals'. His private intelligence army of Soviet officers passing themselves off as Swedes or other foreigners, burrowing away into the fabric of society like invisible woodworm. Underground. Sometimes actively reporting, even breaking into defence establishments where necessary. Sometimes even sabotaging. Others established by the Spetsnaz just 'slept'. Waiting for the call to action.

Yvon's final resource was the Third Department of the GRU itself. The *Spetsnaz.* Drawn in Sweden's case from the Soviet Baltic Fleet. A ruthless unit of undercover special troops who, in preparation for war, would carry out the assassination of key political and military figures, diversionary raids and acts of sabotage to neutralise effectively an enemy before he was aware that he had a fight on his hands. In peacetime, they were used more sparingly, usually for specialist reconnaissance work. Or the occasional 'wet job', when someone had to be disposed of with no questions asked.

Sweden was an interesting posting. Not one of the top like London, Washington, Paris or Bonn. Not one that demanded the control of a full rank major-general, but one that offered more than enough scope for a man like Colonel Yvon. On the surface the place was a placid backwater of Europe. But stir beneath the mill-pond calm and it was a very different story. It might be neutral but it formed the buffer zone between NATO in Norway and Finland, and the Soviet Union. It was the linchpin to the northern flank and, as such, the country was of keen interest to both sides.

The colonel was perfectly aware that, in the event of war, Sweden would be one of the first casualties. There was no way that the Soviet Union would fight its way down through the mountainous spine of Norway, along the one decent road worthy of the name. If it came to the crunch, the Soviet forces would slice in a south-westerly arc, sweeping through Finland and Sweden to hit straight at the important southern heart of Norway. Stockholm would fall even before Oslo.

Yvon gave a macabre grin at his reflection in the mirror. So much for Sven's much-vaunted neutrality. Much good may it do him when the shock troops rolled.

But in the meantime, that same neutrality made it a good feeding ground for the intelligence vultures. People spoke more freely in a country that was on neither side, but where members of both rubbed shoulders frequently.

Colonel Grigory Yvon's eyes swept down to the file open on his desk. Hardly surprising, then, that it attracted men like Ralph Lavender, visa secretary to the British Embassy.

Slowly, the GRU officer lowered himself into the

plumply upholstered leather chair and studied the dossier.

He'd been informed directly from the nine-storey windowless GRU headquarters at Khodinka airfield outside Moscow that Lavender was on his way to Sweden. Some time ago, when he worked on the Russian Desk, the man had been recognised as a rising star in the British Secret Intelligence Service. His posting to Head of Station in Stockholm was tantalising in the extreme. It had happened a month earlier, and Yvon had taken special interest in him. To the extent, in fact, that he had him under almost constant surveillance from the moment he arrived. Newcomers to a posting were, after all, more likely to make mistakes. Strictly speaking, this was a counter-espionage job, the responsibility of the KGB's Directorate K, but Yvon preferred also to have his own man discreetly placed. He didn't trust the KGB to do a thorough job.

Yet so far Lavender had given nothing important away; only one British contact that hadn't been previously known to them. In fact, Yvon had been on the point of agreeing with his hard-pressed staff that it was a waste of time. Just one more week he'd decided. Then this.

A bony white hand reached across the desk top to the intercom.

"Colonel?"

Immediately he recognised the voice of the deputy resident. "Igor, come in will you. I'd like to talk about this business with the British visa secretary."

As usual, Igor Kulik wasted no time. It took only sixty-five seconds to walk the distance to his superior's office, and he arrived in just seventy.

"Sit down, Igor," Yvon invited, interlacing his fingers in a steeple on the desk before him. He studied his deputy carefully from beneath hooded eyelids. "I've read this report, but I'd like you to tell me in your own words."

Kulik nodded deferentially. His face was a bland mask,

158

broad and flat as though chiselled out of hard white rock. The ruthless grey eyes glittered like quartz above a straight thin mouth. He wasn't a tall man, but he had shoulders like a bull and a powerful athletic body that had been trained for its work over many years. His voice was equally powerful, but he kept it to a suitably low pitch in the sombre, panelled room. His GRU chief liked to keep a sense of secrecy in his inner sanctum. "Comrade Colonel, one of our most reliable agents, Göran Hallberg, was on routine surveillance duty yesterday. The British visa secretary, Ralph Lavender. Since just before Christmas he has been engaged suddenly in much activity. He has flown back to Century House in London at least once a week for consultations, and appears to have attended several meetings in the Foreign Office there."

Yvon pursed his lips against his steepled fingers; this much he knew already.

"It suggested something special may be in the wind," Kulik continued. "Then suddenly he made a trip to Norway. It took us by surprise and we nearly lost him. In fact, we did at Otta station. However, our man found the taxi driver who had taken him to his final destination. A place at Sjoa which is used as a Royal Marines base during their annual winter exercise. The unit there is the Mountain and Arctic Warfare Training Cadre. Special ski troops."

Yvon's hooded eyes blinked like a bird's. "Is there any significance in that?"

Kulik shrugged. "It's impossible to say, Comrade Colonel. But what may be an interesting coincidence is that a unit of the Special Air Service was billeted there. I have this from the Third Department, Northern Fleet." He didn't smile but, for once, the quartz eyes gave away a hint of pride at his earnest detective work. "The Fleet had a unit on routine covert surveillance patrol in the area. The SAS officer arrived at Sjoa at the same time as Lavender, who left after only an hour or so to return to

Stockholm. The next day the SAS team packed up and returned to England. I gather it was unexpected."

"And then?" the colonel pressed.

"And then nothing, except another trip to London, until yesterday. Lavender made a deliberate attempt to throw off any follower and went to a private house in Bromma. He had a meeting with some military-looking types. Hallberg could be wrong, of course. He checked with a neighbour. Apparently the apartment is owned by the British Fiscex Holdings company. A discreet enquiry at Fiscex suggested the men there are marketing executives visiting from London."

Yvon raised one finger from the steeple and played it down the long hook of his nose. "So Lavender could have been going there on official business? Something to do with the Visa Department?"

Kulik almost shot a disparaging glance, but stopped himself in time. "That would be unusual, Comrade Colonel. Usually passport holders visit the embassy on consular matters. Or at least Lavender might visit the Fiscex offices. And, anyway, he was clearly covering his tracks when he went to the rendezvous."

Yvon's eyes blazed with ferocious interest although his face remained deadpan. Kulik was getting good, very good. He was becoming an expert at looking at apparent innocence and picking up little, seemingly insignificant clues that didn't quite fit. He would have to watch Kulik, the sorcerer's apprentice was in danger of overtaking the master.

The deputy added: "What really caught Hallberg's interest was the girl who visited. It's in the file. She's also recently been attached to the Swedish office of Fiscex as an interpreter."

All such appointments were routinely investigated in case they yielded agent potential; it was like panning for the rare grain of gold in a mountain stream.

For a moment his chief said nothing. The hoods closed over his eyes and the finger from his steepled hands pressed against his lips. To all intents and purposes 'The Cadaver' was as dead as he looked. Then, suddenly, the eyes opened. They were dark and bright, and very much alive. "You've done well, Kulik. I have decided that we shall maintain surveillance for a while longer on Lavender. And tell me, is there anything on this girl?" He glanced at the file, and pronounced the name with care. "Marsh?"

"We have nothing, Comrade Colonel. I've gone through Moscow."

"What about the KGB?"

"I can check." Kulik's tone was full of distaste. He had every GRU officer's loathing for the political intelligence creeps. Their eternal rivals.

Yvon raised a hand. "No matter. General Badim is due down here any minute. About some visiting scientist. I'll ask him then."

That reminded Kulik. "Oh yes, Comrade Colonel. That scientist Dr Shalayez. I have procured a dossier which I think you should look at. He is a very important man. Perhaps you should be aware that he has been working at Sary Shagan on strategic air defence."

Yvon raised an eyebrow. "Really? Then we must have words with Badim, if there is a military interest there. Thank you, Kulik." Dismissed.

Kulik climbed to his feet in a very agile movement for a man of his bulk. "Comrade Colonel, I was thinking of having the girl watched. And those so-called Fiscex executives."

The colonel leaned back in his chair. "I think not, Kulik, we're very overstretched at the moment. Stick with Lavender and continue your general investigations into the girl and the others. Just keep an eye on the situation."

Kulik nodded stiffly, and retreated towards the door. It swung open as he reached it, the bulk of the KGB station chief blocking his path.

From his chair Yvon watched coolly, hiding his

161

displeasure at the way the new arrival burst in, without knocking. It was all part of the game: General Badim was establishing his widespread jurisdiction, his all-powerful territorial rights. Clearly, he loathed the military intelligence man as much as he in turn was loathed.

Mutual mistrust was encouraged by the Soviet system between the military and political intelligence services – it prevented either from becoming too powerful or complacent. Whilst Yvon was not answerable to the KGB, he was not beyond the unwelcome attentions of the internal security apparatus. For that reason he could not afford to fall out openly with Badim and the KGB general knew it. He enjoyed making their relationship difficult, and delighted in watching Yvon squirm in an effort to maintain the status quo.

"Do come in, General," Yvon said through a plastic smile. "Kulik was just leaving."

Badim rolled into the sombre office in a way that reminded the GRU chief of an overinflated beach ball. His huge belly strained within a baggy grey flannel suit and the thick bull neck bulged at the soiled collar of his shirt as he glanced around. It was the slightly disdainful manner of a policeman: vaguely disapproving whilst the watery blue eyes scanned for the carelessly overlooked clue to some misdemeanour.

The heavy bags beneath Badim's eyes crinkled into an effective impression of joviality which had fooled many people to their cost. His fat lips pushed aside his heavy jowls in a disarming smile.

"Ah, Grigory, I should like you to come down and meet a visitor to Stockholm. Dr Nikolai Shalayez."

Yvon picked a sheaf of paper from his desk and followed the general down to the reception rooms, where the ambassador was just completing a brief conversation with a tall, thin man who appeared ill at ease. As the ambassador left for his private office, Badim made the introductions without referring to either man's rank or actual position.

Yvon ran a professional eye over the scientist, his trained mind making an immediate appraisal like punching data into a computer. The man was a youthful-looking forty, he guessed. Dark boyish features that no doubt women would find attractive. His eyes, violet, were particularly striking. No doubt, too, women would find his undernourished frame appealing to their maternal instincts.

A strong set to the chin, but an expression of uncertainty in those cat-like eyes. Probably romantic; typical of an academic. Evidently uncomfortable in the presence of authority such as theirs.

"Your first time in Sweden, Comrade Doctor?"

Shalayez grinned nervously. "My first time anywhere, thank you."

As I thought, Yvon decided, like a fish out of water.

Badim chuckled throatily. "I have told him that Stockholm is the best possible place to come. The most beautiful women in Europe. Isn't that so, Grigory?"

Yvon refused to respond. The randy fat KGB chief made him sick. Badim was one of the elite minority whose exalted birthright had ensured him a place at the Military Institute and guaranteed him a lifetime of privilege. Yet in gratitude all he ever thought about was an easy life and sex. Yvon knew full well of the man's little lovenest flat in Nybrogatan and the plump Swedish girl who shared it with him. Although God knows what she saw in him; they were an amazingly tolerant race with a taste for the bizarre.

"You like women?" Yvon asked innocently.

Shalayez's expression froze. Instantly he sensed a trap. Quickly he said: "I'm a married man, Comrade Colonel, with a daughter."

It was a cue for Badim to laugh like a drain until his throat rattled with phlegm.

"You are only here for a week?" Yvon continued, ignoring the burst of mirth. "Lecturing at the Rönkä Society?"

Shalayez nodded, anxious to please.

Yvon's eyes focused keenly on his subject. "Then I am sure that you will have little time or interest for distractions outside your work."

Badim was recovering. He dabbed the tears from his eyes with an old handkerchief. Clearing his throat he said: "Come, come, Grigory. All work and no play makes for a dull time. I am sure Dr Shalayez will find a little time for some shopping, some sight-seeing, and maybe – ah, ha – a little relaxation of an evening."

The GRU officer felt a sudden rush of anger. Badim was such a bloody fool sometimes. With an effort he kept his tone moderate. "I wonder if you appreciate the importance of the work on which Dr Shalayez here has been engaged? Top-secret *military* work."

The KGB chief stiffened; he sensed the reproach. "Ah, Grigory, yes. He works on some project at Sary Shagan."

Yvon's eyes glowed darkly. "And are you aware of the importance of that work?" he demanded, ignoring the mathematician's presence.

Badim was caught momentarily wrong-footed. "Er, yes, it is very high priority."

"The highest!" Yvon snapped back. "I am aware, Comrade, that internal security is your department, but here we also have a military matter." He hesitated, selecting his words with care. "If you were to ask my advice, I would say that Dr Shalayez should be protected at all times. And even then should not venture out to places where we do not have the fullest control."

Badim's cheery smile became a little fixed. "*If* I were to ask you, Grigory."

The hooded eyelids lowered slightly. "And *if* you did not ask my advice, I might feel it necessary to record my recommendation in the interests of my own well-being. May I ask who is looking after our good friend during his stay?"

"Jackov is the senior man," Badim answered

smoothly. His chin jutted above the fleshy folds of his neck, daring a challenge.

Jackov! Yvon could scarcely believe it. Jackov was fat and careless, like his boss. He'd gone to seed long ago.

His thin mouth twitched in a polite smile. "Then I must register my view."

For a moment the two security men studied each other with almost open contempt. Then Badim inhaled noisily and turned to Shalayez. "Comrade Doctor, I am afraid I must consider this gentleman's opinion. So for you I am afraid there can be no visits to the cheery fleshpots of Stockholm, you understand."

"I am so sorry." Yvon sounded genuinely apologetic. "But, you realise, one cannot be too careful."

Shalayez nodded, his heart sinking. Such a restriction would surely make any chance of escape impossible.

As Badim turned to leave, Yvon said: "A favour? I wonder if you could check this name on your files? A young lady. We have a security interest."

The KGB chief snatched the paper in a rare show of bad grace. He didn't like being browbeaten by his rival. Not one little bit.

Cherry Brewster was adamant. "I don't trust him, Matt, you know I don't. His eyes are very shifty."

As head of Chancery, responsible for the day-to-day running of the British Embassy, her husband had his own views about the replacement SIS officer. And that opinion wasn't a million miles away from that of his wife.

He said: "In his job you've got to expect shifty eyes." The greying handlebar moustache curled above the smile. "And I suppose you're going to say his eyes are too close together, too?"

Cherry parked herself on the edge of the dining table which was set for four places. Her bright blue eyes peered over the rim of her wine glass. "Well, now that you mention it . . ." she provoked mischievously. "Anyway I think he's definitely creepy."

Brewster laughed easily. "Just because he won't flirt with you!"

He only just ducked the napkin that came flying in his direction.

"Matt Brewster! That was not a nice thing for a diplomat to say!" she scolded, and they both shared the joke.

Nevertheless, he reflected, his wife did have a point. No one could resist Cherry's charm. Just turned forty, she had the bubbly blonde good looks and slender figure of a nineteen-year-old. She was gregarious, happy and was a sparkling conversationalist. In fact, she was the greatest asset a career diplomat could have, even if she was a little outspoken at times. She was definitely the darling of all their dinner-party guests. Never one to duck a sensitive issue, she would innocently draw out a taboo subject into open and lively debate. And in many a quiet tête-à-tête an admiring guest might say a little more than he ought. A useful knack for a diplomat's wife.

Not, however, Ralph Lavender. He was the exception that proved the rule.

Cherry smiled. "I shall work on him tonight. I might read him some of my poetry later on. Get him relaxed."

"You'll send him to sleep."

"Pig!"

Both the telephone and the doorbell of their private suburban residence rang at the same time.

Brewster hoisted himself out of his armchair. "You answer the door, Cherry. I'll get the phone."

His wife flounced gaily to the front door and flung it wide. "Ralph, how lovely to see you!"

Presented with her offered cheek, Lavender had no option but to kiss it. He got it over quickly and thrust the box of chocolates at her. "A little thank-you."

Cherry swooned. "Oh, how lovely! You really shouldn't have, Ralph dear."

166

As they entered the lounge, Matt Brewster met them. "Hello, Ralph. Nice timing. But I'm afraid that was Sir Timothy on the phone. He's had some problem at the embassy and he's only just leaving."

Cherry shrugged helplessly; diplomatic life was often one continual succession of minor crises. Burnt dinners were commonplace. "I'll go and turn the cooker down. I overdid the chicken the last time Sir Timothy came – I daren't risk that happening again."

As she darted for the kitchen, Lavender said: "Actually, Matt, if the ambassador's running late, it'll give me the chance to tell you about something."

"Oh yes?" Brewster sensed trouble. "Like a drink?"

The man nodded. "Gin and tonic. Drowned, if you please."

God damn it, Brewster thought as he went to the cabinet, the man was still like a cat on a hot tin roof. Never relaxed for a moment. I wonder if he even knows how to turn his engine off?

"So what's all this about, Ralph?"

Lavender accepted the drink. "We've got a little something on."

Little something? Brewster groaned inwardly. It *definitely* sounded like trouble.

"There's a Russian scientist staying in Stockholm," the intelligence officer continued quickly, his voice dropping to a conspiratorial whisper. "He's coming over."

"A defection?" It was every bit as bad as he feared.

Lavender looked embarrassed; "defection" was not a word he liked to use blatantly. "Yes, but it won't – *mustn't* involve the embassy."

Brewster was quick off the mark. "You mean there are problems?"

"He'll be heavily guarded and he'll have very little freedom of movement. So we'll have to give him a helping hand."

"I see." The bland response hid the sudden feeling of dread the diplomat experienced. "Well, keep it clean for

167

God's sake. The Swedes get very upset at this sort of thing. Who's involved, the Firm?"

Lavender shook his head. "Only marginally. The Regiment will do the job. Actually, I believe he's an old friend of yours. Captain Mike Ash."

Brewster almost snapped his retort: "No names, I don't want to know." But inwardly he breathed a sigh of relief. At least Ash was a sound man who was level-headed in a crisis. The fact that he knew Sweden well was an additional bonus.

Lavender glanced at the kitchen door, nervous that Cherry might reappear. "Just thought I should keep you in the picture. At least if there *are* any questions, you'll know what you're denying."

"I gather you don't want the ambassador told?"

The SIS man pursed his lips in a pained expression. "I don't think there's any need to bother the Old Man. Let's just keep it all unofficial and off the record."

At that moment Cherry came into the lounge. "I do hope Sir Timothy won't be long, the chicken's starting to curl at the edges."

Matt Brewster downed his whisky. Suddenly he'd lost his appetite.

Everything about the director of the Society was orderly and understated. Like his own mathematic workings, every aspect of his life was neat and precise. Everything, from his personal shopping list to his appointments diary, was arranged in tidy columns. Each minute of each day was planned, as was every direct debit from his bank account, each insurance renewal, and loan repayment. Even his alimony was meticulously detailed. It wouldn't have surprised his closest colleagues to know that he had even arranged for his own funeral in the event of his unexpected demise, so as to spare his wife the distressing task.

In fact the grey-suited, middle-aged figure with the cropped mat of white hair was the complete antithesis of the man he introduced to the line of mathematicians and students.

For his part, Shalayez was bemused by the director's almost sycophantic deference. It would have been embarrassing had he not been enjoying himself so much. In his wildest dreams he would never have guessed that he was so highly regarded by mathematical scholars from so many countries. They seemed to regard him with something akin to awe.

"Since it's been known you were coming," the director had told him in the privacy of his office, "we've been inundated with requests to attend your lectures. I've had to turn down disappointed applicants in their droves. So you really will have to come and visit us again."

Shalayez wished fervidly that he'd had his hair trimmed, or had at least learned the secret of keeping his clothes from crumpling when stuffed into a suitcase.

"Dr Tanaka from Japan," the director introduced.

As he shook hands, Shalayez attempted in vain to keep his frayed shirt-cuff inside the sleeve of his jacket.

"And now," the director said, "we have our small contingent of students. I thought you would appreciate a fair cross-section of academic, commercial and professional interests, so that your lectures are not too elitist."

A pretty young girl with a bun of auburn hair curtsied. He was staggered. Yes, she actually curtsied as though he were royalty. "Mademoiselle Colbert from the Sorbonne."

Next a Nigerian male student.

"And Miss Court-Ogg from Cambridge University in England . . ."

Shalayez was stunned. The name had meant nothing to him, and it took a full three seconds before he realised that the small, delicate hand in his belonged to Lucinda. His mouth dropped as he registered her sad brown eyes and nervous smile.

169

"I've heard so much about you, Dr Shalayez. I do hope we'll have a chance to talk later."

That voice! There was absolutely no doubt. He blinked. Yet she gave absolutely no outward sign that she'd seen him before in her life. Only her eyes seemed to be speaking to him by themselves, urging him not to give anything away.

The director gave a dry little laugh, very controlled. "I am sure you will enjoy talking to Miss Court-Ogg. She speaks Russian very well, you know."

Lucinda's face coloured and she glanced down coyly at the words of praise.

At last Shalayez found his voice. "I look forward to that very much, Miss . . ." He tried to remember the name. She smiled. "Court-Ogg. Lucinda Court-Ogg. Everybody calls me Lucy."

He didn't register the faces of the last two people in the line-up. His heart was trembling uneasily, the blood rushing in his ears so that he could hardly hear the director's carefully modulated voice.

"I am sorry, you say?"

"Are you all right, Dr Shalayez? You look a little flushed . . ."

He managed a smile. "I am fine. It is a little hot in here, that's all."

The director smiled apologetically. "Yes, it is maybe a fault of us in Sweden. Sometimes our houses become a little airless. Now, we will be serving coffee in the first-floor lecture room. Why don't you take the opportunity to relax for fifteen minutes? You are not due to start until ten o'clock."

"Thank you, that will be nice."

The director watched as Shalayez joined the stream of delegates mounting the stairway to the next floor. His assistant Ingrid Segerström joined him. She was a handsome woman in her late fifties with a trim figure which carried the smart cream two-piece well. Her sunlamp tan and lightly rinsed fair hair helped to retain her youthful appearance. She was devoted to the director and his Society, and was the powerhouse that kept it ticking over with a mix of efficiency, friendliness and sheer dedication to the discipline of mathematics.

"He is an odd one, Director," she ventured, peering over her large spectacles. "Not at all what I expected."

The director nodded. "He is a little unkempt. The wild man of mathematics, eh? I suspect that is a nickname that will stick."

"Quite striking in his looks though," Miss Segerström murmured, half to herself.

"Still, he is certainly pleasant enough."

His right-hand woman gave a little snort of derision. "Not like his chaperon, I'm afraid."

Discreetly she indicated the fat KGB minder who had installed himself by the door, sprawled in an easy chair whilst he breakfasted on a large open sandwich. A cascade of crumbs bounced over the spotless tiled floor. Miss Segerström seethed.

"Oh, dear," the director said. "The Russians are usually content to deliver and collect their lecturers. Dr Shalayez must be highly regarded if they insist on keeping someone here all day."

Miss Segerström's eyes machine-gunned the Russian where he sat. "They've also got some oaf in a car at the front gate. I've had complaints he's blocking half the road so people can't drive past."

"Oh, dear," the director repeated. "We'll have to have a quiet word."

The Russian noticed the pair watching him. He swallowed the last of his meal, brushed the remnants from his lap, and ambled over.

"Hey, hello again," he said jovially. "Do I hear you say there is coffee upstairs?"

"Yes, Mr Jackov," Miss Segerström replied stiffly.

He grinned, showing bits of ham stuck between his teeth. "Good, good. I go up and get some, yes?"

She sighed. "I suppose so, Mr Jackov, I suppose so."

171

The first lecture on 'Mathematics as applied to Astro-Physics' lasted until twelve-thirty. During it Shalayez forced himself to avert his eyes from Lucinda to whom they were irresistibly drawn. To make matters worse he kept noticing the omnipresence of Jackov who sat at the back of the room slurping at endless mugs of coffee.

At last Shalayez managed to immerse himself fully in his subject, surfacing only at the end to answer a barrage of questions from an enthusiastic audience. When he finished he actually received a short standing ovation which left him feeling embarrassed but immensely proud. He was quite unused to being treated as a celebrity.

Ingrid Segerström came up to congratulate him. "I cannot remember a more popular speaker, Dr Shalayez. Well done! One of the young students would like to ask one or two more questions."

"Oh yes?"

Miss Segerström tried not to swoon. "Would you agree to talk with her? I know you must be exhausted . . ."

He raised his hand in protest. "No, no, I am fine. I should be delighted."

"How kind. I have allocated you the small office here for your personal use. Perhaps you'd like to talk in there. I'll have some coffee sent in. We have half-an-hour before lunch. The director likes things to be punctual."

Shalayez smiled his thanks. "Thank you. And who is this student?"

Even as he asked the question, he guessed the answer. And as confirmation Lucinda appeared behind Miss Segerström, clutching her lecture notes.

Once inside the spartan office, Lucinda quickly closed the door and turned to face him. "Niki, darling, oh God, it's so lovely to see you . . ." She threw her arms around him and they kissed with a feverish passion for several seconds before Lucinda eased herself gently away. "Niki, I must talk quickly. I don't know what chance we'll get again. You are going to be rescued soon. It's all planned –"

He looked at her curiously. "Is it true? You are a spy?"

She frowned "*What?*" Never had she thought of the term applying to herself.

His eyes hardened. "That you were sent to seduce me? To lure me away?"

Lucinda felt her heart sink. She felt nauseous and a sudden burning resentment against her masters in the anonymous corridors of Whitehall. She shook her head vehemently, her eyes pleading to be believed. She couldn't lie to him the way Lavender had wanted. "It wasn't like that, Niki, *believe* me. *Please*. Maybe in the beginning, but I really fell for you. I love you and I'll do *anything* to help. *Please* believe me!"

He wanted to squeeze her to him, but he felt paralysed. He didn't know what to believe. She certainly sounded as though she meant what she said. He said: "So when will this happen?"

Lucinda smiled awkwardly, uncertain that he any longer trusted her. "In the next day or two."

"Where from?"

"From here, this building." She reached out and touched his wrist. "Don't ask me how. I'll tell you what to do when the time comes."

As he went to speak, the door was thrust open. Jackov stood there, grinning amiably. Quickly, Lucinda withdrew her hand. "Hey, Mr Professor, there you are. You give me a heart attack. I think for a minute you disappear." He glanced knowingly at the girl. "And I understand why." The hungry look was in his eyes again, but not for lunch.

"Just a charming student fan," Shalayez joked.

Lucinda scurried out, averting her eyes from the plump minder.

"And so young, Dr Shalayez."

He laughed half-heartedly. "Aren't I lucky."

Then Miss Segerström appeared at the door. "Gentle-men, the meal will be served in the dining room in a few minutes." She joined Shalayez by the window. "After perhaps you would like to walk around the grounds. We keep the snow cleared from the path. I'd be pleased to show you."

He looked out of the window. "That would be nice."

Jackov joined them and grunted.

Miss Segerström glanced at him with a thin-lipped smile. "And Mr Jackov, of course."

The Russian minder jabbed a stubby forefinger at the glass. "Who are they?"

"What?" She could hardly hide her irritation with him as she looked out. Two men in overalls were unloading two long ladders from an unmarked blue van. "Oh, them? Just workmen. Apparently our landlord wants the guttering looked at. The surveyor says some are in danger of falling with the weight of the snow."

Jackov sniffed heavily and focused suspiciously on the workmen. "Oh, yes?"

Miss Segerström hid her indignation at the man's obvious disapproval. "Buildings *have* to be maintained, Mr Jackov."

"I know that," came the terse reply.

Suddenly she smiled, realising what concerned the minder. Security. "Oh, don't worry, Mr Jackov, they're just leaving their equipment here. They're not due to start work until next week. By that time you'll all be safely back in Moscow. Won't that be nice?"

Jackov gave her a withering look.

Brian Hunt found the Victoria Café without difficulty. Its scalloped roof looked like a snow-covered serpent above the windows which scattered their light over Kungsträdgården, where skaters laughed and shrieked their way around the ice-rink.

He stepped through the wrought-iron arch beneath the red oval sign and made his way through the res-

174

taurant to the bar. At this time of the afternoon there were few patrons. It would fill up later when the offices closed for the day.

Lucinda was the only customer sitting on a bar stool. He passed her and took a stool in the corner, facing into the room, so that he could see anyone else who entered. There was one seat separating them.

While he ordered a small beer he studied her discreetly. He could tell she was nervous. Her skin was ashen and her mouth tight-lipped. She toyed with a half-empty glass.

When the barman moved out of earshot Hunt said: "It's tonight."

She blanched, visibly taken aback. "That's short notice."

His smile was genuinely sympathetic. "I'm sorry, but you've seen what the weather's doing. It's closing in and the forecast isn't too clever. If it's not tonight we might have missed our chance."

Lucinda took a deep breath. "I see. What do I do?"

Hunt lit a cigarette and waited until a new customer was served. The man leered sideways at the girl and went to sit down, but she quickly placed her handbag on the seat. Her disparaging sneer did the rest. The man decided to find another place. Hunt said: "You usually have drinks at the end of play, you said."

"Around five. For half-an-hour or so."

Hunt nodded. "We'll do it then."

She looked horrified. "What if they decide not to have drinks?"

"Why should they?"

She shrugged. "I'm sorry, I'm not looking for problems."

"I know, sweetheart. It's tricky for you, but you don't actually have to do anything. Just tell Ivan to slip quietly up in the lift at exactly five-twenty. Two of our blokes will meet him on the roof and get him aboard the chopper. Safe as ninepence."

Lucinda looked relieved. "Is that all?"

He grinned. "Now synchronise your watch with mine. It's three-o-five and nine, ten seconds." The manoeuvre complete, he asked her if she'd like another drink.

She declined. "No, the sooner I brief Niki, the happier I'll be. It's not easy to get the chance to talk to him."

Hunt understood again. "Any problems – ring through to the apartment. One of us will be there in case of last-minute snags."

"Your boss?"

Hunt grinned. "He's elsewhere. Keep your chin up."

He watched as she slid from the stool and walked towards the door. She looked very small and vulnerable.

Five minutes later, he finished his drink and made his way out to the park. The sky was very dark now and snow was falling quite heavily, spun into rolling clouds by a bitter northerly wind coming down from Lapland.

The weather forecasters had been right.

He looked again at his watch. Three-fifteen. Two hundred and twenty miles away, over the border in Norway, the last minute checks would be under way on the helicopter before takeoff.

Mike Ash, he knew, would be watching anxiously.

Wind moaned across the flat expanse of Gardermoen airfield, raising drifting curtains of spindrift and polishing the hard-packed surface snow until it gleamed.

It was the coldest day Captain Mike Ash could remember as he stood, muffled against the elements, in a secluded corner of the base where the two helicopters were parked.

The numbing cold slowed his senses so that each second of the final pre-flight tests seemed to last an eternity. His teeth ached and his eyes watered with the intensity of the cold, the tears freezing as icicles on his cheeks.

He was thankful when the rotors finally slowed and the pilot clambered out.

Although he only wore an old leather jacket over his flying suit, Flight-Lieutenant Ulrich was impervious to the cold. Adrenalin was pumping round his body and the excitement of the forthcoming mission had kept him warm and glowing ever since he had been suddenly diverted from the four-week pipeline training course up north in Bardufoss two days before.

At forty-two he was a veteran of 846 Naval Air Commando Squadron based at Yeovilton in Somerset. He was fit and keen with an inherent sense of humour and adventure, never happier than when taking one of his Junglies on some seemingly impossible insertion exercise. 'Junglies' was the name given to their MK 4 Sea King helicopters, after the dark green colour which distinguished them from the white 'Pingers' of the Royal Navy's anti-submarine squadrons; 846's speciality was operating with various elite commando forces, especially the Cadre, the SAS and the SBS. But on this occasion the machine had received a white 'overcoat' which obscured all markings.

Ice was already starting to form on the bushy moustache above the wide grin. "She's turning over a treat. Loves the cold does that one. I didn't think we'd need the reserve."

Ash returned the grin. Ulrich treated all machines as though they were human. He maintained that some helicopters were born temperamental; others were thoroughbreds from the start. Conveniently he overlooked that some had inevitably had total engine refits during their lifetime.

Ash tapped his watch. "Ten minutes."

Ulrich nodded. "Come aboard, Mike, and get warmed up."

Ash needed no second bidding and slid open the hatch to the relative warmth of the large cargo body which would normally hold around twenty-two fully equipped troops. But today the weight was pared to the minimum. Stockholm was at the limit of their endurance, and it

177

would be a fuel-guzzling low-level mission all the way in and all the way back. Flying through near white-out conditions with night-vision goggles that even then would strain the eyes until they popped. For that reason the concession had to be made for a relief pilot in addition to the navigator and winchman.

At three-thirty precisely control at Gardermoen gave clearance for takeoff.

In the cockpit second pilot Flight-Sergeant Taffy Hughes twisted the throttle grip on the pitch lever. The thrashing blades gathered momentum, their downblast churning up a blinding white cauldron of powder snow. The engine noise rose to a deafening roar until the machine began to tremble with unleashed power. Then, with a gentle shift of the pitch lever to tilt the angle of the blades, the Sea King rose solidly and majestically. At fifty feet it canted jauntily and roared eastward, skimming low over the pinewood tree-tops.

Operation Wolverine was go.

6

"When did you find this out?" Colonel Grigory Yvon demanded.

His second-in-command didn't flinch; Kulik knew he had done his best. "She didn't turn up for work at Fiscex on Monday. We thought she was probably off sick. Then, when she didn't arrive on Tuesday, I sent Hallberg around to her flat that night. There was no one there. Her neighbour told us she'd said she was going away for a few days to stay with friends in Uppsala. She wasn't at home this morning."

The GRU chief gave a snort of disbelief. "No one's going to give her a week off after only a few days' work."

Kulik agreed. "In answer to some discreet enquiries at Fiscex, the personnel department still maintained she was away on medical grounds."

"And you're sure she hasn't left the country?"

Kulik raised an eyebrow. "Certainly not if she used her own name."

Grigory Yvon lay back in his chair and adopted the steeple-fingered posture he used when he was thinking deeply. "I am afraid, Kulik, you were right. We should have had her put under surveillance. Of course, it could be totally innocent . . ." He looked up suddenly. " . . . What about Ralph Lavender and those other mysterious Fiscex executives of yours?"

Kulik shrugged. "Lavender has been as good as gold. Apparently attending his supposed duties at the embassy. He hasn't returned to the company flat to see those men. And, incidentally, one of them took a flight to Oslo yesterday.''

''Significance?''

''None that I'm aware of, I'm afraid, Comrade Colonel.'' He hesitated before bringing up the subject of General Badim. ''Have our KGB neighbours come up with anything on the girl?''

'The Cadaver' came alive with a sardonic smile. ''Not yet. It can take time when you've a file on half the world's population. No, Badim still hasn't got up off his fat arse. He's probably waiting for me to go down on bended knee. He's still smarting because I twisted his arm over security on that scientist fellow.''

Kulik shared the joke with his superior. ''I'll see if I can't hurry things along behind the scenes.''

''That would be appreciated.'' He had no stomach for another pointless showdown with the KGB chief; it merely served to aggravate his embryonic ulcer.

Colonel Grigory Yvon didn't arrive back at the secure GRU residency within the Soviet Embassy until late in the afternoon.

He had made a rare contact with an important agent whom he had entrapped and recruited many years before. As no documents or money were to be exchanged this time, it was quite legitimate for Yvon to use his cover as a relatively lowly assistant to the naval attaché to meet the man openly for lunch. The agent was a freelance journalist specialising in military and foreign affairs. As such he met frequently with defence attachés from many nations and had excellent contacts within the Swedish military and government. No special importance would be attached to his very occasional lunch with Yvon when the two of them would talk about their shared hobby of stamp-collecting. As usual Yvon would swap Eastern Bloc issues with the journalist's more colourful choice from other nations.

No one would guess that once, when hard up through

his habitual love of hard liquor and soft women, the journalist had been persuaded to write an innocuous appraisal of Swedish defence attitudes for a specialist newsletter which Yvon said he prepared. It was, he promised, a limited circulation internal publication which was highly regarded by the Soviet General Staff and even the Politburo itself. The journalist's experienced and independent views would assist the Kremlin policy-makers to understand Swedish fears and aspirations for peace. Both men had laughed and agreed that the old fogies in the Politburo were *definitely* in need of some enlightenment to see things from the perspective of Sweden! Like no more miniature submarines nosing around, thank you.

Flattered that his personal views would reach the Soviet hierarchy, the journalist had gone to work with a vengeance. And he didn't mince his words. In fact he was mildly surprised when Yvon accepted the paper with delight. Although he couldn't agree on the journalist's interpretation of Soviet intentions, he had to agree that it accurately reflected the unofficial view of the Swedish Government.

The paper, Yvon noticed, was much longer than requested. He quickly spotted paragraph after paragraph of padding. At twice the requested length it commanded twice the already generous fee, and the Russian paid without demur.

A receipt was given, and signed for; the journalist was landed.

Over the next year more innocuous articles were requested and delivered. The fees became ever more generous, allowing the journalist to put his financial house in order, and to invest in a new car. His lifestyle improved gradually but substantially.

Then Yvon suggested that it might be better if they didn't meet so openly; in case it put in jeopardy the journalist's relationships with his other military contacts. That seemed sensible, so the man agreed. Now he was used to conspiracy, as well as an extra income on which he had started to depend.

The screws tightened. Yvon began with a request for a classified military telephone directory – "just for our office use in the Mission". Uncertainly the journalist said he'd see what he could do. Two weeks later it was delivered, borrowed from an old and trusted friend in the Swedish Defence Ministry who understood it would be for the journalist's personal use.

Yvon was grateful, not saying that they already had a full collection of classified directories.

The stakes were increased. Gradually more sensitive documents were requested, lent by friends with access who understood they were to be used for the journalist's background research, and *never* for publication.

And the journalist was as good as his word. He never abused the favours and his prestige soared. The documents were always returned promptly, sometimes borrowed for just a lunchbreak during which time they would be rushed to the Soviet Embassy and photographed.

Of course, ever since his promotion to GRU resident, Yvon no longer took possession of such material. Nowadays that was done by dead-letter drops or brush passes with agents or lesser GRU officers.

Occasionally, like today, Yvon would renew the acquaintance on a purely verbal and open level. Just to remind the journalist what would happen if he stopped co-operating, and to assure him of future rewards for even more ambitious prizes. The carrot and the stick. It also gave him a chance to learn first hand of the latest informed gossip in Swedish defence circles.

Thinking back, Yvon reflected that it had been a worthwhile lunch as his driver sped the dark blue Mercedes through the automatic gates of the Soviet Embassy. He took the elevator to the GRU residency and was surprised to find his first deputy waiting for him.

Kulik acted as though he was standing on hot coals in

his bare feet. "I asked for word as soon as you got back," he explained. "Badim's office has been on the phone every ten minutes for the last three hours."

Yvon's hooded eyes blinked like a vulture's. "What does he want?"

"To see you. He refuses to speak to me alone. Do you want to go right up?"

The colonel smiled faintly. "*Want* isn't the word. It'll be a shame to give myself indigestion after such a good lunch. Nevertheless he must be on the defensive if he wants me to visit him. The *chekist* can never wait to come to us if he's got something against me!"

Kulik smiled at his chief's astute observation and led the way back into the lift and up to the top floor.

Although the KGB residency was much larger than Yvon's with a vast staff, it was organised on much the same lines. Whereas the GRU concentrated purely on military intelligence, that subject was only part of the vast quantities of information amassed by Badim's officers. They were just as interested in politics and its subversion, influence and disinformation, as well as any scientific and technological intelligence or theft which could be of civilian or military benefit to the USSR.

Yet despite the omnipotence and financial resources of the sprawling KGB apparatus, even it failed to match the GRU's limitless funds which were drawn from whichever military department or research institute it happened to be serving on any particular project.

Besides, it was a standing joke within the professional military clique of the GRU that, however brilliant their *chekist* comrades were at harvesting mountains of intelligence data, they weren't always so clever at analysing it. Vastly overmanned, the organisation had more than its fair share of incompetents and was racked by political in-fighting, backstabbing and the scramble to survive, let alone climb to the top of the heap.

In the anteroom of the residency, the duty officer checked on the intercom before opening the steel security door with electronic keys and admitting the two GRU men into the corridor. They first passed the operations room where over a dozen case officers sat at rows of work booths poring over documents and writing reports in earnest silence. It had the hushed atmosphere of a museum library.

Next to it was the office of the chief of Line X who masterminded the theft of scientific and industrial data on behalf of Directorate T. Adjoining was the office of the harassed Line N officer. He looked much older than his thirty-seven years; the harrowing job of organising support for the Illegals scattered throughout Sweden had taken its toll.

They then passed the suite of offices manned by the Department K Group chiefs, each with his interest in a specific country. As always the most important were the American, UK and West German Groups and, here in Stockholm, the Scandinavian Group. Between them they would zealously collect the minutiae of information about the respective nationals living in Sweden in all areas of special interest. Diplomats, businessmen, servicemen, students, academics, engineers, journalists and their families were all methodically put under the microscope: if any could be vaguely useful, today or in the future, plans would be co-ordinated from these offices to make casual initial contact and determine if any could be nurtured with the loving care that a nurseryman devotes to his seedlings. Foreigners would be followed up on their return to their native country through the KGB's worldwide network.

Should any Swedish nationals be willingly or unwittingly coerced into becoming agents, their offerings would be gratefully – and generously – received.

Other Swedes who were in a position of influence, as many were, would be fed with disinformation material to be aimed at 'target' groups. Directly or indirectly journalists would plant the Soviet view in the Scandinavian press; professors would publish papers in learned journals; industrialists and politicians would have the ear of ministers and the military; student movements would protest; activists would activate.

Time and time again it had worked to achieve Soviet goals, both nationally and internationally. The growth of CND, opposition to Vietnam, protests over cruise missiles and now Star Wars were all influenced by the worldwide orchestrations controlled by Service A of Directorate K of the First Chief Directorate of the KGB.

The propaganda weapon had its place in the arsenal. Its role was appreciated even by a strict militarist like Yvon, though he would never admit as much to General Badim, whose office he had now reached.

Colonel Yvon knocked and entered with Kulik close behind. Badim looked up from the teak desk which sat centrally in the spacious but spartan office; an elegant chrome-legged conference table and a feather-filled sofa occupied the left and right sides respectively. A row of retouched portraits of Soviet leaders glared uncomprehendingly across the room at a large Swedish abstract in watercolours.

Badim's fat face crinkled into an automatic welcoming smile, but he made no effort to hoist his bulk from the chair. And his watery blue eyes held no humour. "Have a good lunch, Comrade Colonel?"

"Fine, thank you, General." Unruffled.

Badim's smile stayed. "And how was 'Raven'? Still chirping to your tune, I trust?"

It was a dig, of course. Years before Badim had set his eyes on the journalist code-named 'Raven', but Yvon had beaten him to it. That still rankled.

The GRU resident just smiled thinly. "As sweetly as ever, thank you."

Badim grunted, then picked up a sheet of paper from his desk. "The other day you requested a check on this girl. Lucinda Marsh. British."

Yvon nodded. So that was it.

"Well," Badim said, "she showed up on SCD's computer."

The colonel stopped his eyebrow from rising quizzically. The Second Chief Directorate was responsible for counter-intelligence and the subversion of foreign visitors and residents in Moscow.

"It appears," Badim continued, "that she was seen in the company of known British intelligence officers in Moscow over the New Year. It was believed that she was a relative of one of those agents and being used to add credence to their cover."

Yvon frowned. "Was she kept under surveillance?"

Badim's fleshy jowls reddened. "The Seventh Directorate had her watched, but the file went missing before the results could be put on computer. They're holding an enquiry to find out what happened."

The GRU colonel ground his teeth silently, but held his tongue. It was typical of *chekist* bungling.

"I was wondering, er, if you had a photograph of this woman?" Badim asked hesitantly.

This time Yvon could not suppress his smile. Now we have it! As a routine measure all new foreign members joining the permanent staff of powerful multinationals like Fiscex in Stockholm should have been photographed and investigated by the KGB. For some reason Badim's men had fallen down. Either they hadn't yet got around to it, or hadn't bothered with a mere girl interpreter. Now she was suspect, Badim was anxious to cover himself from his superiors. They tended to lack understanding in such situations, and to seek a scapegoat. Clearly Badim didn't intend it should be him.

But it must have been painful for him to ask. Particularly as he was forever carping at the GRU's independent interest in such matters. He felt it should be purely the KGB's domain and was always accusing Yvon's men of interfering or upsetting his own investigations.

"Here's the file, General," Yvon said reluctantly. He could scarcely refuse a direct request.

Badim grabbed at it like a starving man. He opened it and spread the contents over his desk. The details were sparse.

"It's not much," he grunted.

Yvon said coldly: "You asked for a photograph."

Badim picked up the two glossy prints and squinted at them. Then he frowned, reaching in his pocket for a pair of reading glasses. He settled them on his nose and studied the photographs again. At last he said: "I've seen this face." He paused. "Recently."

"Where?" Yvon asked.

Badim did not reply immediately. He reached for the telephone and dialled through to the section head of Line KR responsible for the control of Soviet citizens abroad. "Bring the photographs of everyone attending Dr Shalayez's lectures at the Rönkä Society. And be quick about it."

Yvon's eyes widened in growing disbelief. The implications of the KGB resident's words were horrifying. However he contented himself with an exchange of glances with Kulik, and waited patiently until the Line KR officer arrived.

Badim looked distinctly pale as he snatched the newly arrived dossier. His pudgy fingers scrabbled feverishly through the sheafs until he found what he was looking for. He extracted the photograph and placed it alongside that of Lucinda Marsh. The hairstyles were distinctly different but Badim's personal delight in beautiful women meant that he rarely forgot a face.

"Lucinda Court-Ogg," he said softly. "They've even kept the same bloody first name."

"Are you sure?" Yvon demanded, peering over the desk.

Badim recited the notes. "Twenty-one. British. Unmarried. Doing a post-graduate course in advanced mathematics at Cambridge University. Invited to Shalayez's lectures following a personal request from a professor in England."

"It stinks," Kulik decided.

Badim removed his spectacles and rubbed his hand roughly over his face. He suddenly felt very tired.

"This Shalayez, what's his Personal Assessment like?" Yvon asked suspiciously.

"Not a blemish," Badim replied. "In fact, now that his special project work is finished, he was being considered for recruitment into Department Twelve." That was the fairly new but already highly successful KGB sector which sent trusted scientists and academics abroad to consort with their opposite numbers in target countries on apparently innocuous exchange visits. "He's a long-serving Party member, happily married with wife and child, and he's got the highest security clearance."

That, Yvon knew, didn't necessarily mean a thing. They'd got it wrong before. "So if the man isn't a likely traitor, what do you think all this is about?"

Badim shrugged. "An abduction?"

Yvon sucked his teeth silently. "Unlikely for the British."

"It has been known," Kulik reminded.

The GRU man didn't answer. Instead he said: "For the moment all that is immaterial. Whatever is planned it has to be soon. Shalayez is due to return to Moscow on Saturday morning. The day after tomorrow. Tell me, how many men do you have guarding him?"

"Jackov is in the Society at all times. Also we have a car and two men at the gate."

"They're armed?"

"Of course."

Yvon thought quickly. "I suggest, General, that we patch up our differences and act together."

Badim blinked and nodded grudgingly. "I appreciate you have an interest."

"Then I recommend we telephone Jackov at once and warn him we think trouble is imminent. Order him not to leave Shalayez's side for a minute, but not to arouse his suspicions. We'll get over there immediately. I'll take

188

a couple of Spetsnaz ensigns off my security staff. Can you get some Department Eight men together?"

Badim nodded. He always kept a small contingent of thugs on hand from the notorious Department Eight of Directorate S.

"Right, let's go." Then he added: "And tell Jackov – under no circumstances to let that girl leave before we get there!"

It was settling in to be a dark and gloomy night. A gusting wind drove leaden clouds low over the land, whipping the frozen snow into icy pellets that stung the skin. Visibility was patchy and rarely more than fifty metres even under the street lamps.

The omens were not good, Big Joe Monk decided, as he completed a precautionary circuit of the Society, using the road which edged the grounds on three sides. Through the trees he could see the lights of the building but its outline shape was obscured by the swirling blizzard. At the gateway he had seen the large black sedan parked on the drive, half blocking it. He didn't need to see the dark-rimmed hats to tell him they were KGB guards. They were so used to doing what they liked back in Moscow that it never occurred to them to behave differently when stationed abroad. He doubted they knew the meaning of discretion. They were taught to behave loutishly in order to intimidate and generate fear. To park where they wanted; where they could be seen. A visual warning.

Probably they were thick-heads from Department Eight. Monk smiled to himself. All square-skulled, flat-faced and no necks, like a cartoonist's impression. Yet not to be treated lightly. What they lacked in mental dexterity they made up for in ruthless determination. Diplomatic niceties meant nothing to them.

He parked the car he had hired that morning in a side street and waited five minutes until Len Pope arrived in his own transport and joined him.

"Did you see anything?" Monk asked.

"No, she's as quiet as can be," Pope answered. "Just the goons on the gate as usual."

Monk peered up through the windscreen at the sky. "I don't like the look of this weather. It's closing in."

Pope nodded. "They won't abort unless it's absolutely necessary."

The other man laughed without humour. "Well, I hope they don't. We'll look a right couple of prats stuck up on the roof if anything goes wrong."

Five minutes later Big Joe Monk left the car carrying a small sports bag. Keeping to the shadows, he walked back down the side street and turned the corner until he was alongside the unkempt hedge which marked the boundary of the Society grounds. He continued walking for fifty metres. When he reached the chosen spot, which was not overlooked, he slipped deftly into the undergrowth.

It took no more than a minute to unzip the bag and slip into the cam-white oversuit. He was adjusting the Velcro fastenings when Pope joined him in the hedge.

Monk waited with growing impatience as his companion quickly donned his camo oversuit, buckled on the lightweight belt-order and checked its contents. Certainly the last three items both men prayed wouldn't be needed. The field-dressing packs, stun-grenades and 9 mm Browning pistols would only get used if things went wrong. In fact Ralph Lavender had at first been adamant that no firearms should be taken, until he was forcefully reminded that Shalayez's KGB minders would most certainly be armed. He finally relented on the strict understanding that they would only be used in a dire situation of life-threatening self-defence.

Sitting crouched in the hedge, it was a battle both men were thankful they'd fought and won. There was only one thing worse than being defenceless in the face of the enemy, and that was knowing that you needn't have been in the first place.

Pope looked up and nodded as Monk tapped his watch.

Monk went first, slipping through the hole in the dense branches with surprising deftness for a man of his bulk. He snaked his way clear of the snatching brambles and began a fast leopard crawl up a slight rise. Before he reached the crest snow had already worked its way into his cuffs, but he was unaware of the discomfort. The sudden burst of physical exertion and the rising level of anticipation had already caused him to sweat, and he welcomed the cooling crystals which whipped at his face as he wormed through the deep snow.

Breathing heavily he propped his back against the tree he had been using to cover his approach. Then, cautiously, he peered over the base roots to where the bright lights of the Society glowed hazily in the churning curtain of falling snow and spindrift.

He cursed silently. It was an eerie, obscured scene that served them well in some respects. But it was unnerving with the shifting patterns of snow creating shapes which formed and dissolved as he looked at them.

Pressing the 'send' button on the Pye Pocketfone radio, which was still favoured for close-quarters work, he spoke into the brooch-mike clipped to his chest. "Target clear. I am advancing."

That was all. It was the sign for Pope, who had been covering him, to come forward to the tree. The message would also have been picked up by Hunt who was in a car positioned to watch the KGB's black sedan at the front gate. No doubt he'd be relieved to hear they'd passed the initial stage without mishap.

A hand tugged at his foot. Pope arrived and slid alongside. Again both men checked their watches. Time to move on.

Just as Monk prepared to cross the next open stretch,

Hunt's terse voice crackled in his earpiece. *"Sunray to Alpha, halt repeat halt. One has left car and is walking up drive. Appears 'equipped'. Over."*

Monk gave two clicks on the transmit button to acknowledge and cursed under his breath.

The two men watched, eyes burning as they strained to discern a shape through the shifting white-out. In unison two 9 mm Browning automatics were unsheathed from their webbing holsters.

Pope nudged with his elbow. The dark shape of the Russian was taking form farther down the path. He was walking ponderously, an extended right arm swinging in an arc before him. He seemed nervous as he pointed his handgun at every shadow that caught his imagination. There was a momentary lull in the wind and the two SAS men could discern the squeak of his shoes in the snow.

The two white-hooded heads dipped out of sight as the Russian moved across their position, his breathing laboured in the face of the wind-driven snow. Then he passed on to be outlined more clearly in the lights of the Society as he approached the front steps. A few seconds later the door was opened by someone and the Russian disappeared inside.

For a moment Big Joe Monk hesitated. KGB goons weren't usually afraid of the dark. That guard had been expecting trouble, he was sure of it.

He'd never been happy relying on the girl's information and the KGB's routine during the week. Two men in the car on the gate and one inside. The balance could have changed at any time, as it just had. The man might just have gone in for a chat with his mate. To grab a coffee, or to have a pee. He could be in there for two minutes or half-an-hour.

But with the time now pressing Monk couldn't afford to wait. He said: "I'm going on."

Pope nodded and Monk set off, this time abandoning cover for speed to take him to relative safety behind the building. A short while later Pope had rejoined him by the aluminium ladders. They had been carefully discarded earlier in the week when Ash and Hunt had delivered them in the guise of maintenance workers.

Monk felt a surge of relief. Despite the girl's assurances, he'd half convinced himself that the ladders would have gone, probably moved by some officious caretaker. Anyway, there they were, half buried in the new fall of snow.

It wasn't easy moving the wavering lengths of aluminium in the gusting wind, and it took all the strength of both men to position them quietly against the low roof of the entrance vestibule. One false move and the scraping of the ladder on the gutter would echo around the building inside. While Pope held the ladder in position, Monk clambered steadily upwards until he was able to stand on the snow-covered flat roof and receive the second ladder.

Pope had just joined him and brought up the first ladder behind them, when strident Russian voices were heard. Instinctively both men dropped to their knees.

Monk edged forward and peered down directly over the entrance. Two KGB guards stood at the head of the steps just fifteen feet below him. They were engaged in an angry exchange of words which were muted by the howling wind. At last the man they had seen earlier started back down the drive towards the car on the gate. This time he was even more cautious.

As soon as he was safely obscured by the deteriorating weather, the two SAS men continued with their task. It was trickier reaching the third-storey roof as the additional height exposed them to the icy brunt of the wind. Twice Monk felt the powerful unseen hand try to pluck him free of the rungs and toss him into the swirling void. He paused, hanging on grimly in the buffeting blast of icy air, his face pressed against the rungs, his eyes closed. His leather gloves had become wet in the snow and the wind cut through them until his fingers burned with cold. The wind eased momentarily and he seized his chance to scramble up again until he could swing over onto the sloping tiles of the roof. He sat down with his heels wedged firmly in the guttering, and attempted to secure the head of the ladder with a length of paracord. But his hands were numb and the operation involved leaning precariously outward. Pope's anguished, blackened face seemed far below.

At last he signalled for his companion to follow. It was an anxious few moments, but the lashing just held until Pope, too, reached the roof.

Both men moved fast and lightly upward, the snow deep and frozen enough to hold their body weight until they were able to huddle in the lee of the machinery tower. It now looked a long way down, beginning with a twenty-foot slide over the roof with nothing to stop them from pitching over the forty-five-foot drop. Even the swaying treetops appeared to be far below. They felt decidedly vulnerable.

The final climb proved to be easier than it had first looked – much to Monk's relief. Drainpiping, coving and a skylight windowledge provided a succession of hand- and footholds to the tower parapet. Whilst Monk set up the Sarbe radio beacon, Pope screwed together a lightweight aluminium shovel and began clearing the snow from the small doorway so that it could be opened when the Russian reached the roof.

Monk glanced at his watch. Just five minutes to go. Swiftly he placed four plastic directional-beacons on the flat roof area to form a T-shaped marker. The battery-driven lamps would only be seen by an aircraft approaching from the correct angle. Although in the appalling weather he was seriously doubting whether the pilot would see them at all.

Finally he looked around for a suitable location to earth the cable-conductor. It comprised a rigid metal end which would be held against the hovering helicopter by means of a wooden handle. From this trailed a length of insulated cable which was earthed to draw off the build-up of static electricity. After such a long journey the approaching helicopter would have built up a powerful charge in the region of two thousand volts. Although Sea Kings were supposed to absorb the electric charge, for their primary anti-submarine role, he'd never yet found someone willing to find out if it worked. And whilst he mused that it might be educational to let the defecting Russian scientist grab the steel flexi-ladder whilst poised above a fifty-foot drop in a snowstorm, he realised it wasn't the best time to experiment.

Pope jabbed a thumb at the television aerial and grinned. "That could be fun."

Monk instantly agreed; it might provide a welcome diversion. Quickly he wedged the discharge pin of the D10-cable conductor in the bracket of the aerial.

There was nothing more they could do now except wait. The two men slid down onto their haunches behind the parapet, thankful to be out of the relentless cutting wind.

Lucinda told Shalayez during the coffee break in the middle of his last lecture of the day.

Although he had been pressing for news every time they were able to snatch a couple of moments together, the final confirmation had come as a shock.

"I don't believe it," he whispered, careful that no one else in the room should hear.

She looked at him intently. "Believe it, Niki. It's today. You're clear what to do?"

He nodded. "But there's so little time."

Lucinda smiled, feeling like a mother giving reassurance to a small boy outside the dentist's surgery. "It's better that way. No time to think."

He smiled nervously. "My palms are sweating."

"So are mine," she confided in a low voice. "And that's with just forty minutes to go."

195

A sudden thought occurred to him. "What will happen to you?"

"Nothing," she assured. "I shall just appear as baffled as everyone else. I'll come back here tomorrow for the last day, if that's what the Society decides. Then I'll return to London at the weekend. I'll probably see you on Sunday."

"I cannot wait, Lucy."

Quickly she pulled her hand away as he went to hold it.

"Ah, spring is in the air, I see!" Jackov chuckled coarsely. Shalayez had not seen him approach, a mug of coffee in his hand and his mouth full of cake.

Shalayez looked pained. "Don't be so vulgar, Comrade. This girl is anxious to unlock the mathematical secrets of the universe. Something a little beyond your comprehension, I think."

Jealousy was written all over Jackov's face; earlier he'd confessed that most Swedish girls didn't want to know him. "All right, Mr Smart-Arse Professor, have it your way. But I know a lecher when I see one. If it goes in my report it'll be the last time you'll be allowed out of the Motherland."

Shalayez's eyes hardened. "Is that a threat?"

Jackov leered. "A promise, Comrade Professor, a promise."

At that moment Ingrid Segerström entered the lecture room. "There's a telephone call for Mr Jackov," she announced primly, her voice scarcely hiding her distaste. "A personal call. I *suppose* you had better take it in my office."

Lucinda's heart fluttered momentarily, and she instantly chided herself. Her nerves were in such a state that anything out of the ordinary was sending her into blind panic.

Jackov gave Shalayez a final sneer and sauntered belligerently out of the room.

"I think," Miss Segerström said, "we'd better get started. I don't want this final session running late. The

196

weather's getting bad and some of you might find it difficult returning to the city tonight.''

The final session was a disaster. Shalayez's voice was flaky and unsure. Several times he lost his place and forgot what he was saying in mid-sentence. His audience of devoted followers were patient, but clearly becoming restless as the presentation disintegrated.

It wasn't helped when Jackov returned from taking his telephone call. Unusually he took his chair right up to the front row and sat glaring up into Shalayez's face. That threw the mathematician even further and he fumbled badly as he tried to explain the myriad equations scrawled over the blackboards.

Finally Ingrid Segerström intervened. "I think, Dr Shalayez, maybe it is a good idea to continue this lecture tomorrow. The snow outside is so bad we should stop now and let everyone go home."

Panic seized at Lucinda's chest. Go home! She glanced at her watch. It was just turned five. Twenty minutes before the helicopter was due to arrive.

Without thinking, she blurted: "Can't we all stay and have a drink?"

Miss Segerström was taken aback. "Oh, I don't think that is a good idea tonight . . .''

Lucinda thought swiftly: "But it's my birthday today . . .''

Miss Segerström hesitated.

Shalayez said quickly: "I must say I could do with a drink. I'm very tired. You notice my lecture is not so good.''

Jackov stepped forward; there was a strange, hostile expression on his face. "That is an excellent idea."

Both Shalayez and Lucinda stared at the KGB minder in astonishment. Such compliance after his particularly hostile attitude earlier surprised them both. He seemed to have changed since the telephone call. Or perhaps it was just his liking for alcohol that had overcome his animosity.

Whilst several of the delegates prepared to leave, Jackov called up the men on the gate on his radio. A few minutes later one of them arrived at the front door. The two exchanged words outside, then Jackov returned alone.

"What was all that about?" Shalayez enquired, trying to sound casual.

Jackov's smile was crooked. The temptation to unnerve the mathematician was irresistible. "I get a telephone message to say to expect trouble."

Shalayez blanched visibly. "What sort of trouble?"

The other man shrugged. "Who knows? I've told one of my men to search the grounds. Just in case."

With a shrug Shalayez tried to make light of it, and ambled nonchalantly into the main reception room. The remaining delegates were gathered around the dining table where the director was struggling to open some bottles of wine.

Jokes and laughter began to flow as everyone relaxed after the long hard day of concentration. The end-of-day social gatherings had become a ritual that Shalayez enjoyed thoroughly. It was a chance to debate subjects and expound theories with fellow professionals he was rarely able to do back home in the Soviet Union. These people from the so-called democratic countries were far less inhibited and more imaginative than his own compatriots. He normally felt comfortable and at ease in their company. But not tonight. His heart was thudding so hard that he heard himself stammer whenever he spoke. His mind was a blank and he searched in vain for the simplest words in English.

The conversation had just reached a natural lull when the roar of a car was heard outside as it struggled to maintain headway on the steep, snow-covered slope of the drive.

Ingrid Segerström smiled benignly. "Has anyone ordered a taxi?"

Evidently no one had and heads turned as car doors

were slammed and running footsteps were heard on the steps outside.

For once Brian Hunt's instincts had been incorrect. As he sat in the black Saab turbo parked halfway up a hill facing the gates of the Rönkä Society, he was convinced that nothing would now go wrong.

The weather had posed the biggest threat but he had every confidence in 846 Squadron. Their crews were a determined bunch and well experienced in coping with the horrendous flying conditions of Norwegian winters. As the time of the rendezvous drew nearer it became less and less likely that they would abort.

Meanwhile he was in constant contact with Bill Mather who, as their signals wizard, was manning both radio and telephone back at the Bromma apartment. Except for a moan about Ralph Lavender's repeated telephone calls for progress reports, there was no news. It all looked good.

There followed a couple of anxious moments when Big Joe Monk and Len Pope infiltrated the grounds of the Society and one of the Russians emerged from the car at the gate. Evidently he went up to the main building. On his return he made a half-hearted inspection of the grounds. Hunt could see him stumbling in the deeper snowdrifts and could imagine the man's curses. After that the Russian contented himself with keeping to the drive and flashing his torch beam haphazardly at the odd bush or tree. But it was a rotten night and Hunt could understand the man wanting to get back to the warmth of the sedan. No doubt they had a flask of coffee in there, or something stronger.

The brief "sitrep" messages from Monk and Pope over the radio kept him up-to-date as they overcame each hazard. At last everything was ready in position. Now there was just a ten-minute wait.

For the first time since arriving in Sweden, Hunt found his mind wandering. Tonight the Russian scientist and

Mike Ash would be safely in Norway, along with Monk and Pope. He and Bill Mather would return to England the next day and, before the weekend was out, the whole team would be together again in Hereford for a thorough debrief.

And, Hunt thought grimly, that meant he could no longer put off his decision. He and Gabby Ash could keep their secret, but there was a price that had to be paid. And it was he who had to pay it.

Perhaps it was a misplaced sense of honour, but he felt he could no longer work alongside Mike Ash, never knowing if his commanding officer knew the truth. Never knowing if Gabby would feel an irresistible urge to unburden herself. She had an open and honest attitude to life which unnerved him sometimes in its naïvety.

For his part he felt an overwhelming guilt at his own betrayal of his friend's trust. Even in Stockholm he imagined a hostility in Ash's tone. And that wasn't good in their business. Hunt resolved what had to be done. A request to move to another squadron would take time, and inevitably mean questions being asked. Rumour and speculation would be rife. Better then to make a clean break.

On the Monday he would hand in his request to be RTU'd. 'Returned to unit'; back to the Royal Green Jackets. Back to a life of the more mundane soldiering he had left behind years before.

It was one hell of a price to pay for a few moments of uninhibited passion, and he wasn't at all sure it had been worth it . . .

Car headlights flashed in his rearview mirror. Instantly he shelved his private thoughts and concentrated as the vehicle sped past. Another followed close on its tail. Both appeared to be full of people, a mass of dark shapes through the fogged-up windows.

Alarm rang in his head like a bell. Instinctively he knew the occupants were Russian; it was virtually confirmed by the CD plates although the spew of slush in their wake made it impossible to discern the numbers.

The lead car fishtailed wildly at the bottom of the hill as the driver changed down and slewed in an arc to negotiate the gateway to the Society. There should have been a collision with a gatepost or the parked sedan, but there wasn't. The drivers were exceptionally skilled.

Hunt's wristwatch alarm began bleeping. It was time.

He spoke rapidly into his mike. "Sunray to Alpha. Any sign? Over."

Static whistled in his earpiece, then cleared. "*Negative.*" Joe Monk's voice was cool and unperturbed.

Hunt's mind raced, but he could see no solution. "Enemy reinforcements just arrived. Two cars, say eight bods. This might get tricky. If chummy doesn't show, get yourselves out. Meantime sit tight. Over."

Monk's voice was without emotion from the rooftop. "*No other place to go. Out.*"

Shit, Hunt cursed beneath his breath. His fingers beat an impatient tattoo on the steering column.

His earpiece squawked again. "*Eagle is approaching. Will proceed as planned. Out.*" This time relief was unmistakable in Monk's voice.

Hunt's involuntary grin died away. This really was going to be touch-and-go. Everything depended on what was happening inside the Society. And that was something he had no way of knowing. All he could do was pray.

Colonel Grigory Yvon was the first to burst through the double doors and march into the reception room. He looked distinctly menacing in the dark coat as he glared at the gathering with hooded eyes. A stunned silence fell over the party as more men trooped in behind him, trailing snow over the tiles.

Lucinda gawped stupidly. Somehow she knew that they were Russians.

201

Ingrid Segerström found her voice. "Just what the hell do you think you're doing?" she demanded indignantly in Swedish.

Yvon ignored her, instead seeking out Jackov who was standing beside Lucinda.

The KGB minder planted a hand firmly on the girl's shoulder. "This is her."

She almost died as she automatically translated the words. Irritably she shook Jackov's hand free and began to protest.

Yvon spoke sharply, addressing himself to Miss Segerström. "Forgive my intrusion, madam." His Swedish was fluent and authoritative. "I am from the Soviet Embassy and I am here on a matter of security concerning Dr Shalayez."

"Your security is no concern of mine," Miss Segerström retorted, drawing herself up to her full height. "We've already had to suffer your men getting under our feet all week. This is an outrage."

The Russian's thin mouth curled into a polite smile. "I do appreciate it is not your concern, madam. But it is *ours*. Dr Shalayez is a very important man and we are obliged to take such matters seriously."

By now the director had overcome his initial shock and, as he was to confess to his wife later, his sheer fear at the sudden arrival of half a dozen Russian thugs. "Now look, gentlemen, I am sure there is no need for this heavy-handed approach. As you can see Dr Shalayez has come to no harm. He is here."

"Things may not be all they seem," Yvon hissed. His patience was running out. "Now is there somewhere here where I can talk to this girl in private?"

Lucinda shuddered. "To me? Why me? What have I done?"

Yvon leaned towards her, his eyes boring into hers. "*That* is what I want to find out!"

"This is all very irregular," the director murmured. His tidy schedule was suddenly shattered. He was un-

202

comfortably aware that Miss Segerström was looking at him for support. For once he realised he had to do something to deserve the respect in which she held him. He struggled to remain calm and rational. "Now, I really don't see that there is any problem. If you just withdraw your men, I am sure Lucy here will be pleased to answer any questions you may have."

"I will *not*!" Lucinda protested. She scarcely had to act the part of a terrified student overwhelmed by events. "Who are these people? What's this all about?"

In the commotion Shalayez had forgotten the time. He had been overcome with such dread that his stomach dipped with the sickening sensation of a lift in a shaft. But his fear began turning to anger as he realised that it was Lucinda who these oafs from the embassy were interested in. On more than one occasion his friend Sergei Chagall had told him how ruthless the KGB could be. Even in foreign countries.

He opened his mouth to intervene, then stopped. The sound was unmistakable, even above the howling of the wind outside. The heavy thud of the aero engine was directly overhead, its reverberation shivering down through the walls of the Society.

Conversation came to a dead halt, and all eyes turned upwards.

"What on earth . . .?" the director began.

Yvon suddenly knew. It took him an instant to recover from the surprise. He snapped across the room to Jackov: "Hold on to the doctor! Keep away from the front door!" He turned to the men behind him. "You lot, get outside and see what's happening!"

Although the Sea King was coming down against the gusting wind, its throbbing clatter was still ear-shattering as it made its final descent towards the glowing T-formation of lamps on the Society roof.

Len Pope dropped the two neon hand-wands from the straight-up 'Come On' position to the cruciform "Hover" signal with both arms held fully horizontal.

Now the dark green hull of the helicopter seemed huge, filling the snow-swirled sky, threatening to crush them. An anxious helmeted face peered down at them from the cockpit. Two more figures were crouched at the open cargo-hatch. The noise drowned out everything as the downdraught of the blades blasted the snow on the roof into a blinding vortex.

The aluminium flexi-ladder unravelled from the hatch, swinging gently some twenty feet above them. Pope lowered the wands slowly and the pilot followed, dropping inch by inch until the edge of the ladder was poised above the tower parapet.

Pope lifted his arms back to horizontal, and the Sea King held its station, shuddering against the buffeting wind.

Joe Monk grabbed the cable-conductor and touched the last rung of the ladder. The discharge pin sparked viciously at its junction with the television aerial as the momentous charge of static coursed down into the building.

The television set in the corner exploded without warning. It disintegrated with a resounding crack and a plume of rubbery black smoke as the screen shattered. Two girls screamed and the professionally trained Russians dived for cover, thinking that someone had opened up with automatic weapons.

Lucinda stood open-mouthed at the pandemonium around her, the thunderous clatter of the helicopter above numbing her brain. She glanced around for Shalayez to tell him to use the diversion to make for the lift to the roof. Then she realised it was hopeless. Jackov had him forced into a corner, the muzzle of a heavy automatic jammed up under his chin.

Already Colonel Yvon had recovered from his surprise and was reordering some of his men outside. His gaze then traversed the room until his eyes met hers. A curious smirk of a smile twisted his thin lips and he beckoned her.

Panic seized hold. Lucinda pushed past the dazed director, and grabbed one of the unopened wine bottles from the table. Without stopping to aim she hurled it at Yvon's head. The Russian ducked, and as he did she weaved her way around the table and the gathering of academics. The bottle hit the window, shattering the first layer of double-glazing. Giant slivers crashed to the floor like falling icicles, bursting on impact. The French girl student screamed in surprise.

Lucinda dived past Yvon towards the front door. But his reaction was fast, and she felt his fingers gouging into the skin of her back as he lunged at her shirt. She skidded on the wine-slopped floor, lost her footing and fell as the Russian got a second hand to her shoulder. She winced at the sharp stab of pain in her knee as broken glass sliced through her denim jeans. An arm descended on her, around her face, blinding her and gagging her mouth. Her arms flailed in vain, unable to find a target. She couldn't breathe.

Then she felt the power behind the shattering glass as Ingrid Segerström wielded another wine bottle at the Russian's head.

The grip around her face relaxed, and she felt the weight of the man's body against her back. In a fit of anger she heaved upwards, pushing Yvon aside. For a second she stood, gasping for breath, as the Russian reeled like a drunkard, clutching at his head. Blood seeped between his fingers.

Miss Segerström motioned frantically towards the door. "Get out, Lucy, for God's sake!"

The girl seized her chance. Staggering to her feet she rushed into the hallway and out into the snow. For a moment she hesitated on the steps as the ice-edged wind whipped through the thin material of her shirt as though she were naked. Catching her breath she blinked

205

through the falling snow to discern three Russians standing on the drive. They were pointing at the roof. Seeing their preoccupation, she tossed aside her indoor shoes and rushed past them.

7

Lucinda stumbled blindly down the slope, hardly aware of the icy numbness of her feet. Angry voices in Russian trailed after her, the exact words muffled by the wind.

Cold air seared her lungs and throat. The sweat of fear froze instantly on her back as she ran. Behind her someone grunted as they attempted to give chase through the fresh fall of snow. She dared not stop to look; she just concentrated on keeping going. Although she was thoroughly familiar with the layout of the grounds, the near white-out conditions were starting to disorientate her.

New snow had obliterated the lines of the drive, drifting in eddies to transform the landscape into an unrecognisable wilderness. She found herself wandering between pine trees where she knew there should be none. Gasping, she leaned against a trunk and squinted through the icy pellets that stung her face. Nothing was familiar. Maybe she was running in a circle? There was no way of knowing. Her sodden shirt was now stiff with ice and she began to shiver involuntarily.

The sound of the helicopter was still in the background, but its powerful heartbeat thud had receded, the sound seeming to echo around the trees from all directions. It gave her no clue as to the way to run.

Dark shapes passed by over to her left. Someone cursed in Russian. She shut her eyes in a bid to clear her mind. She told herself firmly that she must keep going.

Any direction would do, she reasoned; eventually she had to hit the boundary hedge.

The noise of the helicopter rose in tempo, and she was dimly aware of the sharp crack of small-arms fire. Rapidly the engine sound receded, and she guessed the rescue mission had been aborted. The sudden silence was eerie. It brought home just how loud the helicopter had been; it was as though a hidden hand had turned off the background noise of an air-conditioning plant. The wind, too, had lessened until now she was aware of her own laboured breathing and the crunch of the snow underfoot.

All sense of feeling had left her hands and feet, the initial pain of the cold being replaced by a dull nagging ache. Yet she began to feel more relaxed. The immediate danger was past. It couldn't be far now from the boundary and there were plenty of houses in the area she could call on for help. If only she could think of a plausible story when she knocked on the door of a complete stranger!

She had trudged only another ten metres when she heard a rough male voice from her right.

"Hey, English girl! You stay there!"

It was followed by the solid click of a cocking handle.

Dread went through her body like a basin emptying. She wanted to be sick. Slowly and painfully she turned. Her mouth dropped in surprise.

In her confusion she must have been walking around the perimeter for the last hundred metres. She had just crossed the drive by the gate. The black sedan was almost completely hidden under new snow.

There were three of them. Hard-looking men in dark coats and hats. All three were armed with hand guns. Only one of them was smiling.

Her legs refused to move; even if she'd been ordered to she'd have been physically incapable.

The smiling man waved his gun. "Here! Move slowly!"

She couldn't. She just stood stupidly, totally para-lysed.

Something hit the snow between her and the three Russians. Instinctively, she looked down as the card-board cylinder rolled to a standstill. Horror seized her. It was some sort of grenade . . .

The world went mad. Whether the blinding flash came first or the ear-splitting bang she couldn't tell. She was pitched backwards by the blast of displaced air, her vision gone and her ears ringing with pain. Her face hit the icy surface of the snow.

A fast succession of violent movements came from the direction of the Russians. Sudden grunts of pain and violent curses.

She stared, petrified, but unable to see. Her vision was a white blank. Momentarily, she thought it was the effect of the weather; then she realised. She was blind.

A firm hand grabbed her arm and lifted her bodily to her feet as though she was a mere doll.

The gruff voice in her ear was vaguely familiar. "It's all right, it's me, Brian! Don't worry, you're safe."

"I – I – can't see!" she gasped.

"It's only temporary."

Even as he spoke she felt herself being hoisted bodily over his shoulder in a fireman's lift. She felt the sudden violent jolt as Hunt's booted foot landed in someone's face. And then he was running, as though she weighed nothing.

It took several seconds before she began to make out the vague shape of trees and then parked cars. She heard the sound of an engine running, then a door being opened. Warm air blasted against her face.

"Duck your head," he ordered.

Her bottom hit the soft upholstery and the door slammed shut. A second later Hunt climbed into the driver's seat and swung the Saab turbo out of the line of parked cars and up the hill away from the Rönkä Society.

He didn't speak again for a full five minutes while he

swung the vehicle down road after road until he was sure they hadn't been followed.

"How're your eyes?" he enquired.

"Better," she murmured. "I'm starting to see things." Tears began to well. "My hands and feet hurt. Really hurt."

"You're just thawing out, love," he said kindly. "It'll pass."

She felt better for his reassurance. After a moment she said: "I suppose Niki didn't get out?"

"Afraid not. It wasn't your fault."

But it was no consolation. She began to sob.

Brian Hunt said: "We call it the embuggerance factor. Always expect the unexpected."

"If you can," Bill Mather added pointedly.

The words gave no comfort to the SIS Head of Station. Ralph Lavender continued to pace the apartment floor, turning suddenly like a cornered dog. "Well, it's a pity you didn't expect this!"

Hunt lit a cigarette and perched on the sofa beside the girl. "Well, we did our best. We had no way of knowing a bunch of heavies would turn up like that. They were obviously anticipating something. They appeared to know about Lucy here."

"At least we got her out," Mather added. He was trying unsuccessfully to hide his resentment at Lavender's carping. Years of professional training had taught him to make the best of a bad job.

But Lavender just jumped on the words. "Well, I just hope you didn't kill any of them. I don't want a bloody diplomatic incident."

"I told you," Hunt replied evenly. "I just used a stun-grenade and followed up with some unarmed stuff. Headaches and a dentist's bill is the worst those minders will suffer."

"I'm very grateful to you," Lucinda added. She was recovering now, wrapped in sweaters, thick socks and woollen gloves in which she held a mug of hot tea as though her life depended on it. Nevertheless she was still shivering with the effects of delayed shock and cold.

"Yes, yes," Lavender said impatiently. "We're very pleased you got out safely. It was a bit of smart thinking. But it still leaves us with one hell of a problem. Will it be possible to do *anything* for Shalayez now?"

Hunt couldn't sound optimistic. "Well, the only feasible back-up plan involved intercepting his car on the way from the Grand Hotel to the Society. From what Lucy tells us, I doubt he'll be going back tomorrow to finish his lectures. Even if the KGB were willing, I doubt the Society would want him. Not after all that trouble. My guess is he'll be put on the first Aeroflot flight back to Moscow."

Lavender stopped his pacing. "Would you have enough manpower to put it into effect? There's just the two of you now."

"That's not the problem," Hunt replied. "In the event of an abort, it was agreed the helo would drop off our team members at a convenient stop within Sweden. They'll be anxious to be back here by morning."

"The problem is knowing where Shalayez is and where he'll be going tomorrow," Mather pointed out.

Lavender waved the SAS man's concern aside. "We can at least find out *where* Shalayez is now. I've had the embassy and the hotel under surveillance, and it's most likely to be one or the other."

"Then the trick is to be sure of *where* he's going tomorrow," Hunt said. "If we assume he'll be taken to the airport, then we can try to intercept on the way to Arlanda. If they go from the Russian Embassy, it's fast roads almost all the way."

"How would you do it?" Lavender asked.

"With difficulty. It would need quite an elaborate deception. Getting hold of police uniforms and timing a road-check."

Lavender was incredulous. "Jesus, you must be joking!"

Hunt shrugged. "We'd have to find some way of slowing them down at a place of our choosing. That seemed the smartest way. It would all happen pretty quickly, hopefully before the real police realised what was going on." He hesitated. "But we didn't like the risks either, which is why we shelved the concept early on."

"And if he left from the Grand Hotel?" Lavender pressed.

Hunt smiled grimly. "Marginally easier. But it depends which way they go. We can work better in the back streets. In fact, we selected a spot on the route they've been using from the Grand to the Society. Unfortunately, it's not the most obvious route to the airport."

Lavender's face twitched nervously. "And it wouldn't involve dressing up in policemen's uniforms?"

"No," Hunt replied. "But again, even at best it's not a *controlled* situation. There'd be no guarantee that it would work. And if, for whatever reason, they took a different route, then that would be it. Finish."

Lavender sighed. Always thin-faced, his cheeks were markedly sunken, and the skin around the hard dark eyes grey with fatigue. "Then I'd better find out where Shalayez has been taken."

While Ralph Lavender was on the telephone, a taxi pulled up outside. It was a very weary-looking Mike Ash who appeared at the door. Behind him neither Big Joe Monk nor Len Pope looked particularly happy.

"What a cock-up!" Ash snarled, throwing his coat into a corner.

Hunt looked sympathetic. "KGB heavies turned up at the vital moment, Mike. One of those things."

Ash pulled a sour smile. "I know they did, Brian. We bloody well met them. Face to face. Big Joe's expecting Shalayez to come through the roof door at any moment. We wait and wait. The pilot's going spare because we've no fuel to loiter. Still we hang on, and then who turns up, but some slab-faced Slav with a bloody revolver."

"Took ten years off my life," Monk grinned.

"Took twenty off his," Pope quipped. "Never seen my mate here move so fast. Gave him a rapid knuckle-sandwich and slammed the door on his wrist."

"We were damned lucky to get clear," Ash recalled. "They still managed to empty a full magazine into the helo as we pulled away. Thank God nothing vital was hit. I just hope the lads got back to Norway okay. The weather was appalling."

"Where'd they drop you?" Mather asked.

"About three miles from the Society," Ash replied. "In the middle of a bloody field. We were wandering around for an hour before we came across a road and managed to hitch a lift." He sounded really disgusted. "This has got to be the worst bloody op I've ever been involved in."

Hunt said: "It ain't over yet, boss. Friend Lavender wants to have another go tomorrow. A road snatch."

Ash slumped into an armchair. "That's all I need – I'm knackered. Doesn't that bastard know when to quit?"

"Apparently not."

Ash pulled a half-hearted smile. "Okay, we'll feel better after a quick bath and freshen up. Get some grub on, will you, and we can talk it through over a meal."

An hour later, spirits were much improved as the group hungrily demolished a massive tureen of spaghetti and two bottles of red wine. Another reason for the increased atmosphere of optimism was the confirmation that Shalayez was still staying at the Grand Hotel and had not, as feared, been moved to the Soviet Embassy itself. Over coffee Hunt outlined what Lavender wanted to do, and the various drawbacks. The intelligence officer himself was still making telephone calls from the other room.

Hunt concluded: "Personally, I think we should tell Ralph that it's just not on."

Ash poured himself a brandy. "For what reasons?" he asked, stiffly.

Hunt hesitated before replying; he noticed a disapproving edge to his friend's voice. "Well, the whole situation is uncontrolled. We won't know, until chummy's convoy is actually rolling, which route they'll take. And if they do take the right one, there's a million and one things to go wrong. It would be very easy for civilians to get hurt."

"I agree," Monk ventured. "Lavender himself has made it clear how touchy the Swedes are about abusing their neutrality – and what *we're* proposing, well . . ."

"You can't get away with it," Pope agreed. "Not unless the operation is clean and fast – like our job tonight. She was the only way to do it, and even then she blew."

Ash studied the men around the table in silence, then focused his attention on Hunt. "Lavender calls the tune around here, Brian. Shalayez is vitally important, we all know that, so we at least owe it to him to give it a try."

"Sorry, boss, I don't agree," Hunt replied. "We're the specialists with the practical experience. If you say no, he's got no option but to go along with you."

Before Ash could respond, Lavender came into the room. He was obviously in buoyant mood, although he managed to curb the excitement in his voice. "I think I may have cracked the problem. A friend of a friend's got a contact at the Grand. Apparently the Russians are checking out in the morning. One of the KGB minders was moaning in the bar that he was going back to Moscow tomorrow."

"At least we know when," Ash said. "But not which way they'll go."

"I think I've cracked that too," Lavender replied. "I've a Swedish contact who'll phone the Grand's security officer tomorrow. He'll say he's from the traffic police, and that the hotel should advise any of its VIP customers going to the airport that the Nybroplan thoroughfare has been closed because of a major traffic accident. Police advise that traffic is being diverted up Regeringsgatan to join up with Birger Jarlsgatan to avoid long delays. All guests will be informed just minutes before the Russians' departure. There'll be no time for them to query it *if* they want to catch the plane."

Ash downed his brandy. "The simple solutions are often the best, Ralph. Well done."

"That's what I thought," Lavender replied. "There'd be no reason for the Soviets to query the advice, and as they'll not want to be stopped by some zealous Swedish traffic cop, my guess is they'll use the recommended route."

Hunt said: "I still think we're asking for trouble. We've only got a few hours to plan the whole thing in detail. It's going to be a real seat-of-the-pants operation."

Ash rounded on him sharply. "It's my decision that we go ahead, Brian, so let's stop carping, eh?"

Hunt bit his tongue, aware that his colleagues were viewing with curiosity the unusual spectacle of the captain dismissing his senior NCO's objections in a none too friendly tone.

Later, when the maps were being pinned up around the room for the detailed planning session, Monk took Hunt to one side: "What's up with Mike Ash, Brian? He's been moody ever since we got to Stockholm. Quite unlike him. Then the way he shot you down in front of Lavender – I mean he must realise we all agree with you on this. Tomorrow could be a disaster. I can feel it in my water."

"So what do you want me to do about it?" Hunt replied tersely.

"Have another go."

"And get shot down again?"

Monk showed his big teeth. "Better than gettin' shot tomorrow on the streets. Pick your moment, when Lavender's out of the way."

"I'll think about it."

In fact, Hunt had been thinking about it all evening. And the more he thought about it, the more certain he was that Ash had become a changed character since Christmas leave. He had noticed it as soon as the group met at Heathrow; Ash hadn't asked how his Christmas had been, nor offered any of his usual amusing anecdotes about his family's own madcap celebrations. At the time, Hunt had assumed his boss's mind was on the job in hand; on reflection he wasn't so sure. Now he was convinced that Ash had deliberately distanced himself, avoided meeting his eye or engaging in small talk. But then, Hunt reasoned, his own nagging guilt could be making him fear the worst.

He saw his opportunity in the early hours, when the rest of the team turned in to snatch a few hours' sleep after finalisation of the plans. Ash was running a last-minute check over the timetable. He looked up as Hunt entered. "I should throw a few zeds, Brian. It's a busy day tomorrow."

Hunt lit a cigarette. "It's about tomorrow I wanted to talk to you, Mike."

The captain straightened his back and dropped his notes on the table. "Oh, yes? Something we've overlooked?"

"No, not in detail. Just the plan itself. The lads and I think it's a mistake."

Ash's eyes narrowed. "So what's this, a union deputation?"

Hunt half smiled, but the other man's face remained hard-set. "Of course not. If you say do it, it gets done. But Lavender's an ambitious sort, out to make a name for himself. And, if I'm any judge, he's a bit out on a limb with this one. Should anything go wrong, he'll put the blame squarely on our shoulders as his tactical advisers. That's why I think we should reconsider."

"I *have* considered," Ash replied testily.

"I know, Mike, but you've had one sod of a day. Tired and things gone wrong . . ."

Ash had become quite pale with anger, but he kept his teeth firmly gritted.

"And you dismissed my arguments out of hand," Hunt pressed home the point.

Ash said: "It's decided. I've nothing further to say to you, Sarn't-Major."

The use of his rank hit Hunt like the bolt from a crossbow. He felt winded, frustrated and angry. "What is all this, Mike? What the hell's come over you?"

Ash stood up. "I'll tell you what's come over me. For years I treated you as a personal friend. I made the mistake of trusting you and taking you into my confidence – " he hesitated, and Hunt saw the hurt in his eyes " – and into my home."

Hunt felt nauseous, a churning of dread in the pit of his stomach. "So this is about Gabby?"

Ash reached for the brandy bottle and poured a measure, giving himself time to think. "She told me on Boxing Day. Said it was over between you. That you'd ended it."

"I'm sorry, Mike." It sounded lame. "I'd have done anything to turn the clock back, believe me."

"Believe you?" Ash's laugh was brittle. "You're such an accomplished liar, Sarn't-Major, I'm not sure I could ever believe anything you said again."

Hunt stood his ground. "Well, believe this, Mike. I've planned to resign from the Regiment – the only reason I haven't done so is because this operation came up."

"That's very noble," Ash sneered.

"It's just practical. I know the job has to come first."

"We both know that."

"I'll request my posting as soon as it's over. As I said, I . . ."

Ash raised a hand. "Do me a favour, Sarn't-Major, don't say anything. Just do your bloody job tomorrow and then get the hell out of my life."

*

217

Nikolai Shalayez was devastated.

He pressed his forehead against the windowpane of the hotel bedroom. Outside the glittering lights of the ships on Strömmen water and the old island city beyond taunted him. It was all so close, yet just out of reach. The double-glazed window might just as well have been the Berlin Wall with its coils of barbed wire, sentries and landmines.

And how long had it been? Not yet a week. Just a few days. All the time confined to the hotel and the Society. But it had been enough to glimpse another world. Colourful, happy and alive. That much he had learned merely by watching from the window of the sedan that transported him to and from the lectures. A sense of freedom that you could almost smell in the air. He noticed it when he was accompanied to the hotel bar where his minders corralled him into a corner seat, away from other guests. But they couldn't prevent him from seeing and hearing. Then at the Society. The people there had shown the same warmth and total openness that at home you only found over vodka in the kitchen amongst the closest of friends, and with the door shut.

And out there, somewhere, was not only the promise of a new life, but the tantalising hope of a new love as well. Lucinda.

He let the heavy velvet curtain fall back into place and glanced momentarily at the silk bedspread, imagining Lucinda lying there.

It was a vivid and cruel image to conjure with. A harsh laugh came from the other side of the door. The KGB minders had been playing cards for an hour. Playing cards and drinking. Someone was obviously on a winning streak. More laughter and a crude joke.

He turned abruptly away from the sound. It was as though they were laughing at him. Perhaps they were.

Despite the luxury of the best hotel in Stockholm, he was virtually as incarcerated as he would have been in a cell in Lefortovo Prison.

Indeed, he thought grimly, he might even end up there yet. After the helicopter rescue attempt at the Society he'd been treated like a traitor, despite his protests of innocence. The man called Yvon, who he vaguely remembered being introduced to at the Soviet Embassy, had treated him with contempt. Like a common criminal rather than a revered scientist. Had accused him of consorting with a British agent in a plot to defect.

Of course, he'd denied it. He'd protested so fiercely that he'd almost believed it himself. He had pleaded so convincingly that tears had run down his face and his voice had cracked.

All the time that snide Jackov had stood grinning in the corner, adding his four kopecks' worth. Hadn't he been with that girl at every opportunity? Hadn't he been holding her hand? Looking into her eyes like a lovesick youth?

Suddenly, Shalayez had stood up from his chair. He looked the man Yvon directly in the eyes. "I've been a fool, you're right. I met a pretty girl half my age and I was conceited enough to believe she had fallen for me. How stupid! I should have been aware that it could have been a plot to abduct me – especially after all the warnings you had given me. Not to mention the special care you have taken." He held Yvon's unblinking gaze. "I do not deserve the privilege of being allowed abroad. I'm a risk to myself. Please, I should like to be returned on the first available flight to Moscow."

That had shut Jackov up! He'd stared boggle-eyed. Incredulous. Yvon's face, too, was a picture. But it had done the trick, he was sure of it. They believed him.

Unfortunately, they also intended to grant his wish. And it was a hollow victory to be returned to Moscow, certain of facing an investigation over the report Sergei Chagall had so far managed to hush up.

He slumped on the bed and picked up the pack of cigarettes from the side table. It was hours yet before the dawn, but he knew he wouldn't sleep.

His friend's words kept echoing around his head. Sergei Chagall's words spoken on the train. When? A lifetime ago. *"Freedom of choice and action. You stay there a week – no, a day – and you'll understand what I mean."*

Well he had. And now he knew.

Morning broke as clear as a bell over Stockholm. A pale orb of wintry sun glimmered in a cloudless blue sky, coaxing the city into life. The streets were now swarming with people on their way to work, dressed in typically colourful Swedish winter wear. Traffic hurried alongside the glittering waterways, where the white hulls of moth-balled tourist cruisers and ferries dazzled at their moorings. Gulls swooped and squawked overhead whilst others inspected stretches of iced-over water for morsels of deep-frozen protein.

The ochre façade of the snow-topped Grand Hotel stood smugly in its position of prominence on the waterfront, vying for attention with the Royal Palace across the Strömmen.

Beneath the heavily ostentatious chandeliers of the main lobby of the hotel, Bill Mather sat at a table reading a newspaper. Already he'd heard a couple of guests discussing the road crash that had reportedly brought central Stockholm to a halt. He'd had little sleep through the night and had begun to flag, feeling his concentration slipping away. But then his fatigue vanished instantly as a black sedan pulled up outside the main entrance and three black-coated men marched in. Their burly frames and the arrogant swagger of their walk were at variance with the atmosphere of gentle sophistication created by the lush royal blue and gilt decor. While one man took the elevator, the other two made a slow circuit of the lobby in opposite directions. Each scrutinised bystanders so intently that several took exception to their rudeness. Mather shrank behind his newspaper as they passed, lowering it again only when they took up stations by the main door.

Almost immediately Nikolai Shalayez came out of the elevator. He was closely surrounded by four men, one of whom had arrived with the car. They marched swiftly across the lobby, glancing anxiously left and right as they went. In their midst the tall figure of the scientist was just visible. He looked pale and nervous.

As the party bustled out, Mather folded his newspaper and donned a trilby hat. He took care to position it, using the movement to slip the transparent plastic earpiece of the radio into place. He sauntered casually to the door and stood on the top step, breathing the crisp air deeply and smiling.

The doorman shared his delight and nodded in greeting.

Below, the Russian escort had split between the black sedan that carried Shalayez and a dark blue Mercedes parked immediately behind it.

Mather descended three steps, as though unsure which route to take. He scratched his ear with the edge of his newspaper, a gesture which allowed him to bend slightly towards the microphone clipped beneath his lapel.

"Black car leaving now. Chummy plus two. Blue car behind with four. Out."

He watched as the sedan pulled away, then scratched his ear again. "Let's go!"

He took the remaining steps to the pavement just as a white Audi Quattro pulled out of one of the parking bays and cruised to a halt. He opened the door and climbed into the passenger seat.

Brian Hunt didn't acknowledge his companion; he was absorbed in watching the Mercedes and the sedan as they waited their chance to turn into the traffic flow running west alongside the Strömmen.

He edged up behind them.

A gap appeared in the traffic and the two Soviet cars took their opportunity. As they did, a red Volvo backed out of a side alley opposite and turned to get ahead of them.

221

Mike Ash was driving Alpha One. It was first to reach the traffic lights at the north end of Strömbron Bridge. The sedan nudged up to its boot, followed by the Mercedes escort.

Hunt stopped behind the two Soviet cars, now sand-wiched between Ash's red Volvo in the lead and his own Audi. Already his palms were sweating. This was the tricky bit. Their quarry was boxed in neatly, but they still had a considerable distance to go. Even if the Soviets followed the police advice given out at the hotel, at any time an innocent Swede might break the chain. If someone squeezed in between any of the vehicles, it would cause real problems.

Hunt's own job was fairly easy. He could see what was coming and take the necessary action. Ash, on the other hand, was doing everything in reverse, watching everyone through his rear-view mirror. He had to keep the bonnet of the sedan close enough to prevent another car from sneaking in, whilst not making it obvious to the Soviet driver. In addition, he must take care not to break the chain at a set of traffic lights.

Then there was another snag. The bulbs had been removed from the brake lights of Ash's red Volvo, so it was crucial he didn't brake too hard until the moment of the intercept, and reveal the plan.

Despite these problems, the procession had moved easily over Strömbron Bridge, turning right past the Royal Palace, and right again across Norrbro in front of Parliament House. Instinctively Hunt closed up as they approached Gustav Adolf Circus, and prayed the Soviets would continue on the recommended route. He willed them on.

His mouth was dry.

Yes, straight over. Now they were into Regerings-gatan, running north along the two-way stretch.

Farther ahead the street narrowed into a single northbound lane. And once in that one-way system, the chain of vehicles would be locked in. And everything would be set. Side streets ran off to the left and right all the way up through the busy thoroughfare. But towards the far end Regeringsgatan gained height, the streets and shops on either side built on a steep embankment of land. On that stretch the side streets were accessible only to pedestrians who had to descend steep flights of stone steps to the lower level. That was their chosen spot where a car waited on the lower side street, safe in the knowledge that no Soviet vehicle in the procession could give chase.

But first they had two headaches to contend with. The two busy junctions with Hamngatan and Mäster Samuelsgatan to cross. It was touch and go at both sets of traffic lights. At the first Ash made a decision to slow prematurely on approach. It was proved the correct decision as the stop light blinked on; had he continued, the convoy would have been chopped in two.

At the second set on Mäster Samuelsgatan, it was Hunt who was almost cut off from the Mercedes in front of him. He stamped hard on the accelerator, jumping the lights dangerously late.

Ahead of him, the parked florist's van was behind on its delivery round. Its young driver, still suffering a hangover from his previous night's disco dancing, pulled out without looking.

"Watch it!" Mather snapped.

Hunt slammed on the brakes, sweeping around the front of the van, tooting a sharp warning as he went. The youth's reactions were dull. He fumbled his footwork and his shoe flicked the accelerator pedal accidentally. The nose of the van punched into the rear panel of Hunt's Audi.

"Sod it!" Hunt cursed beneath his breath, as he felt the impact and the sickening grind of metal.

"Don't stop," Mather urged.

"I won't," Hunt assured, and glanced in his mirror to see the florist's van stopped where it blocked the flow of following traffic. He put the incident from his mind and concentrated on catching up with the Mercedes.

He did not see the fairly rare sight in winter of a white-helmeted motorcycle policeman. The officer was stationary outside the NK department store on the far side of the central reservation, beyond the road junction. Alerted by Hunt's warning hoot, he had turned his head in time to see the collision. Laboriously he started up his machine and threaded his way across the traffic flow to the reservation, then turned up the northbound carriageway in pursuit of the hit-and-run driver in the white Audi Quattro.

Meanwhile the low winter sun was throwing most of Regeringsgatan into shade, illuminating the stone rendering on the upper storeys of the tall buildings which lined both sides as the street narrowed. Parked cars on either side allowed only one vehicle at a time to pass where the street became a one-way northward flow.

Ahead of him Hunt could see Mike Ash's latest dilemma. Traffic was moving slowly, yet it was essential for the intercept that he braked at speed, while the Soviet sedan carrying Shalayez was close behind.

Ash had slowed to a crawl to allow a long gap to open up between him and the vehicle in front. To any casual observer it appeared that the red Volvo had developed carburettor trouble. Some nimble clutch work started the car kangarooing in fits and starts. Hunt could just distinguish Ash gesticulating his apology to the driver of the sedan behind him.

By now the road ahead was clear almost as far as the intercept point, which was marked by low railings at the mouth of a side street on the right, leading down steps to the lower level. Although he couldn't see them at this distance, Hunt knew that a member of the team waited on either side of the road in doorways. Below, on the lower-level side street, their getaway car waited.

Hunt spoke into his mike: "To all groups. Stand

224

by – " He didn't wait for an acknowledgement. If they weren't in position it was too late now anyway.

The apparently troublesome carburettor appeared to clear itself and Mike Ash's red Volvo began to gather speed. The frustrated Soviet in the black sedan matched him, anxious to get to the airport. A faint smile twitched at Hunt's lips.

The Volvo drew parallel with the railings on the side street on the right. Mike Ash stood on the brakes and braced himself against the column, his head hard back in the rest to prevent whiplash.

There were no brake lights for the Soviet driver to see. He lost vital seconds before he realised that the car in front had stopped. At the last minute he threw the wheel.

The thud and crackle of disintegrating metal echoed up and down the length of Regeringsgatan. Glass and aluminium trimmings tinkled musically onto the hard-packed snow.

A second lesser thud followed as the escort Mercedes nudged the sedan up the rear, stoving in its bumper. Hunt cruised to a halt and waited. Beside him Bill Mather opened the glove box and drew out two 9 mm Browning automatics.

Ash climbed from his car slowly, with a motorist's usual reluctance to confirm that the damage was as bad as it sounded. He looked very Swedish in a two-tone ski jacket, a peaked cloth fishing hat, and sunglasses.

He glared at the driver of the sedan, but the Soviet made no attempt to move.

Then Ash stooped momentarily to examine the damage. He smiled and shrugged at the driver. It wasn't too bad . . .

He continued walking up to the sedan driver's door and leaned down to speak. With reluctance the man inside began to wind down his window.

Hunt snapped into his mike: "GO, GO!"

They came from all directions at once.

Just as an impatient driver behind the pile-up tooted, Mike Ash extracted an automatic from beneath his ski jacket and jammed the muzzle under the sedan driver's chin.

Big Joe Monk and Len Pope came in from opposite sides of the street. The small club hammers they carried took out the rear-door windows with devastating effect, showers of tinted glass bursting in over the startled occupants.

"NIET!" Monk yelled in warning to the KGB guard called Jackov who sat beside Nikolai Shalayez. Jackov withdrew his hand from beneath his jacket, leaving his gun in its shoulder harness.

Pope grinned at the terrified Shalayez. "Open your door quick!"

Shalayez fumbled. "It will not – " he gasped.

"Shit!" Pope breathed. "Central-locking."

Ash heard it. "Release the doors!" he snarled at the driver in Russian.

Meanwhile, all four doors of the escorting Mercedes flew open at once as the security heavies suddenly re-alised what was happening. As legs flailed and feet scrambled to get a purchase on the road surface, the four men were confronted by Hunt and Bill Mather. They covered one side apiece, each aiming a Browning in a solid two-handed grip.

"Very slowly," Hunt said in poor Russian, "throw your weapons out. One at a time. You! You first."

Faces flushed with indignation, the men started to obey.

Mather heard it first. "Police siren."

Hunt glanced up the road at the growing line of queuing cars. He could see the white helmet and pale blue leathers of a motorcycle cop as he weaved his BMW machine towards them.

He looked back to the sedan. Instantly, he recognised the tall figure of Shalayez as Len Pope helped him from the back seat.

226

More angry tooting came from the jam of cars. The driver of the first car opened his door and climbed out. He saw the guns and his mouth fell open.

Mather waved his automatic angrily. "Get back inside!" he ordered in Swedish. The man blanched and nervously obeyed.

The motorcycle cop abandoned his weaving, steered his machine onto the pavement, and raced towards them.

Hunt hesitated. Shalayez was crossing the road. They needed a few more vital seconds. He had no choice. Swiftly he turned his Browning away from the occupants of the Mercedes and aimed above the head of the looming motorcyclist. He squeezed the trigger.

Realisation that he was being shot at hit the policeman as effectively as if the bullet had. Seeing the levelled gun and hearing its sharp report, he was momentarily undecided whether to go on, stop or turn. In blind panic he managed a combination of all three, slewing the front wheel into a sideways skid and tumbling painfully into one of the parked cars.

"WHAT'S GOING ON?" Mike Ash yelled from the sedan.

"Motorcycle cop!" Hunt replied tersely.

He saw Ash curse silently, and then glance over the roof of the sedan to where Len Pope was propelling Shalayez through the gap in the railings and down the steps to the lower level. "Just hang on, Brian! We need another forty-five seconds for them to reach the car!"

Hunt almost laughed despite himself. This crazy slow-motion action was bizarre. Holding up the whole of central Stockholm's traffic at gunpoint. Mike Ash and Monk with guns trained on the sedan; he and Bill Mather doing the same with the Mercedes, whilst Len Pope legged it with a defector. No wonder they'd rejected the idea originally. And now an armed cop frantically calling up help as he lay sprawled in the gutter. He could even hear the radio static hissing angrily from the motorcycle.

It was going to be the longest forty-five seconds of his life! Already he was mentally having to revise their escape plan. Originally Ash and Monk were going to leg it fast up Regeringsgatan, whilst he and Mather raced in the opposite direction – now cut off by an armed Swedish policeman, who was no doubt scared and very angry.

Through the railings Hunt at last glimpsed Len Pope and Shalayez coming into view on the lower level. Although they were running towards the parked get-away car, their movements seemed exasperatingly slow.

Run, you bastards, run, Hunt urged silently.

Inside the Mercedes, time had given the KGB men a chance to recover from their initial shock. Perhaps sensing that things were going wrong for the hijackers, they began whispering to each other.

Mather waved his Browning and yelled at them to shut up in fluent gutter Russian. They lapsed into tense silence.

On the lower level Len Pope and Shalayez had almost reached the getaway car. Relief surged through Hunt as he watched – then his heart lurched sickeningly as he heard the wail of police sirens. Not one but several. The eerie sound seemed to fill the air, coming from many directions at once. Suddenly, a black police Saab with white fenders pulled in across the mouth of the lower level side street. He saw Pope instinctively slow, unsure what to do. The newcomers weren't traffic cops, but crime police.

Hunt made a snap decision, speaking rapidly into his mike: "Len, get the hell back up here! We'll cover you!"

Mather glanced across questioningly. Hunt shrugged. "There's no way out at all down there. At least we're holding the high ground. You'll have to keep this lot covered."

The SAS veteran nodded and pulled back to the pavement so that he could keep all four occupants of the Mercedes in view. Hunt crossed to the railings and looked down. Len Pope and Shalayez were almost back

228

to the bottom of the steps again. Behind them two policemen in leather jerkins and soft uniform caps were giving chase, guns drawn.

Hunt rested his elbows on the railings and fired two rounds towards the policemen. As the lead kicked up chunks of ice and tarmac by their feet, they skidded to a halt. One shouted an obscenity in Swedish, raised his gun. He let rip with half a dozen rounds, peppering the steps with ricocheting rounds.

As he followed Len Pope, Shalayez turned to see what was happening; then tripped and stumbled over the bottom step. Winded, he began crawling up the first flight, hampered by the burning pain in his ankle. He ducked as more bullets were let loose by the second policeman, and he stumbled onto the first landing. The concrete base of the railings offered the only cover. It was just deep enough to protect him if he kept his head down. Driven by fear, he wormed his way along to the shelter of a stone archway which was an emergency exit for one of the main Regeringsgatan buildings. He drew himself into the arch, thankful to be out of the firing line. Gasping for breath he leaned back against the door. To his surprise it fell open under his weight. He peered inside. A darkened passageway.

Glancing back at the mayhem around him, he made his decision. He slid quickly into the darkness and closed the door, muffling out the pandemonium of gunfire, shouting and wailing sirens.

Meanwhile, Len Pope had rejoined Hunt at the railings.

"Where's chummy gone?"

Pope turned. "What? Oh, Christ! He was right behind me!"

At that moment Hunt suddenly became aware of a movement in the traffic queue that now stretched right back down Regeringsgatan. In the corner of his eye he caught a glimpse of a white helmet. As he turned he saw the fallen motorcycle policeman standing, legs astride, with both hands gripping a Walther 765. The expression on his face was one of utter determination.

Hunt heard the crack of Mather's Browning and felt the whistling slipstream as the round flashed past his ear and found its target. With a look of total surprise on his face the policeman staggered back a few paces. For a moment he struggled to keep his balance, then toppled backwards over his own motorcycle.

"LET'S GO!" Mike Ash bawled. He'd had enough. There was nothing more they could do, and the situation was getting totally out of hand.

Together Mather and Hunt slammed shut the doors of the Mercedes, whilst Monk and Mike Ash did the same to the sedan. The move would give them vital seconds before the Russians could give chase. According to the original plan, Ash and Monk raced north ready to disperse down different side streets. Len Pope joined Hunt and Mather going south down Regeringsgatan, passing the policeman who lay moaning in the narrow space between two parked cars.

Mather hesitated but Hunt nudged him on. "C'mon, Bill, he'll survive. His mates will find him in a minute."

The three of them rushed on by the queue of cars. Drivers, who had climbed out to discover what the commotion was all about, quickly retreated to the safety of their vehicles. As each side street was reached, one of the SAS men broke off. Running was abandoned for a less conspicuous brisk walk. Dark alleys were sought where deliberately noticeable top clothes could be either dumped casually into dustbins or reversed to show a different colour. Each man had worked out his own change of appearance beforehand.

Ten minutes later Hunt, minus false moustache and red anorak, was boarding a bus for Bromma. Elsewhere Bill Mather was riding the escalator down to a Metro station, while Len Pope took a taxi. Mike Ash visited the Army Museum on Riddargatan, mingling with the crowds for an hour before resuming his escape, and Joe

Monk began a long leisurely stroll, pausing frequently to take snaps with his pocket Minolta of every likely-looking tourist attraction.

Meanwhile, back amidst the chaos and confusion on Regeringsgatan, a swarm of very nervous policemen closed in on the scene of the ambush. Ignoring the indignant shouts from a group of angry Russian diplomats, they attended to their wounded colleague. At first the thigh wound didn't look too serious. There was little blood loss, but the man looked deathly pale and his pulse was little more than a feeble tremor.

Later, as the Daimler ambulance blasted out its sing-song siren to clear a way through the congested city traffic, the paramedic discovered why the patient was suffering so badly from a light flesh wound. The bullet had evidently ricocheted against the thigh bone and ruptured the femoral artery, causing a massive internal haemorrhage.

But the discovery came too late. As they neared the hospital gates the policeman's fluttering pulse melted away completely. He was pronounced dead on arrival.

8

Forty-five minutes after his disappearance in central Stockholm, Brian Hunt alighted from a taxi in the Bromma suburb. He had already changed buses twice and now walked the final two blocks to the Fiscex apartment.

Len Pope opened the door as he approached down the path. His smile of welcome was uncertain. "Glad you made it, boss." He closed the door. "Ralph Lavender's waiting."

Hunt grimaced. "You've told him?"

Pope nodded. "He already had a shrewd idea. He's been listening in to the police net."

"Anyone else back yet?"

"No, but it shouldn't be long now before the stragglers come in. There's nothing yet about anyone being arrested."

Lavender appeared in the lounge doorway. For once the mohair suit looked dishevelled and his tie hung loosely at his collar.

"And Shalayez?" he demanded. "Do you have news of what happened to him?"

Hunt wasn't used to admitting to operational defeats. He hid his embarrassment with mild sarcasm. "Not unless you have, Ralph."

The intelligence officer's short fuse burned through. "Don't you bloody Ralph me, Sarn't-Major. Are you suggesting he disappeared up his own jacksy?"

"I told you, Mr Lavender," Pope interjected. "He must

have got picked up by those two cops who came after us on the lower level. He was behind me when I started to climb the steps. I guess he stumbled – or maybe got shot – then got picked up by the police."

"Or the Soviets," Lavender murmured to himself.

Hunt said: "What about the Aeroflot flight, did it take off?"

Lavender nodded. "Fifteen minutes ago."

"And?" Hunt pressed.

"No one vaguely resembling Shalayez went aboard. Not even at the last moment. We had someone watching on the tarmac."

"Maybe he's still free then," Pope offered hopefully. "Wandering around Stockholm somewhere."

Lavender shot a scathing look. "Don't talk rubbish, man. He can't have vanished into thin air. Either the police got him or the Soviets did."

"What about the Russian cars?" Hunt asked.

Lavender examined his fingernails intently. They'd been bitten to the quicks. "They went back to the embassy compound. But with tinted windows it was impossible to tell who was in them."

"That's it then," Hunt said. "The Russkies scooped him up. That's why there's been nothing on the police nets. He's back at their embassy. It's all over."

He was aware of the surge of relief as he said it. They could pack up and go home. Chalk one down to experience. And for him, he'd have to face up to the other part of his life that was going just as badly wrong.

"For you lot perhaps," Lavender snapped back. "For SIS it's the biggest intelligence setback of the past decade. Shalayez's knowledge was priceless."

And this failure's got your name stamped all over it, hasn't it, lad? Hunt thought ruefully. Virtually for the first time since they'd met he felt a glimmer of sympathy for Lavender. The man didn't have too many endearing qualities, but no doubt his mother still loved him. But you had to give him top marks for effort. On this jaunt he'd been dealt every card from the bottom of the deck.

Hunt crossed to the drinks cupboard. "Care for one of these?" he asked, pouring a half tumbler of Scotch for himself and Pope.

Lavender, deep in thought, shook his head irritably. Hunt had learned over the past days that, as well as being a non-smoker, he was virtually teetotal, and spent much of his spare time jogging or playing hard competitive squash. By all accounts he usually won.

Hunt crossed the floor and offered his glass. "Ralph, do us all a favour, and break the habit of a lifetime, eh? Look, I might be out of order and I don't know how much front-line work you've been involved in – but we've seen plenty. And when this sort of thing happens you've got to relax and take stock . . ."

Lavender opened his mouth to speak. Then changed his mind. Hunt could read the blazing 'Bloody cheek!' expression in the coal-black eyes. Then the pinprick pupils widened slightly and he almost smiled. "Perhaps you're right, Brian." He took the glass. To Hunt's amazement he downed it in one.

The SAS man said quietly: "I know this business has been a disaster, but at least operationally it was down to us. And we're trained to take it on the chin." Len Pope shared the black joke. "You certainly did your best, and I'm sure we'll say so at our debrief."

"That's decent of you, Brian, I appreciate it. But that won't cut much ice at Century House. They may give forth with soft words of comfort, but the bottom line is that it fouled up. Like all bureaucracies someone has to take the can. Things aren't as cosy as they used to be in the old school tie days. There's a lot of professional rivalry."

"And there's someone who'll see your failure as their way up?" Hunt guessed.

"More than one."

Hunt nodded in sympathy. "So what happens next?"

Lavender gave a snort of self-disgust. "The first of a

234

lot of humble pie. First to tell the embassy what we've done."

"Want me to come with you?" Hunt offered. "Mike and I know Matt Brewster from way back. A bit of moral support?"

Lavender hesitated, but he was obviously a man in need of a friend. "I guess as we didn't get our prize, it'll be okay to come with me to the embassy."

Hunt grinned in an effort to lighten the mood. "I'll put my smart Fiscex exec suit on."

"But no one else. I want everyone else out of the country on the next available flight. Mike Ash won't mind if you come with me?"

Hunt shook his head. "No, he'll appreciate the urgency. And I'm here; he's not." He turned to Len Pope. "Pass the message on when Mike gets back, will you? And contact Peter Burke at Fiscex. Tell him we're leaving and to get all the loose ends tied up, hired cars and the like. Plus a cover story to explain our departure, etc."

"Sure, boss."

Hunt looked at Lavender. "Time, I fear, to face the music."

Music and electronic pulses played continually between the hollow walls of the KGB residency. It created a soundproof barrier that defeated all known means of eavesdropping. It also created an utter quietness within the offices that was quite unnerving to the uninitiated.

The faint wheeze in General Badim's chest was quite audible to Colonel Grigory Yvon as he stood in front of the desk. He waited patiently in the embarrassed silence, whilst the KGB resident thought in vain for a way to talk himself out of trouble.

Yvon bided his time. He was almost enjoying seeing the bastard squirm. Indeed, he'd normally have relished the sight of his complacent rival struggling to justify the incompetence of his staff, had it not been for the gravity of their loss.

At last he could stand the man's floundering no longer, and broke the silence. "There's no point in chastising yourself, General. After all, Shalayez was taken at gunpoint by an obviously very professional team. Evidently, your men were taken by surprise – despite the fact that the helicopter incident at the Rönkä Society yesterday should have put them on their guard."

Badim's fat jowls quivered as he nodded his head in agreement. "You're right there, Colonel. Especially about that idiot Jackov. You said he was useless, and you were right! He'll pay for this."

Yvon's hooded eyes blinked impassively. Typically, the KGB chief was already smelling the scent of a scapegoat. However, he turned his mind to more important matters. Losing the mathematician had been Badim's business; his own role, as GRU resident in charge of the strike arm of Soviet military intelligence, would be to get him back. Or kill him. Either would meet with Moscow's approval.

"You are sure, General, that the British have got him?"

Badim nodded fiercely. "They must have! Our men were trapped in their cars at gunpoint, but they saw Shalayez taken down the steps to the side street by one of the ambushers. That man came back up, but Shalayez was not with him."

"They are sure?"

"They cannot be *sure*, Comrade Colonel!" Badim retorted. "There was a lot of confusion and people racing all over the place. Even that ass Jackov can only report on what he sees, not what he doesn't! Shalayez vanished on the lower level. Maybe he got away in some waiting vehicle. That must have been their plan."

"But you say the Swedish police cut off the road," Yvon challenged.

Badim shrugged, defeated.

"Then he could be in Swedish custody," Yvon surmised.

"I don't think so. The monitoring rooms have picked up nothing to indicate as much."

Slowly, Yvon began to pace the room, his nodding head with its hooked nose resembling the pecking motion of a hungry stork.

That was curious, he thought. Beyond the immediate walls of Badim's office lay the monitoring room where technicians tuned in to radio frequencies used by both Swedish police and counter-intelligence services. It was manned whenever covert meetings were planned with agents, in order to give prior warning of enemy surveillance. Since the abortive helicopter rescue attempt, the room had been operating round the clock. Therefore, they had a full "audio record" of the ambush when it occurred. It consisted mostly of communications between Swedish police units, but also a few short transmissions in English which had used open code. The signals had begun just prior to the ambush but had meant nothing at the time. In retrospect, it was obviously the attackers moving into position.

In addition, on the top floor of the building, banks of radio and microwave receivers, teletypes and other sensors vacuumed the airwaves for all Swedish and NATO communications, eavesdropping on everything from satellites to military installations to numerous individual telephone numbers. And for years they had been patched directly into the teletype circuits of the Swedish Government, including the Defence and Foreign Ministries. All messages sent were copied as a matter of routine.

Surely, Yvon reasoned, if the Swedes had found themselves with a defector on their hands, *something* would have been picked up by the plethora of antennae on the embassy roof. At least in the initial stages after the ambush.

He said: "Would you oblige me by going over the police net recordings again, General?"

Badim nodded.

"And the British and American Embassies, anything from them?"

"No, Colonel, mostly routine open-line stuff. The few coded transmissions were deciphered. Nothing was sent in emergency virgin code that could defy us."

Grigory Yvon took a deep breath. It didn't look good. "Well, General, clearly we can delay no longer. Both our ambassador and Moscow must be informed. No doubt we will both receive our instructions. Now, if you will forgive me, I have work to do."

Badim nodded, but his usual expression of artificial joviality for once refused to manifest itself. "Of course."

The GRU resident turned sharply on his heel and left the office. He was determined that the first news of the scientist's disappearance should come from him and not the KGB or the ambassador. He took the lift back down to the *Referentura*, virtually a fortified keep within the embassy castle, from which all coded material was sent and received. Having gone through the rigorous security procedure to gain entry through two sets of doors, Yvon made his way to one of the cubicles. There he began to write out his signal by hand into the special GRU-only ledger with numbered pages. Handwriting was used to overcome the possibility of eavesdropping equipment picking out the different sounds of typewriter keys being punched and thereby deciphering the signal before it was coded.

Carefully he wrote:

From GRU Residency, Stockholm
To GRU HQ Khodinka, Moscow
Through diplomatic and KGB channels you will be receiving notification of attempted abduction/defection of one Dr Nikolai Shalayez this morning. The current whereabouts of Shalayez is uncertain. Although the abduction attempt was almost certainly made by British agents, it is by no means clear that they succeeded. He may have been picked up by

Swedish authorities or alternatively be freely at large in Stockholm.

In any event it is my opinion that the whole KGB security arrangements were totally inept and inadequate.

Previously I pointed this out to Gen. Badim who ignored my advice with dire consequences.

It is therefore my strongest recommendation that pressure be applied to have the KGB resident replaced with a more competent officer.

In anticipation of your instructions, I am personally putting a GRU plan into operation to locate and secure the said Dr Shalayez with immediate effect.

He scribbled his signature on the bottom of the ledger page and handed it over to the GRU cipher clerk for immediate transmission.

Satisfied, he checked out through the *Referentura* security doors and made his way thoughtfully back down to his own suite. At least if nothing else good came out of this sorry affair, with any luck he'd be seeing the back of that pain-in-the-arse Badim.

He turned his mind to the more immediate action to be taken. Badim, he knew, had already begun to flood the streets of Stockholm with his KGB heavies, looking for Shalayez. However, he had little confidence in their ability.

He would mobilise his own resources with orders not to pussyfoot about. He was also armed with more information than Badim – especially the apartment in Bromma where the girl called Lucinda and five British strangers had rendezvoused with Ralph Lavender of the British intelligence service.

Within the hour he knew Moscow would instruct the ambassador to register their strongest objections about the British abduction attempt with the Swedish authorities. And before that happened Yvon intended to be hot on the trail of Nikolai Shalayez.

When he arrived back at his office he had his plan of

operation already clearly mapped out in his mind. He found his deputy Igor Kulik pacing the room impatiently, ready to be off.

The main manpower resources of the GRU were not at the embassy itself but at the Aeroflot offices and various commercial companies, some co-owned with Swedes to provide more legitimacy.

"I want Shalayez found before Badim gets a sniff of him," Yvon said immediately he entered the room. "I want every officer involved, excepting those on the most crucial of work. I want every port, airport, rail station, bus route and border crossing covered. Alert our agents in immigration, customs and Government offices. Each foreign embassy should be watched, as well as all trade missions and semi-official organisations of NATO nations."

Kulik looked pleased with himself. "It is already in hand, Colonel. I have put in motion my personal contingency plan for just such an abduction. Details are on your desk."

Yvon's eyelids momentarily opened and closed like camera shutters. He really must watch out for his protégé.

But his flat voice gave away nothing of his pleasure at the supreme quality, intuition and eagerness of the organisation he had fused together during his tour of duty in Sweden. Instead he said: "Kulik, I want you personally to take charge of an investigation into that apartment in Bromma. I am sure that it is at the centre of all this. Get together the best available team and head it yourself."

Kulik snapped a salute. "Sir!" He turned to go.

"And Kulik . . ."

The lieutenant-colonel hesitated. "Sir?"

"We've only a few Spetsnaz ensigns here at the embassy. I want some real muscle in reserve – just in case. See what's available, will you?"

For the first time Igor Kulik allowed his smile to break

through his impassive mask, albeit momentarily. "Again, Comrade Colonel, I am pleased to say that has already been done. There is a Staff Company unit attached to the Northern Fleet operating in Norway. They will be here before morning."

"Really, Kulik? Splendid."

Embassies of the largest NATO and allied nations are prudently clustered together on the opposite side of Stockholm to the embassy of the USSR. They are scattered in picturesque grounds around a quiet triangle of tree-lined roads to the eastern extremity of the city centre, just a few yards from the waterside boulevards of the Djurgårdsbrunnsviken. At each corner of this "diplomatic" triangle stands an armed Swedish policeman, protected from the worst of the elements by a glass booth. On the eastern flank of the triangle, set back from the road, stands the sixteen-year old British Embassy, an attractive two-storey building finished in local granite.

It was in the mock-Tudor bar on the first floor that Matt Brewster was enjoying a light liquid lunch, much welcomed after a particularly arduous session with the ambassador. The bar, with its Elizabethan tapestry corner suite and background burble of radio music, always provided a refuge; a moment of off-duty peace and quiet where the "no business talk' rule was enforced with an enthusiastically applied 'drinks-all-round' deterrent for those who broke it.

However, Brewster was in no mood to talk shop. Today was his forty-fourth birthday and his wife Cherry had dropped in for a surprise celebration.

The blonde darling of Stockholm diplomatic circles proffered the extravagantly wrapped package. She loved surprises, especially when she was giving them.

"What is it?"

"Open it and see, silly. I couldn't give it to you this morning because I had to order it from the NK store."

241

She added mischievously: "They didn't have your size in stock."

He twitched his greying handlebar moustache, but refused to rise to the bait. Anyway he could hardly deny that he'd put on a few pounds too many in the last couple of years. He fumbled for a moment with the wrapping before he extracted the sweater, holding it up to the light.

"Do you like it?" she asked eagerly.

It was white with typically Swedish pale patterns in blue and yellow. "It's hideous."

"It's lovely! Look at those nice bright colours."

"You need sunglasses to look at it."

Cherry wasn't hurt; their entire marriage had been one long banter and trade of unmeant insults. "Your trouble is, Matt, you're getting old before your time. Don't be so frumpy. Get with it."

He laughed. "I'd rather be without it, if this is it."

For a moment her laughing blue eyes took on a more serious expression. "Actually, Matt, joking apart, you are looking your age today. You look exhausted."

He lowered the sweater after waving it for sympathy at a cluster of British Council members listening to the radio at the bar. He got no support; they evidently agreed with Cherry's choice. "This morning's been a bit of a sod to tell the truth," he confided, lowering his voice.

"Anything serious?"

Brewster shrugged. "Hard to say. Sir Timothy had me in first thing. A helicopter flew into Swedish airspace last night from Norway. It came all the way in to Lidingo island, then returned. Flying very low, apparently, and was mostly below radar level. Oslo's denied it was one of theirs, but the Soviets have said they've eyewitnesses to say it was British."

Cherry frowned. "How would they know?"

"Good question. They claim it was sent to abduct one of their scientists who's lecturing at some mathematics seminar. They say their security people actually saw it."

His wife's face lit up. "That all sounds very mysterious!" She thought for a moment. "But it couldn't possibly be true, could it?"

Brewster sampled some more of his beer. "Well, I certainly hope not. The Swedes are very convivial whilst you respect their sovereignty and neutrality – but woe betide anyone who oversteps the mark. Anyway, I've spent all morning on the phone to Oslo and Whitehall, but I've come across a blank wall. No one knows anything about it. Sir Timothy's got back to the Swedish Foreign Ministry and given assurances that Britain has no knowledge. But the Swedes clearly don't believe us. It leaves a sour taste."

Cherry touched her husband's hand sympathetically. "It's a shame, darling, but it can't be helped. Just some mistake or the Russians stirring things as usual. After all, it's not the sort of thing we do, is it?"

He smiled. No, of course not. And as Cherry carefully folded up his new sweater, his eyes wandered to the row of shields running the length of one wall. They were mostly unit emblems given by British armed forces personnel who had passed through Stockholm over the years. There were some from ships' companies, a variety of Army units and several airforce squadrons.

"Not the sort of thing we do." Cherry's words swam around his head. Somewhere there was a worrying niggle; the same one that had been with him all morning. And it was a concern that he couldn't put out of his head because Ralph Lavender hadn't been in his office all day. In fact, he hadn't been there for the last couple of days. But Matt Brewster recalled the intelligence officer's enigmatic warning just two weeks earlier.

A Soviet scientist was 'coming over'. And, even at that stage, it wasn't expected to run smoothly. So maybe there was something in this helicopter business after all.

His eyes sought out the unit insignia he'd been searching for. A blue winged-dagger emblem mounted on a teak shield: 22 Special Air Service Regiment.

It had been a gift from Mike Ash when he'd been over advising on security two years earlier. They'd got on well, he recalled, both him and his quiet, rather introspective sergeant-major. What was his name? Hunt! Yes, Brian Hunt. Nice bloke once you broke down his reserve.

Lavender had told him that Ash was involved in the operation; he was probably out there, somewhere in Stockholm, even now.

"You're miles away . . ." Cherry began.

"Hey, Matt!" One of the British Council executives called over from the bar, where the news bulletin was coming over the radio. "Think you might want to hear this. A policeman's been shot dead in the city, and the Soviets were involved – "

"What?" Brewster sprang to his feet. However, the brief summary was finishing by the time he reached the bar. "What did they say?"

The man replied: "I didn't catch it all. Apparently an official car from the Soviet Embassy was ambushed in the city centre. There was some sort of gunfight and a Swedish cop got killed. That was all, really."

"Did they say who the ambushers were?"

The man gave him a curious look. "No, I don't think so. It all sounded a bit confused. It can't have happened that long ago."

There was a growing feeling of dread in the pit of his stomach as Brewster returned to his seat. The bar telephone trilled; one of the drinkers lifted the receiver. "It's for you, Matt. George on the door."

The head of Chancery took the handset. "Yes, George?"

"It's Mr Lavender, sir. He's just arrived with another gentleman. Asked if he could see you in your office immediately."

Brewster's mouth was suddenly dry. "Er – what nationality is Mr Lavender's guest, George?"

"Oh, er – not sure. English I think, sir."

"Thank Christ for that."

244

He hung up, made his apologies to Cherry and promised to be home early, so that they could go out for a celebration dinner at Erik's barge along Strandvägen. Then he made his way to the secure section of the embassy where his office was situated. A punched key-code admitted him through the double doors of bullet-proof glass and into the corridor which led to the Chancery Office. It was a modest and somewhat spartan room, painted cream and dominated by a large-scale map of Scandinavia that covered the wall facing his plain teak desk. A green safe stood in one corner.

The two men sitting in the easy chairs around the coffee table rose to their feet immediately he entered.

Matt Brewster knew instinctively that something was amiss by the expression on Lavender's face.

The intelligence officer made a quick introduction: "I believe you've met Sarn't-Major Hunt before."

As they shook hands, Brewster said: "Can't say I'm pleased to see you, Brian. Your presence here just confirms my worst suspicions."

Lavender raised an eyebrow. "You know what's happened?"

"I've been on the phone all morning over some accusation about low-flying helicopters in Swedish airspace. Then just before you arrived, there was a news flash about a policeman being shot dead in the city during the ambush of a Soviet car. It didn't take a Mensa member to work it out."

The intelligence officer had paled. "Did you say a policeman killed?"

Brewster nodded grimly.

Lavender turned to Hunt. "You didn't mention this?"

"I wasn't aware of anyone being killed," Hunt returned evenly. "There was a lot of lead flying about – mostly from the Swedes. We took care not to actually hit anyone . . ." His voice trailed momentarily ". . . unless . . ."

"Unless what?" Lavender snapped.

Hunt drew a deep breath. "One of our men had to put a round into a motorcycle cop. If he hadn't I wouldn't be here now. But it was just a leg wound – thigh – I saw the damage."

"Christ," Lavender breathed.

"It could have been another cop who picked up an unlucky ricochet," Hunt added.

"That's immaterial for the time being," Brewster interrupted. "The immediate question is, has this Soviet scientist of yours been spirited out yet? And, secondly, how deniable is the operation? Can we take the flak that the Soviets and the Swedes will be heaping on us?"

Lavender's voice was remarkably calm. "I think we'd better sit down, Matt." As they took to the trio of easy chairs, he said: "I'm afraid the operation was a failure. We believe the Soviets have got him back . . ."

Brewster shook his head in disbelief. God, he could just imagine it. The scientist back in Moscow, giving a graphic account at an international press conference of how British agents tried to snatch him from the streets of neutral Sweden. And shot a policeman with a wife and, no doubt, young children . . . They'd have a field day with a propaganda coup like that.

"But," Lavender continued, "it's just a possibility that – somehow – he made a run for it and got away. Or else he was picked up by the Swedish police."

The head of Chancery scratched at his moustache. His celebration birthday dinner planned for that night began to look a long, long way off. "So as yet we just don't know how deniable the operation is? At least until we find the whereabouts of this Russian – the name?"

"Shalayez. Nikolai Shalayez."

"And the weapons?" Brewster pressed. "What happened to them?"

Hunt answered. "They should have been disposed of in inaccessible places, though until everyone's back we won't know the details."

246

Matt Brewster looked and felt uncomfortable; the lunchtime lager was starting to repeat after the sudden mental stress. "You appreciate, gentlemen, that the ambassador will have to be informed. And I have to warn you, he is not going to be at all pleased."

Peter Burke drove from the offices of Fiscex Holdings with growing apprehension.

There had been an odd note to Len Pope's telephone call asking him to come to the apartment immediately. Somehow it didn't sound good.

It sounded even less good when he heard the radio news flash during the short drive to the Bromma suburb. He parked and went straight in to find Bill Mather waiting for him.

"Sorry about this, Peter, but things have got a bit hot. We're off. The others have already left, but I needed to see you first. I've a favour to ask."

Burke beamed his usual ebullient smile, but it was a trifle nervous. "What's the problem?"

"This." Mather held out a polythene package.

The other man took it gingerly. "A gun."

"Fired in anger, I'm afraid. Normally I'd have ditched it, but I can't risk it being found in a dustbin or whatever."

Burke steeled himself. It was like finding that he was well and truly in the middle of one of the thrillers he read so avidly. He was determined to rise to the occasion. "This is the murder weapon?"

Mather's grey eyes narrowed. "Obviously you've heard the news flash. It was a right cock-up, I'm afraid. The mission was a failure. And in the middle of the chaos that gun shot a policeman and that's enough. I don't think it killed him, I certainly hope not."

"But you can't take chances, eh?" Burke understood.

"You can say no, Peter, we'll understand. But I've no time to do a proper job of getting rid of it. If you're willing I'd like you to drive a good fifty miles out of

247

Stockholm to some remote spot in a wood. Somewhere where you won't be seen, and bury it deep where it'll never be found."

Burke smiled manfully. "It's as good as done, Bill. Say no more."

The granite eyes of the SAS veteran glittered with a rare show of emotion. "And don't go speeding."

"I won't."

A car's horn sounded outside. Mather said: "That's my taxi."

"Have a good trip, Bill."

"Ciao."

The front door slammed and the noise of the taxi receded, leaving the apartment unnervingly silent.

Placing the package carefully on the sofa, Burke decided he would leave as soon as it was dark. In the meantime he would clean out the apartment and wipe all surfaces of fingerprints. It seemed a sensible thing to do.

At last he was satisfied that he had thought of everything. Drawing on his overcoat, he thrust the polythene package deep in his pocket. Already he had decided where he would bury it.

He hesitated by the front door. Outside he heard footsteps crunching on the snow.

Was it Bill Mather? Or maybe another of Mike Ash's team? Perhaps they'd found that police were watching all the ports and the air terminal . . . so they were forced to return to plan a new way out of the country.

These thoughts flashed through Peter Burke's mind in a split second. Then he heard low voices talking. They weren't English or even Swedish. Instinctively, he knew they were Russians.

Momentarily, the blood froze in his veins, fear paralysing him to the spot. Scenes from the hundreds of thrillers he'd read raced through his subconscious mind. Calm! Stay calm. That was the first rule. He forced himself to gulp down a deep lungful of air. And again. The movement returned to his limbs. Suddenly, his mind was crystal clear.

Slowly, very slowly, he backed down the hallway, aware that any sudden movement would be spotted through the fluted glass of the front door.

He had almost reached the lounge when a fist began thumping angrily on the door. The noise made him jump, and he retreated hastily to the lounge. Then he heard the glass pane of the front door fracture.

Fumbling in his pocket, he shook Mather's Browning automatic free of the polythene wrapper. He'd never held a gun before, and the weapon was much heavier than he'd expected. He remembered reading about safety-catches, and with surprising clarity of mind he took time to locate and release it.

By the time he heard the hand fumbling with the front door lock, he was already through the lounge and into the kitchen. A plan was forming in his mind: he'd slip swiftly out of the back door, down the small garden and drop over the fence into a neighbour's plot. He smiled to himself, pleased at how well he was coping with this unexpected emergency.

Then the kitchen window exploded inwards, showering glass over the draining board. Slivers of the stuff slid madly over the linoleum to stop at his feet. Outside, he glimpsed pinched white faces peering in at him.

Sweet Jesus! He backed rapidly into the lounge again, twisting awkwardly as he turned to meet the men lumbering in through the front door.

Suddenly, Peter Burke was icy calm. This was the day of reckoning. After years of wondering if he'd ever face adversity with the same courage as countless fictitious heroes, he now knew the answer. He raised the Browning with both hands and levelled it. His palms were clammy with cold sweat. But his aim didn't waver.

There were three of them. Their dark coats and hats gave them an air of menace. Their faces were hard, chins set with a look of determination. Their eyes glittered.

One of them spoke: "Don't be stupid."

The use of English, perfectly spoken without any trace of an accent, shocked Burke for a moment.

"Then don't come any closer!" he snapped. "I know how to use this."

Glances were exchanged. Their leader pulled a rueful face, admitting defeat. He began a backward shuffle, retreating to the front door.

The hammering in Peter Burke's heart eased, and momentarily he shut his eyes with relief. He didn't hear the man approaching from the kitchen. He just sensed his presence a second before the heavy gun butt caught him on the back of the neck.

Pain shot through his head, short-circuiting his brain in a starburst of sparks that exploded in front of his eyes. He felt his balance teetering; the strength in his knees ebbed away. As the pool of red mist opened up like a chasm in front of him, he was aware that he was toppling helplessly in . . .

He came around to the smell of peppermint mouthwash.

"I'm sorry about that, Mr Burke. But you rather left us with no alternative." Igor Kulik's face filled his vision.

Burke turned his head from side to side to see beyond the Russian, and to clear his head of the steady throb. He was sprawled on the sofa in the lounge. Behind the man kneeling before him was a blurred group of dark figures. Again he shook his head, and wondered vaguely why his hands were behind his back? He tried to move them. They were stuck fast.

"A precaution I'm afraid, Mr Burke." Another waft of peppermint.

Burke closed his eyes. "What do you want?"

"I think you know." Kulik's voice was very modulated. Restrained.

The Fiscex executive shook his head. God! That was a mistake! He winced as another bolt of pain flashed from ear to ear.

"I want to know the whereabouts of Dr Nikolai Sha-layez and the men who abducted him. The Britishers who have been staying here in the guise of company workers."

"Shalay – who?" The name meant nothing to him.

"Shalayez," Kulik repeated. "He was abducted by your friends earlier today. A policeman was killed, and our scientist was snatched against his will."

Peter Burke blinked rapidly. So that was what it was all about! But Bill Mather had been adamant that the mission had been a failure. If it had, then why were these Russian heavies asking after this man Shalayez?

"Well, I'm waiting," Kulik said. "We know he was brought here."

Burke felt remarkably calm and rational. Evidently these Russians knew all about Mike Ash's team and their cover as Fiscex executives. It was pointless to deny it. They may even leave him alone if he was co-operative. "Look," he began cautiously. "I don't know what those people were doing here. Or at least I didn't until you just told me. But I do know that it went wrong. If they were trying to snatch your scientist, they failed."

Kulik shot a glance at his companions. One of them shrugged. He turned back to Burke. "How do you know this?"

Peter Burke gave a bland, fat smile. "Simple. One of them told me. He seemed very down."

"Down?"

"Disappointed. He was angry because it went wrong."

Kulik stood up. "And this?" He held out the Brown-ing.

Burke shrugged. "I was asked to bury it. It was obvi-ously used in the ambush."

It was Kulik's turn to smile. "Ah, the gun that shot the policeman. That will be useful."

Burke said amiably: "Well, if that's all, perhaps you'd be kind enough to untie me?"

Kulik's eyes narrowed. "Just one thing, Mr Burke. The

251

names of those Britishers who carried out this atrocity?"

"I don't know them."

Kulik's patience was evaporating fast. "There are some nutcrackers in the fruit bowl, Mr Burke. They can make a nasty mess of the finger joints."

Burke blanched. Fear began to return to his gut. "They didn't use full names."

"No?" Kulik bent down and his breath was heavy with peppermint.

"Well, I think one was called John Billings." It was the first name that came into his head. An old friend from his school days. "But honestly, I don't know the others."

"Try first names."

Christ, Burke groaned inwardly. His mind was a blank. He could hardly think of his own name, let alone any other. At last he visualised the men in the office at Fiscex. He'd use them. "One was Freddy. Another was George. Then . . ."

The GRU man had seen enough men under interrogation to know when they were spinning yarns. He said in a low, menacing rasp: "Had you not thought how I know your name, Mr Burke? Mr Peter Burke. I know all about British residents in Sweden, especially those who work for big companies like Fiscex. You, for instance, are thirty-six years old, weigh one hundred and ninety-six pounds. You live with your wife Joan and daughter Mary in a flat on Storgatan – "

Peter Burke's eyes widened.

"Now perhaps you'd like to try again with the names? Otherwise, my men might feel it necessary to visit your home address."

Burke had no doubt that the Russian meant it. He'd read too many books not to know how ruthless they could be. It couldn't all be make-believe. "Okay, I'll tell you what I know. But it's true about the names. Their leader was a man called Mike. I *think* his surname is Ash. But the others I only knew by Christian names. There was Brian, the second-in-command, Bill and Len. The other man was called Big Joe.''

Kulik looked reasonably satisfied. ''There, Mr Burke, that wasn't too difficult, was it? But if you have been lying to me, just remember that we always know where to find you.''

As the Englishman breathed a sigh of relief, Kulik moved away and began talking to his comrades quietly in Russian. ''I get the distinct impression that neither the Swedes nor the British have Shalayez. That means, I fear, it *was* his intention to defect, and he is therefore roaming about free in Stockholm. And the first place he'll head for will be . . .''

''The British or American Embassy?'' one man suggested.

Kulik nodded. ''General Badim will already have someone in the area, but meanwhile I want you to get down there. The job must be done *properly*. Whatever happens he must not get there alive.''

The row of hard faces nodded in unison. The dogs scented blood. The pack was on the loose.

Sir Timothy Maybush CBE listened in total silence.

He had spent twenty-five of his fifty-nine years in the Diplomatic Service, and there was very little left in the machiavellian underworld of international politics that he had not witnessed. He was rarely shocked, and even less frequently gave way to anger.

Pale blue eyes stared over the half-moon spectacles he perched on the end of his nose. The expression on the clean-shaven face was as bland as that of a professional poker player. Occasionally one of the bushy eyebrows would arch a fraction, or he would thoughtfully run a hand over his lank silver hair. But it was impossible to read anything into the gestures. There was no way of knowing if they signalled surprise, displeasure, or just straight acknowledgement of what was being said.

He reminded Brian Hunt of some crusty old High

253

Court judge. The eyes seemed distant and the nose and cheeks were veined due to an overfondness of port. His obviously expensive suit was now old. It was specked with dandruff and sported a soup stain on one lapel. Living in the past. One of the old colonials left at the Court of St James; out to grass and waiting for his pension. Only the habitual chain-smoking, with long nicotine-stained fingers, ran contrary to the image.

"So that's about the measure of it, sir," Ralph Lavender concluded. Hunt thought he looked relieved. Like a man unburdened.

Sir Timothy didn't smile as he lit a fresh cigarette from an old butt. "And it's *quite* a measure, Mr Lavender. In fact, it's a right old mess you've just dumped on my desk."

"I'm sorry about that, sir."

"So am I, Lavender, so am I. And tell me, why didn't you see fit to advise me of what was going on before?"

The intelligence officer squirmed uncomfortably in his chair. "Century House didn't think you should be troubled with it, sir. Head of Chancery was advised an operation was being planned, but no specifics."

The ambassador cast a reproving eye in Matt Brewster's direction, but his glance was met with an apologetic shrug. Sir Timothy had seen it all before. The intelligence services always thought they had the monopoly on discretion. Don't trust anyone. Especially the gin-and-it brigade of the Diplomatic Service. Just tell the Chancery that something's afoot. But only enough to cover your back. Then they can't say they weren't warned if things blow up.

He knew Brewster well enough to know that he'd been effectively kept in the dark; he wasn't one to have conspired against his ambassador if he'd known the full story.

Sir Timothy looked back at Lavender. "They can be real buffoons at Century House sometimes, y'know.

Knew full well how I'd feel about such a hare-brained scheme on my patch. Yet we're not stupid, y'know. We understand that sometimes things have to be done – however distasteful or undiplomatic. But as soon as the proverbial hits the fan they hand it over to us to sort out. Then distance themselves as fast as possible, leaving us with all the egg on the face." He swivelled in his chair and looked towards Hunt. "And you, Sarn't-Major. You say you're sure the Soviets have got this Shalayez character back?"

"It's the favourite theory, sir."

"And this unfortunate policeman, d'you think one of your men was responsible?"

"Not from what I saw, but you can never be sure in a firefight."

Sir Timothy examined the tip of his cigarette and blew gently on it until it glowed. "That'll be the trickiest thing for us. We can rubbish most accusations the Soviets make, especially if they've got their man back. Governments and public won't know who to believe. But if the Swedes believe we're responsible for killing one of their law officers they won't let us rest."

At that moment one of three telephones on the desk rang. Sir Timothy reached out and put the receiver to his ear. "Yes, who? All right, put him through." He closed his nicotine-stained fingers over the mouthpiece. "It's Wernberg. I think the trouble is just starting . . ." He removed his hand. "Maybush here. Ah, Bertil, how are you?"

Hunt turned to Matt Brewster. "Who's Wernberg?"

"Bertil Wernberg is the new minister for Foreign Affairs. Very courteous and pleasant to meet. But beware the smile on the face of the tiger. Behind that he's calculating and ruthless. He's the prime minister's right-hand man."

All three turned back to Sir Timothy. The stiffened expression on the ambassador's face told them that the Swedish tiger was not smiling today. "Yes, Bertil, I heard it on the news. Terrible business . . . Uha . . . the Soviets claim *what?*"

Hunt and Ralph Lavender exchanged glances.

Sir Timothy was talking again. "I promise you, Bertil, the first I heard about it all was when that radio broadcast was brought to my attention. If we'd been involved in any way, y'know I should have known about it . . ."

Hunt's eyes narrowed at the clever use of weasel words. The ambassador "should" have known about it. "*Should* have" . . . but had been kept in the dark. The diplomat hadn't actually lied.

"Look, Bertil, I promise you, the Soviet scientist is *not* here. I am quite happy for your security people to check. Or come along and see for yourself . . . No, Bertil, certainly not. Must be some kind of unfortunate misunderstanding. Of course I shall, if anything comes to my attention. Rest assured. And my best regards to Lena. G'bye."

Sir Timothy fell back in his padded leather chair. He looked distinctly pale. It took a second or two for him to regain his composure and reach for another cigarette. As he lit it he said: "Well, that was one very unhappy Swedish foreign minister. Apparently the Soviets insist we've got this Shalayez chap. So, Sarn't-Major, I think you must consider your theory well and truly blown."

Half to himself, Ralph Lavender muttered: "So he must be out there on the streets somewhere . . ."

Another phone on the desk sang urgently. Sir Timothy snatched it up, listened for nearly a full minute then replaced the receiver with thoughtful deliberation. "That was George on the door. He said there's been a car parked up on the road outside for the past half-hour. Two more have arrived in the past five minutes. One at each end, in a position to seal off the road if necessary. One of our security chaps has been out to have a look. The vehicle registration numbers are on the Soviet Embassy list."

A chill ran through Brewster and he expelled a low whistle.

"What about the Swedish police?" Hunt asked. He remembered that it was the job of the officers stationed in their glass booths to prevent unauthorised parking in the diplomatic area.

Sir Timothy inhaled deeply on his cigarette. "I can only think Bertil Wernberg believes the Soviets. If those cars aren't moved on, it's because the police are under orders to let us stew awhile. Let's see what happens in the next half-hour. If Wernberg believed me, I reckon they'll get moved."

"A thought has just occurred," Lavender said. "If neither the Soviets nor the Swedes have got Shalayez, then there's one obvious place he's going to make for."

"Oh my God," Brewster said as realisation struck. "You mean – here?"

Hunt agreed. "That's why the Soviet cars are outside. To pick him up if he tries."

With surprising equanimity Sir Timothy said: "Then we must make sure that they don't succeed." He turned to the SAS man. "What d'you recommend, Sarn't-Major?"

Hunt smiled in admiration at the old diplomat's un-hesitating response. "For a start, sir, I'd be pleased if you'd call me Brian. Secondly, is there any weaponry in the building?"

"I don't think we want any more shooting, Brian, do you?" the ambassador replied pointedly.

"If the Russians mean business, you may not have any alternative, sir. We're in no position to combat armed KGB thugs."

"Makes sense, sir," Lavender added.

Sir Timothy grunted, unsure, and turned to Brewster. "What do we have, Matt?"

"The only serious weaponry is a 9 mm Browning kept in my safe with the coding machine. A few of us belong to a small-bore rifle club to give us the excuse to keep some firepower here. Just .22s, I'm afraid."

"I have an automatic in my office," Lavender added.

Hunt said: "They'll do for starters. What about cars?"

"There's a small underground garage for the official diplomatic cars," Brewster replied. "And several vehicles belonging to staff, parked out the front. I should think you can have your pick."

For a moment Hunt turned the possibilities over in his mind. "As the only two here with military training in firearms, I think Ralph and I should take two hand guns and wait in cars at the front. My Saab and one other. We'll also need two chaps who can drive. If Shalayez turns up, we'll then stand a chance of getting between him and the Russians."

Sir Timothy's eyebrows raised. "Won't that be dangerous?"

"Possibly," Hunt replied, "but we're a bit short of options."

Brewster said: "Meanwhile, I'll get onto the police and protest about those cars outside. It's worth a try."

"Any other suggestions?" Sir Timothy asked.

"Just one, sir," Hunt said. "I suggest we try to intercept my friends at the airport before they leave. I've a nasty feeling you might want them here."

Nikolai Shalayez had sat crouched in the darkened office passageway off Regeringsgatan until the shooting stopped.

When it did, all he could hear were voices shouting in Swedish; the words meant nothing to him.

For some time longer he remained with his knees drawn up to his chin, hugging his legs and rocking slightly as he tried to assimilate what had happened. And what had gone wrong.

After the abortive helicopter snatch, this ambush had obviously been a hasty last-ditch attempt to prise him from the hands of his KGB minders.

From outside came the whooping noise of an ambulance siren. Shalayez looked up at the doors outlined in the dark by a faint chink of light. He realised now it was an emergency fire exit with a push-bar release. Normally it couldn't be opened from the outside. Thank God, he thought, that the last user hadn't bothered to shut it properly. Otherwise he'd probably be dead now.

He guessed that the Britishers by this time would have driven away. Or even been arrested by the Swedish police – or worse, shot dead on the streets. If he went out now he could try asking for political asylum, but if Jackov and the others were still there, he'd never get away with it.

No, he decided rationally, he must first get away from the scene. Give himself time to think things through. And he must do it quickly, before someone realised how he'd vanished into thin air.

Using his cigarette lighter to see the way, he fumbled along the brickwork passage until he came to the foot of a staircase which led to the upper floors. As he climbed daylight increased, pouring in from a dirty landing window.

He couldn't resist peering out. There were people everywhere, running around like ants. Police uniforms were much in evidence and white-coated medics. On Regeringsgatan itself the Soviet sedan and Mercedes remained, still crumpled into the pile-up. He saw Jackov gesticulating angrily with a policeman.

That decided him to move on. Fast. He crossed to the landing door and peered into the brightly illuminated office. Only a few girls were working; most of the staff were gathered around the windows, watching the commotion on Regeringsgatan. He slipped off his heavy overcoat, draped it over his arm, took a deep breath, and walked in.

To his surprise no one took the slightest notice of him. One pretty blonde typist glanced up, returned his smile briefly, and went back to concentrate on her work. He sauntered on, trying to look as though he were familiar with the place, as he tried to find the way to the central stairway. Modern partitioning conspired to turn the old building into a confusing maze, and he was starting to perspire as he found himself twice returning past the blonde typist. She was beginning to look curious.

Then he found the door he'd kept missing, and slipped thankfully down to street level. A knot of office workers stood on the street steps, shivering in shirtsleeves, as they watched a policeman being tended by an ambulance paramedic.

No one noticed Shalayez as he stepped out onto the pavement, pulled on his overcoat and set off quietly down towards the waterfront.

Without any real thought about where he was going, he turned corner after corner, working his way deep into the centre of the mainland city area. He was anxious only to be away from Jackov and the other KGB men. At last he found a little café which was empty except for one customer. In English, he ordered coffee and a roll with sausage and lettuce. The surly owner looked a little curious at the Russian's odd pronunciation, but said nothing. Shalayez then lit a cigarette and considered his position.

He only had a few kronor in his pocket; as he'd had little opportunity to spend during his stay, his hosts hadn't considered it necessary to give him much pocket money. So he couldn't rent a room, or try to get to Norway. He'd seen several policemen as he'd walked the streets and he'd had an overwhelming urge to rush up to one and plead for asylum. But then he'd stopped. He'd remembered what his friend Sergei Chagall had warned. The Swedes were as likely to hand him back to the Russians as they were to let him stay.

No, he decided, he had to go to the British Embassy. After all, it was they who had been trying so desperately to get to him. No doubt, they'd welcome him with open arms when he turned up. Lucinda might even be there.

Yes, that's what he must do.

But he'd wait until dark. That would be safest as Jackov and his cronies would certainly be looking for him. Meanwhile, he felt secure in the little café. No one would think to look for him here. He ordered more coffee and settled in to wait. Daylight hours were short, so it wouldn't be long.

Finally, as night fell and a gusting, sleeting wind picked up, Shalayez settled his bill and left, making his way to where he'd seen a taxi rank a few streets away.

During the cab ride the weather worsened. By the time they approached the diplomatic area along Strandvägen hard pellets of snow were rattling on the roof.

"Ja, something going on just now," the taxi driver said suddenly, slowing as they passed the American Embassy. Shalayez leaned forward. A black car was parked right on the corner of the next left-hand turning. An armed Swedish policeman was talking to the occupants.

"Where are we?" Shalayez asked.

The cabbie said: "That's the Norwegian Embassy on the corner. And next to it, farther down, is the British."

Seeing the taxi's flashing indicator, another policeman waved them down.

Fear grabbed at Shalayez. "Stop *now*! Please!"

The cabbie hit the brakes. "What is it?"

But before the man could turn his head, his passenger was out and running, lunging through the snow in an attempt to cut off the corner to the British Embassy and bypass the waiting black car.

The approaching policeman stared in confusion, momentarily glued to the spot. He'd been told not to allow any more Russian cars to park here; no one had said anything about people on foot. But *something* was happening on this filthy night, and the running man was clearly up to no good.

"Stop! Police!" he yelled in Swedish.

The running man paid no heed. He kept going as though the devil himself were giving chase.

At his companion's warning cry, the policeman talking to the driver of the Soviet car looked up. So did the driver.

The policeman hesitated, unsure. The driver did not. The GRU driver instantly recognised the shambling gait of Nikolai Shalayez struggling through the deep carpet of snow towards the road which ran in front of the British Embassy. The GRU driver was an expert and he knew exactly what to do. He'd trained at a special school outside Moscow and had spent hours on a simulator of Stockholm's streets even before he was posted to the city. He had chuckled to himself when a Swedish security car had first followed him. They'd known he was a new boy and had expected an easy time. They'd been in for a rude awakening. He knew the streets even better than they did. He had lost them in just seven minutes.

Now he threw the ignition key, which brought the black sedan roaring into life. Even before the policeman could order him to stop, the electric window was closing in the officer's face. The heavily treaded tyres spat snow as the vehicle leapt forward, the headlamps searching out the running figure.

The driver had no compunction about mowing down the traitor. He'd had his orders, and he wasn't one to disobey. And the presence of a Swedish policeman didn't bother him. They were pussycats. They knew he was in an official Soviet car, and they wouldn't dare shoot. At least, not until it was too late. Besides, he had diplomatic immunity. The worst that could happen was that he'd be expelled and sent home to Moscow – and a hero's welcome.

But such thoughts evaporated from his mind as he accelerated down the road, slowing momentarily, to get his timing right. The chromium-tipped snout of the sedan would crush Shalayez the moment he left the deep snow and stepped onto the road.

Suddenly, the GRU driver was dazzled by headlights. He averted his head, squinting against the blinding aurora. It took a moment to detect its source. Then he realised it had come from a car which had swung out from the drive of the British Embassy. Now it headed straight for him. In that second of hesitation the Russian was obliged to slow.

Then Shalayez was standing right in front of him. A black silhouette in a halo of light. Rigid with fear like a stag at bay. The driver stamped on the gas.

He wasn't sure what happened next. Shalayez leaped aside. The lights of the oncoming car seared into his retinas. All was a confusing white sea of swirling brightness. Then the sedan juddered to a dead halt with the resounding crash of tortured metal. The impetus threw him forward. His skull rebounded painfully off the steering wheel and almost at once he tasted blood on his tongue. His own.

Still reeling, the driver tried to orientate himself. He remained half-blind, aware now that another car had come up behind him, adding to the bewildering array of brightness. Instinctively, he fumbled for the heavy Stechkin automatic pistol beneath his seat. He felt the reassurance of its smooth wooden grip in his hand. He kicked open his door and launched himself out.

He ignored the man who was climbing from the Saab that had hit his vehicle head on. Instead, he turned away, raising the Stechkin as he sought his quarry.

Shalayez was sprawled in the middle of the road, stunned. He lay, confused, in the bright flood of light like a centre-stage actor awaiting a prompt. His eyes stung with the driving sleet and his mouth opened in abject horror as the GRU driver aimed at him.

To stop the execution, Hunt had to hurl himself at the Russian from the Saab's door. It was an awkward manoeuvre on the slippery road surface, and he fell heavily, dragging the driver down with him. Had the man not already been stunned in the accident and been half-blinded by his own blood, Hunt might not have got away with it.

As it was the driver struggled with the strength of an ox until Hunt tightened an arm-lock around the man's throat. He flexed his bicep madly, forcing the lump of hard muscle into the oesophagus, as they both writhed fiercely on the hard-packed snow.

At last the driver stopped struggling, his body becoming limp in Hunt's grip. Sweat stung his eyes as he glanced up. Lavender stood over him with Shalayez at his side.

"Shift yourself, Brian!"

Hunt swung to his feet, grabbed the fallen Stechkin and followed Shalayez to the second car which had closed up behind the sedan. Lavender engaged reverse, backed off, then swung the vehicle back into the drive to the British Embassy.

It jolted to a standstill. Hunt had the rear door open instantly, and bodily jettisoned Shalayez out, propelling him unceremoniously across the covered walkway to the glass doors and the lion-and-unicorn crest.

White-haired George had the doors opened as they approached. "Well done, sir!"

Hunt pushed Shalayez through in front of him, and thrust the Stechkin at the doorman. "If one of those Russian bastards tries to get in here, use that!"

George blinked, and half saluted in his surprise. "Yes, sir!" It was a long time since he'd been in the Army.

Next Lavender came rushing in and, without a word, followed on through into the building. He was white-faced and breathless.

George stood in his bullet-proof cubicle and checked carefully that the automatic machine pistol was ready to fire. Then he put it out of sight beneath the counter.

He glanced suddenly up as a tall bull of a man pushed his way through the glass doors of the embassy. He looked very, very angry.

George's hand slipped surreptitiously under the counter. "Er, yes, sir, may I be of assistance?"

"That man who just came in here!" bellowed the big man.

"Er, yes, sir?"

"He hasn't paid his fare!"

9

Ole Thoresen had just tucked his seven-year-old daughter into bed when the telephone rang.

By the time he returned downstairs he found that it had already been answered by his plump, fair-haired wife Tine.

She looked excited, her cheeks pink.

"Who was it?" he asked with his usual solemnity.

"A call," she replied. "With the code."

Thoresen looked at his wife and blinked. Instantly he felt the adrenalin start to pump.

For ten years now they had lived in the wooden chalet bungalow on the outskirts of the Norwegian town of Trondheim. It was an ideal location for the purposes of the Spetsnaz agents: within half-an-hour's drive of a centre of major strategic importance, yet remote, accessible only by a two-mile track which required a four-wheel drive vehicle. And it was high on a hillside, which made it ideal for radio reception and transmission.

In that decade the Thoresens had earned the reputation, by the few people who knew them, of being a hardworking, somewhat dour family. Like many rural folk they evidently enjoyed their solitude and kept themselves to themselves.

That suited the Thoresens well. Even their nearest neighbour didn't know that they had originally come from Latvia, descended from families with strong Russian blood ties. So no one guessed that their hardworking life was really an elaborate camouflage for their real mission – constantly to update plans for sabotage and subversion in Norway in the event of war.

Occasionally one of the Thoresens would travel to Finland for a holiday when they would 'disappear' for a few days. Long enough to get to Moscow for refresher courses and continuation training.

No contact was ever made with official Soviet representatives in Norway. No KGB or GRU controller even knew of their existence. Their case officers were Spetsnaz only, and rarely got in touch. When they did it was only after the most painstaking precautions.

However the expression on his wife's face told Thoresen that this contact had been distinctly different.

She answered his silent question. "They said that a distant cousin had been in touch and would like to visit us sometime in the spring."

Thoresen tried to remember the meaning of the coded statement.

His wife smiled; Ole's memory never had been as good as her own. "It means we are to be visited by an active unit requiring assistance." She reminded gently: " 'Spring' means soon, within forty-eight hours. 'In summer' means in the next week. 'Autumn' is two to three weeks . . ."

His memory jogged, he joined her for the last: "And 'winter' is next month. Yes, Tine, I now recall."

She said: "It could be as soon as tonight."

And, in fact, it was.

Although they had been watching, Thoresen and his wife failed to see the approach of the four skiers as they traversed silently down the steep slope behind their chalet and into the treeline.

Thoresen jumped and spilled his coffee when the knock came at the door.

He crossed the wooden floor and threw open the bib-and-brace door. It surprised him to see such a diminutive figure standing before him. The dull-coloured civilian duvet made the stranger look heavily rotund.

"I am sorry to surprise you. I think that I may be your distant cousin."

Thoresen stared. It was a woman's voice, soft and slightly husky. He squinted and moved his shoulder so that the inside light played on the newcomer's face. Only the eyes showed between the low fur cap and the fur collar. But he could see now that they were the eyes of a woman.

He took a step back. "We were expecting you in spring. Come in and welcome."

Her shoulders dropped suddenly with relief. His response had been correct. She turned and beckoned to someone, then stepped into the warmth of the chalet. "We are four," she said, glancing quickly around the room. "My colleagues have surrounded your home in case of trouble."

Thoresen smiled nervously. "As you see there was no need. I am Ole and this is my dear wife Tine."

The woman pulled off her hat and shook off the snow. Her hair was short and flattened, greasy from her days spent out in the field. Her face was oval and pleasant, if a little flat-featured for Thoresen's taste. Her eyes were hard and suspicious which detracted from her looks.

She shook Tine's offered hand as though she was mildly irritated; clearly she wasn't used to such civilian niceties. Thoresen's wife looked a little in awe.

"I am Captain Valia Mikhailovitch," the newcomer announced. "But just call me Valia."

She turned as the first man tramped in. He was tall and broadshouldered with the cynical look of a professional soldier. "This is Petkus, my second-in-command. And this is Litvinov." A younger man entered, again tall but with black curly hair and sly eyes. He was followed by a fair-haired youngster who appeared to be hardly out of his teens. "And lastly Yuri Popov."

The young man nodded his acknowledgement.

"And don't drop snow all over these comrades' floor," Valia scolded him. "Have some respect."

268

Popov looked sullen, and returned to the door to shake the snow off his boots.

The woman captain removed her duvet jacket and Thoresen was surprised that under all the winter wrapping she had a slim but powerfully built figure. The shape of her thighs in the snug black ski pants suggested someone who spent a lot of time skiing and climbing.

"How can we assist?" Thoresen asked.

"We have to get to Stockholm by the morning," she replied.

"Ah," he responded thoughtfully. "Maybe you can fly from Trondheim."

She shook her head. "No, we have personal equipment we need to take. It would not go down well to try and take it by aircraft." Was there just a hint of a smile on her face?

"Train, then?" he suggested.

"We cannot wait for timetables," she retorted. "Do you have a car?"

"But of course. Nevertheless it is a very long drive."

"We are four. We'll drive in relays. Two asleep while two do the driving. I should like to leave in an hour."

Thoresen nodded. "I'll check the car, and fill it up with petrol."

Tine stepped forward. "You will have time to eat? And maybe a bath?"

For the first time Captain Valia Mikhailovitch's face broke into a full smile. And for the first time she looked more like a woman than a soldier. "A bath! Ah, that would be so wonderful."

"Welcome to British soil, Dr Shalayez," Sir Timothy Maybush said.

The Russian clutched his brandy nervously. His eyes darted across the desk to the British ambassador and then to Hunt and Lavender. He raised his glass. "Yes, thank you."

He swallowed hard, downing it in one. He was in desperate need of its kick and the comforting afterglow. Fifteen minutes ago he thought he had reached his goal, but now he wasn't so sure. Although everyone had been stiffly polite, it was obvious that his presence was really far from welcome.

He'd been through enough for one day; he decided to be direct. "You do not want me here, is that right?"

His challenge was thrown down to Sir Timothy. "Oh, not at all, Dr Shalayez. You are most welcome on British soil." The ambassador smiled benignly. "It is only a pity that you have landed on this particular patch."

Shalayez frowned. "Please?"

Hunt dropped down on his haunches beside the Russian's chair. "You must understand that a defection is a very delicate political matter. Especially when it takes place in a neutral country."

Shalayez blinked. Defection? He hadn't really thought of it like that. He'd just been running for his life. Is that what these people *really* thought of him? A defector? In Russian there was not an equivalent word. The nearest was traitor. Traitor to one's homeland. To one's own kith and kin.

Hunt said: "We had planned originally to spirit you straight out of the country by helicopter. It would have been over before anyone knew anything about it."

"And now?"

Hunt tried to look reassuring. "And now we have the problem of getting you out of here unhurt."

Shalayez didn't follow. "So we just go to the airport. I am here of my own free will."

"The Russians will say otherwise," Hunt said. "And the Swedes may believe them."

"Then I shall tell my people to their faces."

Lavender stepped in quickly. "That's not a good idea, Dr Shalayez."

"Why not?"

"Because they have ways of applying pressure to

make you change your mind," the intelligence officer explained cautiously.

Shalayez shrugged. "Then I don't speak with them. We just go to the airport. A plane to your England."

"You won't get far," Lavender muttered.

Sir Timothy threw daggers at the SIS man. There was no point in putting the fear of God into the poor wretch.

But Shalayez had caught the tone. "You think I would be in danger from my own people?" He was angry. "Please, who do you think we Russians are? That my own people would kill me in a public place? While in your – what is the word – custody? In front of Swedish police?"

The ambassador looked uncomfortable. He smiled awkwardly and offered Shalayez a cigarette before lighting one himself. Carefully he said: "You must understand that, from what I have heard from Mr Lavender here, you are most highly regarded by your own people. But the scientific knowledge you have is of immense value to strategic defence decisions. In such matters governments – all governments – sometimes act in a way that they would not normally consider. Sometimes they will go as far as acting totally illegally, even downright criminally."

"Does *your* government do such things?" Shalayez challenged.

Sir Timothy raised one bushy eyebrow. "We flew in a helicopter illegally. And then the car snatch attempt . . ."

Shalayez swallowed hard. He hadn't quite thought of it like that.

Sensing that he'd got through, the diplomat continued: "All four of us in this room have first-hand knowledge of how far your people will go if a matter is that important to them. And, frankly, I cannot imagine *anything* more important to them than your return. For them, and for us, you could affect the entire strategic arms balance for the foreseeable future."

As the words sank home, Shalayez lapsed into stunned silence.

Hunt said quietly: "So you see, Dr Shalayez, your life really could be at risk. You saw what happened outside here. That man had been sent to get you back. He was prepared to kill you."

Shalayez's eyes were moist. He nodded numbly. He couldn't deny what he had seen himself, although he didn't want to admit it. That was already how his own countrymen saw him. A traitor. To be shot in the street like a rabid dog. "I have not thanked you for saving my life, er . . .?"

Hunt grinned. "Brian. And I'm just pleased I was in the position to do it."

Shalayez smiled. This was the one Britisher he'd met, apart from Lucinda, whom he felt instinctively he could trust. That reminded him. "Is Lucy here in the embassy?"

"Who?" Sir Timothy asked.

"Lucinda Court-Ogg," Lavender replied. "She came over recently to work with Fiscex Holdings. She used the name Marsh."

"She is a spy?" Shalayez asked.

"She works for me," Lavender confirmed.

Shalayez's eyes hardened. "You make your spies to prostitute themselves?"

Lavender's cheeks reddened. Stiffly he said: "Her orders were to make contact with you, nothing more. I am sure that anything else that happened between you was completely – shall we say, spontaneous?" Then he added: "I understand she has grown fond of you."

The Russian gave a dry laugh. "That, at least, is good to hear." He drew thoughtfully on the English cigarette. It was strangely mild and smooth after his usual rough-tasting brand. He inspected its glowing tip. "Very much I should like to see her."

Sir Timothy glanced at Lavender. "Is that possible?"

"I really don't think it's a good idea at this stage."

"I must see her," Shalayez persisted. It was clear to all three men that he was trying to set a precedent. To establish how far any demands he made would be met.

Lavender reluctantly decided to give ground. "She went back to England yesterday to await your arrival, but I'm sure she'd agree to fly back here."

"Tomorrow?" Shalayez pressed.

"I expect so."

Shalayez relaxed visibly and smiled. "That is good. That I would much like."

At that moment there was a knock at the door, and Matt Brewster entered. He looked distinctly unhappy. "I've just been on the phone with the chief of police," he announced. "And taking all kinds of flak. He's demanding to know just what the hell's been going on here."

"And you told him?" the ambassador asked.

Brewster was uncharacteristically irritable. "I didn't really have much choice, Sir Timothy! I said that the Russian had just turned up, being chased by half a dozen Soviet thugs. We had no option but to intercept him before he was killed."

"And what did he say to that?"

"Started giving me the third degree. Like how did we know what the man looked like? How come we were prepared with men in cars? Not really the actions of people who knew nothing about the Soviets' accusations over the ambush." Brewster looked to Hunt. "That was what he was really after, if you ask me. It was our involvement with the killing of that policeman this morning. To tell the truth, I don't think he's bothered about Dr Shalayez here, his defection, or how the Soviets try to get him back. But now he's convinced of our involvement in the murder and he's hopping mad. He's clearly taking the Soviet side in this."

"And I can hardly blame him for that," Sir Timothy muttered. "So how were things left?"

"I just stonewalled," Brewster replied. "Said we were

looking closely at the situation. What else could I say? Well, he wasn't satisfied with that. Said, under the circumstances, he could hardly prevent the aggrieved party from parking outside our embassy."

"It's hardly just parking," Sir Timothy growled. "It's more like a damn siege."

Brewster shrugged. "Anyway, the Soviets can stay, he says, provided they keep within the law. And he wouldn't agree to armed police protection at the entrance. Just the usual guys at the end of the road."

It was with some difficulty that Shalayez had followed the rapid conversation, but he understood the gist. "I am very sorry to have caused all this problem."

Hunt smiled tersely. "No problem, Dr Shalayez. It's not your fault." He turned to the ambassador. "I suggest, sir, that we keep our guest in the embassy's secure area, just in case of an attempted break-in."

Sir Timothy weighed up the seriousness of the threat for a moment, then looked to Brewster for verification. It was not something that would normally be considered.

"We can put up a camp bed in the spare office," the head of Chancery said with obvious reluctance. "Our guest will be comfortable enough."

"Meanwhile I'll keep watch on the front door with George," Hunt announced. "Okay if I keep the Browning?"

The ambassador nodded, his eyes closed. This really was turning into the worst kind of nightmare.

"And I'll stay with Dr Shalayez," Lavender added. "Someone should be with him at all times."

"Will you be going home tonight, Sir Timothy?" Brewster asked.

The British ambassador lit a new cigarette from the butt of the old. "I don't think any of us will tonight, Matt, do you?"

Brewster twitched his handlebar moustache and forced a grim smile. "No, Sir Timothy, not really."

"Oh, by the way . . . many happy returns."

It was almost midnight before journalist Björn Larsson was able to get to the exclusive Café Opera. A story had broken at midday concerning the ambush of a Soviet diplomatic car in central Stockholm. A policeman had been shot dead.

The authorities had been very secretive about the whole business. The police were being unusually non-committal and refused to speculate. No one was available for comment at the Soviet Embassy. It made piecing some sort of story together for the morning edition very difficult and time-consuming. All there was to show for the numerous telephone calls and endless rewrites was a highly speculative piece.

Normally Larsson, a dedicated newspaperman, would have accepted it all with good grace. All part of the job. But tonight he had a date with the lovely Birgitta, and he planned to persuade her to go skiing with him in a few weeks' time. His plump young face glowed pink with the effort of rushing to reach the rendezvous on time.

The queue at the doorway was shorter than usual, but that didn't concern him. He was one of the few hundred well-known Swedish jet-setters to have received an unsolicited lifetime membership when the restaurant had first opened. Which was just as well, because he did not share the trendy nightclubbers' desire to queue to be allowed in. The longer the queues, it seemed to Larsson, the more fashionable the nightspot became.

The restaurant was, as usual, heaving with people, but Birgitta had caught his attention by waving from the bar. He breathed a sigh of relief that she hadn't become impatient and allowed herself to be picked up by one of the many narcissistic playboys who frequented the place. Perhaps, after all, a well-known by-line journalist did have a certain romantic attraction.

They had just ordered drinks and were contemplating the merits of the Janssons Frestelse, a potato and sprat casserole with onions and cream, when Larsson saw a familiar face.

Threading his way through the mass of people was Tord Jensen, a journalist for a rival newspaper. Tall, dark and thin, Jensen was a thirty-eight-year-old who'd never come to terms with the fact that he was approaching middle age. Nor had he learned to accept that his perpetual lascivious sneer was a turn-off to the young girls he tirelessly tried to chat up. Even if the liberated Swedish female did find older men attractive, few would have been seduced by Jensen's display of gold fillings which gave him a distinctly unsavoury air.

Larsson was sure the man was making straight for him. Normally he would have steered Birgitta into the nearest crowd and disappeared. Otherwise Jensen would hang on all night like a leech, constantly ogling the girl's substantial figure.

But Tord Jensen also had superb contacts with the Soviet Embassy. With the mysterious affair of the ambush still fresh in his mind, Larsson decided to discover if his rival had any inside information on the business. As it turned out, he was not to be disappointed.

"Björn, my old friend!" Jensen's teeth glittered devilishly. "Wondered if you might be here tonight! Surprised you're not beavering away on that Russian kidnap story." The fathomless black eyes alighted on Birgitta's freckled cleavage. "Ah, what a charming lady! I don't believe I have had the pleasure."

Larsson noticed his girlfriend take an involuntary backward step. Her full lips curled with disdain as her hand was taken and pressed to the gold teeth.

"Birgitta, this is Tord," Larsson said uncomfortably. "Tord – Birgitta. Tord's a rival of mine. A freelance on one of the weeklies. Writes the same sort of material as I do. Military, parapolitics, espionage – all the intriguing stuff. Only he has better contacts!"

"You're too kind, Björn. Too kind!"

Larsson noticed that, unusually, Tord Jensen did not

appear to be drunk. And for once, his eyes didn't linger obscenely on the nearest pretty woman. In fact Larsson was now sure that the journalist had deliberately singled him out. "So about this kidnap story, Björn, haven't you been working on it?"

Larsson suddenly realised he'd missed a trick. "Did you say *kidnap*?"

"Yes, my old friend. God, was I envious of you. It's a swine being freelance. By the time I let rip with all I know, you daily guys will have bled it dry. Found out all I discovered today."

The younger man took a chance. "I thought that was a terrorist ambush today. Maybe some right-wing crackpots like the Grey Wolves."

Tord Jensen cackled with mirth. "More like the Mangy Lions, my old friend!" He thought his own joke very amusing. "And it was a kidnap, not a terrorist attack."

"I don't understand."

Jensen hesitated momentarily, then appeared to come to a decision. "Oh, why not! You'll find out before I can use it on Sunday. I was talking this evening to an old contact at the Soviet Embassy. Chap called Yvon. D'you know him?" Larsson shook his head. "He's only some junior defence attaché, but he knows what's going on, all right. Couple of aquavits and he tends to talk a bit too much."

"What did he say?" Larsson pressed. He was vaguely aware that Birgitta was becoming bored.

"He said the Soviet Embassy's in uproar. Reckons a major international incident is blowing up. The Russians reckon that the kidnap attempt was made by British secret agents acting on behalf of the Americans. He told me they've got proof that the policeman was killed by one of these British thugs."

Larsson's mouth went slack with amazement. "Good God!" If it had come from anyone but the respected Tord Jensen himself, he wouldn't have believed it. "But *who* did they kidnap?"

It was his rival's turn to look amazed. "My old friend! You mean you don't *know*? I'd have thought of all people . . . It's your pet subject, Star Wars . . . the Soviet mathematician, Nikolai Shalayez – "

Björn Larsson was in the middle of sipping his lager. He missed his mouth, the drink slopping down his shirt. "Christ, Tord, you're joking!"

The man was evidently pleased with the effect his revelation had. "Not at all, my old friend. It's absolutely true . . . But apparently the kidnap went wrong and Shalayez ended up roaming Stockholm with everyone out looking for him. No one knows where he is."

At that moment a barman leaned across the counter. "Excuse me, Björn."

"Yes?" the journalist muttered, still brushing the spilled drink from his shirt.

"An urgent telephone call for you. The editor of *Expressen*."

Larsson nodded his thanks and turned to Jensen. "Sorry, Tord, I must take the call. Perhaps you'd buy Birgitta another drink for me."

The girl pierced Larsson's back with her pale blue eyes as he made quickly towards the telephone. Tord Jensen watched him go with a certain amount of satisfaction. Colonel Grigory Yvon would have been proud of him. The story had been beautifully placed. There would be just enough time to prepare a front page and inside spread for the early evening editions of tomorrow's paper.

It was fifteen minutes before Larsson returned. He was smiling widely. "The editor wants me back at the office. Something's happened down at the British Embassy."

"Shalayez?" Jensen asked.

"I think so. We've picked up something on the police wavelengths." He didn't mention that the police radio frequencies were constantly monitored to pick up an early break on new stories.

"Good luck," Jensen said. For once he meant it.

Björn Larsson suddenly realised that Birgitta was no longer there.

"She made apologies and left," Jensen explained. "Didn't say why. Just that she'd be in touch – sometime."

Larsson cursed, swallowed the last of his drink, and left.

Three separate taxis arrived at the British Embassy that night. They arrived in fairly close succession, each travelling more slowly than the last as the snow filled the night sky, and was blown into deep drifts by the strengthening wind.

Mike Ash was the first to arrive. "What in God's name is going on out there, Brian? It's like Piccadilly Circus on a bad night."

"The Russkies are camped on our doorstep," Hunt explained. "Our friend Shalayez turned up earlier this evening."

"Oh, God," Ash said as he removed his coat. "No wonder you recalled us. I was just about to board my plane."

"We also got hold of Len and Big Joe; they're on their way. But we didn't stop Bill Mather. The police are talking about a murder rap."

"Sweet Jesus," Ash muttered. "They really think it was one of our rounds?"

Hunt nodded. "I'm afraid it looks like it. Must have been a freak shot. Anyway, they're convinced we British are behind it all. That's why they're letting the Ivans sit outside."

Ash ran a hand over his bald head. "Can't say I blame them. Has there been any trouble?"

"Only when Shalayez arrived. They tried to negotiate him right outside."

"This is getting worse!"

Hunt lit a cigarette. "Fortunately we were able to get

to him. He's shocked but otherwise okay. They've tried nothing since."

He knocked on Matt Brewster's door and showed Mike Ash in. It was a dishevelled head of Chancery who sat behind the desk with a club tie hanging loosely at the collar of his crumpled shirt. A tumbler and half-empty bottle of Scotch stood like a lighthouse amid a raging sea of paperwork.

"Great to see you, Mike," Brewster said as he rose to shake hands. "Sorry it's all such a mess, but as you've gathered we're in the middle of a political storm."

Ash nodded. "So Brian's been telling me."

"Sir Timothy's just had the Swedish minister for Foreign Affairs on the phone again. *Second* time this evening. Bertil Wernberg is one very unhappy man. He's got his police chief hammering on one door, and the Soviets hammering on another – demanding to know what they're going to do about it. Gave Sir Timothy a right ear-bashing. 'I can't believe any accredited member of your diplomatic staff could be involved in such chicanery', et cetera, et cetera."

"So what happens next?" Ash asked.

"The ambassador has been summoned to the Foreign Ministry for first thing tomorrow morning."

"And what about the Russians?"

Brewster went to the window and lifted the blind to peer out into the road. "God knows, Mike. In London the Soviet ambassador has requested a meeting with our foreign secretary. He won't get it, of course; we'll fob him off with a junior minister. But here . . . well, I *hope* Shalayez will be okay until we try to move him. Then I suspect that they'll stop at nothing."

"That's where we come in?" Ash guessed.

Brewster left the window. "I'd like you to look at ways of getting him out in one piece. Any subterfuge you like. But the sooner the better. For all concerned."

Ash nodded. "We'll get to work. Meanwhile I think

we ought to take the precaution of getting some firearms in."

Hunt said: "I've already suggested that, Mike. The ambassador's agreed to have some delivered in tomorrow morning's diplomatic bags."

"With great reluctance," Brewster reminded darkly.

Colonel Grigory Yvon had not slept all night.

He had kept awake on a cocktail of nicotine, black unsweetened coffee, and adrenalin.

By early morning the deep shadows under his eyes gave him an even more pronounced corpse-like look than usual. His skin had drawn even more tightly over his high cheekbones so that the flesh beneath them sank around his jawline.

The air was thick with stale tobacco smoke and a faint smell of perspiration when the deputy resident entered.

"Good morning, Comrade Colonel," Igor Kulik said, glancing round the office. "If I may say so, you look as though you have had a busy night too."

The hooded eyes blinked like those of a bird of prey. "The telephone hasn't stopped. And see the pile of cables I have to deal with from Moscow."

Kulik waved the sheet of paper he was holding. "Well, here is another to add to the collection. But I don't think you will be unpleased. It is a response to your request to have General Badim removed."

As Yvon studied the cable, Kulik said: "Shall I turn up the airconditioning?"

"Is it that bad?" the GRU chief murmured, only half listening. Suddenly he looked up. "This is excellent news, Igor!"

Kulik's grey eyes glittered. "Badim is not to be replaced."

It was unusual to see such a bright smile on the face of 'The Cadaver'. "Ah, but you must read *between* the lines. The KGB will not be seen to respond to a request from us. But they are sending out a man to handle this

281

Shalayez affair over Badim's head. You mark my words, Badim will not be with us long. When this business dies down and the dust settles, our friend will be quietly recalled to Moscow. Those *chekists* always have to save face."

"Then I am pleased."

Aware that he'd been indulging in personal emotion, the colonel's facial expression stiffened. "So bring me up to date, Igor, on the latest developments since our man fumbled the execution of Shalayez last night."

"A valiant effort, Comrade Colonel," Kulik commented. "So nearly successful."

"You are starting to talk like Badim," Yvon scolded. "In my book near success counts as failure. And this operation is down to us from now on. We have carte blanche from Moscow so there is no excuse for failure. None."

The other man conceded the point. "At least we now know where Shalayez is. The Swedes believe us and are taking no special steps to protect the British Embassy. If they make any effort to remove Shalayez, he will not survive. I promise you that, Comrade Colonel."

The dark eyes burned with anger. "I should point out that they can keep him there for months, Igor, and we can hardly sit outside until the spring. Despite Moscow's priority directive we can hardly storm the embassy either. Don't we have anyone on the inside?"

Kulik nodded. "Yes, Comrade Colonel, but in a very lowly position at present, although we have high hopes of promotion in the next few years."

"Well, put some pressure on. See if this recruit can't find out exactly where Shalayez is being kept and if something can't be done to have him eliminated. Please act on it, Igor."

Kulik stiffened subconsciously to attention. "I shall do, Comrade Colonel."

"Now," Yvon continued, "what other steps have been implemented during the night?"

"As you know, we have our own teams in cars at the front of the embassy and now the police are making no attempt to move them on. But the rear of the embassy is a problem. It backs onto Ladugårds Gärdet."

"The park?"

Kulik nodded. "A large expanse of undulating grassland with a few trees. It is a difficult area to cover and would provide the Britishers with an ideal method of escape. The waterway is only some two hundred metres away and the ferry docks are only two kilometres to the north."

Yvon blew a silent whistle. He knew the area well. In the summer months he enjoyed walking amidst the wild flowers and watching the children sailing dinghies down on the water. In winter it was deep in snow. "So what have you done?"

"I've isolated seven of our men who are competent on skis to patrol the area. They will pose as citizens taking their recreation."

"That is not many for such an area."

"Even worse when they are split into shifts. In these temperatures it isn't practical to have them out for more than four hours at a time. So really it is only two or three at one time."

"What about the Spetsnaz team from Norway?"

Kulik shrugged. "Another four would make little difference with the shifts. Besides, you may need them elsewhere. Instead we have other men patrolling the roads on the perimeter of the park. As you are aware Kaknästornet is also in the park . . ."

A hint of a smile crept over Yvon's face. He indeed knew the ugly square communications tower well. At 385 feet it was the tallest building in Scandinavia. On top was a restaurant and public observation platforms. In event of war it was the task of Yvon's organisation either to take over or destroy the tower.

" . . . It gives us a bird's-eye view of the rear of the British Embassy. In daylight we can use the public telescopes. At night I intend to send in men dressed as engineers with night-vision devices. We have detailed plans of the layout and also forged security passes – if I have permission to use them?"

Yvon nodded. "As I do not expect us to be at war for a year or two yet, I think you can. Moscow will approve. There will be time if the Swedes review security after this."

"Good." Kulik seemed well satisfied. "Our observer teams will be in constant radio contact with our men on the park perimeter and the skiers. Meanwhile I also have our men posted at all railway, bus, ferry and air terminals and a private helicopter standing by at Bromma airfield. We also have more Spetsnaz teams coming over on the Helsinki ferry."

Yvon pushed back his chair and stood up. Casually he rubbed the stiffness in his legs and walked to the window. "So, Igor, that is that. Comrade Nikolai Shalayez is like a rat in a trap."

"What are the chances that the British will relent and return the traitor?" Kulik asked.

Yvon returned to his chair, relaxed and steepled his fingers in the usual posture he adopted when deep in thought. "If he gets away to London, I'd have thought not much. But whilst he's in the British Embassy we can apply diplomatic pressure on both Britain and Sweden. Already I have planted a story in the Swedish press that will break tomorrow – revealing the truth of what has happened. Badim's people will organise a spontaneous protest march of students in Stockholm the next day."

"And then?"

"For once Badim and I are in complete agreement. We shall continue to crank up the pressure steadily until both British and Swedish eyes water." He studied his fingertips. "When we have finished with them I hope they will decide that Nikolai Shalayez is not worth the candle. They will look to a way to save face, and we shall give it to them."

Suddenly the telephone trilled, shattering the solemn silence of the dark-panelled office. Kulik took the call. The Spetsnaz team from Norway had arrived. The deputy resident asked for their leader to report immediately in person.

"Captain Valia Mikhailovitch." Colonel Yvon rolled his tongue around the pronunciation. "A woman. How intriguing."

"There are several female officers in the Spetsnaz," Kulik said helpfully.

"I do know that, Igor. It is just that I have not met one before."

The knock on the door was short, sharp and loud. The woman who entered was not what either GRU man had been expecting.

For someone who had just driven the six hundred miles from Trondheim in Norway in fifteen hours, she looked remarkably fresh. Although cut fairly short in a severe style, her soft auburn hair had an attractive sheen and framed a pleasant face which was devoid of make-up. The wind-burnt skin gave way to distinct white patches around the serious hazel eyes where ski goggles had been worn. She was small, but hardly doll-like in the dark anorak and trousers. Her body looked solid and capable.

She introduced herself briskly, standing to attention.

Yvon noted that she did not salute. She was respectful, but her lack of the strictest etiquette appealed to him. It showed an independent streak.

"You have made good time, Comrade Captain. Congratulations," he said. "No doubt your team would appreciate some sleep before you go to work."

Her eyes narrowed fractionally. Was it a look of indignation? "We've taken shifts on the drive, sir. None of us is too tired. We're ready to start immediately."

Yvon nodded appreciatively. "Good. Lieutenant-Colonel Kulik here will brief you on the situation at the British Embassy. I want your team to be responsible for the elimination of the traitor Shalayez if any attempt is made to move him."

"May I ask what opposition we might face, sir?"

Yvon blinked. This one didn't mince words. She was going to ask her questions when and where she wanted to.

He said: "We believe that members of the British Special Air Service Regiment were responsible for an attempted abduction of Shalayez yesterday. We cannot be certain, but four men returned to the embassy during the night. Positive identification was difficult, but we're fairly sure they were members of that same SAS team."

Captain Valia Mikhailovitch's lips moved imperceptibly. For a moment a ghost of a smile could have passed over her face.

"Now," Yvon continued, "I suggest you grab some breakfast in the canteen and report back to Lieutenant-Colonel Kulik here for your briefing in – shall we say, thirty minutes?"

Her heels snapped together. "Sir." Again no salute.

As the door closed, Kulik murmured: "An impressive woman."

Yvon remained impassive. "We have work to do, Igor. First someone must meet this new KGB man from the airport."

"Do you know him, Comrade Colonel?"

"I don't believe so. But the cable says he was Shalayez's political assessment officer where he worked. What was his name?"

"Chagall, Comrade Colonel. Sergei Chagall."

Brian Hunt felt shattered. The small smoke-filled room they'd been allocated as a billet had left his eyes red and gritty; even the endless cups of coffee had done nothing to stop his mouth tasting like a sewer.

He didn't complain. He knew full well that Mike Ash must be feeling similarly on the edge of exhaustion after hours of going over every map and guidebook they could find on Stockholm. In a long 'Chinese parliament' session with Len Pope and Big Joe Monk, they had turned over every possible way of getting Nikolai Shalayez out of the country unharmed.

There were not many options. And of those, few were really practical.

Had the inlet not been frozen over, the most attractive would have been a quick dash to the waterfront, a few hundred metres away, and a getaway boat. Only, sadly, feasible after the spring thaw.

A helicopter from a Royal Navy carrier or frigate would have been favourite, but Matt Brewster had scotched that from the start unless the Swedes agreed. And at present there was no chance of that.

They even considered using a powered microlite, the military uses of which were being explored by a group at Hereford; but a brief exchange of coded telexes with the experts decided them against the idea.

"So we're back to getting him out by car again," Mike Ash said. He sounded deflated.

"I've made out a list of delivery vehicles that call," Hunt said. "But there's nothing regular except the laundry van every Monday. Groceries and booze wagons call when there's a delivery wanted. The stationers deliver once a month, and office equipment maintenance is again when required."

"Could we persuade any of them to let us hijack their van, I wonder?" Ash murmured thoughtfully.

"Do we have to involve anyone else? We could buy a van and dummy up the livery. Photocopier sales or somesuch."

"It's an idea," Ash conceded. "If we arranged for various types of delivery to occur in a short period."

"Maybe also have half a dozen vehicles all leave the embassy at virtually the same time," Hunt suggested.

"Ivan would have his work cut out following them all," Ash agreed, warming to the idea.

For an instant it was like old times, thrashing out a

solution to the insoluble, their recent animosity momentarily forgotten. Grins were exchanged. Then suddenly the spell was broken as the door opened, and Big Joe Monk entered. Above the padded anorak his hair and moustache glittered with ice crystals. "It's bleedin' brass monkeys out there," he said with feeling.

Len Pope pushed him aside. "Get in, you big oaf." He glanced at Ash. "Hi, boss, worked out the conundrum yet?"

"We're getting there. Thinking of getting him out in a delivery vehicle."

"Then it'll have to be a bloody armour-plated one," Monk growled. "We've just recced the outside and the park round the back. The place is stiff with KGB. I've never seen so many people taking a stroll in a blizzard before. They've even got skiers posted at the back."

"Most of them were carrying heavy-looking bags too," Len Pope added. "Bags long enough to carry lethal hardware."

Mike Ash was about to respond when there was a gentle knock on the door. Monk opened it and an instant smile came to his face as he saw the secretary standing with a tray of four steaming mugs of coffee.

"Mr Brewster told me to keep you topped up," she said with a slight giggle in her voice. She was petite and dark and scarcely twenty. "I noticed two of you had just come in. You looked like yetis. You must be frozen!"

"Getting suddenly warmer, love," Monk leered. A big hairy paw took one of the proffered mugs. "And what's your name?"

"Barbara. Call me Barbi."

"You Matt Brewster's secretary?" Len Pope asked. He wasn't going to let his oppo steal the advantage.

The girl blushed. "No such luck. Just a secretary in Visas. But Mr Brewster called for volunteers to help out in the emergency and stay over."

"And you drew the short straw?" Monk suggested.

Another giggle. "It sounded like fun. Nothing ever

happened here like this before. I wanted to help." Her face suddenly clouded. "Oh, I have got a security clearance, you know. We *all* have who work here."

Hunt laughed. After all the anguish of the past few days it was good to see the innocent, willing face of youth.

"No boyfriend who'll miss you then?" Monk pressed.

"Leave it out," Ash said reproachfully.

She didn't appear to hear. "Yes, he's Swedish. But to tell the truth he's been taking me a bit for granted lately. It'll do him good if I'm here for a few nights."

"It'll certainly do us good," Pope murmured.

"Anyway, thanks for the coffee," Mike Ash interrupted, deliberately cutting off the SAS men's chat-up line. The others got the message and lapsed into silence. As soon as the girl had gone he said: "Right now we've a lot of work to do, but we'll do it a lot better if we catch up on some sleep. Brian and I will be on hand in case of trouble, whilst you two grab an hour's catnap. As soon as the offices are open in the morning, I want you to see about getting hold of a van and getting someone to signwrite it for us. The longer we have to keep Shalayez here, the worse this bloody farce is going to become. You can bet your bottom dollar that Ivan is thinking of everything he can to get their man handed back."

"How soon can we try?" Hunt asked.

Ash frowned. "I'll put the idea to Matt Brewster this morning. If it gets the go-ahead I'd like to have Shalayez out of here within forty-eight hours. At the latest."

Alf Nystedt, senior adviser to the prime minister, was an intensely worried man as he was driven through the early morning Stockholm traffic to Rosenbad.

He had not slept well. The late evening phone call from his old and trusted friend Peter Öhman in the Ministry of Foreign Affairs had guaranteed his insomnia. He had tossed and turned for hours beside his wife until she had kindly but firmly suggested that he get up and

289

make himself a coffee. As a working wife, she too wanted to be fresh in the morning.

He had followed her advice as he had many times before. Usually, when sitting in his dressing-gown with a hot drink in the early hours, the problem that had been haunting him would melt away. Or at least a solution would quickly begin to form in his mind.

Not so last night. The more he thought about the gathering diplomatic storm clouds, the more insurmountable the problem seemed. The prime minister would be demanding a carefully thought-out policy to be recommended, covering every contingency before his Cabinet meeting. But for once Nystedt doubted that he'd be able to give it. He thought of phoning Peter Öhman back and airing his fears. But he dismissed the idea. They were the same age and shared the same interest in government and politics, but to get Öhman out of bed like that would be pushing friendship too far. It would have to wait until the morning meeting.

The black Volvo eased to a halt between the small triangular gardens and the entrance to Rosenbad which housed the Ministry of Justice as well as the prime minister's office.

His chauffeur took the usual precaution of checking the back seat – Nystedt was notoriously forgetful about his personal possessions. For the second time that week it was his reading glasses; yesterday it had been his trenchcoat.

The automatic glass doors opened obediently to let him into the vaulted lobby where his footsteps echoed on the grey and white marble floor. He passed by the four figure statues to reach the security booth.

The two private armed guards from Abab, in uniform brown shirts and green trousers, recognised the dark, stocky figure dressed casually but smartly in slacks and sportsjacket with a blue shirt open at the throat.

One of the guards was a girl and she smiled as she opened the bullet-proof glass security doors. She liked

Nystedt. He wasn't pompous and full of his own importance like so many senior civil servants. Nystedt was not too proud to stop and exchange a friendly word with the likes of herself.

But today Alf Nystedt did not ask after her husband or her small son. He scarcely acknowledged her as he passed through to the inner lobby and took the lift to the seventh floor. Once there he used his coded security card to gain admission to the prime minister's office.

His personal secretary was waiting for him in reception. She was an attractive woman in her late thirties, although the pageboy hairstyle, snug denim jeans and casual check shirt conspired to make her look ten years younger.

"Good morning, Mr Nystedt." She had long ago learned to distinguish when he was in one of his rare bad moods. Immediately she recognised that this was not going to be a good day. "Mr Öhman and Mr Fellén are already here. They are waiting in your office."

He nodded his acknowledgement. Ove Fellén was a gruff forty-nine-year-old official from the Ministry of Defence. He had to be in on this one.

His secretary stepped deftly in front of him and led the way through to his personal office which was decorated in light birchwood panelling and pale blue upholstery. An unhappy combination of old oil paintings and modern Scandinavian abstracts decorated the walls.

Both men were seated on the soft floral settee which was set to one side of the desk. The tall lanky frame of Öhman was first on his feet. "Morning, Alf. I'm sorry to have been the bringer of such bad news." He offered his hand in an unnecessary shake; a gesture of personal friendship and solidarity.

Ove Fellén's bulk slowed him down and he was only just standing as Nystedt turned to him.

"Thank you both for coming," the prime minister's adviser said tersely. "Perhaps between us we can make some sense of all this."

"Shall I pour the coffee?" his secretary offered.

"No thank you, we'll manage. It's best that we're left alone on this matter."

The woman smarted privately, but gave no outward sign of annoyance. Smiling politely she left Sweden's most senior civil servants to get on with their affairs of state.

As soon as the door closed, Nystedt said: "Peter, you had best bring us both up to date with events."

Öhman nodded. "The missing Russian has turned up at the British Embassy. Their ambassador claims that the man went there voluntarily, but the Russians say he was abducted against his will."

"The *Ryssdjävlarna* would," Fellén growled. He had finally lost patience with the Soviets back in 1981, when one of their *Whiskey*-class submarines had got itself stranded on the rocks off the Karlskrona naval base. They offered no explanation and no apology. Since the 'Whiskey-on-the-Rocks' incident, as the press had dubbed it, the Russians would always be the 'Russian devils' to the Defence Ministry's Fellén.

When the other two sat down, Nystedt remained standing, shifting his weight from one foot to the other, impatient as Öhman continued: "But this time there is evidence to suggest the Soviets might be right. We're as certain as we can be that British agents were involved in that car ambush yesterday. And by implication it was one of their men who killed our police officer." He lifted a hand to halt the protestation that Fellén was about to make. "Now I'm sure it wasn't deliberate. In fact I got the autopsy report from the chief-of-police this morning, and death appears to have been caused by an unlucky ricochet which ruptured the femoral artery. Nevertheless it is still murder."

Nystedt nodded his terse agreement.

"Now the foreign minister will be seeing Sir Timothy Maybush at ten," Öhman continued. "He will leave the British ambassador in no uncertainty as to how we feel about the situation. We hope he may have some explanation."

Fellén meshed his pudgy chipolata fingers together over his grey-suited knees. "Let us be realistic, Peter. What *possible* satisfactory explanation can Sir Timothy offer? If it's true, the best he can do is to offer us a private admission and an apology. He certainly won't do that publicly."

"The public don't know about it yet," Öhman pointed out. "They think the ambush was some sort of terrorist attack."

"Thank God for small mercies," Nystedt muttered. "But how long before the press finds out? Once there's a hint that the British Government is implicated, they'll be baying for blood. You know how unpopular Mrs Thatcher is with your average Swede! They'll have a field day."

"We must try to preserve the secrecy for a day or two," Öhman thought aloud.

Nystedt wasn't so sure. "You know how the prime minister feels about honesty with the press, Peter. The worst thing we can do is remain silent and let the newspapers take the initiative."

Fellén shook his close-cropped head. "Let's think this through. Do we really want a major row with the British?"

"I think we already have one," Nystedt replied testily. "And the Russians certainly aren't going to let matters rest."

Peter Öhman agreed. "They're already demanding that we take action and put pressure on the British to return their man."

The big man grunted his disgust. "I say we keep quiet. Say nothing. Like the Russians did in '81. Know nothing and say nothing. Then try and help get the British off the hook. Smuggle this damn Russian trouble-maker out to Norway."

"No!" Nystedt was adamant. He was a highly

principled man and he knew the prime minister would share his view. "The British are clearly at fault in this, however sorry they may be now. Whilst I agree that we should do nothing to further aggravate relationships, I do not see that we should assist them. That would be as good as condoning the crime." He began pacing the room as his indignation grew. "And I'll remind you, gentlemen, that this crime is murder. And the entire episode was *indeed* tantamount to an act of terrorism. The prime minister will refuse to countenance that on the streets of Stockholm. If we are seen to condone it, such activities will only increase. Everyone will see Swedish territory as the place to commit their atrocities and get away with it. Our streets will not be safe to walk."

Anger was like electricity in the air. Nystedt's words hung, charged thunder about to explode.

"The police say the Soviets with the scientist were armed too," Fellén pointed out. "Apparently the ambush scene was littered with discarded Russian weapons."

Öhman added softly: "There are other considerations. The Soviets are very angry. If they get no satisfaction, they may take matters into their own hands. I have reports that the British Embassy is virtually under siege. The KGB and GRU are all round the place. All we have are two armed policemen on the street corner."

"They wouldn't dare," Nystedt murmured.

"I wouldn't bank on it," Fellén grumbled throatily. "You know the contempt with which they've treated us. Not only in '81, but in all the mini-submarine incursions since. They *expect* us to do what they demand."

"Then they'll be out of luck," Nystedt retorted defiantly. "For a start we'll have those Russians at the ambush expelled for carrying illegal firearms."

"And they tried to kill the defector on the street last night." Öhman's quiet words went off like a landmine.

"What!" The prime minister's aide was shocked.

"Reports are unconfirmed," the Foreign Affairs Ministry official added. "But a policeman on duty reported that first a Russian Embassy car tried to run down the man believed to be the defector. Then the driver attempted to shoot him. Someone from the British Embassy intervened just in time."

"I'm not surprised at the Soviet reaction. Typical!" Fellén said flatly. "However, such behaviour by them may be even worse for Sweden's reputation than one dead policeman. We'd be ridiculed world-wide."

Peter Öhman sniffed heavily. "Then maybe this time it would be better to stand firm. Put pressure on the British to hand this Russian back."

"And soon," Nystedt agreed. "I shall recommend to the prime minister that we do so before the story reaches the papers. Tell Sir Timothy in no uncertain terms. The British will get no assistance from us. And no special protection. Let the Russians put on the pressure for us."

All three men agreed.

10

Nikolai Shalayez awoke with a start.

He had been dreaming that he was incarcerated in the labyrinth of cells in Lefortovo in Moscow. His tortured mind had pictured it as evil and dank with water trickling down the brickwork and rats nesting in the straw.

Every so often the steel door would open. A KGB guard would be standing there with someone he knew. His wife Katya. Then his daughter. Another time it was his friend Sergei Chagall. Once it was his long-dead parents. Each time they would point an accusing finger. "Yes, that's him." They would spit in contempt and the door would slam shut.

The knock came again as he sat up on the camp bed in the darkness.

The door swung open and a shaft of daylight illuminated the small room. It took a moment for him to realise that he was no longer dreaming. Then he recognised the voice of Brian Hunt.

"Good morning, Niki. Had a good sleep?"

Shalayez disentangled himself from the twist of bed-clothes. Cold sweat had drenched his pyjamas.

"It is not so good," he mumbled.

Hunt switched on the light. "Barbi here's got you a cup of tea. I thought you'd prefer it Russian-style. No milk." The SAS man stepped aside to allow in the small, dark-haired girl. She smiled coyly and placed the tray by the bed.

"There's some biscuits too. The ambassador's favourites. He guards them like a state secret."

Shalayez half smiled. He did not really understand the joke, but took the cup thankfully.

As the girl left, Hunt said: "I shouldn't be too long getting dressed, Niki. You've got a visitor coming in half-an-hour."

The Russian's face clouded. "Who?"

"Your friend Lucinda. She arrived at the airport on an early flight."

The cloud passed and Shalayez smiled. "That is good."

"Thought you'd be pleased."

The Russian leaned forward. "Tell me, Brian, you have been good to me."

"Tell you what?"

"Lucinda." He lowered his voice. "Can I trust her?"

Hunt gently closed the door. "I think so, Niki. I've only met her a couple of times, and she struck me as being very genuine. To tell the truth, I think she got involved with more than she bargained for."

"With me?"

"With you, yes. I don't think she expected to get emotionally involved. And I think this whole business was way beyond her experience. She's very young still."

"But she *is* one of Mr Lavender's spies?" Shalayez challenged. The venom in his voice took Hunt by surprise.

"She's not a professional, Niki. She was recruited to help because of her fluent Russian and good grasp of mathematics. And her good looks, of course."

"Her duty to her country?"

"Something like that."

"Yes, I can understand." He gulped down his tea in quick successive swallows. Then he looked up, a much happier man.

"Thank you for talking to me, Brian. It is good. I

297

cannot talk to Mr Lavender. He does not like me and I do not feel that he is to be trusted."

Hunt half smiled, and offered a cigarette which the other man took eagerly. As he lit it for the Russian, the SAS man said: "Mr Lavender does have an unfortunate manner. But he's just doing his job. He is under a lot of stress at present."

"That I begin to understand. It also makes me very worried."

"We'll make sure you come to no harm," Hunt assured.

"I do not mean that." The violet eyes took on a distant look. "If I have to stay here, and there is much trouble, then perhaps Mr Lavender will hand me back. To the KGB."

"I promise you, Niki, there is no chance of that."

But, when Hunt left the room a few minutes later, Shalayez felt far from convinced. The Englishman could have no real concept of the intense political pressure the Soviet Union could generate. He'd heard his friend Sergei Chagall boast how the KGB could manipulate international affairs to get their way. If they were determined enough they could achieve almost anything. And since arriving at the embassy, he'd learned just how determined they were to get him back.

He tried to put the thought from his mind as he showered and shaved in the washroom along the corridor. The clean shirt and trousers that Hunt had brought him were not a bad fit, although the trousers were a trifle short for his lanky frame.

Finally, he peered closely at his face in the mirror. Perhaps it was his imagination, but he appeared to have aged ten years in as many days.

"Nikolai Shalayez," he spoke to the mirror in disgust. "Just what do you think you are doing with your life?"

As he returned to the cramped office that was serving as his temporary home, he found Lucinda waiting for him. She was much smaller than he remembered.

298

Vulnerable and unsure. And he had almost forgotten her striking resemblance to his wife Katya.

"Niki?" Her smile was uncertain.

He felt a constriction in his chest. The sheer joy of seeing her again lifted his heart. Even as he stepped forward to greet her he was aware that he had never felt like this about any woman. Ever.

He failed to find the words he wanted. Instead he just hugged her to him, squeezing her close until he could feel the butterfly flutter of her heart against his.

"I am so afraid for you," he managed at last. "At the Society I think they will kill you."

Her smile was radiant. "They may have, Niki, but Brian managed to save me."

"You too, eh?" He chuckled. "He is a good man. Apart from you, I think he is the only one I can trust amongst these Britishers."

She stepped back and adjusted her hair. "You're just not used to them, Niki, that's all. They're all nice people. They're just very worried about you. Even Ralph Lavender is all right under that cold-fish exterior of his."

"You have spoken with them?"

"Just a couple of minutes before I came in here. They suggested we might like to have breakfast together. Alone." Her eyes sparkled. "I thought that was a *very* good idea."

He nodded. "And they ask you to give me reassurance, yes?"

She looked hurt. "*You* asked me to come, Niki." She half laughed in disbelief. "I was awfully flattered, and very pleased. And now . . . why *did* you ask me to come?"

He slumped against the wall then, his violet eyes peering sideways at her from beneath the wild fringe of black hair. "Because I have fallen in love with you. And I am frightened of the future. Frightened I will be sent back . . ." He hesitated . . . "Frightened I will lose you."

She clasped his hand. "Dear Niki. All *that* and still you don't trust me?"

He stared at the floor.

She squeezed his fingers tight. "I've never met anyone like you, Niki. I'd do anything for you. Anything. You're the first real man who's come into my life. Trust me when I say I would die for you."

He stared hard at her for a moment, and then the boyish grin broke through. It had been a long time since she'd seen it. A long time. "I hope that will not be necessary. To die for me to prove your trust!" His teeth glistened.

They laughed together. Like lovers.

Events that day were to move quickly at the British Embassy. Shortly after Lucinda's arrival, the ambassador returned from his meeting with Foreign Minister Bertil Wernberg.

For twenty minutes Sir Timothy Maybush had sat in the wood-panelled room with its magnificent chandelier and antique patterned carpet and listened to the tall man at the other side of the ornate heavy desk.

Twenty minutes. It could have been for as many hours that he endured the verbal onslaught from Wernberg. He had never known the usually mellow minister to be so angry. The Swede's usual self-control only just held in check, he spoke rapidly with the brusque assurance of a prosecuting counsel who knew he was on a winning case. It was quite a grilling, each calculated question breaking down the British diplomat's vague defence.

At last, Wernberg stopped and it was as though someone had switched off a pneumatic drill. On the mantel shelf an antique clock chimed the hour.

Wernberg levelled his eyes at Sir Timothy's. "So you are still saying that you know nothing about the ambush and the murder of our police officer?"

The ambassador fenced. "We have been in communication with Whitehall all night, and no one can confirm such an operation."

Wernberg's eyes hardened. "Does that mean no one can deny it, either?"

A wan smile. "I don't believe for a moment that it was anything to do with us. But anyway, such operations would clearly be the province of our Secret Service and, as you are no doubt aware, such people are not given to admitting anything to anyone."

"Even to their own elected Government, it seems. Perhaps like Sweden your intelligence people should be answerable to someone."

Sir Timothy rode the thrust. "Indeed, Bertil, perhaps they should."

"And your SIS head of Station in Stockholm. What does he say?"

"He knows as much as me." That, in its way, was true. "That's what makes me wonder if the ambush was organised by outsiders. Mercenaries."

"Ah, that is a new one!" The foreign minister relaxed back in his chair with a cynical smile on his face. "Perhaps someone who seeks to capture Shalayez and use his knowledge for personal gain? I see. Maybe hired by some American defence conglomerate?"

Sir Timothy shrugged. "It's possible. What do you think, Bertil?"

Wernberg leaned forward bullishly. "I shall tell you what I think, Mr Ambassador. I think that you are wriggling. I have seen enough men lying in my political lifetime to know when someone is wriggling. And you are wriggling."

The British diplomat's cheeks coloured. He felt the sweat in the small of his back. He fumbled for his comeback. "I am trying to *help* you, Bertil."

"Well you can help by telling the truth. And spare me the cock-and-bull fairy stories. After the ambush, Shalayez turns up at your embassy. Was it coincidence he turned down the wrong street? Why did he not go to the American Embassy? He had to *pass* it to get to yours! So what does he have to say about that? Does he say he was in collusion with the ambushers?"

Sir Timothy took a deep breath. "It is not in my remit to debrief defectors, Bertil, you know that. That is a job for our security experts."

"And they won't tell you?"

"Not everything, no."

"That is not very satisfactory."

"I'm sorry."

"So am I," Wernberg said, wearily. "I am also sorry that your SIS head of Station has been unable to enlighten you in any way."

"Perhaps there is nothing to enlighten me about."

Wernberg's eyes held steady. "And perhaps that situation might change if your Mr – " He consulted his notepad, just to let it be known he was on top of the situation. " – Mr Lavender were to be declared *persona non grata* . . ."

The veins in Sir Timothy's cheeks reddened. Whether it was at the threat or at having to defend the slippery bastard, he wasn't sure. "Mr Lavender has my fullest confidence."

"Be under no illusion, Sir Timothy, should that confidence prove to be unfounded, we will have no hesitation in having him expelled. And that goes, too, for the four burly gentlemen who appear to have settled in at your embassy."

The ambassador batted straight. "You mean our security staff?"

"The first of whom arrived only shortly before Shalayez himself."

"You are very well informed, Bertil, as always."

"And don't you forget it, Sir Timothy," Wernberg replied, then deliberately changed tack to catch the other man off guard: "By the way the Soviets are demanding consular access to Shalayez."

"It's too soon," Sir Timothy snapped back quicker

than he'd intended. That was one thing they didn't want, and certainly not while the defector was still on neutral soil. "He needs to find his feet; settle his own thoughts."

"This conversation is not getting us very far, Mr Ambassador. And I am not satisfied with the answers you have given to my questions. So would you please convey our extreme displeasure at this affair to your Government, with a request that the matter is resolved as a matter of utmost urgency if relations between our two countries are not to be seriously – if not irreparably – damaged.

"I have here a note from the Ministry of Justice, detailing your request for additional police protection at the embassy. In view of the fact that you claim to have nothing to do with yesterday's ambush, I see no grounds to fear undiplomatic behaviour from the Russians. Therefore, that additional protection is unlikely to be forthcoming."

Crafty bastard! Sir Timothy thought. But he said, in a conciliatory tone: "If there were any involvement by my country in that ambush, Bertil, then here and now I give my unreserved apology for the action and the unfortunate death of one of your policemen."

"*Murder*, Mr Ambassador," Wernberg reminded. "And only a diplomat *par excellence* could get away with apologising for something that his country knows nothing about. However, rest assured, you have not heard the end of the matter. Good day, Mr Ambassador."

By the time he returned to the British Embassy, Sir Timothy's pulse had only just returned to normal. It rose again at the sight of half a dozen Soviet cars parked along the avenue and not a Swedish policeman in sight. It was further aggravated when his chauffeur said he suspected their car had been trailed on both journeys to and from the Foreign Ministry.

He had his fourth cigarette going since the traumatic meeting by the time he reached the Chancery Office. He wasn't surprised to find Matt Brewster's room full of people, anxiously awaiting his return. Hunt and Mike Ash were there, as well as Ralph Lavender and Brewster's wife, Cherry.

"How'd it go, sir?" Brewster asked.

"How'd you think – bloody diabolical! Half-an-hour listening to a verbal ear-bashing, and not *one* thing I could say in our defence!" He took a deep breath and brushed the hair from his eyes, glancing awkwardly at his captive audience. "I'm sorry, I'm forgetting myself. But y'know it was all very unpleasant. And there'll be no police protection." He glared pointedly at Lavender. "As I expected, they're leaving us to stew."

The intelligence officer studied his gleaming toecaps intently.

"Any fresh direction from London?" Sir Timothy asked.

Matt Brewster shook his head. "Same as before. Placate the Swedes, stall the Russians and get Shalayez the hell out as soon as possible. On no account admit complicity in the ambush or anything else. And meanwhile, keep a low profile."

Sir Timothy simmered. "And how long do they think we can keep the lid on this one?"

"It won't be long," Brewster confirmed. "I had a call from a reporter on *Expressen* earlier. Asking about reports of an attempted murder outside the embassy last night."

Sir Timothy raised his eyes to the heavens. That was all he needed.

"I told him we knew nothing about it," Brewster assured. "He didn't press the matter and I got the feeling he didn't have many facts."

The ambassador grunted. "Unless he just wanted a quote without alerting you."

Brewster shrugged; he just didn't know.

Sir Timothy turned to the two SAS men. "And how are your plans going to get this Jonah out of here?"

Ash said: "Our lads are getting hold of a van today. It'll be sprayed and signwritten this afternoon. We thought office equipment manufacturers. Then we can put chummy inside a steel filing cabinet for additional protection."

"So he can be out tonight?" Sir Timothy asked eagerly.

"Afraid not, sir," Hunt interjected. "The Russians will definitely smell a rat if we start moving office equipment at night. It'll have to be done in working hours, and once we've established a period of normality to fool them."

"And first there will have to be a test run," Ash added.

Sir Timothy groaned.

"I'm afraid so, sir," Lavender confirmed. "We've got to see what the Russians do if they suspect. Can we get as far as a warehouse on the outskirts of Stockholm, or even farther? Can we effect a switch?"

The ambassador was getting lost. "A switch?"

"To another vehicle."

"You plan to get him out by road?"

"To Norway," Hunt replied. "It's just too risky to use ports or airports. Even worse to use some remote airfield. Ivan can get up to all sorts of tricks there. We plan a succession of switches to get him close to the border."

"And won't crossing-points be watched?" Sir Timothy queried.

"Yes, but we'd cross at a remote area, unofficially. We're all from the Regiment's Mountain Troop, so we can take a day or two to leisurely ski across. We've requested all our kit be sent across from Hereford."

"What about Shalayez, can he ski?"

"I've spoken to him about it. He was quite accomplished in his teens."

"That was some moons ago," Sir Timothy observed. "Still if you think that's the best option."

"It's the best we've got," Mike Ash said.

"Oh, by the way," Brewster interrupted. "A chap from the MOD in London arrived this morning. Name of Dinton. He's a tame psychiatrist from the Intelligence Corps. He's in with Shalayez now."

"Good grief," Sir Timothy muttered. "It's a bit late to discover we've a nutter on our hands. Couldn't we have checked his mental state before we helped him defect?"

"It's just routine," Lavender retorted. He'd decided it was time to start re-establishing his credibility after the chain of disasters. "This is a period of great stress for a defector. Conflicting loyalties, anxieties about facing the unknown. Dinton will help him out there. Also examine his motivation. Just the start of his debriefing really. Shalayez is no good to us if he's going to change his mind and go back to Moscow in a few weeks. Even worse, if he's helping us on projects and *then* decides to do a bunk three years on – taking all *our* secrets with him."

Sir Timothy stubbed out his cigarette. "Well, I suppose you know what you're doing . . ."

Mike Ash said: "There is one other aspect of security, sir, that we think you ought to consider."

"And what is that?"

"That of personal security of embassy personnel. Everyone is being followed by Soviet agents and if this drags on, there's a chance they'll be tempted to intercept one of our people and quiz them on what's going on."

The ambassador blinked. He opened his mouth to reject such a preposterous suggestion. Then he remembered that he himself had been followed according to his chauffeur. "So what do we do?"

Ash smiled. "Well, not get unduly alarmed. Luckily, sir, your wife's visiting London; so I suggest she stays on there. And I've asked Mrs Brewster here to move into the embassy for the duration."

Cherry, who had been silent but attentive, acknowledged the decision. "Had to bring our cat too, I'm afraid," she apologised. She knew the ambassador hated cats.

"And I've told other key personnel to ask their wives to do the same," Ash continued. "I'd suggest any other non-essential personnel return to London. Or at the very least be sure they never travel or stay away from the embassy alone. Always be with small groups."

"Isn't this all a bit drastic?" Sir Timothy asked.

"It's our job to think of the unexpected," Ash returned evenly. "We've spent the morning playing Ivan. Putting ourselves in the Russians' shoes, and seeing what we might do in their position. We don't want diplomats' wives going missing."

"London won't like staff going back," Sir Timothy demurred.

"I can get the recommendation made to Whitehall direct from Hereford," Ash said. "It'll carry more weight that way."

"Very well," the ambassador agreed resignedly.

It was then that Matt Brewster's telephone rang. He answered it, then covered the mouthpiece with his hand. "Your office, Sir Timothy. The American ambassador has called to see you. Urgently. He apologises for not having an appointment."

"Now what does he want? Okay, I'll go through to my office now. Have him shown up."

Sir Timothy Maybush straightened his back and left the room for his own office at the end of the corridor. He met his secretary and the handsome silver-haired American at the head of the stairs.

Walter Bream smiled charmingly with pearly white teeth which were capped to perfection. His voice was a soft, cultured Bostonian accent. "Nice to see you, Sir Timothy. Sorry about the short notice."

The two men shook hands briefly and the secretary retired to let them stroll to the office together. They were old friends – surprisingly, perhaps, considering their widely different styles.

Once the door was closed, Walter Bream came straight to the point. "We've got wind of your little problem. I

307

just wanted you to know that if you want any help at all, you just have to say the word."

Sir Timothy lit a cigarette before pouring one bourbon and one port from the cabinet. "That's kind, Walter. Y'know the gesture is much appreciated."

Bream's eyes crinkled with sincerity. "Of course, we could spare a couple of marines in plain clothes. Maybe organise a little mischief to keep the Soviets off your back. Even get this guy Shalayez out the country for you."

The British ambassador handed over a tumbler with a straight face. He didn't let his raised hackles show. "Out of ice, I'm afraid, Walter."

Bream grinned. "So what's new? It's no problem . . . As I was saying, anything . . ."

Sir Timothy slumped on his sofa. "You seem to know a lot about this. I'd have thought you'd have wanted to keep well clear. There's a lot of diplomatic flak about."

"You know who your real friends are in a crisis."

"True," Sir Timothy murmured and spun his port around the glass. "But we're well protected with our own people and I really don't think we want to antagonise the Russians unnecessarily."

Bream nodded. "No, of course not. But we do have a frigate in the Baltic with a helicopter aboard . . ."

Sir Timothy could hide his smile no longer. "This wouldn't have anything to do with the fact that Shalayez is one of the Russians' top Star Wars experts would it, Walter?"

The teeth dazzled. "I should have learned by now never to play poker with you. Sure, it's to do with Shalayez's specialist knowledge. It's something of a coup to have landed him. We just wouldn't like to think that there might be any slip-ups."

"There won't be." There was a hard edge to the Englishman's voice.

Bream raised his hands in apology. "No, of course not! I appreciate it was just pure bad luck your plans have gone wrong already." A barbed reminder. "But if we're in the position to take him off your hands . . ."

Sir Timothy savoured the bouquet of his port. "I've a feeling, Walter, that if that happened, *we* would never see him again."

The American shrugged. "He's coming to us eventually anyway, you know. We've wanted to lift someone off the Soviet's Sary Shagan project for years. It's just that he's the first one to come along and he happened to be your contact."

A gentle smile. "Then I think we'll keep it that way for a little while longer, Walter. But thanks for your offer."

Nikolai Shalayez stared at the window where the Brewsters' ginger tom had curled in the patch of sunlight. "I suppose it will always be like this?"   "Don't get seen," Dinton warned. "Not too close."

Shalayez turned slowly to face the MOD psychiatrist who was perched on a typist's chair in the narrow office. "In case I am shot at?"

Dinton smiled kindly. It was the sort of kindly smile one expected from a psychiatrist and it sat well on the calm face which showed no expression except sympathy. The glittering dark eyes projected sincerity and intense interest at every word and nuance being spoken. "We must take precautions."

"In case I am shot at?" Shalayez repeated. He hated the quiet grey suit and the man's overlong hair and sideburns grown to compensate for the bald pate, that glistened with perspiration in the confines of the airless room. He hated Dinton's soft, patronising tone. He resented the coaxing, probing questions. It was all a mask, he knew, yet he seemed unable to resist saying more than he intended. "Shot at by my own people?"

"They don't understand what you *had* to do," Dinton assured.

Shalayez raised an eyebrow. "They do not? How

surprising that is. You know, in their position, I don't think I would understand either. My country has never done me harm. I know you in the West think we are all suppressed and spied on by our secret police. But in reality it is not like that. I have been treated well. A good education for a boy from peasant stock. A good career to follow, a home of my own. A beautiful . . ." His voice faltered.

"You are saying?" Dinton encouraged.

The Russian looked darkly at the psychiatrist. "I was about to say a beautiful wife and daughter."

"You miss them?"

Shalayez drew in his breath with a hiss. "You think because I am Russian I have no feelings? What do you think? Of course I miss them." He felt in his pocket for some cigarettes; the pack was empty.

Dinton offered one, and reluctantly the Russian accepted. "Niki, why don't you sit down? Try to relax and tell me about things. Tell me how you feel. I am here to help."

"*Help, help*," Shalayez mimicked. "Everyone here is trying to help! All I want to do is get out of here."

"These things take time."

"So all these *helpful* people tell me."

"I understand you're anxious to start a new life."

"Huh!" Shalayez dropped onto the edge of the camp bed. It was low for such a tall man and emphasised the length of his legs. He supported his wrists on his knees and toyed with the cigarette. "I will tell you, Mr Dinton. I was quite happy with my old life. It was only when your people contact me that I am in trouble with the KGB."

"Ah, Lucinda." He sounded almost wistful.

"I did not even know what she was! I walked right into it. Compromised – I think you say – with my own people. If it had not been for the Britishers I would not even be here."

"A friend tipped you off?"

310

"Yes, I – " Shalayez stopped dead, and the violet eyes blazed. "Yes, a friend in the KGB . . . How do you know that?"

The kindly expression returned with a vengeance. "It is our job to know these things. And this friend of yours, he warned you of the consequences if you stayed in Russia?"

Shalayez drew heavily on his cigarette. "Interrogation followed by life in a prison or labour camp. That is what he said. But . . ." His words trailed away.

"But?" Dinton persisted.

"But since then, I have wondered if he was right. I cannot believe that, if I went back and told them it was all a terrible mistake, they would not pass a more lenient sentence. Let me work out my days somewhere, far away in the country."

Very quietly Dinton said: "Is that truly what you'd like to do?" His voice was very soothing.

A slow grin spread over the Russian's face. It made him look years younger and quite handsome. "It is a dream, Mr Dinton. If Katya and Yelina were still with me, then I would think it worth the chance. But they are not. The only one who cares is Lucy."

"You said earlier you weren't sure about her."

Shalayez turned towards him, and Dinton noticed that his eyes were moist. "I have to be sure of *something*. Something I can hold on to. Yes, I must doubt because of who she is. But I think now I believe what she says. She is so young, and not very good at lying."

"You love her?" A whispered question.

Instinctively the Russian recoiled and his eyes narrowed. "That is a very – personal? – question."

"You can tell me."

"I have never felt about a woman as I feel for her. Not since I first met Katya, and maybe not even then." He stared at the ceiling. "Between us it is like a mathematical equation."

Dinton nodded. "You mean a chemistry?"

Shalayez inclined his head. "That is a good description."

The intense silence was broken by a gentle rap at the door. Dinton climbed to his feet and opened it.

"I've brought Dr Shalayez some lunch."

"Barbi, isn't it?" Dinton stepped aside as the petite secretary entered and placed the tray on the table. She smiled at the Russian. "I hope you like it. It's *Köttbullar*. Swedish meatballs. Very popular."

"You must be tired," Dinton said to Shalayez. "I'll leave you to eat in peace. We'll talk again later."

"Thank you, but I am not hungry."

That afternoon Brian Hunt telephoned the Fiscex office and asked for Peter Burke. The personnel manager took his time coming on the line, and sounded uncharacteristically reticent when Hunt said he needed some more assistance.

"I can't talk on an open line," Hunt said. If the Soviets weren't listening in, he was damn sure the Swedish security services would be. "Let's meet. Say in an hour?"

Burke was hesitant. "It's difficult. I've got meetings . . ."

Hunt sensed trouble. "Is something wrong, Peter?"

"No, no." The protest was too pronounced.

"This *is* important."

"I'm sure it is. I'll put off my meeting. Where do you want to meet?"

"The apartment."

Burke was horrified. "Certainly not there!"

Now Hunt was certain there was a problem. "Okay, Peter, then how about that café where we ate on our first night with you."

"I'll be there."

"An hour. But hang on if I'm late."

"I'll be there," Burke repeated. But he sounded far from pleased.

312

With a nagging worry still at the back of his mind, Hunt telephoned for a taxi to pick him up from the embassy. Ten minutes later, it was speeding into the centre of Stockholm with a black limousine trailing one car behind them all the way. He paid the cabbie off outside Åhléns department store and rushed inside. Quickly he mingled with the crowd, stripping off his distinctive white raincoat as he walked and stuffing it into a plastic carrier bag. He now wore a fleece-collared brown bomber jacket, and added a cloth trapper's hat with earflaps before slipping out through a different exit. Immediately, he hailed another taxi to drive him to a nearby Tube station.

It was almost deserted as he descended by escalator into the cavernous depths hewn out of solid rock. Momentarily he thought he heard the sound of hurried footsteps echoing behind him on the upper level. But as he waited for his train only an old woman appeared, loaded down with shopping. Mentally he registered her worn red overcoat before turning his mind to the other evasive measures to be taken on his route to the rendezvous.

He changed trains twice more, then took a further taxi to within two blocks of the café. He walked the final half mile, pausing after each corner to see if anyone hurried around it in anxious pursuit. He noticed nothing. Satisfied, he strolled on to the café.

Peter Burke was toying with a cold coffee. Frightened dark eyes darted towards the door as Hunt entered and crossed to his table.

"Nice to see you again, Peter."

The returning smile was strained. "Thought you lot had all gone home."

After the waitress took the order, Hunt sat back in his chair and studied the Fiscex executive. The man was like a scared rabbit. He was perspiring heavily and his usual constant smile was now like a shorting neon sign.

"What's happened, Peter?"

Burke took a deep breath. "This isn't going to sound good."

"Try me."

He hesitated, searching for the words. ". . . Just after you left I got a visit. A bunch of heavies from the Soviet Embassy. They knew all about you . . . and me. They started putting on the pressure . . ."

"What did you tell them?"

"I tried to fob them off. They wanted your names. In the end I'm afraid I told them . . ." He raised his hand. "Only what I knew, of course. Mike Ash, I'm afraid. But the rest of you I only knew by your first names."

Hunt's mind raced, trying to evaluate the damage. What use would their names be? Probably not much. All they could do was check Ash's service career. That wouldn't help them much. It was unfortunate, but not catastrophic. At best they'd know the calibre of man they were up against.

"Anything else?" Hunt asked.

Burke paled, staring at his coffee. "Your friend's gun, the one used in the shooting. I was just leaving to bury it when they turned up."

"They took it?"

Burke nodded helplessly.

Hunt cursed beneath his breath. "That *could* prove embarrassing in the wrong hands . . . But why in God's name didn't you tell us?"

The executive looked sheepish. "They threatened my family, Brian, if I said anything. And they meant it . . . Besides you'd already left, so I didn't think it mattered too much . . ."

Hunt nodded his sympathy. "It must have been scary, Peter, and I can see your reasoning under the circumstances. As a volunteer we can hardly ask for more than you've already done."

"I feel such a bloody coward," Burke muttered miserably.

"Well don't," Hunt replied. "You helped us a lot. And, if you want to, you can help us again."

"Would my family be in danger?"

Hunt shook his head. "The Soviets have got more on their plates than frightening housewives, Peter. Besides, they won't even know your involvement. What we need is a series of safe houses en route from here to Åre and a change of vehicle at each. Different types. Cars or vans, even a truck. At fifty- or seventy-mile intervals."

Burke nodded slowly. "I could get our Estates Department to work on that."

Hunt grinned. "That's good. Start with a secluded warehouse in the north of Stockholm. Something that's self-contained and detached. I'm sorry to have to ask you to do this, but everyone from the embassy is being followed, and it's certain the phones are tapped."

"How soon do you need this set up?"

"Two days. We've got to do a dummy run first, and if that works we want to move as soon as possible on the real thing."

"That's not much notice," Burke reflected. "I'd better get cracking."

Hunt placed a restraining hand on the man's arm. "And if you get any problems – even threats – let me know. I'll be at the embassy. Just ask for Brian and use open-line code. If it's anything serious we'll talk face-to-face. We'll make this our rendezvous for any future meetings."

This time Burke's smile was more relaxed. "Couldn't we choose a place that has better coffee?"

They parted company after that. Peter Burke left first; Hunt had a second cup of the appalling coffee before following him out into the cold grey afternoon. Again he slipped into a routine of throwing off anyone who might be shadowing him. Alternating taxi trips with Tube trains and buses, he finally arrived at a back-street garage near the dock complex in eastern Stockholm.

Vivid blue flashes burst fitfully from the black mouth

315

of the open double doors of the workshop. The smell of oil and rubber hung heavily in the narrow street. As he stepped inside the burly Swede with the oxyacetylene torch noticed him and switched off the burner. The muscled biceps straining the cutaway sports vest were slick with sweat despite the bitterly chill air. He jerked up the steel visor and eyed Hunt suspiciously.

"I've come to see the van," Hunt said. "Is this it?"

The Swede's unshaven chin jutted. "English, eh?"

Before Hunt could reply he heard a familiar voice above the heavy clank and hiss of air pumps.

"Thought you weren't going to make it, boss." Big Joe Monk emerged from the shadows, the rangy figure of Len Pope behind him.

"I had some things to attend to," Hunt replied. "How's it going?"

"She's lookin' good." It was Pope who answered. As an ex-REME engineer, he had taken a special interest in the project. "I'm having a second sheet of steel fixed alongside the walls of the van inside."

"A sensible idea," Hunt observed peering into the open rear doors.

"We couldn't use very heavy-gauge stuff," Pope added. "Otherwise, the damn thing wouldn't manage more than a crawl – despite the uprated engine we're putting in. Don't want to sacrifice too much speed for protection."

"It won't stop any high-velocity lead," Monk interjected. "But a double skin will slow down any parabellum rounds which are the most likely to be used. And given the metal cabinet chummy's going to be in . . . well, at least he stands a better chance of survival."

The big Swede watched on bemused. "So you are the boss of these crazy people, eh? What you doing with this thing?"

Monk's lips formed a snarl around his tombstone teeth. "I've told you, Sven, no bloody questions. You're being paid well and in cash. So stow it."

For a moment the granite-faced mechanic stared at the large SAS man, then shrugged. The Englishman was right; it was nothing to him. He'd prepared many vehicles for Stockholm's villains; it wasn't his style to ask questions if the money was right. And this money was very all right. Defiantly he snapped down his visor and relit the torch.

Amid the noise Len Pope showed Hunt around the van. Its flanks had been carefully signwritten with the name and telephone number of an office equipment company. That number was, in fact, a spare embassy line which would be manned for the benefit of the opposition if they decided to check. It all looked very convincing.

Outside in the street again, they could once again hear themselves speak.

"Will it be ready by tomorrow morning?" Hunt asked.

Pope nodded. "She'll be ready, boss. No problem."

"Good. Then we'll set up the dummy run."

He turned and retraced his footsteps down the narrow street. As he went he noticed the Swedish housewife who just happened to be going in the same direction. He decided he hadn't seen her before.

But Captain Valia Mikhailovitch had, in turns with the three male members of her Spetsnaz team, been with Hunt for the entire afternoon. The last time he had seen her, the reversible blue coat had been red, and she had looked like an old woman travelling down the escalator to the Tube.

Now she radioed up the taxi which had been waiting discreetly farther down the road. She hailed it as it passed and climbed in.

She spoke briefly to the driver. "Petkus is taking over now. Get me back to our embassy as fast as you can."

"Yes, Comrade Captain," replied blond-haired Yuri Popov. The young ensign had learned a lot today.

*

317

In the late afternoon the bar in the British Embassy was almost deserted. After a gruelling night and day of diplomatic activity, Sir Timothy Maybush sought its sanctuary during a lull in telephone calls.

He wasn't altogether surprised to find Matt Brewster there, talking to Lucinda.

The head of Chancery looked desperately tired. Not one to mince words with his staff, the ambassador told him so.

"I'll try and get some sleep tonight," Brewster promised. "We'll have another taxing day tomorrow if I'm any judge. Including the trial run in that van."

Sir Timothy poured himself a glass of his favourite port, its smooth texture calming his nerves. "Think it'll work?"

Brewster fingered his handlebar moustache. "The van? Frankly, sir, no. I've never known the Soviets as upset as they've been over this. If they suspect we're smuggling Shalayez out, they'll stop at nothing to prevent it."

Lucinda had been sitting quietly, only half listening as she toyed with a glass of tonic water. Her mind was on other things: considering the very real possibility of spending the rest of her life as the wife of a Russian defector. Two months ago it would have seemed ludicrous. An absurd girlish fantasy dreamed up in a moment of wandering concentration during a university lecture, on a drowsy summer day. Even now she found it hard to grasp the reality of the situation. But not – she knew – the reality of her feelings for Niki. They grew each time she saw him. What had started as a glowing ember had been fanned at every encounter, until she now felt her passion for him burning out of control like a forest fire.

She'd long forgotten the age gap between them; if anything, that was part of the attraction. He had welcomed her into his adult world as an equal. And every time she saw the anguish in those angry violet eyes, she felt drawn to him. Flattered that he needed her to ease

318

his torment. She could only guess what he had been through since they had first met. She was also painfully aware that his suffering had been largely due to her, and the impassive manipulations of Ralph Lavender.

Matt Brewster's talk of the van had broken into her thoughts. She hadn't considered before the very real dangers that would face Niki, if he was driven out of the embassy through lines of waiting Soviet agents.

"There's no chance that Niki would be hurt is there?" she asked.

Brewster smiled reassuringly at her concern. He admired the quiet courage of the girl who was young enough to be his daughter. "We'll make sure he comes to no harm, Lucy. That's why we've got Mike Ash and Brian working on it. They're the experts. Besides, we'll do a dummy run first, just to see how the Russians react."

His words only partly allayed her fears. It struck her that there was no guarantee that, just because the trial run had worked, the real escape would go without a hitch.

Before she could express her doubts, Ralph Lavender entered the bar with the psychiatrist who'd flown in from the Ministry of Defence in London.

Dinton nodded amiably to those already in the room. "I see this is the favourite retreat of us British when things get rough."

Sir Timothy raised an eyebrow and exchanged glances with Brewster. Neither man had taken to the quietly spoken newcomer. He was a little too friendly, a little too sincere to be true.

Brewster overcame his instinctive distrust. "Well, how did your talks go with our defector?"

Dinton hedged. "I'm not sure, to be honest . . ."

"You know better than to ask that, Matt," Lavender said sharply. He handed the psychiatrist a small brandy and poured a mineral water for himself. "Dr Dinton's findings are strictly confidential."

319

It may have been tiredness, but Brewster found himself irritated by the intelligence officer's attitude. "Look, Ralph, you don't hold the patent on confidentiality. If you had shared your plans with your fellow professionals, we might not be in this situation now. Whilst Shalayez is in this embassy, his attitude of mind and his state of mental health is of great concern to us. It could colour decisions *we* have to make."

Sir Timothy hid his amusement as he added his weight to his head of Chancery. "Matt has a point, Ralph. I'd certainly like to know how the poor chap's faring under all this. Don't want him snappin' under the strain."

Lavender gritted his teeth. Under the circumstances he could hardly countermand a directive from the ambassador himself.

"Niki isn't likely to have a breakdown is he, Dr Dinton?" Lucinda asked innocently. "He seems such a strong character."

Dinton enjoyed being the centre of attention. It was as though he relished the opportunity to study a group of diplomats under pressure. A perfect case study.

He took a seat. "My dear, the strongest of men have their breaking point. We all have. But to put your mind at rest, I don't think we're going to find Niki reduced to a gibbering wreck overnight." He turned to Sir Timothy. "However, you should be aware that he is – at this moment – a man of conflicting loyalties and emotions."

"You mean about betraying his country?" Brewster asked.

"Well, you see, he hasn't *actually* betrayed his country."

"He's defected," Brewster reminded.

Ralph Lavender shifted awkwardly.

Dinton smiled benignly. "The only act of treason our friend Niki has committed is, after being subjected to a street ambush, to wander into the British Embassy whilst his mind was disorientated. He is aware of that. And, rightly or wrongly, he believes he could go back to Russia tomorrow. He knows he'd never work on a defence project again. He accepts that he could be sent to a labour camp or psychiatric hospital for a while. But he thinks he would eventually be allowed back to ordinary life, although he'd never attain the career ambitions he used to have."

Sir Timothy grunted. "So his leaving was in no way ideological? It doesn't sound like a very stable basis for a defection."

"About as stable as nitroglycerine," Dinton confirmed softly.

"So why did he leave in the first place?" Brewster asked.

"A combination of events. Most important was that his wife left him. He was emotionally shattered. Then the real turning point was when Lucinda here came on the scene. A friend in the KGB warned him that she worked for British Intelligence and that their liaison had been reported. He was advised to get out."

Lucinda shivered. It sounded as though it was all her fault.

"So what's keeping him?" Sir Timothy asked. "Why doesn't he just tell us he wants to go back?"

"Because he's not *certain* how safe he'd be. He wants to believe his own people wouldn't harm him, but he witnessed that attempt on his life, so he treats our warnings seriously . . ."

"And?" Brewster prompted.

"And he's very in love with Lucinda here," Dinton said, and touched her arm reassuringly; she withdrew instinctively. Unperturbed he continued, "In fact, I would go as far as to say that she is the real and only reason he doesn't get up and walk out of the front door."

Lavender could hardly disguise his anger at Dinton expressing himself so freely in front of the ambassador. He didn't want it to sound as though Shalayez's return to the Soviets was at all likely. He said testily: "Well,

321

we'll make damn *sure* that thought is furthest from his mind, won't we, Lucy?"

The girl blinked. "Will *we*, Mr Lavender? What do you mean?"

Lavender managed a smile which sat awkwardly on his face. "I don't have to spell it out, do I? You'll just have to turn up the heat a little. Keep his mind occupied."

Lucinda couldn't believe what she was hearing. She had never liked the intelligence officer. Her distrust of him had been instinctive from the very first time they met. Yet since then she had obeyed his instructions without question. She had held him in a kind of awe that was more akin to fear. Fear of the unknown, and fear of the considerable power he undoubtedly had. Her sheltered academic life had in no way prepared her to handle people like him; before she had been recruited, she had no idea that men as ruthless and omnipotent really existed with the blessing of governments.

And now to have her loyalty thrown back in her face was shattering. To talk to her in front of others as though she were a common slut or a hired prostitute . . .

"Mr Lavender, I don't know *who* you think you are," she challenged icily. "I'll remind you that I *volunteered* to help in this business after *your* department approached me! But my personal relationship with Niki is none of your bloody business . . ."

Sir Timothy and Matt Brewster were stunned.

Lucinda went on undeterred: "It strikes me that I've been used to trick Niki more than persuade him to come over to us. Just about everything you've told me about the situation has been half truths or complete fabrication. And I am not going to be used like that again. He's a decent, sincere man and deserves better from us!"

"Have you quite finished, Lucy?" Lavender hissed. His face was pinched white with anger at her outburst. "Whether you volunteered for this operation is totally irrelevant. When you agreed to work for us you signed away all your rights. It's as well you understand that quite clearly. And when it comes to high-ranking Soviet defectors, I'm afraid your personal relationship is very much our business. You're not talking about some principal ballet dancer from the Bolshoi, but a leading defence scientist. So your relationship with him becomes a matter – not of personal – but *national* interest. International even. I expect that was made quite clear to you at your initial induction course!"

She opened her mouth, turning her head from side to side in a vain attempt to find words to express her feelings.

Lavender sensed victory. "I'm very sorry to be blunt. But you're no longer a university student. It's time to grow up and get wise to the ways of the world. It is absolutely imperative that you play your part in keeping Shalayez content in our care until he has related to us his full technical knowledge on the Soviet defence projects he was involved in."

"Enough!" Sir Timothy snapped suddenly. "I hardly think this is the time or place to talk like this to Miss Court-Ogg."

"I think you may all be wasting your time," Dinton observed. "My reading of Shalayez is that coming over to us is one thing. To his mind, relating Soviet secrets with which he was entrusted will be quite another!"

"We'll see about that," Lavender said darkly.

Matt Brewster looked hard at the intelligence officer. "So what will you do? Threaten to send him back? From what Dr Dinton says, he might even welcome the idea. If you ask me we should all save ourselves a lot of trouble and surrender him. Maybe arrange it through the Swedes and win back some of the goodwill we've managed to lose."

"That's not an unattractive idea, Matt," Sir Timothy agreed.

Lucinda was bewildered. She went to speak then thought better of it.

Lavender said impatiently: "Well, thankfully that's

not a decision that's down to us; one way or another, Whitehall will have the final say."

The ambassador lit a fresh cigarette. "But no doubt they'll take into account any recommendation I make on the subject."

"No doubt," Lavender conceded stiffly.

It was a welcome relief when Cherry Brewster came into the bar to break the mounting antagonism. The respite, however, was short-lived. In her hand she held the early edition of *Expressen*.

"I think you ought to see this." Gone was her usual gaiety. "You aren't going to like it, I'm afraid."

Sir Timothy took the newspaper unhurriedly, his face already a mask in preparation for what he might find. But even he was stunned by the headline splashed across the front page:

> *POLICE MURDER WEAPON FOUND*
> *SOVIETS CLAIM BRITAIN ABDUCTED TOP*
> *SCIENTIST AGAINST HIS WILL*

"That's all we need," Brewster groaned.

Sir Timothy raised a silencing hand as he tried to read the story.

Lavender turned to Cherry. "What does it say?"

She looked sympathetic. "I've only glanced at it, Ralph. But the gist is that the Soviets claim to have found the murder weapon and have handed it over to the police. They also claim that the fingerprints on it will identify an executive of a major British investment house in Stockholm as the killer."

For a moment Lavender was puzzled, until realisation dawned. "Oh, my God, that bloke from Fiscex . . ."

"They say he was a British agent who set up the ambush," Cherry added. "The others fled the country, but the executive is attempting to maintain his cover. God, Ralph, it's not true, is it?"

"Peter Burke an agent!" Lavender snorted contemptuously. "Of course, it isn't. But it hardly matters, does it? The crafty bastards. In a way this is even worse. They can't get our chaps or know who they are, but they've got a scapegoat who's still in the bloody country! He hasn't even got diplomatic immunity. Christ, if it's true about the fingerprints, there could be a trial. Excuse me." The intelligence officer climbed to his feet. "Sir Timothy, I have to try and get Burke on the phone. Persuade him to go into hiding."

The ambassador laid the newspaper on his lap. "Of course, Ralph. But for goodness' sake be discreet. I don't want to put any evidence into the hands of the Swedish police that links us directly with that policeman's death."

Lavender gave a cursory nod of agreement and left hurriedly. A stunned silence had fallen over the embassy bar. Their worst fears confirmed, there was nothing they could do now but await developments.

Cherry decided to change the subject. "Matt darling, I know you've other things on your mind, but I suppose you haven't seen Copperfield have you?"

Brewster wrenched his thoughts away from the newspaper report. "What's the confounded cat up to now?"

She shrugged. "I can't find him anywhere. He was very unsettled when I brought him in. I wondered if he might have got out."

"I doubt it," Brewster muttered absently. "All windows and doors are being kept shut at all times. Maybe he's hunting mice in the cellar. Now, for goodness' sake, Cherry, I've got more important things on my plate."

After the meeting with Hunt, Peter Burke drove slowly back towards his flat in Storgatan. He checked constantly in his mirror, but he didn't really know what he was looking for. No particular vehicle appeared to follow but then, he reckoned, if they were professional he wouldn't notice anything anyway.

Despite Hunt's assurances that the Soviets were unlikely to have any real interest in his family, he had decided to take no chances. His earlier confrontation had convinced him that they could turn really ugly if it suited them. Therefore, he would persuade Joan to take their daughter, Mary, back to Britain for a few weeks' holiday.

By the time he parked his car and reached the door of his apartment block, he was chiding himself for being so paranoid.

A neighbour waved him a greeting as he breathlessly climbed the carpeted stairs.

Everything was perfectly normal as he put his key in the lock and opened the door. "Joan, I'm home! Decided to take the rest of the afternoon off . . ."

Through the open lounge door he could see his wife sitting on the edge of the sofa, her hands clasped in her lap. There was a curiously bland expression on her face and an unmistakable questioning look in her eyes as she turned her head towards him.

His heartbeat increased in tempo. He swallowed hard and forced himself to step forward.

"There are some gentlemen here to see you." His wife's voice was hoarse. "They're from the police."

Gingerly, he pushed the door wide. He wondered if they'd be the same Russians he'd met before. Would he recognise them again? He was sure he would.

"Good afternoon, Mr Burke."

Relief ebbed through him as he heard the distinctive Swedish accent.

He blinked rapidly at the two men, trying hard to be certain that he hadn't seen them before.

By the window was a tall man in his early thirties. His huge shoulders were hunched as he stood with his hands thrust nonchalantly into the pockets of fashionable baggy trousers. Pale blue eyes gazed unblinkingly at Burke through a pair of modern, square-framed spectacles. The full impassive lips, set in a handsome angular jaw, suggested pure Scandinavian stock.

But it was the second man who had spoken. He was

seated on an armchair, delicately holding a cup of coffee between thumb and forefinger. In complete contrast to his companion, he was much older; small, dark and black-suited. A black beard framed a very pale face that gave him the look of an academic who rarely ventured out of doors. When he scrambled to his feet in a series of quick, jerky movements, Burke was reminded of a small black spider that had been suddenly disturbed.

"Commander Vinberg," the man introduced himself, unsmiling.

Burke frowned. "Police?"

"OP5," Vinberg replied without offering further explanation. It may have been accepted by others as a police department, but Burke knew different. As an avid reader of thrillers, including those written in Swedish, he knew that OP5 was the Military Intelligence Service. The equivalent of Britain's MI5 counter-espionage organisation.

Burke tried to brazen it out. "Of course, I'm willing to be of assistance, but I can't think how."

Vinberg held him in a steady inscrutable gaze. "Can't you, Mr Burke? I'll explain on the way to headquarters, if you have no objections."

"Headquarters? For what purpose?"

"For an informal chat to help us with some enquiries. And also to take fingerprints. Just routine procedures, you understand."

"Not really."

Vinberg's eyes narrowed. "Do you really want me to spell it out to you, here?"

Burke glanced at his wife, who was looking puzzled and anxious. "All right. But I want to telephone my firm first."

A flicker of a smile passed over Vinberg's face. He nodded towards the blond giant. "Mr Reis will do that for us."

Burke shrugged; the Swede wasn't going to make it easy.

Then the telephone began purring on the coffee table.

327

Instinctively his wife reached for it but Reis, moving fast for a man of his size, reached it first.

He lifted the receiver but said nothing. *"Peter, are you there? Hello?"*

Burke recognised Ralph Lavender's voice, distant and distorted.

Reis smiled silently and replaced the receiver. "Your caller, he has hung up."

Vinberg said quietly: "Shall we go?"

11

"Lucy, something is wrong." Shalayez's voice quavered as he spoke.

Alarm seized her as she stepped inside his room.

The tiny face on the floor was a grotesque mask of agony, capturing the moment of death. The open eyes gazed in sightless horror. Its mouth was open, too, drawn back in a snarl of torment. Unchewed meat hung from the row of tiny sharp teeth.

"Copperfield?" she breathed.

Shalayez didn't understand.

"The Brewsters' cat," she explained. "I think it's their cat. My God, what happened?"

Her eyes travelled across to the low table where the food tray was in disarray, its contents spread around with abandon, traces hanging over the edge.

As she stepped forward the Russian restrained her. "Don't go near it, Lucy. It must be poison. I do not know what sort. Maybe one that transmits through the skin."

"Poison?" she repeated, incredulous. "Oh, my God."

"The cat just started to eat my dinner," he explained. She saw he was pale with shock. "Then the cat . . ."

She stared at him in horror. "You didn't eat any, did you?"

He shook his head. "If I had, I think you find me like that also. I left it because I was not hungry."

"It's horrible," she said, unsure what to do. "I must get Mike Ash." She rushed to the door and called down

329

the corridor to where the armed SAS captain was taking his turn on guard duty.

She pointed into the room. "The cat, Mike! It's been poisoned. It ate Niki's meal . . ."

Ash glanced at the two in turn, sharing their own initial disbelief. "Are you sure?"

"Look for yourself," she invited, a note of desperation creeping into her voice.

He crouched down by the plate and sniffed at it cautiously. Thoughtfully he climbed back to his feet. "I can't smell anything, but then I'm no expert on poisons. But at first glance, I'd say you were probably right. Who brought the food?"

"The secretary," Lucinda replied. "The little dark-haired girl. Barbara, I think her name is."

"Barbi?" Ash shook his head. "Surely it couldn't be her?"

"Maybe the chef?" Shalayez suggested.

Ash smiled thinly. "No such luxuries here, Niki. I expect Barbi prepared it herself. I saw her in the kitchen earlier."

"Then, if it is not her," Shalayez said, "perhaps it is done by one of your others. Maybe Mr Lavender?"

"That's ridiculous," Ash retorted. "You know he's been responsible for getting you here in the first place."

Shalayez narrowed his eyes. "Maybe now he wishes he had not, eh? I am proving much embarrassment. Lots of problems for you. You cannot make me go back alive. So it is easier to send back a corpse."

"Don't talk rubbish," Ash snapped.

"Oh yes?" Shalayez's eyes blazed accusingly. "So it is a conspiracy. You and Mr Lavender. Maybe Lucy too – "

"Niki!" the girl protested. "How can you say such a thing?"

The Russian turned on her. "Because *someone* tries to kill me. And I no longer know *who* I can trust."

She clasped his arm. "You can trust *me*, Niki, you know you can."

His expression softened, and he patted her arm.

At that moment, Brian Hunt arrived at the door. "Could I have a word, Mike . . .?" he began. His voice trailed off as he sensed trouble. "What's the problem?"

Ash said: "It looks as though someone's made an assassination attempt. Poisoned Niki's meal – luckily the cat ate it. Or unfortunately for the cat. I don't want anyone leaving this building until we get to the bottom of it."

Hunt paled. "Bit late for that. I just passed Barbi as I was coming in. She was taking a cab into Stockholm."

"Alone?"

"Yes. I reminded her about the security ruling, but she said she'd spoken to you about it and you'd made an exception because something was wanted urgently."

"And you believed her?" Ash challenged.

Hunt shrugged. "Under the circumstances I didn't have much option."

Ash turned back to Shalayez. "Unlikely as it seems, it looks suspiciously like the girl. We'll know soon enough if she doesn't return. I'm afraid your people want you back, or they want you dead."

The Russian nodded soberly.

Ash looked at Hunt, and both men knew just how close it had been. It was unnerving to feel that the Soviet presence had been in this room just minutes before. There had been an agent in their midst and they hadn't had the slightest suspicion. The Soviets had struck through the most unlikely of people.

Ash said: "Get rid of that bloody cat will you, Brian. And from now on we'll prepare and deliver the food ourselves. They may have lost their person on the inside, but we can't afford to be complacent. I want to review our security measures to cover *every* eventuality. I don't want George left alone on the door any more, even if he is armed. One of us must be there whenever possible, and there must *always* be one of us guarding the secure section. And I want a regular security patrol checking all windows and fire exits against a break-in. Round the clock."

"I'll draw up a roster," Hunt promised.

"By the way, how are the preparations going for tomorrow?"

"It's looking good," Hunt replied. "We're all set for the dummy run."

Ash touched Shalayez reassuringly on the shoulder. "Not long to go now, old chap." He moved towards the door. "I'll let everyone know what's just happened."

Hunt watched him go. He didn't envy him the job.

Her heart felt as though it was trying to hammer its way out of her chest. Never in her whole life had she been so terrified. Even now, sitting in the back seat of the taxi as it raced towards her boyfriend's flat, she could still feel it thudding.

But as the tension slowly subsided, it was replaced by a newer and greater dread of what would happen next.

Her boyfriend Manfred would be praying for her return. His life depended on it.

Until two days before she had been happy to supply him with little titbits of information from the embassy. She had come from a strongly socialist Welsh family and had been weaned on the evils of exploitative capitalism by her father and several uncles. In her late teens she had developed a social conscience of her own, although she never took much interest in politics.

All that changed, however, when she came to Stockholm to work at the embassy. At a private party she met Manfred and fell passionately in love. Blindly in love some might have said.

Manfred had been out of work since his days as a radical left-wing college student. He felt as passionately about socialism, the environment and ecology as he did about her. Yet she found his sincerity a refreshing change from the artificial world of diplomacy where people rarely said what they meant.

By contrast, Manfred was always writing painfully honest articles for socialist magazines and the newsletters of various radical movements. However, it hardly earned him enough to live on. All that would change, he promised, when he'd finished his book. His masterpiece of revelation about the decadence and deceit of modern capitalist societies.

To that end, he had persuaded her to tell him things that went on at work. Little examples that would serve to illustrate the points he wanted to put across in his book. She thought it would be a harmless exercise, and yet would help vindicate the views of her father which still echoed in the recesses of her mind. It became a regular occurrence, in the warm afterglow of their lovemaking, for them to share a joint of marijuana. As he stroked her hair she would giggle as she recounted events at the embassy that had amused, annoyed or frustrated her.

Indeed, she found their intimate conversations decidedly therapeutic. It was only three days ago that she learned the savage truth. Manfred had long ago been recruited by the KGB.

However, Manfred's controllers clearly believed that neither he nor his live-in lover would have the stomach for the very special assignment they had in mind: assassination. So they had come at night. Three of them, hard-faced men in dark coats who had begun as they intended to go on. Manfred had been brutally beaten up in front of her eyes, on the very rug in front of the fire where they had so often made love, and where she had so often told her lover diplomatic secrets.

Finally, they had propped his semiconscious naked body in a kitchen chair. One of them had yanked up Manfred's shoulder-length hair until she could see his bruised face.

"Listen carefully to me, Barbara," the leader had

hissed. "It will take just one skilled blow by one of my men to break Manfred's spine in such a way that he will be paralysed from the neck down."

She gulped, her eyes bulging in horror, mesmerised by the thin worm of blood that escaped her lover's nose. It dripped from his chin and over the contours of his tortured body until it was soaked up by his thick bush of pubic hair.

"That is what will happen to him if you do not do exactly what we say." The man paused. "Then we will come after you, wherever you are. Because we operate in every country in the world. Do you understand?"

Numbly she had nodded.

"Don't think you are betraying your country, because you are not. You are just righting an injustice. We Soviets are not always the villains of the piece. And to prove it, afterwards we will see you and your lover set up under a new identity in the country of your choice. You will never want for anything again." A very sincere smile creased the lipless mouth. "If you do exactly what we say, you will be in no danger of being caught. We will wait here and look after Manfred until the job is done."

Well, now the job was done, and she was still terrified. There was nothing she could do but place herself at the mercy of the men in black.

In her hurry to get back to Manfred she nearly forgot to pay the taxi driver. Then she overtipped him, hurriedly telling him to keep the change.

Once inside the apartment block, she ran the two flights of stairs to the front door. It opened as she approached and the leader of the men stood there, grinning. Light played on a gold filling as he beckoned her.

Hesitantly she moved towards him. Fear had turned her legs to jelly.

"It is done?" he asked.

She nodded, unable to find her voice.

"That is good. Come in. It is our turn to keep our side of the bargain."

She glanced quickly around the room, alarm bubbling up inside her like a spring. "Where's Manfred? What've you done with him?"

The gold filling glittered. "Relax, relax. He's just resting, look – " He pushed open the bedroom door. The shaft of light widened to reveal a sleeping figure lying on the mattress. She thought how peaceful he looked; almost like a little boy.

"Have a drink," offered the man. He poured a measure of aquavit into a tumbler.

She shook her head. "I don't want anything."

"Don't be silly. Look, you're shaking. It'll steady your nerves. Go on."

He was not an easy man to disobey. Besides she could do with it, he was right there. She shut her eyes and swallowed hard, grimacing as the fiery liquid burned her throat.

The last thing she remembered was slumping in the armchair as the room began to spin.

The man in black wasted no time. He stripped her naked and carried her limp body into the bedroom, dumping it unceremoniously on the bed beside her lover. Squeezing her nose, he jerked back her head to force her mouth open. With his other hand, he reached for the bottle of pills on the bedside table and tipped the contents down her throat, a few at a time. It took a few minutes as he poured in aquavit and pills in turn.

Satisfied, he turned over the girl's body, draping one arm around her lover's shoulder. Thoughtfully he lifted her left leg and hooked it over the man's thigh.

Artistic touch that, he thought, as he stepped back to admire his handiwork.

Finally, he covered the bodies with a duvet quilt and placed the note Manfred had been "persuaded" to write by the bedside. Then he silently closed the door and left the lovers alone to their suicide pact.

By the time he reached his companions waiting outside in their car, he had already forgotten about his young victims. He had no time for agents of sympathy like Manfred. Just another *govnoed* shit-eater.

And as for the girl, he knew little and cared even less. To him she was just a name on a list of "wet" jobs to be done. All in a day's work for the man from Executive Action Department Eight of the First Chief Directorate.

That night lights burned in many different locations throughout Sweden. At the British and Soviet Embassies. At Rosenbad, in both the prime minister's office and the Foreign Office, diplomatic activity had become frantic. With the passing of each hour the flow of messages between Moscow, London and – more recently – Washington increased until it was a veritable torrent.

Journalists, too, were working late into the night to prepare their follow-up stories on the arrest of a quiet British business executive on a charge of murdering a Swedish policeman. Reporter Björn Larsson, who had again been the first with the story, had his work cut out answering the flood of calls from newspapers and television and radio news teams from all over the world.

The offices of Scandinavian Airlines System were inundated with requests for flight tickets from all over Europe and the United States. Demand was fast outstripping supply and an urgent meeting was called to discuss adding extra flights on certain routes.

At the headquarters of OP5, Commander Vinberg was trying to put together a jigsaw of disparate pieces. The executive Peter Burke had been placed in police custody, whilst they attempted to gather evidence to substantiate the murder charge. The Englishman was saying absolutely nothing, but Vinberg was convinced that he was no murderer. The real mystery was how the Soviets had managed to come up with forensic evidence to the contrary. Fingerprints. *Somehow* Burke had been involved, and that was enough to vindicate the shouts of foul from Moscow. A trial was now inevitable.

During the night, Vinberg also learned that a secretary at the British Embassy had been found dead in what had all the signs of a lovers' suicide pact. The information was routinely copied to him because the girl was the employee of a foreign embassy.

More disturbingly the dead man, known as Manfred, was listed on Vinberg's own files as a possible subversive who had, on occasion, been seen in the company of known KGB agents.

A pattern was emerging. A pattern that he did not like.

Something very strange was happening.

At nine o'clock, he received a personal call from an intelligence liaison officer in the Royal Swedish Air Force. A number of RSAF pilots had reported having been called upon at their homes by Polish ex-servicemen, selling reproduction prints of famous aircraft for charity.

By midnight, it was clear that over thirty pilots had encountered these strange callers at their doors.

A tingle of apprehension ran down Vinberg's spine. Similar instances had happened before. Previously investigations had established that the callers were operating on behalf of the Soviet Spetsnaz special forces. The purpose was to update their files on the addresses of airforce pilots. In the event of war, the plan was to assassinate the flyers on their doorsteps. By means of one ruthless pre-emptive strike, the mighty Viggen and Draken aircraft fleet would be left standing impotent in its secret underground hangars.

The last time such an address check had been conducted, it had been carried out over a period of months. It had been low-key and exceedingly discreet, and had only been discovered by chance.

But now? Vinberg sucked at the end of his pencil and stared into the darkness of his office beyond the table lamp. This time the message was clear. The Soviets could not have issued a more definite statement: they wanted the Swedes to take action on Shalayez and they were losing patience; they meant business.

At ten to one, Vinberg decided to finish for the night. His mind was hyperactive but it was just taking him round in circles. In the morning, after the mere five hours' sleep that he needed, his brain would be sharper. He gathered his papers together and placed them in the combination safe. Just as he reached to switch off the table lamp, one of the bank of telephones on the desk began to ring. It was the direct line to the *Flygvapnet* Air Defence Command.

With a sense of foreboding he picked up the receiver and listened. There had been an incursion of Swedish airspace over the island of Gotland in the Baltic, between Sweden and the coast of the USSR. An aircraft believed to have been an SU-24 had buzzed a Scandinavian airliner in a dangerously provocative manner.

A pair of Viggen interceptors had been scrambled from Uppsala air base just north of Stockholm, but by the time they had rocketed across the intervening hundred and sixty miles, the intruder had fled.

Deep in thought Vinberg hung up. The message had been underlined.

He came to a snap decision, and dialled through the scrambler line direct to the home of Alf Nystedt. Although Vinberg's department was officially the responsibility of the Home Office, he preferred to go through Nystedt direct on his one.

If Nystedt had been disturbed from sleep he gave no sign. His voice was unusually brusque.

"Vinberg here, sir. I think the prime minister will want to know there's been an incursion of airspace over Gotland by a Soviet aircraft; one of our airliners has been buzzed. Also I'm getting reports that some of our pilots are being contacted by foreigners believed to be working for the Soviets."

Nystedt cleared his throat. "Anyone hurt?"

"No, sir. But I'm reading both incidents as signals from Moscow."

"This damn Shalayez business?"

"*Is* there any other at the moment?" The silence at the other end told Vinberg his mild sarcasm was not appreciated. "Anyway, I feel a meeting with you for first thing would be advisable."

Nystedt grunted. "It'll have to be early. Eight o'clock."

"That's fine by me, sir."

Vinberg hung up. Now his mind really was racing. He held up his palms in front of his face. They were damp with perspiration.

He was certain he wouldn't sleep between now and the eight o'clock meeting at Rosenbad.

Commander Vinberg stood respectfully in Alf Nystedt's office while the senior advisers to the Government studied copies of his report.

He was a shy man and did not enjoy the limelight; he really only felt at home in the shadows, behind the scenes in his own secret world. Standing before his superiors like this, he was painfully aware that all eyes were on him. It made him acutely conscious of his squat, hunched frame and his awkward, jerky body movements. It was a curse to be ugly in any society, but particularly so in a land where almost everyone was uniformly tall with striking Nordic looks.

Yet strangely he drew solace from the knowledge that behind his back they called him 'The Troll'. To another, it might have been considered an insult to be likened to the mischievous mountain dwarfs of Scandinavian legend. But Vinberg warmed to the idea that it was really a term of affection amongst his colleagues. Recognition that he worked in dark and magical ways in his murky undercover world. That he had a real place in the land of blond giants; he might be different, but he was still one of them.

As the civil servants read in silence, Vinberg could

339

sense the charged atmosphere in the room. Instinctively his eyes darted from one to the other, studying the expression on each face.

Unfortunately, Alf Nystedt had left his reading glasses at home and had to hold the report awkwardly at arm's length.

His old friend, Peter Öhman from the Ministry of Foreign Affairs, sat beside him with his long legs at an acute angle as he sat uncomfortably on the low cushions of the sofa. He had already read the report once and now, typically, he began again, carefully studying the implications of each line.

On the other hand, the bullish Ove Fellén had skip-read through at a fast pace and now sat meshing his pudgy fingers together, impatient for the others to catch up. As Defence Ministry representative he had been fully informed of events at the same time as Vinberg. He'd had plenty of time to think about it and he was anxious to make a decision.

Nystedt had finally managed to work his way through to the final paragraph. The grim expression on his face left no doubt as to his concern; he looked to his colleagues.

"Well, gentlemen, this makes very distasteful reading. I can tell you the prime minister is worried sick. What are your reactions?"

Fellén didn't hesitate. "They're doing it again, aren't they, Alf? Those damn *Ryssdjävlarna* are treating us like one of their own satellite republics. Using us like door-mats. If we don't do what they say when they say, they start making threatening noises. Rattling their accursed sabres."

"You don't think it's more than that?" Nystedt asked.

The question had hardly occurred to Fellén. "Well, I don't think they're going to go to war over their wretched defector, if that's what you mean. But they're definitely trying to show us who's boss. Letting us know that, if it came to it, they'd treat our neutrality and our defence

340

forces with total contempt if it suited them." Then he muttered under his breath: "And that would be a *big* mistake."

Nystedt understood his colleague's offended pride. "Well, Peter, what's your reading?"

"The Soviets are obviously trying to win over public opinion," Öhman answered in his usual calm and deliberate tone. "Look at all the detail that appeared in last night's *Expressen*. That can only have come from official Soviet sources. Even we did not know half of it. So now they've stirred up anti-British feelings to establish them as the guilty party. Now the Soviets come in with their next weapon. Fear. I will stake my office that the contents of Commander Vinberg's report will be public knowledge by the end of today." He added with dry sarcasm: "I'm surprised they didn't organise a press photocall when their Spetsnaz people knocked on the doors of our airmen."

The prime minister's aide nodded sagely; he always appreciated the steadying influence of his old friend in viewing everything with a cold and dispassionate eye. "So, Peter, if they are going for public opinion, will they win it to their side?"

"So far," Öhman conceded. "And they're holding a press conference in half-an-hour. Also I understand there's going to be a protest rally in Stockholm today – no doubt orchestrated by young University radicals. But they might be making a mistake with this latest move. I think the public mood has changed over the past few years. Fear of the Soviets is being replaced by indignation at the way they always try to intimidate us."

Fellén disagreed. "If they apply enough pressure the public will start to get worried. And I'm sure this is just the beginning. You believe the Soviets won't be satisfied with incursions into our airspace, and knocking up airforce pilots?"

"The alert status of both navy and airforce has already been increased," Fellén stated gruffly.

Nystedt refused to be panicked. "Let's see what happens first." He turned to Vinberg and smiled apologetically. He didn't like outsiders like the OP5 chief witnessing disunity amongst senior civil servants. "Well, Commander, as our military intelligence adviser, I think we should ask for your expert opinion."

All eyes turned on the small black-suited man with the neat black beard.

Vinberg cleared his throat. "The Government's policy so far, Mr Nystedt, has been to keep us clear of this situation. No help has been offered to the British until they come clean over the killing of the police officer. And you have virtually given the Soviets free rein to put pressure on the British for the return of their man." He paused to ensure that everyone agreed with his assessment. "To date that has worked reasonably well. In their desperation to get something to happen, the Soviets have unearthed the murder weapon and a prime suspect – although I very much doubt he was directly involved in the killing. Nevertheless whilst he is in custody, it gives us the excuse to offer the British a way out."

"*Excuse?*" Nystedt questioned.

Vinberg nodded. "The British obviously have no intention of admitting to anything. They'll say you've got your man so ask *him*. It's nothing to do with us. And as the suspect is clearly not working directly for their intelligence people, he won't be able to tell us anything anyway . . . But at least we have the *excuse* to defuse the situation."

"And let Britain off the hook?" Nystedt didn't think the prime minister would like the idea.

"Things have changed, sir," Vinberg reminded. "The Soviets are no longer content with putting pressure on the British; as events last night have indicated, it is easier for them – both politically and geographically – to put pressure on us to persuade the British to hand this scientist back."

342

"What exactly are you suggesting?" Fellén intervened.

"Let me visit the British Embassy and find out exactly what they plan to do. This situation can't be allowed to drag on, especially now that it is starting to threaten our own national security."

Nystedt exhaled in a low, silent whistle. "It's tantamount to letting the British get away with it."

"I think perhaps they have learned their lesson," Öhman observed. "The priority is still to get Shalayez out of the country – to Britain or back to Russia, it hardly matters to us."

"And we still have that Englishman to put on trial," Fellén added. "We can still make the British Government's eyes smart during that."

Nystedt reluctantly submitted. "All right, Commander, I'll suggest to the Prime Minister that you go to the Embassy and see what can be done. But on no account offer assistance that implies that we condone what they have done."

At that point a sharp knock came at the door. "Come!" Nystedt called out.

It was the prime minister's under-secretary. "I'm sorry to interrupt your meeting, gentlemen, but I thought you'd want to know immediately. A submarine has been sighted off the Karlskrona naval base, well inside our territorial waters."

Commander Vinberg blinked rapidly as he heard the news. Just as he feared, it had begun.

By the time the meeting at Rosenbad was finished, the SAS team at the British Embassy had already been at work for an hour.

It was adrenalin that gave the men their much needed kick-start that morning. They were short on sleep after a long discussion the previous night with Sir Timothy, Matt Brewster and Ralph Lavender. The long and often heated debate was over what to do following the Soviets' attempt on Shalayez's life.

343

There was little doubt that the KGB would be pacing in circles, anxious to know the results of their handiwork. Lavender, his devious mind seeking to turn the event to advantage, suggested that Sir Timothy should announce that the Russian had in fact died. Perhaps, he suggested, they could smuggle the live Shalayez out in the coffin.

It was then that Hunt pointed out that neither the Soviets nor the Swedes were going to be satisfied until they saw a corpse for identification. And the KGB certainly were as unlikely to allow a coffin out of the country as they were a living defector. They would certainly claim their right to the body of a Soviet citizen.

After hours of debate it was agreed to stick to the original plan, but to keep a strict silence on Shalayez's fate.

The Soviets' anxiety to find out was confirmed by the appearance of a small news item in the morning paper. An unattributable source suggested that the defector had suffered a heart attack whilst in British care. As a ploy to draw out the truth it worked like a charm. By eight-thirty the telephone lines were jammed with phone calls from news reporters asking for confirmation. The pressure to issue a statement would soon be irresistible.

However, just as disturbing as the report of Shalayez's heart attack was the major story to which it was linked. Around the country, in the course of just twenty-four hours, there had been sightings of no less than five Soviet submarines within Swedish territorial waters.

Each sighting had been confirmed by independent eye-witnesses who in each case stated that the submarine had made no obvious effort to conceal itself.

Everyone at the embassy realised what it meant. Normally Soviet forays into Swedish waters were confined to the summer months when the coastal waters were safely ice-free. Sightings were fleeting and therefore usually difficult to corroborate. Not so this time.

The underlying message to the Swedes was unmistakable – do something about getting Shalayez returned – or else.

It all gave fresh impetus to the after-breakfast briefing Mike Ash held to go over the plans for the day.

Big Joe Monk and Len Pope were to leave the building separately, taking three hours to reach the garage where the van was waiting. Every precaution would be taken to ensure that they weren't followed all the way. Experience over previous days had established that the Soviets would attempt to keep close on their tracks. Both men had their elaborate evasion plans memorised to the last detail and were confident they would work.

Meanwhile, those remaining at the embassy would patrol the road outside and the parkland at the rear to ascertain the strength and location of Soviet deployment.

At precisely eleven forty-five, the van would leave the garage in Stockholm on its journey to the embassy. On board would be a new filing-cupboard, supposedly replacing the one that was going to be removed.

The van would trundle innocently to the front door of the embassy in full view of the road. The new filing-cupboard would be taken inside and the old one brought out and loaded.

The driver and his mate would begin their return journey to a used furniture warehouse where the old cupboard would be sold for a few kronor in cash.

Mike Ash hoped the Soviets would just accept that the van was part of a legitimate business, and ignore it. At worst, they would satisfy themselves that the Russian was not aboard. If that happened they would develop a regular pattern of a delivery a day, suggesting that a complete refurbishment was in progress.

When the actual exfiltration attempt was made, Ash had it in mind to have virtually every embassy car out on the road, minutes before the arrival of the van, in order to swamp the Soviet resources. In addition, once it had left the immediate vicinity of the diplomatic area, it would be supported by armed escort cars.

345

However, Ash was painfully aware that day was still some time off. It was now Thursday and it would be impossible to put it into effect tomorrow. For a start, it left no time to incorporate any lessons learned from the dummy-run, and the untimely arrest of Peter Burke had set back plans to establish a series of safe houses. Ralph Lavender had made a second approach to Fiscex, who now flatly refused to assist until something was done for the release of their personnel manager. Lavender could offer nothing on that count and an impasse was reached. The intelligence officer now had the laborious and time-consuming task of making the arrangements himself.

Mid-next week had been the most optimistic estimate. The news did not go down well with Sir Timothy and Matt Brewster. Their relationship with Lavender became even more visibly strained than usual.

A similar atmosphere prevailed between Hunt and Mike Ash. For the past few days there had been plenty to occupy them both, and each man had deliberately avoided being alone with the other.

Now, with nothing left to do except wait, they found themselves in each other's company, perhaps inexorably drawn together by the mounting tension. It was almost like old times, but not quite. And Hunt felt a deep sadness that a barrier now existed between them. One that couldn't be climbed and which would never allow things to be the same again.

It was Ash who spoke first. "About what I said the other day, about you and Gabby . . ."

Hunt stiffened.

Ash made a lame attempt at a smile. "No, I don't want to rake it all up again. It's just that I said some things in the heat of the moment . . ." He hesitated. " . . . Look, Brian, this is bloody difficult for both of us. I've hardly been able to concentrate on this business since I found out about you and Gabby. And I don't have to tell you I've been antagonistic to all your ideas. Like that road snatch – you and the lads were right, of course. I should have said no. I can see that now."

Hunt lit a cigarette. "It *could* have gone either way."

But Ash was adamant. "No, you were right. And that's not just hindsight. That's why we've got to sort something out. If we don't it could jeopardise this assignment further – and God knows it's tricky enough as it is."

Hunt nodded. "I know that. I've told you I intend to resign from the Regiment. If it had been practical I'd have done something immediately."

"I appreciate what you're saying. And I admit, under non-operational circumstances I'd find *some* bloody reason to have you recalled. There's no way I could have you serving with me under normal circumstances."

Hunt's face was a mask. "I know that."

"Well, at least we understand each other. Meanwhile, we've got to get through this together. And I can't pretend it will be easy. You betrayed my trust and that is unforgivable."

Hunt stood, silent.

"But I've been thinking things over," Ash continued. "And I appreciate temptation was put in your path. I mean, I know what Gabby can be like at times. In some ways she's never really grown up. Maybe it's partially my fault that the two of you got together. It's easy for a woman to feel neglected when her husband's in the Regiment. If you listen to the wives, they reckon it's easier coping with a mistress . . ."

Hunt held his tongue. He just wanted to shout at Ash. To tell him not to be so bloody patronising. That his affair with Gabby hadn't been some trite adolescent adventure. It had been an irresistible fusion of spirit and flesh. It had fulfilled a carnal need in Gabby that her husband could have satisfied if he hadn't always spent most of his leave climbing his beloved mountains.

Hunt wanted to say all those things, but it would have been difficult enough to say them to the closest of friends. And now he could think of Ash only as his commanding officer.

"So let's put the matter behind us for the duration," Ash added. "Salvage what remains. Keep things on a professional level and get it over with."

"I thought that's what we had been doing," Hunt said.

Ash looked candidly at the man who had cheated on him. "Let's try it without the acid? When we're not avoiding each other, we're snapping like a couple of old stags in rut. Let's remember the good years before this happened. Just consider this mission as that last mountain we'll be climbing together, eh?"

Hunt recognised the reference to the Flecker poem that had become part of the Regiment's heritage, and he couldn't resist a wry smile. It was appropriate for Ash to bring mountains into the conversation somewhere. And somehow Ash's phrase had suddenly put things into perspective. Everything had changed and yet nothing had. Just one last mountain and they would go their separate ways. Without hatred or jealousy, and on Hunt's part, not without a little shame.

He accepted Ash's offered hand. Both men understood and felt happier for it.

They didn't hear the door open. "Oh, sorry to interrupt –" It was Matt Brewster.

Ash said: "We're just settling a difference of opinion, Matt, that's all. So what is it?"

"We've a visitor upstairs. 'The Troll' – " He glanced at the uncomprehending expressions. " – Commander Vinberg, head of OP5, Swedish Counter-Intelligence. I think you ought to sit in on this." Hurriedly they followed the head of Chancery to the ambassador's office. On the way they passed Lucinda, who looked concerned at the sudden flurry of activity.

"What's going on?" she asked. "Is that man from the Swedish Government?"

Brewster was unusually irritated at the girl's interruption. "He's from their secret service."

"Why's he here?"

Brewster shrugged. "Perhaps he wants to offer some sort of deal, who knows?"

He went to ease past her, but she placed a restraining hand on his arm. "Do you want me to come too, Matt?"

Taken aback, he said: "Oh, I don't think that's a good idea. Anyway, why should you want to?"

"So I can keep Niki updated on what's happening, of course." She was clearly puzzled that Brewster didn't realise why.

He smiled politely. "That's not a good idea, Lucinda. This is all highly confidential."

Her eyes hardened, and her mouth formed into a sullen pout. "And I'm not to be trusted – " she nodded in the direction of the two SAS men " – unlike just about everyone else in the place."

"It's not like that – " Brewster began.

"Don't bother to explain," she blazed suddenly. "I'm beginning to know *exactly* what it's like!" She turned on her heel and marched angrily down the corridor.

Brewster shrugged, mystified. But Hunt felt sympathy for the girl. Everyone was quite happy to use her when it suited them, even when she might be in danger. However, she was never allowed to feel as though she was one of them. Never trusted with more than the bare minimum of facts she needed to know. And the closer she became to Shalayez, the more the embassy staff appeared to distance themselves from her. It was hardly surprising she was feeling isolated.

Ralph Lavender was already with Sir Timothy Maybush. Both were waiting in awkward silence in the presence of two strangers. One was a squat, dark-suited man whose arms and legs seemed too long for his torso. A neat black beard framed a pale and serious face.

He was introduced as Commander Vinberg, and then he in turn introduced his companion. "Mr Reis is one of my field agents."

The tall blond man in a fashionably baggy suit inclined his head benignly. Hunt's instant assessment of him was that he was deceptively relaxed. Behind the modern square-framed glasses, the pale blue eyes were alert and constantly moving; he wasn't the sort of man to miss a trick.

"Ralph and I have just been bringing the commander up to date with developments," Sir Timothy mumbled as he lit a cigarette. "I've explained how we don't seem to have got very far regarding the unfortunate shooting of their policeman. Nor, it seems, in getting Dr Shalayez on his way to London."

"We were pleased to hear you've made an arrest." Lavender spoke the words deadpan, like an automaton. There was no expression on his face.

Sir Timothy smiled wanly. "Although it *is* a shame he's a British subject."

Hunt hid his amazement at the front they were putting up; it almost had him convinced.

Vinberg, however, was not so easily fooled. He toyed absently with a pencil as he spoke. "But *not* a shame he has no connection with your embassy, I expect?"

"That is a relief," Sir Timothy conceded.

The commander's eyes were hard bright coals. "I hope it will continue to be a relief during the trial. The newspapers seem to think he was working for your Government."

Sir Timothy's eyes crinkled as he smiled. "They're just reiterating Soviet propaganda. Besides, the trial is some time away yet."

Cat-and-mouse, Hunt mused. Both sides were testing each other, seeking out strengths and weaknesses, assessing the other's tactics.

"Meanwhile, there is Dr Shalayez," Vinberg said. "His

presence here in Sweden is causing much unpleasant-ness. No doubt you've read this morning's news-papers?".

Sir Timothy studied the tip of his cigarette. "The Soviets can overreact when they don't get their own way, can't they, Commander? Calling on your airmen and causing an incident over Gotland – I don't see a stoutly independent country like Sweden bowing to such bully-boy tactics, do you?"

Vinberg ignored the provocation. Unsmilingly he said: "We understand each other, Sir Timothy. None of us wants to give in to intimidation, but the Russians have some grounds – albeit unjustified, you might say – for being upset. It is sometimes wise to move with the wind, rather than be too rigid." The pencil in his hand broke with a sharp snap. For the first time a smile of uneven white teeth showed. "Grant the Russians their request for consular access to Dr Shalayez. If, after talking, he still says no to going back – then that will have to be the end of it."

Sir Timothy leaned back in his seat and studied the Swede through the pall of smoke of his own making. "Commander, y'know there's nothing I'd like more. But my Government is adamant. No access until he's in London."

Vinberg shrugged, the smile persisting. "What harm would it do?"

Lavender stepped forward. "Commander, let's not play games. You know very well what damage could be done. The Soviets only have to imply threat to kith and kin back home and a vulnerable defector will go running back. It's almost a foregone conclusion. It's happened time and again as, I am sure, you are perfectly well aware."

Vinberg leaned forward, his beard jutting belliger-ently. "Then put him on an aeroplane *out* of here!"

This time Ash spoke. "I'm afraid there's already been an attempt to shoot him when he arrived here. And, sir,

351

you must be aware that the road outside is full of armed KGB thugs."

"People of diplomatic status," Vinberg replied blandly. "One doesn't want to exaggerate the situation."

"Then give Dr Shalayez a full police escort to the airport," Sir Timothy suggested.

Vinberg shook his head. "That is as good as taking sides. My Government will not do that under these circumstances."

"What *will* they do?" Lavender challenged sharply.

Vinberg raised his eyebrows and looked up; he knew all about this ambitious and abrasive young intelligence officer. He'd studied his file before he'd left headquarters that morning. "Anything that will bring this to a speedy conclusion. Preferably today. And nothing that will appear that we are assisting in any way."

Ash said: "Give us permission to fly in a helicopter. The Royal Navy has a frigate standing by in the Baltic. Or one could come from Norway. It could land behind the embassy here."

Vinberg's eyes blazed. "You are joking with me! *Another* of your blessed helicopters. After all that has happened? The press would crucify our Government if that was allowed. And the Soviets would be even angrier than they are now."

In the stunned and angry silence that followed, the trilling of one of the battery of telephones on Sir Timothy's desk came as a welcome interruption.

He excused himself, lifted the receiver and listened. The veins in his cheeks reddened as the seconds ticked by. Finally he replaced the receiver with great deliberation. All eyes were on him as he fell back in his chair like a man close to accepting defeat.

"What's happened, Sir Timothy?" Brewster pressed.

The ambassador regained his composure. "Something quite extraordinary has just happened at the press conference at the Soviet Embassy."

12

The atmosphere in the wood-panelled room on the ground floor of the Soviet Embassy was charged with anticipation as the deadline neared.

Björn Larsson had never seen so many pressmen at an event in Stockholm before. There were representatives from all the major nationals and the provincials. He recognised faces from the staffs of *Dagens Nyheter*, *Kvällsposten*, *Svenska Dagbladet*, *Aftonbladet* and the TT Swedish newsagency, all vying for the best position in front of the rostrum under the huge red flag that dominated the far wall.

Organised chaos reigned as the radio and TV people tried to dominate proceedings with their arc lights and tangled snakes of cable which waited to trip up the unwary. Larsson was surprised to see an American NBC crew as well as one from the BBC in England. Clearly the story of the Shalayez defection had created world-wide interest and, with the overnight news of submarine sightings, everyone anticipated that something big might break at this hastily called press conference.

Larsson was briefing his female photographer about the importance of a good close-up shot of the Soviet ambassador for the big spread he had planned, when he heard a familiar voice.

"Good morning, Björn! I think congratulations are in order."

Tord Jensen. Involuntarily Larsson felt himself cringe as he recognised the syrupy tone. He looked up to see his rival freelance looking very pleased with himself.

"I should have expected you'd be here, Tord."

The gold fillings glittered sharply. "But of course. I've already let you steal the march on me with this one. I gather you've become quite the newspapers' hero over the Shalayez story. Can't let you have it all your own way." He glanced around him. "This is your first time in the embassy?"

Larsson sensed the put-down. "Can't remember the last time they held a conference in here. Their PR men aren't exactly sunshine and smiles."

Jensen smiled sweetly. "They're all right. Just not used to having to be nice to people. Or having the imperialist press hordes trying to run the show for them." He glanced up. "Looks like they're about to start."

"I'll be seeing you then."

"Don't forget you owe me a drink."

With that parting shot Jensen disappeared into the mêlée. Flash bulbs began popping as the Soviet ambassador entered the room flanked by grim-faced men in dark suits. Talk died away as he climbed the steps and took his seat on the rostrum.

A tall middle-aged man with a slightly less than solemn expression on his face introduced himself as Andrei Tarasov, the embassy's public relations officer.

"Ladies and gentlemen of the press, you have been invited here to listen to a very important statement to be made by our ambassador. I would thank you not to interrupt. Afterwards there will be an opportunity to ask me questions. I should like to point out that there are telephones at the rear of the hall which may be used by any of you to file your stories after the conference – with the compliments of the Soviet Embassy."

As the urbane Tarasov sat down all eyes switched to the Soviet ambassador. He was a large, rotund man in a slightly crumpled grey suit which matched his expression that morning. His florid jowls hung heavily each side of his thick lips, which were compressed in concentration as he peered over his heavy horn-rimmed glasses, awaiting his moment. Perspiration glittered on his scalp beneath the sparse grey hair that had been combed in brilliantined tramlines straight back from his forehead.

At last he rose to his feet, clutching a prepared statement in his hand. Then in a flat, monotone voice he went straight into his speech.

Russian politicians and diplomats are past masters at lengthy, convoluted speeches that have very little substance. For the first few moments Larsson had little idea what he was rambling on about. He felt disappointment settling in and his concentration began to slip. Then suddenly he began to realise the importance of the message within the tiresome diplomatic language.

" . . . It is with apology and no little regret that the good relations between our two great nations should become overshadowed by events from not far without these walls. Also it is of much regret that the chief protagonists to these events claim to be striving to achieve a climate of peace and understanding with us at a time when our very planet is threatened by nuclear weapons and now the dangerous possibilities of war in space."

The ambassador did not look up, but continued reading in a steady humdrum tone: "We further regret that these events should now come to cast a shadow over all that is being achieved in arms reduction talks, and that the Government of the Union of Soviet Socialist Republics has been obliged to take carefully considered diplomatic steps in its own interest of national security, following the abduction of one of its scientists whilst visiting this very country on a mission of scientific goodwill . . ."

Larsson was aware of the heat and mounting tension in the room that had become almost oppressive. He loosened his collar, straining to hear every word as the

Soviet ambassador's voice deepened with determination: "It has been noted – I regret to say – that at least one attempt at armed abduction was with the connivance of an independent society of mathematical learning that is essentially Finnish-run. This may be construed as an act of aggression on the Soviet Union through Finnish territory as defined by Article One of the 1948 Treaty of Friendship, Co-operation and Mutual Assistance between Finland and the USSR . . ."

A stunned and total silence had fallen over the room. Every face stared in blank disbelief at the speaker on the rostrum as he concluded his statement. "By definition, in order to defend its neutrality, Finland must not behave in a provocative manner and must avoid actions that might offer incentives for military threat against the Soviet Union. Clearly that requirement has been breached in this case . . . Therefore, under Article Two of the treaty, the Government of the USSR is calling for urgent consultations with Finland. A demand to this effect will be passed to the Finnish ambassador in Moscow at 11 o'clock this morning."

The Soviet ambassador finished abruptly, sniffed heavily, and resumed his seat amongst an erupting scene of total uproar. A buzz of excited conversation swept through the rows of the audience as leading journalists left hurriedly for the nearest telephone to file the story. Angry questions were raised from the floor as Tarasov rose to give his well-prepared answers.

The Soviet Union had just signalled its intention to deploy its troops along Finland's western border, as a prelude to going to its assistance to meet a perceived outside military threat.

It was the stuff that nightmares were made of for the governments of all Scandinavian countries. The vision of Russian tanks rolling into Finland. A prelude to war. The shock waves would rock the Western world. Moscow had found its lever.

*

Commander Vinberg found it difficult to contain his mounting anger. "You see now the damage you are causing. None of us expects the Soviets actually to go into Finland, but the mere threat will create total hysteria in the press and amongst all the Scandinavian peoples. Finland and ourselves will have at least partially to mobilise as a precaution. It will cost millions of kronor for every day the emergency lasts, and the Soviets could protract it for weeks. Something *has* to be done."

Sir Timothy was not about to be stampeded. "We have plans, Commander, but these things do take time."

"Tell me," Vinberg snapped. "What are these plans?"

The ambassador glanced at Ash and then looked to Lavender for approval. The intelligence officer nodded reluctantly.

"This afternoon we're making a dummy run," Ash began. "Using a reinforced van for furniture removals. If it works, we'll try for the real thing next week."

"Next week," Vinberg said emphatically, "is too long."

"We have to set up a series of safe houses," Lavender interrupted, irritated at the Swede's criticism. "And a succession of suitable vehicles. We've limited resources to organise such an operation at short notice."

Vinberg tugged at his beard. "What route do you intend to use? West to Norway?"

"That's too obvious," Ash replied. "We'll go north. Up to the Åre ski resort, then go cross-country over the border. The Russians will be watching the roads."

The Swede looked surprised. "That can be rough country at this time of year."

Ash smiled thinly. "That's why we'll use it. It's not something the Soviets will be expecting. Besides there's a reasonable route through if the weather is good. We've had all the necessary equipment flown here already."

Janne Reis spoke for the first time. "Beware of the Swedish mountains, sir," he warned quietly. "They may

357

seem small by comparison with others, but they grow in winter."

Vinberg gave his assistant a withering glance. "That is not our concern."

Reis didn't appear to hear. "I know the area well. It can be very treacherous. Back in history our King Charles XII retreated from an attack on Trondheim in Norway through that territory. His army froze to death on the march."

"We'll be prepared," Ash assured, but the young Swedish officer's words left an almost tangible chill in the air-conditioned warmth of the ambassador's office.

Vinberg appeared to come to a sudden decision. "I am authorised by my Government to give you *limited* assistance." He glanced at Reis for acknowledgement. "I am sure Mr Reis can organise your route plan for you within twenty-four hours if you are satisfied with your trial run. And, when your vehicle leaves, I shall set up an apparently routine police roadblock to stall any Soviet attempt to follow. Also I can have all known Soviet cars marked by Swedish police cars. They would, of course, only be able to act if they believed an actual crime was about to be committed. For instance, if the Soviets tried to force you off the road, or to shoot up your vehicle." He held Ash's gaze steadily. "Of course, I appreciate that may be too late. But the police presence should act as a limited deterrent."

Ash looked sideways at Hunt; both men smiled. It was a major breakthrough and a massive increase in manpower to cope with the Soviet numbers. "It's a much appreciated gesture, Commander."

But Vinberg's reply was scathing. "Read nothing into the gesture, gentlemen. It is offered merely for expediency. When a respectable nation resorts to virtual terrorist tactics expected of the Libyas and Irans of this world, it is a sorry state of affairs."

Matt Brewster tried to keep the mood of co-operation going. "Commander, there is one more thing that would positively help. If our request for a police cordon around the embassy could be reconsidered. Now we not only have Russians parked outside our front door, but also half the world's press and television. A little breathing space would be welcome."

"It would also make it less easy for the Russians to observe what's going on," Ash added.

Vinberg suddenly scrabbled to his feet. "Very well, it shall be done. Meanwhile give Mr Reis here full details of all the assistance you need." He nodded curtly towards Sir Timothy and made no attempt at a handshake. "Perhaps someone will kindly show me out."

Reis watched impassively as Matt Brewster left with the Swedish security chief. "You see The Troll at his best in a crisis," he muttered sideways to the two SAS men. "Now let's go over your plan. Tell me, when does your trial run begin?"

Hunt looked at his watch. "In just over ninety minutes."

The entire Soviet Embassy had taken on the atmosphere of a wartime operations bunker. There was a log jam of urgent cables waiting to pass in and out of the communications suites, and all radios were fully manned in an attempt to cater for the hefty increase in both military and political intelligence traffic. Every available officer of both the KGB and the GRU – their numbers now swollen by Spetsnaz teams arriving from Leningrad and Moscow – was out on the streets. Every main metro station and the railway Central were under surveillance, as were every port and air terminal. Every usable water inlet had someone watching, and at every small airfield within fifty miles of Stockholm there was an armed agent on the lookout.

Crack members of all intelligence arms were allocated to the stakeout of the British Embassy itself with back-up reserves of vehicles parked in nearby side streets. Taxis and motorcycles had been purchased to supplement numerous hire cars which had already swollen the regular Soviet vehicle fleet. Half a dozen skiers patrolled the Gärdet park behind the embassy, each in radio contact with observers on the Kaknäs tower and the surveillance teams parked outside the front of the embassy.

Everyone who left its grounds was followed by a four-man shadow team, at least until it was ascertained that Nikolai Shalayez was not amongst them.

But the massive drain on manpower was having its effect. Men who had been out on full sixteen-hour patrols would stagger in and fall onto their makeshift camp beds, too tired to eat. After a few hours' snatched sleep they would be awoken by comrades coming in from the cold. Turn-and-turn-about. With eyes glued with exhaustion and denied sleep, the teams would grab coffee and biscuits and return to the biting chill of Stockholm in the grip of winter.

Colonel Yvon was proud of their achievement, and particularly at the organisational prowess of his second-in-command Igor Kulik. Yet he was aware that this state of affairs couldn't continue for much longer. Now that Moscow was stepping up its military threat, Yvon's resources were straining at the seams with additional responsibilities.

For that reason alone, he had welcomed the news of the Soviet ambassador's statement at the press conference that morning. If anything was likely to bring matters to a head, that was. And not before time.

He also welcomed the arrival of Shalayez's KGB assessment officer who was to take on overall command of the operation. He just hoped the *chekist* wasn't another in General Badim's mould.

At least first impressions, as Colonel Sergei Chagall entered the sombre office of the GRU chief, were encouraging.

Clearly Chagall was not of the old school. Hardly in his forties, he evidently looked after himself. The neat Finnish suit showed off his broad shoulders and disguised the slight thickening of the midriff. The wavy brown hair was neatly trimmed and the pleasant well-scrubbed face had a healthy bloom to it. If he drank, like so many of his *chekist* comrades, he hid it well.

"My congratulations, Colonel Yvon, on mounting such an effective blockade of the British Embassy," he began. "Kulik has brought me up to date on the drive from the airport."

Yvon's hooded eyes blinked impassively. "Thank you, but it is no more than is expected of us. Much of the credit goes to Kulik himself."

A flicker of pride passed over his aide's face as he stood in silence beside his master.

"Firstly, let me say how I understand the difficulties that can arise when we KGB people attempt to co-operate with our neighbours the GRU," Chagall began amiably. "I appreciate that we are essentially different animals. But have no fear on that score. You have set up such an effective system that I should want you to continue as before my arrival – acting in conjunction with General Badim as best you see fit. I just ask to be consulted."

This was too easy, Yvon thought. And he was to be proved right in Chagall's next sentence.

"But I must insist that ultimately the requirements of the Centre are met. During my discussions before I left Moscow, it was agreed that enough political pressure has been applied to make any attempt to eliminate Shalayez unnecessary."

Yvon crooked one eyebrow. "Dead traitors are known never to repeat their treason, Comrade Colonel," he growled sardonically.

Chagall's good humour remained. "We are entering a new enlightened age under General Secretary Gorbachev. It does not do to be seen running around shooting political dissenters, however much they may deserve it. So please let us have no more gunning down people in the street. Or sleeping draughts administered like

361

something out of the medieval ages." He smiled brightly. "I assume Nikolai Shalayez *is* still alive?"

"Regrettably," Kulik murmured. "The British would be quite anxious to announce Shalayez's death if it happened. They cannot be enjoying this situation."

"Could he be ill as a result?" Chagall asked.

Kulik shrugged. "It's possible, but no medical help has been summoned."

"You would know?"

"All communications are monitored," the GRU aide explained in a slow and patronising way. "And all new visitors are checked out by our teams."

That seemed to please Chagall. "Then he is alive, so let us keep it that way. The Centre is satisfied that we have mounted sufficient pressure for the British to find an excuse to return him. Meanwhile, we just don't let up. Any elimination of Shalayez will be the very last resort."

The Cadaver steepled his fingers and slowly closed and opened his eyes like an owl. "Why this sudden concern for a traitor's life?"

Sergei Chagall smiled ruefully. "Between these walls, the Americans have threatened disruption of the Geneva conferences if anything happens to Shalayez that is of our doing."

"And we give way to this intimidation?" Yvon asked hoarsely. Surrendering to threats was anathema to his military outlook.

Chagall said: "I repeat, this is an enlightened age, Comrade Colonel. We can afford the spiralling costs of Space Wars even less than the West. If we make peace talks now, we stop it whilst we are way ahead of the Americans. In an atmosphere of renewed détente, Congress will not be so inclined to fund billions of dollars for their SDI project to catch up with us. Shalayez becomes irrelevant."

"Not if he passes on his knowledge," Yvon pointed out acidly.

Chagall's smile melted. "You do not know Nikolai Shalayez. As a brilliant scientist, you will understand that he is no fool. But on political matters he is a little naïve. His defection is not ideological; it is personal. Done in the heat of the moment. He will think long and hard about betraying his country's secrets to our enemies."

Slowly, with thoughtful movements, Yvon lifted a cigarette from the onyx box on his desk. He inspected it carefully. "You, Comrade Colonel, were his political assessment officer at Sary Shagan, I understand?"

Chagall nodded as Yvon flicked on the lighter flame and inhaled.

He blew a long steady stream of grey smoke into the centre of the room where it coiled upward resembling a cobra poised to strike. "And was it *your* assessment that this top scientist of ours was a potential defector – for *whatever* reason?"

Chagall's eyes narrowed like a cat's.

"And based on your assessment, did you recommend that Nikolai Shalayez could safely be trusted to visit Stockholm?"

The cloud of smoke swirled around the KGB colonel.

Chagall replied stiffly: "I have much work to do with General Badim. You will forgive me."

Kulik's impassive mask crumpled before Chagall was fully out of the door. He could scarcely hide his delight at the way his master had out-matched the KGB newcomer.

Yvon noticed his aide's expression. "Don't be complacent, Igor, that is one dangerous man. He obviously has contacts in high places, and a great deal of influence. No doubt, if this business is not concluded to the satisfaction of Moscow, he will try to ensure we take the blame . . ."

"And if it succeeds, he takes the credit," Kulik suggested.

Yvon killed his cigarette. "Let us know our enemy."

Kulik nodded. "It shall be done."

At that moment one of the GRU chief's telephones shrieked urgently. His aide snatched up the receiver and spoke for several seconds.

He put his hand over the mouthpiece. "A signal from Captain Valia Mikhailovitch. The office furniture van has just arrived at the embassy. This could be it."

Yvon sat upright in his seat and for once the thin lips curled into a tight smile. "So she was right! Excellent. Tell her to proceed."

"And if Shalayez is aboard . . .?"

"Kill him."

Kulik frowned. "But what Colonel Chagall just said – "

"An operational hazard." The sunken eyes stared into the middle distance. "Kill Shalayez."

Brian Hunt felt the dull ache of tension in his kidneys as he watched the white van back up the drive of the embassy.

His eyes flickered sideways to Mike Ash. The taller man stood impassively; he showed no visible signs of nerves as he scanned the bullet-proof glass of the entrance vestibule. Outside the black cars of the Soviet embassy had gone, along with the gathering of pressmen and television camera crews. The Troll had been as good as his word. Since early afternoon, a police cordon had been thrown around the embassy, the onlookers held back to either end of the approach road. Only those on official business were allowed through after a telephone check with the appropriate embassy within the cordon. Protection had also been extended some two hundred metres behind the building, with armed policemen warning away anyone who ventured too close.

Not a breath stirred the late afternoon sky of black velvet which provided a contrasting backdrop to the steady fall of large snowflakes.

"It is looking good just now," a voice said laconically.

Hunt turned to the big blond Swede who stood behind

them. "Your boss has kept his word – we're grateful for that, Janne."

Reis winked. "The Troll is a real good guy when you get to know him. He likes it when something's going on. All this stuff, you know, he gets a kick."

Hunt grunted, and wondered if Vinberg would enjoy it so much if he were in the firing line like Big Joe and Len Pope, who had left the front seats of the van and were moving warily to the rear doors.

He watched anxiously as the two men opened them and began manhandling the filing cupboard. Neither were recognisable, wrapped in thick jackets and peaked snowcaps with earflaps down. Hunt smiled when he noticed that Big Joe's bandido moustache had gone. It transformed his face, emphasising the size of his teeth. That must have been a great personal sacrifice.

The two men struggled in through the glass doors which Hunt and Ash held open.

"Straight upstairs with it," Ash said.

Relief showed on the straining faces of the SAS men as they entered the warmth of the embassy and started manoeuvring the steel cupboard up to the first floor.

"Any trouble?" Hunt asked.

"None to speak of," Monk gasped as he struggled with the load. "Worst thing was getting through the cordon at the end of the road. I don't like being photographed at the best of times and we were blinded by bloody pressmen."

"Not to mention people sticking microphones in our faces," Pope added. They'd already planned their roles as surly delivery men. Len Pope spoke limited Swedish and Big Joe had taken the precaution of learning a few choice words suitable for his part. Swear in gutter slang in any language, and people inevitably took you as the real thing and were deterred from further questioning.

They dumped the cupboard on the first floor landing beside the furniture due to be replaced.

"Any sign of Ivan?" Ash asked.

365

"There were some black limos parked the other side of the cordon," Monk said, "but there were so many bods around, God knows who they were. Half the press could have been Ivans for all I know. They were all trying to see into the back."

"But the police were keeping an eye on them?" Ash pressed.

Monk was clearly uneasy. "Look, boss, the cops were keeping the crowd in check, sure. But any one of them could have opened up with an automatic and riddled the bloody van with rounds. The police wouldn't have been able to do a damn thing before it was too late."

Reis touched Ash on the shoulder. "You sure you want to go ahead with this just now?"

"No," Ash answered tersely, "but we don't have any option." He turned back to Monk and Len Pope. "There's a brew on in the kitchen. Grab a quick wet and be ready to go in fifteen minutes. Brian and Janne here will follow after you at a safe distance, but they won't interfere unless there's a life-threatening situation."

"Janne?" Len Pope queried.

"He's from Swedish security."

Pope exchanged a brief glance with Monk; obviously something had changed.

With last minute amendments to the plan settled, Hunt showed Reis the way down to the small underground carpark beneath the embassy. He opened the door of a black Saab turbo with dark tinted windows and an array of spotlights fitted to both the front and rear fenders.

"A real fancy car," Reis observed. "A 9000."

"We've made a few modifications," Hunt conceded. Len Pope had once been a driver-mechanic in the squadron's Mobility Troop. He'd never lost his fascination for squeezing a little bit of extra power from conventional engines. "Those lights have already saved Shalayez's life once."

"I can imagine," Reis said, shutting the door.

"There's cellular foam in the fuel tank to prevent it being set off by a stray round," Hunt added. "We were going to rig a device to lay a smoke screen, but we ran out of time."

The Swede was impressed. "Like James Bond, you have rockets too?"

Hunt laughed. "Not quite. The nearest we have is that box of tricks by your feet. Different types of smoke grenades and flares."

Reis lifted the lid of the tin tool box with his toe. "And the Browning pistol, like the one that killed that policeman in Stockholm?"

Hunt winced, immediately regretting he'd taken the man into his confidence. "Standard British Army issue. Commonplace."

"I suggest if there is any shooting to be done," Reis replied easily, "it is I who do it. Don't look so apprehensive, I am a champion marksman. Besides, your people are in enough trouble already. Sweden is not such an open society that its security agents do not have a few privileges."

"Like shooting people?"

Reis's grin was positively boyish. "Ja – like shooting people."

Hunt gunned the car into life. "I'll remember that."

"I suggest you do."

It was then that Mike Ash's signal came over the radio to confirm that the van was on its way with Joe Monk and Len Pope. He was relieved to be moving at last and, as he swung left down the road towards the cordon, he could see the bright brakelights of the van.

By the time he reached the crowd of pressmen and onlookers, the other vehicle had gone. He scarcely slowed at all, forcing overeager photographers to leap aside as he carved a way steadily through them. A policeman banged a protesting fist on the roof, but Hunt kept going.

Strandvägen was almost deserted, the soft fresh

blanket of snow making driving difficult until the next routine tour by the municipal snowplough. The van's rear lights remained visible until the road splayed out into a dual carriageway boulevard that ran along the waterside towards the city centre.

"No sign of the *Ryssdjävlarna*," Reis observed.

"Don't speak too soon," Hunt grunted. He nodded, indicating ahead to where a motorcyclist, clad in black leathers, had appeared from nowhere. It settled in behind the van, its rider manoeuvring skilfully in the treacherous conditions.

"A motorcycle? The *Ryssdjävlarna* like their comforts."

"Maybe these aren't the *Ryssdjävlarna* you're used to, Janne. I expect they've brought in special people." He sat upright in the seat, and cursed his lack of an extra vital inch or two. "I can't see what's in front of the van."

Reis peered ahead. "I can't tell – ah, ja, it is just a taxi."

Hunt relaxed. The taxi had already been on the road when the van had caught up with it. However, it was still ahead when Monk swung a right up Skeppargatan towards the north.

The motorcyclist went straight on. "He's gone," Reis said with a smile.

Hunt shared his mood as he swung north after his companions. It was beginning to look as though they would get away with it. Maybe the extra police presence had been a deterrent after all.

He settled down to maintain a discreet distance from the van as it cruised around the mess of Östermalm one-way streets to get to Karlavägen, cross it, and reach the broad, tree-lined lanes of Valhallavägen.

His earlier sense of relief began to dissipate as he felt a grub-like doubt gnawing away at the back of his mind. It was Janne Reis who pinpointed the source of his concern.

"That taxi is still in front of your friends. Is it a coincidence? We have taken many turns."

368

"Too many," Hunt murmured. "They can't know the route unless they've had Big Joe and Len under surveillance for the last couple of days." He spoke into the brooch mike on his lapel. "Sunray to Alpha One. Taxi may be hostile. Suggest you take discreet evasive action. Over."

Almost instantly Monk's voice crackled in his earpiece. *"Roger to that. Reading my mind. Taking next left without signal. Follow me. Out."*

As he drew level with the next turning, Monk hit the brakes, slithering to a speed slow enough for the van to drift into the narrow side street. Hunt paused to watch what the taxi would do. If anything it accelerated, a tell-tale puff of exhaust escaping its rear.

The Saab nosed into the side street after the van, which had reached the far end and was turning left to resume a course parallel to the original street. As Hunt followed, slipping briskly in front of an angry lorry driver, he looked ahead. The van was there. And, just pulling in front of it from another side street, was the taxi.

"It's them," Hunt decided.

"They must know the route," Reis said. "When your friends turn off, they know where to pick them up again."

Hunt's earpiece crackled into life again. *"Alpha One to Sunray. Looks like we've caught one. Passenger in back seat is taking interest in us. Shall we evade again? Over."*

"Roger," Hunt replied. "But not too obvious. Remember, if anything happens, do not resist. We will intervene only if situation is life-threatening. Over."

"Grateful for that, Sunray," came the sardonic reply. *"Am taking next right. Out."*

An opening between two blocks of office buildings loomed suddenly. Awkwardly, the van took the corner, fishtailing as it turned, the rear wheel clipping the hard kerb beneath the mound of snow. As the Saab followed, Hunt realised it was a bad move. It was a long, very narrow back street with trash bins stacked along one side, so that it was scarcely wide enough for one vehicle. The surface was rutted with ice and as slippery as a skating rink. He changed down cautiously, using finger-tip pressure to control the skittish steering.

Ahead, the van had slowed to a crawl along the endless concrete and brick corridor which had closed in on them like a tunnel. Snow was now falling hard, obliterating vision as the wipers struggled against the weight.

A single headlight appeared beyond the van, illuminating the narrow street with its dazzling brilliance.

"A motorcycle," Reis breathed.

Hunt slowed, killing his lights. "And no guesses which one. The same we picked up just after we left the embassy. He must be in radio-contact with that taxi."

Hunt watched nervously from the stationary Saab as the brakelights of the van came on. The motorcyclist had left his bike and was walking forward, silhouetted in the halo of his own headlamp. Gigantic shadows played over the walls of the street.

"He's armed," Reis hissed, reaching for his shoulder holster.

"Do nothing!" Hunt warned. "Joe and Len will just play dumb. If he wants to search, they'll let him. All they'll find is an empty filing cabinet."

Reis swallowed hard; he just hoped the Englishman was right.

Monk was climbing from the driver's seat, his hands half-raised in a gesture of submission. The motorcyclist waved a machine-pistol at him. Len Pope emerged from the other side of the van and moved warily to the rear.

"Does that Russian know we're here?" Reis asked.

Hunt nodded. "I expect so. If he didn't see us, his chums in the taxi would have told him we are following." He reached to the tin box at Reis's feet and fumbled for a flare. Just in case.

Monk opened the rear doors of the van under the

direction of the motorcyclist, and motioned Pope to help him slide the cabinet out. Monk opened the cupboard door and the motorcyclist peered in.

Apparently satisfied, he said something to the two SAS men and waved the machine-pistol at them. Cautiously, with their backs to the wall of the street, they inched away slowly in the direction of Hunt's Saab.

The motorcyclist tossed something into the open window of the van, then turned and ran back towards his parked machine. At the same time Monk and Pope broke into a panic-driven sprint, skidding and sliding over the corrugated ice in their haste to reach the Saab.

They were almost there when the van blew. The force of the explosion lit up the sky like daylight as a mighty maelstrom of displaced air rushed down the alley with the awesome power of an invisible locomotive. Its sheer force bowled over the two running men like skittles. Instinctively Hunt covered his face as debris cracked against the Saab's windscreen like shotgun pellets.

Flying panels of bodywork spun through the air, grotesque, twisted bats striking blindly against the alley walls before crashing into the snow.

Within a split second Hunt had grabbed the Browning pistol from the box and was out of the Saab's door. Ahead, the remains of the van had become a raging pyre as the upholstery spat and crackled brightly into the night sky. He ran to the prone bodies of his two companions.

Monk was visibly trembling with shock. "I'm all right, boss. Just winded."

As Reis joined them, Pope too sat up and twisted round, looking on at the burning wreck of the van.

"Did the Russian say anything?" Hunt asked.

Monk had a strange expression on his face. "*He?* It wasn't a bloke. It was a woman." He rubbed grit from his eyes. "Uncanny. Almost spoke perfect bloody English. Like a girl from Roedean. Just told us to get out and open up. Then just said: 'Tell Brian it was a nice try.' "

Hunt's mouth dropped. "Don't be ridiculous – "

But Len Pope's eyes said it all. He'd heard it too.

Ralph Lavender felt a growing sense of foreboding as he walked along the deserted street, muffled against the snow which was falling fast and heavy. His footfalls were deadened by the thickening white carpet that obliterated the pavement.

As though things were not bad enough already, he thought grimly. His career lay in tatters now, he knew; it would take years to redeem himself. What had begun as the promise of the intelligence coup of the decade had degenerated into a tacky international incident which had exposed his country and his service to the gaze of the world's press and television. How many quality Sundays would relish exposés in the months to come? How many hours of television documentary would be devoted to probing into the strange events in Stockholm?

For him it was a total personal disaster. If Shalayez didn't get out of the country soon, Whitehall would almost certainly be forced to give him up. And then the demand for his own resignation would be a foregone conclusion.

He was scarcely aware of the icy kiss of the snow on his face as he trudged on. His thoughts returned to the brief telephone call he'd received at the embassy.

It had come out of the blue – totally unexpected. And it had thrown him into panic. Perhaps he should have said no. Shut it off. But on the spur of the moment he'd agreed to the meeting. It just added to his problems. As if he didn't have enough.

He paused by the flight of steps that rose steeply to the narrow entrance of an hotel. Half the lights were missing in the cracked illuminated sign. A bed-and-breakfast pension for students and manual labourers living cheap away from home.

Then again he wondered if there wasn't a chance to make up his losses. To regain the initiative.

He climbed the steps and pushed through the door into the mean warmth of the lobby. His senses were assailed by the clang of a bell and the distinctive smell of cabbage cooking. The tatty wallpaper was disfigured with tiny notices of house rules which had been added over the years. 'No smoking', 'Door shuts at 11', 'Don't use all the hot water', 'No female guests', 'Keep the lavatory clean'.

"Yes?" A sour-faced woman peered from the under-stairs cubbyhole which served as her office. "We've no rooms."

"You've a Mr Heinrich staying here?"

"Oh him. Is he German? He sounds more Russian to me."

Lavender ignored her question. "I'd like to speak to him."

"Who wants him?"

"It's a personal matter."

Her hostile gaze held him momentarily, undecided whether or not to be difficult.

Lavender said: "I think your cabbages are boiling over."

She too heard the sizzle of water on the gas ring. Struggling to get her fat hips out of her chair, she said irritably: "Room 5." She hesitated at the kitchen door. "All guests out by ten."

Lavender smiled thinly and climbed the worn stair carpet to the first landing. He found the room at the end of the cramped corridor. He knocked.

Immediately he heard the clink of glass on glass, followed by a mumbled curse. A bedspring groaned as someone hastily got up and stumbled to the door.

"Yes?" The voice was thick with drink, the accent distinctly Eastern Bloc.

"Open up, it's Lavender."

After several fumbled attempts the key turned noisily in the lock and the door opened a fraction. An eye peered through the gap. It blinked. A grunt followed and the door lurched wide, squeaking on unoiled hinges.

By the time Lavender had closed it and turned around, Heinrich was back on one of the two single beds which had been squeezed into the long, narrow room, either side of the window. The yellowing curtains flapped fitfully.

"It's freezing in here," Lavender said.

"I'm hot."

"That's the booze."

Heinrich gave a harsh laugh. "It is my nerves. Fear makes you hot."

"I'm not surprised. This is a bloody stupid thing to do. Risky for both of us."

Again Heinrich laughed hoarsely and proffered the bottle. "A drink, Comrade Lavender. There's a tooth mug by the basin."

Lavender shook his head. "Do you know what you're doing here? You can blow everything."

The smile vanished from Heinrich's face. "It's all right. I've covered my tracks. The room's booked for the night – payment in advance. I'll slip out a few minutes after you've gone. That miserable *babushka* won't ask questions, she'll be too busy counting the few kronor I'll leave behind in my room."

Lavender removed his hat and sat on the edge of the bed opposite. It was too cold to take off his coat.

"So what do you want?"

Heinrich drained his glass. "We have a deal."

"I know that."

"I've kept my side of the bargain."

"So that's why you're in Stockholm?"

Heinrich smiled slyly. "It isn't the reason, but it should make it easier for you to keep your side of the bargain."

"Shalayez isn't home and dry yet."

"I know." The other man looked suddenly angry. "An *unbelievable* mess! But that is not my problem."

"It is if we don't get him to London."

"You are a bastard."

374

Lavender flinched. He wasn't used to such direct talk. "If Shalayez doesn't get to London the deal's off."

"Because I am not worth it without him?" Heinrich goaded.

Lavender ground his teeth.

The other man slopped more brandy into his glass. "Then it is good for both of us that we meet like this."

"Oh yes?" Lavender replied boredly. He didn't like Heinrich much, and could stand drunks even less. It might have been different if he hadn't 'inherited' Heinrich from his predecessor.

"Because if you don't make a move tonight it will be all over!" His voice was slurred with drink. But the burning passion in his eyes was unmistakable. "You know about the submarines and the threat at the press conference today? Well, your Government can't resist much more."

"Meaning?"

Heinrich stared into his glass as though he had found something obnoxious at the bottom. "Something is due to happen tonight that will apply the final pressure. Already your Government is wavering. By morning they will decide to send him back."

Lavender leaned forward, ignoring the fumes on the other's breath. "What will happen?"

"I can't tell you."

"Won't tell me, you mean."

Heinrich shrugged. "Have I ever lied to you? Take my word for it. It's as much in your interests as mine. If you don't get Shalayez out tonight your career is finished, and my life."

"Your life?" Lavender pressed.

Heinrich stared at his half-empty glass. "It may be years before I have another chance like this – so for God's sake GET HIM OUT TONIGHT!"

The intelligence officer was taken aback by the sudden shouted plea. Anxiously he motioned the man to lower his voice. "Heinrich, you *have* to give me *something* to go on."

The man downed the remainder of his brandy in one long, last burning swallow. He wiped his mouth on the back of his hand. *"Mokrie dela."*

"What? 'Wet affairs'?"

Heinrich nodded. "Department Eight. It's something for Executive Action. It'll happen tonight."

"What will happen tonight?"

Now Heinrich shook his head, already regretting what he'd said. "I've told you too much already, Lavender. More than you deserve to know. Act on what I said or go and piss on yourself. Because if you don't do something that's what you'll be doing – pissing on both of us! Now – " his voice lowered to a hoarse whisper – "get out of here!"

Ralph Lavender was hardly aware of his journey back to the embassy by taxi. His mind was in turmoil, filled with indecision. Should he heed the warning he had just been given? And if he did, what the hell could he do about it?

His mind still wasn't made up as he crossed the shallow, snow-covered steps to the entrance vestibule. George didn't look happy when he saw him.

"There you are, Mr Lavender! Everyone's been screaming for you. No one knew where you were."

"I was out on private business," he replied testily. "What's gone wrong?"

George shook his head. "Easier to ask what's gone right, sir. They're having a pow-wow in the Chancery, if you want to join them."

Lavender removed his coat and took the stairs three at a time. He let himself in through the glass security doors and made his way to Brewster's office.

The head of Chancery looked up as he entered. "Ah, Ralph, just the man! You'd better sit in on this."

Lavender glanced at the four SAS men seated on easy chairs around the coffee table. "How did it go?"

"With a bang," Big Joe Monk answered quickly.

"The van was followed and intercepted," Mike Ash added. "A woman motorcyclist at gunpoint. She checked over the van."

For a moment Lavender's spirits lifted. "Well, if they found it clean, we can still go ahead – "

"No, Ralph," Brian Hunt interrupted. "She blew it up. Then and there. Just like that. They knew *exactly* what we were up to."

"We *assume* that," Ash corrected. "Maybe they just weren't taking chances."

"Nobody hurt?" Lavender asked. "Well, thank God for that."

"It means we're back to square one though," Hunt pointed out. "With no quick way of getting Shalayez out."

Matt Brewster moved round to the front of his desk. "The thing is, gentlemen, I think this matter is coming to a head. We've had a signal from Whitehall to stay our hand for twenty-four hours anyway. They've had Dinton's psycho report and they've studied Sir Timothy's view of the danger this incident is causing to the Scandinavian balance of power. There've been Soviet troop movements towards the Finnish border and a massive increase in military radio traffic picked up by GCHQ. If you've read the early editions of *Expressen* you'll see that there's been an embarrassment of submarine sightings all around Sweden. And there've been several Foxbat reconnaissance flights at high altitude – that hasn't been reported."

"What are you saying?" Lavender demanded.

Brewster looked awkward. "I may be jumping the gun, Ralph, but I think we'll hand Shalayez over to the Swedes."

"Christ!" Lavender's white cheeks had pinked with rage. "You know what'll happen – they'll grant the Soviets consular access and – bingo! – that'll be it."

"I know how you feel, Ralph." Brewster sounded genuinely sympathetic. "If it's any consolation the Americans are pulling all the stops out to persuade our Government to hold on to him. Ambassador Bream's in with Sir Timothy at the moment, reading the riot act. Even demanding that Shalayez be transferred across to their embassy."

"Do you think we might?" Lavender asked.

Brewster pulled a bitter smile. "Too much loss of face, Ralph, you know how it is. Not a chance." He wiped a finger over his moustache, curling one end. "Well, that's the situation. We wait and see. At least it's a chance for you all to catch up on some sleep tonight. Nothing will happen until midday tomorrow. And I'll let you all know as soon as I hear anything."

A depressing air of defeat hung in the air as the meeting broke up.

Hunt felt unaccountably sorry for Lavender. Always a cold fish, this humiliating failure meant far more to him than to the SAS men. For them it would probably mean a brief spell back at Hereford, or Norway, before a posting to Kuwait, where preparations were being made in case of an Iranian breakthrough in the stalemate of the Gulf war. Or maybe some continuation training in the Cameroons. Even covert operations in Latin America. But for Lavender, this would be an end to all his career hopes. And as for Shalayez – the likelihood of the decision made Hunt feel as though he'd turned on a friend.

He said: "Sorry, Ralph, we did our best."

Lavender accepted Hunt's hand. "I know, you all did. Can't win 'em all, I suppose."

"Come and join us for a drink in the bar, eh? Drown your sorrows."

Lavender smiled awkwardly. "I'm still no drinker, Brian. I've got things to get on with."

The intelligence officer shouldered past the knot of

people at the door, and made his way to his small secure office for which he had the only pass key.

He shut the door and fell back against it, his eyes closed. He didn't turn on the light of the soundproofed room. Instead he breathed in the sterile air in the confined space that was just large enough to take the grey steel desk with its scrambler telephones, the shredding machine and filing safe.

Opening his eyes again, he crossed to his desk and slumped into his chair, feeling crushed and humiliated. For a full half-hour he stared blindly into the darkness, thoughts tumbling around his mind in disarray.

Then slowly, very slowly, a pattern began to form in his mind. He reached forward and switched on the desk lamp, its sudden brightness hurting his eyes.

No, he had nothing to lose. Not now. Nothing.

Unusually, he made a snap decision. He stretched for the safe and spun the dial through the release-code number. As the heavy door opened under its own momentum he took out a small, weighty cardboard box. Closing the safe again, he placed the box in the pool of light on the desk and prised it open.

The black gunmetal of the M67 Yugoslav pistol glinted dully amidst the crumpled wrapping paper. To his knowledge it had never been used. He had acquired the gun for his self-protection, but he had never used it, except when they'd been half-expecting Shalayez's arrival. Should he ever have fired in anger, he would have the satisfaction of knowing that the weapon was untraceable. Its country of origin would point any police force in the wrong direction – or indeed any direction. Yugoslav arms were available world-wide.

Deftly, he thumbed six rounds into the magazine, palmed it into the grip, and checked that the safety was on. He dropped it into his jacket pocket and placed the box of spare 7.65 mm cartridges into the other. His decision made, he switched off the lamp and went to the door.

It was a short walk to where Len Pope was seated with a commanding view of both the inner glass doors of the secure section and the door to Shalayez's room. A buttless Heckler and Koch carbine rested across his knees.

Lavender smiled sympathetically. "You must be all in."

"Not every day you get blown up," Pope admitted. "I'm due for a relief in an hour."

"It'll soon all be over. I'm just going to have a word with Shalayez."

Pope nodded. "Better knock first. Young Lucy's in there."

A fleeting expression of doubt passed like a cloud over Lavender's face. "I will."

The room was fetid with sweat and stale cigarette smoke. Shalayez was sprawled on the bed in tracksuit trousers and singlet, propped against the pillow. He looked pale and tired with deep rings around his eyes as he toyed with a glass of vodka. Half a dozen empty bottles beneath a chair testified to what had become his main way of passing the waiting hours.

Lucy sat by the Russian's feet with a text book on mathematics open on her lap. Her eyes were dark and sullen, clearly resenting Lavender's intrusion.

The intelligence officer tried to be informal; something he wasn't very good at. "Ah, teaching our Lucy some of your tricks of the trade, eh, Niki?"

Lucinda scowled. "Do you have to be so damn patronising, Mr Lavender? What d'you want?"

A tic flickered beneath Lavender's right eye. "You've changed, Lucy, do you know that? You seemed a different person when we started this."

Her mouth moulded into its familiar pout. "I *was* a different person then. That was before I learned that people like you would use *anyone* for their *own* ends."

Lavender replied stiffly: "Only in the national interest, Lucy. Only that."

She raised her eyes heavenward in exasperation, and Shalayez placed a consoling hand on her arm. "Leave it, little Lucy. Mr Lavender only does his job."

"And it may be his job to send you back, Niki," she retorted. "You've heard the rumours."

Shalayez's violet eyes narrowed on Lavender. "Is it true, what is being said?"

"That's why I've come."

"*Is* it true?" Shalayez persisted.

"It's up to you."

The Russian gave a harsh laugh. "Since when is *anything* up to me any more?"

Lavender lowered his voice. "As from now." He turned to the girl. "You, too, Lucy. I'm afraid this has to involve you, because I doubt you're keeping any secrets from each other."

Lucy's eyes blazed. "I *haven't* been sleeping with Niki here, if that's what you mean!"

Lavender waved a dismissive hand. "No, no. Forget that. It's just that you must both listen to me and then decide."

"Decide what?" Lucinda demanded.

He took a deep breath. "Whether you want to risk taking matters into your own hands." He hurried on quickly: "Look, I'm levelling with you both. As things stand there's a worse than fifty-fifty chance that my Government will throw in the towel tomorrow. I'll be asked to pressure you to hand yourself over to the Swedes. And, from what I've heard, the Soviets plan something tonight that will make that a certainty."

Anguish contorted Shalayez's face like a mask. "It's true then . . .?"

"Listen!" Lavender hissed. "That's why your only chance is to take affairs into your own hands. Get out – tonight."

Shalayez sat bolt upright, his interest suddenly roused. "Tonight? How?"

"Out the back. To be precise, through the window of

381

the bar. I know the room's usually locked, but I have a key. It's not difficult to get down to ground level, and then over the railings into the park."

"The KGB – " Shalayez began.

Lavender waved the protest aside. "There's now a Swedish police cordon. It'll give you time. You can ski across before they know what's happening."

The Russian was incredulous. "Ha! Yes, I ski – as a small boy. I have talked with Mike and Brian about it for a crossing into Norway. They say we go real slow and they teach me all over again."

"For God's sake, Niki, I'm *serious*! Skiing cross-country is like walking – even I know that! All you have to do is to *keep going*! There are only four Soviets covering the whole park area. You have a good chance."

Shalayez sneered. "You wish to teach *me* about mathematical odds, Mr Lavender!"

The intelligence officer dug in his pocket and drew out the lightweight pistol.

"Oh my God!" Lucinda gasped. For a second she thought Lavender was going to kill both of them.

"This will lengthen those odds, Niki," he said evenly. "And they won't expect a single person – unescorted – to be you. It's a vast area out there, it's pitch black, and the snow is falling heavily."

Shalayez shook his head doubtfully.

"And I'll create some sort of diversion," Lavender added. "In the confusion you have every chance."

Lucinda said: "You mentioned this involved both of us. What did you mean?"

At last Lavender felt he was getting somewhere. "I don't think Niki can manage this alone. He doesn't know the country and he'll need someone who does. And you're the only one Niki really trusts. I'll make sure he gets to Central Station. You will meet him there with rail tickets for the north. The trains are packed with skiers. A couple of lovers will pass unnoticed."

Lucinda's face was white with fear and bewilderment.

"But you know yourself the KGB will be watching the station – "

Lavender nodded. "I know, I know, it's a risk. But they'll be looking for someone surrounded by a bunch of heavies. Someone well-protected. Not just another couple of skiers. Your chances are good – I know, I've been trained in this sort of thing."

A sudden thought occurred to her. "Wouldn't Mike or Brian be better doing this?"

Lavender sighed. "They don't *know* about it, Lucy. It's just between you and me. It would *never* get official sanction. They'd say it was too risky. But I've thought about it, and it can be done."

She frowned. "God, is this some kind of set-up?"

He shook his head, exasperated. "No, it's just your last chance, that's all. It's up to you. Just get him to Åre and book into an hotel. If it's successful that far I'll tell the others and we can revert to the original plan. Mike's people can escort Niki cross-country to the border."

Shalayez and Lucy looked at each other long and hard. Slowly, he reached out his hand for hers and clasped it. Both felt a sense of numbing fear mingled with a curious sensation of relief.

Lucinda turned sharply. "Why are you doing this?"

Lavender was momentarily thrown by the direct question. To hell with it, he thought, he may as well tell them. "Because if I lose Niki back to the Soviets, my career is finished. That's the simple truth. And I think I'm worth more than that to my country. I deserve more than being thrown on the scrapheap, just because my department will want a scapegoat!" He stopped suddenly, realising that he had spoken with more anger than he'd intended.

The girl bit her tongue. Then she said slowly: "At least your motive would seem to be in keeping . . ."

Lavender scowled.

Her full lips spread into an insipid smile. "Self-interest."

Shalayez pointed to the gun that lay on the bed. "One thing, Mr Lavender, that I will not need. I have no intention to shoot my fellow countryman.'

Ralph Lavender stood up. "Niki, from now on you will do *everything* I tell you. And you will bloody well take it!"

13

A sense of profound relief mixed with bitter disappointment had settled over the small group drinking in the embassy bar. And the likelihood that Shalayez would be handed over to the Swedish authorities had created an atmosphere of anticlimax.

Somewhere in Whitehall lights would be burning as politicians and the intelligence hierarchy debated where their own best interests lay.

It was an unsatisfactory conclusion for Mike Ash and Brian Hunt as they shared a bottle of consolatory whisky with Cherry Brewster.

Hunt echoed all their thoughts when he said: "At least it's out of our hands now."

"Thank God," Cherry murmured with feeling.

"Personally," Ash added, "I don't envy anyone having to make the decision. To weigh one man's life against our entire relationship with Scandinavia. Not to mention the Soviets' threats."

Cherry tossed back the fringe of blonde curls from her forehead. "I know Matt feels terrible about recommending Shalayez be sent back. He's really got to like the man. But he felt he had to agree with Sir Timothy's view on it."

Ash was sympathetic. "It's their job to put our relationship with Sweden first, Cherry. That's what he's paid to do."

"It doesn't make it any easier," she replied, more sharply than she'd intended.

Hunt said: "We all feel bad about it. But I just wonder how Lucy's going to take it? She's really keen on him."

"She doesn't know yet?" Cherry asked.

Ash shook his head. "No, Lavender's taken care to keep her in the dark. But I bet she's heard the rumours. She's a smart kid."

"It's a pity she didn't join us for a drink," Cherry said. "We might have been able to break it to her gently."

Hunt lit a cigarette, deciding it would be his last for the night. "Maybe that's what Lavender's doing now. They left together earlier, and they're not back yet."

"Rather him than me," Ash reflected. "It's just a pity she ever had to be involved. She's much too young and inexperienced to handle this sort of business."

Hunt stood up. "If you'll excuse me, I've got to relieve Big Joe, and do a security check of the building."

As he reached the door, he collided with Matt Brewster. The head of Chancery looked pale, his voice breathless after his sprint down the corridor. "Have you heard?"

"What?" Ash asked.

"Alf Nystedt's been shot."

Hunt blinked. "Say again?"

"Alf Nystedt. One of the country's top civil servants and adviser to the prime minister," Brewster gasped. "There's been an assassination attempt."

"Jesus!" Ash breathed. "When did it happen?"

Brewster fell onto the sofa. "About forty minutes ago. Reports are all very confused, but apparently he was taking his dog for a walk. He was in a park near his home when some bastard just stepped out and shot him."

"How serious is it?" Cherry demanded, aghast. She'd met Alf Nystedt many times at dinner parties and considered him to be a personal friend.

Brewster shook his head. "I don't know for sure, but I gather it's pretty bad."

Hunt's eyes narrowed. "Do they know who did it?"

386

The head of Chancery bit into his lower lip in an attempt to stop the emotion that was threatening to choke him. "They haven't arrested anyone yet. No one knows who was responsible."

At precisely that moment doctors at Sabbatsberg hospital pronounced Alf Nystedt dead. The time was six minutes past midnight.

Nikolai Shalayez was totally unaware of the devastating events that had taken place in a park just a few miles away.

His mind anyway had been preoccupied since the moment he had agreed to Lavender's suggestion. At first his thought processes had been paralysed with apprehension. But after the initial blind panic subsided, the thought of freedom started to flow through him like an elixir.

He was doing something for *himself*, at last! Suddenly Ralph Lavender soared in his estimation.

He glanced at his watch. It was nearly 2 a.m. Time to start. He patted the pockets of his trousers and jacket to check that he had all his important personal possessions. Beneath his clothes he had pulled on a set of long thermal underwear to protect himself against the icy cold outside. He could make no more preparations until he located the kit that the SAS men had prepared for him in readiness for the cancelled escape plan.

He eased open the door. As usual he could see the back of his guard who was seated on a chair which gave him a clear view of the bullet-proof glass doors of the secure section. He felt a flutter of regret that this was the turn of the man called Brian. But it had to be done.

Lavender had advised Shalayez not to creep up from behind, so he sauntered up, deliberately clearing his throat as he went.

"Hello, Niki," Hunt greeted. "Not insomnia again?"

Shalayez smiled. "When you have so much on your mind, it is difficult to sleep."

387

"I can believe that."

The Russian said: "It gets lonely, too."

"No Lucy?"

"She goes back to her flat until tomorrow." Deliberately Shalayez made his words sound a little slurred. In fact he had never felt more sober in his life. "Maybe you join me for a drink, yes? Like last time. Perhaps then I sleep."

Hunt laughed. "*Not* quite like last time, Niki. The idea is *you* sleep, not both of us. After that last session I could hardly keep awake until I was relieved. Bad form."

"A small vodka then. I have some *starka*."

Hunt moved the Heckler and Koch from his lap and stood up. "Now that *is* an offer that's hard to refuse."

The two men went to Shalayez's room and sat on the edge of the bed while the Russian poured out two generous measures. It was then that he appeared to fumble, letting Hunt's glass bounce onto the carpet and roll into the far corner.

Hunt shook his head. "What a waste, Niki. How much of this stuff have you already tucked away tonight?"

He crouched over to retrieve the glass. As he did so Shalayez rose swiftly to his feet behind him, the half bottle of drink in his hand. Momentarily he hesitated. He had not harmed anything since the days of his childhood when he was taken hunting in the forest. To hurt anyone, least of all a friend like Brian, was . . .

He shut his eyes and put his full weight behind the downward thrust. The heavy glass struck Hunt's cranium with a sickeningly dull thud, the power of which prised the bottle from the Russian's grasp.

Hunt was poleaxed. Already on his knees, now his shoulders pitched forward like a man at prayer. Then, slowly, he keeled over on his side. Still.

Shalayez opened his eyes. Horrified at what he had done, he nervously reached out to Hunt's head. A trace of blood came away on his fingers. He just hoped that the after-effects would be no worse than mild concussion.

Reaching under the bed, he pulled out the roll of heavy-duty plastic packaging tape that Lavender had left him. Following his instructions precisely, he wound the stuff around Hunt's wrists and ankles. Then he strapped a final length around the man's mouth.

He was sweating profusely by the time he finished manhandling Hunt's heavily muscled body. Already he noted stirrings that suggested his victim was beginning to come round. It had taken Shalayez much longer than he had planned and he began to rush, afraid he would miss the diversion that Lavender had promised would occur.

After locking the door to his room, he moved stealthily down the corridor to the store cupboard. It was there that the gear for their planned escape had been stashed in readiness for instant use. He slipped inside and closed the door.

Using the faint glimmer from a heating tank pilot light, he stripped off his top clothes and slipped on a pair of windproof trousers and a fibre-pile jacket. Over that he zipped up a green windproof top with a hood. He recalled that his pack contained a pair of casual civilian slacks and a two-tone duvet ski top which would be more in keeping with the holidaymakers going north to Åre. But for the moment he wanted to merge totally with the bleak surroundings outside. After a few moments' search he found a set of cam-white overalls, and pulled them on, turning up the hood.

Next he searched for his footwear, stoutly made Lundhag ski-march boots with squared-off toes to take cable bindings. That done he quickly located his skis. They were easy to find amongst the broad white "pusser's planks" of the SAS men. They had selected him a pair of lightweight Rossignol Chamois touring skis with steel edges suitable for rough cross-country work. They were a far cry from the crude hickory affairs of his youth with just leather straps for binding to the feet.

He wondered if he'd forgotten anything, but by now

his mind was a complete blank. He pushed his way into the deserted corridor, dragging out the hefty bergan. Struggling, he hoisted the load onto his back, wincing at the weight of it as he tightened up the padded hipbelt and shoulder straps. That eased the pain as the weight was distributed equally around his torso.

Picking up the skis and poles, he moved swiftly to the glass security doors and waited, listening.

A mumble of voices came from the direction of the ambassador's office. But thankfully no one was on the landing beyond the glass. He released the catch to let himself out and moved quietly down the stairs.

On the next landing he turned right, along the corridor past the British Council offices, until he reached the door to the bar. He extracted the spare key given him by Lavender and twisted it in the lock. Gingerly he moved inside, shut the door, and promptly stumbled into one of the low tables. Cursing under his breath, he made his way across to the window.

Outside icy white petals floated steadily down from the windless sky. Reflected light from the undulating expanse of snow gave feeble visibility for some fifty metres; he could even make out the skeletal outlines of a row of hibernating trees which denoted the footpath. That path, he knew, would lead him north to the road.

But the real menace was out there, unseen. A mile and a half away the giant Kaknäs tower dominated the parkland, invisible behind the falling curtain of snow. Lavender had warned that the enemy would almost certainly try to use it as an observation post with night-vision devices.

It was an unnerving thought and he pushed it brusquely from his mind, concentrating instead on releasing the security catch on the double-glazed windows. In his haste it took an age, and when it swung open he wasn't prepared for the stinging indraught of icy air that took his breath away. After days confined to his room, he'd forgotten just how cold Sweden could be in winter.

Through smarting eyes he discerned the six-foot drop onto the roof of a covered terrace which ran the full length of the rear of the embassy. Having lowered himself from the roof, he would have just a low wall and then a six-foot spiked fence to scale.

He smiled to himself. *Just!* God, he must be mad.

Two forty-two a.m. Lavender's diversion should have happened a couple of minutes ago. Had it? There was no way of knowing. The Englishman hadn't been specific – he just said to trust him. When it happened, he would be in no doubt.

Shalayez frowned. Should he wait or go? It was becoming bitterly cold by the window, and he decided rashly to wait just two more minutes. Then he would go, regardless.

Those two minutes took a lifetime to pass. He listened intently, but heard nothing. There was a passing scare when he heard footfalls in the corridor outside and voices talking earnestly. But whoever they were, they kept on walking and he breathed again.

Firstly he dropped the bergan down onto the terraced roof, following with the tied bundle of skis and poles. They clattered noisily together when they hit, but he realised the building's double-glazing would have muted the sound. At last he scrambled onto the sill, took a deep breath, and jumped. It was the softness of his landing that surprised him. He'd been bracing himself for a hard crash, but instead was gently absorbed into a deep bed of snow.

He repeated the process to the next level, tossing his kit from the roof to the grounds below. Then he worked his way to the corner of the building, where he could use the roof support pillar to let himself down until his feet touched the terrace railings.

It was trickier than he'd imagined and, despite his height, he found himself hanging by his upstretched hands which clutched the roof cornice. His boots were still several inches above the railings.

That was when the explosion blew.

In the hushed white world the noise was devastating. The deep, rolling pulse of the soundwaves caused his heart to jump like the heavy basso vibration in an enclosed discothèque. His fingers lost their grip and he felt himself slipping through space. The explosion was still echoing around the open space of Gärdet as he scraped the snow from his face and struggled to stand in the knee-high drift.

Then irrationally he laughed. He was down and he was safe. And that bastard Lavender had been as good as his word. Late, sure, but he had *kept* his promise. The explosion must have been heard for miles around – it wasn't the sort of noise you could ignore even if you were asleep.

Gathering together his bergan and ski-pack, he sat on the low wall and twisted around until his feet touched the snow on the far side. It was really deep here where the unchallenged wind from the park had piled it up against the stonework. As he staggered awkwardly forward, he became alerted to flashlights on the far side of the railings. A dog barked.

He half slid, half fell into the lee of one of a row of large boulders that ran parallel with the perimeter. Hunt had explained to him earlier that they had been placed to stop the sort of suicide lorry-bombers who had decimated the US Marines' headquarters in Beirut.

Now they served his purpose well, enabling him to shelter from the probing beams of the flashlights. He could hear the voices clearly, conversing in Swedish. Two armed policemen emerged from the shifting white haze, one pulled by a powerfully built dog on a chain leash. He guessed they were making their way to the source of the explosion.

Holding his breath until they had vanished, he advanced rapidly to heave his bergan and skis over the spiked railings. They proved more difficult to scale. It was only after five attempts that he managed it, and even then the trouser leg of his cam-whites caught on a spike, ripping the material as he launched himself over. Again the snow saved him from a nasty injury.

Making himself as small as possible, he hunched over to unpack and fit on his skis. Once more he shouldered the bergan and hauled in the straps. It was difficult because his hands were wet and cold, and he realised that in his haste he had overlooked his mitts.

Earlier Lavender had explained to him that the embassy was situated in a depression. The ground rose about three metres in height between the perimeter of the building and the footpath which was some thirty metres distant. It provided convenient dead ground which could be used to avoid anyone watching from Kaknäs tower.

Experimentally he pushed one foot forward and then the other. The skis slid easily over the ice crust and offered no resistance. He wobbled like a novice as the things began to run away with him, and he cursed beneath his breath. But after a few strides of kick and glide he became used to the feel of it. The sense of movement and balance came rushing back from his childhood. He even grinned to himself and the cold air made his teeth ache. But he didn't care. After all these years he could still do it, he *knew* he could! Maybe it was like riding a bicycle: once you learn, you never forget.

Gaining in confidence, he launched himself at the slope up towards the footpath. He splayed out the fronts of his skis, turning his ankles inward so that the steel edges bit into the crust to prevent him running back. With poles behind him, he thrust himself forward, leaving a trail of herring-bone marks in the snow.

Ah, yes, it was all coming back! The use of unfamiliar muscles made his legs ache as he mounted the rise and levelled out through the trees which lined the footpath. However it was his hands, not his muscles, that caused him concern. They were starting to throb with cold.

If anything the snow was coming down thicker and faster than ever now. He could see nothing and no one. Even the black bulk of the embassy had been swallowed up. But he also knew that he was now at his most vulnerable.

Turning his skis northward, he kicked off down the pathway. Fresh snow hid the iced-over tramlines created by previous skiers and it was an uncomfortable ride as his ski tips nosed their way through as if they had a mind of their own.

The path began to fall away rapidly and he gathered speed down into a shallow valley. Ahead he discerned a further rise on the far side, and he doubled into a crouch to gather sufficient speed to carry him out of the dip again.

He was so concentrating on keeping his skis in line that he completely missed the two grey shapes coming from the opposite direction.

Only a short way from the base of the valley did he spot the two skiers, their snow-covered grey coats making them almost indiscernible from their surroundings. Afterwards he realised that they must have been as surprised as he was – perhaps even more so, because he was wearing actual cam-whites. He merely registered a fleeting expression of astonishment on their faces as he thundered through the gap between them, bottomed into the valley and carved up the other side with the combined momentum of speed and the heavy pack on his back.

Gravity pulled him to a standstill on the upward slope, and he threw himself into a vigorous herring-bone walk to reach the next stretch of level ground. Perspiration broke out on his skin following the sudden exertion, and then became a flood of sweat as it dawned on him that no one goes skiing at three in the morning. And the two phantom skiers he had nearly run down had not been in police uniform.

He cast a glance over his shoulder. The vague grey

394

forms of the men could be seen manoeuvring with kick turns on the far side of the dip as they prepared to come after him.

His eyes glazed with determination, Shalayez began pumping uphill with every ounce of strength he could muster. Somewhere ahead he knew there were tall housing blocks, but before he reached them he should come to the road which cut across the open parkland.

It seemed an age before he bridged the rise and the long, undulating slope was before him, hidden by the white murk. He risked a last look behind, and was shocked at the distance the grey skiers had made up. They were herring-boning up the long rise behind him at a furious pace with arms and legs going like pistons. He could even distinguish the breath clouds obscuring their faces as they laboured.

Shalayez turned back to the slope and began double-poling as hard as he could. Soon he'd reached a speed so fast that it was all he could do to hold the crouch and keep his balance as he hurtled through the night. He was a spacecraft pulsing towards infinity with snowflakes flashing past like galaxies of stars, as he bounced over the uneven ground into the unknown.

The road emerged with stunning suddenness, its solid band of compacted snow clearly defined against the rolling white dunes of the parkland.

He went into a fast skating turn, unweighting each ski in turn to take him in a new direction, running parallel with the road.

Somewhere ahead he knew there was a bus shelter. That's where Lavender would be.

He powered on, throwing all his resources into a last effort before the men in grey caught up. But each kick and glide seemed to take him no closer to his goal. Nothing emerged in the opening tunnel of his vision except metre after metre of ice-ribboned road.

Then he saw it, half buried in a drift on the far side. He slewed his ski points together into a stopping plough and squinted into the stinging confusion of swirling flakes. No one there.

He bent and released his skis. Hastily gathering them into his arms, he shambled forward on the harder snow of the road to get a better view.

He was only ten metres away now and could make out the frozen colour picture of an advertisement hoarding at the back of the bus shelter.

Then his heart skipped a beat as a figure detached itself from the shadows. He noted the long overcoat and trilby hat trimmed with ice crystals. In his hand the man was holding a radio transceiver with a short rubberised aerial.

"Niki?" the man called out. "Over here!"

Thank God, Shalayez thought. It's Lavender! Relief ebbed through him and he realised that instinctively he had been holding the butt of the automatic pistol in his windproof pocket.

Behind him he could hear the hiss of skis as his pursuers gained ground, and he hurried on clumsily under the weight of the bergan and the awkward bundle of skis and poles.

His eyes became fixed on the smile on the face beneath the trilby hat. No, that wasn't Lavender's face –

Beyond the man, a car suddenly flashed its headlights from the darkness, twice.

Oh, my God, Shalayez thought, *that* must be Lavender.

The man in the hat was moving forward, grinning inanely.

"Hello, Niki, this is the way to the ferry-port." He laughed, now not bothering to disguise his Ukrainian accent. "You are planning to catch a ship back home via Helsinki, yes?"

Shalayez was aware of the scrape of skis on the hard road ice behind him. At the same time he noticed the black shape of an unlit car, moving like a phantom behind the man with the hat.

"I save you the price of the ferry ticket, Niki," the stranger's voice goaded. It was then Shalayez saw the top-heavy shape of the pistol with its long silencer in the man's hand.

In desperation his numbed fingers tried to close around the butt of his own M67 in the pocket of his anorak. But he could feel nothing except the pain in his joints, his fingertips without sensation.

The stranger levelled his pistol, still grinning.

Shalayez tried to pull the M67 free. It caught fast in the lining. He tugged again.

A look of stunned surprise came over the stranger's face and he staggered back as the muffled detonation blasted through Shalayez's pocket. Gawping in amazement, Shalayez saw his adversary stumble back against the wall of the bus shelter. A cascade of snow showered from the roof, half burying the body. The shimmering white crystals began to glow crimson as blood seeped through from the wound.

Shalayez stared. He'd fired by accident and hadn't even aimed. What had he done! He turned quickly to see what had become of the skiers. Evidently the sight of their comrade being shot had shaken them. They'd abandoned their skis and were now approaching much more cautiously. One on each side of the road.

The sound of the black Saab turbo looming out of the darkness without lights jolted Shalayez's head back the other way. As the vehicle drew alongside, the driver reached across and threw open the door.

"For Christ's sake, get in!" Lavender shouted. "Just throw everything on the roof rack!"

Shalayez needed no second bidding. He'd have cheerfully abandoned everything, but he forced himself to take vital seconds to jam the skis and bergan together so that they wouldn't fly off as soon as the car moved.

"C'mon!" Lavender urged.

The second Shalayez's backside hit the passenger seat, Lavender hit the accelerator.

The two skiers had been taken by surprise with the arrival of the Saab. They had wasted time deciding what to do, shouting to each other across the road. Realising their quarry was in danger of slipping from their grasp, they leapt into the road with guns held in solid two-handed aiming positions.

They weren't expecting the battery of heavy-duty spot-lights which fired an incandescent blast of dazzling light that was like looking directly into the sun. Self-preservation took over as the blinding aurora swept towards them. Shots went wild as they dived aside and the Saab roared through, its body slithering from side to side as the snow-tyres fought for grip.

The two men recovered quickly, swinging round to get well-placed shots at the rear wheels and window. The secondary blast of light from the rear-mounted spotlights was another surprise. Filled with self-anger, both men loosed their entire magazines blindly at the receding halo that trailed like a glowing meteor across the park road in the direction of Stockholm.

Lavender switched off the spots, and reverted to normal dipped headlamps which were proving inadequate at probing the thickening fall of snow. "Are you hurt?"

Shalayez's thumping heart had returned to something nearer its natural rhythm as he now struggled out of his cam-whites and slipped on a civilian anorak. "No, I do not think so. I feel, in fact, quite good."

It was true. After the exhilarating downhill ski chase, and the shock of shooting a comrade, the relief of the sudden rescue had made him feel quite light-headed. Almost intoxicated. He had heard it said that the closer you lived to death, the more you cherished life. Perhaps it was true.

Strangely he felt no remorse at shooting dead a fellow countryman. And even that didn't worry him. He just didn't care.

Lavender concentrated on the road. "They'll be out in

force now, Niki. It'll be more dangerous than ever. The trouble is, in this stuff, we could be on top of a Soviet ambush before we realised it. You'll be safer on foot. Besides, this car is known to them."

"What happens next?"

"Lucinda has got two rail tickets for Åre. That's a ski resort not far from the Norwegian border. You'll catch the early morning train. When you've arrived safely, she will telephone to let me know. Then you stay in your hotel room until I can arrange for you to cross the border under escort."

"You will be in big trouble for this?" Shalayez suggested.

"I have a wide discretion in my job." A ghost of a smile passed over his lips. "But if this succeeds, then there will be no recriminations. Some minor token punishment to show my masters' displeasure, but a success is a success. My future will be assured."

"And if it fails?"

"No one will know what was done."

Shalayez didn't follow. "There is me and Lucy."

"Be under no illusions," Lavender snapped more harshly than he'd intended, "there are unlikely to be any survivors if this fails. Neither you nor Lucinda. I explained that was the risk you would be taking. It was your choice."

Shalayez's admiration for the intelligence officer had been shortlived; he felt his animosity return with a vengeance. But he held his mouth in check. At least the bastard had been as good as his word, so far.

Lavender's next words, spoken in a lighter tone, echoed his thoughts. "But it needn't fail, Niki. Already you are over the worst – out of the embassy and on your way."

Before Shalayez could reply, Lavender hit the brakes. "Sod it!" he cursed, peering ahead. "A police road-check. Niki, just keep quiet and let me do the talking."

He wound down the window as the policeman approached, bowed against the sheeting snow.

"What's the problem, officer?"

The policeman squinted against the icy wind. "English?"

"Ralph Lavender, Visa Secretary to the British Embassy. I'm taking my friend here to the station. Lucky beggar's off on his holidays."

Despite the weather the officer managed a grin. "I saw the skis. I'd tie them down if I were you. British Embassy, eh? There was trouble near there earlier. Some explosive device in a patch of wasteland. Curious because there's nothing there. So no one was hurt."

"Thank God for that," Lavender replied. "Had me worried for a moment. You see, I haven't been in tonight. No doubt it'll be all the talk tomorrow. Is that why you're stopping vehicles?"

The officer looked sad. "I wish it was, my friend. A top civil servant was shot dead tonight."

That came as a real jolt to Lavender. "What?"

"I am afraid so. You have heard of Alf Nystedt? Gunned down in a park while walking his dog. We are looking for a man of dark complexion aged between thirty-five and forty."

Lavender smiled thinly and handed over his ID. "Do I fit the bill?"

The officer shook his head, and handed back the document. "I don't think it is something a British diplomat would do. Besides, you are going the wrong way. We are really looking for someone *leaving* Stockholm. You have seen nothing suspicious on the road?"

Lavender shook his head, and the policeman waved him on. "Don't miss your train now."

Thankfully the intelligence officer followed the previous car through the gathering of policemen. Despite the relief of being safely on their way again, he remained stunned at what the policeman had told him. Alf Nystedt assassinated. Was that what Heinrich had been referring to back in that sleazy hotel? Was that the final twist in the Soviets' spiral of intimidation? God, even he could scarcely believe that . . .

Then another thought occurred to him. Central Station was bound to be full of Swedish police looking for the gunman trying to make good his escape. That could actually work in their favour. If Shalayez was spotted, any KGB goon would be reluctant to take action when the place was stiff with armed cops in vengeful mood.

Police cars seemed to be everywhere during the remainder of the drive. The sound of their sirens echoed endlessly through the hushed white city streets, their flashing lights constantly seen in the distance.

At last Lavender pulled into the kerb. He handed Shalayez a polythene package. "This is the new identity we'd planned for you in Sweden. It's a false British passport for a Soviet émigré called Alexander Barskov. You are over here for the skiing. Your travel documents say you've been staying at the Mornington Hotel on Nybrogatan, and there's the return half of your air ticket to Heathrow. If you're questioned by police, use a mixture of English and Russian. Should the questions get difficult, lapse into Russian, smile a lot and look stupid. Hopefully they'll get bored with you."

"What about Lucy?"

"We hadn't planned any cover for her, so she'll just have to be herself. You met her at the bar at the Mornington and discovered you both planned a ski trip at the same time. Okay?"

Shalayez shrugged. "Yes, it is good, I think. I can remember that."

"You'd better," Lavender warned. "Your life may depend on it. Now get out and cross the road. Lucy will meet you. And for God's sake, stuff that gun of yours down the bottom of your rucksack until you've cleared Central Station. You might not fit the police description of that assassin, but if they search you and find a gun they'll take you in for sure."

Shalayez smiled and offered his hand. Irritably the other man shook it. "Thank you, Mr Lavender, for everything."

He was left standing on the snow-piled pavement as the Saab pulled away in a cloud of spindrift and vanished into the night. When the car had gone, it was eerily quiet in the amber glow of the street lights in the deserted ghost city.

Shouldering his bergan, he carried the ski-pack in his right hand as he slid and skidded across the ploughed channels of snow to the far side of the road. He climbed over the discarded mound of rotten snow debris to the pavement and sheltered in a shop doorway. Alarm began to rise in his chest. There was no sign of Lucy.

It took just two minutes for that alarm to turn to stark panic. He twisted left and right, peering anxiously up each street of the empty crossroads for some sign of her. Nothing. He could have been the last human being alive in the world.

Then he noticed the illuminated sign of a taxi coming towards him from the direction he knew the station to be. It cruised to a halt at the pavement and the rear door swung open.

"Niki! Here!"

His heart momentarily skipped, and then he recognised the soft brown eyes peering from inside a bundle of fur.

"Lucy!"

The driver got out and stowed his gear as Shalayez climbed into the taxi's welcome warmth.

She threw her arms around him and kissed him full and hard on the mouth. "Thank God you're safe. I was terrified for you." She laughed. "Your face is so cold!"

He was infected by her pleasure at seeing him again. "And my nose runs in this warmth, see! But my heart is *never* cold now."

She squeezed his hand and huddled against his

shoulder. "I know it isn't, Niki, I know! Tell me, how did it go?"

"I talk about it later."

She looked unsure. "Whatever you say – Anyway, we'll be at the station in a few minutes. Here's a hundred kronor, it'll look better if you pay the driver." She pulled back. "And for goodness' sake comb your hair, Niki. You look so *recognisable* like that."

"I have a hat somewhere."

He fumbled in his pocket and pulled out a large American baseball cap with a peak and perched it roughly on top of his mass of black hair.

"Niki, you're incorrigible!"

And they laughed together.

"Here, mate, have a wet!"

The mug of steaming hot tea was thrust in Hunt's hands. "Thanks, Joe."

Monk watched as his friend sat on the edge of the bed and gulped down half a dozen mouthfuls in quick succession. "How's the head now?"

"Bloody terrible." He grinned without humour. "And that bloody tape felt like it pulled half the skin off my lips."

"Rotten stunt to pull. Just goes to show you can't trust the bastards."

Mike Ash pushed open the door. "Well, he's gone all right. We've scoured the place from top to bottom."

"I discovered the bar window when I was doing the rounds," Monk explained. "That must have been the way he went."

Ash said: "The Saab's missing from the car park."

Hunt waved a hand. "No, Ralph Lavender asked me if he could borrow it earlier."

"Then chummy *must* have legged it out the window," Monk said. "Len's gone down to check. Maybe the bloody KGB got in and dragged him out."

Ash shook his head. "I can't believe that. Anyway

there'd be no reason for Niki to wallop Brian here. No, I reckon he got wind of the way things were going and simply did a runner."

"He won't get far," Monk muttered darkly. "The bleedin' KGB goons will pick him up, no problem. He's probably lying out in the park somewhere, stiff as a board. Serve him bloody right, too."

"Lavender's going to be thrilled about this," Ash added thoughtfully.

"Stuff Lavender," Monk growled. "Those two bastards deserve each other."

Hunt had revived and began to marshal his thoughts. "What about that explosion earlier?"

Ash snapped: "Well, Shalayez can hardly have been responsible for that!"

Monk slapped Hunt on the back. "One of life's little mysteries that. The police reckon it was the Sovs just adding a bit of pressure."

"What, like bumping off Nystedt?" Hunt sneered.

"No one knows the Russians did that," Ash retorted. "And it's not something any of you should suggest to the Swedish security people when they come round."

"They'll have to be informed about Shalayez, I suppose?" Hunt asked.

Ash nodded. "Matt Brewster's already decided and he's sure to get clearance from London. If Shalayez isn't found dead outside, then we'll need Swedish resources to track him down."

Len Pope arrived at the door, his anorak encrusted with snow. "He went out the back, boss, that's for certain. Big yeti holes in the snow all over. He took that bergan we had for him and the skis."

"Crafty sod," Monk chuckled. "Gotta hand it to 'im."

Len Pope caught the mood. "Can't be too many people skiing down Stockholm high street."

Ash became irritated by the jocularity; it was clear the men were almost relieved that Shalayez had gone.

"Before we actually start congratulating ourselves that

chummy's gone walkabout, I suggest we start thinking about where he might have gone."

"That's a bit academic, boss," Monk pointed out, "if he's a corpse out in the park."

"Point taken, Joe. That'll be our priority at first light. And, of course, if the KGB or GRU don't get to him, there's always a possibility he'll get picked up by the Swedish police. After all, they are on the lookout for Alf Nystedt's killer."

"He might have decided to go home and try his luck," Len Pope suggested. "You know, either try the Soviet Embassy or take the Helsinki ferry."

Hunt took the opposite view. "Or take a train or bus to Norway."

Monk agreed. "He knew the dangers of going back to Russia – we'd made that quite clear, and I'm sure he believed us. But he also knew the Soviets would be watching all border crossing points to Norway."

Hunt said slowly: "You don't suppose he had in mind to do what we had planned – but going it alone? You know, ski backcountry over the border."

"I shouldn't think so," Ash retorted scathingly. "If you recall, he hadn't skied since he was a kid. The idea of doing it with us terrified him; he's hardly likely to try it alone."

"True," Monk agreed. "But if he did, it's one hell of a long border. He could be anywhere."

Ash came to a decision. "We can go over all these possibilities with the Swedes tomorrow – *if* we don't find his body in the park, or the police haven't picked him up. The one thing that could still be on our side is that the Soviets might not know he's gone. That'll give us an edge." He glanced at his watch. "Well, there are some hours to go until first light. I suggest the rest of you turn in and grab some kip. Tomorrow's going to be busy."

As the men began to leave, Ash called to Hunt. "I'd like a word before you go."

"Yes, Mike."

The SAS captain waited until the other two men had gone. His expression was deadly serious. "Right, Brian, I want to know just what the hell you thought you were doing with Shalayez earlier?"

Hunt was taken aback. "Doing? You know what I was doing – keeping the bastard company."

"You were supposed to be guarding him."

"I was. No one was going to break through the front door *and* into the secure area without me hearing it."

"You were drinking with him," Ash challenged.

"You know I was, Mike. Hell, we've all shared a jar with him to keep him company."

"No one else managed to get coshed."

Hunt stared at his commanding officer. He realised what it was all about – Ash's seething anger over Gabby had once more broken through, despite their agreement. Yet under such stress, Hunt could understand it all too well. He decided it was better to say nothing.

"It's going to look brilliant in my report," Ash went on. "A senior NCO in the Regiment gets ko'd by the man he's supposed to be protecting. We'll be a bloody laughing stock, let alone any disciplinary action that's taken. Not to mention we've lost the most important defector this country's had in years."

"So important that we were all set to send him back," Hunt retorted.

Ash's eyes blazed. "Don't be glib with me, Brian. You know as well as I do, that isn't our concern."

Hunt remained cool. "Is there anything else?"

Ash's lips tightened. "No, except that I can't promise how Hereford will view this, or the MOD. It'll be on your head." He uptilted his chin, staring at some spot above the other man's head.

Without a word Hunt left the room and shut the door.

By contrast with the rest of Stockholm, Central Station was buzzing with activity. Holidaymakers were arriving by bus and taxi, unloading skis, rucksacks and suitcases as the time for the departure of the north-bound train neared. The high vaulted roof echoed to the chatter and occasional laughter of the passengers who thronged the beige marble concourse. People lined the rows of seats and queued to purchase tickets, or rushed to buy last-minute confectionery and magazines for the journey. Boisterous children shrieked in excitement as they played tag around the legs of adults who did not share their sense of fun at such an early hour.

Nikolai Shalayez hugged Lucinda closely as they entered via the locker rooms like engrossed lovers, constantly kissing as they walked.

"Can you see any of them?" he whispered in her ear.

"Don't be silly, Niki, they're not going to wear labels," she replied tersely. "And keep smiling. We're supposed to be on holiday."

He glanced casually around, his grin unnaturally fixed. "Our KGB people are not so good at hiding themselves," he said out of the corner of his mouth. "They are used to being seen. They like you to know. See, there – "

"Where?" Casually she scanned the concourse.

"By the fountain. He pretends to read a newspaper, but all the time he looks and scowls."

"In the black coat?"

"Yes. It is not a very favourite colour with Swedes, I think."

She had to agree. The man had a distinctly surly expression, and had an angry dark mole on his cheek. And, as she looked carefully around the concourse, she spotted two other likely-looking candidates. She shivered. "Come on, I've got the tickets."

Keeping amongst other passengers as much as possible, they checked the departure board, then joined the queue for the platform.

Two policemen were talking to selected passengers as they went through.

Lucinda exchanged a nervous glance with Shalayez, smiled bravely and walked on, hugging his arm.

"Excuse me, sir. Are you a Swedish national?"

Almost too quickly, Shalayez blurted: "I am a Britisher. I stay at Mornington Hotel where I meet my girlfriend. Do you want to see my passport?"

The other officer looked curiously at Lucinda.

"Thank you, sir." He studied the document carefully. "That's an unusual English accent you have."

"Ah, I am from Russia once. Now I am British residence."

"On holiday, Mr Barskov?"

"Yes, I go to ski."

"Where are you going to ski?"

"I, er, I think – " he began to stumble.

"We are going to Åre," Lucinda said quickly.

The second policeman said: "You do not ski?"

She laughed. "I don't have my own skis. I'll hire some when I get there."

The first policeman had lost interest, and the second waved them on.

"I think I am so red in the face," Shalayez said when they were out of earshot. "I think I am wet with the sweating."

She squeezed his arm. "It doesn't matter, we've *done* it! God, I never thought I'd say it, but I could kiss Ralph Lavender right now."

Shalayez laughed. "Don't you *ever* let me catch you doing that!"

A large area around the bus shelter had been taped off as the police photographer took a succession of photographs of the dead body from a variety of angles.

Behind him stood the tall frame of Janne Reis, his blond hair covered in an astrakhan hat. He stepped forward.

"So this is not Nikolai Shalayez?"

Both Mike Ash and Brian Hunt peered at the figure half-covered in snow.

"Definitely not," Ash confirmed.

Hunt nodded his agreement.

"As I think," Reis said. "But I have to be sure just now. There is no identification. The clothing has been disturbed, I think someone clears out the pockets."

"Who would have done that?" Hunt asked.

Reis shrugged. "Whoever shot him. There is much shooting last night." He pointed to where a team of policemen were laboriously scouring the snow-covered road and verge. "We find like two heaps of spent cartridges there. But it is a different calibre to the one that shoots this man."

"What have the ski-tracks told you?" Ash asked.

Reis removed his spectacles and wiped them over with a handkerchief. "They are much filled in with fresh snow, but our tracking expert tells me they lead from your embassy. There are others, too, made at about the same time, but they double back on themselves. Very confusing. All I can say for certain is that your Russian was here. Maybe *he* shoots this man. But maybe it is someone else."

"Shalayez didn't have a gun," Hunt pointed out.

Again Reis shrugged. "Well, someone did. Maybe the Russians have their defector back just now."

"It seems to me, Shalayez is making a habit of disappearing with no one knowing where the hell he is," Hunt commented.

"*Déja vu*," Ash agreed.

Reis smiled thinly. "I think the *Ryssdjävlarna* will take much delight in telling everyone if they have him back."

"When it suits them," Ash added. "And that could be *after* he's out of the country. Meanwhile, we cannot assume anything."

"You want our help in finding this man?" Reis asked, scarcely hiding his cynical amusement at the turn of events.

"It would be in everyone's best interest, Janne," Ash said. "We are obliged to look for him. So are the Russians."

"We cannot take sides."

"He's a willing defector, despite propaganda to the contrary. It would be better if we got him."

Reis's smile remained. Quietly he said: "Correction, Mike, it would be better if no one found him. One way or another he is big trouble."

"If you help us get to him, Janne, you'll never hear of him again until he turns up in London," Ash promised.

Reis kicked thoughtfully at a pile of rotten snow. "Commander Vinberg is involved with the police over the assassination of Alf Nystedt just now. So it is for me to decide on this. I will have details circulated and see what we come up with."

Ash was relieved. "Thank you, Janne, I appreciate that. But perhaps we can do it discreetly."

The Swede raised a quizzical eyebrow. "You mean without alerting the Russians that you have lost him?"

It had been the most confusing twelve hours that Colonel Yvon could remember.

Events had begun at 1 a.m. with the urgent ringing of his bedside telephone in his apartment situated in the Soviet Embassy's accommodation block. The news had stunned him; one of Sweden's leading civil servants had been shot dead in a Stockholm park.

The ambassador convened an immediate conference of diplomats and chief representatives of both the KGB and the GRU. Tired men with exhausted minds and bodies debated tetchily what had happened. It was an acrimonious meeting with accusations flying like arrows across the table.

Yet the final conclusion was that neither the GRU nor KGB in Stockholm admitted having had any part in the affair. If the murder were related in any way to the build-up of pressure on Sweden over the Shalayez defec-

410

tion, then it had been organised direct from Moscow. And no one in the Kremlin was saying anything.

However, the immediate effect had been a standing down of their provocative presence around the British Embassy. The ambassador wanted no excuse for the Swedes to think the tragic loss of their top civil servant had any bearing on the defection. Patrols in the area had been halved, and the technician secreted in the Kaknäs tower with long-range surveillance equipment was withdrawn.

Yvon had only just returned to his rooms when he received the second slice of bad news that night. One of Badim's KGB agents had been shot dead by a man identified as Nikolai Shalayez.

The only remaining ski patrol in the area had attempted to intercept him but he was picked up by a car, the registration of which tallied with a vehicle hired to Fiscex Holdings. That same vehicle had been used by embassy staff.

The KGB ski patrol members had stripped the body of all identity before withdrawing.

So far neither the car nor its occupants had been found.

As Yvon waited in his office for the morning meeting with the new man sent from Moscow to oversee the Shalayez affair, he sensed that it would be a stormy ride. He was to be proved right.

"Well," Sergei Chagall began arrogantly as soon as he entered the GRU chief's sombre office, "just what the hell went on last night?"

The Cadaver sat calmly, bolt upright in his chair behind the desk. "You have read the report. It was your people involved – mine had been withdrawn on orders following last night's meeting."

"You have overall operational responsibility," Chagall reminded.

"It was still your clowns who fouled up. If my people had been involved, you'd have a corpse on your hands for the next Aeroflot flight to Moscow."

Uninvited Chagall slipped into the upright chair facing the desk. "All right, Comrade Colonel, now we know what *would* have happened. As it is, Nikolai Shalayez would appear to be back safely in the hands of the British. He was picked up by a car known to be used by their embassy. Am I right?"

Yvon didn't answer. He reached forward and pressed his intercom. "Kulik, have those prints been developed yet?"

"This moment, Comrade Colonel. I'll bring them in."

"And send Captain Mikhailovitch."

"What is this?" Chagall demanded.

Yvon's heavy eyelids half closed. "*My* people have been looking after Central Station, whilst yours have been running around like children playing snowballs."

"And – ?"

Kulik knocked and entered without waiting for a reply. Behind him was Valia Mikhailovitch, her well-built figure flattered by the trim grey business suit and black court shoes. The neatly combed auburn hair framed a scrubbed face that glowed with good health and the outdoor life.

Yvon said: "We've had a man with a telephoto lens on the balcony of the station since first thing this morning. Photographing all passengers who could possibly resemble Shalayez."

Kulik fanned out the prints on the desk. "A couple. The man was very careful not to show his face, as you see. A half-profile here – very blurred. And a full face here, but half hidden by the girl. Now look at her."

"That's the one from the file," Valia Mikhailovitch said.

Yvon looked up. "You indeed have a photographic memory, Captain." He didn't quite succeed in hiding his admiration.

Her eyes danced with pleasure in an otherwise deadpan face. "Just training, Comrade Colonel. But that is Lucinda Court-Ogg. Or Marsh."

412

"And the man?" Yvon pressed.

The woman allowed herself a discreet smile. "While one cannot be sure, nothing in those features does *not* resemble Shalayez. See – the strong nose in the profile." She jabbed a finger. "The line of the jaw. And on the full face shot, see, the dark ring of colour around the iris."

"Let me see," Chagall demanded, snatching up the photographs. He glared at them contemptuously. "As I thought, these bear no resemblance to Shalayez at all! I should know, I worked with him for three years!"

Yvon's eyelids opened and closed in a slow blink. "Indeed you *should* know what Shalayez looks like. We *all* have photographs of him."

Chagall shrugged uneasily under Yvon's hostile glare.

"This man could be a decoy," Valia Mikhailovitch said. "On this evidence, one cannot be sure. But for certain that *is* Lucinda Court-Ogg."

Chagall appeared lost as to the significance.

"Miss Court-Ogg – or Marsh – works for British Intelligence," Yvon explained. "As you will know – *if* you've read the files. She was heavily involved in his abduction."

Chagall shifted uncomfortably.

"So what moves have been made, Kulik?"

His deputy resident said: "They took immediate precautions of putting someone on the train at the last minute. All seats are pre-booked so he will not have a seat – "

For the first time in a week Yvon laughed aloud; an unpleasant sound. "I think our trained agents are able to cope with such discomfort."

"Quite," Kulik smiled. "He will keep an eye on them. The train goes north, then at Östersund veers west through the ski resort of Åre, then over the Norwegian border to Trondheim."

Yvon grunted. "They will not get that far."

"The man on the train?" Chagall asked.

413

"Certainly not," Yvon retorted. "This is a job for professionals." He turned to the woman. "Captain Mikhailovitch, you will join the train in good time before the border. With your own team."

She inclined her head. "Understood, Comrade Colonel." He noted with pleasure her first use of his title. "An aircraft is waiting. Nikolai Shalayez will not reach Norway."

14

The long brown caterpillar of a train, with its yellow trim and crown-and-hunting-horn emblems, shrugged away from the low platform.

Lucinda squeezed Shalayez's hand. "We've done it, Niki my love," she whispered.

He grinned at her stupidly. This was a dream come true.

The overhead cable spat and sparked as they crossed points and gathered momentum. Shalayez lay back in the plush red seat with its padded headrest and looked around him. He had a Russian's love of railways.

At home people treated rail journeys as an adventure. From being dour and uncommunicative they would suddenly become transformed by the heady sense of freedom the train gave them. Total strangers in the compartment would become like long-lost friends. Vodka and packed lunches would be shared over the latest anti-Politburo jokes. Had you heard the one about Gorbachev and the Ukrainian farmer? Or the commissar and the knicker factory? Black-market deals would be struck and goods exchanged during a steady supply of tea from the bubbling samovar.

But Shalayez had seen nothing like the Swedish train before. It was so smart and luxurious with thoughtful extras for the convenience of passengers: a row of coat hangers on a rail by the door, and a water container with plastic cups in each carriage. And the lavatories were spotless, unlike the evil-smelling units on Soviet trains.

His spirits soared as he soaked up the luxury and enjoyed the soft-sprung vibration of the train as it sped away from the suburbs of Stockholm. Houses gave way to an endless vista of snowfields and ranks of silver birch glistening beneath a breathless blue sky.

Villages of clapboard bungalows and chalets with stylish canted roofs would suddenly flash past, splashing their primary colours against the ice-white backdrop. Then, as quickly as they had appeared, they would be swallowed up by swathes of frost-feathered pine. Then a frozen lake, mist wreathed over its flat silvery surface. Another village, another startling blur of colour.

Lucinda could see the joy in his eyes as he watched through the window and it made her heart sing. Suddenly she realised how hungry she'd become. "C'mon, let's find the restaurant car and have something to eat."

After buying coffee and expensive open sandwiches from a pretty but offhand waitress, they settled down again to watch the passing landscape.

"It's quite beautiful," Lucinda said.

"It reminds me of Russia," Shalayez murmured as he cupped the hot coffee in his hands. "The silver birch tree is the symbol of Russia – also here in Sweden they say."

"It was the first tree to grow after the Ice Age, apparently."

He raised an eyebrow and laughed. "What a wise head on such young shoulders."

"I wish it was," she replied ruefully. "So much has happened to me in the last few months that has left me confused and unsure."

"Like me?"

She touched his hand. "You're the one thing I am sure about, Niki. I'd never have believed I would fall in love with a man who is – yes, I suppose you are old enough to be my father."

He looked pained.

Lucinda dismissed his expression with a shake of her

head. "No, no, Niki. I've grown up since then. Age means nothing when two people fall really in love. I know that now. Tomorrow either one of us could be dead. Love is too precious to waste. What others think doesn't matter. Besides, I wouldn't want you to be younger."

He laughed. "They say a man reaches the peak of his prowess when he is nineteen – only no one told me then. What a waste!"

She shared his mood. "I remember nothing wrong with your prowess."

He looked serious. "There was a time – when I do my work on the project at Sary Shagan – I lose my appetite to make love. It disappoints my Katya, but there is nothing there."

"Maybe you just didn't love her so much any more. Or perhaps she didn't love you as much as I do."

He didn't reply. There was a sadness in his eyes as he looked out at a passing river as it swirled fitfully between two snow banks.

"You never talk about her, Niki. You can, you know. I'll understand."

"There is no point. It is all in the past." He looked back to her. "Now we have a future. That is what I must think about."

"A future with me?"

"If that is what you want?"

"I want."

They held hands for a long moment. Then he reached out and plucked one of the linen alpine flowers from the table display and tucked it behind her ear. "There. A symbol of our love."

"You're more like your old self. Like when we first met in Moscow."

His face lightened at the recollection. "Ah, golden days, little Lucy. You remember we eat those kebabs in Gorky Park?" They laughed at the shared memory.

She said: "Since you arrived at our embassy we've

417

had no time alone." She looked steadily into his eyes, studying his reaction to her. "When we get to our hotel at Åre . . ."

"Yes?"

"The first thing I want to do . . ."

"Yes?"

"Is to make love again."

"Yes?"

"Yes."

His grin was wide and boyish. "Yes."

Following Shalayez's disappearance, Brian Hunt had shared the others' sense of futility. They were all at a loose end now, just waiting until Janne Reis came up with some news.

The consensus amongst them was that the Russian was back in the hands of his countrymen. If so, it might be several days before they received confirmation, and the thought of sitting on their hands until then was frustrating in the extreme.

It was worse for Hunt. Now it was over he had to face the future. That last mountain was crossed and his request would have to go in to be returned to his old regiment. His SAS days gone forever.

What a price! Yet still he couldn't bring himself to hate Gabby for what she'd done. In fact, he could hardly get the mental picture of her face out of his mind. Still she haunted him.

He downed another Scotch in the embassy bar.

"Knockin' 'em back a bit, Brian," Big Joe Monk observed as he strolled in. He nodded at the half-empty bottle on the table. "And drinkin' alone? Bad sign that."

Hunt made light of it. "Antidote to boredom, Joe, that's all."

"Like Christmas all over again?"

Something jarred. "What?"

"You were smashed out of your skull over Christmas, remember?" Monk showed his big teeth. "Till I saved you from yourself. Is there some problem? Anything you'd like to talk about?''

Hunt was irritated. "What's this, your new job as the Regiment's padre?''

"Yeah, ask Auntie Joe.''

"Piss off, Auntie Joe. I'm bored, that's all.''

"Happen you won't be if old Janne Reis turns up with Shalayez. It'll be all hands to the pump again.''

"Not much chance of that.''

Monk joined Hunt on the sofa and helped himself to a modest splash of whisky. "Old Ralph Lavender seems to think there's a chance. Mike wanted to get us out on the next flight, but old Lavender insists we stay around in case something turns up.''

Hunt welcomed a topic that would drag his mind away from his personal problems. "Lavender's been very cool about the whole thing. I thought he'd blow a gasket when he heard about it. He treated it all very philosophically. Actually asked about my headache.''

"He's an odd fish and no mistake.''

"I doubt we'll cross his path again. He won't be operational after this little fiasco.''

Monk sniffed. "But they're a crafty bunch some of these Int. boys. Fall in a cow pat and come up smellin' of roses, some of 'em. It's all down to the old school bit.''

"Lavender's *new* school, Joe, or hadn't you noticed?''

"I still wouldn't trust him not to pull off some stunt.''

"As long as it doesn't involve us.''

Monk shrugged. "Say, Brian, when you've finished your liquid lunch, Len and I were thinking of doing some skiing in the park. Fancy joining us?''

"You're on. Bugger all else to do.''

The instant he awoke, Nikolai Shalayez knew that there was something different. He could smell it in the atmosphere, sense the unease in his mind.

Yet everything appeared the same as before he'd

drifted into sleep, except that outside it was almost dark. Opposite him Lucinda was dozing like many others in the carriage. Some were reading.

The train had slowed as it approached a town and the crossing-bells chimed a sedate warning as they passed through. An endless line of timber wagons groaned by in the opposite direction.

He tried to relax. Still he couldn't.

Outside the light had gone and he studied his reflection in the glass. Then he knew what it was. In the mirrored image of the compartment he saw a face that hadn't been there earlier. A man with dark hair and scowling eyebrows was reading a newspaper in a corner seat across the aisle. There was a dark mole on his cheek.

Shalayez twitched involuntarily, as though he'd accidentally touched a live wire.

Lucinda stirred and opened her eyes. Immediately she noticed his discomfort and leaned forward. "What is it, Niki? What's the matter?"

He motioned her to keep her voice down. "The man who I see at the station. He is on this train."

"What man?"

"The man with the black coat and the mark on his face. Remember?"

She was puzzled momentarily, then she recalled. "Oh, *him*, vaguely, yes. Why?"

Shalayez looked horrified. "Why? I tell you why. I tell you then who he is."

"I thought you were – well, sort of guessing. Had you seen him before?"

He shook his head. "No, but I know his type. He is one of them."

"Don't be ridiculous, Niki! You can't possibly know. You're letting your imagination run away with you."

"I tell you, Lucy, you don't live in the Soviet Union, so you do not recognise such people."

She tried to be patient and understanding. "He's per-

420

fectly entitled to travel on this train like everyone else."

"And in *this* carriage?" Shalayez hissed.

"A coincidence?" Even as she suggested it, she experienced a sudden doubt herself. Niki seemed so sure; so much so that perspiration had broken out on his forehead like a fever.

"When we get off the train, he will see us. They will know where we are."

"Mr Lavender will send help. Anyway, that is only one man. You can't get to Åre faster than the train. Your enemies can't get anyone else there quicker than our people."

Shalayez gave a derisory laugh. "That man may be a professional assassin."

"There's nothing we can do now." She still didn't believe he was right.

He thought for a moment. "At least I can see if it is just in my mind."

"What are you going to do?"

"We are at a station," Shalayez replied, climbing to his feet. "I shall see if he follows me. He will have to find out if I get off."

Lucinda paled. "For goodness' sake be careful, Niki."

"I will," he whispered, and was gone.

At the end of the carriage, he stopped to extract something from his bergan in the luggage rack before continuing to the next car.

Glancing back through the window of the inter-carriage door he could see no movement. He breathed a sigh of relief. Perhaps, after all, he was wrong.

Opening the outer door, he negotiated the high steps down to the platform, slipping and sliding a few paces over the hard-packed snow. Then he paused for a few minutes, enjoying the icy sharpness of the air after the confines of the compartment. From the corner of his eye he noticed another door open farther down the train. A figure in a dark coat climbed out and stamped his feet for warmth. It could so easily have been just another

421

passenger snatching the opportunity to stretch his legs.

Shalayez wandered slowly back to the steps and climbed aboard. He shut the door, then hesitated for a moment, deep in thought. Then he came to a decision. He edged his way rapidly down the corridor until he came to a toilet that was vacant. He slipped inside and slid the bolt home.

Shortly after, the train jolted into life without warning, and smoothly gathered speed on the next leg of its journey. That would be Åre. Shalayez looked at his watch. Under an hour to go. And it was likely to be his last hour of freedom. At the ski resort he would be trapped. Unable to go on to Norway until help arrived, and unable to escape the all-seeing eye of the watcher with the mole on his cheek.

To get so far and fail! It would have been better if that man at the bus shelter in Stockholm had shot him dead.

A cold shiver ran through his bones and he braced himself to carry out his decision. He stood up and opened the bolt. Peering both ways down the corridor he was surprised to find it deserted. There was no sign of the man with the mole on his cheek. His plan receded. It *had* been his imagination after all.

He stepped out awkwardly, unable to keep his balance as the rocking train gained speed. Walking like a sailor on a rolling ship, he made his way back towards his carriage.

He'd passed before he realised, stepping through the concertina-joint between two cars. The man with the mole was reading his newspaper in the side exit alcove.

Shalayez stepped back. The man was hastily stuffing the paper into his coat pocket.

"*Kotoriy chas*?" Shalayez asked casually.

"No," the man answered spontaneously, taken by surprise. He hesitated, fumbling his words. "I'm – I'm sorry, I don't understand?"

But he was too late. A slow smile crossed Shalayez's face. "That is some special newspaper, comrade. You

422

have been reading it all day," he continued in Russian. "Don't play games with me."

The volume of the train noise seemed to grow as the men confronted each other. The man's scowl deepened. "All right, Shalayez," he said at last, giving up the pretence and replying in Russian. "But you may as well know *your* game is up. My job was just to follow you, but now you give me no choice. Our orders are to shoot you or persuade you to return. You had better make your choice *now* – and be quick about it!"

Shalayez could almost read the man's eyes. Evidently he had been assigned only to watch and report, but now he had the chance of greatness thrust upon him. His eyes glinted with thoughts of the glory he would have if he took the traitor back himself.

As the watcher reached inside his coat, Shalayez drew the M67 clear of his anorak pocket and fired one round into the man's chest.

The sharp bark of the pistol was absorbed by the noise of the train as the force of the shot slammed the man back against the door. There was a look of total surprise on his face as he slid down to the floor, his legs outstretched. The head lolled and a small gurgling noise came from his throat. A thin trickle of blood crawled down from the corner of his mouth.

Shalayez was stunned by his own action. But abhorrence was quickly consumed by panic. A thick snake of stinking blue cordite smoke twisted slowly around the confines of the corridor.

He looked quickly both ways. Miraculously there was no one about. But in the next carriage a blue-jacketed ticket inspector was working his way slowly down the aisle. Shalayez estimated he had a minute. Perhaps more, but probably less.

He stepped over the body and released the window, thankful as the blast of sub-zero air swept in and sucked out the acrid stench of death. Shalayez stooped, hooking the man beneath the armpits with both hands. Strug-

423

gling, he managed to lift the body up to the window. But the weight was too much, and he dropped it again.

This time he opened the outer door which threatened to wrench his fingers from their sockets as it caught in the slipstream. The body leaned sideways half protruding. Terrified that he'd lose his grip on the door, Shalayez pushed his boot against the man's torso. A few more inches slid grudgingly through the gap. He began stamping furiously as though on an insect. He kicked madly, again and again, until suddenly there was more weight outside the train than in. A final kick and the body was gobbled up by the slipstream, vanishing into the night.

Shalayez felt the vomit clawing at his throat. He slammed the door shut, heaving at the effort.

In the next carriage he heard the inspector asking for tickets.

Shalayez opened his eyes and looked down. A single shoe.

Gingerly, he picked it up like something contaminated and hurled it out of the window, as far as it would go.

He slammed the window shut and fell back against the corridor wall, still not believing what he had done.

"Ticket please, sir."

Shalayez gulped and smiled weakly. "I am sorry . . .?"

The inspector repeated in English, adding: "You do not feel well?"

"I am good, fine. Thank you." He handed over his ticket.

Outside, the frenzied cloud of spume that trailed in the wake of the train was whipped high into the air. Only slowly it drifted back down to earth. The mantle of white crystals settled over the smashed body on the track side, obliterating all traces.

A solitary black shoe hung on the stark skeleton of a bush like an obscene fruit. As the toe filled with snow the twig snapped under the weight.

Before morning there would be nothing to be seen.

*

424

Captain Valia Mikhailovitch watched as her three-man team loaded their kit and skis onto the single-engined monoplane.

She had taken the precaution of approaching the free-lance mercenary pilot at Bromma airfield the day she had arrived in Stockholm.

He was on Yvon's 'special agent' list, known to fly occasional loads of marijuana up from Spain. It gave the GRU the hold it needed to ensure his co-operation. Still there was no way she would trust the cynical Swedish pilot with his obvious love of canned Pripps. She distrusted men with beards and the long blond hair which curled at the shoulders was anathema to her military outlook. Yet, although she failed to admit it to herself, she quite liked his steady blue eyes. She didn't object to his silent lascivious stares when she was around.

But still she would not trust him. For money he would do what was required, but no more. Probably less if he could get away with it. However, he had been as good as his word to date: the aircraft had been on constant standby every day for an event such as this.

Her enthusiasm to get under way showed itself in a tight-lipped impatience. Already, the opportunity to recapture Shalayez had been deprived her, by the bungling bureaucrats at the Soviet Embassy who had withdrawn her team at the vital moment, in panic over Alf Nystedt's assassination.

She had already fired an effective shot across the bows of the SAS team by blowing up their van; now she was certain they had successfully put a back-up plan into operation to extract Shalayez from the embassy. She wasn't sure of the details, but she did know that Hunt's black Saab had been involved.

Deuce, she conceded, thinking in terms of the tennis she enjoyed playing in the summer months back home. But the match was far from lost yet.

And it was a match that had become unusually personal. A strange twist of fate found her pitted once more against old adversaries. Although she doubted that they themselves knew.

The information that Kulik had extracted from the Fiscex executive Peter Burke was to confirm what she had suspected. There had only been one full name to go on, and the Christian names of the others. But it had been enough for the Ryad computer at GRU head-quarters, which did its best to track the activities and careers of the cream of NATO special forces, and to build up dossiers on individuals. Their strengths, weaknesses, and preferred tactics. Know thine enemy was the maxim.

And Valia Mikhailovitch knew this particular enemy far better than she guessed they would ever have imagined.

She herself had never grown up with any aspirations to a military career. Although looking back, she realised she had always been a bit of a tomboy, preferring the company of the young lads of the village to that of her girlfriends. And even then, eager to be accepted as one of them, she would often be the first to climb the highest tree in the orchard or to swim the river in summer. It was not long before the boys came to regard her as their leader, although it was never put in so many words.

At school she was academically bright, showing an early flair for foreign languages. And in all types of sport, too, she excelled, and joined the local branch of DOSAAF, the military-sponsored sports club for Soviet youth. There she continued to prove her prowess in skiing and mountaineering, swimming and rifle-shooting, and even parachuting.

It was only a matter of time before the branch principal recommended her for entry to the Central Army Sports Club, the ZSKA. If she had any hesitation it evaporated when she learned that, not only would she be well paid and have the opportunity to travel and other privileges, but she would also be awarded the rank of lieutenant. This was in order to qualify her as an 'amateur' in international competition events.

She attended an officer-training course at the Lenin Komsomol Higher Airborne Command School at Ryazan before returning to ZSKA, where she joined a special unit of women athletes who specialised in skiing, mountaineering and freefall parachuting events.

She led her team in the 1976 Winter Olympics at Innsbruck, and personally won the silver medal for the Nordic Combined Individual Event. But it was no longer the tomboy village girl with a simple love of sport who mounted the rostrum.

By now, Captain Valia Mikhailovitch was a full member of the *Spetsialnoye Nazhacheniye* – 'Special Purpose' Forces of the USSR. The Spetsnaz. With the wolf as their chillingly appropriate unofficial emblem.

And a new range of less sporting skills had been added to her repertoire: radio-communications, ciphers, survival training, interrogation techniques, explosives and the art of *samooborona bez oruzhiya*, the ruthless 'sambo' discipline of self-defence.

In early 1979 a mixed team of Soviet athletes completed a series of spectacular high-altitude parachute jumps, using new techniques, onto some of the highest mountains in the Urals. The achievement received considerable coverage in the Soviet internal media. The team's leader was Captain Valia Mikhailovitch.

It was no coincidence that within the year the USSR had invaded Afghanistan, and specialist Spetsnaz units were parachuting into remote mountain areas to conduct intelligence-gathering and surveillance operations against the *Mujahideen* resistance fighters.

It was there that she first came across her shadowy adversaries, members of the British SAS.

In 1980 there were constant rumours of a three-man team of Britishers assisting the rebels to direct and carry out demolitions and ambushes in classic guerilla-warfare style. Two such operations in particular were a spectacular success, but resulted in the Soviets moving into the region in force.

Due to the increased risk of discovery, the British team was evidently ordered to withdraw. Although they hadn't known at the time, they had made the correct decision. Twelve hours after they had fled their latest village base, Captain Valia Mikhailovitch led an assassination squad of Spetsnaz troopers. They landed by freefall parachute on the high peaks above the village. Two of their number died in the attempt, and a third was paralysed for life. But the survivors successfully stormed the village at first light, when twenty rebels were killed and ten were taken to Kabul for interrogation.

Nevertheless, the escape of the elusive Britishers left a bitter aftertaste.

Later, with the benefit of the interrogation results from Kabul, and information culled by GRU intelligence officers operating over the border in Pakistan, the identity of two of the three SAS was established by comparing the information with existing computer data at GRU headquarters in Khodinka.

The names were Captain Michael Ash and Sergeant-Major Brian John Hunt.

Three years later one of the SAS men returned alone and this time, it later transpired, his Government had placed no restrictions on his activities in assisting the rebels. For nine months he wreaked havoc on the Soviet occupying forces. It was almost possible to locate his presence merely by following a line of map pins indicating scenes of the latest disruption: sabotage of power supplies and convoy ambushes.

Valia Mikhailovitch was given the task of locating and destroying the thorn in the side of the Soviet and Afghan armies.

Only once more fate was to take a hand and, at about that time, the Britisher vanished, just as quickly and mysteriously as he had come.

His identity was never confirmed, but Valia Mikhailovitch had no doubt. That man was Brian Hunt.

Now honoured with the distinguished Red Banner

medal, she had been transferred to the headquarters Spetsnaz company of the Northern Fleet. For the past three years she had spent her time training fellow officers in advanced Arctic warfare techniques, and in studying Scandinavian languages. Except for four months of each year, from December to March. That time was devoted to providing high-risk surveillance studies of the annual NATO manoeuvres in Norway. Her particular task was to report on the deployment and techniques of the West's special forces in the area. Her team achieved this by posing, with false identity papers, as hunters or winter-sports enthusiasts, whilst making full use of their camouflage and concealment expertise.

Last year, her Fleet HQ had identified one particular SAS team's identity from intercepted Morse transmissions and by cross-referencing 'fingerprint' tapping patterns on computer. They matched those monitored in Afghanistan in 1980. The names of Ash and Hunt came up on the print-out.

It was perhaps an indication of the calibre of her old adversaries, she thought, that they had been the first team ever to discover that they were under her surveillance.

Valia Mikhailovitch felt no bitterness, no need for vengeance. Just a natural respect for a proven equal and a fellow professional. But she did feel that she almost knew the man Brian Hunt personally. Now she would even recognise him in the street if she saw him. He and his team would prove an interesting match against her own, should they ever be put to the test. And, if Brian Hunt's men *were* guarding Shalayez, then that test of strengths was likely to occur within the next few hours.

Her most trusted ally in her team of 'wolves' was Sergeant Ustin Petkus, who was now supervising the loading of the aircraft. Petkus was a *stariki*, a Spetsnaz veteran who had seen action at the time of the Czechoslovakian uprising; then in Angola, El Salvador and Nicaragua before he joined her team. Their missions together in the mountains of Afghanistan had forged them into a partnership of steel. A hard and cynical professional, with iron-grey hair and a body built like a tank, Petkus was also a total opportunist who worked the Soviet Army system as though it had been invented for his own personal pleasure and comfort. It meant that she and her team were never short of the best rations and best equipment.

An unspoken fondness had grown between them, yet the one-time heptathlon champion never said a word out of place. Just his eyes sometimes let her know that he would be willing to bed her if ever she wanted it.

It was a situation that Stepan Litvinov assumed had already happened, she knew. And that really galled her. In fact, more than once she had been tempted to take up Petkus's unspoken invitation, and only the fear of giving Litvinov the pleasure of being proved right had decided her against it.

Litvinov was a corporal and downhill ski medallist who was surprisingly well-educated for an NCO. He was tall, dark and with a slim athletic build. He was also the most politically motivated soldier she had ever had the misfortune to work alongside. She found it loathsome and disconcerting the way his coal-black eyes would burn with an inner passion when he spoke of political ideology. But Valia Mikhailovitch daren't be too scathing in her reluctant conversations with him, as he was widely suspected of being on the payroll of the KGB's Third Directorate, whose job it was to spy against dissent within the armed forces at all levels.

Instead she left the goading in Petkus's big and capable hands. Fearlessly he would delight in winding up or shocking the uptight Litvinov with his outrageous statements. In his turn the corporal would tend to clam up, quite aware that the sergeant would have no compunction in crushing him like an insect if the need arose. On the plus side Litvinov was a competent and efficient soldier, if a little short on imagination for the special forces.

Frustrated by Petkus, he would more usually vent his ideological lectures on the baby of the pack. In his mid-twenties, the Lithuanian-born Yuri Popov had the bright open features of an innocent. Always smiling, he had crinkly blond hair that fell over his lineless forehead in what Petkus provokingly described as 'kiss curls'. The youngster took the ribbing in the same way that he did Litvinov's endless ideologue – with a boyish good humour. More than once she had the chance to admire secretly Popov's handsome physique; he was an accomplished gymnast and still never missed an opportunity for a punishing work-out or circuit training programme.

Now Petkus crossed the snow-covered apron to her. "All is loaded, Captain Mikhailovitch," he grinned knowingly. "We are ready to hunt down our quarry, eh?"

Her eyes sparkled for she knew he shared her mood. But she didn't smile, and spoke with a very level voice. "Thank you, Petkus. Let's just hope our pilot is sober enough to get us there in one piece."

"You are saying?" The big Swede shambled over, huddled in a leather flying jacket with a huge sheepskin collar.

"What is the flying time to Åre?" she asked.

Per Kronlund sniffed and squinted up at the clear sky. "It is a little over three hours. But there is a strong wind from the north that we fly into. So – maybe – that slows us down a lot."

"We'll arrive before the train?"

Kronlund gave a sneer of a smile. "Ja, I sure hope so. We land on the lake, see. It is not a proper equipped airfield like here, see, and no radar. Do you like the idea of landing through mountains in the dark?"

She frowned. "We arrive before dark?"

He laughed at the subtlety of his own humour. "That is why we must arrive before the train."

Valia Mikhailovitch smiled stiffly. "Then let's go."

Kronlund said: "I must tell you, the weather report is not so good from the north. It is due to get real bad."

"When?"

"Tonight."

Her eyes were wide. "Then, as you say, we had better get there before the train, hadn't we?"

"I was mistaken," Nikolai Shalayez said.

"You mean he wasn't KGB?" Lucinda asked.

"No, you are right. I make the big mistake," he said dismissively. "See, he must have got off at that last station."

"He got up and left as soon as you did. Just like you said."

Shalayez sounded unusually tetchy. "Yes, but he is not there now."

"He didn't pick up any luggage."

A shrug. "Maybe he did not have any."

"Why didn't he get off as soon as we got to the station? That's usual. That's what most people would do."

"Questions! Questions! My little Lucy, what does it *matter*?"

"What's wrong, Niki? You seem very on edge."

He leaned back against the headrest and closed his eyes. "No, Lucy, I am just tired. Very tired. It has been a long day."

She looked at him curiously but said nothing. He was in a very strange mood.

The train began to slow and the passengers suddenly came alive with activity, collecting their possessions and wearily sharing jokes. Minutes later the train was panting into Åre station where Shalayez and Lucinda filed off onto the low platform area with the rest of the ski-laden crowds.

"It is very beautiful," Shalayez said.

On the other side of the track, the illuminations of the resort threw shimmering coloured reflections over the vast frozen flatness of Åresjön lake, already wreathed in tendrils of rising mist. Echoes of their voices carried across its immense stillness.

Behind them the resort itself crawled up the lower slopes of the Åreskutan peak, the lights from its hotels, shops and restaurants twinkling enticingly between the snow-dusted firs. The fourteen-hundred-metre crest itself, and the twin shoulders of Västerskutan and Blåsten, were reduced to a towering dark presence against a night sky livid with sprays of stars.

"Where do we go?" Shalayez asked.

"The Sunwing Hotel."

"We take a taxi. See, look, there are people waiting."

Lucinda shook her head. "No, we will walk. If we take a taxi or bus someone may remember us."

He looked surprised. "You learn your spy business quickly."

"It's mixing with the likes of Lavender," she answered tersely.

"Wait a minute! Lucy, see there." He jabbed a ski-pole in the direction of the train. "Those people talk to the railway guard."

Lucinda squinted. The light on the platform was patchy and the place was still filled with holidaymakers. "A woman – and three men."

"Do they look like skiers?" he demanded.

She had to admit they didn't, although they actually did carry skis. They were darkly dressed and the men seemed heavily built and menacing.

"One of them's getting on the train," she said. "Not the others."

"How could they know?" Shalayez breathed. "And how can they get here so soon? Our train just gets in."

Lucinda was uncertain whether or not to share the Russian's paranoia. The people did seem oddly out of place, and one of them appeared to be looking for someone on the train. Yet they were almost certainly entirely innocent.

"Look, Niki, if you're right or wrong, the best thing we can do is get away from the station as fast as possible. The sooner I can put that call through to Lavender, the safer we will be."

He nodded agreement, unable to tear his eyes away from the train.

"C'mon," she urged.

Reluctantly he followed her, sweating under the weight of the heavy bergan, skis and poles. She led the way, taking a short cut up steep paths through snow-covered hotel gardens towards the line of flagpoles which marked the vast Sunwing. It was a gruelling, hot climb despite the bitter night air for which neither were prepared. Thankfully they reached the hotel basement level – only to be greeted by the steamy heat of the swimming pool and sauna complex.

It took a supreme effort to climb further to check in at reception and then find the way to their room. Lucinda was pleased to see the double bed but immediately felt incensed and cheapened. Lavender had arranged the booking.

As Shalayez unburdened his load and fell back on the pillows, she threw open the curtains and stared out at the lights reflected on the vast expanse of frozen lake below them.

She said: "If you *were* right about those people at the station, Niki, then I know how they got here so soon. There are half a dozen skiplanes on the lake. It must be used as an airfield in winter."

Shalayez sprang to his feet and joined her at the window. From their elevated position he could just distinguish the ghostly white shapes of a rank of private aircraft. He slapped his forehead. "Why did I not think of that? So stupid!"

"Well don't go *convincing* yourself that those people were KGB," Lucy chided. "We're safe here until Lavender arrives. In the meantime all you have to do is stay in this room."

He stared out at the lake and lit himself a cigarette. "Another prison, eh? Just like back at your embassy."

She didn't have the strength to argue with him. Instead she dropped onto the edge of the bed, picked up the telephone and got a line.

The number rang three times before Lavender's familiar voice snapped: "Yes?"

"It's your long-lost cousin," Lucinda said. "We're here."

"Thank God for that," breathed the voice at the other end. "Any trouble?"

"None to speak of. But our friend keeps on seeing unfriendly faces."

"*Are* they?"

"Are they what?"

"Unfriendly!" Lavender snarled with impatience.

"How should I know?" she retorted angrily. Then she added: "There were some suspicious-looking characters at the station here. They *may* have been searching the train."

There was a brief pause. "It's probably nothing to worry about. Just sit tight and don't let Shalayez out of your sight for a moment. Nail the bastard to the floor if necessary."

"When?" she asked. "When will you get here?"

"By the morning. One way or another."

"Not before?"

"The morning," Lavender repeated brusquely. "At this precise moment I'm the only one who knows where you are."

Her voice was small. "I'm afraid."

"Don't be. You're as safe as houses. Just have a hearty meal in your room, get Shalayez to soak up some vodka and crash out. By the time you wake up it'll all be over."

The earpiece went dead in her hand and the dialling tone cut in. She hung up.

435

"Well?" Shalayez asked.

"He says someone will be here by morning."

The Russian smiled. "Then at least you have your wish."

"Wish?"

"That we make love."

Realisation dawned as her face lit up brightly. "I'm sorry, Niki, my mind was on other things."

He moved swiftly to the bedside, quickly putting out his cigarette in the ashtray. The sudden and overwhelming relief of being safe and undetected, for at least the next twelve hours, had released in him a sudden surge of passion.

"I'm rock-hard for you," he whispered, laughing in her ear.

"Niki!" Lucinda protested with a giggle, as she fell back against the bedspread beneath his weight.

"I have a confession to make, gentlemen."

It would have been possible to have heard the proverbial pin drop in the expectant hush of the ambassador's office, as Ralph Lavender addressed the hastily convened meeting.

It was bad timing for Sir Timothy Maybush, who had been about to return to his home for the first time since the crisis broke. Similarly Matt Brewster was shortly to leave for his belated birthday celebration.

However, for Mike Ash and Brian Hunt, the news was to be oddly welcome. The daunting prospect of another week or so sitting idly in readiness melted instantly with the intelligence officer's next words:

"Nikolai Shalayez did not depart this building unaided. It was part of a last-ditch intelligence plan to salvage the situation. And I have just received a signal that he is safe on neutral ground, well clear of Stockholm."

If he'd been expecting a round of applause, he was to be sadly disappointed. His announcement was met with

436

the shocked silence of incredulity. Expressions were frozen in amazement, faces slowly darkening as the implications registered.

Sir Timothy was the first to speak, in a low angry hiss: "And just on *whose* authority did you take this action, may I ask?"

"I acted on my own initiative," Lavender replied blandly.

"Good God, Lavender!" the ambassador thundered. "You really are something else!"

"I'll remind all concerned," Lavender whipped back sharply, "that as head of Station in Stockholm, I *do* have adequate authority to act as I see fit."

"An authority you have clearly exceeded," Sir Timothy retorted. "This is not just a case affecting the Swedish Desk, Lavender, it has major international repercussions. To act like this without approval of Century House is total lunacy."

"That will be for my peers to judge," Lavender snapped. "My brief was to get Shalayez to London with the minimum of fuss. That failed due to the incompetence of other parties, thus forcing me to take this extreme – and, as it turned out, highly successful – action."

His eyes avoided both SAS men as he casually cast the blame at their feet. Ash flinched silently at the barefaced nerve, while Hunt seethed at the man's obvious attempt to ingratiate himself with his masters at the expense of everyone else involved.

"So I suggest," Lavender continued quickly, "that we address ourselves to the job of getting our Russian friend into Norway without further delay – and this time *without* mishap."

"Just hold on a minute," Matt Brewster intervened. "Before you start telling everyone what they're going to do, let's just get one thing straight. You say *you* assisted in getting Shalayez out?"

"Correct."

Brewster's handlebar moustache bristled with suppressed rage. "And did that include the brainwave of coshing his guard?"

Lavender averted his eyes from Hunt. "Of course not, Matt," he replied placidly. "That was his own idea. He was supposed to choose his moment and just sneak out."

Hunt knew it was a lie, and no doubt everyone else in the room did too. From their sentry position at the only entrance, it was impossible for the Russian to get out undetected. And an SAS trooper wouldn't leave his position for any reason.

"And that dead body by the bus shelter?" Brewster pressed. "Was that anything to do with you?"

Lavender hesitated.

"We're waiting," Sir Timothy growled.

"Shalayez shot the man. He was a Russian," Lavender said quickly. "I could do nothing to stop it. I arrived with the Saab just too late."

"Shalayez was *armed*?" queried the ambassador.

"Yes, sir. I felt it was only prudent under the circumstances. And the very fact that he had to use the weapon vindicates my decision."

Sir Timothy rose behind his desk in a tower of rage. When he spoke his voice was constrained only with the greatest effort: "Ralph Lavender, I am taking this to the highest level with our Government. I shall demand that you be relieved of your post with immediate effect."

Lavender's eyes blazed back. "Sir, that is your privilege. But I would remind all of you that this is a *covert* operation. Nothing should be done to jeopardise Shalayez's chances of survival."

The ambassador blinked at the challenge. "Wait until you've got away with it, is that the idea, Lavender? Wait until you've scored your success before I rock the boat? Well, no way. I want you out of my embassy and out of Sweden. You're a menace to all of us."

Ash said: "Sir, whatever the rights and wrongs of this,

438

Mr Lavender is right about one thing. Shalayez's safety must be our most immediate concern."

Sir Timothy lowered himself back into his seat. He nodded and reached for his cigarettes. "Yes, Captain, of course, I appreciate that." He flicked his lighter, drew on the flame, and turned to the intelligence officer. "Okay, Lavender, what have you done with the poor bastard? And this had better be good."

Lavender toyed with the lapels of his suit. "He's in the ski resort of Åre. He's quite safe in an hotel. It's the area Mike's people had decided to use anyway."

"How did he get there?" Ash asked.

"By train, mingling with the other skiers on holiday."

"That's why he took all his equipment?" Hunt suggested.

Lavender nodded. "He needed the skis to get across the park, then all the stuff to pass himself off as a *langlauf* skier – it also means he's got all his kit for a cross-country escape with you."

"By God, you took a chance," Ash said. "It's a miracle he hasn't been found by the KGB."

The man allowed himself a conceited little smile. "I sent Lucinda with him."

Ash gaped; this was unbelievable.

"I knew the Russians would expect him to be protected by a bunch of heavies – they wouldn't be looking for a couple."

Hunt grudgingly admired the chances Lavender had taken – even if it was with someone else's life.

Lavender was saying: "They're expecting someone in the morning. The idea is for you to put your original plan into operation and ski with him over the border."

"You mean we do have *some* use for you after all," Hunt sneered.

"Cut it out, Brian," Ash scolded quietly. He turned to face Lavender. "So how do you propose we get to Åre?"

"You can hire an aircraft from Bromma to fly you up at first light. I'll make arrangements tonight."

439

"Just one moment," Sir Timothy intervened. "I've promised Commander Vinberg we'll take no further action without consulting with them. We're in enough damn trouble with the Swedes."

Lavender looked scathing. "I don't think that's very wise – "

"In the wisdom stakes, my friend, you are a positive non-starter," Sir Timothy growled. "I don't want the Swedes claiming we're doing anything behind their backs. I'll sound them out without giving details. If I can get their co-operation, I want it."

"It might slow things up . . ." Lavender began.

"Does it matter if we lose a couple of hours?" Brewster asked.

Lavender shrugged. "The girl did say there were some suspicious characters at Åre station."

"Suspicious?" Ash asked.

"Maybe KGB."

"Sometimes, Ralph," Hunt said, "I get the impression you're just an accident looking for somewhere to happen."

She watched the smoke spiral towards the ceiling. "It's never been like that for me before, Niki. Never."

He was propped on one elbow, looking down at the taut contours of her belly. Slowly, he traced a finger over her breast, finishing in a circular motion around her nipple. "No? Then you are now truly a woman."

She chuckled and handed back his cigarette. "You make it sound as though I've really achieved something."

"Some women never do, you know."

"They haven't had you as a lover then, have they?"

Shalayez gave a soft grunt and swung his legs from the bed. "It is not always like that."

"Not with Katya?"

She saw the muscles of his back tense and realised she shouldn't have spoken.

440

Quickly she said: "I'm sorry, Niki, I was curious. I shouldn't have asked."

He stood up and padded across to the window. She thought how lean and strong he looked naked. You wouldn't have expected it when he was dressed; his height tended just to make him look thin. "I told you the past is finished, Lucy."

"I know, I'm sorry."

He turned to face her and his expression had changed to one of adolescent mischief. "I am really hungry now. So much exercise. Let's eat!"

"We can't go to the restaurant. I'll order something for the room."

"And some good vodka maybe. To celebrate."

"Your freedom."

"Your womanhood."

They shared the joke together, and then Lucinda attempted to ring reception. It came up engaged, and again the next two times she tried.

At last she said: "I'll have to go down. It won't take a minute."

"You must be careful."

"I will, Niki, I promise. I shall remember all my training in how to be one of Mr Lavender's ace spies."

He watched contentedly as she pulled on her pants and dressed quickly in snug corduroy jeans and a patterned après-ski sweater.

Running her fingers through her dishevelled hair, she peered quickly at the mirror. Then, blowing him a kiss, she slid quickly into the corridor and took the stairs down to the reception area.

Although her spirits were high, warning bells suddenly began to ring in her mind. She remembered her promise to Shalayez, and slowed at the foot of the staircase. Cautiously she peered around the pillar.

Her heart stopped.

Instantly, she recognised something about the woman talking to the receptionist. She was short and muscular, and there was a familiarity about her stance. Lucinda was certain it was the same woman she had seen at the station earlier.

Instinctively, Lucinda drew back up the staircase, her mind racing. No, don't panic, she told herself. Check again.

She edged forward and scanned the lobby. Three men in dark ski clothes stood in a silent group, studying each hotel guest who passed.

There was no doubt.

15

They came at midnight.

They were very professional. Although Lucinda had been waiting for three long hours, when the moment came it took her by surprise. Of course, it may have been that she never really thought it would happen; such a thing was quite beyond her comprehension. Or it may have been because of the nagging fatigue that her guard had slipped.

Without warning the door splintered. Such force was used that the lock was wrenched from its mounting. As the door swung open she expected there to be a split-second of delay before anything happened. But there wasn't, because a second man was already crouched in the corridor with both hands clasping the heavily silenced pistol.

She had thought she would have the chance to talk to them, stall them.

Her lips parted to speak, and the first round blew off the roof of her mouth, shattering her teeth. Her body jumped involuntarily back against the bedhead, the rear of her skull exploding in a vermilion spray. A grey slime splashed over the expensive wallpaper and began to trickle slowly down towards the floor.

Another shot ripped a hole in the ski-jacket that hung on the stand, the dark shape mistaken for Shalayez.

Young Yuri Popov swung in first while Petkus and Litvinov remained covering from the door. He kicked open the bathroom door. "The room's clear. He's not here."

Petkus followed in and crossed to the window, throwing aside the curtains. The balcony was deserted and there were no tell-tale footprints in the snow.

As he turned back to face the room, Captain Valia Mikhailovitch entered.

"The bird has flown," Petkus announced matter of factly.

She glanced at the ugly mess on the bed and flinched inwardly.

Young Popov stood looking down at the remains of the girl, his skin quite pale. "Did you have to shoot her in the face?"

Petkus shrugged. "I'm still not used to this thing." He lifted up the new issue PRI automatic pistol with its cumbersome silencer. "I was aiming for her body-centre."

Popov shook his head.

"Learn, Yuri, learn," Petkus growled and pushed the body aside. The M67 pistol was half-hidden beneath the pillow. "Didn't anyone ever tell you the female was the deadliest of the species?"

Valia Mikhailovitch said: "Don't stand gawping, Popov. Cover it up with the bedspread."

Litvinov struggled to force the damaged door back into its frame. "We shouldn't have waited so long," he muttered.

"I didn't ask you," Mikhailovitch replied tetchily. She turned to Petkus. "If Shalayez left the hotel, it wasn't through the front."

"I know, Captain. One of them must have spotted us. Probably at the station when we farted around after that clown who was *supposed* to be on the train. What *did* happen to him?"

"It doesn't matter," Mikhailovitch said dismissively. "The point is, Shalayez has taken flight. We must alert our people at the border in case he's made a dash by car."

"He wouldn't be that stupid," Litvinov opined. "Besides, he had skis with him."

"His cover for the train journey," Petkus replied sarcastically.

"Not necessarily," the captain cut in. "Why get off the train here, so close to the border, if it wasn't to cross by some other method? Why not ski?"

"Alone?" Petkus wasn't impressed.

"The people at Central Station said only *he* carried skis, so maybe this girl wasn't going with him," she said thoughtfully, pacing the room. "Besides, she clearly wasn't very experienced and would hardly be escort material . . . unless . . ."

"What?" Litvinov pressed.

Valia Mikhailovitch stroked her chin. "I think we interrupt them here. Before they are ready to go. Maybe tomorrow our friends of the SAS arrive to take Shalayez over the mountains."

Petkus frowned. "It would be a good idea. We would never find them off the roads. These Swedish mountains are the last wilderness of Europe."

"See, his skis are not in the room now," Popov pointed out. He knelt and picked up two discarded ski-straps used when the equipment was being carried. "And his rucksack is missing."

"You think he panics and tries to go alone?" A slow smile broke across Petkus's granite face.

The captain made a decision. "There are two choices. Either he is hiding in this resort or he makes his bid for freedom. And if he does that, which way does he go? To the north of the road, or to the south?"

Petkus chuckled, jerking a thumb at his shoulder. "He won't climb *that* mountain, for sure! Not until the ski lifts operate in the morning."

She nodded her agreement. "Then it would be south. Sergeant, take Popov with you to the lake and see what you can learn. I'll make inquiries here. We'll meet in one hour."

*

Nikolai Shalayez was still in a hot sweat when he reached the lakeside, despite the fact that the night temperature had plunged to an intense thirty below zero.

All the time he had negotiated the pathway down from the Sunwing swimming-pool complex to the edge of the lake, he had been glancing over his shoulder. But there had been no sign that he was being pursued.

As soon as the metal edges of his skis began to hiss on the sheet ice of the lake he felt relief ebb through him. For the first time he began to believe he could make it after all. He pounded on in long easy strides across the hard snow crust, until he was swallowed up by the ghostly vapour that hung suspended in the still frozen air above the surface, and his confidence soared.

An uncanny silence pressed in around him in the icy fog, so that he was aware only of his laboured breathing and the scrape of his skis. His mind wandered as he pushed on into a blind grey world. He began to question if he was doing the right thing. It had been Lucinda's idea. She had insisted that she would be perfectly safe; after all, it was not she the Russians wanted. If there was a confrontation, she would simply tell them lies about where he had gone. They'd have to accept her word and, by the time they found out, it would be too late for them to do anything about it. Help would have arrived.

Meanwhile, he would make for the far side of the lake and climb up to the treeline of the high hill. Once there he would dig an open snowhole beneath the spread of a fir tree. Thankfully he had everything in his bergan that he needed to survive: warm clothes, an Arctic down sleeping bag and some emergency ration cans. He could kindle tree bark for a fire to give himself a little warmth and as for water, he was surrounded by it.

From his hideaway, he would watch the lake and wait until he saw Mike and Brian before making himself known. He had to admit it was a simple but clever plan.

For safety's sake he had given Lucinda his gun for her own protection in the last resort. Personally he never wanted to see another gun as long as he lived. The shooting of the man at the bus shelter in Stockholm had been bad enough, but at least it had happened by accident in the heat of the moment. It had been over in a trice. It was the killing of the man on the train that had truly sickened him. From now on, no matter what, he would manage without the gun.

At last the vapour thinned and the thick ice skin gave way to deep powdery drifts of snow beneath a lightly frozen rind. His throbbing muscles told him that the incline of the hill had begun and soon he was having to herringbone strenuously. The sweat once more broke out beneath his layers of clothing. He'd had enough when he found himself at the edge of the dark line of firs. He removed his skis and fell down exhausted to unstrap the aluminium-and-leather snowshoes from the side of his pack.

Having regained his breath, Shalayez fixed a ski to each side of his bergan, then humped the deadweight onto his shoulders. He'd forgotten just how cumbersome "elephants' feet" snowshoes were as he waddled upwards in a muscle-straining, bow-legged gait. It took an agonising ninety minutes threading between the dark cathedral columns of firs before he reached the edge of the treeline. Above him were the wind-polished dunes of the upper peaks.

A short search located a suitable site for him to make camp. Once out of his snowshoes, he sank up to his thighs in soft snow, and had to wade through its icy wet grip to get to the base of a spreading fir. He screwed the handle onto the lightweight aluminium shovel and set to work, clearing a pit around the tree trunk. He piled the snow debris to make a firm wall against the gathering wind.

He sweated heavily as he worked for an hour to clear a space big enough to spread out his sleeping bag. As soon as he stopped he felt the perspiration start to freeze against the skin of his back, and he cursed his own folly. But by now cold and exhaustion were fogging his mind and he could think of nothing but sleep.

He discarded his anorak and crawled inside the bag, zipping its feathered bulk around him. He waited for the warmth to spread around his body, but it didn't. The ice on his skin turned to cold water that soaked into his bag. His gloves had become wet and now the pain as his fingers thawed brought tears to his eyes. He shivered and dozed fitfully, waking many times to memories that might have been a nightmare or might have been reality. He didn't know and he didn't care.

Dimly he wondered if he would survive the night.

It was the last thought of his confused mind before he was jolted awake.

He sat bolt upright, his whole body trembling and his teeth chattering uncontrollably. For a moment he thought it was still dark, but as he twisted around to peer out of the pit he could see the snowfield above the treeline. Spindrift trailed like smoke across the dunes under a bitter wind, and a myriad pinpoint diamonds dazzled in the pale saffron wash of first light.

Then he heard the steady double throb of helicopter rotor blades echoing around the mountains. Slowly the noise receded, until it was lost beneath the sound of the wind moaning across the peaks.

He felt little better for the snatched few hours' sleep, although his mind was sharper. He made an instant decision. If he didn't act immediately, he could die of hypothermia. He struggled from the sodden sleeping bag and, ignoring the freezing air, stripped himself naked before extracting the change of clothes from his bergan.

The cold swiftly ate into his mind and body. He could

never remember it taking so long to get dressed. The simplest movements defeated him, and buttons and laces proved near impossible. Finally he shook out his board-stiff windproof and struggled into it.

At long last a meagre warmth returned to his torso. His stomach ached with hunger and he began devouring a pack of oatmeal biscuits as fast as he could. He scooped a handful of snow and sucked at it to wash down the last of the dry crumbs, spitting out occasional pine needles.

Sanity, inch by inch, was creeping back. He took the pair of lightweight 8 x 21 binoculars from his pack, strapped on his snowshoes, and plodded up through the trees. There he had a clear line of vision down to the lake and the still sleeping resort of Åre on the far side.

The first thing he noticed was the giant twin-rotored helicopter parked on the edge of the lake. Even at that distance the blurred camouflaged tones were visible together with the Swedish Royal Air Force roundel. But the figures huddled around it were indistinguishable.

He breathed a silent prayer of thanks. Its arrival had awoken him from a sleep that might have gone on to eternity. But otherwise the aircraft's presence meant nothing to him. He tracked his binoculars across the sparkling sugared surface of the lake until he found his own ski-tracks. They were blue-shadowed scars, picked out in relief by the low angle of the light. They were deeper than he'd have thought. He scanned closer in towards the near shore.

Suddenly he understood the surprising depth of his tracks. The four dark skiers were spread out single-file, moving fast along the tramlines he had created during the night. Already they were starting the long climb up to the treeline.

He knew who they were.

At the very best he had a two-hour start.

Ralph Lavender dropped the red blanket back over the shattered head of the corpse. "Yes. That's her," he

449

said quietly. Always pale, his face now appeared totally bloodless.

With a nod Janne Reis indicated for the two ambulance men to wheel the stretcher out of the hotel room. "I am very sorry, Mr Lavender."

The intelligence officer acknowledged the sympathetic words with a terse grimace. Behind him Mike Ash and Brian Hunt looked on silently, their own personal grief at the horrific scene hidden behind expressionless faces. In the short time they had known the girl both had grown to admire her refreshing innocence and simple courage. Her tragic death, in circumstances such as these, was devastating.

Reis said: "If it is any consolation, you could not have reached here in time. The police say it happened at around midnight."

"I'm afraid it isn't much consolation," Lavender said, "but thanks for the thought."

Hunt watched on with a savage anger. How in God's name could the SIS station chief live with himself after this? The girl must have been like a lamb to the slaughter, up against the people who had done this. Lavender had gambled with her life and the Russian's – and lost.

Ash said: "I guess it's a safe assumption that the Soviets have finally got Shalayez."

No one replied; there was nothing much to say.

They filed slowly out of the room and began making their way down to reception.

"You won't be calling for a postmortem?" Reis asked.

Lavender shook his head. "No. But won't your police – ?"

"Not under the circumstances," the blond Swede replied. "Our Government wants this affair closed. My department will take over this matter from the police in the interests of national security. A suitable cause of death will be entered on the certificate. We'll arrange for her body to be flown to Heathrow, if that is your wish?"

"Thanks," Lavender said.

At the bottom of the stairs, Big Joe Monk and Len Pope were talking to a group of Swedish police officers gathered by the reception desk. Seeing the others appear, the two SAS men detached themselves and crossed to meet them.

"The worst?" Monk asked.

Hunt nodded. "She's dead and chummy has gone. They must have him back."

Monk wagged a finger. "Don't jump to conclusions, Brian, not yet. We've been talking to the cops. They've just interviewed a bunch of Swedes who said they saw some crazy skier charging off across the lake about nine o'clock last night, when they were on their way to a disco."

"Shalayez?"

Monk waved aside the interruption. "On their way back to the hotel in the early hours, they bumped into a couple of foreigners who struck them as behaving oddly. They were asking everyone who was about if anyone had been seen crossing the lake – so the Swedes told them about the guy they saw earlier."

"Any description of the foreigners?" Ash asked.

Monk grinned. "The kids were pretty blitzed after a night at the disco. Lucky they could remember their own names. All they said was they were big guys and spoke a sort of impeccable English that didn't quite sound natural. And they both looked pretty mean."

Hunt said: "You remember as we flew in this morning, there was a party of four skiing across the lake?"

"You think that could have been Lucinda's killers going after Shalayez?" Ash asked.

"It's possible."

"It would certainly tie in," Monk conceded.

Ash turned to Reis. "Any chance your friendly pilot could fly us on a recce over the hills on the far side of the lake?"

The big Swede shook his head. "A blizzard is coming this way, Mike, and he has orders to head south. Otherwise maybe he is caught here for days. I'm sorry – "

Len Pope said: "We've got all our kit, boss. Let's take a look-see for ourselves. If it is the Russkies, they've only got a few hours' start."

Ash raised an eyebrow. He clearly liked the idea. "What do you think, Ralph?"

"What about the weather?"

"No problem," Hunt interjected. "If it gets bad we dig in until it passes. If we can't move, neither can the opposition. Nor Shalayez for that matter."

"Then I think it's worth following up," Lavender decided.

"In that case," Reis said, "I shall come with you."

That idea didn't go down well with Ash. "Thanks for the offer, Janne," he said politely, "but there's little point. We'll have to move fast – "

"I am afraid I must insist." The Swede spoke with the utmost good humour, but it was unmistakably an order. "I stay by your side until you are out of the country. No more mishaps." He smiled. "And don't worry about speed. We Swedes can ski before we can walk. Also I serve in the Army, so you have no problems there."

Reluctantly it was agreed. The SAS men would have much preferred to operate without the inhibitions of a Swedish official in tow – even if Reis had proved a more than capable operator so far. They all knew that if the Russians were out there, there was a more than even chance of a confrontation. And in those circumstances they would want the freedom to act without looking over their shoulders.

Lavender was obviously unhappy about it, too, as he watched the party unload their kit from the helicopter before it returned south.

For the intelligence officer it was worse. He couldn't ski and therefore couldn't go with them. He was relegated to waiting and listening for radio reports of their progress, feeling useless and frustrated that he could contribute nothing. And all the time knowing that the

Swedish presence could sway the outcome. He was convinced that Reis would in no way allow the SAS team to engage the Russians. If the Soviets got to Shalayez first, then that would be it.

"Mr Lavender?"

He turned at the sound of his name. The pretty fair-haired receptionist was holding up a telephone handset.

"There's a call for you, Mr Lavender."

Frowning, he nodded his thanks and took it. "Hello?"

"Mr Lavender! How are you? It is Heinrich here."

"What?" He blanched. "How in God's name – ?"

A laugh. "Did I know where you were? Simple really. I, too, am in Åre. But I can't talk now – I want to see you."

To his own surprise Shalayez found his mood of desperation lifting once he was under way. The steep climb to the upper edge of the treeline warmed his body to a comfortable temperature. Even when he mounted his skis there was still no sign of his pursuers. He realised that, if only he could maintain a steady pace, there was no reason why he should not continue to evade them.

He set off westward around the level contour of the hill, his skis slicing a firm grip in the brittle ice crust that had formed overnight. The sunlight was bright and cold in a transparent blue sky. But the fair weather also meant little improvement in the raw air temperature.

His technique improved by leaps and bounds as he progressed. A long-forgotten sense of balance returned from the recesses of his mind where it had lain dormant since childhood. Indeed the modern skis and bindings made it easier than he remembered as he negotiated the series of challenges thrown up by the variable terrain. There were long steady traverses across treacherously steep and ice-encrusted slopes; then plummeting narrow descents between trees which loomed at him from both sides. The snow here was soft and yielding and his skis refused to obey his commands.

453

At one point his slowing snowplough posture broke away, the tips pointing straight down the fall-line of their own accord. He had a choice of deliberately throwing himself to the ground, or going for it. Fear drove him to the latter course and he crouched over, knees bent against the jolts, as his skis bounced skittishly on their downhill run.

With no runout at the bottom he pile-drove into a deep drift. Sprawled upside down and breathless, he found himself laughing crazily at the madness of his predicament.

At least, he mused, no one could have come down the hill faster!

Brushing the ice crystals from his clothing, he re-mounted his skis and set off up a diagonal traverse climb of the next hill.

It was impossible for him to tell how far he had travelled. Although he had been on the move for five hours, the range of low hills had forced him to make many detours. He had to pick his way along river valleys, where unwelcome black holes of icy water gaped beneath the snow bridges. Then he had to take the lowest passes between each pair of hills, and seek the most level contour he could find.

He hadn't been going long before he realised his biggest mistake. Although there were both maps and compass in his bergan, he had been under too much pressure when he started to check his position. Now when he stopped for five minutes to scoff more oatmeal biscuits, and pore over the maps, he realised he was hopelessly lost. He had never seen a close-detailed survey map before – such items were rare in the Soviet Union – and even his mathematical mind found the proliferation of contour lines and symbols totally confusing. He was in a river valley where he sat. But which one? It could be any of half a dozen. He realised too late that to be sure he should have checked his position many times as he'd travelled.

He told himself that he must simply head westward to the Norwegian border, but all the time veer slightly south to take himself farther and farther away from the main road and the most likely source of danger.

A solitary snowflake landed on the map. He glanced up. The clear sky under which he'd started had been swallowed by a bubbling low tide of grey cloud which radiated a pale coral hue. It now filled the heavens, pressing down like the lid on a pressure-cooker, the surrounding peaks melting as though wiped out by an artist's watercolour wash. While he had been on the move he hadn't noticed the gradual lift in temperature to around minus twelve.

By the time he'd repacked his bergan and mounted up, the snow was falling steadily. It landed on the ice crust and began swirling in eddies in the face of the gathering wind. One last glance at the sky and he decided he would not make the mistake of the previous night. Indeed now he couldn't, because he had discarded his sodden sleeping bag.

He sped on, happier in the knowledge that the fresh snow would hide all traces of his ski-tracks. Hopefully that would decide his pursuers to give up the chase.

With visibility fast becoming a total white-out, he slid into the gloomy, eerie shelter of the treeline. Fifteen minutes found a gully sheltered from the wind, and he set about constructing a shelter. Without the fear of the previous night he could think more clearly. His mind returned to his days in the Soviet Army many years before, when he had slept out in the snow as a humble conscript. Surrounded by companions with their crude humour it had been endurable, even enjoyable at times, even though such luxuries as sleeping bags were not considered necessary; greatcoats and a blanket-roll must suffice.

An hour's hard work with the 20-ounce survival knife and he had managed an adequate lean-to shelter of fir branches, lashed together with paracord. He then constructed a low timber wall in front of the shelter to act as a reflector for the fire he would build. The fire itself proved difficult to start, even using the stripped bark from a nearby birch, and the flint-and-magnesium device. After much coaxing it took hold and he began melting snow to make his first hot drink of the day. It took a lot of snow to make, but it was worth the wait while he sucked and grated his way through several bars of rock-hard chocolate.

Sleep became irresistible and his eyelids heavy. The protection of the trees and his shelter could no longer keep out the probing fingers of the blizzard blowing in through the trunks. But he was past caring. He threw more logs on the fire, positioned himself as close as possible, and settled down. He was asleep the instant his head touched the bergan he was using as a pillow.

The blizzard had died away by the next morning, but the steady fall of light snow persisted for the next two days and nights. It obliterated all ski-tracks only minutes after they had been cut.

Meanwhile, on the first morning the SAS team, with Janne Reis in tow, had located the remnants of Shalayez's makeshift first camp. And his discarded sleeping bag. It was an ominous sign.

Equally ominous were the ski-tracks that followed those of the Russian. After a couple of hours Hunt was convinced that there were indeed four pursuers. One of the ski-tracks was also considerably lighter than the other three. It tallied with what they had been told by witnesses back at Åre. That there were four skiers and, yes, they were sure one of them was a woman.

The news had given Hunt an uncomfortable feeling. He remembered the motorcyclist in Stockholm and the strange incident of 'Volga Olga' back in Norway before Christmas.

Was it possible that they were not only up against a

Spetsnaz team, but also the same one they had encountered then?

And as he skied steadily on for hour after hour, his mind kept drifting back. Over the years. To Afghanistan. To the rumours then. The wolf-woman, the *Mujahideen* had called her. The she-wolf. He tried to shake the image of her from his mind, but still it lingered like a bad dream.

He attempted instead to concentrate on the more immediate practical problems they faced. For a start, the team's provisions were adequate but no more. As each man would burn up a full 4,500 calories a day, it meant that the food would weigh an unacceptable amount for such an open-ended journey. They'd decided on sufficient for each man for only three days; they would just have to pare the daily ration to the bare minimum in case it took longer. Speed, after all, was of the essence and additional weight would defeat the object. Fortunately they were spared the curse of heavy quantities of ammunition. Each man took only two spare magazines for the Heckler and Koch HK33 carbine he carried. The weapon had been selected for its lightweight and telescopic stock, which made it ideal for concealing in a bergan. A bonus was its ability to throw a high-velocity 5.56 mm stopping round effectively to around three hundred metres.

It was always known that communications were going to be a problem in the mountains, so they'd opted for one manportable frequency-hopper radio with burst-transmission, via the Skynet 2B satellite, to Hereford in an effort to overcome the problem. It did, however, mean that any communication with Lavender in Åre would have to be relayed from the UK. The unwelcome load of the equipment fell to Pope as the signals wizard, although the others took reluctant turns at carrying the spare battery. For short-distance communications between the group each carried a super lightweight Clansman PRC 349 with earpiece and throat mike attachments.

457

The others had allowed Len Pope to select their civilian windproofs and, as usual, he'd turned up trumps. They were non-military green, lightweight and with ample cargo pockets. On the move no more than a zip-up Norwegian army shirt and thermals would be worn beneath the windproofs. A fibre-pile jacket would be added if it was exceptionally cold, or the going very easy. At night a feather duvet top and padded Mao trousers would be needed when the temperature sank below minus forty. With a sleeping bag and tent sheet added, the entire weight was kept to a modest thirty pounds.

With such a light basic load for personal kit, it was more comfortable to accommodate the other necessary items of survival: each man a lightweight snowshovel or snow saw, heavy-duty survival knife, ice-axe, crampons and 'elephants'-feet'. Pieps location beacons and avalanche-probes also added to the necessary paraphernalia, which included lightweight climbing harnesses, and two sets of 'talking-rope' with communication wire running through its core.

As a result the SAS men found the going fairly effortless, although Reis's lack of recent practice began to tell. Although a more accomplished skier than all the others, with the exception of Mike Ash, his stamina was beginning to fail him towards the end of the first day.

He was more than happy to stop and set to work scooping out a snow-trench, using branches to form a roof which was overlaid with hard-packed snow. The entrance was then sealed until it formed a hole no bigger than the circumference of a man's body. It was less warm than a fully dug snowhole, but was far quicker to build.

He joined the others who were already boiling up beefsteak and dumplings on their naphtha stoves and, unaccountably, adding apple flakes.

Rubbing his hands together, he asked: "No fire tonight?"

"We don't want to attract attention," Ash replied. "Especially if it's a Spetsnaz team out there."

Reis nodded and indicated the gathering momentum of the blizzard. "They won't see much tonight."

"I'm not taking that chance. They might send out a recce patrol. That's what I'll do if the weather gets no worse."

But, to Reis's great relief, it did. They had scarcely finished their meal before they felt the full brunt of the blizzard, lancing through the shelter of the trees like pellets blasted from a shotgun. Each man scurried into his individual hole as the site became obliterated with a fresh deep layer of snow. It was with blessed relief that the big Swede fell instantly into a deep and dreamless sleep.

Two days of steady snowfall followed. Whilst it was not bad enough to prevent travel, it caused distinct disadvantages. All features were erased from the landscape, creating a white haze without dimension which reduced visibility to no more than fifty metres. Disorientation set in, playing tricks on the eye, until each man felt giddy as though he were floating through cloud.

It put the SAS team in a quandary: Shalayez or the following Spetsnaz, or both, could be holed up. The SAS team could ski right past their positions without knowing. If the Russians were of a mind, Ash's men might also ski straight into an ambush.

By radio via Hereford and Stockholm, Janne Reis arranged for another helicopter to overfly the area. But the pilot reported nothing, which was only to be expected given the appalling visibility. With more bad weather threatening, the air search was abandoned.

It was decided to follow the easiest, most natural route towards the Norwegian border as being the most likely course for Shalayez to choose. That was a very hit-and-miss arrangement, but there was no alternative.

Meanwhile they learned from Hereford that Whitehall had granted permission for additional SAS Mountain

Troop teams, and elements of the Mountain and Arctic Warfare Cadre, to mount observation posts in the heights along the Norwegian border. Grid references for the OPs were duly noted. Shalayez may avoid the Russians, it was pointed out, but if he slipped through the net he'd probably die in the wilderness on the other side of the border. They wouldn't find his remains until the snow melted next spring.

It was a sobering thought.

The third day broke bright and clear, but stunningly cold.

Shalayez had only been on the move for an hour when he came across the lake.

From his vantage point on a high peak he could see the vast expanse of sheet-ice glittering below for as far as the eye could see. It was breathtaking in its magnificence.

He extracted his map and studied it. This was the first major lake he had come across, so surely it was Kölsjön? But then, he reasoned, he could easily have missed it if he'd travelled farther south than he'd realised. In which case this could be the even bigger lake of Ånnsjön! Either way, it was impossible to tell . . .

He slumped down, suddenly depressed. He'd had no concept of how vast this wilderness was. Hundreds of square miles of inhospitable, empty mountains with only the remotest hamlets marked on the map – and even those he daren't go near for fear of his pursuers already being there.

Disheartened, he delved into his bergan and pulled out his provisions bag. It offered little solace. Only one pack of dehydrated food remained and a couple of bars of sickly sweet mintcake. Scarcely enough to keep him going for another day.

Already he was aware that he was weaker in himself, despite the fact that his muscles were becoming attuned to the hard, unfamiliar exercise. But he thought he knew what it was. He noticed how dark his urine had become,

on the rare occasions that he went at all. The words of
warning about dehydration that the man called Brian
had given him returned. They'd been talking about the
intended escape across country: You sweat gallons, so
you must drink. Dehydration is a killer!

Yet there was little he could do. He had no stove in
his pack, so he was reduced to melting snow over an
open fire, which took forever. He had to melt a ton
of the stuff for a teaspoonful of precious water. He
despaired, making do on the move with just sucking a
handful of the snow to slake his thirst. At least this day
he had determined to melt enough for half a hot flask of
chocolate to be drunk at midday.

He squinted out at the shimmering white plate of the
mysterious lake. That was another thing! His goggles
kept steaming up and he'd abandoned them in a fit of
anger. Now his eyes hurt and he had to endure a thumping headache. Would it never end?

Again he squinted. Far below he could just determine
four ant-like figures moving steadily west across the lake
surface. Ant-like that was, except that they were wearing
white so that they were almost indistinguishable from
their surroundings.

Could it be? Was it possible that his pursuers had
overtaken him? He frowned. Could they have overtaken
him without knowing, perhaps even kept going at night?
He nodded to himself. Yes, in this icy godforsaken
wilderness it was quite possible. Even as he looked he
was envious of the way they were eating up the miles.
Effortlessly sliding into the shimmering infinity until his
eyes could no longer follow them.

Whilst they were far below it would be best now to
keep to the high ground, he decided. With renewed
vigour he started around the rolling mountain contour,
keeping the lake far below on his right.

Out of the blue he discovered where he was. It was
some eight kilometres later that he stumbled across a
road as the steep slope forced him nearer to the lake

edge, where the going was more negotiable. Pausing to consult the map, he realised this time that he *had* to be on the southern flank of the vast Ånnsjön lake, which stretched some ten kilometres in each direction. Ahead of him the Bunnernäset isthmus, which probed into the seemingly endless white flats, confirmed it.

He'd been lucky to have realised. So easily he could have wandered south into the desperate peaks of the Bunnerfjällen range, which even now were funnelling him back to the lakeside by their mighty presence. With food running low and his strength ebbing, his life expectation would have been numbered in hours.

But he now faced a new problem. His pursuers were ahead of him, gliding fast across the lake in a westward direction. To what purpose, he asked himself? He forced his cold-dulled mind to concentrate as he tried to put himself in their position. For the past two days they'd had no ski-tracks to follow, and no idea whether he was travelling or holing up. What they undoubtedly *did* realise was that they were far more expert skiers. They could move faster, maybe even travel through some of the night deliberately to get ahead of him – it was the one advantage they could be certain of.

He smiled to himself. Mathematical odds. Q.E.D.

His fingers traced along the edge of the lake westward. It paused at the little hamlet of Handöl on the west bank. That must be their destination, it must!

They had reasoned that they could get ahead of him and wait at the first outpost of civilisation. Correctly they assumed that, as a man travelling alone, his supplies would be limited and his morale low. And how right they were! If he had not seen them from his vantage point earlier, Handöl was *exactly* where he would be heading now.

In fact he could still see no alternative. He removed his bergan, and rested thankfully on it as he studied his map closely. Then, after several minutes, he saw a possible solution. There was a fell-station at Storulvån, which lay some eleven kilometres south of Handöl in a remote river valley. The red legends indicated accommodation and, more importantly, a telephone.

Taking Handöl as the apex of a triangle, the fell-station was on the baseline with his current position, allowing him to bypass the hamlet completely. It would take him up a long steady climb over a pass between two peaks. That pass eventually fed down on the other side to the Handölåan river valley and, farther south along its bank, the fellstation.

Satisfied with his decision, he humped the bergan back onto his aching shoulders, mounted his skis, and set off with fresh determination.

*

The Täljstensvalen peak dominated the village of Handöl some 740 metres below, and offered a commanding view over the vast Ånnsjön lake and all approaches from the east.

It was reached by what in summer was a tough but popular climb for hardy hillwalkers. In the depths of winter it was a muscle-searing, tortuous ascent wading up to the knees in soft snow. It sapped the energy, all the time acting to pull against the climber and defeat his best efforts.

Even for Sergeant Ustin Petkus it was hard going, but years of training and dogged determination to allow nothing to defeat him kept him moving relentlessly upwards. Every now and again, when he was well ahead of young Yuri Popov, he would pause, breathe in the fresh clean air and grin down inanely at his trailing comrade.

"Bracing this, eh, Popov?" he would laugh.

Popov, eyes bulging with effort, was unable to speak. He would struggle on, longing to be standing beside the veteran sergeant so that he, too, could take a moment's respite.

But, just as he thankfully reached the older man, Petkus would grin again, turn and set off. Popov, heart throbbing and muscles screaming, bowed his head and followed like an obedient puppy.

"This will do," Petkus said.

He was sitting comfortably on a mound of snow when Popov, drenched in sweat, surmounted the crest. The sergeant seemed none the worse for wear, smiling and breathing normally as he scanned the magnificent white-and-silver vista of lake and snow-dusted forest. He even had a cigarette going, discreetly cupped in his hand.

"We're here?" Popov gasped.

"Fine view. We'll pick up old Niki Shalayez whichever way he comes. Cigarette?"

The young man almost threw up at the thought; he shook his head. "It'll be exposed if the weather changes."

Petkus nodded. "That's why you can start digging a snow-pit as soon as you have your breath back. I don't want our beloved comrade captain coming up here to find us slacking."

Valia Mikhailovitch had been summoned to the hamlet of Handöl, much to her annoyance. The place of her team was in the wilderness where they could plot the likely course of Shalayez. Move and counter-move, gradually boxing him in like wolves stalking a prey. If he was stupid enough to go to Handöl – fine! They could move in for the kill. But in the mountains they could cover *every* contingency.

But that new *chekist* monkey, Colonel Sergei Chagall, had ordered her over the radio to attend the briefing. And she had no alternative but to obey, as he was now in overall charge of the operation to recapture Shalayez. Petkus had suggested that she feign radio failure and just ignore him. That's what he'd have done. But Valia Mikhailovitch didn't work that way. Instead she'd taken that slimy *stukach* Litvinov with her to Handöl. That was the trouble working with women. Even one as capable and good-looking as she was.

"There is no sign of the Britishers," Popov observed.

Petkus sucked on his cigarette. "They'll not be far away. We're sending up that *govnoed* Kronlund this afternoon."

"The one who flew us up here?"

"Yeah, the Swede who looks like Jesus Christ. He's taking his plane up this afternoon, as soon as they can wean him off the Pripps."

"So he'll locate the Britishers – and Shalayez?"

"That's the idea." Petkus looked at the clear sky. "But they'd better look sharp, because I sense this weather is not going to last."

He settled down with his binoculars to scan the landscape below. In the same way that he was sure the weather was due to change, he also trusted his other instinct. Shalayez was nearby. There was the scent of the quarry in his nostrils and that made the hairs at the back of his neck bristle. He could smell him.

It was two hours later before Yuri Popov sat down exhausted by the cavern he was creating in the nearby snowdrift. The skin beneath his white waterproofs was drenched with sweat.

"If you're having a rest," Petkus called out, "then you can put a brew on. Don't waste your time."

Bastard, Popov cursed beneath his breath. But it lacked venom; he had spent too long in the Soviet Army not to be well used to being put upon by senior soldiers and NCOs. The unspoken privileges of rank were all part of the pecking order. Besides, Ustin Petkus was a good man beneath that veneer as hard as an old walnut.

Petkus, too, had come up the hard way and deserved his respect. It wasn't easy to be selected to the ranks of the *razvedchiki* or "scouts" as the Spetsnaz were more popularly called. In its elite formations a code of conduct was demanded that would have been alien to the average Soviet serviceman. It never reached the informality of its Western counterparts, but the very nature of its work required its members to get along together in trying circumstances. Petkus never abused his rank – well, perhaps he did, but he was as likely to craftily put down some superior with a smell under his nose, as he would intimidate one of the soldiers under him. The sergeant had saved Popov's own life more than once, yet he never mentioned or even hinted at it. No debt was owed.

Popov knew he could trust the wily old crustacean, which was more than could be said for that insufferable Party-liner, Litvinov.

He scrambled up to Petkus's vantage point and handed over a mess-tin full of sweet black tea. The sergeant lifted its taped edge to his lips and slurped at it noisily.

"You really think we will stop this scientist, Sergeant?"

Petkus laughed as he drained the hot liquid down his throat. He wiped his mouth on the back of his hand. "You can rest assured of that, Yuri. Our madonna will not stand for failure on this – even if she has to pursue him back into Norway."

"It must be a strange feeling to be a traitor," Popov murmured, staring down at the lake. "To turn against your people."

Petkus shrugged. "There's a good life to be had over there for some." He jerked a thumb in the direction of Norway. "It tempts a lot of people. You've seen it for yourself. You don't believe all the pigshit you are told about the West, do you? Unemployed and starving people, mass strikes and people dying in queues to get into hospitals." He raised his binoculars again. "I wouldn't mind a life there, I can tell you."

Instinctively Popov glanced over his shoulder. "Careful, Sergeant, Litvinov could be back at any time – "

Petkus belly-laughed. "Even on top of a mountain with your balls frozen you are worried about the likes of that *stukach*! See what I mean?"

The younger man smiled at his own timidity. "You have never thought of doing it, then? Of going over? You've had many chances over the years at your athletics meetings in foreign cities."

Petkus took away the binoculars and turned to face his comrade. His eyes were smarting with the cold. "That's no question to ask, arsehead! I said earlier it was a good life for *some*. But what would I do over there? The Army is the only life I know – it's food and drink, even air to breathe. I'd just drink myself to oblivion in such luxury."

But Popov was curious. "But if you were younger – ?"

"For a start I'd stop asking such damn fool questions," Petkus snarled, returning to his surveillance. He added under his breath: "Or maybe just put up my hands when we come across the Britishers . . ."

"But you wouldn't let Shalayez do that?" Popov pressed.

"Shalayez is a traitor. That's different. I'd track a traitor to the ends of the earth." He grinned lustily to himself. "Especially with Comrade Captain Mikhailovitch by my side."

"Sergeant, aircraft!" Popov climbed onto his knees. "Eleven o'clock. About two thousand metres!"

Petkus lowered his binoculars and screwed up his eyes at the speck in the vibrant blue sky, his attention attracted as much by the distant, insect-like buzz of the monoplane as he was by Popov's directions.

He focused his binoculars. "It's the Jesus Christ Swede. They must have sobered him up. Quick, get him on the net. And, remember, use your schoolboy Swedish."

The monoplane circled low over the lake twice, then broke off in a line directly towards their elevated position. It banked right, pulling in a tight circle, round and round again.

The engine noise and the icy buffeting wind prevented Petkus from hearing the conversation Popov was having on the radio. He waited until the trooper had scrambled back up to him. "Yes, that's Per Kronlund. He says he thinks he's located Shalayez's ski-tracks coming in this direction along the lakeside, but he loses them in the trees."

"How does he know it's Shalayez?"

Popov said earnestly: "He says no one is out today, not with the weather that's forecast – but, listen, he thinks he also finds the Britishers about seven kilometres behind. They are making fast progress, but disappear as he approaches."

Sergeant Petkus arced his binoculars away from the lake to the slope below them. He adjusted the focus with his thumb, its feeling almost non-existent after several years of annual frost-nip in Norway.

"Aaah," he breathed. "What have we here?"

Three kilometres distant a tiny figure in torn cam-whites struggled up the pass, just clear of the tree-line.

The unmarked truck was parked at the side of the road on the outskirts of Handöl.

Captain Valia Mikhailovitch approached cautiously, her skis sliding over the hard-packed snow of the track. They hissed noisily as both she and Litvinov edged them to slow their approach.

Ahead the big lamps of the lorry blinked once. Then twice more.

She exchanged a glance with the corporal and nodded. They both had PRI automatics stuffed inside the open fronts of their windproofs – just in case. She would go in first; if there was any trouble Litvinov would take everyone out, even using a grenade if necessary.

The weather-scarred truck was a dull red beneath the grey dribble of slush that had splashed all over its sides and bonnet. Snow was encrusted in the wheel arches, thrown up by the giant cross-country tyres. It could have been any anonymous commercial vehicle, plying any one of a dozen different trades. There were a set of transfers on board to cover each contingency. Only the exceptionally tall short-wave aerial suggested it was anything other than a perfectly legitimate vehicle.

The driver wound down the window. "Yes?" he asked in perfect Swedish.

"Mikhailovitch," she snapped.

"Go round," the driver said and wound up his window.

She removed her skis and stuck them into the snow debris at the roadside by the rear doors. No handles were fitted on those doors which fitted flush so that it would be impossible to prise them open with a crowbar. She knew someone was watching through the tiny fisheye viewing lens hidden in the rear light cluster.

"Mikhailovitch," she repeated irritably, feeling foolish at addressing the doors of a lorry.

A clank of steel bolts came from inside and one door opened slightly.

She stepped up and pushed her way inside, followed closely by Litvinov. The mobile covert communications centre was as compact as it was well-designed. In the dim red light she could determine the layout of the radio consoles at the far end for long, short-wave and satellite transmissions.

A familiar figure sat at the grey steel work-station by the door, and the cigar in his hand explained why the place stank of tobacco, flouting the 'No Smoking' signs.

The rosy-cheeked face beamed benevolently. "Nice of Colonel Yvon to lend me use of this splendid vehicle, don't you think, Captain?" Sergei Chagall asked with a smile. "I am most impressed with the GRU's ingenuity."

Valia Mikhailovitch hid her disdain behind a mask of inscrutability.

Chagall turned abruptly to the two communications technicians working at their consoles. "You two, get out! I expect you could do with stretching your legs for ten minutes."

The captain raised an eyebrow. "That is strictly against

procedure, sir," she said sharply. "No personnel are to leave the vehicle."

The KGB colonel watched her in silence as the two men left. "It is kind of you to tell me what I may or may not do, Captain."

"The rules are clear, Comrade Colonel," she returned, standing her ground. "This is a command vehicle for covert operations. If someone should be seen leaving a supposedly commercial vehicle then suspicions will be aroused. It would be necessary to detonate the emergency charges to prevent it falling into the hands of the Swedes – "

Chagall raised his hand. "And I would remind you that this GRU vehicle is currently under my jurisdiction. Nevertheless, I take your point . . . However, I wish to speak to you in privacy."

Still standing rigidly to attention, she spoke to some point in the middle distance. "*My* team is under the jurisdiction of the GRU, and any questions should be asked via Colonel Yvon in Stockholm. With respect, we are not answerable to the KGB."

Chagall sighed. "Why is it we always find it so difficult co-operating with you people? Captain Mikhailovitch, I am in supreme command of this operation to locate Shalayez, and in effect Colonel Yvon is subordinate to me in this matter. Now do I have to go through the tiresome procedure of radioing him just to instruct you to talk to me?"

Mikhailovitch's eyes flickered down to the KGB man. She was standing on principle, defending her organisation and its professional reputation. As a matter of pride, she realised. Probably misplaced pride, because it did not do to upset the *chekists* too much. It could damage her career.

"Very well, Comrade Colonel," she relented.

"Good. Now tell me, how close are you to getting hold of this delinquent scientist of ours?"

"I think quite close. We have almost certainly overtaken him and we are now in the position to seal off his escape route to Norway."

Chagall waved his hand. "But these Britishers – what if they get to him first? I understand that Swedish security is giving them tacit support – although, of course, the two-faced buggers are denying it."

"If it is necessary, we will take care of them."

"You're sure? How would you stop them?"

"That depends. Probably by ambush. We've been able to raid an emergency cache for ski-mines. We each carry one. So it wouldn't be difficult – even if the Britishers get to the traitor first. We would take them all out – no trace would ever be found."

"Ah," Chagall said. "That is a thing I must talk to you about. Shalayez must be taken alive."

"Sir?"

"Alive, Captain Mikhailovitch."

She was puzzled. "All this time our orders have been dead or alive. May I ask why the change?"

Chagall smiled. "I am in charge now. My people in Moscow have to take a political overview in international terms. We have received a bad reception to our press conference statement and sightings of our submarines. That, of course, does not worry us. But we must be seen to be justified in the end. If Shalayez is dead, everyone will say it is those barbarous Cossacks again! If he is taken alive, he will appear before the television cameras in Moscow and say how he was abducted against his will. General Secretary Gorbachev is anxious that our actions should be seen to be vindicated."

God save us from politicos, she thought, but said nothing.

"So I charge you with his safe return," Chagall continued, nodding in Litvinov's direction. "With your comrade here as witness. *And* I want Shalayez handed over to me personally."

At that moment one of the radio sets began to hiss

and crackle. Chagall looked embarrassed. "Do either of you know how to handle these sets?"

Mikhailovitch nodded curtly to her corporal, and Litvinov stepped briskly forward to don the headset. After a few brief moments' conversation, he looked up. "The traitor has been located to the south of here. He appears to be making for the fell-station. Petkus requests permission to pursue. He also says the Britishers are some seven kilometres behind and closing."

A sly smile crossed Chagall's face as he turned to Valia Mikhailovitch. "Tell your sergeant to follow discreetly so we don't lose him. Meanwhile, we will drive to the fell-station. Shalayez was once a friend of mine – before he betrayed his country. I think it is time that we renewed our acquaintance."

16

Mike Ash had set a blistering pace. During the past three days, progress had been hampered by the need to make compass checks at regular intervals, with back-bearings to confirm their position in frequently white-out conditions. Now at the Ånnsjön lakeside, that became unnecessary.

Moreover they had picked up clear fishscale tracks that almost certainly belonged to Shalayez. They were fresh and unfrozen, and there was no one in obvious pursuit.

As they approached the Täljstensvalen peak, where the tracks branched off towards a high pass, Ash slid to a standstill and waited for the others.

"He's making for the fell-station," he said as Hunt pulled up alongside. He didn't need to look at the map; it was etched indelibly in his mind. "I'm sure of it."

"What happens next?" Janne Reis asked.

"I think we've got him," Ash replied. "Shalayez is almost certainly heading for the fell-station at Storulvån. We'll try to catch him up there."

"That is good." The big Swede grinned. "But let's get on. It is my responsibility that . . ." His voice trailed away.

"What is it?" Ash asked.

"Up there. Two skiers in whites." Reis jabbed his ski-pole in the direction of a long, undulating spur that ran off the commanding peak of Täljstensvalen.

"Christ," Monk muttered. "No guesses who those jokers are."

"They must have been using the peak as an OP," Ash said, his eyes only just able to pick up the skiers against the slightly lighter white of the snow, as they traversed deftly down towards the pass in a continual zig-zag pattern.

"And they will have our friend before we get to him," Reis observed.

The group of SAS men looked at each other, questions unspoken. Ash confirmed it. "Get tooled up. And full comms."

It took no more than three minutes to unload the bergans and break out the HK 33s, or Hocklers as they were called for simplicity. Rapidly checked and loaded, they were then clipped onto the chest for comfort and fast accessibility.

Satisfied that everyone had their radio ear-pieces plugged, Ash pulled down his goggles and began powering up the incline like a man possessed. The others, spurred on by the anticipation of trouble, were close behind, kicking furiously.

Soon they had bridged the pass and were gliding fast downhill, alongside a wooded area on their left which dominated the valley floor. Far ahead, a tiny speck came into view, now virtually clear of the pass and entering the south-running river valley that would take him to the fell-station. There was no sign of the two mysterious skiers.

Ash instantly smelled danger. He'd been in too many tight spots over the years not to trust his instincts absolutely. They rarely let him down. He lifted one pole up in the signal to stop. Four sets of skis scraped to a halt behind him and an eerie silence fell.

No sound came from the trees to their left. To the right the spur crept away up to the dominating peak from where the plaintive sound of the moaning wind just reached them.

Slowly he pointed one pole skyward and moved forward, the team obeying the unspoken order to advance in single file. Without a word being exchanged, each man gathered his poles in his left hand, and unclipped his Hockler with the right. Reis followed their example and cocked his automatic pistol. Alternate members of the group covered the woods on the left and the slope on the right, where avalanche snow debris and occasional rocks offered plenty of hiding places.

Cautiously the column slid forward, one step at a time.

The muzzle-flashes and the distinctive sharp report of Kalashnikov AKS 74s broke simultaneously. They came from the left, in the dark labyrinth of fir trees. And from the right, high up on the spur. The echoes swirled around them, and icy spray whipped at their faces as rounds tore into the surrounding snow.

"TAKE COVER!" Ash yelled, and dived for the snow as the rest of the group broke to the left and right. He pulled round his ski-poles to support his elbows from sinking as he levelled the Hockler. He loosed off three controlled two-round bursts into the woods, then followed up with three more at the spur to provide covering fire as his team spread out.

To his left, Len Pope was already moving into the edge of the wood, removing his skis behind the cover of a massive pine trunk. Janne Reis was contributing with steady, well-placed single shots from his automatic. Meanwhile, Big Joe Monk was out of his skis and scrambling up through the crumbling slope of snow to gain the high ground.

An uneasy quiet descended over the pass, the echoes of the gunfire reverberating away around the surrounding mountains.

Hunt slid forward full length on his skis, using them under his body like a sledge. He found better cover which gave him a clearer view. There was no movement from the scree of frozen snow chunks on the spur. Not a rustle of material or tell-tale clink of metal as a magazine was reloaded. Nothing.

High above him, Monk settled in, confident he was unseen by the enemy – waiting for that enemy to make the first move. Ready. The trigger finger of his mitt poised. Waiting for the other's mistake.

The woods were equally silent. Hunt could just determine Pope, his body concealed in shadow amidst fallen pine fronds. No doubt listening for a footstep on a brittle twig. But the silence was deafening. No one stirred.

Silence. Just silence, made all the more intense by the distant whine of the wind over the peak.

The digits flickered noiselessly by on Hunt's wristwatch. He tried not to blink, afraid of missing the vital moment. His eyes strained and watered. He felt the cold seeping up into his legs, into his groin.

A cascade of snow fell from an overburdened fir branch in the wood, its sudden soft patter causing an increase in pulse rate. Eyes diverted, throats dry. Fingers tightened on triggers.

Pope shook his head. False alarm.

Another five minutes pulsed by on Hunt's watch. How long was it now? Fifteen, twenty minutes. Both sides waiting for the other to make the first move. And for every second they waited, Shalayez slid another metre away from them. The whole pursuit held up by two men.

Two men? No woman. Christ, Hunt thought suddenly and savagely, the cold must be addling our brains! The two skiers blocking their path hadn't made a move, and had no reason to. They'd sit there until kingdom come, because they had two more in their team who were in full pursuit of Shalayez – while the SAS team sat like idiots watching the snow freeze.

Hunt moved his hand to the send-button of his radio.

In a low voice, he said: "Mike, this is Brian. Listen, I think our friends are just trying to stall us."

"What?" Ash was irritable, concerned their voices might be heard.

"They could have taken us out like ninepins," Hunt said. "And they're not using silencers – in these conditions shots will be heard for miles. They've taken the risk because they *wanted* us to hear. Wanted us to go to ground and stay here. It doesn't make sense otherwise."

Ash was silent for a moment. "*You could be right,*" he conceded, at length.

"I'm sure I am. Whilst we're stuck here, that woman and the other one will go after Shalayez. Let's play them at their own game. Leave Joe and Len here just to keep them happy, whilst the rest of us pull back into those woods. We can make our way across country to the fell-station. It's a slower route, but not as slow as waiting here until they decide they've had enough of playing silly buggers."

Ash hesitated. There was a movement up on the spur as one of the Russians attempted to change position, and slipped on the ice. Two shots hammered from Monk, demolishing the snow ridge the man had been using to conceal himself. The return of fire was way off target.

"If you don't call off Big Joe," Hunt said, "someone's going to get hurt."

Mike Ash agreed.

Nikolai Shalayez heard the distant shots, and came to a dead halt.

The echoes went on endlessly, bouncing from summit to summit, coming closer in a mocking illusion. He cocked his head to one side. What in God's name did it mean? Was it some kind of hunt, for reindeer perhaps?

Whatever the reason his previous feeling of elation evaporated in an instant. Somehow the noise reminded him more of his time in the Soviet Army than of days hunting in his childhood. The sound was distinctly different to that of a hunting rifle.

He pressed on with a renewed sense of urgency.

Nevertheless he decided on caution rather than speed, keeping clear of the roads on either side of the south-running river. There were sufficient trees to offer him cover, but they were not dense enough to slow him down. At one point he saw a colourful group of skiers along the roadside, moving with some haste in the direction of the fell-station. He understood their apprehension.

Nightfall was fast approaching and the sky was now laden with livid bruised cloud. It raced under a stiffening wind which cut with a razored edge. At least it was behind him, billowing out his jacket like a sail to urge him forward. But there was no comfort. Any rise in temperature was more than counteracted by the freezing gusts which kept blowing him off course. Despite his exertion, the cold was beginning to creep inside his windproof.

The last of the light faded from the landscape, and the blizzard began to howl.

It came bellowing down from the frozen northern tundra in relentless stinging waves, gathering momentum and anger with each second that passed. Dancing devils of spindrift rose from the dunes, swirling and twisting in torment, blasted into great clouds that totally obscured visibility. He felt himself pushed along by the unseen hand, an unnerving experience as trees and branches loomed suddenly and dangerously out of the maelstrom like black skeletons in a ghost train. It was impossible to judge the gradient and frequently he found himself rapidly accelerating out of control downhill. He fell frequently; the effort of remounting his skis from waist-deep snow, with the heavy bergan on his back, drained his last resources of energy. Exhaustion dragged at his mind and body.

He shuffled doggedly on, frequently peering at his compass and travelling on dead reckoning, aware that the slightest error and he could pass by the fell-station within a few metres and never even know.

For safety he edged back nearer the road, but it was now impossible to discern exactly where it was. Fresh drifts had totally disfigured the terrain and the road had virtually disappeared. It would only re-emerge when the rangers were able to get the snowploughs running again.

Fatigue was setting in deeply now, and the cold gnawing into his bones. Snow managed to find its way into his cuffs and around his throat. The hair on his forehead and his eyebrows had formed into icicles. He was aware that his pace had slowed, his strength sapping away. Every step became a painful effort of determination. His mind thought only of sleep. How easy just to curl up in the lee of a pine and shut his eyes until it was all over. Sweet, sweet oblivion.

Then he saw something. It happened so quickly he thought he was hallucinating. He peered through strained, red-rimmed eyes. Two wraith-like figures had flashed suddenly across the slope in front of him. In the swirling white vortex he almost missed them as they skied across his path, travelling fast and confidently in the beam of head torches. Then, as quickly as they had appeared, they melted into the billowing spindrift. He rubbed his eyes. Was it all his imagination? The feeble daydreams of a mind on the very edge of consciousness.

He couldn't be sure. Uncertainly he edged forward. No, there were the ski-tracks, fast being covered even as he looked at them. In desperation he began along the tramlines, welcoming the respite from breaking fresh snow.

Those men had to be heading for the fell-station. They had to be, because he knew there was nothing else out there. Except the rolling mountain wilderness. But who were they? They'd been dressed in cam-whites like his own, so he reasoned they were either hunters or soldiers. The Britishers? Or? – his heart sank with the realisation that they were almost certainly his pursuers.

He was still churning the possibilities over in his numbed mind when he stumbled into the fence. It was half-buried in a fresh drift. Spitting out a mouthful of snow, he sat up and slowly tugged off his skis. Through the streaming white veil he became aware of a blurred aurora of light. Around it was the dark shape of a building. He shrugged off the dead weight of his bergan and crept forward on hands and knees.

A dozen half-buried cars and a giant caterpillar snow-plough told him it was the fell-station carpark. He crawled on, hidden between the vehicles until he reached a window. Scraping away a patch in the frost, he peered through the glass.

It appeared to be a canteen: orderly rows of tables and red-upholstered chairs filled the room which had a serving bar at one end. Display boards were decorated with a selection of skis and bindings through the ages. The place was deserted, except for three people who sat at a corner table, talking over cups of coffee. Facing him was a woman, who might have been attractive but for the fact she wore no make-up and her hair was flat and matted, and a granite-faced man with grizzled hair.

The third man had his back to the window. Shalayez frowned. There was something familiar about the head and the attitude of the shoulders. But he couldn't quite place it . . .

Then Sergei Chagall laughed and turned his head, giving Shalayez a clear profile. The shock of it sent him reeling.

Sergei here! Heavens be praised, his old friend was *here*. It was unbelievable. He scraped away at the ice that was already re-forming under his breath. Yes, he was sure. It was Sergei Chagall.

Then slowly it came to him that there could only be one reason why his trusted friend was here. He would have been sent by the KGB to persuade him to go back. Sergei Chagall must be with the pursuers. That woman would be the one he saw back at Åre station.

His heart sank and he withdrew warily from the window. Ducking below the sill, he worked his way along the building until he reached the corner. At the covered entrance porch a skier was stamping his feet impatiently, while his companion was removing his cam-white overalls and stuffing them into his rucksack. They must have been the two skiers who crossed his path a few minutes earlier. A long, bulky object had been wrapped in sacking and was strapped to the side of the pack. Shalayez had little doubt what it was: the men could hardly walk around ski resorts or public fell-stations with Kalashnikovs openly displayed.

He drew back and slid down onto his haunches, burying his head in his hands, and tried desperately to think. To go on would be to die in the blizzard that was now tearing away at the fell-station as though intent on demolishing it, plank by plank. He must find somewhere, perhaps a garage or timber store, to give him shelter. At least until the wind died down enough for him to continue on his way. It was a terrible risk, he knew, because the moment visibility improved, he would again be at the mercy of his pursuers.

Wind was rattling at the wooden doors of an outbuilding with maniacal force, shaking them until the hinges looked as though they might spring free at any moment. Snow around the bottom edge of the doors was sweeping in as fast as he could kick it aside. It took some minutes before he cleared it sufficiently to edge open one door and squeeze between the gap.

The wind slammed the door behind him, the noise instantly muted. And the meagre warmth from an oil heater overwhelmed him, causing an involuntary gasp of relief. Stooping over its tiny flame, he rubbed the circulation back into his hands and face. He gritted his teeth at the pain as his skin thawed.

For half-an-hour he sat, until the agony subsided and his mind had sufficiently defrosted from its stupor to begin to think clearly again. His eyes had become accustomed to the gloom and he hobbled to his feet. It was a spacious building used to house bicycles that were hired out to tourists in the summer. But at the front lay three gleaming motorised skidoos, like open-topped motorcycles which ran on a caterpillar track.

He unscrewed the filler cap of one. The immediate stench of petrol filled his nostrils. He felt with his hand. It was nearly full. The ignition key was in. No doubt on fine days the rangers would use the machines to tow parties of skiers to some of the remoter mountains in the area.

Now his brain was turning over fast. If he stayed or if he left, he would still have no access to food. But should he remain he would surely be caught. And he doubted that Sergei Chagall would be able to do anything for him – however much his friend might want to help.

So his first priority must be to get as far away as possible. There were only two ways to travel in these conditions, and he knew he was physically incapable of skiing another kilometre. But a skidoo offered possibilities; certainly no other vehicle could cope with the conditions outside, especially away from established roads and tracks. Hastily he consulted his map.

There! Another remote fell-station. It lay some fifteen kilometres to the south, in the shadow of a horrendous maze of contour lines that marked the giant Sylarna mountain complex which straddled the border with Norway. If only he could reach that under cover of the blizzard, then his pursuers would be left far behind with no idea where he was. There he could eat and rest. When the weather cleared he would travel south, and pick up the State-run track that skirted the southern slopes of Sylarna and cross the border into Norway. By this time tomorrow he could be there.

That decided him. He set to work immediately clearing the snow from the shed doors so that he could open them. Enthusiasm triggered a surge of energy. He was almost oblivious to the lashing icy torrent as he struggled to get the red skidoo out onto the snow.

Carefully he strapped his bergan and skis to the machine. He hesitated. One more thing. He must make certain that no one could follow. A few moments' search in the shed revealed a petrol can, the contents of which he poured over the remaining two skidoos.

He then returned to his own machine, mounted up and threw the key-switch. It started immediately, its ugly burring sound drowned by the wind. He experimented until he felt he understood its controls. Then he extracted a lifeboat match from his pocket, struck the flame and tossed it back into the shed.

The utter force of the following explosion took him by surprise. Its searing heat momentarily warmed his face as the steel fragments of the skidoos demolished the shed as effectively as a bomb. He ducked as a pair of handlebars swooped over his head.

Burning timbers from the roof collapsed into the raging conflagration, fanned by the savage wind and fed by the fuel tanks of the wrecked skidoos.

He turned the throttle and the caterpillar teeth bit hard into the snow, jolting him forward. The machine bucked like a steel bronco, racing away with him as he tried to slew it around the corner of the fellstation.

Momentarily he caught sight of two of his pursuers. They were rushing from the entrance at the sound – only to be confronted by the gleaming red shape bearing down on them. Shalayez yelled abuse at the top of his voice. The men leaped from his path as the skidoo tore between them with the wail of a banshee.

Then they were gone, devoured by the gyrating columns of spindrift. And suddenly he was alone, the metallic shriek of the machine resounding in his ears while he clung on for dear life as it bounced headlong through the white eternity.

It had been his intention to keep to the track, but he simply couldn't find it. Instead he had to content himself with droning onward in what he took to be a southerly direction. One moment the skidoo would be nosing its way sedately over level ground then, without warning, it would plunge down an unexpected slope. Then, just

483

as suddenly, it would be grinding uphill, the tracks scrabbling for grip.

For two long hours he continued his helter-skelter journey into the unknown. Then, almost as quickly as it had begun, the blizzard cleared. Within fifteen minutes the buffeting wind had dropped, and the freshly con-toured landscape revealed itself, glowing dully in its own reflected light.

Shalayez grinned. Against all odds he had made it. True, he had no real idea where he was; but, more importantly, neither did his pursuers.

He found himself on high ground and, as he looked around for some identifying landmark, he noticed a light far below him. A cluster of trees half obscured the shape of the timber chalet, wind-driven snow banked high against one side. A curl of smoke issued from the chim-ney stack.

The fell-station? No, he decided, that would be too much of a miracle to hope for. Besides it was too small. It probably wasn't even marked on the map. But at least it was inhabited, and would provide shelter and food.

He revved the engine and cruised cautiously down a steep defile, until he reached the main valley which ran alongside the chalet. Here the snow was deep and thick, causing the skidoo to labour for purchase. He cut the engine and decided to approach on foot. Although he could think of no way his pursuers could have overtaken him, it would be stupid to take a chance. Perhaps there were other groups in the area searching for him. He would take a discreet look first.

But, even as the engine noise died, he realised he'd left it too late for that. The sound of the barking dogs drifted loud and clear through the icy stillness.

As he swung his leg over the seat, he froze. He felt the snow creak and shift beneath his foot. Without warning the skidoo lurched sideways. And both man and machine went down like a lift in a shaft, as the fresh riverbed snow collapsed under the weight.

A split second's sensation of falling through space was all he felt before his body plunged into icy water so cold that he wanted to scream. His cry came out in a gurgle of bubbles as the turbulent surface closed in above his head, shutting out the stars.

The skidoo landed on his left leg, pinioning him to the fast-flowing black current that tried to wrench it free. But he had no idea what was holding him. His mind was filled with nothing but blind panic. He knew only that he had mere seconds to live. With all his might he tore and clawed at the obstacle, totally unaware that his fingernails were gouging his own flesh around his exposed ankle.

He could see nothing, the sound of rushing water screaming in his ears. He tried again, grabbing at the obstacle with both hands. Something shifted and miraculously he was free. Almost instantly he broke surface, his lungs heaving in great draughts of icy air as he spluttered and groped for the sheer sides of the hole through which he'd fallen. His fingertips clutched at snow but there was no feeling left in them.

The racing flow sucked at his legs, pulling against his feeble grip. Beneath his fingers the snow began to crumble. He dug in again. But without sensation his grip was useless and he was aware of his skin dragging over slippery ice. He felt himself going, the water now tightening its vice-like grip around his waist.

He opened his mouth to scream, and he was gone. The water closed in over his head again, and he was tumbling helplessly along like a weightless man in space, not knowing which way up he was.

Then he bounced on the rocky bottom, and for an instant knew the direction of the surface. With tortured muscles he forced himself upward, his arms outstretched.

At the surface his palms touched the solid pane of sheet-ice. He jammed his feet into the embankment, standing rigid against the flow.

Above him, through an inch of scratched ice, he was dimly aware of a wavering aurora of light. And then a distorted face pressed against it, peering down at him, eyes wide with horror.

He was entombed and he knew his sixty seconds must be up.

Mercifully his world went blank.

Mike Ash reached the fell-station first, with Hunt and Janne Reis close behind.

It had been a long and frustrating night since the blizzard struck. They had kept going for as long as they dared, until they were finally obliged to seek temporary shelter amongst the trees. The interminable wait was aggravated by their anxiety over the safety of Monk and Pope, who had been left behind to keep the two Russians occupied.

As soon as the weather began to lift, Ash's team pressed on until, as a steely dawn light spread over the virgin white landscape, the wooden buildings came into view.

Hunt and Reis slid alongside Ash outside the fell-station and began removing their skis.

"Looks like they've had quite a fire," Ash observed. The gutted outbuilding shed still smouldered, its charred timbers in stark contrast to the surrounding snow. "Let's get inside and pray that Shalayez is still here."

The three of them walked around to the main entrance where a ranger in a fur-hooded anorak was shovelling snow away from the porch.

He looked up irritably. "How did you get here? Didn't you see the snow-barriers were down on the road?"

"We came across country," Ash answered in Swedish. "We were caught out in that blizzard last night."

The ranger shook his head. "You should listen to the weather forecasts. I don't know why we bother! Then we have to put our lives at risk coming out to rescue you."

Ash glanced at Hunt, who managed to suppress his grin, then asked: "We have a colleague who went on ahead, a tall man with long black hair. Probably spoke English with a strong foreign accent. Is he here?"

The Swede shook his head. "No one's here. There were three skiers last night – they were foreigners, Finns they said – but they left when the blizzard lifted – more fools them. Totally ignored my warnings."

"Was the tall man with them?"

"Tall, you say?"

"With untidy black hair."

Another shake of the head. "No, I noticed that – the men in the party had short hair."

"You mean there was a woman?"

"Yes, one with two men."

"Volga Olga," Hunt breathed.

"And no one else?" Ash persisted.

The ranger was getting angry. He jabbed a thumb in the direction of the outbuilding. "Not unless he was the bastard who stole a skidoo and set fire to that lot!"

Hunt said quickly: "No, our friend wouldn't do that. No point . . ."

"Point?" The Swede glared. "Huh! Who *would* have a point in doing that, I ask you? I still don't believe it. It must be the work of a madman."

"Which way did this madman go on the skidoo?" Hunt asked.

The Swede shrugged. "Who knows? It was a filthy night, as you know. There are no tracks left to follow."

Ash said: "When will the road south be opened?"

"Not until midday when we get the plough down there to the next fell-station." He looked up at the grey unpromising sky. "But more blizzards are coming, so maybe it's not worth it."

"Thanks," Ash said. "We'll push on to see if we can find our friend."

"You may find him at the next fell-station. I can't check for you because the telephone line is down. But if you're going, don't hang about. It's seventeen kilometres and I'm not sure the weather will hold for that long."

Ash thanked the ranger again, and the three men returned to their skis and bergans, leaving the disgruntled Swede to continue his shovelling. He had never met so many crazy recreational skiers in one night for as long as he could remember.

The brightness was blinding. He tried to focus, but all he could see was the vague outline of two people moving around.

"I think he's awake now," an elderly woman said in Swedish.

"Then he's a very lucky man," muttered a male voice.

A gnarled brown face with a bulbous nose and fleshy jug ears emerged from the brilliance, inches from Shalayez's eyes. A white blond fringe protruded below the black leather fishing hat. "Ja, he is coming round."

The woman pushed the old man aside. "Here, let me. Don't go peering at him like that, Jonas, you'll scare the daylights out of him."

Shalayez's nostrils detected the floral scent of eau-de-cologne. A soft, pudgy hand soothed his forehead. "There, dear, you are safe now."

"English?" Shalayez breathed. "I am Russian, but I speak a little English. I do not understand what you say."

"Ah, English," the woman said. "I speak not so much. I learn some from my daughter."

"Water? Do you have some water?" he croaked.

She understood and shortly a ladle of sweet-tasting spring water was pressed to his lips. He sucked at it greedily. She laughed cheerily to see him revive. "I have some hot meal for you. Then you feel real better."

Later, over a meal of reindeer steaks with dumplings

and potatoes, she explained that her name was Lena. She and her husband had retired to the remote mountain chalet to spend their twilight years hunting and fishing, and working their dog-sleigh team. It was those dogs, she said, who had alerted them to the sound of the skidoo the previous night. Not used to visitors, Jonas had hastily gone outside to see if some lost skier might be in trouble after the blizzard. He had arrived at the riverbed to find nothing but a gaping hole, eight feet deep. Even as he looked, the bobbing head disappeared beneath the ice.

"Jonas is not a young man no more," she explained. "But last night he move real fast. Like when he is a young man." She patted his knobbled hand affectionately. "I am real proud of him. He moves along to where the ice surface is clear of snow, and there he sees you looking up at him like a goldfish. He is very shocked, but he breaks the ice and pulls you out."

"I am very grateful," Shalayez said as he finished his meal. With his belly now full to bloating he felt an inexorable tiredness creeping over him. He stifled a yawn.

"You will need to sleep," Lena said. "And while you do, Jonas will take the dogs to the fell-station and get help. You must have a doctor see to your eyes."

"My eyes?"

"They hurt you, I see."

He nodded. "Yes, my vision is not clear and they are very sore and gritty. And a bad headache."

She smiled kindly. "You have the snow-blindness. All the brightness burns the eyes. You should wear goggles."

He shrugged. "I lose them way back, I'm afraid. But, listen, Lena, when your husband goes to the fell-station. Please you ask him to telephone the British Embassy in Stockholm? Tell them I am here."

"But you say you are *Russian*?"

He shook his head slowly; he was too tired even to

think of an explanation. "No longer. Please, do not ask questions."

Lena smiled and stood up, wiping her hands on her apron. "Okay, we do that. No more to eat?"

He shook his head.

"Then you rest some more now."

He pushed back his chair and staggered across to the pine bed and the soft bliss of the down duvet. He took one last look round the cosy warmth of the little chalet. The stone hearth crackled fitfully with birch logs. He shut his eyes and was instantly asleep . . .

The ear-splitting sound of rending timber stunned him back to consciousness. His eyes were instantly wide.

Jonas was standing by the fire in his dungarees, lighting his pipe from a spill. His mouth dropped open and the force of the three rounds from Petkus's PRI folded him over at the belly and sent him crashing into the fire.

Litvinov's shot blew the old woman out of her rocking chair and halfway across the room. She lay face-down, twitching for several seconds before she fell still.

The momentum of her chair kept going until Yuri Popov reached out a hand and stopped it. Petkus hauled the old man's body from the fire and stamped out the smouldering material with his boots.

Shalayez was in shock. He sat bolt upright in the bed, his body trembling like a tuning-fork, his eyes staring with disbelief. The blood pounding around his heart, threatening to burst its arteries.

Captain Valia Mikhailovitch stepped slowly into the room, taking in the carnage around her. She looked first at the old man on the hearth and then the dead woman. Then she turned to face her quarry.

She lifted her dark goggles and stripped off the white silk ski-mask. Her eyes were dark and angry, but when she spoke her voice was as icy cool as the weather outside. "We've come to take you home, Nikolai Shalayez. Before you cause any more trouble."

He swallowed hard. "You are butchers," he breathed, and inclined his head towards the dead couple, his eyes moist. "Two old people, who have done no harm to anyone . . ." His voice trailed away, choked with emotion.

Mikhailovitch didn't move. "Yes, Comrade Shalayez. Their only crime was unwittingly to give shelter to a traitor. How many more people have to die because of you?"

His eyes tore at her face. How could a woman behave like that? "*I* did not butcher them."

Petkus stood alongside his officer. "We had no choice," he grated. "Anyone could have been in here with you. Maybe Swedish security, or your Britisher friends."

"We do not take chances," Mikhailovitch added, and reached forward to strip the duvet from his body. Brusquely she pushed him aside and checked beneath the pillow. "He is not armed," she said. "Check there are no weapons in his rucksack, and get the old man's shotgun stowed in the kitchen."

Petkus took a finely engraved Sako Hunter from its rack above the fireplace and admired its walnut butt. "A handsome souvenir, Comrade Captain."

"Get on with it," Valia Mikhailovitch snapped. First the death of a naïve young girl, even if she were a British agent, and now a helpless old couple did not rest easily on her shoulders.

"Do you want me to call up the KGB colonel?" Litvinov asked.

The woman hesitated. "It is a temptation to shoot this traitorous dog now and take the consequences," she said, eyeing Shalayez with contempt. She regained her composure and allowed her professional mask to slip back into place. "Get on with it, Corporal. But tell him he must get here fast. Tell him there is a small lake where he can land a light aircraft. Give him the co-ordinates. But if the Britishers get here first, Shalayez dies."

Litvinov stiffened. "I cannot say that to a KGB colonel, Comrade Captain."

"What's the matter with you, Stepan?" Petkus jeered. "Since when is a mighty *razvedchiki* warrior afraid of a fat *chekist* slob? I wonder who pays your miserly pay, the Navy or those creeps in Lubyanka?"

Litvinov rose to the taunt. "One day, Sergeant, your mouth will get you court-martialled."

"Just get on with it," the captain repeated wearily. "And do as I say, unless you want to volunteer to stay behind alone to defend Shalayez if the Britishers come."

Litvinov blanched and saluted. Petkus watched with amused despair, and shook his head as the corporal set about rigging his R-350M radio set to send a burst-transmission.

"What happens now?" Shalayez asked.

"We wait until transport arrives," the captain said. "Then we can wash our hands of you – even if it takes a lot of hard scrubbing to get off the blood you've had us shed. Now you shut up and ask no more questions."

Her order was issued in a tone that said she did not expect to be disobeyed. Shalayez clammed up, alone with his thoughts of darkest despair, hardly aware of the discomfort as Sergeant Petkus roughly trussed him up like a chicken.

Meanwhile, young Popov had the most distasteful job, dragging out the dead bodies and throwing them into the hole created by the crashed skidoo. The current would drag them out of sight and they wouldn't be discovered until the thaw. He was then sent out as picket on nearby high ground which had a clear view of all directions of approach.

As he shivered in his snow-pit and made regular radio reports, Sergeant Petkus took delight in telling him how warm it was in the hut, now that they had repaired the damage they had caused. A larder full of provisions had been found. They were making short work of them and *hoped* there might be some hot food left for him.

"You are very quiet, Captain Mikhailovitch," Petkus said through a mouthful of buttered bread as he prepared the next slice with his survival knife.

"I am thinking."

"Yes?" It didn't do to press her when she was in this sort of mood. She may be a woman, but she was no ordinary woman. No ordinary woman would ever have earned such respect from Ustin Petkus.

She pulled a wry smile. "I am thinking maybe I have had enough of this sort of life."

"It has its compensations."

She frowned. "Like killing little old ladies and men?"

Petkus shrugged. "One of the unfortunate accidents of war. We've seen enough civilian casualties in our time. Remember the villages in the Panjsher Valley?"

"This is not a good time to remind me of Afghanistan, Ustin," she warned darkly. "Maybe it is because I'm a woman, but I find it painful to see old folk and children killed and maimed."

It was a rare admission of what Petkus regarded as essentially a female weakness; yet he respected this unusual glimpse of the hidden side of her personality. It made him want her all the more.

She stared into the mug of soup which she held with both hands. "Maybe it is time for me to leave and find myself a husband . . ."

Petkus chuckled.

She looked up. "And what is so funny? Don't you think there will be a man who would want me? Or has the snow and ice destroyed my complexion and frozen my heart, eh? Is that what you think?"

The sergeant acted on impulse and took the biggest gamble of his career. The mere gesture terrified him more than enduring a stonk of *Mujahideen* mortar fire, or clinging by his fingernails to a sheer ice slope: his rough hand closed over hers on the soup mug. "I know there is one man who would want you, Valia."

A look of astonishment crossed her face. "Sergeant,

I think you forget yourself!" But Petkus thought he discerned a softness in the dark brown eyes.

The intimate, whispered moment was shattered by the discordant buzz of static from Litvinov's communications equipment. He'd been checking his gun in the corner, and reached across to the radio, replaying the taped message at normal speed. He listened, then turned to his officer. "Colonel Chagall is flying with that Swede pilot. Estimated arrival is in fifteen minutes."

"Very good. We'll mark out a landing-strip on the lake."

The three Spetsnaz soldiers went out to prepare for the aircraft's arrival, whilst Yuri Popov was called in from his observation post to guard Shalayez and to have some food. Petkus had been as good as his word: only one potato was left in the pot.

Popov stabbed it savagely.

The aircraft swung in low over a pass between two glimmering white mountains, swaying slightly in the cross-wind before it turned into the weather, and dipped for a final approach.

Brian Hunt tracked it all the way down through his binoculars. In the last moments he lost it behind a ragged fringe of pines on the lakeside.

"It's down," he said.

All five members of the team were lying on reversible foam kipmats, hidden beneath a patch of snow-dusted shrub on high ground to the south.

"It's a pity we can't hit them now," Mike Ash murmured. "There's only one with him now in the hut."

"Don't worry, boss. We can handle them," Big Joe Monk assured.

"Just as well we caught up," Len Pope added. "otherwise you *would* have had a problem."

That was true enough. And it had been a real relief to have them rejoin the team.

Apparently the two Spetsnaz members, who had been

holding them up, hadn't been seen again after the others left.

After an hour Monk and Pope had retreated cautiously and taken the long route to the fell-station.

"I wonder how many are on the plane?" Ash asked.

"Just two," Hunt answered. The dark figures had emerged from beyond the pines. "Looks like the pilot and one other."

Ash jabbed a finger in the direction of a high rise between their position and the chalet. "If they're still manning that OP tonight, we'll have to make a wide circular approach. Use the dead ground of that river."

The others nodded their agreement. Monk said: "We'll have to take out the OP. Who's got the short straw?"

Ash grinned. "You want the privilege?"

"Not bothered." But he was a bad liar.

Pope laughed. "Whoever does it, he'll have to be careful. Rumour has it they're even trained to use entrenching spades like spears. Sharpen her edges like razors. Can snap someone's spine with her at twenty paces."

"Bollocks," Monk rejoined.

Janne Reis didn't like the sound of it. "Listen to me, there is to be no unnecessary killing."

Ash felt an unreasonable flash of anger. "D'you want to do it yourself, Janne?"

The Swede looked affronted, then squared his shoulders. "Okay, if you like," he said stiffly.

Hunt patted him on the back. "Attaboy, Janne. But you're talking about specialist Spets troops. They'd eat you for breakfast and not even bother to spit out the bones. Leave it to Big Joe and Len. They were weaned on this sort of stuff."

"How would you do it?" Reis asked.

Monk patted the blackened Fairbairn-Sykes commando knife on his webbing. "My trusty friend. More than a match for any rusty shovel."

"You'll have to wait until dark?"

Mike Ash said: "Afraid so, but it's not long to go."

"Maybe the plane takes off before then."

Len Pope chuckled. "And maybe she doesn't!" He knew Hunt well enough to know what he had in mind.

It took Hunt half-an-hour to negotiate the dead ground to the lakeside. Once safe in the pine copse he was able to move swiftly to a position where he could see the light aircraft. After landing, it had been taxied close to the trees for the Spetsnaz team to cut pine fronds to act as temporary camouflage.

This served Hunt's purpose well because it meant he didn't have to risk exposure on the ice flats. They had discussed several methods of temporarily disabling the aircraft, but were restricted because any damage had to appear accidental.

He moved swiftly in under the wing and opened the cockpit door. A moment later he'd located the pilot's fuel control valve and selected 'both' to allow a free flow from both wing tanks. It took a few seconds longer to open the engine cowling and lift the fuel-strainer. The stench of gasoline was overpowering in the freezing air, as the blue liquid gushed onto the ice. As soon as the tanks were drained, he released the plunger and shut down the cowling.

Hunt was halfway back to the team when the Russians emerged from the chalet, with an addition to their number.

Nikolai Shalayez. It was good to see him again and to know that, after the tortuous chase, he was now only a few hundred metres away. Hunt realised then that he'd come to regard Shalayez almost as one of his own team. He'd even started to forgive him for the sore head.

As he expected it took the party very little time to discover their fuel leak – indeed they could hardly have missed the stench. A heated debate followed with the Swedish pilot protesting that a fuel line must have cracked in the extreme temperature. He searched for it for five minutes then gave up, announcing that anyway he didn't have anything to repair it with. Irritably the group began trudging back to the chalet.

Two soldiers were this time sent to reman the observation post whilst the others went inside. The door shut and soon smoke was pumping from the chimney as fresh logs were added to the fire. With nightfall fast approaching it had clearly been decided that nothing more could be done until dawn.

Finally, Hunt rejoined the SAS group who had, in the meantime, been discussing and planning details of the coming night's operation. Janne Reis had vetoed several ideas on the grounds that the death of the Russians would be the inevitable result. That, he declared to Monk's obvious chagrin, was politically unacceptable. Eventually a compromise solution was struck which offered Shalayez's abductors at least a chance of surrender.

Although there was no wind, the clear sky heralded a cold night of shimmering intensity. During the long wait to the early hours the temperature plummeted to minus forty. Ski-masks were donned together with duvets and Mao trousers. Even so, it was miserably cold. Eyes smarted and noses ran, the liquid freezing uncomfortably on unshaven skin.

As the hour approached, the party stripped off their additional bulk and prepared for the attack. A final weapons check was made and they moved off in single file. At a chosen point, overlooking the Spetsnaz observation post, Ash and Reis dropped off at a position from which they could provide covering fire, if things went wrong.

Meanwhile, Hunt fell in some metres behind Monk and Pope as they worked their inimitable double-act, inching along gullies and indentations in the snowfield, until they were between the chalet and the OP. Then they turned, worming their way back to approach the Spetsnaz picket from the rear. The least expected line of approach. All three men carried silenced Hocklers in case of accidents. If it was necessary, Reis's plea for a bloodless result would be ignored.

The night was breathlessly still and the temperature continued to fall until now the brittle cold was painful to breathe. The stars were as sharp as needles in the black velvet sky so that the hushed silvered landscape glowed with its own luminosity. These were not the best conditions for a covert approach.

Hunt stopped moving forward, unclipped his Hockler and settled into a convenient depression in the snow. His finger slipped the safety. Ahead the shapes of his two oppos merged into the white of the dunes as they slithered forward an inch at a time. They were nearly there.

Hunt lifted his Hockler, and held his breath.

17

Hunt saw the hand signal. Saw the two phantom figures growing swiftly like snowmen out of the drift behind the OP. Sensed their urgency as they leapt the last few metres. Felt his own adrenalin pumping. Willed them on.

His own muscles contracted and sprang free. And he was launched, up and scrambling through the deep white powder. Hard on their heels.

Heard the muffled sounds of violent movement. Heard the grunts of exertion. Split-second timing. He jumped into the pit.

He was there, the Hockler's deadly snout threatening instant annihilation.

Dark faces. Twisted and upturned towards him by the forearms strapped rigidly across their throats. Eyes white and bright from near strangulation. Eyes that glowed with sudden fear as the razor edge of a Fairbairn was felt prodding at the jugular vein.

Eyes that registered the Hockler, and decided it was an unequal fight. The struggling stopped.

"Joe," Hunt snapped. "You first."

Monk had the man's hand up his back, had the plasti-cuffs snapped on. Fast, but slower than usual because of the goddamn cold.

Hunt nodded to Pope. The second sentry was secured, both men gagged and blindfolded.

Monk was grinning beneath the ski-mask. "Not a bloody spade in sight."

"Stow it," Hunt said. He flashed the green penlight three times. The signal that the opposition had been overcome.

Sixty seconds later Mike Ash and Janne Reis appeared. The Swede was given the job of guarding the bound prisoners. He'd been warned, knew how dangerous they were, and had promised he'd have no compunction about blasting them with the silenced automatic. They seemed to sense it, too, and lay still.

The rest of the team advanced on the chalet in accordance with the plan. They approached along the edge of the river gully, protected by the screen of trees and skeletal scrub.

Three of them settled down, covering, while Ash went ahead, making a circumference of the chalet. Then he closed in to the far side of the building, where the blizzard had swept snow into a huge drift that almost reached the roof.

No one had argued with Ash's self-appointment to this task. He was acknowledged as the most skilled and stealthiest climber of the team. And he proved it again, by negotiating the tricky slope of loose soft snow without mishap. Once on the roof he advanced up the slope on elbows and knees. He kept his boots clear of the timber, spreading his weight to reduce the inevitable tell-tale creaking. On reaching the stone chimney stack, he raised one hand.

"GO!" Hunt said, and the three men moved in low and fast to the front of the chalet.

Monk waved and jerked a thumb in the direction of an outbuilding. Six dark furry shapes were half buried in snow, their leads still fixed to the hitching rings. Only one head was visible, its mouth frozen open in a snarl of pain and surprise, its eyes glazed. No doubt the Spetsnaz team had taken out the dogs with silencers when they'd arrived at the chalet earlier.

Hunt positioned himself on one side of the door. Monk took the other. Both men pressed themselves flush

500

against the timber cladding. Len Pope positioned himself to one side with a clear field of fire. If anyone managed to make a break for it, he would have to make the snap decision whether or not to cut them down. He was acutely aware of the risk of shooting the very man they had come to rescue.

They waited, edgy and impatient. The adrenalin was pumping again. Palms were damp with sweat. All knew that Ash had draped a windproof over the chimney stack. That it was only a matter of minutes before the small building filled with smoke. He was now stationed at a rear window and would attack that way if they met resistance.

"Oh, shit!" someone oathed in Russian. "We've got a bloody chimney fire!"

Another voice, this time a woman's, said: "Wake up Shalayez and get him out."

"Let the bastard die in his sleep – it's better than he deserves."

There was a sudden rush of movement.

"Get that damn door open!"

The latch rattled and the door swung inward. A thick cloud of smoke burst out into the crystalline night air. With it came the Swedish pilot, his face covered with a handkerchief. He staggered out, head bowed, and fell onto his knees, retching violently into the snow. The SAS team ignored him; it was vital to neutralise the two Spetsnaz troopers first.

The civilian who had arrived by plane emerged next – the man who they'd decided was probably a Soviet KGB or GRU officer. He stumbled blindly into Len Pope's arms, and was promptly handcuffed before he knew what had happened.

Shalayez was bundled out next. Monk seized him by the collar and threw him clear, around the corner of the chalet.

Hunt snatched the arm of the Russian who had pushed Shalayez out. It was fast jammed up into the spine in a

501

fierce armlock whilst Hunt's other arm snapped around the throat, tightening into the gullet.

The last man out was alerted, but seconds too late. Monk swung the butt-end of his Hockler up into the Russian's jaw, sending him reeling into the door jamb.

The pilot had recovered. He looked behind him in bewilderment and decided it wasn't the place for him. Throwing himself forward, he began pounding through the snow in the direction of the OP.

Len Pope raised his carbine.

"Leave him!" Hunt yelled. "No more dead Swedes – besides, he ain't going no place."

Pope looked disappointed, and lowered his weapon. He shouted towards the OP: "Janne! Pilot's coming your way!" Then he froze. "Christ, the bugger's armed."

The man stumbled to a halt halfway up the slope as Reis emerged from the OP. Instinctively the pilot aimed his pistol. A sharp crack resounded as Reis practised his marksmanship. The round blew the pilot off his feet and propelled him back down the slope. He rolled over and over, and came to rest at the bottom.

Monk jeered as Reis approached the chalet. "I thought you wanted no Swedish casualties?"

Reis smiled gently. "Not if you cause them, Joe. But Sweden is my patch, as you say. And here I have a privilege or two."

"Hey," Pope said suddenly to Hunt, "d'you know what you've got there?"

Hunt frowned. He was aware that the trooper he held was smaller than he'd expected, but he couldn't see the face from behind.

"You've got the star prize!" Monk breathed. "That must be bleedin' Volga Olga!"

It took some minutes for the windproof to be removed from the stack and for the smoke to clear. It left a pungent sooty stench as the group assembled in the centre of the main room.

Shalayez was busy shaking everybody's hand and

502

thanking them profusely. "It is wonderful to be free again!" His laugh had an almost hysterical edge to it. "And tell me, how is my Lucy? She is so brave, it is she who says I must go while she stays." He grinned at Ash, who looked at Hunt for inspiration.

The sergeant-major said: "I'm sure she's fine, Niki."

The Russian nodded. "And my good friend, Brian. I am so sorry what I do to you back at your embassy – "

"Think nothing of it."

"It is good now to be amongst all my friends. And also I can now speak with my dear friend, Sergei – "

Ash glanced at the civilian in the grey overcoat. "You know this man?"

Shalayez grinned. "Yes, he is my greatest friend. I cannot say anything in front of these *razvedchiki*, but it is he who warned me to get out of Russia." He threw his arms around Chagall and hugged him closely. But the KGB colonel looked rigid and distinctly uncomfortable.

Hesitantly Shalayez stepped back; he could not understand his friend's coldness.

Chagall addressed Ash: "You are the senior British officer here?"

The SAS captain was taken aback by the man's excellent English. "Yes," he replied cautiously.

"Then I wish to speak with you privately."

Ash considered for a moment, then turned to Hunt: "You'd better be in on this, Brian. I might want a witness."

"We are still on *Swedish* soil," Reis reminded gently.

Ash smiled thinly. "Of course, we can't really expect to keep secrets from you."

Monk said: "I'd best get a brew on. We've a lot of thirsty Ivans to look after."

The four men moved into the main bedroom, the only other room in the chalet, and shut the door.

Chagall seated himself on the bed and wrung his hands. He seemed unsure how to begin. "Do you have a cigarette?"

503

Hunt obliged and stepped forward.

Chagall drew a deep lungful of smoke and exhaled. "Listen, please. What Nikolai Shalayez says is true, but I cannot speak in front of those *razvedchiki* – it is important that Moscow does not know the full story."

"What story is that?" Ash asked.

Chagall toyed nervously with his cigarette. "About a year ago I am on an assignment in Moscow. Sometimes I am brought back to renew old acquaintances with foreigners I have known many years. In this case it was two British agents – two old ladies, Alice Tate and Daphne Withers. Both sides we play a pretending game which suits us all. You know them?"

The names meant nothing to the others in the room.

He shrugged. "Anyway, I tell them that I want to come over. I think about it for many years – I have had good times in your West. But now I am stuck in Sary Shagan – a godforsaken hole in the middle of Asia – and I have no opportunity to travel abroad no more. The ladies say they will think about it and let me know.

"After a month I am contacted by a man from your embassy in Moscow. Plans are laid. Then – suddenly – there is nothing. Eventually I am contacted again. It is said a new man takes over as my controller in London. This man does not think I am worth the trouble. I can bring little information they want. Mostly my work is internal security of no interest. To get me out causes much trouble and expense – huh, your capitalist system at work, yes? – and it will sour good relations under that sweet-smiling tiger Gorbachev."

Chagall shook his head as he recalled the conversation. He sucked greedily on his cigarette again before continuing: "I did not understand. But I am no fool, I know that some in your Whitehall has thoughts about it. How to make me pay my way! They say – *but* – if I can get out a scientist working on Sary Shagan – *then* they will do me the *big* favour, and take me, too. Bastard!" He looked up. "So I decide that my friend Shalayez will be the easiest to turn, because I know his personal thoughts and circumstances."

Hunt was puzzled. "We've got to know Niki pretty well, Colonel. He seems the least likely person to defect, so how did you manage it?"

Chagall pulled a wry smile. "You British may think I am not worth the trouble, but I am a good operator. First I set what you English call a honey-trap for his wife, so we can put pressure on her to leave him. I have considerable *blat* in my own department. My men do as I say without question. Then we tell Nikolai Shalayez he is in big trouble with the KGB. Meanwhile, the new controller in London gets the Swedish academy to invite him to speak in Stockholm, and for a new woman to enter his life – one who bears a striking resemblance to the wife who has deserted him. Defection suddenly looks very attractive. An only way out."

Hunt and Ash were speechless. All the suffering and personal anguish that Shalayez had been through was due to the savage manipulations of this would-be KGB defector and his London controller. Now both knew that Lucinda's apparently uncanny resemblance to his wife had been no accident. That likeness had eventually led to her death.

Janne Reis said: "What was the name of your controller in London?"

Ash started to protest, but Reis waved him to silence. As he'd said earlier, this was his patch.

Chagall said: "The bastard's name is Lavender. Mr Ralph Lavender."

Ash and Hunt exchanged glances. The revelation was hardly a surprise: the description of the controller's methods fitted exactly with everything they had come to expect from the SIS man.

Ash said: "Was your controller expecting you to be in Sweden?"

Chagall laughed. "No, my friend. That was my good fortune. I was only brought in because, as head of personnel security at Sary Shagan, I knew Shalayez well. I am now responsible to get him back. So you see, now you have him it is imperative that I come with you."

"Why?" Ash asked.

"Because," Chagall replied testily, "once Shalayez is out of the country, I'll have to return to Sary Shagan. And I think Lavender may choose to let me rot there if it suits him. I will never have such a chance again. No, I have kept my side of the bargain. Now it is Lavender's turn to keep his. I shall come with you."

The very thought of having Shalayez's betrayer with their party turned Ash's stomach. The man had happily destroyed his own friend's life for his own ends. "I'll have to get clearance before I can agree to it."

"I come anyway," Chagall threatened.

Hunt, too, was seeking a way out. "Do you ski?"

"What?" the Russian asked. "Ski? No, skiing is for the youngsters – or the village peasants. I am neither. But I guess I can shuffle, eh?" He laughed.

"Our route takes us over bad terrain," Ash said, catching on to Hunt's theme. "You need to be competent or you'll put everyone in jeopardy."

Chagall became alarmed. "Then what do we do?"

Ash said: "We'll think of something before the night's through."

Pope rigged up the radio, running out the three hundred metres of compatible aerial wire from the spool. Having first carefully warmed the battery in front of the fire, the ciphered morse message was keyed into the electronic memory. It was then fired in a condensed split-second burst through the 'squirt-box' by low-power HF transmission. An hour later Lavender's reply was received via Hereford, and the signal 'stretched' and deciphered.

Lavender agreed that, when the rest of the party left for the border, Len Pope should escort Chagall to the fell-station at the foot of Sylarna mountain. Lavender would meet him there and arrange to get him out of the country separately.

Meanwhile, the Spetsnaz team should be left bound in the chalet with sufficient supplies to keep them alive until everyone was out of the country within forty-eight hours. Then their people at the Soviet Embassy would be told where to collect them.

The Swedish Government, Reis explained, would not want murder charges brought against the Spetsnaz wolves, as it would serve to antagonise relations between Stockholm and Moscow still further.

The remaining hours of darkness in the cramped chalet were strained. Reis vetoed the SAS men's plans to take the Russians' radios, equipment and cipher books, false papers and documents which Hereford would find interesting. He insisted everything should be left, although he agreed that their communications equipment be put out of action.

Shalayez and Chagall sat at opposite ends of the room in tense silence, one out of choice, the other in puzzlement.

Throughout, the expertly secured Spetsnaz members sat on the floor, resentful and uncommunicative. They accepted black tea and cigarettes, but refused to utter a word despite attempts to put them at their ease.

As the bleak dawn light spilled over the landscape, the Spetsnaz team were ordered to strip down to their thermal underwear. They were then carefully resecured in different corners of the room so that they could not assist each other. Plates of cooked meat and water containers were placed within reach of each prisoner. Eating would be difficult and uncomfortable but they would not starve. Their clothes were thrown on the fire, together with all other materials in the chalet which could be used for makeshift clothing, including curtains and duvets. Their skis and poles were broken up and thrown into the river. Finally, a stack of fresh firewood was placed alongside the man secured nearest the hearth.

The team prepared to leave and Hunt took one last look round the place.

"You'll be all right," he said to the woman. Strangely, he found that he didn't hate her for the murder of Lucinda or the old couple. The blame for that ultimately rested with Chagall and Lavender. She'd just been doing her job.

She looked back at him quizzically.

He dropped down on his haunches in front of her. "Look, I'm sorry you won't speak, but I understand. Neither would I, if the situation was reversed. But I'm curious to know if our paths have crossed before? Maybe, a long time ago, in Afghanistan? Or back in Norway before Christmas?"

He thought he detected a faint flicker of humour in those dark eyes. "If it was you," he said, "I'd like to thank you for the vodka."

Suddenly she spoke, and it made him start. "That is something you will never know." The words were said in beautifully enunciated English. The accent would have been at home in Cheltenham Ladies College.

"C'mon, Brian!" Monk was at the door. "We're ready."

Hunt stood, and looked down once more at the mysterious, almost mythical enemy that had been the subject of numerous lectures at Hereford. They had even played the Spetsnaz role themselves during home-defence manoeuvres. Yet, despite all that, it was difficult to grasp that they existed in flesh-and-blood reality. Until you came across them like this. Face to face. Close up, they seemed remarkably ordinary.

He reached into the cargo pocket of his windproof and extracted a plastic flask of whisky. He'd been saving it for a celebration when the mission was completed. He placed it within reach of the woman. Hell, it was only extra weight anyway. And they'd won, so let the Ivans drown their sorrows.

Her eyes followed him as he turned and left.

As he closed the door, he thought he heard a voice say quietly: "Thank you, Brian." But he couldn't be sure because the wind was gusting noisily around the chalet, filling the air with a haze of spindrift.

Len Pope and Colonel Sergei Chagall were already trudging laboriously into the white murk, the Russian trying to get used to the kick-and-slide rhythm. He would find it a long journey to the fell-station.

"All right, let's get moving!" Ash shouted above the wind and, heads bowed, they moved off in single file, a near-invisible white snake working its way steadily across the bleak and desolate landscape.

By mid-morning the wind had lessened and a reluctant brassy sun made an occasional appearance, adding welcome definition to the landscape. The temperature rose to around zero and the going became almost leisurely. Once or twice the distant sound of an aircraft was heard.

Shalayez had slowed considerably. The sheer exhaustion of his ordeal had taken its toll. But for once the SAS men themselves were happy to slacken the pace. They, too, were suffering the effects of the past few days. Thoughts inevitably travelled ahead of them, anticipating the mission's end. A steaming bath and a hearty meal. A round of drinks and then crashing out for a long and blessed sleep.

By two o'clock everything had changed. As is the way in mountain areas, the weather altered dramatically and without warning. A savage wind picked up, filling the air with hard, stinging darts of ice crystals, and the temperature took a dive.

There were no shadows in the diffuse light and the white murk merged land and sky, destroying all sense of perspective and distance.

The terrain had become noticeably more rugged and unpredictable. Ash ordered everyone to switch on their Pieps avalanche-beacons, as traversing even a modest

509

slope could result in disaster if the previous night's fresh snow began slabbing off the surface.

At three they pulled into a sheltered gully in preparation for the fast-approaching night, and the task of lacing together the individual tent sheets began while Monk set up the radio to receive the transmission scheduled for three thirty-five.

Despite his best efforts to keep the battery warm, reception was poor, leaving distorted gaps in the incoming signal. But the overall message was clear, and was unwelcome in the extreme.

The OPs set up on the Norwegian side of the mountains, by both Royal Marine Cadre and SAS units, had picked up hostile contacts over the Swedish border during the earlier clear weather. The opinion was that several small groups of unidentified skiers were attempting to seal off the passes to the south and west. Boxing them in. Clearly Volga Olga's wasn't the only Spetsnaz or GRU team in the area.

The final part of the signal was even more chilling. Without stating its source – the obvious assumption being by collusion with Sweden's OP5 – it mentioned local covert radio traffic from a mobile transmitter which appeared to be co-ordinating the hostile operation. By monitoring these it was believed, but unconfirmed, that a hired civilian helicopter had landed in the vicinity of the chalet Ash's team had left that morning.

Meanwhile, Lavender would rendezvous with Len Pope and Chagall at the Sylarna fell-station as soon as the snow-barriers were lifted to give road access.

The signal petered out at the end. Monk acknowledged but doubted it would be received.

He looked at Ash sympathetically. "Sorry, boss."

The captain pulled a tight smile and glanced at Reis, leaving the Swede in no doubt whose fault it was that Volga Olga's team were possibly in pursuit again. No wonder the Spetsnaz team had been so calm, cocky almost. They knew that transport had already been called up. Probably they had radio'd as soon as they had discovered the skiplane's fuel loss.

Reis realised too. "I think, Mike, that is something maybe we all should have thought of."

While the group had been preparing the tent and receiving the transmission, Hunt was positioned back along the track, covering their meandering trail across the low hills.

In a momentary lull in between squalls of wind, the air cleared of spindrift and visibility increased sharply. Somewhere, in the far distance, he wondered if he detected movement.

He refocused his binoculars. It was difficult to see, to be certain. His eyes smarted with the strain. Then, for a fraction of a second, he caught sight of the ghostly figures. Definitely one or two; perhaps it had been three or four. Before he could confirm, the wind began gusting again, stronger than ever. The shroud of spindrift closed again, sealing him into his own seething white world.

He mounted up and slid down the track until he found the others. He was surprised to find that Ash had been half expecting his news.

"How far, Brian?"

Hunt shrugged. "Five klicks maybe. But double that in terms of travel distance."

Ash turned to the others. "Sorry, lads. Take that tent down. We've no *option* but to push on regardless."

Hunt read Ash's meaning. Had Reis not been chaperoning them, the temptation to set an ambush would have been irresistible.

Ten minutes later the crocodile moved off with a pressing need to gain time and distance. The wolves were closing.

It was a horrendous and dangerous journey. Night had fallen quickly and brought with it a raw and unforgiving wind that got into the bones. Frenzied spindrift created a palpitating fog which head-torches could penetrate no more than a few metres. Dead reckoning was the only way to navigate, taking whatever the treacherous terrain cared to throw up.

There were constant falls. No one was immune. A sudden slope, an uncontrolled skid, and down. Everyone waited, miserable and frozen, whilst the hapless victim sorted himself out. Pack off, skis off. Stand up. Skis on, pack on. Moving again. Just a few minutes. Then stop. Another bastard has taken a tumble. Another tired, shivering wretch looking like a bloody yeti. Covered from head to foot. On again until someone falls through a hole in a stream bed. Life's full of surprises and now the poor sod's got wet, frozen feet. Wait again. Wait, wait, wait. The wind deadening the brain, petrifying the body. Genitals shrunk to nothing, seeking warmth, finding none.

Then Monk went down. Through a cornice on a narrow ridge. Thought he was standing on solid ground, but it was wind-blown snow held up by fresh air. It was a bad fall.

It decided Ash they had to stop. That and the fact that the anemometer gave a windspeed reading of 50 kph. Combined with a minus twelve temperature it meant that even ski-masks could no longer protect the flesh of their faces.

"We'll have to dig in!" Ash announced reluctantly, yelling his words in Hunt's ear as the wind was shrieking through the snow dunes, carving a bizarre new moonscape. "Take Joe ahead on decoy up this hill and join us later!"

Hunt nodded slowly, his head heavy under the accumulation of ice on his hood and goggles, and beckoned to Monk with his mitted hand. They bowed their heads and turned into the wind, their pace reduced to a slow slog against the blizzard's onslaught.

Halfway up the slope Ash chose a spot where dead scrub edged the trackside. There the group 'jumped off', removing skis and donning elephants' feet before picking their way into the birch trees, careful to leave no trace on the broken snow surface.

Hunt, meanwhile, led Monk on up the incline, both men pounding vigorously with their poles to leave numerous impressions that suggested the full party was still on the move. Two miles later they themselves 'jumped off', and skied their way back to where Mike Ash had decided to locate the night's hide.

It was a good position, a deep drift of snow into which the others had already begun tunnelling. The entrances couldn't be viewed from the track they'd created; an ideally sheltered spot for an observation post. It was concealed amongst trees just above the route any pursuers would take.

Monk grinned at Hunt in the shared horror of stripping naked in the vicious wind and redressing in their reversible waterproofs as fast as numbed fingers would allow. The hard work of digging a snowhole in normal clothes would have built up a sweat which would have turned to a layer of ice even as they worked, and to have attempted to sleep in freezing wet clothes would have been to invite death.

They went to work with a vengeance, one carving out snow blocks while the other began digging a cave into the drift. Thankfully, the snow was relatively soft and much of it could be compacted, rather than laboriously dug out and the snow debris carefully spread around. It still took an hour before the cave entrance was sealed with the snow blocks, and the access tunnel finished.

The other construction was already completed and, after changing back into gloriously warm, dry clothes, Hunt and Monk crossed to Ash's hole where the naphtha stove was hissing out heat and fumes. Mess-tins of lamb, rice and appleflakes were devoured with a vengeance, followed by AB biscuits to fill in the gaps. It was washed down with sticky mugs of hot chocolate.

They had scarcely finished when their personal radios crackled weakly with static. Janne Reis was manning the

513

OP and his voice was faint: *"Some people approach on track, maybe a hundred metres."*

"Out!" Ash snapped, dousing the survival candle. Hunt and Monk were already on their feet and worming down the six-foot-long entrance tunnel. "Stay put, Niki, and don't even breathe," Ash ordered before he left.

Outside, the stunning intensity of the cold took Hunt's breath away after the meagre warmth of the shelter. He grabbed his webbing and weapon, which couldn't be taken inside because condensation would freeze it, and edged forward to Reis's position. Although the wind had eased, the raw air was still full of floating spindrift.

He winced and swore silently as the ice-coated gun-metal stripped the skin from his fingers. In his haste he'd left one of his contact-gloves behind.

Monk slid silently alongside him and waved the missing garment with a reproving shake of the head. Hunt gave him a friendly V-sign and slipped it on.

As Ash joined them the click of ski-poles became quite audible, echoing across the eerie landscape.

The four men watched with deadly fascination as the four skiers passed, condensation trailing as they panted up the tramlines in a determined, steady rhythm. They passed silently, just thirty metres distant. Pulses quickened, fearful that the 'jump-off' point would be discovered.

It wasn't, and the pursuers went on up the decoy trail. There was little doubt that Volga Olga and her team were back in business. If all went as planned, when the decoy trail ran out, the Russians would assume that it had been obliterated naturally.

As the tension ebbed, Ash and Monk relieved Reis who took to one snowhole, whilst Hunt joined Shalayez in the other. He relit the stub of the survival candle which provided a surprising amount of light and heat.

"We are safe now, Brian?"

"Most probably. They'd have their work cut out to find us before daylight," he replied, rolling out his 'green

514

maggot' bag and kipmat on the ice slab beside the Russian.

Shalayez looked at the slippery iced dome above his head. "And we are safe in here?"

Hunt laughed. "Don't suffer from claustrophobia, do you? You know, enclosed spaces?"

The Russian shared his humour. "It is maybe too late to ask me that, I think. But I will not sleep."

Hunt reached out and waggled the ski-pole which had been pushed through the vent-hole to the outside of the drift. "Just make sure the airway's free. And if you see the candle go out, wake me immediately."

The SAS man smiled his reassurance, then removed his boots and peeled off his socks. His feet were pinched and numb with the onset of frost-nip. "How are your feet?"

Shalayez shrugged. "I don't know, I don't feel them."

"Mike pushed it today. As well we did, but it was risky – Here, take those socks off. Now get your feet up under my armpits. C'mon, I'll do the same." Hunt laughed again at the shocked look on the Russian's face. "We call it the buddy-buddy method. It may look bloody stupid but it'll save your toes from dropping off!"

After a painful thirty minutes' thawing out, they settled into their respective bags. It had become quite warm and cosy in the candleglow. Outside, the blizzard had returned with a vengeance, but in the snowhole its howling anger was hardly discernible.

Hunt smashed a grubby piece of sweet mintcake and handed a fragment to Shalayez.

The Russian sucked at it, the sweetness getting to his teeth. "How long now, Brian? You know, I am very tired."

"Yes, we all are. But maybe tomorrow." He hesitated as he said it, and Shalayez picked up the nuance in his voice. "Trouble is, Niki, our Spetsnaz friends have overtaken us. That might cut off our last chance of an easy pass over the border. We're being forced onto the mountain."

Shalayez looked apprehensive. As well he might.

"Yes, it's a bloody great mountain." He laughed thinly. "Well, big enough if you're the poor sod who's got to climb it. But don't worry. Our *biggest* battle in this place is the weather and terrain, not the enemy. That Spetsnaz team have kept going at some minus forty degrees – they're not doing themselves any favours. They could be dead by dawn." It was wishful thinking, he realised, however true. Somehow he didn't believe they would perish. No way.

"I will be pleased to get to Norway," Shalayez murmured. "Only then, maybe I think it is all worthwhile. All this pain and suffering. That poor old couple at the chalet. When again I am with Lucy, then it will all be worthwhile, yes, Brian?"

There was no reply, and he realised then that Hunt was asleep, the uneaten piece of mintcake still between his fingers.

Shalayez lay back, hands beneath his head, and stared at the ceiling of the ice cave inches above him. It was strange, he thought, he could not picture Lucy's face. It was the first time.

At dawn the air was still alive with spindrift. The wind was gusting, but nowhere near as viciously as the previous night. A low rolling ceiling of cloud shed a steady fall of light dry snow.

The icy blast of morning came as a shock after the cosy silence of the snowholes. It was decided to leave them intact; normally they would have been collapsed for safety's sake. But the men might need a fall-back RV if they found their route blocked by the Spetsnaz team who had overtaken them the previous evening.

As a precaution against that eventuality, Hunt and Monk went on ahead. Keeping within the half-mile range of their personal radios, they reconnoitred the safest route and potential ambush points.

By mid-morning the wind had finally exhausted itself.

The air became uncannily still, the sky remaining oppressively dull and overcast. For the first time in days the temperature nudged above freezing.

Hunt halted to consult the map. Reports the previous day from the British observation posts on the Norwegian border, and from OP5's reconnaissance, had suggested that the easy routes to the south and west had been effectively sealed by the Russians, forcing them into the mountains which formed a natural barrier between the SAS team and freedom. It was an inhospitable area with no obvious easy way through.

Geologically the mountains represented two horseshoes butted side by side, with the open ends facing east; to the west lay freedom.

Hunt was now standing a kilometre from the uppermost of the two horseshoes, through the centre of which ran a glacial tongue. The frozen river of molten ice poured from the high plateau, the translucent sheen of its surface clearly visible. The broad sweeping slopes of the ice field were broken at intervals by sudden drops. Petrified waterfalls descending almost vertically, a cathedral organ of viridescent ice which culminated in a confusion of gigantic, jagged ice blocks and scree. And if those steep icefalls were not formidable enough, the edge of the glacial tongue was guarded by an extensive crevasse field, a disfiguring maze of electric blue veins in the distance.

Enticingly, Norway waited for them at the top.

But it was not the sort of climb to be taken lightly by experts with back-up and an extensive range of equipment. To attempt it with Shalayez and Reis, relying solely on ice-axes and crampons, would be unthinkable.

"Don't like the look of that one, Brian," Monk observed, adding: "Wouldn't mind giving it a crack in summer, mind."

Hunt didn't share his friend's enthusiasm for climbing, unless it was strictly in the line of duty. "Let's move on and see what else there is on offer."

They set off around the towering spur where the two horseshoes joined. Again the climb looked horrendous, being even more sheer than the main ice field of the glacier. The lower horseshoe opened into a wide flat valley some two kilometres deep by one kilometre wide, surrounded by steep-sided heights in every direction. A frozen river and two lakes ran through the centre.

"That's home," Hunt said. "The border runs right through the centre of the valley. Just two klicks away."

Monk grinned. "Two kilometres, eh? Our blokes have got an OP up there somewhere." He pointed to beyond the centre of the horseshoe where the glaciated side of the mountain rose steeply on the Norwegian side of the frontier.

Hunt was deep in thought. Once inside the horseshoe there was no other way out. The far end may be Norwegian territory, but it was virtually an enclave cut off geographically by the surrounding heights.

He said, half to himself: "If we could make a dash down there, they could fly in a chopper. They wouldn't even have to leave Norwegian territory."

"No sign of Ivan," Monk said in support.

Hunt wasn't so confident. "I'm sure Volga Olga hasn't decided to pack up and go home. She could be anywhere up on the mountains. Or in the valley itself. And we've already had reports of other groups in the area. It just needs one marksman with the old Dragunov sniper-rifle and we're sitting ducks."

They found a sheltered spot and settled down with binoculars to quarter the valley inch by inch for signs of clandestine occupation. Whilst one watched, the other coddled the radio battery using chemical handwarmers to coax life back into it before the next scheduled transmission time.

When Ash and the rest of the party caught up, there had been no visual sighting of a hostile contact in the valley or the surrounding heights.

518

Hunt put his suggestion about the helicopter pick-up to Ash.

"It sounds plausible," the other agreed. "And there's no sign of opposition?"

Hunt shook his head. "Bare as a moonscape. But then they're not going to advertise. Ivan could have OPs in the valley or anywhere in the mountains. If anyone's seen anything, it'll be our blokes up on the Norwegian mountains. They've got a commanding view."

Ash consulted his map. Although it was unmarked, as standard SAS practice, it served to remind him of the positions of the British OPs which he'd been given during earlier transmissions. He indicated the Norwegian mountain at the far side of the valley. "That's a Cadre OP," he observed.

"All we need," Hunt quipped. "Bloody bootnecks at a time like this."

But the SAS captain was in no mood for humour. He couldn't believe the Soviets didn't have the valley covered; reports suggested they'd already cut off every other route. They must realise, too, the possibilities offered by the Norwegian enclave of level ground at the end of the valley.

"It would have to be done at night," he said finally, and glanced up at the sky. High smoky cloud was shredding with the promise of a cold clear night ahead. Not the best weather for crossing such exposed territory which might be under surveillance.

It was galling that, with Norway under three kilometres away, an 'accidental incursion' into Swedish airspace couldn't be arranged. If only they could be picked up from where they stood. But he'd already fielded the idea and the Foreign Office had curtly vetoed any such notion.

"We can put the idea forward on the next transmission," Hunt suggested. "It'll be easier to decide once we've had an updated sitrep."

Ash agreed. "Meanwhile, let's get comfortable. I

suggest we dig in for a lengthy wait and get some hot grub on the stove."

No one argued with that.

Hot food and drink improved morale dramatically, but the optimism was short-lived. The exchange of transmissions raised as many questions as it answered. While the request for exfiltration by helicopter from the Norwegian enclave was immediately agreed, it came with an unnerving warning. Hostile contacts had been reported from the Cadre OP overlooking the valley two days earlier. Movement had been detected on the far slopes and along the central river valley.

The time for the lift was fixed at 2300 hours.

"What range has a Dragunov rifle got?" Ash asked.

Hunt considered. "With a nightscope in good conditions, effective to three or four hundred metres. Maybe more."

"So anyone in the centre of the valley could prevent passage on both sides?"

Hunt nodded. "And make the landing zone untenable."

"And what about Volga Olga?" Monk asked. "She can't have been in the valley for two days. She was only a few hours ahead of us. So where's her mob disappeared to?"

Ash said: "Let's hope we don't find out. Meanwhile, I think we ought to enter the valley by traversing along the north slope – put as much distance between us and any snipers in the river valley. Rely on speed and surprise."

No one could disagree; there just wasn't an alternative.

As the hours dragged by and the time for the off approached, adrenalin was pumping and an air of optimism returned once more. It was, after all, the final push.

Even Shalayez found himself sharing the soldiers' black humour, enjoying the mood even if he didn't always understand the jokes.

520

For Hunt the end of the mission would be the end of an era and the thought depressed him. But he did his best to concentrate on what would be the longest and most anxious three-kilometre ski of his life.

Ash's hooded figure approached Hunt, his white windproofs already accumulating a rime of frost. He tapped his watch. Hunt acknowledged, and slid into the lead position of the column.

It was hard work gaining height on the steep northern slope, side-stepping through deep, crumbling snow as he edged towards the start position. From there the plan was to make a long, steady downhill traverse with skis edged into the northern slope. By gaining height before they started, they would be able to maintain a reasonable speed all the way to the rendezvous with the helicopter.

When the party was in position Hunt led off, keeping his poles in his left hand and the Hockler carbine in his right. Once he was several hundred metres ahead, the centre party of Ash and Reis with Shalayez would follow whilst he waited, prepared to return fire should they come under attack. Joe Monk travelled similarly as a 'tail-end Charlie'. At all times at least one of them was ready to offer instant protective fire.

Progress, however, was far slower than they'd anticipated. Although it was a brilliantly clear night, a vicious wind was whipping the spindrift at them, making visibility patchy on the ground. The slope was also far more precipitous than they'd anticipated. Only the edging of the skis, jammed horizontally into the gleaming ice crust, prevented any one of them from skidding down into the valley. Thank goodness, Hunt thought, that they had allowed a full half-hour for contingencies; they were likely to need every precious moment of it.

They were halfway across when Hunt stopped, went down on his haunches, and turned the barrel of his Hockler out into the void of the valley.

It seemed forever that he waited, perched precariously

on the slope, for the figure of Ash to emerge from the swirl of spindrift.

Christ, where are they? he wondered impatiently. Time really was beginning to run out. He squinted into the darkness. Finally the lead skier emerged, head bowed against the wind.

It was then that Hunt thought he heard the sound. A sudden sharp report, momentarily audible above the wailing wind. Was it his imagination? As though in confirmation he felt the ground beneath his feet tremble. The entire mountain appeared to shake. Anxiously he glanced around him for some kind of explanation. That noise wasn't natural. He looked back, puzzled, towards the approaching party. Ash had stopped and was staring up at the invisible peak towering above them.

Another sound joined the wind, a low resonant note.

It began with a deep background bass hum, hardly discernible. Then it grew like a gathering tidal wave of sound, drowning out the wind in its might and anger. It rolled inexorably on, louder and nearer until it resembled the deep-throated boom of thunder. Only it went on, and on. Louder and louder, interspersed by the sharp snap of timber as trees and bushes were uprooted.

Then he knew. In the split second that it took to register, it all flashed into place. He had dug the avalanche-pit himself before they'd crossed the slope. He'd checked the snow layers in the hole and the risk was minimal, the old snow plastered to the mountain face like cement and then glued with the night's ice. That first noise he'd heard was high explosive. God, if anyone should have recognised it, he should!

They had just walked into the most effective trap of all, the avalanche ambush. Suddenly the whereabouts of 'Volga Olga' was no longer a mystery – her team was somewhere up there on the heights above them . . .

Discarding his poles, his fingers tore at the bindings of his skis. Frantically he kicked one free; the other stuck. He kicked again and again, simultaneously scrabbling at the buckle of his bergan with mitted fingers. Only at the last moment he remembered to face up the mountainside.

"AVALANCHE!" he screamed at the top of his voice.

18

There was no visual warning when it hit.

It came out of the night with the deafening roar of a waterfall and the awesome power that only a hundred thousand tons of snow on the move can have.

Hunt was struck with the mighty deadweight of a sledgehammer, crushing the air from his lungs as the onslaught swallowed him up greedily and plunged on down into the valley.

He knew to swim into an avalanche, to try to break surface. But the white beast of the mountain would have none of it. Scornful of theory it tossed him around at its will, a rag doll in the raging torrent. The jammed cable-binding was torn free at the heel, wrenching his bones until he felt something snap with the strain. The white lava flow clawed the bergan from his shoulders, ripping buckles and straps with total contempt. He spun in a blind weightless world, all sense of gravity lost, totally disorientated as he cartwheeled through the seething white space at the mercy of its whim.

Suddenly, he hit something solid and stopped. The moving wall poured in on top of him, pulping his body with its consistency of wet sand. He was plastered into the landscape, with more and more leaden ballast rolling on top. Squeezed like an insect between thumb and forefinger until its abdomen popped.

Then it stopped. First the movement, then the noise. There was nothing. Just absolute silence, and blackness. Hunt had tried to protect his head with his arms, and now he attempted to clear a breathing space around his mouth as he felt himself coming to rest. But it had only partly worked. One hand was trapped behind his neck, immovable and stuck fast as though set in concrete. The other hand was free; he could wriggle it and feel the tip of his ski mitt against his nose, but he couldn't see it. He tried one leg and then the other. They were totally compacted; there was no movement and no feeling except for a burning sensation in one ankle. His chest was so constricted he couldn't even fill his lungs, reducing them to mere millimetres of expansion.

Even had he been able to move, he had no idea which way to dig. Up or down? Which way was the sky? And which way would he have found himself just digging in deeper? He forced some saliva into his mouth and let it trickle out of his lips. But the silk ski-mask prevented it from dribbling anywhere.

He knew then he was going to die.

At least, he consoled himself, it was warm. And, apart from his ankle, he wasn't in any great pain. His breathing was uncomfortable, breathless, but then it hardly mattered because the air wouldn't last for long. He moved the fingers of his right hand, describing a circle in an effort to find out how large a gap he had managed to create. But his elbow was wedged firmly, restricting movement, so there was still no way of knowing.

Twice he summoned his energy to free all or any of his limbs, but he remained stuck fast. An ornamental butterfly sealed in a glass paperweight.

He closed his eyes and tried to accept the inevitable. It was frighteningly easy, and for a moment that revelation shocked him. He never thought he would be one to surrender life so willingly. It was against every natural instinct he'd ever had, let alone his training. There was only the chillingly calm acceptance of the inevitable.

He wondered about the others; could any of them have survived? Or were they all out there, like him? Splattered under the crush of snow, wondering the same thing. All lying there, imprisoned and immobilised, all hoping against hope that there was a survivor who would find them. At least they all carried a Pieps avalanche beacon – not that it did much good when you were all buried.

He thought of Mike Ash and Big Joe Monk, both dying a slow suffocating death. Men so alive and vital and fearless, it had seemed that they were indestructible. And the good-humoured, laconic Swede: Janne Reis had kept up with them during their race across the snows, never once complaining and always willing to help out. Yet it must have been agony for him at times. Such an end was poor thanks for such determination.

Then there was that poor bastard Shalayez. All that suffering and manipulation by others and all for what? To be frozen alive on some godforsaken Swedish mountain. He didn't even know that the love of his life was no more than a bullet-shattered corpse. That, Hunt's wandering mind reasoned, was maybe something to be grateful for.

Inexorably his thoughts were drawn to memories of Gabby. He could visualise her standing at the door of the ramshackle farm with Baby Walt in her arms. Watching, knowing, as the officer from Stirling Lines opened the front gate and patted the dog that came to greet him. Hunt's mind zoomed in like a camera to a close-up of her face. The wispy blonde hair and the translucent skin with scarcely a trace of make-up. And those distant blue eyes, somehow showing that they knew what the officer was going to say before he opened his mouth. Instinctively, her free hand went down to the child in pigtails who clung to her skirt. A reassuring hug. Because, like mother like daughter, Jessica knew too.

For the first time he felt tears in his eyes. And he didn't know if it was sorrow for their loss, or self-pity . . .

Something sharp bit into his neck, and he winced.

Then again, this time poking into his shoulder.

His eyes widened, his mind suddenly pulled back from the soporific trance into which it had been coaxed. A probe! A bloody avalanche-probe!

He yelled at the top of his voice, but there was no air in his lungs and his utterance was reduced to a painful croak.

Then he heard the sharp decisive grate of aluminium slicing into snow. Then again and again, working into a frenzy. Suddenly, he was aware of laboured grunts and the squeak of boots nearby.

He'd been expecting the breakthrough to come from above his head, but it didn't. The shovel struck once more and suddenly there was a hole underneath him. Totally confused, he found he was staring up at the night sky, the air flickering with spindrift. Sweet icy air rushed in to sear his lungs.

"Hold on, mate," Big Joe Monk gasped as he wielded his shovel. "Have you out in a jiff."

The weight lifted from his legs and the pain shot into his ankle. He ignored it, kicking his limbs free, wrestling to tear his trapped arms from the icy grip.

He struggled to sit up and Monk hugged him like a lost son. "You lovely, lovely bastard! Thought I'd lost you. Any bones broken?"

Hunt wriggled his ankle and felt the sparks of pain. "Don't know. I'll survive."

Monk staggered to his feet. "I've got to get on to the others. Give us a hand if you can. I tried you first because you were on the edge of the slide like me. I got a chance to leap clear. God knows how deep the other poor sods are buried though."

Monk turned and waded frantically off into the thick broken carpet of snow debris, leaving Hunt to get his wind back and climb groggily to his feet. He looked around for signs of his bergan, Its dark green top protruded from the snow some thirty metres away. Wiping the pain from his ankle aside, he plodded across to it, up to his knees in snow, and extracted his shovel and

527

collapsible probe. He tried to move fast across to the main site of the slide, but his pace was reduced to agonising slow motion.

He took the orange plastic Pieps transceiver from his windproof pocket and joined Monk in the search. In practice the system worked well, but now the methodical task seemed endless. First you walked down the fall-line of the avalanche, listening for the tell-tale bleep of a buried transmitter. As the sound became louder you slowed until the volume began to die; then back until you'd established the best reception. Then horizontal across the slide: first left, sound fading. Go right. Ah, better – louder, clearer, clearer, fading. Back – louder, louder. Got it! In with the probe. In, in, in. Nothing! Try again, that's it. Something soft. Just hope you haven't poked the poor sod's eye out. Start shovelling for all you're worth. Ignore injury pain, screaming muscles and pounding heart. Just dig, dig, dig . . .!

"GOT ONE!" Monk bawled, his booming cry of triumph diluted by the unforgiving wind.

Hunt kept digging, his heart rising as he uncovered the outline of a leg. It twitched. Thank God! There was some life yet. More frantic wielding of the precious little aluminium shovel. Another leg, now the body. Shoulders rise like a yeti in some horror movie and the man stands, snow cascading from his back and head.

Shalayez's bloodshot eyes blinked at him, a tired smile creasing his face. Hunt grinned back and hugged him for a moment. It was no time for words. Then the SAS man turned to see who Monk had unburied. It was Janne Reis.

The search then began in earnest for Mike Ash. All four spread out across the uneven tide of debris and began a systematic search. They took twenty minutes working down the slope, and there was nothing.

Fighting exhaustion they struggled back up, looking at the highest level, and started gridding out the area again.

Hunt found him, but it took the four of them to dig him out. He was twelve feet deep. When they cleared off the snow they saw that three of his limbs were at grotesque angles. His head was laid flush with his shoulders, his neck broken.

The four men stood, silent. Just looking. Four snow-covered figures with heads bowed. Hunt felt the tears well. Mike Ash, mountain man and man mountain. Who loved the high peaks and the adventure of it all. Who couldn't get enough of ice and snow which he could challenge and conquer. It was his life blood and it had coursed through his veins with a passion. A gentle man who was never slow to offer the hand of friendship. A man who hated the death and destruction of his trade; preferring, when he could, to emphasise its positive aspects. More at home converting an enemy by example and persuasion, than by the bullet or the bomb.

A mitted hand touched Hunt's elbow. Monk's be-goggled head nodded in the direction of the valley. Dark shapes were moving snake-like across the snow in their direction.

Hunt squinted. There was no doubt in his mind who they were: Russians from one of the hidden OPs coming to see what damage had been done. Ready to finish off any survivors who might have a tale to tell. Another squall blew and the spindrift obscured the view.

Hurriedly they collected together all the pieces of kit they could find. Between the four of them there were six skis; Hunt and Monk made do by skating on one ski apiece, pushing themselves along with an elephant's-foot on the other leg.

Slowly they edged back to the mouth of the valley, to where the night's events had begun. If the Russian search party had seen them, they never knew.

At last they located the snow-cave they had built earlier. Monk got a stove going to brew tea. It was a long, long time before anyone spoke, each man alone with his thoughts.

Finally Hunt said: "The bastards who did that are up there. On the mountain behind us. That woman and her mates. While they're up there and the other Russians are in the valley, we can't get out."

Monk slurped his tea thirstily. "What are you suggesting, Brian?"

"That it won't take them long to find us in the morning."

"We'll give 'em something to think about," Monk growled.

Hunt shook his head. "We didn't have much ammunition to start with, Joe. And we've just got two Hocklers left."

"And my pistol," Reis added.

"With a magazine apiece," Hunt pointed out. "It would make the Alamo seem like a tea-party." He stared out into the thrashing spindrift beyond the open cave. "We're out of provisions, only proper skis for two, and the radio's somewhere under an avalanche. The only way to get out of this alive is to do the unexpected. And we *have* to do it now – before the Russians can confirm that we weren't all killed in the avalanche."

"Do *what*?" Monk pressed.

Hunt could hardly believe what he was suggesting himself. "Scale the glacier. Scale the glacier and get the jump on that bloody woman and her team."

Monk let out a long, slow whistle.

"It's the only way," Hunt said. "We're boxed in and they think they've got us. The last thing they'll be expecting us to do is to hit back. The top of the mountain is virtually a plateau. Once we're there, we just ski along the flat into Norway. With any luck we can bypass Volga Olga's team. They're bound to be on the south side. We can pass to the north."

"You make it sound so simple," Monk muttered sarcastically.

Janne Reis watched on with amazement: the idea was daring and he could see the sense it made. However he did not cherish the thought. Shalayez clearly didn't understand the implications of what was being proposed.

Hunt said decisively: "Right, let's see what kit we can muster between us."

It was, in fact, precious little. The survivors' bergans at least yielded one set of crampons each, but only Monk's ice-axe hadn't been wrenched off and lost in the avalanche. Hunt had one length of climbing rope. More rope, together with harnesses and a small selection of ice-screws, belays and anchors, had been in Ash's kit which had not been found with his body.

Nevertheless it would have to suffice. They restowed their equipment in silent apprehension at what lay ahead. Mounting up on the unorthodox mixture of skis and snowshoes, Hunt led the forlorn column into the freezing night.

The going was hard, awkward and slow as they made their way doggedly up the spur of the northern horseshoe to give themselves access, through the crevasse field, to the main tongue of the glacier.

When the time came, each man's crampons took an age to strap on. Exhaustion was already setting in and fingers had lost all sense of feeling after mitts had become sodden during the avalanche. Hunt ordered all heavy equipment to be ditched. There would be no shelter on the peaks, and without sleeping bags there would be little protection from the elements. Emergency plastic bivi-bags would have to suffice as protection against wet and wind. Likewise only solid-fuel hexamine stoves and the bare minimum of food and essential survival items could be taken as they could be carried in pockets. It was a difficult decision.

But equally Hunt was aware that, with weighty bergans to haul, Shalayez and Reis might not make it at all. Their only chance, he reasoned, was to travel light and fast while their energy reserves held out. And the last thing he wanted was for them to be caught out, strung across the glacier when morning came. Spetsnaz snipers would be able to pick them off at their leisure.

Monk led the way into the crevasse field. He groped his way across the zig-zag path of snow bridges which, in places, spanned seemingly bottomless chasms. At each crossing he moved slowly, prodding ahead of him with an avalanche-probe. He was roped through the group's only remaining ice-axe, which was anchored deeply to form a belay, with Hunt feeding out the slack. But if a bridge collapsed under Monk and he plunged into one of the fissures, there was no guarantee that the axe would hold. And no one knew the depth of each inky void that yawned beneath them.

Visibility was fair, the route marked by the white reflected crystals of the snow crust against the blackness of each crevasse. Monk inched forward on hands and knees, probing the surface as he crossed. Some sections held firm, soft snow on bedrock or solid ice. Others threatened to crumble under his weight. Still other sections were slippery, wind-polished ice moguls which fell away sharply to the subterranean depths.

Panting heavily with relief, he would sit after each crossing, untie their only rope and watch it being pulled back across the bridge. Reis would then tie on the rope and pluckily crawl across, expecting each step to be his last. Shalayez would then repeat the process, which was then reversed for the final man – if there was a rock suitable to act as a belay. Frequently there wasn't, and Hunt would have to cross on a prayer with his heart pounding in his chest like a drum.

As they negotiated fissure after fissure, threading their way inexorably toward the glacier, Monk's skills at recognising unstable bridges grew rapidly. He would detour continuously until he found a safer, stronger span.

But even then he sometimes got it wrong. With a yelp of surprise he found himself plunging through a solid crust that had collapsed under him. Only fast reaction saved him as he jack-knifed his body to spread his weight and managed to scramble clear of the weakest point of the span.

Each man watched, transfixed with bated breath. All knew that anyone sliding into one of the bottomless crevasses would likely never be found.

However, Monk's persistence paid dividends and at last the lacerated snowscape was crossed, and they had reached the glacial tongue itself.

It was comforting now to feel the bite of the crampon teeth in the translucent ice film beneath their boots, holding them to the glassy slope that fell away behind them. Again Monk led, swinging his ice-axe rhythmically to chisel holds in the smooth surface. He moved in a series of steady upward traverses, negotiating the shambolic scattering of glaciated rock.

At last they came to the main sheer ice-fall, columns of frosted white marble fluting the cliff face for a hundred feet. Starlight played on the glistening black ice piping that dripped all around them.

Shalayez took an instinctive backward step.

Hunt took his arm. "It's all right, Niki. It won't be as bad as it looks. You've got crampons, just dig them in. Joe's cutting handholds. You can't fall unless you let go."

The Russian stared at him as though he were mad.

Above their heads Monk was already edging steadily up a chimney formed by two towering ice-columns. Chisel, move, crampon points in, chisel, move . . .

Wordlessly Reis followed, numb fingers gripping the holds made by Monk.

Shalayez shook his head. "There is nothing to hold . . ."

"Yes, there is," Hunt assured. "You don't need big holds. Just keep an upward momentum. Keep going. Don't look down."

"I-I-can't," Shalayez stuttered, fear draining into his groin.

533

"It's like climbing a tree when you were a kid," Hunt hissed. "Don't think, just do it. Now *GO!*"

Trembling, the Russian stepped forward into the ice-chimney and stretched out his hands for the first chis-elled handholds.

"Feet and hands," Hunt whispered in his ear. "Not knees or elbows. Keep upright. Understand?"

Shalayez nodded dumbly.

"Don't reach your hands too high or you'll get into trouble. Take your time and *look* where you're going."

Swallowing hard, the Russian tentatively began the climb, Hunt immediately below him to offer advice.

Hunt knew that Shalayez would be applying his deadly powers of concentration, normally reserved for mathematical problems, to sticking to the polished ice like a fly to a wall. Hunt also knew that the scientist's heart would be pounding with fear and his body slick with perspiration despite the intense cold. He could even see the tension in the Russian's rigid body posture as he inched his way up, his fingers nervously seeking the next chiselled handhold. He would pause frequently, gulping great draughts of icy air. Relief flooding through him that he had managed another few feet. Forehead pressed against the transparent ice; fingertips in his mitts throbbing with the pain of clutching the thin shelf of ice no more than an inch deep. Above him came the steady crunch of Reis's crampons into ice, sending down a cascade of crystals. And beyond that, the rasp of Monk's ice-axe carving the next set of handholds.

Shalayez forgot himself and chanced a look below. He wanted to see how far he'd come. Hunt's begoggled face looked up anxiously, a hand waving him on. He felt suddenly sick and giddy. The faint first light of the false dawn illuminated the ice wall and the jagged profusion of debris, blue-grey and angry, ready to devour anyone who fell.

He felt the vomit in his throat, fought the nausea. He shut his eyes, shaking his head to clear the dizziness.

534

Felt the agony of his fingertips and knew he was going to fall.

"Keep going!" Hunt's voice urged. "Go on, Niki."

Shalayez pressed his cheek against the ice again, paralysed, and thought how much easier it would be to just let go.

Cramp began gnawing its way up his calves, the muscles rigid from the pressure of keeping the crampon points pinioned to the ice wall. A rush of tiny numbing pinpricks worked along his tendons, deadening all feeling. Now he had lost all sensation in his hands and legs, staying fixed only by some magical act of will.

In that moment he died a thousand times. He had never, ever experienced sheer blind total terror before. He was mortified, a split second's drop from death, and totally unable to move. His heart was thudding with such massive resonance that he thought the vibration must shake him off. Sweat poured from him, freezing his heated body instantly, between his shoulders, and in his armpits and groin. His goggles fogged with condensation until he could scarcely see.

"Niki, go *on*!" Hunt shouted again. "You can't stay there forever! Go *on*! Look, there's a handhold to your left."

Shalayez had his eyes tight shut. "I cannot let go. I will fall."

Hunt's voice was patient. "No, you won't. You're quite safe. Feel for it."

Tentatively the Russian moved one hand, anticipating his fall. To his surprise he didn't.

"Left a bit," Hunt instructed.

His hand crawled gingerly over the polished ice. It found nothing.

"You got it!" Hunt called.

Numb fingers felt the cleft. The original chiselled hole had been crunched by others' crampons.

"It is too small!" Shalayez wailed miserably.

"No it's fine!" Hunt insisted. "Go for it!"

Shalayez shook his head and began to sob.

By now Monk and Reis were far above, leaving the other two motionless on the ice wall. Frozen, white specks against a vast glistening rampart.

Minutes passed as the two men clung on, buffeted by the wind. Minutes that seemed like hours. Shalayez's mind was as exhausted as his body. His will had gone, he knew it. He could not even conjure a picture of Lucinda in his mind and wondered whether it would spur him on if he could.

He opened his eyes at the sudden sound beside him, and found himself staring into the sinister black lenses of Hunt's goggles. The man had clearly risked everything to get alongside, leaving the safety of the ice-axe holes, relying on crampons alone.

Shalayez felt at once thankful and ashamed.

"Come on, old lad," Hunt said. "We can do it. Give me your hand."

He took the mitt that clutched at the broken ledge and placed it for a better grip.

"Now move your left foot. Up, and kick in again. Hard."

Feeling safer now, Shalayez obeyed. He felt the sensation return to his calf as he moved, and was instantly relieved. Under Hunt's coaxing he began the upward momentum again.

To his own surprise he found himself gaining confidence. He knew then he was going to make it, and felt curiously elated at the danger he was in. There was even a sense of pride that he had done it, and he edged up the giant skirt of corrugated ice with rapidly increasing skill. Above, the masked faces of Monk and Reis looked down on him, growing ever closer.

And then his crampon gave.

The adjustment bar of the articulated fitting worked free, the front points flexing down under his weight. And the grip was lost. His mitts slid over smooth black ice as his fingers tried in vain to grip.

536

All he was aware of was the sudden cold rush of air as he went. He felt Hunt grab for him, or push him. The briefest touch. Gone, falling. Then the shock of impact blasted the breath from his lungs as he landed on his back.

For a split second he was stationary, as though caught by the outstretched hand of God. A miracle. But then he felt himself begin to slip, gravity pulling him helplessly sideways down the tilted ice shelf that was scarcely a metre wide. Instinctively he stabbed his remaining crampon into the hard silk crust. He began to pivot, feeling one leg waving out over the void. With every last dreg of energy he clawed his fingers into the glassy indentations of the surface. His slide grudgingly slowed, stopped.

How long he clung on in mindless desperation he didn't know. All he knew was that he shouldn't open his eyes. Shouldn't confirm the steep angle of the shelf. Shouldn't know how precarious was his grip on life. Shouldn't see the tortured debris at the foot of the ice-fall.

He just clung. Mind blank. Fear pointless, just fatalistic acceptance of what was inevitable.

Then he heard the chunk of crampons in ice and once more recognised the reassuring sound of Hunt's voice. Telling him to be calm. To hold on. Dear sweet God, how he intended to hold on!

Suddenly Hunt was there, securing their only rope in a harness cradle around his waist and thighs.

Hand on his shoulder. A pat of assurance. He was safe, and only now dared to look around him. It was then he realised just how lucky his escape had been. A seven-metre fall had been broken by the only lateral protuberance large enough to hold a man. He wondered if Hunt had deliberately pushed him in that direction as he'd fallen. Otherwise it was pure good fortune.

Hunt stood with the other end of the rope that snaked up to where Monk and Reis stood twenty metres above, at the head of the ice-fall. There it had been belayed around a hefty embedded ice nodule, and then back down to the Russian's harness. The SAS man anchored himself to a jagged rock outcrop and motioned Shalayez to begin his climb back up.

To his own surprise Shalayez found his courage return. After this nothing could stop him. Cautiously but steadfastly he started upward as Hunt took in the slack to hold him if he slipped.

But the Russian went up with renewed confidence and agility, determined that this last effort would not fail.

Willing hands grabbed him, hauling him bodily up the last few feet, and he fell back, eyes closed, as Reis and Monk waited anxiously for Hunt to appear.

It took the SAS man little time and, expert though he may have been, he was clearly relieved to be over the worst of it. He looked around to see that they were in a sheltered cleft, at the top of the glacier where it flattened out onto the plateau peak.

The first fingers of light were in the eastern sky and definition was returning to the landscape. They'd done it.

"What happens next?" Monk asked.

"Next?" Hunt said, unable to think. There was just one thing on his mind. "Next? We eat, that's what!"

And everyone laughed. Tension evaporated with the morning, and life had suddenly never seemed more glorious. The sheer unadulterated joy of conquered fear. And for one fleeting moment Hunt understood the unbreakable addiction that Mike Ash had had for the mountains.

They dug into pockets to find scraps of biscuit and mintcake bars and shared everything equally with each other. The water bottles on their belt orders were half-frozen, but there was enough icy liquid to slake the worst of their thirst.

With the improving light the extent of their achievement in scaling the glacier became apparent. Their victory was only slightly marred by the discovery in daylight that an ice-path ran gently up the side of the tongue, and could have afforded a less hair-raising ascent. Monk, typically, felt obliged to point it out with obvious relish. It was not appreciated.

"Joe and I will go ahead onto the plateau to do a recce," Hunt decided at length. "We'll try and pinpoint Volga Olga's team, and then take steps to avoid it."

"I should come, too," Reis said. "We are still in Sweden."

"Just," Monk added. "By a few hundred metres."

Hunt said: "Someone has to stay with Niki."

"I do not like the idea of us splitting up," Reis said emphatically.

"Look," Hunt replied patiently, "if anything happens to us, you two still stand a chance. Please don't argue."

Reis grinned. "And spoil a beautiful friendship, eh?"

Hunt shared his humour. "You got it."

There was no more discussion. Feeling much revived, the two SAS men checked over their Hocklers and set off over the undulating snow dunes of the peak, using the wind-worn gullies for cover. They moved cautiously and swiftly in classic leapfrog style: one covering whilst the other advanced, until they were out of sight of the others. Deliberately they worked their way towards the highest ground where they would have a clear view of the plateau. There appeared to be absolutely no sign of life. It was another planet, shimmering in the crystalline air of morning. The strengthening sun ignited a trillion specular pinpoints until the quartz-like snow surface dazzled with brilliance, and electrified the blue of the shadows. A bizarre alien landscape had been fashioned by the ever-moaning wind: smooth turrets and ice spires of the high ground giving way to staggered terraces of eddying spindrift and the purple jaws of the crevasse fields.

For a moment both men were stunned by its magnificence. Then Monk pointed a finger. "Brian, look!"

Two hundred metres away, in a deep drift, the steely morning light caught the lips of two snowhole entrances. Outside, a collection of small arms, skis, and a radio had been stowed in an open pit.

"We've found 'em," Monk murmured with satisfaction. "And we don't even have to go past their position. We can slip over into Norway before they're even awake."

Hunt hesitated.

"C'mon, Brian," Monk hissed. "Let's get out while the going's good."

"No," Hunt said.

"What'ya mean –?"

"They killed Mike last night. We've already let them get away with murdering Lucy. And that old couple at the chalet." He turned to his friend. "But not Mike. They won't get away with that."

Monk shoved his goggles onto his forehead. "What you said to Janne – about locating them and avoiding them – you didn't mean a bloody word of it, did you?"

Hunt didn't answer immediately. After a moment he said: "Janne's got his job to do. He wouldn't allow us to do anything."

"So that's why you told him to stay with Niki?"

"Some," Hunt said.

Monk shook his head. "Now that he trusts us – you take advantage."

"You don't have to come with me. This is personal."

"Don't talk wet, Brian. 'Course I'll come. But it's too late to do Mike any favours. I'd like to blow a hole in Olga's knickers same as you, but – "

"Then stop gassing. They could be awake at any moment." But as he spoke, Monk's words sank in. He wondered just what he was trying to prove. To purge himself of his guilt over his personal treachery to his best friend? To avenge Mike and earn absolution in some way? Savagely he pushed the thought from his mind.

Monk was considering the problem. "They'll have a bloke on stag."

Hunt nodded. "Maybe. Or maybe they think we're all dead. They can't be sure till their mates examine the avalanche in daylight. We'll work around separate ways. If there is a guard, one of us will find him. It shouldn't be difficult. They won't think we've climbed the glacier."

"That's true," Monk laughed harshly. "No one would be that daft."

"We'll approach over the snowhole together from the rear and let them have a full magazine through the top."

The idea appealed to Monk. "Melt down, eh?"

They split up then, each selecting a route that would provide continuous cover from any lookout. Both knew the sort of location the enemy would choose for an outpost: good cover plus an open field-of-fire. It would probably also be close to the snowhole so that the occupants could be silently alerted by a tug on a communications cord.

But in the event they found nothing. At last their enemy had made a fatal slip-up. Asleep, exhausted. Vulnerable like babies.

Hunt's heart was pounding as he approached the final leg and he could feel the adrenalin flowing. He mused how strange it was that the fear of anticipated action evaporated the instant the real thing started.

He rounded the dune behind the snowhole. Monk was waiting, anxious. They looked at each other long and hard. Perhaps it was a silent question. To go on or not? It was too late now for Hunt. He raised his hand. Standby, standby. His hand dropped like a guillotine.

In unison they rose up on the drift with Hocklers primed. The air was suddenly shattered by the vicious hammering of the guns as they went into action, the steady bursts lacing the snowhole beneath their feet. A rain of death pouring like leaden stair-rods into the unprotected bodies of the Spetsnaz team below the surface.

They stopped together as the sudden heat caused the water vapour in the air to crystallise. They waited impatiently for the ice fog that the weapons had created to drift away. To reveal the holocaust.

Without exchanging a word, they slid down the front slope to the entrance holes, ready to cut down anyone who attempted to escape.

Hunt stared at the hole in disbelief, and his mouth dropped stupidly open. They were decoy holes, no more than three feet deep. And they led nowhere. It was one of the oldest tricks in the book.

"PLEASE DO NOT MOVE!"

The woman's voice carried sharply in the crisp air from behind. It was accompanied by the metallic clack of cocking handles.

"NOW YOU DROP THE WEAPONS! MOVE!"

Hunt and Monk let the Hocklers fall, and raised their hands.

The woman lowered her voice. "Now you may turn, please!"

Obediently they turned. There were four of them. Ghostly white figures plastered in frost, their outlines dark against the gleam of the morning sky. A shaft of sunlight broke like a silver starburst on the ice turret behind them, glinting sharply on the four short-barrelled Kalashnikov AKS 74s.

"*Khuligani!*" taunted the large, granite-faced soldier. And obliged them with a mocking translation. "Hooligans, like they say. The hooligans of Hereford!"

The woman snapped an angry word at the big soldier; he stopped talking but his grin stayed, and all the time the snout of the AKS arced slowly back and forth between its two targets. He looked eager to pull the trigger.

Hunt's mouth was dry. He swallowed hard and silently cursed his own stupidity.

"Listen to me, Britishers," the woman demanded. "We are sorry about last night, but it had to be done. You were lucky to escape, but our comrades in the valley

542

saw you. They have been in radio contact with us. So we monitor your progress up here." Hunt thought he detected a note of genuine sympathy in her voice. "It is very brave. Now you are tired, you have enough."

"Like shit – " Monk spat beneath his breath.

"Shut up!" Hunt ordered.

"Now there is another way," the woman said, her voice softer. "No one else needs to die. You are soldiers and you do your job with honour. But is time to concede defeat. Just tell the traitor Shalayez to surrender himself to us. That is all we want."

"So you can murder him?" Hunt challenged.

The woman shook her head. "No. We are told to take him alive – *if* that is possible."

"Then why the avalanche?" Hunt sneered.

"That was last night, when we think there is no other way. Today is different." Her voice sounded impatient; clearly she wasn't used to explaining her actions. "Now you come with us and tell Shalayez to give himself up."

"Get stuffed!" Hunt snapped.

"Co-operate or you are dead," the woman said. "Then maybe Shalayez and the Swede both get killed when we go to get them. Is that what you want?"

Hunt drew a deep breath. He didn't want to die, and once dead he could do nothing to save Shalayez anyway. He owed the poor bastard something, he thought. The big Russian with the granite features shuffled impatiently, the trigger-finger of his mitt making a delicate caressing movement.

Monk caught Hunt's eye and nodded. To agree was at least to stall for time. "Okay."

The two SAS men were spreadeagled and searched. Knives and webbing were removed, roughly by the two older male Russians, but more politely by the fair-haired youngster.

"Get up and walk," the woman ordered. She and the granite-faced NCO covered them, while the other two followed carrying the party's skis and the discarded Hocklers; they seemed pleased with their new acquisitions.

Wearily Hunt and Monk trudged back through the deep snow, following their own deep footprints to where Reis and Shalayez waited.

"Where are they?" the woman demanded.

Hunt pointed his mitt. "In that depression. About sixty metres, at the top of the glacier."

The three Russians looked uneasily around them. High winds had shaped the snow into a maze of gullies and carved grotesque castles out of solid ice, like a child's fantasy adventure playground. All around they glistened and twinkled sharply in the sunlight. It offered concealment in every direction.

"Right," the woman said. "Just you, Hunt, advance thirty paces. Then stop. If you don't stop yourself, Petkus here will do it for you."

The big sergeant grinned malevolently.

Hunt sniffed heavily and moved reluctantly on, counting every awkward movement as he sank to the knees with each step. His injured ankle began to scream in protest.

He'd only reached twenty-five when the single, solitary shot cracked through the brittle air like a bullwhip. Instinctively he threw himself down.

"STAY THERE!" The Swedish accent was unmistakable. "NOT ONE MORE STEP!"

Feeling slightly foolish, Hunt stood up and brushed the snow from his cam-whites. He looked around, uncertain where the voice had come from.

The woman yelled: "Hunt! Tell him!"

He shrugged and spoke to the deserted white landscape. "Janne, they want Shalayez! If he goes with them no one gets hurt."

For a moment there was silence. Ice creaked eerily all around as the sun gathered strength. Then: "WHAT GUARANTEES?"

Hunt shook his head. Still he could not place the direction of Reis's voice. "No guarantees."

"AND YOU COME ALL THIS WAY FOR *THAT*?" There was an edge of disgust to the voice.

The woman suddenly shouted: "Tell Shalayez I have a note here from his wife! From his Katya! She wants to go back to him!"

Hunt turned. "You bloody bitch – "

The man called Petkus swung his AKS angrily, and the SAS man's mouth clammed shut.

A mocking laugh echoed around the ice pinnacles. "I think Dr Shalayez will not fall for that, dear lady!"

The woman stood her ground. "But does he know his lover is dead?! The girl called Lucy?! Have you told him *that*?!"

Reis's voice came back loud and clear; Hunt was now sure the Swede was moving each time he spoke. "I REMIND YOU THAT THIS IS *SWEDISH* TERRITORY! I AM A GOVERNMENT OFFICER, AND YOU ARE UNDER ARREST!"

Petkus laughed, pointed his AKS at the sound of the voice and pulled the trigger. Five rounds shattered the icy stillness and chewed into the base of an ice pinnacle, so that it toppled into a gully. It fragmented like a porcelain ornament, shattering in all directions.

Hunt scarcely followed what happened next. He was momentarily aware of the *swish-thud* of a grenade launcher and the instant bright crackle of small-arms fire. The entire plateau seemed to disintegrate in a cloud of blue cordite and ice like flying glass. Transparent shards lanced the air in all directions, swallowed up by the drifting gusts of displaced spindrift. And then suddenly, everywhere, the air was filled with the thick, choking contents of smoke grenades.

Picking himself up from the snow, he ploughed back in the direction of the Russians. A big figure loomed towards him in the stinking murk. He lunged, head first at the belly, carrying the body backwards with his momentum. His hands grabbed at the throat.

"For Christ's sake, Brian!" Monk croaked. "Leave it out!"

Hunt gasped as the smoke seared his lungs, and he rolled off the prone figure, unable to mouth his apology. As he staggered to his feet, someone in white thrust a Hockler in his hand.

A vaguely familiar voice said: "Follow me, Brian."

Roughly a hand grabbed the sleeve of his smock and hauled him through the ebbing smoke.

At last he was out of it and he opened his stinging eyes, hardly able to see, let alone comprehend the meaning of the white figures running to the right and left in the total confusion of the scene.

Dusty Miller grinned at him. "I think this evens the score with the Cadre, Brian."

"What the – ?"

Miller dragged him down into the snow. "Keep down, old lad. A couple of Russkies have gone to ground."

His eyes still smarting, Hunt was able to see a little clearer now. Miller's men had fanned out in a defensive semicircle. Beyond them someone was firing from the fairytale ice pinnacles.

A few feet in front of him a body lay sprawled on its back, the legs thrown wide and one arm outstretched as though reaching for help. The mouth was distorted with anger and surprise, the upturned eyes still open in death, trying in vain to see where the bullet had entered the forehead, caused a neat red puncture.

"Did you – ?" Hunt began.

Miller shook his head. "The Swede shot him. Stone dead at fifty metres."

Hunt couldn't cope with the speed of events. "How in God's name did you get here? This is sodding Sweden."

"After you didn't meet the chopper last night, we took a leaf out of your book, old lad. Map-reading error. And all our radios went on the blink, so we couldn't contact HQ. Funny effect the mountains have . . ."

"You mean – ?"

Miller feigned horror. "You don't mean we *are* actually in Sweden do you?" And he managed it with a totally straight face.

"Watch out! Left flank!" a voice bawled suddenly.

Both men turned to see two Russians making a dash for freedom, firing from the hip as they ran. Obviously they were unaware of Hunt and Miller's position, hidden in a snowy pit created by the grenades. They were running straight towards it.

Suddenly the older man with the face like granite saw them. His reaction was instinctive, born of the training galleries with pop-up targets, and he fired straight and level without hesitation.

It is easy to forget in a split second that snow or timber, or even brick, offers no kind of protection. Movement is the only solution, fast and unpredictable enough to throw the enemy's aim. Hunt and Miller dived in opposite directions, the SAS man rolling hard and fast over soft snow for several feet. Then he jammed in the tips of his boots to stop the momentum, his legs spreadeagled and the Hockler in the firing position.

Petkus's gun followed Hunt's roll, the snout passing over its target as the SAS man stopped suddenly. Petkus overcorrected and fired. Two geysers of snow sprayed over Hunt as he pulled the trigger. The squab butt jolted into his shoulder, twice. He heard the sharp snap of the rounds as the gas ejector spat the spent cases from the breech. Petkus kept on running towards him, momentarily checked by the bullets pumping into his abdomen, then on again. Hunt fired once more and the Russian pitched forward in a last determined effort. The big body twitched involuntarily once, twice. Then lay still.

The second Russian stood crouched over his weapon, his short fair hair tugged by the breeze. He appeared to hesitate in that moment; it was something in the stance of his body. Hunt thought how young he looked. Young, almost innocent. And confused. The barrel of the AKS dipped a fraction. It crossed Hunt's mind that he was about to surrender; there seemed to be a half-smile of relief on the unlined features.

In that millisecond of indecision it was over. The sound of the shot and the round striking home was simultaneous. A look of curiosity came over the young face, the body jolting as though it had received an electric shock. Then the legs just appeared to give way and the young man's torso twisted as he went down, giving the macabre illusion that he was screwing himself into the snow.

Chalky Appleton scrambled up from his position on the flank, his black face gleaming with sweat. His eyes were white and wide with apprehension. "He wasn't – ?"

Hunt shook his head. "I don't think so."

Miller slapped the young Marine on the shoulder. "Well done, son. I owe you a pint."

Appleton smiled nervously; he didn't know whether to feel proud or ashamed. The young fair-haired Russian was the first man he'd ever killed.

Miller turned to Hunt. "That's all three of them accounted for."

It took a second for Hunt's tired brain to register. "Three?"

The Marine sergeant-major nodded. "The three Russians."

Hunt's mouth dropped. "There were four. The woman's missing."

Miller was aghast. "Four? Oh, Christ – " He looked around.

The angry clatter of the Sea King distracted them as it circled overhead, homing in on the streaming coloured cloud from the smoke-flare.

"WATCH OUT!" a voice yelled suddenly.

All eyes turned to the Marine who'd called the warning. His mitted hand was pointing to one of the surrounding ice turrets, where a white-shrouded figure had emerged from behind a jagged shield of ice spires. It moved with an awkward shuffling gait towards the top of a steep slope that ran down to the main level of the plateau.

Hunt registered the poles and the skis, and knew in that second who it was and why she'd done it. In the confusion and the smoke, she had somehow got to her equipment. Now she had the high ground. Had the run she needed. He saw the Kalashnikov strapped across her chest, saw her head lower as she kicked off.

"Jesus!" Miller breathed. "What the hell does she think she's doing?"

The words died on his lips as she rocketed down the incline, gathering a fantastic speed that spat out ice chips in her wake. Powering with her poles, crouched low at the end of each downward stroke.

She flew the last few feet, using a jutting outcrop to launch herself. In a cloud of spume, she landed amidst the startled Marines who instinctively leapt aside, gaping after her in astonishment, too stunned to react.

Appleton raised his rifle, but Hunt pushed it aside. Perplexed, the soldier dropped the muzzle.

She was speeding towards the glacier now, carving her way deftly through the difficult broken snowscape with seemingly effortless skill.

"My God," Miller murmured. "She'll bloody kill herself."

Hunt knew she was at the depression where they'd sheltered earlier after the glacier climb. Winced as he anticipated the drop. Perversely willing her on. Then she was airborne, her graceful shape momentarily silhouetted like a bird in the sun's gilded rays. And she was gone.

Half a dozen men rushed to the brink. Hunt and Miller followed.

As they reached the group of astounded Marines, one was saying in awe: "Fucking roll on!"

Hunt looked and saw she'd taken the ice path down

the edge of the glacial tongue. A fast, helter-skelter journey to the depths, across a treacherous ice surface on which it was near impossible to control skis. Yet she made it seem so easy.

The receding figure skidded around a tight outcrop bed, spraying ice as her steel edges bit, and disappeared from sight.

"She'll never make it," Miller said. "A bleedin' Olympic champ couldn't make that."

Monk joined them, overheard. "Don't take bets, Dusty, don't take bets."

Slowly, still too stunned by events to talk, they turned and trudged back towards the helicopter.

Janne Reis emerged from the main group of Marines with Shalayez in tow. The Swede looked pleased with himself.

Hunt said: "I'm sorry about all this, Janne." He indicated the helicopter that was making its final approach, the downdraught sending up a blinding fountain of loose snow.

Reis shook his head, and smiled. "The border is hard to define in this area. Maybe I am wrong and we stand in Norway." He offered his hand.

Hunt took it, and for a moment they shared the feeling of two men whose friendship had been forged in adversity, and who both knew they would never see each other again.

Reis's smile melted. "Don't ever come back, Brian. You or your friends. You will not be welcome."

Hunt nodded. "A lift?"

"Your Mr Miller is calling up our defence net. There is a helicopter at Åre which can collect me."

"And the Russians?"

Reis looked across to where the three bodies had been laid out in a neat row by the Marines. He said: "I'll take their equipment back with me. Their bodies will be found in the spring. I'll arrange it, together with the autopsies. A mountaineering accident. It happens all the time."

"And the woman?"

"Our police will look out for her." He paused. "Somehow, I do not think they will find her."

Hunt smiled thinly. "No, Janne. Neither do I."

"It has been good to know you – despite the circumstances."

"Thanks for everything," Hunt said lamely.

The Swede nodded solemnly and moved away.

Hunt beckoned Shalayez and pointed to the helicopter.

"Time to go to your new home, Niki."

The Russian looked grim. "What the woman said, about Lucy? It cannot be true?"

Hunt averted his eyes, staring at the helicopter with intense concentration, unable to find the words.

Monk said: "I'm sorry, mate." He placed a consoling hand on Shalayez's shoulder, and nodded towards the row of bodies. "They killed her."

The Russian's face contorted in disbelief. "My own countrymen . . .?"

Hunt said hoarsely: "They were doing their job, Niki. It's what they're trained for. Now go to the helicopter."

He shook his head. "I can't go. Not now."

"Go," Hunt repeated. "Don't let Lucy's life have been in vain."

Monk said gruffly: "She died for you, mate. Don't let her down now."

The two SAS men watched in silence as the tall lonely figure struggled through the snow towards the helicopter; he was better left alone.

By now the remaining Royal Marines had gathered and stowed their kit, ready to embark. Dusty Miller hastened over to Hunt and Monk.

"C'mon, you two. Don't like Sweden that much, do you? Got a brew on back home." He looked around the deserted plateau with its three corpses and the lone figure of Reis.

"I gather Len Pope's coming back with Ralph Lavender," he said. "So I guess Mike Ash is with him?"

551

The innocent words were like an electric shock. Hunt grimaced momentarily, and then turned to the Marine. He said slowly: "Mike's not coming back, Dusty. The clock beat him."

The helicopter rotors began to thrash, impatient to be off.

Len Pope watched from the entrance of the fell-station as the two cars bumped their way down the snowy track.

The Volvo and the dark blue Mercedes had been the first two vehicles to arrive since the snowplough had managed to get through.

His hand crept into the pocket of his civilian anorak and felt the cold comfort of the 9 mm Browning pistol. His Hockler had been carefully concealed in his bergan, his cam-whites stowed. He now wore a chequered huntsman's hat with ear flaps.

He watched with apprehension as the two cars stopped. Both had darkly tinted windows, so it was with relief that he recognised Ralph Lavender as he emerged from the Volvo. The intelligence officer was wrapped in a thick sheepskin coat, the collar turned up against the cruel morning chill. No one else left the cars which remained stationary, their exhausts still belching to keep the heaters working.

"Is Chagall inside?" Lavender asked. No niceties, no greeting. No enquiry about how their journey had been from the chalet.

Pope looked at him coldly. Sod you. "He's inside having a coffee."

"Wait here," Lavender ordered, and went inside.

The cafeteria was deserted except for a lone figure hunched over a cup at one of the tables. He looked up and smiled nervously. "Am I glad to see you! This bloody Swedish weather lasts forever."

"Hello, Heinrich." Lavender sat down.

"Can we stop using that stupid name now?" Chagall glowered. "I remind you I am a colonel of the KGB.

From now on I think you can use my real name. And a little respect, huh?''

"Yes, Colonel Chagall."

He seemed satisfied. "That is better." He had suddenly lost interest in his coffee. "Shalayez is safe?"

"He arrived in Norway two hours ago. He'll be on his way to London by RAF transport."

"Then my side of the bargain is complete."

Lavender nodded, and he sensed the other man relax. "You want a coffee?"

"No thank you, Colonel."

Chagall smiled. "I cannot believe my time has come. It has been so long. Shall we go now?"

"In a minute," Lavender replied. "I just want to ask a question."

"Yes?"

"That night in Stockholm when you called me. In your hotel room. You warned me that something would happen that would persuade my Government to hand Shalayez back."

A sudden concern clouded Chagall's face. He smiled nervously. "I was drunk."

"Not that drunk," Lavender said darkly. "You knew an assassination attempt was to be made?"

Chagall's face dropped. "Believe me, no! I just get the rumour that something really big will happen, but that was nothing to do with us in Stockholm."

"Nothing else happened," Lavender reminded coolly.

Chagall shrugged. "Maybe the plan was cancelled after the assassination. After all, the killing of a senior civil servant is a fairly important event. Nothing Moscow could dream up could equal that."

"But it wasn't Moscow?"

The Russian smiled thinly. "I would not think so, but in any event, the secret of such things is not shared outside those directly involved." He drained his coffee. "I believe the Swedes are looking for Croatian separatists, a group calling themselves Ustasha."

Lavender's eyes were dark and cold. "In London the Holger Meins Commando claim responsibility – connected with Baader Meinhof and the Red Army Faction."

Chagall's smile showed genuine relief. "You see! Already there is much confusion."

"These assassins were *exceedingly* professional."

Don't play games with me, you bastard, was what Lavender wanted to say. Instead he obliquely reminded the KGB colonel that the Kremlin had once made use of the right-wing Grey Wolves in its attempt to kill the Polish Pope.

Chagall appeared to miss the insinuation. "Maybe, sadly, these killers will never be found. And their motives will never be known."

Ralph Lavender stood up. He had made his decision a long time ago. It had been his brainchild to use this man to hook a Star Wars scientist; he alone had colluded with the KGB colonel to enmesh the most suitable candidate. The short list had been narrowed to three. Shalayez had been selected; Sergei Chagall knew him best, knew which strings to pull and when. He had acted alone because he was young and ambitious, and because he wanted the glory. He wasn't prepared to climb to the top of his profession in dead men's shoes. He knew he wasn't widely liked, but he also knew that his superiors would be obliged to recognise his brilliance if he landed a coup such as Shalayez.

Chagall, of course, had always been expendable. Only the KGB colonel knew the risks of the methods being used in manoeuvring the victim into defection. If the scientist ever learned the truth of how he had been manipulated and abused, he would invariably turn on his new-found homeland. And, probably working on some top secret project in Britain or the United States, he would be in a position to do the utmost damage. Lavender's own superiors would recognise it too.

A man like Chagall would be aware of that, and Lavender realised his knowledge would hang forever over him like a Damoclean sword. For in Chagall he recognised an ambitious, like-minded soul.

That had been the position before Shalayez came to Stockholm. It was going to have been easy to cut Chagall off then: a stranded, disconsolate and disillusioned man slowly drinking himself to an early grave in some remote research outpost in Asia. After all, he could scarcely complain to his superiors.

But Chagall's arrival in Stockholm had changed all that. It forced Lavender to keep his side of a bargain he had never had any intention of keeping. If he refused, then Chagall could hand himself over to any Western embassy and beg asylum. No doubt he'd be taken in.

Worse still, was that Chagall might have had pre-warning of Alf Nystedt's assassination in Sweden's capital. Inevitably it would come out in the routine debriefing. The interrogation of defectors was very professional and *very* thorough.

He could almost see Chagall ingratiating himself with his questioners, gaily telling them how he'd given advanced warning of the plot to the British agent, who had ignored his words.

Now Lavender had no real option.

"We are going now?" Chagall asked, standing too.

Lavender smiled lightly. "An Englishman is as good as his word, Colonel."

The Russian's step was light beside the intelligence officer. "I wait so long for this."

At the lobby Len Pope was keeping watch. The two cars were still outside.

"All right?" Lavender asked.

Pope looked concerned. "I'm not sure, sir. The cars – "

"It's all right, Len, the colonel here is going to Norway straight away in the Mercedes. I have to clear up things in Stockholm."

Chagall rubbed his hands together eagerly. "I go now?"

Lavender nodded and waited while the Russian briskly shook hands with him and Pope before leaving the entrance.

"The Mercedes," Lavender said. "The driver knows where to go."

As the bulky figure of Chagall slipped and slid in his haste to reach the car, Pope said anxiously: "I must have a word with you, sir."

Lavender didn't take his eyes from Chagall. His face was grey. "Not now, Len!" he hissed savagely.

The Russian had reached the blue Mercedes. He opened the rear door, bent his head and began to climb inside. He faltered halfway. Then quickly he disappeared, as though someone had grabbed him by the collar and hauled him in. Even before the door had slammed shut, the vehicle was on the move, bouncing over the rutted ice of the carpark and onto the track that led back to the snow-barrier.

Len Pope knew then that his near photographic memory for names and numbers hadn't let him down. It was the absence of the diplomatic plates that had thrown him. The registration number was on the list of those belonging to the Soviet Embassy in Stockholm.

"Not a word," Ralph Lavender warned softly, watching the trail of exhaust whipped away by the stiffening wind on its way down from the tundra. "Come on, I'll take you over the border to Trondheim. You can catch a train or a flight from there."

The two men crossed to the remaining grey Volvo. Moments later it edged its way cautiously onto the track.

By the time it had disappeared from view, the sky had clouded over. The barometer on the outside wall of the deserted fell-station was dropping fast.

Another blizzard was on its way.

Epilogue

The news that Nikolai Shalayez had reached London was worthy of a celebration. Even more so when they learned that the Swedish prosecutor had released Peter Burke due to lack of evidence. Sir Timothy Maybush insisted on Matt and Cherry Brewster joining him and his wife for dinner at the exclusive Old Town restaurant.

At the time the ambassador was pondering which bottle of vintage port to select as the crowning glory to the meal, on the other side of Stockholm the journalist was putting the finishing touches to his story.

Björn Larsson was tapping furiously at the typewriter in the study of his small flat. He wanted to finish it by eleven so he could meet Birgitta at the Café Opera before midnight.

For that reason he did not welcome the interruption. At first he ignored it, but the doorbell rang again. Louder and more insistent.

He didn't know the tall good-looking man with blond hair who filled the door frame. Behind the modern plastic frames of the spectacles his eyes were blue and smiling. Larsson guessed he was just a few years older than himself.

"Mr Larsson?" Very courteous. "I'm sorry to disturb you. My name's Reis. From security. May I come in?" He showed his ID.

Instantly the journalist was both alarmed and intrigued. He offered coffee then wished he hadn't, be-

557

cause the security man would say nothing more until they were both seated with the cups in front of them.

"You have made quite a name for yourself over the past few weeks," Reis observed. "Many coups for your newspaper. You must have very good contacts?"

Larsson gave a nervous laugh. "You know how it is, we journalists never reveal our sources."

"Quite," replied the other, and rose to his feet. He hadn't touched his coffee. "But you managed to give a very detailed account of the abduction of the Russian scientist, and events during the British Embassy siege."

There was nothing Larsson could say to that. His one-time rival Tord Jensen had supplied a wealth of information. His eyes followed Reis as he ambled nonchalantly around the study, peering at the books on the shelf.

"The inside story of it all, eh?" Reis said absently, as he picked a volume at random and flicked idly through it. "But, I think, very much the Soviet version."

Larsson shifted uncomfortably. "It was the only version available," he answered defensively.

The stranger replaced the book. "Know Tord Jensen well, do you?"

"Fairly. We've been rivals for years."

"Yet lately he has been helping you a little, yes?"

Larsson clammed up tight.

"Well, here's a little exclusive for you. Jensen has a friend in the Soviet Embassy. An assistant military attaché by the name of Grigory Yvon."

"So?"

"Colonel Grigory Yvon, in fact. Not so lowly, you see. The GRU chief in Stockholm to be precise. Tomorrow that gentleman will be expelled for activities inconsistent with his diplomatic status." A meaningful pause. "You know what I mean?"

Larsson blanched. Again he said nothing.

"One thing surprises me, Mr Larsson . . ." He paused

by the typewriter. " . . . Your story is incomplete. You have not written what happened after the scientist escaped from the embassy."

The journalist was on his feet, but too late. Reis had the thin sheaf of typed manuscript in his hand and was reading it carefully.

Larsson watched miserably.

After ten minutes Reis looked up and smiled. "Very interesting. But, to be honest, not exactly accurate."

"Oh no?" Incensed.

"You see," Reis explained gently, "I was there."

Larsson frowned.

"Yes, I know exactly what happened." He replaced the papers on the desk. "I tell you what, how would you like the exclusive story of what *really* happened?" He sat down again and this time sipped at his coffee. "Of course, for security reasons I will have to leave out some details. But there will be enough facts for you to verify."

Björn Larsson felt himself relax. "That I should like very much."

"Of course, you must understand that this must be totally unattributable . . ."

The journalist grinned widely. "I never reveal my sources."

Birgitta had a long wait in vain that night.

There were wild daffodils beneath the fence that bordered the rough track leading down to the farm.

It was almost April and Hunt could smell the expectancy of spring in the air as he negotiated the MG roadster around the puddled ruts. The birds sang boisterously and he noticed that the hedgerows were in bud, and the patch of unmown lawn in the cottage garden was a lush green.

Yet there was a solemnity surrounding the rambling farmhouse as he drew up outside. A goose appeared half-heartedly from one of the outbuildings, flapped its wings and squawked a couple of times, then seemed to lose interest.

Biff rose from his position in the porch, barked and wagged his tail. But even he seemed to lack the enthusiasm Hunt remembered from his visit at Christmas. He seemed an older, sadder dog.

The door opened before he reached it. Gabby stood there, a distant look in her pale blue eyes. He noticed the skin around the tiny laugh-lines was red from tears, and the long fair hair unbrushed.

"Hello, Brian." She didn't seem surprised to see him. Not pleased, not angry.

He searched awkwardly for the right words; he never had been the most articulate of men. "I wanted to come, Gabby. But I didn't know if I should . . . I – I hoped that I . . . that is, I thought I should be the one to tell you – "

She smiled tightly. "Major Fraser called last week. As soon as they knew."

"We only got back today – " he said lamely.

"He was sweet. Understanding."

"I'm very, very sorry."

She stepped to one side. "Come in, Brian. I was about to make some tea."

He noticed her waddling gait as she moved, and the grossly swollen belly beneath the maternity dungarees. It was intensely quiet inside like a mausoleum, and dark, illuminated only by the shafts of sunlight through the deep-set mullioned windows. The air was rich with the smell of beeswax polish and he guessed it had been how Gabby had exorcised her grief. The furniture gleamed.

"Where's Jessica? The children?" he asked as he followed her through to the kitchen. It was a relief to step out of the oppressive gloom into the pine and sunshine of the kitchen.

"They're back at school; I thought it best. The boys have returned to boarding school, there was no point in letting them hang around with time to get depressed.

560

They'll be back for the funeral on Monday." She sighed wearily. "And Baby Walt's asleep. Thank God he's nearly over his teething now."

Hunt looked at his watch. "I'm sorry, it was a stupid time to call. You'll be having to pick the girls up from school, I suppose . . .?"

She put her hand on his wrist; her skin felt very soft and cool. "There's time for a cup of tea first, Brian. I'm just pleased you came." The tapwater gushed noisily into the kettle. "I'm also glad you were with Mike when he died. It makes it seem less lonely, somehow."

Hunt swallowed hard; he didn't want to disillusion her.

"Did he say anything?"

A shake of the head, not trusting himself to speak.

She put a match to the cooker and gave a small, half-hearted laugh. "I suppose, if he'd had a choice, he would have chosen that way to go. In the mountains."

Hunt remembered the moment he himself had come to terms with death in the aftermath of the avalanche. "The snow's very warm. Very comforting."

"That's nice." But he wasn't sure she was listening.

Gabby Ash put out some home-baked muesli biscuits on a plate and they watched the tea brew in silence.

Then, as she poured his cup, she said slowly: "I told Mike, you know? About us."

Hunt said nothing.

"I felt I had to, you see. After the things you said. I am sorry."

"Why?" Hunt asked. He wanted to add, why did she have to punish her husband? But he couldn't bring himself to say the words.

Nevertheless he felt he got the answer to his unasked question. "I think I wanted him to know that someone else cared. That I meant more to someone than some remote mountain." Her voice had dropped to a whisper, as though talking to herself. "And I think I wanted his forgiveness."

He couldn't pretend really to understand, but he felt his heart going out to her. He felt an overwhelming urge to crush her in his arms and tell her everything was all right.

"Did he say anything about it to you?"

Hunt shook his head.

"No." She smiled. "No, he wouldn't. Dear Mike."

She winced suddenly, and placed a hand on her stomach, her eyes closed against the pain.

"Are you okay?"

Her eyes opened wide and she gave a gasp of a smile. "Sorry. It's been very active the last two days. I don't think it will be long now."

Hunt shifted awkwardly; he was unused to such situations. "Look, would you like me to pick up the girls from school?"

She smiled and reached out, squeezing his hand. "Oh, would you, Brian? Jessica especially would love that – but don't you have to get back?"

He grinned at her. "Two weeks' leave."

That smile that belonged to him alone. "That's lovely. Then you'll be around when the little chap arrives?"

"You know it's a boy?"

"I've never been wrong. I wonder if he'll look anything like you – " She'd let it slip before she realised.

To her surprise Hunt missed it. Instead he just laughed. "God forbid! I wouldn't wish that on anyone." He glanced at his watch. "I'd better go and pick them up."

"Thanks for calling, Brian."

She watched him as he strode out and climbed into his beloved old wreck of an MG. As it worked its way up the track, she was sure he hadn't realised.

Perhaps it was just as well. Maybe, one day, she would tell him.

The roses in the little garden of the cottage on the outskirts of Christchurch were Daphne Withers's pride

562

and joy. They'd been planted by her beloved late husband and she tended them with a devotion that others might lavish on a grave.

She climbed unsteadily from her knees and wiped her brow from the effect of the heavy August sun. The ice in the limewater on the patio would have chilled the drink nicely now. With half a dozen blooms in her trug, she crossed the lawn. Her knees, she realised, ached more each year. She really must think about hiring a gardener; maybe for just a few hours a week.

Alice Tate let herself in unannounced through the side gate. She did not spare the immaculate garden a glance. Horticulture had never been a subject anywhere near her heart.

"In time for a cool drink, my dear!" Daphne called. "Perfect timing."

Alice sat down, hot and flushed. "I've just got back from London. The train was packed with mums and their snotty, screaming kids on day excursions! Horrific!"

"So you did go to see that Mr Lavender?" Daphne challenged.

'That Mr Lavender' said it all; she didn't like the hard-faced little man. He reminded her of a ferret. Or was it a weasel? She never was sure which was which.

"He wanted to sound me out about a job in Leningrad."

"Oh really? How interesting! What did you say?"

Alice sipped her lime, and her lipstick bled into the fine pucker lines around her mouth. "I said no."

"Really?" Daphne was astounded. "Why?"

"Because I asked about meeting Colonel Chagall, and he said it wasn't possible because the man was doing life in a hard-labour camp in Yakutsk!"

Daphne was horrified. "Oh, that nice Mr Chagall! How awful!"

Alice frowned disparagingly. "He was an awful two-faced little toad, Daphne, and well you know it!"

She smiled gently. "But he was very good-looking. And such charm."

"When it suited." Alice crunched on ice. "Anyway, apparently he was taken away in Sweden by the KGB during that Shalayez business."

"Goodness."

"And something else, I learned. That little gel, Lucinda something – she was killed by the KGB around the same time. Shot in the head. She was in Shalayez's bed at the time."

Daphne Withers felt her heart palpitate. Little Lucy? The girl whom she had almost begun to believe really was her own granddaughter. Hadn't she even instructed the innocent young thing how to seduce a man?

"Yes, my dear," Alice said. She knew exactly what her old friend was feeling. "So I said no thank you, Mr Lavender, I think we really are getting too old for this sort of caper."

"And what did he say?" Daphne murmured vaguely.

"He was very pompous, of course. He's been promoted, you know."

Nikolai Shalayez had passed through the spring and summer in a kind of trance.

Everyone had been extremely hospitable and considerate to him. There had been kind words about Lucy; much English tea and sympathy.

It was a lush, beautiful country, England. He had seen much of it as he was moved, at frequent intervals, from safe house to safe house during the period of his debriefing. A cottage in Wales, a flat in Birmingham, and a mansion in the West Midlands.

Yes, lush and beautiful, but it was not home.

He'd asked for a photograph of Lucy. They'd promised it faithfully, but it never had arrived. There was always some reason.

The nightmares had stopped now, at last. Suffocating under snow had been even worse than reclimbing the ice wall. He would literally wake up in a cold sweat, his bed drenched. The tablets had worked and he no longer needed to take them.

He was like a man recovering from an anaesthetic.

His reception in Britain had been so friendly that he had told his questioners most things they wanted to know; many were extremely pleasant men, fellow scientists who shared his passion for his subject.

He'd also talked with some Americans, and it was on the cards that he'd be invited to the Lawrence Livermore Laboratory in the United States in the near future.

It was an exciting prospect, but even that did nothing to help the crushing feeling of personal loneliness he had. Female companionship had been discreetly offered, but he'd rejected it out-of-hand for what it was. More and more he thought of Katya and wondered what sort of life she and little Yelina had together now.

He liked this latest safe house. It was a smart little detached house in a Hertfordshire town, the name of which he couldn't quite pronounce. It was just one of many similar suburban dwellings in a tree-lined residential street. In summer it was almost like being in the heart of the countryside.

He had shared each of his temporary homes with an armed detective called McGarry who was with him at all times. They got on well together now after an uncertain start. The policeman and he would watch television together, when various British customs, jokes and lifestyle would be patiently explained to him. The two of them would sometimes go for a drink together at the local pub. A strange new experience. He'd also taken a liking to cricket, and McGarry had promised him a visit to the Oval.

There was a noise at the door, and the letterbox clattered.

"I'll get it!" McGarry called down. He was having his ritual bath.

"It's all right," Shalayez answered from the lounge. "It's just my magazines."

He'd been waiting all week for the latest edition of *Nature* to arrive from the local newsagents. There was an absolute feast of scientific journals available in the West which he had rarely had a chance to see in Russia. It was a wonderful bonus.

He crossed to the hallway and stooped to the mat. As he lifted the copy an envelope slipped from between the pages. He frowned; they didn't usually put the bill in an envelope.

Retracing his footsteps to the lounge, he thumbed it open. There was a short, typed note and another envelope. It was addressed to him. Immediately he recognised the neat handwriting and his heart began to pound.

He ripped it open.

My dearest Niki,

They have let me write to you to explain what has happened. It was all a terrible mistake and your so-called friend Sergei set it all up to drive you to leave your beloved Motherland. I gather he was collaborating with Westerners.

I was threatened by him until I agreed to leave you for the sake of our little mother, Yelina (who is well and sends all her love to her papa). How can you ever forgive me! Can you ever?

My dearest, I want you home. I've always wanted you.

They say you can speak to a man at the Soviet Embassy in London who will explain to you how the British and Americans worked this evil plot on us.

They also say we have a new flat waiting for us in Moscow and there is a position for you at the University. They promise there will be no recriminations.

Please, please, my dearest, come home to me and your Yelina.

Hugs and kisses,

Your own Katya

He gulped and began to read it again. Upstairs he heard McGarry's bathwater gurgling away. Hurriedly he scanned the terse note. It told him to visit the lavatory on the first floor of Selfridges in London next Wednesday at twelve midday. A diversion would take care of his minder – all he had to do was be there.

"Anything interesting?" McGarry asked later as he entered in his dressing-gown, still rubbing at his hair with a towel.

"What?" Shalayez looked up from his magazine. "Oh, yes, always there is something good."

McGarry grinned. "Too intellectual for me, I'm afraid . . ."

"Tim, I was wondering . . ."

"Yep?"

"I have not been to London for many weeks. Maybe it is time I buy some new clothes."

"Shopping spree, eh? Why not? I'll have to get clearance, mind. But I don't see no problems."

"Next Wednesday?"

SCIENTIST IN DEATH CRASH

By Our Moscow Correspondent

THE MATHEMATICAL SCIENTIST Dr Nikolai Shalayez, who caused a world-wide sensation earlier this year during his defection and subsequent return to the Soviet Union, was today reported killed in a road crash on the Moscow ring-road.

His wife Katya, who was with him at the time, is said to be stable after a night in intensive-care.

Shalayez was apparently on his way to take up an appointment at the Moscow University when the accident occurred.

Obituary – P14.

TERENCE STRONG

DRAGONPLAGUE

A DISTURBINGLY AUTHENTIC THRILLER WHICH
LAYS BARE THE PLOT BETWEEN IRA AND LIBYAN
TERRORISTS TO FLOOD BRITAIN WITH HEROIN.

Ex-Royal Marine Billy Robson is determined to go
straight after serving a five-year sentence on a robbery
charge.

Anxious to make things up to his wife and child, he
takes the one legitimate job on offer – unaware that
he's stepping into a nightmare.

He finds himself in a desperate fight for his freedom,
his family – and his life. Against an evil force of cor-
ruption, addiction and perversion that consumes all
before it . . .

DRAGONPLAGUE

ITS TENSION WINDS TO BREAKING-POINT AS THE
ACTION STRETCHES FROM THE MIDDLE EAST,
THROUGH BRITAIN, TO AMERICA.

ITS REVELATIONS CHILL TO THE MARROW.

POST A LITTLE HAPPINESS

Post·A·Book

A Royal Mail service in association with the Book Marketing Council & The Booksellers Association.
Post·A·Book is a Post Office trademark.

TERENCE STRONG

CONFLICT OF LIONS

The pulsating inside account of an SAS peace mission that finds itself pitted against the insidious forces of Colonel Gadaffi.

DATELINE: WEST AFRICA '82

A vicious assassination attempt is made on the President of a fragile African democracy by Libyan terrorists. The call for an advisory training team goes out to 22 Special Air Service Regiment:

WHATEVER THE COST – KEEP THE PEACE

But is it already too late? Beneath the sleepy surface of the 'friendliest nation in Africa' the dark forces of a secret enemy advance inexorably. Hampered by diplomatic ineptitude the crack SAS team struggle against the odds. Emotions and passions run high as they battle to stop the sweep of revolutionary fervour and bloodshed . . .

HODDER AND STOUGHTON PAPERBACKS

TERENCE STRONG

WHISPER WHO DARES

An action-packed, nerve-biting inside account of a
crack SAS team sent to cut the jugular of the IRA . . .

DATELINE: ULSTER '76

The British Government is worried. The new monster
in the IRA's armoury must be destroyed at birth. A
top-secret, top-priority order goes out to the 22 Special
Air Service Regiment:

SEEK AND DESTROY – NO MATTER WHERE.

For the four-man Sabre team of the legendary SAS this
will be their toughest mission . . . probing the inner
sanctum of the IRA's terror machine, fighting in the
bloody carnage and chaos of Ulster – never before has
so much been at stake. They encounter both triumph
and disaster – and the cruellest twist of fate.

HODDER AND STOUGHTON PAPERBACKS

TERENCE STRONG

THE FIFTH HOSTAGE

A pulse-racing inside account of the SAS rescue they said couldn't be done. Afterwards they said it should never be told.

DATELINE: TEHERAN '80

He is held in revolution-torn Iran. His secret could shatter NATO unity like a megaton blast. Khomeini wants him to talk. Britain does not. 22 Special Air Service Regiment receive their top priority order:

REGARDLESS OF RISK – GET HIM OUT!

The crack team disappears into the hostile turmoil of Iran to snatch Britain's most wanted man . . . and a devastating Nordic beauty. It is a nerve-shredding rescue bid that makes the blood run cold, and which turns into one of the most gruelling ordeals in the secret annals of the SAS.

HODDER AND STOUGHTON PAPERBACKS

GAVIN LYALL

BLAME THE DEAD

'There was just the one shot, and maybe I heard the thud as it went into his body. Then I was on my face in the roadway, gun held straight in front . . .'

Just one shot on a snowy Sunday in France, but it spoilt James Card's professional reputation as a body-guard – as well as leaving him with a body he hardly knew and a pistol he didn't want to explain.

That was when he knew the time had come to take a look into the ex-life and times of Martin Fenwick, sometime Lloyd's underwriter and deceased man of many parts . . .

'First rate . . . the writing, like a Hitchcock movie, instantly transmits the flavour of each new face, each new scene'

The Guardian

HODDER AND STOUGHTON PAPERBACKS

GAVIN LYALL

SHOOTING SCRIPT

'I don't know if you're working for Jiminez or not. But either way, the general made a mistake. You should've been in jail. Now you're loose, and that worries me. Because you're still a killer . . .'

Flying charter around the Caribbean wasn't quite the same as flying high cover against Migs in Korea. But it was a living. A flying living.

Carr had been careful, kept his hands clean, built up a solid reputation. In this part of the world you couldn't be too careful. So why, all of a sudden, did everyone look at him as though he was working for the rebels?

Maybe it was the film company who'd hired him. And the plane. Why did the plane have to be a B-25, an old World War Two bomber . . .?

'Caribbean politics made even more turbulent by one of the most compelling of contemporary storytellers'
The New York Times

HODDER AND STOUGHTON PAPERBACKS

GAVIN LYALL

UNCLE TARGET

It wasn't just *a* tank. It was the prototype, next generation, Main Battle Tank, with a radically new gun. And now it was missing, presumed about to fall into hostile hands.

Secretly loaned to the Jordanian army for desert evaluation tests, it has vanished in the confusion of a revolt by an entire armoured brigade.

From the bloody evidence of a London hotel seige it is clear that the events are deliberately connected. The MBT90 must be found and if necessary destroyed, to preserve its secrets.

SAS-trained Major Harry Maxim is sent in. But what starts as a simple demolition job is about to turn into a desperate run for freedom as their tank is hunted across a desert wilderness.

'The action never flags'

Financial Times

HODDER AND STOUGHTON PAPERBACKS

MORE TITLES AVAILABLE FROM
HODDER AND STOUGHTON PAPERBACKS

TERENCE STRONG

☐	41089 2	Dragonplague	£2.99
☐	38310 0	Conflict of Lions	£3.50
☐	32120 2	The Fifth Hostage	£2.95
☐	27908 7	Whisper Who Dares	£2.95

GAVIN LYALL

☐	42976 3	Blame the Dead	£3.50
☐	42975 5	Shooting Script	£3.50
☐	48841 7	Uncle Target	£2.99

All these books are available at your local bookshop or news-agent, or can be ordered direct from the publisher. Just tick the titles you want and fill in the form below.

Prices and availability subject to change without notice.

Hodder and Stoughton Paperbacks, P.O. Box 11, Falmouth, Cornwall.

Please send cheque or postal order, and allow the following for postage and packing:

U.K. – 55p for one book, plus 22p for the second book, and 14p for each additional book ordered up to a £1.75 maximum.

B.F.P.O. and EIRE – 55p for the first book, plus 22p for the second book, and 14p per copy for the next 7 books, 8p per book thereafter.

OTHER OVERSEAS CUSTOMERS – £1.00 for the first book, plus 25p per copy for each additional book.

Name ....

Address ....

....